FOREIGN POLICY
ON LATIN AMERICA
1970–1980

Edited by the staff of
**FOREIGN
POLICY**

Westview Press / *Boulder, Colorado*

The Carnegie Endowment / *Washington, D.C.*

Copyright © 1983 by the Carnegie Endowment for International Peace

Published in 1983 in the United States of America by Westview Press, Inc., 5500 Central Avenue, Boulder,
Colorado 80301; and the Carnegie Endowment for International Peace, 11 Dupont Circle N.W., Washington, D.C.
20036

Library of Congress Catalog Card number: 83-50492
ISBN: 0-86531-704-6 (HC); 0-86531-705-4 (PB)

Composition for this book was provided by the editors
Printed and bound in the United States of America

CONTENTS

ACKNOWLEDGMENTS

FOREIGN POLICY EDITORIAL STAFF 1970-1980

FOUNDING EDITORS

Samuel P. Huntington	1970-1977
Warren Demian Manshel	1970-1978

EDITORS

Richard H. Ullman	1978-1979
Charles William Maynes	1980-

MANAGING/ASSOCIATE EDITORS

John Franklin Campbell	1970-1972
Richard Holbrooke	1972-1976
Sanford J. Ungar	1977-1980
Leigh H. Bruce	1978-1983

FOREWORD

The attitude of the United States toward Latin America is paradoxical. For long stretches of U.S. history, the Western Hemisphere has been among Washington policy makers' lowest world priorities. As recently as the 1970s, both the Ford and the Carter administrations paid more attention to black Africa than to Central America.

At the same time, few foreign events evoke such panic-stricken reactions in the United States as unfavorable developments in "America's own backyard." When the United States suffers a major political setback in this hemisphere, the country tends to plunge into paroxysms of anger or fear. The policies of even such a tiny country as Grenada can suddenly be accorded international importance. The consequences of foreign-policy failure are portrayed as ominous in the extreme for the United States. Reflecting the national neurosis regarding this hemisphere, President Reagan recently warned that if the American effort in El Salvador failed, U.S. prestige would decline and U.S. alliances would crumble. The president, in effect, suggested that the fate of a small country in Central America could shift the entire balance of world power.

Further complicating the present U.S. approach to Latin America is the so-called Vietnam syndrome, the popular fear that the United States will be dragged into a misguided military adventure in a previously little-known part of the Third World. At first glance, the comparison would seem completely misplaced. The countries of concern this time are small, close, and traditionally susceptible to U.S. influence and control. The North Vietnamese had China as a friendly neighbor and a secure source of supplies, whereas the guerrillas in El Salvador have only tiny Nicaragua as a sanctuary. U.S. interest in Vietnam developed suddenly, while U.S. involvement in Central America is long-standing and expected by the rest of the world. Thus the problems of El Salvador and/or Central America seem manageable in a way that events demonstrated the conflict in Vietnam was not.

Yet time is not on the side of the United States in Central America. The pro-U.S. governments in power there seem increasingly on the defensive. The U.S. position does not even enjoy the support of major powers such as Mexico or Venezuela.

Nor is the overall U.S. position in Latin America much brighter. The Reagan administration moved early to improve relations with the right-wing dictatorships of Argentina and Chile, both of which are now in serious political difficulty. U.S.-Cuban relations have reached their lowest point since the early 1960s. Many of the regional giants—Brazil, Mexico, Venezuela—are experiencing the kind of grave economic trouble that in almost any political system leads to popular unrest. Few Latin American governments are comfortable with the key international policies pressed by Washington.

To help explain how U.S.-Latin American relations came to this unhappy pass is the purpose of this volume, which brings together articles on Latin America that appeared in FOREIGN POLICY in the 1970s. One virtue of the volume is that the issues that have surfaced prominently in the early 1980s were repeatedly adumbrated in the pages of the magazine during the previous decade.

The disastrous misreading of national character that took place in both Washington and Buenos Aires during the British-Argentine war over the Falkland Islands, or Malvinas, should have been no surprise to the readers of Mariano Grondona in FOREIGN POLICY.

In the middle of the Carter presidency, FOREIGN POLICY contributor Abraham F. Lowenthal warned that nowhere was the gap between announced policy and actual decisions more notable than in U.S.-Caribbean relations. Articles on Mexico warned of the looming problem of external debt.

A persistent theme runs throughout these essays as does a recurring controversy. The theme is the steady decline in U.S. control over the politics and economies of Latin America. The controversy is whether the explanation for this decline is to be found in poor policies in Washington or in trends in Latin America that no U.S. administration can expect to control.

The decrease in U.S. influence, of course, is a worldwide phenomenon; the causes are many. In this volume, Norman Gall points out in his important essay on the Brazilian-West German nuclear agreement in 1975 that U.S. international domination after World War II rested on three pillars: U.S. command of strategic nuclear weaponry; the role of the dollar in assuring monetary stability; and U.S. control through U.S. firms of the world's fuel supplies of oil and uranium. In the 1970s all three pillars were shattered with consequences for the U.S. position in the world far more serious than those resulting from the American misadventure in Vietnam.

In Latin America itself, however, there seemed to be another dimension to America's problems, and the first article on Latin America published in FOREIGN POLICY—Lawrence E. Harrison's "Waking from the Pan-American Dream"—expressed it cogently. Harrison warned in late 1971 that power in the region was passing from the oligarchy into new hands—"if not the hands of the masses, at least hands increasingly influenced by or catering to the masses." Harrison also noted that "anti-Americanism," heretofore largely confined to far-left-wing circles, was spreading to the "moderate left, to businessmen, to the military, and to the church."

The 10 years since the publication of that article have confirmed this observation about Latin American public opinion to the great distress of policy makers in Washington. Washington's response to the challenges of Latin America has not been very effective, however, both because of powerful political currents in Latin America itself and because the traditional tools of U.S. policy toward its hemispheric neighbors have been blunted. A congressional mandate to concentrate U.S. foreign aid in programs designed to help the poorest of the poor has had some unintended consequences. U.S. foreign aid to Latin America, overall the richest area of the Third World, has declined sharply. Denied this tool, many U.S. leaders, particularly in the executive branch, were also distressed to recognize that the vigorous nationalism of Latin American countries effectively raised the cost to the United States of using force to impose its will. Then, rising protectionist pressures began to limit the ability of administrations in Washington to use trade as a positive instrument of policy.

Despite vigorous efforts by the Reagan administration to refurbish some of these policy tools, the likelihood is that the United States will have to live in the future with a Latin America much less subject to its will than in the past. For the 1980s, therefore, the key problem for U.S. foreign policy in Latin America will be to manage and even to accommodate this change. Specifically, the United States will have to decide what kind of radical regimes it can tolerate in the Western Hemisphere. The effort to prevent their rise altogether will almost assuredly fail. The United States will have to find ways to meld its diplomatic efforts with those of the regional powers such as Mexico and Brazil, which now demand a much larger voice in hemispheric affairs than they sought in the past. Finally, the United States will have to accept that its overwhelming dominance in the postwar period was unique. Because the European powers were so weak after World War II, their influence in Latin America was temporarily but sharply diminished. Now they have regained their prewar strength and have returned to the hemisphere in a major way. Never again will the United States be able to formulate its policy toward Latin America without taking into account several new actors on the scene—West European friends, who again have extensive interests in the region, as well as the Soviet Union.

Sometime in the 1970s, in other words, the underpinnings of the Monroe Doctrine eroded badly without anyone calling attention to the damage. These essays plot the consequences of that fundamental change in America's hemispheric fortunes.

June 1983

Charles William Maynes
Editor, FOREIGN POLICY

WAKING FROM THE PAN-AMERICAN DREAM

by Lawrence E. Harrison

Pan-Americanism, at least under U.S. leadership as it was understood by Presidents from Franklin Roosevelt to Lyndon Johnson, is in its death throes, if, indeed, it ever lived. The ties that bind together the nations of North and South America become fewer and weaker; the policies and actions of the countries south of the Rio Grande become increasingly independent of U.S. influence. The vision of two great continents, joined by common liberal values and aspirations as well as by geography, marching hand-in-hand into a better future for all is distorted almost beyond recognition by the events of the last several years. Many idealists and pragmatists alike among U.S. observers are alarmed, feel frustrated, and are searching for explanations.

In the short run, only the most optimistic can foresee any strengthening of hemispheric solidarity. A large majority expects further deterioration. In the longer run, many think that the attitude of Latin America toward the United States will range from Third World indifference to Communist hostility. For this state of affairs, scapegoats abound: the Eisenhower Administration's lack of concern, the Kennedy Administration's lack of realism, the Johnson Administration's lack of restraint, the Nixon Administration's lack of commitment. Very rarely does one hear, however, what may be a far more accurate explanation of the disintegration of Pan-Americanism: that its basic concept is so flawed as to have assured the failure of virtually any U.S. policy in its pursuit. An appreciation of these flaws will not only help to explain the disintegration. It may also help illuminate some foundations for a new, more promising and durable inter-American relationship, but one which cannot be expected to materialize for many years yet.

Two Different Worlds

The differences between North America and Latin America are enormous, covering virtually all aspects of human life. They go deeper than geography and language. The North American and the Latin American have differing concepts of the individual, society, and the relationship between the two; of justice and law; of life and death; of government; of the family; of relations between the sexes; of organization; of time; of enterprise; of religion; of morality. These differences have contributed to the evolution of societies which are more unlike one another than our past policy-makers appear to have appreciated. In fact, it can be argued that there are some Asian societies (Japan is an obvious candidate) which have more in common with the societies of North America than do most of the societies of Latin America.

One crucial result of the disparate value structures of the two Americas has been a dramatic difference in the pace of modernization. Differing economic and population growth during the past few decades may mean that the average Latin American today is less well off compared to the average North American than he was when Franklin Roosevelt announced the Good Neighbor Policy in 1933. North America even in the Great Depression was so much more "modern" that the definition of "Neighbor" inevitably had to be a limited one. The chief significance of the Good Neighbor Policy was its rejection of the Big Stick in hemispheric relations. One cannot expect a truly neighborly relationship to develop between poverty and affluence, between traditional and modern societies. In fact, what should have at least in part been expected—and what probably in part materialized—was a new dimension of Latin-American bitterness, self-doubt, and self-reproach to add to the psychic problems precipitated by the era of intervention. Where Latin America had earlier been intimidated by the might of the United States, it now was being intimidated by North American virtue and accomplishment.

Few Americans appreciate how intimidating our culture can be for all but the most vigorous and integrated Latin-American societies. Many Latin Americans see the Colossus of the North not only in terms of physical greatness but also in terms of a super-society inhabited by supermen. And although the recently increased Latin-American awareness that the United States has its own serious problems may have attenuated the impact somewhat, the Latin American's ego is still likely to be jolted when he objectively compares conditions in his own country with those in the United States. Or, as has happened with the extreme left in Latin America, he may simply refuse to look objectively at the United States at all.

The facts are that the average North American is something like 10 times better off economically than the average Latin American; he has twelve grades of education as compared to three; and he regularly gets a chance to pursue his interests within a political system which, although at a less than ideal pace, has nonetheless demonstrated irrefutably its capacity for change. The contrast was not significantly different in 1933. Yet, the success of the Good Neighbor Policy had inevitably to depend on common values, goals, and interests.

World War II added a further artificiality to the myth of inter-American solidarity. The hand-in-hand image was transformed into a locked-arm defense of the hemisphere against Axis totalitarianism. While there was a considerable Latin-American identification with the Allied cause, there was also a twofold irony: the economic backwardness of Latin America rendered it militarily impotent, and dictatorship—in various forms and degrees, to be sure—was at the same time flourishing in Latin America, where it had found fertile ground ever since the first Latin-American countries achieved independence. The irony

was intensified by the existence of at least some Latin-American sympathy for the Axis cause. While this sympathy was principally rooted in Latin Americans of German and Italian extraction, there may also have been a more generalized secret hope for the satisfaction of seeing Uncle Sam get his nose bloodied.

It is difficult for us today to comprehend how our Latin-American policy of the 1930's and 1940's, at least in its long-term projection, could have been so out of touch with reality, so obviously based on an imagined mutuality of aspirations and interest. To some extent, the myth was probably explainable by the special romantic qualities of that period of U.S. history, qualities in some ways similar to those that appeared in the early 1960's. Perhaps the pragmatists of those years saw the reality but advocated the myth as a means of protecting our interests as they saw them. Also relevant may have been the kind of view of Latin America we were getting: through the eyes of diplomats who had never heard of Mao Tse-tung, rising expectations, or racial violence, and whose contacts were often confined to the educated, frequently English-speaking oligarchies, the military, and the clergy, all of whom had something to gain from American favors and who were prepared to pay lip service to democracy if that were the price; through the eyes of U.S. businessmen who were sometimes not above buying their way to influence and profits; through the eyes of tourists who looked at extreme poverty and injustice and saw something picturesque. Whatever the explanation, Pan-Americanism moved into the 1950's with its Northern component growing increasingly conservative, its Southern component increasingly restive, and much of the glue being supplied by alleged Soviet threats to hemispheric security, the Panama Canal, and "our way of life."

The First Taste of Reality

When anti-American demonstrations surged around Governor Nelson Rockefeller's 1969 fact-finding mission, few informed Americans were surprised. Many expected worse. Yet, when Vice President Richard Nixon made a similar trip 11 years earlier and encountered hostility and violence, the United States was shocked and incredulous. Even informed Americans were taken aback by the intensity of the hostility in an area of the world that had always been considered "safe" and "friendly."

It was alleged following the Nixon trip, and, especially, as events in Cuba grew more ominous, that "Latin America had been neglected." The United States, in attending first to the enormous problems of European reconstruction and then to an Asian land war, had forgotten its good neighbors and was paying the price—or at least so the deterioration in hemispheric relations was frequently explained.

In many ways, the deterioration had little to do with the United States. Above all else, anti-Americanism was a side-effect of a social ferment so intense and widespread that the late 1940's and the 1950's will probably be viewed as an historical watershed in Latin America: the years when, throughout the region, power started shifting leftward, at least in the sense of moving out of the hands of the oligarchy, the traditional military, and the traditional church, toward new hands—if not the hands of the masses, at least hands increasingly influenced by or catering to the masses. While the modernization process had started before, and while it was relatively advanced in a few countries, it was the post-World War II period when the process really began to take hold.

At the root of the unrest, the willingness to look for new solutions and new relationships, was the same internal malaise which had made a true good neighbor policy unattainable: extremes of injustice, poverty, ignorance, and national indignity, and the indifference of the ruling classes. The relationship of the United States to the ferment has been indirect. We provide a standard against which, consciously or otherwise, shortcomings are measured (which does not necessarily make us any more popular); our diplomacy and overseas business interests have on occasion identified us with the national power elites, who have for the most part shied away from social responsibilities in their pursuit of personal interest. And, for those who would prefer to look for the explanation of Latin America's social problems outside of Latin America, we are handy. The role of scapegoat was more justified in the case of the few countries which had suffered the humiliating trauma of U.S. military intervention. But even in these countries, the goads to revolutionary action existed before—and after—the interventions.

Because so much of the Latin-American problem is internally rooted, there is real doubt that, even if begun in the 1930's, any reasonably conceivable U.S. trade and aid programs could have deterred the ferment or channeled it into significantly less violent, less anti-American manifestations. The credibility of this assertion gathers strength when one considers how difficult it would have been to develop a constituency in the United States for a major effort in Latin America during the Depression, the Second World War, European reconstruction, or the Korean war. Some might argue that, by the time the United States had both the will and resources to mount an effort of the proportions of the Alliance for Progress, it was too late. What is indisputable is that the Alliance for Progress has failed to make Pan-Americanism a reality.

The Alliance That Stumbled

The Alliance for Progress was the expression of the first broad U.S. awareness that there was something fundamentally amiss in Latin America, something which threatened our vision of a secure, progressive hemisphere. The Alliance was one of the most idealistic and at the same time arrogant undertakings in the history of U.S. foreign policy. The Charter of Punta del Este, signed on August 17, 1961, is the complete liberal democratic, free enterprise prescription for modernization: "This

Alliance is established on the basic principle that free men working through the institution of representative democracy can best satisfy man's aspirations, including those for work, home and land, health and schools. No system can guarantee true progress unless it affirms the dignity of the individual which is the foundation of our civilization." It is a compelling, even moving declaration which Americans would do well to reread from time to time for its relevance to our own society.

However, it had limited relevance to most Latin-American societies in 1961. Parts of it may have more relevance today, and, hopefully, all of it will have more relevance tomorrow. But while the Charter of Punta del Este may have meant a great deal to the New Frontier United States, it was fashioned not for our benefit but for the benefit of Latin America. It is now clear that, for many Latin-American governments, Punta del Este was important not for its explicit liberal philosophy but for the implicit promise of major new resource flows from the United States.

It is currently fashionable to criticize the Alliance for Progress for its overambitious goals, its general lack of realism. When it comes to economic development and some aspects of social development (e.g., education, health, population growth), this criticism may be little more than carping: what was scheduled to take 10 years may take 15 or 20. But even over the longer period, the progress is still likely to be impressive and significant. What was truly naive—and arrogant—was the belief that Latin-American societies should and could be transformed into mirror images of modernized Anglo-Saxon societies *at all,* to say nothing of doing it in a period of a decade or two.

What was even more arrogant was the belief that the United States government knew so much about Latin-American societies, not to mention the development process, that it could play a major role, through carrot and stick paternalism, in bringing about the modernization of Latin America. United States

government activism and interventionism—well-intentioned to be sure—often influenced decisions involving basic questions of national policy and sovereignty for several years after Punta del Este. It is true that progress occurred during this period in Latin America, and it is also true that some of the progress was attributable to the activism of representatives of the United States government. But in many instances, the progress might well have occurred without the intervention; in some cases, the intervention backfired; and without exception, two costs had to be paid: (1) further loss of Latin America's confidence in its own capacity to solve its problems, the kind of confidence which is so closely linked to better hemispheric relations in the future; and (2) annoyance and, at worst, alienation of Latin-American officials who couldn't help but ask themselves, "Where does this representative of a foreign government get off telling my government—and me—what to do?" On occasion, the simple fact of the United States government's promoting a policy has resulted in its rejection by officials and interest groups who might otherwise be sympathetic to it.

In the Alliance for Progress, then, the United States government created (it was done largely on a unilateral basis) a mechanism which responded to our first real appreciation of Latin America's problems, but a mechanism, nonetheless, which, in its simplification of the problems and its overestimate of U.S. power to precipitate change, inevitably fell far short of what it set out to achieve.

The first U.S. Coordinator of the Alliance for Progress, Teodoro Moscoso, a person who saw the Alliance in its early years as a noble crusade and communicated that sense of purpose to his colleagues, had the following to say less than seven years after Punta del Este: "The Latin-American case is so complex, so difficult to solve, and so fraught with human and global danger and distress that the use of the word 'anguish' is not an exaggeration.

"The longer I live, the more I believe that,

just as no human being can save another who does not have the will to save himself, no country can save others no matter how good its intentions or how hard it tries. The Latin-American countries have been too dependent on the United States, while the United States has been too nosey and eager to force down the throats of its southern neighbors its way of doing things."

And, as part of his prescription for how the United States can "assist as much as it can its southern neighbors in helping them to solve their own problems," Moscoso suggests, "Extend all economic and technical aid only through multilateral agencies . . . . Dismantle the United States aid apparatus in Latin America."

To the extent, then, that the Alliance for Progress was designed to restore hemispheric harmony by modernizing Latin America along North American lines with the United States government leading the way, it has failed and will continue to fail. Nonetheless, the Alliance must be viewed as an important step forward. For the first time, U.S. policy reflected an appreciation of the need for change in Latin America if satisfactory hemispheric relationships were to be achieved. It has provided major new resources to help accelerate the process of change. It has given the United States government its first real opportunity to perceive the depth and breadth of the Latin-American "anguish" and at the same time develop some humility about our capacity to influence the process of change.

For all that, 10 years after Punta del Este, Pan-Americanism seems farther out of reach than at any other time in the history of inter-American relations.

Down the Drain

In the past, we have tended to judge relationships between Latin America and the United States on the basis of Latin America's responsiveness to or acceptance of our policies. The inter-American community we have sought has been one in which the U.S. voice would be dominant on such matters as relations with the Communist world, hemispheric trade policy, even hemispheric development policy. This is the kind of hemispheric order, so often identified as Pan-Americanism, which is in the process of going down the drain.

There is compelling evidence that the disintegration is occurring. Perhaps the most significant indicator of the past few years has been the emergence of CECLA (a Spanish acronym for the Latin American Special Coordinating Commission), a body whose principal reason for existence is to develop positions reflecting purely Latin-American interests with which to confront the developed world, and particularly the United States. CECLA came into being without the least encouragement from the United States; in fact, for those Americans clinging to the vision of Pan-Americanism, CECLA was viewed, quite rightly, as a serious threat to "hemispheric solidarity." Notwithstanding the lack of U.S. enthusiasm, CECLA has acquired a special vitality, evidenced by Latin-American enthusiasm for it and its impact on U.S. policies and programs, which suggests that CECLA is likely to be with us for quite some time.

Other inter-American institutions, in which the U.S. voice is loud—and which, in fact, were created largely at U.S. initiative—do not seem to possess CECLA's vitality and responsiveness to what Latin America sees as important in hemispheric relations. While the Organization of American States has acquired new vigor under Galo Plaza, its genesis, its role in the 1965 Dominican intervention, and the fact that it has virtually become a symbol of a U.S.-dominated hemispheric community, have tarnished its respectability in many Latin-American countries. In part because of increasing resource infusions by the United States, the Inter-American Development Bank has grown both in developmental impact and prestige over the past decade. But Chilean Felipe Herrera, its president for 10 years, was not welcome on the campuses of some Latin-American universities, in large part because of the Bank's identification with the United States.

The foreign policy of Latin-American countries is increasingly independent of ours, particularly when it comes to their relations with Communist countries. The number of Communist diplomatic and trade missions has grown rapidly over the past few years, as have trade relations. Finally, the tone of our bilateral relations has become unprecedentedly strained in the cases of Chile, Peru and, until the recent overthrow of the Torres government, Bolivia. There are few observers who expect that the trend towards increasingly difficult bilateral relationships will be stemmed, at least during the next several years.

This is not to say that U.S. relationships are uniformly bad. At least for the time being, Brazil, Argentina, Mexico, and Colombia, which together dominate Latin America in terms of population and area—and are all relatively self-assured—are more or less favorably disposed toward the United States. But even in the case of these countries, to say nothing of Chile and Peru, there is a new willingness to carry issues to a confrontation, to run greater risks of giving offense, to pursue independent foreign policies. Expropriation of U.S. investments and the seizure of fishing boats are clear manifestations of this new wave of nationalism. While the pattern of nationalism is far from uniform, the trend is apparent in most countries. The burden of proof rests upon those who foresee developments which move toward rather than away from Pan-Americanism.

Four Future Trends

The disintegration of our vision of hemispheric solidarity is viewed by some with alarm. It is argued that forces hostile to the United States will exploit the resulting vacuum, as has happened in the case of Cuba; that we will be cut off from important raw materials, markets, and investment opportunities; that we will no longer be masters in our own house.

There can be little doubt that the disintegration will carry with it—and indeed already has carried with it—costs to the United States. But there is also a chance, at least in the long run, that there will be some benefits for us, too. In fact, it is possible that from the ashes of Pan-Americanism will emerge a more rational, durable set of hemispheric relationships, one which is more consistent with our own tradition, or at least vision, of how relationships should be ordered within a community. While the parallel has to be stretched somewhat, it is not irrelevant to cite the case of our relations with Western Europe. Twenty years ago, our influence there was much greater than it is today. That does not mean, however, that the relationship today is either unhealthy or unstable, or that the old relationship is to be preferred to the new.

While only the rash would attempt to forecast developments in Latin America over the next two or three decades with any real specificity, there are certain trends for which the antecedents are sufficiently apparent as to warrant their use at least as working hypotheses:

1. *It is unlikely that the internal political changes that occur will follow a uniform pattern beyond a continuation of the general shift to the left.* Diversity is the current norm for Latin-American politics. While military governments predominate, there is considerable difference between what is happening in, for example, Peru and Paraguay. Some countries, e.g. Costa Rica, Colombia, Venezuela, may be in the process of finding durable solutions through representative democracy. The Mexican one-party experiment has proven thus far to be both lasting and capable of bringing about change. Chile searches for its solutions in the direction of a socialism which may or may not remain within Chile's democratic tradition.

Aside from the wide variety of political forms, economic and cultural factors also point toward diversity. On the basis of per capita GNP, Venezuela and Argentina are approaching the ranks of the developed countries. Haiti is as poor as some of the poorest Asian countries. The different mixes of European, Indian, and African cultures have had much to do with past diversity among Latin-American countries and are likely to influence the Latin America of the future toward diversity. Size will also contribute to diversity in national evolution: we must remember that Brazil is larger than the United States without Alaska; Argentina is almost the size of India; and El Salvador is just slightly larger than Massachusetts. It is indeed difficult to foresee any single pattern crystallizing out of this mélange beyond the continuation of the movement leftward which started after World War II. And even this general movement is likely to be manifested in diverse ways and at widely varying speeds.

2. *There are likely to be frequent political changes.* With a few exceptions, Latin America is an area of political instability. Mexico, Chile, Uruguay, and Costa Rica are the only countries that have known continuity within a constitutional framework for 20 years or more. In almost every other country there has been at least one violent change; in several countries, political violence has been commonplace. When one considers, against the backdrop of political volatility of recent years, that the process of power transfer which started in the late 1940's is, in several countries, in its incipient stage; when one reflects on the length of the road the process has to travel in many countries; and when one ponders the implications of the apparently growing gap between expectation and realization, it is difficult not to conclude that instability is going to continue to be widespread during the next few decades. The internal instability is likely to be accompanied by instability in international relations, particularly relations with the United States.

3. *Economic and social development are likely to proceed at least at the pace of the last 10 years, quite possibly faster.* Latin America is an area of ample resource endowment. The principal obstacle to development has been a shortage, at all levels of the public and private sectors, of people with the attitudes and preparation demanded by the development process. Education made important strides in the 1960's, both in terms of preparing people as well as in terms of building institutions. The institutions will be producing more and more better-prepared people in the future, and it is from these people that a more effective development process can be expected to emerge. Reinforcing this hopeful expectation are three other factors of importance: (1) Although population pressures are currently acute, family planning programs are likely to reduce perceptibly the population growth rate in several —perhaps most—countries, thereby improving chances for greater degrees of individual well-being and at the same time reducing some of the pressures for investment in social services; (2) Major technological improvements are likely to make development easier to achieve in the 1970's and 1980's than it was in the 1960's; and (3) There is at least a fair chance that regional economic integration schemes will reach levels of sophistication and efficacy which will add a major impulse to economic development as markets broaden to permit production at optimal scale.

In addition to Venezuela, whose per capita GNP already approximates $1,000, Argentina, Chile, Costa Rica, Mexico, Panama, and Uruguay could all have reached—or at least be close to—the $1,000 per capita GNP level by 1990. And most other countries could be approximately where Mexico is today (about $600 per capita). What is more, as politics drift leftward, income distribution is likely to become more equitable.

4. *Nationalism will continue to be a dominant political theme, often at U.S. expense; Latin America will look increasingly outside the hemisphere; but there is also likely to be an increasing feeling of community among Latin-American nations.* While unrest in Latin America in the past 25 years has been importantly related to social injustice, the failure of several Latin-

American countries to develop a broad national integration, and the consequent feebleness of the idea of nationhood, has also played a role. Both kinds of shortcomings have shaken the Latin American's confidence in himself, and this lack of confidence has contributed to some of the manifestations of the new Latin-American politics of the past several years: the search for new ways of organizing societies; the persistence and shrillness of calls to national unity; and anti-Americanism.

As suggested before, Latin-American anti-Americanism is probably more reasonably explained by problems internal to Latin America than by the inadequacies or provocations of U.S. policies and actions. This does not make anti-Americanism less real or less in the ascendancy. While it was confined largely to far left-wing circles in the mid-1950's, it has since spread to the moderate left, to businessmen, to the military, and to the church—surely not all elements of these sectors, but to unprecedented numbers within them.

The quest for national identity and purpose which is likely to occur over the next decades will probably sustain, if not broaden, anti-American sentiment. But there is some reason to expect that the fulfillment of this quest, with its resultant boost to Latin-American self-confidence, may reverse the tide, just as Latin America's lack of self-confidence has largely caused it to flow. Several of the countries where anti-Americanism is relatively muted are countries that have found, or are finding, a place in the sun, e.g. Argentina, Brazil, Costa Rica, Colombia, Mexico, and Venezuela. While the pattern is not sufficiently uniform to justify the axiom that national confidence is inversely proportional to anti-Americanism, there is at least some evidence that this is true.

Strengthened relations, particularly trade relations, with other areas of the world are likely to evolve, motivated in part by the psychological impediments to relationships with the United States but particularly by a wholly legitimate economic self-interest. Yet geographic and economic realities will place important limits on Latin America's ability to turn away from the United States; trade will be expanded not only with Communist countries but also with Western Europe and Japan; and it is unlikely that any of the new trading partners will develop a dominant position, except in special cases such as Cuba.

The quest for national identity and purpose is likely to be paralleled, although probably not as vigorously, by a quest for regional—Latin American—identity. The sense of regionalism, which in a way has been reborn with CECLA, and the sense of nationalism are likely to be mutually reinforcing. And while, in the short run, the emergence of subregional groupings (e.g. Central America, the Andean Group) may impede broader identification, experience with subregional groupings may make the formation of a regional grouping easier in the longer run.

If it is true that Latin America in 1990 will know less poverty, more social justice, less economic dependence on the United States, better national integration, and better regional integration, it will be an area both less troubled and more confident, an area with which a more truly neighborly relationship—a relationship more nearly of equals—should be possible.

It would be fatuous to expect that the millennium in hemisphere relations will arrive 20 years hence. The problems of Latin America will not have vanished, although they should be less acute. There may well be one or more countries which are intransigently hostile to the United States because of ideological incompatibility. There will still be great inequality between North America and Latin America. Latin America will doubtlessly still be sensitive to any suggestion of U.S. dominance or intervention. And we may still have our own problems of national integration, to say nothing of difficulties with other parts of the world. But for all that, both Latin America and the United States should be finding it easier to live with ourselves, both at home and in the hemisphere.

The Difficult Decades

At best, the relationships of the United States with Latin America over the next decade or two are going to be difficult. If it is true that significant trends are largely beyond our control, then U.S. policy-makers are going to be operating within a narrow margin of options and a wide margin of frustrations. The choices that we make can, however, influence the pace of maturation of hemispheric relationships and the extent to which additional stresses appear.

Our goal is something comparable to our relationship with Western Europe, one in which Latin America is no longer our "responsibility," one guided by enlightened self-interest. Latin America's ability to participate in this kind of community with us depends on its self-confidence, and this in turn depends importantly on its success at modernization.

The kind of U.S. policy which is likely to be most helpful will combine restraint, disengagement, and expanded assistance. The tide of nationalism is flowing in Latin America, and history and proximity dictate that its force will often be directed against the United States. Provocations are likely to increase; a failure on our part to exercise restraint will usually aggravate matters.

The United States government and its officials should give wide berth to the policy and decision-making apparatus of Latin-American governments; the recent downtrend in U.S. representation in Latin America is encouraging on this score. Disengagement is also preordained in the private sector, and U.S. investors and entrepreneurs have to reconcile themselves to a new ball game in Latin America, one which will remain open to them only if they are able to adapt to an increasingly nationalistic psychology on the part of their public sector hosts and private sector competitors. (Hopefully, both of the latter will recognize the inability of their countries to save enough to achieve adequate investment levels and will not make the adaptation impossible.)

The style of our relationships with Latin America will be particularly important. Paternalism is not going to be tolerated, nor is a language of diplomacy which communicates overtones of U.S. national power. It will be more important than ever that care be taken in the selection of our representatives in Latin America.

These are not propitious moments in the United States for liberalization of trade and expansion of foreign aid. Yet the need is no less great, and there is substantially more capacity to make good use of additional resources. While we cannot live comfortably in a poor neighborhood, we at least stand a chance in a middle-class one. We would, however, be deceiving ourselves if we concluded that, even with the end of the war in Southeast Asia and headline-gathering changes in the structure of our aid program, we are going to be able to achieve substantially more liberal trade and aid policies. Until the link between these policies and U.S. self-interest is more demonstrable—and widely appreciated in the United States—we shall have to live with more restrictive trade policies and smaller aid budgets than we might like and with the inevitable Latin-American criticism that we are not doing enough.

To some extent, trade and aid are substitutable. Because aid is always somewhat demeaning, it is preferable to find trade solutions. We would do well to press for policies which will promote Latin-American exports, in the best of circumstances within a world-wide scheme of preferences for all less-developed countries.

There will, nonetheless, be an important role for foreign aid, particularly when technology as well as physical resources must be transferred. The style of our aid-giving is highly important, and we would do well to move in the direction suggested by Teodoro

Moscoso: phase down our bilateral aid programs and increasingly channel aid resources (hopefully in greater overall amounts) through international institutions. By so doing we will attenuate a friction-inducing reminder of U.S. dominance and "superiority." We will also mitigate the problems which attend the inevitable proximity of bilateral programs to short-term U.S. foreign policy considerations, prominent among them the dilemmas which flow from our direct identification with authoritarian governments. It will then be easier for us to stand more firmly on the Charter of Punta del Este, which is, after all, where we must stand if we are to avoid the schizophrenia which comes from domestic and foreign policy values that are not harmonious. We need not and should not preach the ideological principles of the Alliance for Progress; but it must be made unmistakably clear to all that we are committed to the democratic process and to the pluralism enshrined in the Charter of Punta del Este, and that our relationships abroad as well as at home will be governed by these principles.

The "mature partnership" policy of the Nixon Administration has been frequently criticized by those who allege that the United States is turning its back on its Latin-American "responsibilities," its economic interests, and the vision of a U.S.-dominated, "safe" hemisphere. These critics do not perceive the reality of Latin America today. They cling to an illusory vision that has guided our thinking for almost two generations; and their proposals would perpetuate the errors of the last decade. Restraint and realism born of the often painful lessons of the past are being confused with inaction and apathy. It would be most unfortunate if this misunderstanding, partisan politics, or anything else detoured us from the admittedly difficult route staked out by the new policy: toward hemispheric relationships more consistent both with reality and our national commitment to pluralism.

*Can We Do Business
With Radical Nationalists?*

CHILE: NO

by James F. Petras & Robert LaPorte, Jr.

The I.T.T. documents and memoranda which Jack Anderson has published raise a number of critical issues in assessing the true nature of U.S. policy toward economic nationalists. In the Chilean case covert political action was an element of U.S. foreign policy—although there were substantial tactical differences between the C.I.A., the State Department, and the White House over the measures to be adopted and over the timing of events. Nixon's position and the measures, speeches, and behavior of the lame-duck Frei administration were intended to create economic collapse over a *protracted* period of time—while the C.I.A. and I.T.T. seemed to see that as their *immediate* goal. The political assessment in Washington of the relationship of forces in Chile appears to have been more realistic than the C.I.A.'s. The prudent course chosen—limited to economic pressure—was based on a long term strategy of political and economic attrition. Key U.S. policy-makers were and are firmly opposed to the Allende government. However they firmly rejected the "adventurist" proposals to upend Allende because they felt that a coup was premature and its failure would trigger a move to the left. This assessment was essentially correct: the abortive rightist coup leading to the assassination of the Commander in Chief of the Chilean army, General Schneider, contributed to the increase of leftist support from 36 percent in September 1970, to 50 percent in April 1971.

While the extreme "military" measures proposed by the C.I.A. and I.T.T. to policy-makers were rejected, many of the economic proposals were put into practice by private businessmen and public policy-makers. Banks have not renewed credits and/or are delaying any new decisions. Companies are not making new investments. Delays of deliveries and shipping of spare parts have occurred. Technical assistance has been withdrawn. In a word the Anderson Papers provide us with further evidence to substantiate the thesis of this paper (written before the I.T.T. memos were released) that U.S. policy was and is trying to do everything possible short of military intervention to keep Allende from succeeding.

The Chilean decision to nationalize U.S. property is the most recent direct confrontation with U.S. business interests and the most significant challenge to U.S. policy since the Cuban revolution. What happens to U.S.-Chilean relations as a result of the struggle over the Chilean copper industry will have repercussions for U.S.-Latin American relations during the rest of the decade. The Chilean situation can be viewed as a "test" of U.S. commitment to defending U.S. investors or as an "opportunity" to develop a new set of relationships with nations in Latin America as well as the rest of the world.

The recent measures taken by the government of Chile in nationalizing the Anaconda and Kennecott mining properties emerge from and are a logical extension of a pattern followed throughout the region by regimes with significant social, political, and economic differences. Rather than viewing the Chilean government's actions as sinister ideological moves engineered by Marxists, their actions should be seen as part of the regional response to deep-seated national needs to direct and control their own resources. What we are seeing in Chile is much more than the action of a single government; it is a Latin-American phenomenon with both long and short range implications for the industrialized nations of both East and West.

A great variety of regimes, with differing approaches to internal problems, have adopted nationalist measures in recent years. The modernizing Peruvian junta nationalized the International Petroleum Corporation (IPC) in 1968. The conservative Ecuadorian government seized U.S. fishing boats which violated its 200 mile limit (an action to exert control over maritime resources). The rightist as well as populist Bolivian juntas (under Ovando and later Torres) nationalized Gulf Corporation assets (1969) and a number of other U.S. owned mining enterprises. In Colombia rightist President Pastrana signed the Andean pact restricting foreign investment. In Argentina the Peronist labor unions have pressured the military to adopt a nationalist posture (buy Argentine campaigns, takeover of the Swift packing house, abstention on the China question in the U.N., friendship agreements with the Allende government, etc.). In addition, the Andean countries have signed an investment code which purports to restrict areas and terms of foreign investment. The pro-business Social Christian COPEI government of Venezuela has passed a law leading to the gradual expropriation of all major oil resources and has forced the major oil companies operating in Venezuela to accept more government control.

Meanwhile, Back in Chile . . .

When Dr. Salvador Allende Gossens was elected President of Chile in September 1970, U.S.-Chile relations entered a new phase. The Nixon Administration proclaimed that it would adopt a "low-profile," wait-and-see policy towards the Chilean "experiment" with democratic socialism, but it was not long before President Nixon announced a tough stand on expropriations, aid, credits, and other financial agreements which, while not explicitly aimed at Chile, were widely understood to be a clear warning to the new government in Santiago.

It was clear, even during the election campaign, that the United States was hostile to Allende. The American Ambassador preferred the rightist Alessandri but could have lived with the Christian Democratic Tomic.

After the election, hostility towards Allende was evident not only in the behavior of U.S. officials but also in the liberal American press, including the *New York Times*, which contended editorially on September 6, 1970, that the election was "a heavy blow at liberal democracy."

During the administration of Allende's predecessor, Eduardo Frei, the United States had presented Chile to the world as a "showcase" country—an example of what the Latin countries could do with U.S. technical and economic assistance. Chile had received the highest per capita U.S. aid of any country in the hemisphere. Chile was going to be the liberal alternative to "Castro-Communism." Now, in 1970, the situation was to change drastically.

The result, despite some internal debate in the U.S. government and the business community, seems in retrospect to have been foreordained—in favor of the hard-line conservatives. Their victory, and the implications of the anti-nationalist U.S. foreign policy, are far-reaching: an increasingly close and vastly expanded relationship with the pro-U.S. military junta in Brazil, tacit support of rightist military coups such as occurred in Bolivia, and economic isolation and pressure on nationalist governments such as the one in Chile.

Despite the appearance of a pluralistic decision-making structure with competing viewpoints, the over-all thrust of U.S. foreign policy is largely in the direction of supporting U.S. business interests abroad. Policy tends to follow the line favored by a single interest—the U.S. investor community. U.S. economic interests appear to be the only concrete, specific, and visible reference point to which policy-makers refer. U.S. corporation images of political reality have become the point from which policy-makers begin to define their positions.

Congress has increased its efforts to influence policy, but with limited success. Congressmen continue to press for specific interests—individual firms or lines of industry which have had problems with Latin governments. Congress serves as a forum for airing dissident and critical opinions, but has been of little importance except where the position of Congress coincides with that of the executive branch and the business community—in which case congressional opinion is perceived by the executive branch as a "pressure" to get things done quickly. Thus Mr. Nixon's announcement of a "hard line" on expropriations; his aides revealed that it was intended to "head off congressional action." But, as we shall soon see, Nixon's top appointees had already adopted harsh policies opposed to expropriations long before Congress had taken a poll of its own members.

Rhetorical and Symbolic Response

U.S. policy toward the democratically elected Socialist president is in stark contrast to its policy to the authoritarian military dictatorship in Brazil—toward the former unmitigated hostility, to the latter lavish praise and aid. The strategy of U.S. opposition to Allende operates on three levels of policy making: (a) an "outsider" strategy; (b) an "insider" strategy; (c) a regional strategy.

The "outsider" strategy includes basically three types of policy moves: (a) symbolic hostility; (b) veiled threats; (c) overt hostility. Symbolic hostility has taken the form of not extending to the Allende government the usual courtesies on ceremonial occasions: for example Nixon snubbed Allende after his electoral victory.

The speeches of Rogers, Laird, and Connally regarding Chile's nationalization policies have been full of threats of U.S. economic reprisals. The purpose of these speeches is to make other countries aware of possible negative reactions from the United States if they follow the Chilean route.

President Nixon and other policy-makers have repeatedly stated that the U.S. objective was to "have the kind of relationship with the Chilean government that it is prepared to have with us." Charles Meyers, Assistant Secretary of State for Inter-American Affairs, has emphatically insisted that the U.S. government has taken a neutral position, refraining from any hostile acts. More direct and serious actions have been taken to underscore U.S. displeasure toward Chile's President. Short of economic blockade a number of economic measures designed to pressure the government have been adopted; thus far, U.S. policy-makers have avoided the more extreme policies adopted vis-à-vis Cuba, such as freezing of assets and other massive global pressures.

Economic pressure on Chile has taken the form of cutting U.S. and "international" lines of credit to the Allende government. Two examples of this response present themselves. Chile's application for a small loan from the Export-Import Bank for the purchase of commercial passenger aircraft from Boeing (a U.S. firm) for the Chilean National Airlines was denied. As a result the United States has forced Chile to consider alternative European producers, perhaps a minor inconvenience. U.S. representatives within the Inter-American Development Bank reacting to threats to reduce or withhold U.S. funds to IDB because of its willingness to listen to Chilean requests for development loan funding have "delayed" Chilean requests (which has the same effect as an overt denial). U.S. AID funds have not been either requested or suggested in the case of Chile since the end of the Frei regime.

A third form of U.S. pressure on the Allende regime has been in the area of diplomatic relations between the United States and other Latin nations. This can be seen in U.S. relations with Chile's two neighbors, Peru and Bolivia. United States relations with Peru have improved considerably during the past year with State Department officials attributing the "change" to a shift in Peruvian politics from a nationalist to a more "open" position regarding foreign

investment. According to one State Department official, Peru was a "dirty word" two years ago; now that has changed. In Bolivia, the United States now has a new rightist regime which in part owes its existence to U.S. Air Force personnel who "advised" Colonel Hugo Banzer and his associates. This regime can be counted upon to facilitate U.S. policy toward Chile. With Brazil the United States enjoys close to a "model" relationship, according to State Department officials we interviewed. Brazil considers Chile's experiment with Democratic Socialism to be a "threat" to its own aspirations for regional hegemony. Thus, the Brazilian government is actively supporting U.S. efforts to diplomatically "isolate" Chile in Latin America. Given Chile's dependence on meat and grain imports from Argentina, a successful blockade in Latin America can have economic as well as political consequences over the short and long run.

The regional strategy that U.S. policy-makers are developing has two basic ingredients: (1) strengthening Brazil as a counter-revolutionary center and possible source of military intervention—if not directly in Chile at this time, at least on bordering countries (Uruguay) if they should decide to go the Chilean route; (2) isolating Chile on its borders—especially with regard to Peru, Argentina, and Bolivia. In part this strategy has already brought about some immediate payoffs: two days before Chile and Bolivia were to open relations, the U.S. military and embassy (along with Brazil and Argentina) provided logistical support, intelligence reports, and medical supplies to aid the Bolivian army in its overthrow of the nationalist-populist Torres government. The United States now has a loyal government in Bolivia led by Hugo Banzer which can increase border pressures on Chile as well as provide a passageway from Brazil through Bolivia to Chile. Regarding Peru, the United States has moved in the direction of closer relations— there are agreements on most issues which have been pending, especially since the "nationalist" Peruvian military has come around to seeing the "need" of foreign investment for economic development. If U.S.-Peruvian differences narrow, the United States may be able to push the Peruvians into a more distant relationship with Chile.

The over-all purpose of U.S. policy is to create economic dislocation and provoke a domestic social crisis that could lead to either the overthrow of the Allende government by a civil-military coalition made up of the Army, the Christian Democrats, and the extreme right-wing National Party, or the discrediting of the government and its defeat in the 1973 congressional elections, thus undercutting the basis for future changes.

The Copper Issue

The U.S. dispute with Chile over the copper issue must be viewed within this hostile atmosphere of U.S.-Chilean relations. The copper issue itself is not new—the Frei government felt compelled to begin to "Chileanize" copper—and the idea of nationalization of copper was no surprise to U.S. policymakers. Furthermore, the notion of uncompensated expropriation has precedent in other Latin contexts. The reaction of the U.S. government toward Chile can best be understood through a discussion and analysis of the attitudes of congressmen, State Department and other Administration officials, as well as policy advisers.

These include two executive agencies (Treasury and State), the Congress (Senate and House Committees and Subcommittees and individual members), the "international" banks. Also, the actions of the Chilean government trigger, in turn, further U.S. actions. Finally, the policy inputs of U.S. business—the individual firms (commercial/financial as well as extractive and manufacturing) who do business and/or have financial investment or other economic ties with Chile and other Latin American countries—have very important consequences for U.S. policy.

The Department of State

On October 13, 1971, Secretary of State William P. Rogers stated:

"The Controller General of Chile announced his findings on October 11 that no compensation would be paid for the U.S. copper mining investments expropriated on July 16 except for modest amounts in the cases of two smaller properties.

The U.S. government is deeply disappointed and disturbed at this serious departure from accepted standards of international law. Under established principles of international law, the expropriation must be accompanied by reasonable provision for payment of just compensation. The United States had made clear to the government of Chile its hope that a solution could be found on a reasonable and pragmatic basis consistent with inetrnational law. . . .

Should Chile fail to meet its international obligations, it could jeopardize flows of private funds and erode the base of support for foreign assistance, with possible adverse effects on other developing countries. . . ."

This statement, the official policy of the Department of State, is an explicit endorsement of the position of the U.S. copper companies. The State Department's claim that it holds a "position of moderation" is hardly convincing. This policy statement also obliquely refers to and warns against other countries following the Chilean example. This was the first officially stated concern not so much about Chilean actions *per se* but concerning action that might be taken against all U.S. business holdings in Latin America. Thus, the statement is clearly directed not only at Chile's ability to garner U.S. public and private loans and investment but is also directed toward other Third World countries. By wielding the weapon of economic sanctions and exhibiting the capacity to manipulate international financial funds the U.S. can, in the Secretary's words, produce an "adverse effect on the international development process."

Despite the blunt language and obvious threats explicitly stated, officials continued to argue that the State Department is the voice of reason and moderation between both Chile and U.S. decision-makers.

The State Department's influence over Administration decisions affecting Latin-American affairs appears to have been greater prior to the rise of Secretary John Connally in the Nixon Administration. Latin America was a low priority area in the eyes of most officials in the Nixon Administration. Apparently the Nixon Administration was fairly satisfied with the configuration of regimes in Latin America, in part the product of the Johnson Administration. The nationalization of U.S.-owned copper interests in Chile coincided with a shift in the Nixon Administration decision-making structure. A major part of the responsibility for Latin-American policy shifted from the State Department to the Treasury Department and Secretary Connally. To the outsider it appeared that State and Treasury were making independent policy contributions; nevertheless, it appears that even statements by Rogers were agreed upon by Connally and the Treasury officials.

While legal forms of opposition existed and while the United States can effectively apply "diplomatic pressures," U.S. officials did not feel that irreversible changes would be brought about. Not all officials interviewed agree in their evaluations of present and future prospects for Chile, Allende, or U.S.-Chilean relations. Privately, officials express a range of attitudes toward all three subjects. The negative appraisal of some State Department officials is not shared by others. Some reject the idea that the United States should "write off" Chile as a result of the nationalization of copper.

However, the "hands-off" viewpoint carries little weight in policy-making circles. The input of the State Department to the making of U.S. policy toward Chile under Allende has not been great. By their own admission, other executive department officials have "the ear of the President" and the State Department has not been frequently consulted since the copper nationalization crisis.

The Department of Treasury

It appears that the decisions as well as the decision-makers in the U.S. Department of Treasury are more closely linked to U.S. corporate and business interests than is the Department of State. In any case Treasury is more likely to articulate and defend U.S. private economic interests than other agencies within the executive branch. This is all the more significant in light of the above observations that in critical moments involving conflicts between U.S. private interests and Latin nationalist governments it is Treasury that emerges as the spokesman of U.S. policy.

According to a *Business Week* writer who interviewed Secretary Connally (July 10, 1971):

"The Secretary is especially miffed when foreign nations expropriate U.S. assets. Under his orders, U.S. representatives have taken to abstaining from votes on World Bank and other loans to expropriating countries, and Connally is forcing the reopening of debate at top levels on what U.S. policy should be. He is particularly bitter about Latin-American hostility toward U.S. investment. . . ."

What has emerged publicly is a business-oriented Secretary of the Treasury who has not been reticent about expressing opposition toward Latin-American nationalist leadership and the Chilean leadership in particular. Once policy has been defined through Connally's initiative, the State Department has moved toward the more extreme position, shedding its reservations and "flexibility."

The input of the Treasury Department to executive policy-making regarding U.S.-Chilean relations does not end with Connally's access to the President. Treasury Department officials claimed Treasury control over other public institutions (Export-Import

Bank, the World Bank, the International Monetary Fund, and the Inter-American Development Bank) in carrying out their anti-Chilean position. According to one high Treasury official we interviewed:

". . . Treasury is having an input (to U.S. foreign policy) that it hasn't had in the past. The National Advisory Council passes [on] credit programs, Export-Import Bank loans, [the] whole range of Federal Government financial activities abroad. Connally [has an] increasing input in financial aspects which other agencies sometimes tend to play down. Executive Directors of the IMF and the World Bank are both under the Secretary of the Treasury so we have a considerable punch in both of those. . . ."

Treasury control over the international public lending agencies was claimed by Treasury officials interviewed and substantiated by State Department officials.

In short, the Treasury position and input to policy regarding Chile has been to exert as much pressure on Allende as possible. The strategy of outside influence (the denial of direct loans, credits, and aid) has been directed to force a favorable settlement for U.S. business interests. Equally important has been the action taken to isolate Chile by increasing the "external" costs, thus discouraging other Latin nations from following the example.

The Congress

The range of congressional opinions concerning U.S.-Chilean relations and the copper issue appears to parallel the diversity of opinions and attitudes in the State and Treasury Departments. Congressional "hard-liners," "moderates," and a few "liberals" are present in the hearings and congressional activities concerning U.S.-Chilean relations. Up through the early part of 1972 no House position existed. Individual congressional members presented their positions and indicated their pleasure or displeasure over U.S. policy on an individual basis. Neither House nor Senate leadership has enunciated a specific policy toward Chile. Congressional activity has taken shape through committee hearings and reports and through the efforts of individual congressmen. The differences between the Senate and House membership on this issue are sufficient to warrant a separate discussion.

The Senate

An interesting facet of the Chilean copper crisis has been the extent to which some Senate liberals have responded in a very unliberal fashion. Senator Javits of New York has been especially hostile to economic nationalism not only in Chile but in other Latin American countries as well. At the same time he has been one of the most outspoken defenders of foreign investors. On May 10, 1971, Javits defended foreign investment:

"The role of private foreign investment in Latin America is one of the most pressing questions of the day, and one that must move toward resolution. . . .The lack of a logical coherent policy works to the detriment of Latin-American growth objectives. This 'no policy' approach or 'highly restrictive policy' approach—such as the one just developed by the countries of the Andean group—not only impedes foreign capital flows, but also *threatens to exacerbate the economic and political relationships between the United States and Latin America.*"

As a senator who has outspokenly supported the multinational, U.S.-based corporations, Javits represents the view that American capital should not be infringed upon even when foreign political leadership has a democratically-based consensus to limit exploitation of national resources by these corporations. The Javits' position exposes the marginal differences that exist between conservative and liberal U.S. political leadership on a key foreign policy issue. Javits' stand is indicative of the inflexible congressional posture—a position corresponding closely to that advocated by the major copper corporations. Not surprisingly, the Javits-corporate position was the one adopted by the Nixon Administration.

Other, more identifiably conservative senators chose different means of expressing their hostility toward Chilean and Latin-American economic nationalism. Their positions and attitudes, and the techniques that they advocate to intimidate the Chileans, are illustrated in the Senate debate over the U.S. contributions to the Inter-American Development Bank Fund in October 1971. Senator Byrd (I-Virginia) opened the debate by arguing that American taxpayers should no longer support the "giveaway programs that the Federal Government has engaged in over the last 25 years." Senator Dominick (R-Colorado) wanted to be assured that the U.S. control of the Bank would prevent loans going to Chile.

It was clear from this debate, however, that conservative and liberal opinion was united in the desire to take all actions necessary in support of U.S. business interests. The key question was not whether a pro-business policy was to be adopted but to select the measures which would be most *effective*.

The left-liberals in the Senate approached the Chilean situation from a different standpoint. Senators Church and Kennedy have expressed opinions and attitudes quite different from the bipartisan liberal-moderate-conservative coalition which dominated the Senate on this issue. Both Senators agree that the current government of Chile was "a decision of the Chilean people" and that the copper issue is "a matter between the companies (Anaconda and Kennecott) and the Chilean government" and not an issue in which the U.S. government should interject itself.

Kennedy has publicly gone on record in support of the present Chilean Government:

"A wise Administration policy would have recognized that the Chilean experiment in socialism had been decided by the people of Chile in an election far more democratic than the charade we saw last week in Vietnam. But the Administration response was brusque and frigid, colored by its attachment to the ideology of the Cold War. We can never know whether a more sensitive policy toward Chile might have helped to avoid the expropriation decision, which we learned of today. . . .We should halt the tendency to identify U.S. Government interests with the interests of U.S. private investment." (Oct. 12, 1971.)

The "hands off Chile" position of both Church and Kennedy, however, represents a small minority in the Senate and, for that matter, in Congress as a whole. Most senators of both parties who have spoken on this issue take the position that the Chilean expropriation of U.S. copper corporations is a "threat" to U.S. public interests and that the U.S. government must undertake all steps to ensure that these actions do not become habit-forming in other Latin-American or Third World nations.

The House

House attitudes and opinions, as a body and individually, reflect a high degree of unanimity regarding the policy the U.S. should adopt toward Latin-American governments (such as in Chile) which challenge private U.S. business interests in their countries. Given the importance of the committee structure of the House, the attitudes and opinions of members of the two House committees most involved in Latin-American policy determination—the Committee on Foreign Affairs and the Committee on Banking and Currency—demand the greatest attention. The most important hearings in the House to date have been organized by the Inter-American Affairs Subcommittee of the Committee on Foreign Affairs, chaired by Dante Fascell (D-Florida).

According to one staff member, the position of the majority of members of the Inter-American Affairs Subcommittee is "moderate"—a position and role which has "counseled moderation" to both the Treasury and State Departments as well as to other members of Congress. It has attempted, also, to preach "moderation" to the government of Chile so that Chile would not become a victim of economic "repercussions" that would certainly occur if Chile does not change its compensation policy. The difficulty with this description lies in what is, indeed, "moderate" as opposed to "immoderate." An examination of the recent Hearing on U.S.-Chilean relations, reveals that Representative Fascell is "hopeful" as well as "disturbed" by the nationalization of copper.

The Hearing included testimony and memoranda from leading executive branch officials involved in U.S.-Latin American relations, including Charles A. Meyers, Assistant Secretary of State for Inter-American Affairs, Marshall T. Mays, General Counsel for the Overseas Private Investment Corporation (OPIC), Walter C. Sauer, Vice-Chairman and First Vice President of the Export-Import Bank of the United States, and John W. Fisher, Director of the Office of Bolivian-Chilean Affairs, Bureau of Inter-American Affairs, Department of State. For the most part, the testimony of Administration officials was directed toward defending the hostile Nixon position toward economic nationalism in Latin America and Chile with terse and/or ambiguous responses to congressional queries.

The general drift of the House Subcommittee was that harsher measures should be adopted to pressure for a favorable compensation settlement. The congressmen, far from being concerned with parochial economic interests, were concerned with all U.S. private investments and the possible impact of Chilean policy.

Perhaps the final measure of House attitude toward Chile and Latin-American nationalism can be seen in the House version of the bills to fund the international lending agencies for 1972-74. The total authorization was for $1.96 billion for the World Bank, the Inter-American Development Bank, and the Asian Development Bank. The Senate approved the same dollar total; however, House amendments have forced a House-Senate conference to resolve the differences. The House amendments to the three bills require U.S. representatives to the banks to vote against loans to any nation that expropriated American property without just compensation. These amendments were very similar to the defeated Brock-sponsored amendment to the Senate bill.

The role and nature of the international lending agencies had been discussed during the Senate debate over additional funding for both the World Bank and IDB; likewise, the House discussed similar issues in its debate over similar funding proposals. What emerged was an assessment of the World Bank and the Inter-American Development Bank as transmission belts of U.S. policy. Congressional control through appropriations coupled with U.S. representation in sufficient numbers on the Boards of Directors of both institutions (40 percent in the case of the World Bank) insures that loans to countries out of favor with the United States will not be granted. The U.S. representatives on the Inter-American Development Bank, the Executive Director of the World Bank, and the U.S. representative on IDA are directly responsible to the Secretary of the Treasury.

Several recent incidents further illustrate the role of the international lending agencies (World Bank and IDB in particular) as implementers of U.S. policy. The case of Peru best illustrates this. After the Velasco government nationalized the International Petroleum Company, U.S. aid dropped from $60 million to $9 million in 1969, causing the Peruvian President to accuse the Inter-American Development Bank "of being used as a weapon of political pressure."

In terms of formal decision-making structure of the International Banks overt U.S. control is not always manifested because, as the historian Mark Chadwin has pointed out, "to date the U.S. never has voted formally against a loan request either in the World

Bank or the IDB but that is partly because the bank boards operate by consensus; issues on which there is disagreement are not brought to formal vote."

Protestations to the contrary, the public and private statements of Administration officials illustrate the degree of control that the Secretary of the Treasury has over the Export-Import Bank. His willingness to *use* this control to retaliate against countries such as Chile merely underscores the fact that political values have first priority over banking criteria in shaping loan decisions.

It is clear from the record that the "international" lending agencies are mere appendages of the U.S. government. Contrary to the preoccupation of some conservative congressmen, there is no danger that these institutions will deviate from the official, articulated, hard-line position taken by the Nixon Administration.

U.S. Business Interests

In many ways the most important input to U.S. policy-making in Latin America is that of U.S. business interests—a collage of private sector operations, major and minor, which have direct investments of between $10.4 billion and $11.7 billion in Latin America. U.S. private investments are distributed in a variety of sectors roughly corresponding to overlapping historical periods. Investment and direct ownership in extractive industries (mining and petroleum) and related service industries (utilities such as electric, other power, and telephone) was characteristic of the period up through the 1950's. In the last 20 years U.S. investors have shifted toward manufacturing, trade, and banking.

The pattern of U.S. investment for Latin America as a whole is maintained in Chile. Table I indicates the date of initial investment and the type of U.S. investment and activity in selected major industries prior to copper nationalization. It is clearly discernible from this table that pre-World War II investments were basically those in extraction of raw

materials or in basic utilities. With the end of World War II, the growth of a large internal consumer market and high tariff walls, U.S. private investment began to "diversify." The

TABLE I

Selected U.S. Firms with Majority Investment in Chile Prior to Copper Nationalization: Ranked by Date of Operation

Firm	Date of Operation in Chile	Principal Activity
W. R. Grace	1881	Transportation
Bethlehem Steel	1913	Iron Mining
Anaconda	Circa 1916	Copper Mining
First National City Bank (N.Y.)	1916	Banking & Finance
Kennecott	Circa 1920's	Copper Mining
Dupont	1920	Explosives
I.T.T.	1927	Telephone
R.C.A.	1942	Radio & Television
I.T.T.	1942	Radio & Television
Kaiser (Argentina)	1946	Iron & Steel Products
Oscar Kohorn & Co.	1948	Textiles & Fibers
Englehard Minerals & Chemicals	1955	Iron Mining
American Cyanamid	1955	Pharmaceuticals
Standard Oil (N.J.)	1959	Oil Distribution
Parke, Davis & Co.	Pre 1960	Pharmaceuticals
Chas Pfizer	Pre 1960	Pharmaceuticals
Sterling Drugs	1960	Pharmaceuticals
Armco Steel	1960	Iron & Steel Products
Mobil Oil	1961	Oil Distribution
International Basic Economy Corp.	1961	Banking & Finance
W. R. Grace	1961	Food Manufacturing
CPC International	1961	Food Manufacturing
General Motors	Pre 1962	Auto Assembly
Simpson Timber Co.	1965	Pulp & Paper
Sperry Rand Corp.	1966	Office Equipment
Singer Sewing Machine	1966	Iron & Steel Products
General Mills	1967	Food Manufacturing
Ralston Purina	1967	Food Manufacturing
Dow Chemical	1967	Petro Chemicals
Firestone Tire & Rubber	1967	Rubber Tires
Northern Indiana Brass	1967	Copper Fabricating
Bank of America	1967	Banking & Finance
Ford Motor Co.	1968	Auto Assembly
Monsanto Co.	1969	Petro Chemicals
General Tire	1969	Rubber Tires
IRECO Chemicals	1969	Explosives
Cerro	Late 1960's	Copper Mining
General Telephone & Electronics	1970	Radio & Television
Chemtex Inc.	1971	Textiles & Fibers

Source: North American Congress on Latin America, *New Chile* (California: NACLA, 1972), pp. 150-168; "Recent Developments in Chile, October 1971," *op. cit.*, p. 18; and D. Lynne Kaltreider, "A Tale of Two Interventions and Other Related Actions," unpublished paper, November, 1971.

1960's witnessed a rather wide variety of investments designed to tap and exploit the potential Chilean consumer market which had developed as a result of the boom in the copper industry during the Korean conflict. The "appetite" of the Chilean middle class for U.S.-type consumer goods is well known; investments in the 1960's reflect the attempt of U.S. firms to cash in on this Chilean tendency to use precious foreign exchange to produce middle class consumer items.

Despite the diversification of investment, the bulk of U.S. direct investment in Chile remained in the mining and smelting category (53.4 percent—see Table II). The balance of U.S. investment was in consumer-type industries (34 percent). The critical area of manufacturing accounted for only 7.7 percent with trade making up the remaining 4.8 percent.

TABLE II

U.S. Direct Foreign Investment in
Latin American Republics and Other Western
Hemisphere (Excluding Canada)

(book value at end of 1969 in millions U.S. dollars)

Percentage Breakdown by Sector

Country	Total	Mining & Smelting	Petroleum	Manu-facturing	Trans. & Utilities	Trade	Other
Latin America	11,667	11.5	26.4	34.9	5.3	11.2	10.6
Mexico	1,631	8.3	2.1	67.9	1.7	11.7	8.2
Panama	1,071	1.8	22.3	8.4	5.2	32.2	30.1
Other Central America[1]	630	1.3	24.4	17.9	20.5	6.8	28.9
Argentina	1,244	*		63.4	*	5.5	31.1
Brazil	1,633	6.1	6.1	68.1	1.5	11.5	6.6
Chile	846	53.4	*	7.7	*	4.8	34.0
Colombia	684	*	50.0	23.2	4.2	9.2	4.4
Peru	704	62.9	*	13.8	*	8.4	15.1
Venezuela	2,668	*	66.4	15.6	.7	10.3	7.0
Other[2]	554	9.0	34.3	12.1	9.9	5.9	28.7
Other Western Hemisphere[3]	2,144	26.9	30.0	12.6	3.5	4.6	22.6
Total	13,811	13.9	26.9	31.5	5.0	10.2	12.5

Latin American
Republics &
Other Western
Hemisphere

*Combined in other industries.
[1]Includes Costa Rica, El Salvador, Guatemala, Honduras and Nicaragua.
[2]Includes Bolivia, Dominican Republic, Ecuador, Haiti, Paraguay and Uruguay.
[3]Includes all of the Western Hemisphere, except Canada and the 19 Latin American Republics.

Source: U.S. Department of Commerce, *Survey of Current Business,* October 1970.

Only Peru has a higher proportion of foreign investment concentrated in the mining sector, and Chile has the lowest percentage of foreign investment in manufacturing of any Latin-American country. A nation-by-nation examination suggests that in each country foreign investment is concentrated in one sector rather than diversified throughout the economy. Taking Latin America as a

whole there appears to be a greater dispersion. This sectoral specialization, while perhaps the result of the profit-maximizing behavior of investors, leaves their investors *isolated* and vulnerable to nationalist coalitions which embrace or cross socio-economic sectors—as was the case in Chile.

Table III reveals that U.S. investments spread throughout the industrial sector remain after the nationalization drive and disinvestment that occurred since the election of Allende. These firms represent, perhaps, the type of foreign investment that the Chilean government desires, will permit, and possibly even encourage in the future. From the political standpoint, these firms are enmeshed in the sector of the economy most closely linked to the middle class and to the political opposition.

TABLE III

Remaining U.S. Investments in Chile, Not
Nationalized, Bought Out, or in Process of Buyout

Firm	Principal Activity
Continental Copper & Steel	Steel Products
Crown Zellerbach	Manufacturing
Dow Chemical	Petro Chemicals
Ensign Bickford	Manufacturing
Firestone Tire & Rubber	Rubber Tires
General Cable	Copper Fabricating
General Electric	Electrical Equipment Manufacturing
General Motors	Auto Assembly
I.T.T.	Hotels & Electrical Equipment Manufacturing
IRECO	Chemicals
Xerox	Photo Reproduction Equipment

Source: "Recent Developments in Chile, October 1971," *op. cit.* p. 18. These firms own either a part or all of their Chilean operation—they account for $75 million direct, U.S. private investment in Chile.

As a result of the long private investment ties to Chile, U.S. business groups, particularly the large copper concerns (Anaconda and Kennecott), have staged rearguard legal action in Chile attempting to receive compensation for their investments. The copper companies even will seek compensation from the U.S. government and taxpayers.

More important, U.S. copper companies may be acting to seize Chilean markets by increasing their sales from the U.S., thus driving the Chileans out of established markets.

In addition, AID loans have been extended to Yugoslavia to develop copper mines to be jointly owned with foreign investors. It is clear that the U.S. corporations will concentrate their struggle in the international commercial arena—an area where the Chileans may be at a disadvantage.

The principal lobbyist for U.S. business interests in Latin America has been the Council of the Americas—an interest group with a membership of some 210 firms representing 90 percent of all U.S. investments in Latin America. Originally, this organization was more descriptively called the Business Group for Latin America. Through formal and informal meetings at regular intervals the Council and key U.S. government officials work closely in shaping U.S. policy. The Council's activities and the ability of its members to secure sensitive decision-making positions within the executive branch of the U.S. government assures corporate representation and decisive influence over major governmental decisions in areas which affect them.

The Nixon Administration's hostile policy toward economic nationalism in Chile and Latin America is substantially shaped by officials in government who are or were the representatives of U.S. firms in Latin America.

The Council on Foreign Relations

The range of policy options open and under consideration to U.S. policy-makers was discussed at a series of meetings held by the Council on Foreign Relations (CFR) during 1971. Corporation executives, international functionaries, State Department officials as well as academics and others with an interest in Latin America attended. The free and uninhibited discussion which occurred presents an unusual opportunity to examine the position of opinion leaders from influential segments of "public opinion."

The general impression left after a reading of the CFR "confidential" minutes (which were published in the *Newsletter* of the North American Congress on Latin America) is the lack of any innovative thinking and of any coherent proposals to meet the key problems discussed but hardly explored in any depth. The participants did not pose any specific alternative policies to confront the problems of mass marginality, dictatorship, the growing gap between the United States and Latin America, and the failure of the Alliance for Progress, nor did most of the participants seem to understand the dynamic forces underlying the growth of the nationalist challenge. The best that some of the participants could come up with was either a return to a revised version of dollar diplomacy or a policy of "disengagement." The few participants with a relatively clear set of ideas around which to focus U.S. policy were mostly the executives from private corporations—they defined U.S. policy and interests in terms of promotion and protection of U.S. business and more specifically corporate investments in Latin America.

A spokesman for Standard Oil called for overt direct action: "The U.S. should frankly acknowledge the role of senior partner and should take some initiatives." He then went on to suggest the establishment of "international" machinery to defend private investments as well as a unilateral policy which would not tolerate "economic aggression." More specifically, he urged that "U.S. policy should aim at protecting and promoting U.S. interests (investments) in the region but within an international context." Underlying the corporate viewpoint was a general malaise and growing discontent with the behavior of Nixon's foreign-policy-makers: U.S. policy was attacked as being the "antithesis of protector and promoter of U.S. interests"; the government was accused of being "passive" toward Chile and Peru, Nixon was attacked for not encouraging U.S. investment where it was not welcome (presumably the implication is that Nixon should make the proper political arrangements in Latin America *to make* investment welcome). Rather than using the inter-American councils as active instruments to promote and protect U.S. interests, the U.S. representatives are perceived as "passive." Projecting current problems in Latin America into a global context, the corporate spokesman warned that failure to act against nationalization in Latin America could generate a "ripple effect" in other areas—a point of view taken up and supported by others during the discussion. A spokesman for the State Department suggested sanctions against uncompensated expropriation, fearing the "demonstration effect of Peruvian and Chilean actions on the rest of Latin America." Most government advisors—public and private—felt that the Latin Americans perceived the United States as "wavering as to whether it will take up the cause of private investors." An executive from Standard Oil called for the U.S. government to "make its position clear before incidents arise."

On January 19, 1972, Nixon announced the tough U.S. stand on expropriations, backing the strong position advocated by the overseas investors and their supporters in the Treasury and State Departments. The Nixon announcement terminated loans and aid to countries nationalizing U.S. property. The proviso calling for "prompt, adequate and effective compensation" is a euphemism for opposition to nationalization since few, if any, underdeveloped countries have large sums of hard currency available to divert from socio-economic development to U.S. corporations. The key passage of Nixon's speech reads:

"When a country expropriates a significant United States interest without making reasonable provision for such compensation to United States citizens, we will presume that the United States will not extend new bilateral economic benefits to the expropriating country unless and until it is determined that the country is taking reasonable steps to provide adequate compensation or that there are major factors affecting United States interests which require continuance of all or part of these benefits."

The gradual escalation of U.S. pressures against economic nationalism in Chile took a new turn when a U.S. court in New York blocked the bank accounts of 14 Chilean agencies. Despite Chile's agreement to pay over 90 percent of the Kennecott debt which had purportedly caused the attachments, the Federal judge refused to lift attachments against nine Chilean enterprises. Chile's agreement to pay the enormous debts incurred by past regimes has led to efforts to renegotiate the payments schedule. Once agreeing to renegotiation, Chile has become increasingly vulnerable to external pressure which may have adverse internal social, economic, and political effects on the Allende government. For example, part of the price Chile has to pay to obtain refinancing of her debt is the agreement to allow the International Monetary Fund to periodically "review" Chile's monetary, credit, and trade performance. Part of an IMF "review" are "recommendations" that usually include credit and wage freezes, which if not heeded by the host country can result in an unfavorable "review" and new credit restrictions. If past experiences are any indication, Chile's acceptance of IMF recommendations could lead to undermining the Allende government's social basis of support. The involvement of the IMF in Chilean politics along with the blocking of the Chilean accounts in the U.S. reinforce the notion that the Chilean government is being economically encircled in order to create the necessary and sufficient conditions for the internal opposition to take power.

What Low Profile?

Dominican-style "gunboat diplomacy" has been replaced by "credit-diplomacy"—for now. The low profile approach suggests that U.S. policy-makers will give increasing importance to indigenous military elites and oppositionists in dumping the economic nationalists; this has already occurred in Bolivia and more recently in Ecuador. By confining themselves to maintaining credit pressure from the outside, U.S. policy-makers allow their national allies inside the country to mobilize on internal issues—a strategy which appears to be paying off in Chile.

The more immediate experiences concerning U.S. policy and overseas investment suggest that when a crisis situation emerges—when a major U.S. investor group in a Latin country is endangered—there is an increasing convergence of U.S. government and business responses. Once the crisis passes the two major interests may diverge. The overlap in policy is largely a result of the career patterns and prior socialization of many of the leading policy-makers; individuals who have come from corporate or corporate-related careers and/or who may be headed for such a career, but who in any case share many of the key beliefs associated with business enterprise ("foreign private investment is essential for the development of underdeveloped countries"—and similar beliefs).

Whatever the value of any particular enterprise affected by economic nationalism, it has been shown how U.S. policy-makers have a tendency to view the particular problem from the standpoint of the impact on the whole overseas investment community. Hence, the constant preoccupation not only of high Administration officials but of seemingly "parochial" congressmen with the so-called "ripple effect."

U.S. policy-makers perceive the real challenge to be neither the Soviet Union nor China but economic nationalism and social revolution in these Third World areas under U.S. hegemony. Thus, while the U.S. policy-makers propose an opening to China they heighten pressures on Chile and the rest of Latin America. While the U.S. "opening" toward China is a major new development in U.S. foreign policy, the objectives are not very different: recognition of a Great Power is the first step toward mutual agreement in defining traditional spheres of influence. It is within this framework that we can under-

stand why the United States can open relations with the major Asian Communist power, China, but not with revolutionary Cuba. We can also understand why the United States plans to increase trade with an authoritarian Communist regime in Asia while limiting credits and eliminating loans to a parliamentary, Democratic Socialist government such as governs Chile.

Despite the hostility of U.S. policy-makers and private investors toward economic nationalism, there are important factors which should encourage some restraint on U.S. public activities. The large foreign debt which Latin nations (including Chile) owe to U.S. financial institutions is a double-edged sword; while it provides the creditor nation leverage to pressure for favorable policies, it also provides the debtor nation with a bargaining weapon which can be expressed in the form of a threat to repudiate the debt and thus influence important financial interest groups in the creditor country. Conservative but prudent bankers who still have hopes of recuperating their loans may wish to moderate the extremist demands of U.S. private investors whose properties have been nationalized. While the non-nationalized U.S. economic groups continue to have an economic stake in Chile and feel that there is some hope for partial or total recovery, it is to be expected that bargaining, negotiation, and some agreements can be reached regarding specific areas. More specifically, it is likely that Chile will be allowed to refinance the debt in exchange for guarantees that the Allende government will make prompt, complete payment. Thus, within a framework which locks U.S. private interests and government in combat with Latin-American economic nationalists, the possibility of short-term arrangements are possible and probable, given the loss of U.S. omnipotence in this hemisphere and the emergence of somewhat "durable" nationalist regimes in Latin America.

THE CHALLENGE OF VENEZUELAN OIL

by Norman Gall

Each year we, the countries which produce coffee, meat, tin, copper, iron or petroleum, have been handing over a larger amount of our products in order to obtain imports of machinery and other manufactured goods, and this has resulted in a constant and growing outflow of capital and an impoverishment of our countries. . . . To cite the particular case of Venezuela, petroleum prices showed a steady decline for many years, while our country was obliged to purchase goods from the United States at ever-higher prices, which, day after day, restricted even further the possibilities of development and well-being for Venezuelans. The establishment of the Organization of Petroleum Exporting Countries (OPEC) was a direct consequence of the developed countries' use of a policy of outrageously low prices for our raw materials as a weapon of economic oppression.
—President Carlos Andrés Pérez of Venezuela, September 24, 1974.

With these words in an open letter to President Ford, published as a full-page advertisement in *The New York Times* last fall, the new President of America's leading foreign supplier of oil hurled a now familiar challenge to the United States. But the nation was not in the Middle East; the Israeli question was not remotely a consideration; and the nation in question, Venezuela, has traditionally been regarded by the U.S. and Latin-American Left as a strategically vital province of U.S. imperialism.

Within a few months, Venezuelans are expected to nationalize their oil industry. How successfully they do it—the exact details and the nature of the relationships which come into being after nationalization—may help decide the degree of future U.S. dependence on Middle East oil, the structure of the international petroleum industry, and the prospects for democracy in Latin America.

For years, Venezuela has played an important role in the formation and growth of the oil cartel, OPEC. As an outsider, Venezuela was to play a leading role in unifying the squabbling states of the Middle East. Despite her backwardness in other respects, Venezuela had a far more sophisticated and progressive political leadership that the other states that formed OPEC.

A "Devilishly Difficult" Problem

It is one of the many ironies of the present oil panic that OPEC might never have come into being if the United States had protected Venezuela from the economic hardship resulting from the oil import quotas imposed by the Eisenhower Administration in 1959 to protect domestic producers and the oil majors against the flood of low-cost Middle East crude then glutting the world market. Venezuela was then emerging from a decade of military dictatorship in an economic slump that grew out of the U.S. recession of the late 1950's, aggravated by a loss of oil revenues due to the price-cutting in the Middle East. In this atmosphere Venezuela spent much of the 1960's pleading with Washington for "hemispheric preferences" for access to the U.S. market along lines similar to those given Canada. Indeed, at one point, President Rómulo Betancourt (1959-1964) thought that he and John F. Kennedy had worked things out. Kennedy "promised me that this Venezuelan aspiration for preferred entry to the U.S. market would be satisfied before the end of his mandate and mine," Betancourt recalled. "He told me the problem was 'devilishly difficult' because of the special interests involved. But he assured me that justice would be done to Venezuela." [1] The gunshots of Dallas left this explicit promise unfulfilled.

To the credit of Venezuela's young democracy, never has the public debate over nationalization of a great extractive indus-

---

[1] *Rómulo Betancourt, "Un recurso energético que no tiene igual,"* Visión, *February 12 & 26, 1972.*

try taken place in a more open and peaceful political climate. The possibility of nationalization, distantly contemplated for about 1984 when most of the concessions were due to expire, became an imminent reality with the October 1973 war. The discussion intensified greatly after the war and the landslide election, two months later, of Carlos Andrés Pérez as President of Venezuela. Since then, Venezuela has moved to nationalize its oil and iron industries and take a leading role in hemispheric politics.

The main question is no longer whether Venezuela will nationalize, but what the future modus operandi of the oil industry will be. The central issue of the nationalization debate is whether at least some of the 16 foreign companies—Exxon and Shell subsidiaries alone account for more than 80 per cent of Venezuelan production—will be allowed to remain in Venezuela as operating or marketing contractors to the new state holding company, Petroleos de Venezuela, in return for some share of future production, or whether the government will try to run the industry itself. Some companies have been quietly trying to play upon the percolating fears of mismanagement and to promote jobs for their employees in the future state marketing organization. This would give the present concessionaries more leverage in the future production of a nationalized industry. Expecting some kind of amicable dissolution of the old concessions, companies seem less interested in indemnification for installations already heavily amortized and depreciated than in some role in the Venezuelan industry's future.

At stake is the most important source of non-Arab oil for the United States, a source that becomes all the more critical during periods of threatened or actual embargo. And, as in the past, developments in Venezuela may affect events elsewhere.

Democratic Solidarity

Venezuela became the world's leading oil exporter in 1929, and held this position for the next four decades. Since the end of the long dictatorship of Juan Vicente Gómez (1908-1935), oil and democracy have been closely linked in their development.[2] The flow of oil money into the cities has generated such enormous urban-rural income differentials that the countryside has been depopulated in one of the most intense internal migrations of this century, transforming Venezuela from a nation that was nearly 80 per cent rural in 1920 to one 80 per cent urban today. Meanwhile, Venezuela has moved fitfully toward creation of a complex and broadly based social democracy, with the economic leavening of oil revenues.

Venezuela received especially gentle and considerate attention in Washington after Mexico kicked out the foreign oil companies in 1938. Venezuela became a primary target for the Good Neighbor policy, and the State Department put heavy pressure on the oil companies to make their policies and personnel less offensive to Venezuelans, as well as to give in to Venezuela's demands for more oil money in order to avoid a repetition of the Mexican nationalization. By the 1960's, democratic solidarity had developed to the point where the Kennedy Administration viewed Venezuela as a test of its own hopes for the Alliance for Progress, and, later, as its only clear success in promoting reform, counterinsurgency, and private investment in Latin America.[3]

When Betancourt became the first popularly-elected ruler in Venezuela's 150-year republican history to finish his constitutional term of office, it was a triumph of his own

[2] *For a view of this relationship and of the structural weaknesses in Venezuelan society that have impaired the rational use of oil revenues, see my* Oil and Democracy in Venezuela, *American Universities Field Staff Reports, East Coast South America Series, Vol. XVII, Nos. 1 & 2, 1973.*

[3] *The Roosevelt and Kennedy policies toward Venezuela contrasted strongly to the official decoration given dictator Marcos Pérez Jiménez by Secretary of State John Foster Dulles in 1954 at the Caracas conference of the Organization of American States. However, the medal was awarded to the dictator over the objections of high State Department officials and only at the insistence of the U.S. military that anti-Communist rulers in Latin America must be given visible support.*

tenacity and of the people's awakening democratic vocation. To do this, Betancourt had to survive armed insurrections from the Left and the Right. He put down an outbreak of guerrilla warfare far more sustained and bitterly fought than Fidel Castro's Cuban insurrection. Two of his aides were killed and his own hand mangled in a 1960 assassination attempt by henchmen of Dominican dictator Rafael Trujillo, who rolled a car full of explosives into Betancourt's motorcade. This attempt was one of the considerations that led Washington to allow the CIA to supply arms to the men who killed Trujillo in May 1961.[4]

Venezuela Forms OPEC

As Venezuela's internal violence escalated, Betancourt's Minister of Mines and Hydrocarbons, Juan Pablo Pérez Alfonzo, was traveling in 1960 among the capitals of the Middle East to persuade the rulers of the oil-producing nations to form OPEC to defend their economies against the price-slashing being carried on by the companies and to find markets for the low-cost crude that was flooding the international oil trade in ever-increasing quantities. Pérez Alfonzo knew that only control of supply would enable Venezuela to influence price levels. If the oil-producing countries could unite, then the power of the integrated majors could be curbed. Later, a bargain could be struck with the United States and Canada to parcel out the hemispheric oil trade, giving Venezuela more security of access to its main markets.[5]

When Betancourt and his Acción Democrática (AD) party first ruled Venezuela in a reformist regime in the 1945-1948 period, the imaginative Pérez Alfonzo already had achieved much toward reversing the tendency of the oil companies to enrich rulers rather than governments. Under his leadership, Venezuela in 1947 pioneered establishment

of the 50-50 principle of profit sharing between companies and governments. AD governments in the 1940's and again in 1959 were the first among the oil-producing countries to formulate a policy of "no more concessions" to foreign companies. Trying to prevent her higher tax-paid costs from making her oil uncompetitive in world markets, Venezuela, in the late 1940's, began explaining to Middle East governments the terms of her new 50-50 deal with the companies, which led to the establishment of the 50-50 principle there as well.[6] By then, Venezuela had become so important to Jersey Standard (now Exxon) that half of its worldwide profits in 1948 were generated by Creole Petroleum, its Venezuelan subsidiary and the world's largest producing company, which supplied the crude for half of its worldwide refining capacity.[7]

The financial concessions that were wrung from the major companies by the host governments in the 1940's and 1950's, under Venezuela's leadership, did not disrupt the majors' cartel-like marketing arrangements, but only began a continuing escalation of the producing countries' share of the companies' profits. The next major mutation in the system came in 1960 with the formation of OPEC in response to the price erosion of the late 1950's. The U.S. import restrictions had created such an oil glut on the world market that British Petroleum (BP), with an oversupply of crude and rela-

---

[4] See my "How Trujillo Died," The New Republic, April 13, 1963.

[5] See Franklin Tugwell, The Politics of Oil in Venezuela (Stanford: Stanford University Press, 1975).

[6] *The Iranian Ambassador to Caracas, Manoucher Farmanfarmaian, who was Iran's Director-General of Mines in 1949, recently told a meeting of the Inter-American Press Association that the 1949 Venezuelan mission to Teheran "opened our eyes, showing us and discussing the contracts between Venezuela and the oil companies that were based on the 50-50 principle. This was the first time Iran got to know about these contracts. This shows how much influence the companies had. . . . In the following years, the Venezuelan system became our goal. The 50-50 was our objective but the resistance was so tenacious that finally there was no other solution but to nationalize."*

[7] *See "Creole Petroleum: Business Embassy," Fortune, February 1939, p. 180. The 87 cents per barrel earned by Creole in Venezuela compares with the return for the seven majors of 78 cents for lower-cost Middle East oil in 1957, during the post-Suez oil emergency.*

tively few marketing outlets of its own, unilaterally cut prices in 1959 for Iran, Kuwait, and Qatar production. Since the British government was then the majority shareholder in BP, the Venezuelan government addressed a memorandum on the price cuts to the British Embassy in Caracas, arguing:

> BP, the largest producer in the Middle East, has by this action brought prices below the 1953 level. Since that year, all the factors affecting production cost have increased substantially and the general level of prices in international trade has also risen. In the United States, the largest world producer, not only did costs rise, but the country also failed to discover sufficient oil in the past two years to replace the production of that period. The United States appears to have reached the depletion curve within a relatively short time, and other important producing centers of this irreplaceable natural resource will also reach a similar situation. In general, the costs of exploration and drilling are increasing throughout the world and the more widely dispersed the search to find new reserves for human needs, the more each new barrel will cost . . . the additional lowering of prices, by encouraging consumption, could very soon bring oil to the historic cycle of scarcity. This would force consumers to pay much higher prices to finance the exploration and discovery of new areas. It is evident that for the good of mankind, a stable situation would much better guarantee the interests of all concerned.[8]

Pérez and Oil

Since then, despite recurrent political crises, Venezuela has gone far toward consolidating her constitutional democracy. Today, flush with oil money and votes, President Carlos Andrés Pérez has embarked on a series of popular domestic reforms, including general wage increases, under special powers given him by his AD majority in Congress. A tough Andean politician who, as Betancourt's Interior Minister, had taken the lead in crushing the Castroite guerrilla insurrec-

tion of the 1960's, Pérez became a prime mover behind the efforts to end the Organization of American States' diplomatic sanctions against Cuba last November. Failing to marshal the two-thirds majority needed to lift the sanctions, Venezuela then established diplomatic relations with Cuba, and, in other actions, championed higher prices for Latin-American primary products.

Venezuela is also trying to use her excess oil income to finance more rapid economic development in Latin America. After the tripling of her oil revenues between 1973 and 1974, Venezuela is recycling abroad more than one-third of her trade surplus, or about one-tenth of her whole GNP, in $500 million loans to both the World Bank and the Inter-American Development Bank, and in another $125 million distributed among the Andean, Central-American, and Caribbean development banks. Another $500 million was lent to the International Monetary Fund's oil recycling facility. Discussions are being held for lesser projects like financing a paper factory in Honduras, and an oil refinery in Costa Rica. This is more public money than the United States ever committed to the Alliance for Progress. In December, President Pérez met with the six Central-American presidents in the Venezuelan iron and steel center of Puerto Ordaz to announce that Venezuela would pay up to $80 million to Central-American coffee producers to enable them to withhold part of their crops from the market in an effort to support declining prices. Pérez announced that the six republics would only have to pay $6 of the $12 selling price of Venezuelan oil in dollars. The rest could be paid in local currencies into counterpart funds for soft loans such as those the United States made for decades to countries like India and Bolivia in the Food for Peace program.

In this way, Venezuela was able to advance her long-cherished ambitions for influence in Central America, and project her image throughout the Caribbean. A leading Dominican economist wrote recently that

---

[8] *The memorandum was reproduced in* Venezuela and OPEC *(Caracas: Imprenta Nacional, 1961), p. 99.*

"1974 probably represents the close of a period that began in 1961, of great dependence of our country on the United States, and unfortunately the beginning of another period of economic dependence on Venezuela and other nearby oil producers." [9]

Venezuela's oil power gave President Pérez center stage in Lima, at the December celebration of the 150th anniversary of the Battle of Ayacucho that won independence from Spain, where he urged the assembled military dictators of Bolivia, Panama, and Peru, and envoys of other Andean nations, to stop squabbling in ideological and border disputes. It also helped him in seeking to transform Venezuela into a democratic counterpoise to the influence of Brazil's military regime in Latin America and into a champion of economic justice for all underdeveloped countries.

Crisis of Democracy

But Pérez's trendy Third World rhetoric and some policy initiatives of his first year disguise much Venezuelan discomfort about how the oil revenues of the past two decades were wasted. How can they now absorb the much greater flood of oil money into what is essentially a rentier economy—some $10 billion in 1974, which is triple normal budgetary needs? Venezuela entered the 1973 election campaign in a mood of crisis due to the erosion of public faith in the parties that have run the country since the overthrow of dictator Marcos Pérez Jiménez (1948-1958).[10] The two big parties, AD and the Social Christian COPEI party of President Rafael Caldera (1969-1974), were able to dominate the election only through lavish advertising and by

---

[9] *Bernardo Vega, "1974: Año del Cambio en Nuestra Dependencia Económica Externa," in* Listín Diario, *November 22, 1974.*

[10] *The Kennedy Administration extradited Pérez Jiménez from his Miami exile in 1963 at the request of the Betancourt regime. He was finally released from jail in August 1968 and went to live in Madrid. Four months later, he ran, in absentia, for a Senate seat in Caracas, sweeping all but one of the city's 16 parishes. He gained the most votes in the poor workers' districts, where people had poured into the streets to overthrow him a decade earlier.*

changing the constitution a few months before the balloting to rule out a possible presidential candidacy of the ex-dictator, who had made a sensational political comeback in the five years since his release from jail for stealing public funds. The Yom Kippur war and the overthrow of Chilean democracy occurred within three weeks of each other at the height of Venezuela's election campaign, providing at once the economic impetus for oil nationalization and concern among Venezuelan leaders for the consequences of mismanagement of nationalized industries as under Allende. Many responsible Venezuelan politicians realize that their democracy could be washed overboard by incompetent handling of the nationalized oil industry or the tidal wave of oil money now pouring into the country. As Pérez himself said in a speech in Maracaibo three weeks after sending his public message to Ford:

> We have immense economic resources that the economy cannot absorb. We have the traditional and insatiable voracity of public spending, and the negligence with which the public and private sectors have used oil income. We are either at the beginning of an ascent toward consolidation of our nationality, or at a precipice that could leave us, not in catastrophe, but at a point back where we would have to start our development all over again.

In the same speech, Pérez attacked mismanagement of the state petrochemical industry, in which Venezuelan governments over the past two decades have invested roughly $2 billion, much of which has been squandered because of corruption and political interference. The new President said that, in its first six months of operation, the huge El Tablazo petrochemical complex near Maracaibo had some 50 breakdowns "from deficiencies in diligence and supervision." Previously, audits of the costs of building the $92 million El Tablazo complex found suppliers' and contractors' overcharges variously estimated at $20 million and $35 million. A few days after Pérez's speech, the head of the state petrochemical industry was fired amid charges of price-rigging that allegedly cost the Venezuelan government $3 million in a deal with a U.S. firm.

Venezuela's difficulties in developing her state petrochemical industry, and in managing other state enterprises, have led to considerable self-doubt as she develops plans to nationalize oil, which before 1973 produced 90 per cent of her foreign exchange earnings and two-thirds of her government income, and today produces much more of both. While Venezuelan politicians have been talking for nearly four decades now about "sowing the petroleum" to diversify the economy, and despite widely publicized investments in modern infrastructure, heavy industry, agricultural development, and social programs, Venezuela has become more rather than less dependent on her oil revenues. The decision to immediately nationalize the oil and iron industries came in the weeks before and after the December 1973 elections, when the Arab oil boycott stimulated leaps in the posted price of Venezuelan crude to $14.08 per barrel, compared with the January 1973 price of $3.10. Although Venezuela's two big parties, AD and COPEI, had quietly agreed not to debate oil issues in the election, all but one of the 14 presidential candidates in the race had vaguely backed an "early reversion" of the industry to the state before the scheduled expiration of the concessions.

Doubts about Nationalization

Pérez began fulfilling this promise in May by appointing a 36-man Presidential Commission on Oil Reversion, representing the full range of political parties, professional associations, universities, and business and labor groups concerned with nationalization. As it was working on a draft nationalization bill last November, one member, Carlos Alberto Piñerua, president of the oil workers' union FEDEPETROL, expressed the growing nervousness of both politicians and the public over nationalization when he told me: "This is a kind of forced nationalization because of what is happening in the

Middle East. Without the rise in oil prices, Venezuela would not have moved so swiftly. The oil companies have started a campaign to frighten workers about the future. There is much more fear among the engineers and white-collar people than the workers, who want to conserve their social benefits, as well as technology and markets for Venezuelan oil production."

Pérez will be under great pressure to articulate policies in line with the conservative nature of his electoral mandate, with the feeling that Venezuela's rentier economy depends on one commodity that Venezuelans, lacking sufficient organizational and technological capacity, know they cannot produce and market alone. Many politicians privately say that the movement to nationalize comes not from any public clamor, but from pressures from within the smaller community of politicians, and from recent dramatic changes in the oil industry outside Venezuela.

Alternative to Middle East Oil?

One of the stakes is the degree of future U.S. dependence on Middle East oil. While Venezuela was overtaken in the ranking of oil exports by Iran in 1970 and Saudi Arabia in 1971, she remains the leading oil supplier to the United States. In 1973, Venezuela produced 35 per cent of net U.S. imports, mainly as heavy fuels for heating and electric utilities along the Eastern Seaboard.[11] However, Venezuelan production peaked at 3.7 million barrels daily (MBD) in 1971 and, according to both government and company projections, is expected to decline to below 2.0 MBD by 1984 from presently existing fields, mainly around Lake Maracaibo, many of which have been operating continuously for more than 50 years. This process of natural decline of the traditional producing areas has been temporarily obscured in 1974 by the conservationist production cutbacks of about 11 per cent of a government swim-

---

[11] *This includes the heavy oil exported by Venezuela to Canada's maritime provinces, offset by oil exported by Canada to the U.S. north central states.*

ming in oil revenues it cannot use. These cuts were made at the suggestion of the companies, which told the government that world demand had declined at the 1974 price.

If current predictions of rapid decline in Venezuelan oil production come true, then the United States will have to search elsewhere for supplies of heavy oil for her largest energy market, the Eastern Seaboard, or revert to greater use of coal. If the controversial conversion to coal is not made immediately, and the United States continues to rely on oil imports for its needs, then the international rivalries for access to Middle East oil may intensify. While world oil consumption continued its rapid rise over the past decade at an annual rate of 7.7 per cent, the volume of oil moving in world trade during the 1963-1973 period rose even faster, at 10.8 per cent annually. Because of steep rises in domestic demand, the role of U.S. oil imports since 1970 in world oil trade expanded even more dramatically, at more than twice the rate of international oil sales in the rest of the world. Between 1972 and 1973, U.S. imports rose by nearly one-third—to 6.2 MBD—while the volume of imports from Arab countries nearly doubled.

The relative immunity of the United States from the economic consequences of political convulsions in the Middle East has been based largely on U.S. domestic production and Venezuelan oil, both of which were taken for granted. Just as in the U.S. domestic oil industry, supplies from Venezuela are imperiled by the exhaustion of the reservoirs that have been producing now for several decades. Moreover, the anticipated production declines in Venezuela could be greatly accelerated by mismanagement of politicization of the nationalized industry. On the other hand, productivity could remain high if certain conditions are created. These are efficient management of the industry, and effective short-term investments in secondary recovery—gas and water

reinjection systems to maintain underground pressure in the older wells. These investments in high-cost recovery techniques have become more attractive after the tripling of Venezuela's oil prices during 1973. Moreover, any major exploration program probably could enable Venezuela to remain an important exporter at least for the rest of this century. To develop these new production possibilities soon, new tradeoffs will have to be devised to provide incentives for Venezuela, already overflowing with oil revenues, to at least maintain present production levels.

The strategic value of Venezuelan oil to the United States was again illustrated during the 1973 Arab oil boycott. Exxon's worldwide production of 6.3 MBD was cut by 20 per cent between the third and fourth quarters, but her 48 per cent share of Venezuela's 3.5 MBD production flowed normally to the United States. According to Exxon's 1973 annual report: "Supplies of heavy fuel oil . . . were not affected as seriously by the Arab embargo. Virtually all of Exxon USA's heavy fuel oil supplies are imported from refineries in Venezuela and the Netherlands Antilles operated by Exxon's affiliates. . . . Venezuelan crude supplies utilized in these refineries were maintained at normal levels." On the other hand, the tripling of the price of Venezuelan heavy fuel oil has had a major economic impact on the Eastern Seaboard.

Geologically speaking, there are promising prospects offshore in the Caribbean, in the 150-mile-wide delta of the Orinoco River, and in the Gulf of Venezuela, which is practically contiguous—separated only by a strait and some sandbars—to the great oil-producing basin of Lake Maracaibo. Apart from these conventional oil prospects, Venezuela contains one of the world's largest petroleum reserves in the Orinoco Tar Belt, estimated by geologists to contain 700 billion barrels of heavy oil. If only 10 per cent of the volume were recoverable, Venezuela could produce, from this basin alone, five times her present reserves. Because this heavy Orinoco oil contains large amounts of nickel and vanadium, new technologies will have to be developed for large-scale lifting and refining operations by the 1990's. However, though the problems may be formidable, they may be less costly than producing oil from Colorado shale or Canada's Athabasca tar sands—the other major prospective sources of nonconventional oil in the Western Hemisphere.

The Future of the Majors

Beyond its role in determining the degree of future U.S. dependence on Middle East oil, the Venezuelan oil nationalization also may help shape the way the major oil companies will operate over the next few decades. Last November I talked with the government's chief economic negotiator, Manuel Pérez Guerrero, a soft-spoken, fragile-looking former Minister of Mines, who was one of OPEC's leaders in the mid-1960's. He said:

> We want this nationalization to be acceptable as an act of sovereignty within the law. Our greatest political problem is management capacity. We will need help from foreign technologies, but the reins of the business must be in our hands. We are not nationalizing buns and cakes, but important strategic commodities that cannot be left entirely in the baker's hands. We will be the owners and must make the basic decisions ourselves. We feel an obligation not to bring about any upheavals, nationally or internationally. . . . Under these new conditions, the major companies will be reduced to the role of traders, intermediaries, refiners, and providers of technical services. This is no small thing, but much less than before, when they had what seemed unlimited supplies of crude under their exclusive control. We must force the majors to be more aboveboard than secretive, and this will be good for the industry and the world.

In the worldwide wave of oil nationalizations that began in 1971 and is expected to reach its climax this year, two-thirds of the production of the seven major oil companies outside North America, or an amount roughly equivalent to more than half of the 34.1 MBD that moved in world trade in 1973, will be taken from the proprietary control of these companies with the end of the old concession system. Although much of this oil will continue to move through the majors' marketing network as a result of new production and purchase agreements with the exporting countries, the security of abundant and low-cost supply that was the basis of an integrated industry now may be a thing of the past. Saudi Arabia, Venezuela, and the Persian Gulf sheikdoms, with a combined 1973 production of 15.8 MBD, are expected to announce the terms of their state takeovers this year. With the old structure of the international industry badly shaken, today's high prices and the insecurity of future supplies have made the oil contingencies less of a question of entrepreneurship and more of a question of state. The stresses caused by oil payments and supplies have led the governments of consuming as well as producing countries to consider taking a stronger hand in the management of the industry, just as the British government did on the eve of World War I, when Winston Churchill, First Lord of the Admiralty, told the House of Commons in 1914:

> Nobody cares in wartime how much they pay for a vital commodity, but in peace . . . price is rather an important matter. . . . I cannot feel that we are not justified . . . in considering how in years of peace, and in a long period of peace, we may acquire proper bargaining power and facilities with regard to the purchase of oil. The price of oil does not depend wholly, or even mainly, on the ordinary workings of supply and demand.

The occasion was the British government's purchase of a 51 per cent share of the Anglo-Persian Oil Company (now British Petroleum) as her navy's warships were converting from coal to liquid fuel. Today, consuming governments are pressed more urgently to reconcile the dual character of oil as both a strategic resource and a commodity traded throughout the world.

Through tax policies, Washington favored the oil companies with depletion allowances and credits for taxes paid governments of producing countries, and indirectly stimulated consumption by using a gasoline tax to finance the building of an interstate superhighway system. Now other tax policies are being discussed to limit oil imports. Going beyond this kind of fiscal improvisation, Walter J. Levy observed recently that "the problems of oil have become matters that in many key respects can only by handled directly between governments," adding that oil prices must remain high so as not to endanger the economic viability of expensive alternatives, such as development of tar sands, shale, and coal gasification as energy sources. Levy wrote that "avoiding dependence on foreign oil dictates public support and a substantial measure of price guarantees by individual countries, notably the United States . . . acting . . . in coordination." [12] During the Arab boycott another leading oil analyst, Edith Penrose, saw the possibility of the companies becoming "public utilities with appropriate public regulation," arguing that "it will no longer be possible for the governments of the oil-importing countries to leave the international companies as free a hand in the industry as they have had in the past in view of the fact that the governments of the exporting countries will be deciding the major issues affecting the terms on which oil is sold." [13]

A U.S. Government Share in Big Oil?

These arguments seem to provide strong reasons for U.S. government purchase of large minority stockholdings in one or more of the major American oil companies. First, the capital accumulation and reduced levels of consumption that will soon be needed in the energy field to lower oil imports and develop alternative sources of energy will require a strong public guarantee that the oil industry's "obscene profits" will actually fulfill the stated purpose of energy investment and not be diverted into unrelated activities (such as Mobil's attempted purchase last year of Montgomery Ward, as part of its efforts at corporate diversification, to relieve its dependence on an increasingly regulated yet unstable industry). Second, with the oil companies losing their control of foreign supplies of crude, their self-advertised role as buffers and intermediaries between producing and consuming governments has become less meaningful. What do remain important are their managerial and technological skills. Third, such direct government leverage in the industry would facilitate long-term government-to-government arrangements on price and supply that repeatedly have been urged by producing countries, especially Venezuela.

In the coming months, Venezuela will be faced with a choice between two kinds of nationalization: the Latin-American tradition of the operating state oil company, such as PEMEX of Mexico and PETROBRAS of Brazil, or the developing Middle East pattern, now working in Iran, by which the state owns the industry but foreign companies continue to operate under varying degrees of government control. The Iran formula may soon be applied, with modifications, in Saudi Arabia and the Persian Gulf sheikdoms, and the major concessionairies in Venezuela have expressed hope that they will be able to remain on similar terms. The Middle East formula is a variant of the "service contract" concept first formulated in Venezuela in 1959 but not applied there until 1970. In its 1973 annual report, Exxon said it was "optimistic that whatever changes may take place and whatever relationships may evolve, there will be a basis for continuing operations" in Venezuela.

While the state oil company has been the dominant operating entity in Chile, Argen-

[12] *See Walter J. Levy, "World Oil Cooperation or International Chaos," Foreign Affairs, July 1974, p. 699.*

[13] *From Edith Penrose, "Origins and Development of the International Oil Crisis," Millenium, Vol. III, No. 1, 1974.*

tina, Uruguay, Bolivia, Peru, and Colombia as well as Mexico and Brazil, none of these countries has a major export industry like Venezuela's. Moreover, some repeatedly have called in foreign companies to find oil that their state enterprises have lacked the financial and technical resources to discover. While the producing countries agree that the technical and organizational services of the majors and large contractors will be needed for at least the near future, the Middle East formula remains an anathema to many Venezuelan nationalists.

In Venezuela, the draft law approved by the nationalization commission prohibits "creating mixed enterprises or participation in profits for activities reserved to the State." However, toward the end of 1974, the AD government showed many signs of moving away from this restricted definition of nationalization to allow itself much more flexibility in running the industry. In the final months of the commission's deliberations, the AD party and government representatives pointedly stayed away from the sessions to allow President Pérez and his advisers more room for maneuvering before presenting the final version of the nationalization bill to Congress. Pérez's attack on the management of the petrochemical industry has been seen as an effort to reinforce the public's fears that the government cannot directly manage the oil industry and that some deal with the companies should be made. Moreover, in December, when he announced the negotiated nationalization of the iron mining operations of U.S. Steel and Bethlehem Steel, Pérez called it "a magnificent solution that opens very favorable prospects for the more difficult and complex situation that will arise with the expiration of the oil concessions that will occur by Venezuela's sovereign decision in coming months."

The iron nationalization arrangement calls for the companies to run the mines during a transition period of one year, in exchange for a continuing supply of ore to U.S. steel mills, and leaves the way open for future technical assistance in mining and joint ventures in intermediate stages of processing. Significantly, all the opposition parties refused to support the iron nationalization deal in Congress, arguing that it was too generous to the companies, and only AD's parliamentary majority and a small party sympathetic to ex-dictator Pérez Jiménez voted for approval. Since there were persistent rumors of oil company support for AD in the election campaign, the debate over oil nationalization may prove to be even more bitter if a formula is presented that would enable the companies to continue operating the industry.

Once nationalization is approved, difficulties are anticipated by conservatives and Jacobins alike. For one thing, automation and a sharp decline in exploratory drilling since Venezuela's "no more concessions" policy was announced in 1959 have resulted in a halving of the industry's work force over the past 15 years to 21,000, or less than 1 per cent of all persons employed in the country. The fact that so small a proportion of the labor force is employed in the capital-intensive industry on which the country is so dependent has permitted a pervasive ignorance of the oil business among even educated Venezuelans.

Scared Workers and Scarce Technicians

Automation and attrition have left the oil industry with a work force composed largely of middle-aged men (averaging 45 years old and 19 years on the job) who are economically privileged, politically conservative, and, on the whole, deeply worried about their future. Said a Marxist union leader, "both the iron and oil workers are against nationalization. They're afraid of what will happen to social benefits like company medical care and their retirement plans. The iron workers want all of their retirement payoff now, but if they were to get it they'd all leave the iron mines and never come back." The government has promised to place the retirement money of the oil and iron workers in a special fund in the Central Bank. But unrest in the industry is likely to continue until the government provides strong proof that the nationalized industry will be effectively managed in the interests of both the workers and the country. Otherwise, both the iron and oil work forces will become hosts to agitation by opposition political parties that will make the transition to state ownership much more difficult.

While Venezuela proportionately has more of her own professionals in the oil industry than any other OPEC nation, she is still short of technicians to run the nationalized industry without outside help. Although the companies have made an effort in recent decades to put Venezuelans in high-level jobs, there are still 635 foreigners in key technical and executive positions. While many of these foreigners, if encouraged, would stay on after nationalization, many middle-level Venezuelans already have taken early retirement from the companies with the approach of a state take-over.

High Venezuelan officials have said many times that, after nationalization, they will maintain intact the organizations of the four largest concessionaires—Exxon, Shell, Gulf, and Mobil—and will gradually consolidate the operations of the smaller companies into larger production units. But there will be a continuing need for something like the logistical and technical support that always has been provided by the majors to their overseas subsidiaries. Moreover, most of Venezuela's oil has been sold abroad by the majors' marketing organizations outside Venezuela. While some of these limitations can be overcome with time, any attempt by Venezuelans to overreach these limitations now could prejudice their nationalized industry.

Curiously, some of the most important nationalizations since World War II[14]—Iran-ian oil in 1951, Bolivian tin in 1952, and Chilean copper in 1969-1971—seem to have occurred when world prices for the commodity have peaked and begun to decline. Instabilities in the supply of oil can be anticipated from the wave of nationalizations now taking place throughout the world and from possible political conflict in the producing areas. Because of new oil from non-OPEC countries that probably will be available for marketing in the late 1970's, just as consumption restraints in the industrialized nations begin to take hold, it may be reasonable to expect dramatic fluctuations in the price and supply of oil for the rest of this decade. Despite their recent success in driving up oil prices, the OPEC countries have a long history of bickering among themselves, and, until 1974, have been especially unsuccessful in limiting production, as any cartel must, to protect prices. With most big producers now operating below capacity because of consumer response to high oil prices and the spreading world recession, coordinated production cuts by OPEC may be needed in the near future. Mexico's recent decision against joining OPEC indicates that new oil-producing areas may not be easily absorbed into the cartel.

Not that OPEC, of itself, is a bad thing. One of the most ardent advocates for primacy of the majors has argued persuasively that, in an inherently unstable industry given to boom and bust cycles and to gluts and scarcities of supply, "the oil industry, to exist at all, calls for concerted effort and, however often a cooperative structure may have been disturbed or broken up, it will soon begin to form again." [15] The problem is that OPEC has attempted to justify its 1974 price levels as being below competing sources of energy. This is a fallacious argument because, in the short term, there are no competing sources of energy, and OPEC could just as well charge $40 or $50 per barrel as $10 or $12. But many oil analysts in the consuming

---

[14] *On the Chilean and Bolivian nationalizations, see my* Copper Is the Wage of Chile, *and* Bolivia: The Price of Tin: Part I, *American Universities Field Staff Reports, West Coast South America Series, Vol. XIX, No. 3, 1972, and Vol. XXI, Nos. 1 & 2, 1974.*

[15] *P. H. Frankel,* Essentials of Petroleum *(London: Cass, 1969), second edition, p. 97.*

countries now believe it would be more tragic for humanity than for the OPEC countries for the price of a barrel of oil to fall back to the pre-1970 price of $2, thus stimulating a return to wanton consumption that would hasten the exhaustion of the world's limited petroleum reserves. A return to low oil prices also would undermine the shaky financial structure supporting worldwide oil exploration, into which consuming countries poured upward of $10 billion in 1974.

Given future market uncertainties, now may be a good time for Washington to enter into long-term price and supply arrangements with Venezuela, which could thus continue as a pioneer in developing new relations between producing and consuming countries. While Venezuela's unsuccessful quest for hemispheric preferences has been forgotten in the upward surge of prices over the past few years, such favored access to the U.S. market, coupled with price guarantees, could be extremely helpful to her should oil prices again become unstable. Extending preferences and guarantees to Venezuela, which could be done unilaterally by Washington, would be in the U.S. interest in that they would stimulate Venezuela to expand her oil production capacity despite worldwide economic uncertainty, and to remain an extremely valuable supplier. In addition, price and market guarantees could be coupled with technical and educational support to the nationalized oil industry to give Venezuela more economic autonomy and stability over the long term.

This kind of cooperation is certainly not going to be achieved through economically meaningless and politically counterproductive reprisals such as the denial to OPEC members of most-favored nation status under the new U.S. foreign trade statute, a provision that has led Venezuela and Ecuador, the two Latin-American OPEC members, to force cancellation of the Buenos Aires hemispheric foreign ministers' conference in March.

In the end, the United States must meet the challenge posed by President Pérez's letter to President Ford. If not for reasons of sympathy or justice, then a decent respect for the future price and supply of a wide range of raw materials should dictate a new departure in U.S. policy toward nationalized industries. This would mean a reversal in U.S. economic diplomacy, since these industries traditionally have been treated as pariahs by international aid agencies. However, the stability of supplies of oil, copper, tin, iron, bauxite, and even bananas will depend, to a considerable degree, on the performance of nationalized industries in Latin America. To ensure a rational flow of these products into world markets, it may be in the self-interest of consuming countries to provide facilities in Latin America for the training of people from these nationalized enterprises in such varied skills as management, marketing, cost accounting, and specialized engineering operations. If the United States could provide continual training for more than a decade for police and counterinsurgency operatives in Latin America, then Washington surely could support, along with other industrialized countries, a public sector manpower training program implemented by some international agency. Beyond this kind of training, it may be advisable to provide design, engineering, and capital assistance to these industries to expand their capacities, especially in the processing of raw materials, and reduce the polarization between producing and consuming countries that is at the heart of the oil crisis. In this connection, perhaps as counterpoint if not refutation of former President Nixon's public expressions of support for the military dictatorship in Brazil, it might not be amiss for Ford to voice solidarity with Venezuela's democratic institutions and with her economic defense of the hemisphere's more vulnerable republics.

CUBA:
TIME FOR A CHANGE

by Abraham F. Lowenthal

For the first time in years, the United States and Cuba have a chance to break the deadlock which has kept such close neighbors so far apart. The outcome of the San José meeting of the Organization of American States (OAS) this July means that the United States is now free to determine its own stance toward Cuba. For its part, Cuba is ready to compromise to achieve rapprochement with the United States. "Normalization"—mutually respectful and profitable diplomatic, commercial, and cultural relations—is at last possible, perhaps within two or three years.

The road to normalization will be long and cannot be one-way. Traveling it successfully will require patience, skill, and flexibility on both sides. Neither country desperately needs improved relations, though each nation would gain substantially, both in bilateral terms and in the broader framework of inter-American and international relations. Each country will encounter formidable internal problems as it moves toward nonhostile relations. Each (especially the United States) must contend also with allies who will be unenthusiastic about a U.S.-Cuban rapprochement. But the will to face internal and external difficulties to achieve normalization exists in Havana, both at intermediate and at high levels of government. In Washington, a similar spirit prevails at intermediate levels in the executive, and is gaining increasing strength in Congress.

Despite some signs in Havana and in Washington that normalization is desired, however, U.S.-Cuban relations are still logjammed, if not icebound. Each side waits for the other to make concessions before direct negotiations begin. Cuba has already taken several significant steps toward the negotiating table, but the United States has yet to respond clearly; ambiguous, even contradictory, signals emanate from Washington instead.

To move beyond the impasse, therefore, the U.S. government should clearly demonstrate its interest in normalization. The United States should take the next symbolic step by lifting at least part of its long-standing blockade of Cuba and by expressing its intent to end the remaining sanctions as soon as direct negotiations with Cuba permit. And Washington should act now, before the electoral campaign deprives the Administration of flexibility.

These are the main conclusions I draw from recent and extensive conversations in Havana and in Washington. I would not pretend, of course, that 11 days in Cuba and two days in Washington this June make me an authority. But the more interviews I have, the more clearly these conclusions emerge.

The Revolution Is Here to Stay

Recently published reports about CIA involvement in attempts on Castro's life remind us how intensely hostile relations between the United States and Cuba became in the early 1960s. The captured Sherman tanks at Giron (the Bay of Pigs) impressed that point on me most vividly. Over 200 Cuban soldiers died there in 1961 in defeating a heavily armed force, trained by the CIA, convoyed to Cuban waters by U.S. Navy destroyers, and aided (however ineffectively) by temporary U.S. air cover.

Despite its humiliation at the Bay of Pigs, the U.S. government continued its ardent efforts to topple the Castro regime. American radio broadcasts wooed the Cuban populace, periodic U.S. airdrops supplied anti-Castro groups in the Escambray mountains, and American intelligence operatives reportedly helped carry out sabotage operations. But all these tactics failed.

Even in retrospect, the triumph of Castro's movement was impressive. The few surviving veterans of Moncada and *Granma* had only an outside chance to oust Batista, much less to purge the island of U.S. influence. The American presence in Cuba—once described by a Cuban nationalist as "no more independent than Long Island"—was overwhelming. But, however implausibly, the Cuban revolution did triumph. Cuba's political, educational, and economic systems have been transformed. Many of its national habits and values have been profoundly altered. After several false starts, Cuba's economy seems to be on a successful course: national income is going up, the balance of payments was favorable in 1974 for the first time in 15 years, and heavy investments in infrastructure, public health, and education are beginning to pay off. Above all, perhaps, Cuba's historical relationship with the United States has been thoroughly overturned.

A fundamental reversal of Cuba's revolutionary achievements is most unlikely. The regime faces no serious threat from within. A large share of the country's dissidents were among the approximately 650,000 persons who left after 1959, mostly bound for the United States. Half the island's current population has been born since Fidel took power. The populace is fully mobilized, mainly through the Committees for the Defense of the Revolution, in which 80 per cent of adults are said to participate. Finally, the government has shown its will and capacity to control and even suppress dissent. There is, therefore, no need for an obtrusive military presence in Cuba, nor for the obvious surveillance of foreigners which marks the Soviet Union. The traffic control posts outside each Cuban town still remain, but no one bothers to stand guard inside the booths. The revolution is here to stay.

A Policy of Restrained Hostility

And yet the U.S. government, at its highest levels, seems never to have fully ac-cepted the presence of a Socialist state in Cuba. True, Washington's attempts to subvert the Cuban government were slowly abandoned, but only as it became clear that Castro's hold is firm, and as U.S. dealings with the Soviet Union sharply reduced the military security problems Cuba poses for the United States (and limited what the United States can do to Cuba). But even after dropping its direct efforts to end the Castro regime, the U.S. government tried hard to isolate Cuba. The policies of diplomatic nonrecognition and "economic denial" which the United States pressured its allies to support were avowedly aimed at thwarting Cuba's "export of revolution" and at forcing Cuba to cut its military ties with the Soviet Union. More important than those two stated goals, however, was the desire to undermine Cuba's appeal as a development model by minimizing the successes of the Castro government and by limiting Latin-American access to Cuba. And there was long a fourth reason, a wishful thought (especially among many Cuban immigrants) that the Cuban revolution would eventually abort, if only the United States did not recognize or support it. These four reasons—reinforced by personal pique and by psychological stress, no doubt—have undergirded U.S. policy toward Cuba since the mid-1960s, a policy of restrained hostility.

In September 1975, none of these four concerns provides a defensible basis for U.S. policy (if, indeed, they ever did). Yet America's hostile policy, symbolized by the total embargo, continues.

Cuba began to disengage from its previously active attempts to "export revolution" in 1968 after Che Guevara's storybook failure in Bolivia. By 1969, Cuba was supporting the reformist Peruvian military regime, even though the Peruvian junta was led by army officers who only a few years before had commanded counterinsurgency units to combat the spread of Cuba's influence! By 1971, Cuba was being sharply criticized by rebel leaders like Douglas Bravo of Venezuela for failing to provide effective support to revolutionary movements. By 1975, Cuba had re-established diplomatic relations with Venezuela, which had proposed the OAS expulsion of Cuba in 1964; Cuba has also developed correct to cordial relations with Argentina, Colombia, Panama, and a number of Caribbean states. All these countries seem reasonably confident that Cuba is neither engaging in nor planning armed subversion in Latin America. The U.S. government, which maintains constant air surveillance of Cuba, is in a position to be sure of this as well. Cuba's extensive military build-up over the years has been defensive in character; short-range fighter-interceptors, rather than bombers, compose most of Cuba's air force purchases, and Cuban military training emphasizes defense of the island, not attacks on others.

As for Cuba's relations with the Soviet Union, U.S. efforts to isolate and punish Cuba have done absolutely nothing to limit the considerable (though hardly visible) Soviet presence in Cuba; on the contrary they have surely increased Cuba's incentive to remain close to Moscow. The United States has a legitimate interest in trying to limit Russia's capacity to use Cuba as a base for hostile actions. But the 1962 missile crisis showed conclusively that the main actors can and will deal with each other directly. That lesson was reinforced in 1970 when a sharp American reaction to Soviet naval movements and construction activity at the port of Cienfuegos led the superpowers to clarify (or perhaps to extend) their agreement that bars Russia from introducing a strategic offensive capability into Cuba.

Normalizing U.S. relations with Cuba will not immediately weaken Cuba's links with the Soviet Union. But there is absolutely no reason to believe Soviet influence will increase with normalization, and there is some reason to think it may decline over time. One can reasonably speculate, at least, that Cuba's capacity to act independently of the Soviet Union should expand if Cuba enters a triangular relationship involving both superpowers.

The long-standing U.S. aim to isolate Cuba in order to limit its appeal to Latin America is both forlorn and misguided. It is forlorn because Cuba has already broken down the blockade. Not only has Cuba in recent years established or re-established relations with innumerable countries of Latin America, the Caribbean, Africa, Asia, and Europe; it has also joined the Latin American Group at the United Nations, been elected to the U.N. "Committee of 24," hosted several important international meetings, and become an obligatory stop for distinguished statesmen and aspiring politicians from all parts of the world, near and far. It is misguided because Cuba's appeal in most of Latin America has been, and is, strictly limited. Cuba's revolution may have shattered the myth of "geographic fatalism," but the "second Cuba" feared by U.S. officials a decade ago never appeared, and shows no sign of doing so. Highly placed Cuban authorities freely concede that a second Socialist revolution in the Americas is not easily foreseeable. The Colossus of the North has nothing to fear from Cuba's full entry onto the hemispheric stage.

Finally, the unstated hope that the Cuba issue will eventually disappear simply cannot be sustained. Not even the Cuban community in Miami still really holds on to the belief that the revolution will be reversed. Richard Nixon, whose involvement with Cuban exiles eventually did him in, apparently maintained to the end his conviction that the present Cuban leadership could be ignored. Gerald Ford, the fifth American president to rule since Fidel took over in Havana, should not cling to this illusion.

"No Virtue in Perpetual Antagonism"

The long-time U.S. policy of restrained hostility toward Castro's Cuba is clearly being eroded, as was signaled by Secretary Kissinger's statement in March 1975 that the United States sees "no virtue in perpetual antagonism" between this country and Cuba. But various pronouncements, including President Ford's subsequent interview with Pierre Salinger in June, suggest that the U.S. government may delay undertaking any significant shift in the U.S. posture. The Administration's view has long been that "it takes two to tango," and that the United States proposes no move toward the dance floor until it is convinced that its putative partner is willing. Even after the OAS meeting at San José, therefore, the U.S. government waits, either because it feels it has no real interest in rapprochement with Cuba (beyond having partially defanged the Cuba issue as a problem in inter-American relations), or because it is not sure whether the Cuban regime really wants normalization, or because it does not wish to give up —or appear to give up—any "bargaining chips" without gaining something concrete in return.

An impasse has thus been reached; the Cubans want the United States to drop (or at least clearly to begin to drop) its obviously hostile blockade of Cuba as a precondition to discussing other bilateral issues. The U.S. government waits for a "change in Cuban attitudes"; Cuban gestures to date are dismissed as not dealing with "basic issues."

This impasse should be broken now. Moving beyond the impasse will require some elegant steps in a minuet (if not a tango), a minuet which has already begun. A less hostile tone in diplomatic discourse and public statements between the two governments has been noted, for instance. So have a few American gestures, primarily the slowly evolving U.S. position on the Cuban issue within the OAS forum, the liberalized restrictions on the travel of Cuban diplomats posted at the United Nations, and the decision to permit a few Cubans to enter the United States for cultural or religious purposes. But, despite some Administration indications to the contrary, all the major steps toward normalization so far have been taken by Cuba: the 1973 hijacking agreement (belatedly recognized this June by Assistant Secretary William D. Rogers as having been a significant gesture by the Cuban government); the invitations extended to important members of Congress from both parties and to congressional staff persons; the treatment accorded visiting journalists and scholars; the content of various Cuban government statements, especially Castro's television interview with Dan Rather in October 1974 (with his skillful, if subtle, praise for Presidents Kennedy and Ford and for Secretary Kissinger and his careful distinction between the American people and U.S. government policy) and his remarks to Senator George McGovern in May 1975; the release of several U.S. prisoners; the invitation to exchange baseball teams; and the announced intention to return a $2 million hijacking ransom confiscated some years ago by the Cuban government. Thus, the logical next step, if our government genuinely desires normalization, would be for the United States unambiguously—if only partially—to begin ending the embargo of Cuba, the continuing embodiment of official American hostility.

Why the United States Should Act Now

Arguing persuasively that the U.S. government should set in motion the dynamics of rapprochement by beginning to lift its embargo of Cuba requires showing: (1) that it is in our national interest for normalization to occur; (2) that the Cubans themselves now seek normalization and are therefore willing to compromise to achieve it; and (3) that there is no reason to think that the United States will achieve normalization on more favorable terms by further delay.

Normalization of relations with Cuba— on negotiated terms which are responsive to legitimate U.S. concerns—would be in our national interest for several reasons. First, ending official American hostility toward Cuba would help make it clear that the United States is adopting the new approach toward Latin America persuasively recommended by the recent report of the Commission on United States-Latin American Relations (the "Linowitz Report"): an approach "respectful of the sovereignty of the countries of the region and tolerant of a wide range of political and economic forms." As the Linowitz Report emphasizes, the United States—in its own self-interest—should cooperate with the countries of Latin America to build a more equitable, stable, and mutually beneficial structure of international relations. Efforts by the United States to make the "management of interdependence" a positive fact, not merely an ambiguous slogan, will depend for their success in part on securing the active help of the Latin-American countries, nations which share our primary interest in improved economic security and which exert increasing international influence.

No "new dialogue" to achieve this vital objective will have even a remote chance to succeed, however, if the United States appears to prolong its overbearing attitude toward Latin America. We can no longer expect to veto change in Latin America and elsewhere in the Third World. The days of unquestioned U.S. domination of the hemisphere are over. U.S. policy toward Cuba thus takes on a special significance, as it often has in the past, as a test of this country's attitudes and assumptions. A creative attempt to resolve outstanding problems with Cuba and with Panama would be understood in Latin America as testimony—far more eloquent than official rhetoric or state visits—of this country's desire to improve its hemispheric relations. And failure by Washington to change its policies in these key instances could convey exactly the opposite message.

The second set of reasons for the United States to seek normalized relations with Cuba involves economics. Given the size of the U.S. economy, no one would contend that the benefits the United States would gain from eventual trade with Cuba are overwhelmingly significant in aggregate terms. The Cuban market could be very attractive, however, for specific U.S. corporations trying to recover from a prolonged international recession. Cuba might import from the United States fairly substantial quantities of such products as automobiles and automotive equipment; agricultural commodities (corn, rice, wheat, cattle and poultry feed, vegetable oils, and fertilizers); farm machinery; food processing, textile manufacturing, construction and port equipment; computers and computer technology; and general know-how in agriculture and specific industries. A significant market for spare parts of U.S.-produced goods also appears to exist. Cuba's imports of consumer goods are rising, too, and American products are still the standard by which Cubans shop. Cuban officials emphasize that import decisions will be based on the quality and price of goods, on credit terms, and on delivery date; their repeated mention of the last criterion suggests that their experience with the distant and centrally planned economies of Eastern Europe may make Cuban managers long for the day when they will be able to call Miami or Chicago and obtain rapid delivery of needed items.

Trade with Cuba would not necessarily be one-way. Cuba's major exports—sugar and nickel—are products the United States imports; Cuba's known reserves of nickel, a raw material in scarce supply, are among the world's largest. Cuban cigars are still remembered in the United States with fond nostalgia. Cuba's hoped-for expansion of the tourist trade would find its greatest potential source of customers in the United States. A major Cuban project, supported by the United Nations Development Program, promises to achieve a breakthrough in lowering the cost of producing paper from bagasse (a sugar by-product), thus opening up the possibility that Cuba could help alleviate this country's paper shortage. Though none of these prospective Cuban exports to the United States is of crucial importance, each would be of some benefit.

A more speculative but potentially very important benefit of a U.S.-Cuban rapprochement would be that it might help Cuba lessen its dependence on the Soviet Union. Cuban officials explicitly reject this as a possible motive for their interest in improving relations with the United States; they invariably refer, as do numerous billboard posters, to Cuba's "unbreakable" bonds of friendship with the Soviet Union, the only foreign country singled out for mention in the draft constitution now being discussed in Cuba.

"Cuba wants and expects normalization, is striving to achieve it, and *is* ready to compromise to gain rapprochement with the United States."

My own guess, however, is that Cuba's official line "doth protest too much." Cuba's foreign trade statistics are suggestive in this regard. In 1957, the United States accounted for 64 per cent of Cuba's foreign trade. Although diversifying its international relations was a leading aim of Castro's movement from the start, 13 years of revolutionary foreign policy had, by 1972, succeeded only in reversing the statistics; 64 per cent of Cuba's trade in that year was with the Socialist countries (and overwhelmingly with the Soviet Union). Only since 1972 has Cuba been able to diversify its trade pattern more extensively; in 1974 (admittedly an exceptional year, due to the record high price of sugar), Cuban trade with non-Socialist countries climbed to nearly 42 per cent. 1975 and 1976 may see some slippage, but Cuba's commercial agreements since 1973 with Argentina, Canada, Spain,

France, England, Italy, and West Germany —agreements for lines of credit totaling over $3 billion—suggest a keen desire to move away from its nearly exclusive reliance on the Comecon countries for both imports and exports. Cuba's sugar sales to Japan have been extraordinarily high for several years. Normalizing relations with the United States is part of this long-term strategy. And lessening Cuba's dependence on the Soviet Union should be a key aim of U.S. policy, for Cuba's only plausible threat to the United States is as an instrument of potential Soviet ambitions.

In sum, normalized relations with Cuba on negotiated terms which protect legitimate U.S. interests would be desirable. Arguing that these relations should now be actively sought by the United States depends on showing, however, that Cuba's interest in normalization is sufficiently strong to warrant thinking that direct negotiations would lead to reasonable compromises on outstanding U.S.-Cuban problems.

Cuba Wants Normalization

Perhaps the most important impression I obtained on my visit was that Cuba wants and expects normalization, is striving to achieve it, and *is* ready to compromise to gain rapprochement with the United States.

Officials and others with whom I talked were willing to guess, for instance, that most well-informed Cubans think normal diplomatic and commercial exchanges with the United States are possible within two years, and certainly within five. But Cuba is not merely waiting for history to take its course. The number of Foreign Ministry personnel working on the United States has nearly doubled in the past year, and the professional competence of Cuba's America-watchers is impressive. One Foreign Ministry specialist asked detailed questions about the Kansas City reforms in the Democratic Party's convention delegate selection process, for instance, and three members of the University of Havana's government-linked study group on the United States grilled me on the role of nonprofit institutions in U.S. foreign policy-making. The skillful campaign Cuba is waging to influence American opinion clearly expresses Fidel's interest in normalization.

With regard to each of the major issues outstanding in Cuban-American relations, I came away from Havana with a sense of Cuban willingness to bargain flexibly, provided that the United States is willing to do so.

On the difficult issue of compensation for expropriated American companies (and of possible Cuban counterclaims, which Cuban officials have indicated might amount to three or four times the U.S.-certified claim of $1.8 billion), a fairly detailed conversation with Carlos Rafael Rodriguez, Cuba's First Deputy Prime Minister, convinced me that Cuba is prepared to reach a realistic settlement. Such a settlement would involve not only recognition of the principle of compensation (which Cuba has already paid to several European countries) but some net transfer of funds from Cuba to the U.S. government, with our government acting as trustee for the expropriated firms. The Cuban desire not to pay "a single cent" to any American company could easily be taken into account by an arrangement similar to the one the United States and Peru devised to resolve the imbroglio involving the expropriated International Petroleum Company (IPC); a U.S. government claims commission could distribute a lump sum Cuban payment according to criteria decided by the United States alone. Exactly how much Cuba would pay the United States obviously remains subject to detailed negotiations. The price of sugar would be one relevant factor in these negotiations, and a specific understanding regarding Cuban access to the U.S. market would clearly be another.

As for Cuba's aim to oust the United States from the anomalous and unneccessary Guantanamo naval base, Cuba is deliberately letting this issue remain on a back burner until a later stage in the normalization process, after we have dealt with the Panama problem. Cuban officials understand that their chances of ending the U.S. presence at Guantanamo will increase if an American withdrawal cannot easily be represented in the United States as unseemly capitulation. Cuba seems prepared to wait, therefore, until the Guantanamo issue can be discreetly resolved in a mutually satisfactory manner.

Regarding nonintervention in the affairs of other countries, Cuban policy pronouncements and Cuban practice over the past several years appear nearly to coincide—something that cannot be said about our own government's statements and actions. Assurances against foreign intervention should not be difficult to secure from Cuba on a reciprocal basis.

"The embargo no longer serves to isolate Cuba; the country being isolated is the United States."

The one "sleeper," potentially the most difficult issue between Cuba and the United States, concerns the future of Puerto Rico. Cuban officials openly express their support for Puerto Rico's independence movement but claim that their support is restricted to "legitimate" activities and does not include terrorism, armed subversion, or other internationally proscribed acts. (I know of no hard evidence to the contrary, though it would not surprise me to learn of some.) Whatever the current facts, I suspect that trends in Puerto Rico will bring that territory's problematic status to the fore in years to come. If Cuban-American hostility continues unabated, Cuba's incentive to exploit this country's Puerto Rican problem will heighten. If the United States and Cuba normalize their relations, Cuban sympathy for Puerto Rican *independentistas* may still produce continuing friction. In that case, however, tacit or perhaps even explicit limits on the character and extent of Cuban activity should be possible to work out. Mutual restraint of propaganda efforts should be feasible, for instance, and mutual control of subversive groups should be possible.

Cuban assurances that its links with the Soviet Union will not be threatening to the United States are unlikely to be made public, but the tacit mutual understandings which have evolved since 1962 regarding the Soviet military presence in Cuba and U.S. restraint of anti-Castro Cuban exiles can probably be reinforced and made more explicit. The United States can probably not exact in advance a specific commitment from Cuba to reduce the Soviet military presence on the island (though such an arrangement may be feasible in the larger context of U.S.-Soviet negotiations). What can be accomplished, however, is to create conditions in U.S.-Cuban relations which would encourage Russian withdrawals from the island. To the extent that Cuban-American tensions are reduced, the Cuban desire to reduce Russia's presence should increase.

The desire of Cubans on the island and in the United States to be able to exchange visits from time to time is another item on the bilateral agenda. No commitments have yet been made by Havana, but the Cuban authorities understand that one way to reduce Cuban refugee opposition to normalization will be to ease the agonies of divided families by allowing such visits to take place.

Other pending issues range from Cuba's postal debt on the one side and blocked Cuban assets in the United States on the other to U.S. concerns about Cuba's violations of fundamental human rights, particularly in the cases of political prisoners, believed in Washington to number several thousand. Some questions can surely be settled early in the normalization process; Cuba's track record in resolving specific problems in its negotiations with France, Spain, and Switzerland is encouraging in that re-

gard. Other problems—the plight of political prisoners is a painful example—may well seem as far from satisfactory solution three years from now as they do today. What can be said, however, is that the leverage the U.S. government can exert on an issue like this, limited at best, is even less in a situation of mutual hostility than it would be under conditions of some openness in U.S.-Cuban relations.

The Time Is Now

Our government's bargaining strength will not improve if the United States continues stubbornly to prolong the hostile posture symbolized by the continuing embargo. On the contrary, the embargo was for some years a wasting asset, even on its own terms; by now it is undoubtedly a mounting debit. The embargo no longer serves to isolate Cuba; the country being isolated is the United States, whose policy and practice toward Cuba is every day further removed from the realities of the 1970s. Indeed, it is ironic (or worse) that the United States continues to impose its coercive Cuban embargo while bitterly protesting OPEC and particularly Arab oil diplomacy. Our pleas for an end to raw displays of commodity power might be more convincing if the United States ended its own politically motivated sanctions against Cuba.

There are reasons to think that the point of greatest U.S. leverage in its negotiations with Cuba may well be now. Cuba's first five-year plan, covering the period 1976-1980, is currently being drafted; assumptions about the availability of U.S. goods might affect immediate Cuban decisions with operational consequences two or three years from now. Unless the United States acts soon to make it clear that normalized relations are being sought, Cuba may well find itself forced to make commitments which will severely limit American access to a market in which the United States would otherwise have considerable competitive advantage. And this would, in turn, sharply reduce Cuba's incentive to compromise.

Similarly, international economic and political circumstances make this a good time to break the impasse in Cuban-American relations. Having enjoyed the benefits of record high sugar prices and having seen these prices fall back down to about 12 cents a pound in mid-1975, Cuba would undoubtedly value the increased economic security that improved relations with the United States would afford. If the United States drags its feet, however, Cuba will either find itself in a stronger bargaining position in the future (assuming that sugar prices stabilize at about 20 cents a pound, as many experts predict) or else more dependent than ever on the Soviet Union; in neither case will the United States be more likely than it is at present to reach advantageous compromises with Cuba.

A final reason why the United States should act now is the imminence of the Panama issue as a congressional and political focal point. A positive and flexible American posture toward Cuba would clearly reinforce the stance the Administration is taking on the Canal issue. At the same time, importantly, it would defuse criticism of Washington's fruitless policy on the Cuban issue without giving away anything of real consequence prior to detailed negotiation. The Cuban issue would be taken out of the limelight and allowed to percolate on the back burner through the election campaign, while greater public attention could be devoted to the potentially explosive Panama question.

Despite all these reasons to end the embargo, some well-informed Washingtonians feel that the U.S. government may not act soon. The reason most often cited is an alleged White House perception that a positive U.S. gesture would risk adverse domestic political consequences outweighing any national or international gain. The problem is said to be compounded by the relative lack of sustained high-level attention which

the Cuban issue can command from top decision-makers beset with accumulating domestic and international problems. The President and the Secretary of State are said to believe that the costs of our long-standing Cuban policy are not demonstrably great and will decline now that the OAS action has taken place. The presumed benefits of normalization are thought to be remote and speculative, while its domestic political costs may seem immediate and concrete, especially for a President bent on winning his first national election. The President is thought to fear that significant numbers of the American electorate would interpret even a partial end to the Cuban embargo as a sign of national weakness.

I hope, and suspect, that this analysis underestimates President Ford's capacity for creative leadership in foreign affairs. An alert President concerned with the national interest and not primarily with partisan political advice will recognize the scope he has for a well-conceived Cuban policy. By now the American people as a whole are ready for U.S.-Cuban rapprochement. 63 per cent of Americans polled by Gallup in October 1974 favored normalization; the percentage may well be higher now after the visit in May of Senator George McGovern and a flock of journalists, including Barbara Walters. According to a State Department analysis, 79 per cent of the leading newspapers which had expressed themselves by June 1975 favored normalization. Senators Kennedy and McGovern among Democratic leaders, and Percy and Javits among Republicans, have proposed a U.S. initiative to end the embargo.

The President need not fear that such a largely symbolic gesture of the Administration's interest in negotiating with Castro's Cuba will be understood as a sign of weakness. On the contrary, an Administration decision to begin the normalization process could very persuasively be presented as an example of President Ford's realism, and of his refreshing willingness to cut unnecessary losses, in contrast to three Presidents before him. The President inherited a number of bad policies; one important measure of the Ford Administration will be its capacity to end anachronistic and unjustified measures.

Indeed, if the Administration does not seize the initiative on Cuba during the six months after San José, it might find itself on the defensive in the electoral campaign, vulnerable to what could be a telling criticism that it has not adjusted to a changing world but rather has prolonged Cold War attitudes which no longer have any place (if they ever did) in hemispheric relations. A Republican Administration which has sought détente with the Soviet Union, promoted negotiation in the Middle East, and wants to travel to Peking in search of better understanding might appear to be hung up over outmoded concepts or hostage to special interest groups if it shied away from talking with Cuba. The political costs of this image could turn out to be much greater than the resentment thought likely to be stirred up among some Cuban immigrants by a conciliatory U.S. government attitude toward Castro, especially if the Cuban community is—as several observers believe—far less monolithic in its opposition to U.S.-Cuban rapprochement than it is usually represented.

But perhaps the whole Cuban issue is simply not worth the time of the highest U.S. government officials, faced with the Indochina debacle, the Korean powder keg, the Middle East conundrum, the crisis of democracy in India, and Communist gains in southern Europe. U.S. government officials working on Latin-American affairs undoubtedly have a hard time getting the President and the Secretary of State to focus for long on the question of normalizing relations with Cuba, a relatively small country which poses no urgent or critical problem for the United States.

Our top officials cannot, of course, afford to spend much time on the Cuban issue, nor on any of a number of other potentially important foreign policy problems from Angola to Zaire. No one individual, not even Henry Kissinger, can be expected to deal with every problem. But the process of foreign policy-making must not be limited by the attention span of the Secretary of State. Kissinger has assembled at State perhaps the ablest group of individuals ever to work together on U.S. policy toward Latin America. These officials seem ready to face the fascinating challenge of protecting U.S. interests on the road to normalization. The time has come for the President and the Secretary of State to give them a chance to do so.

What Should We Do Next?

If and when our highest officials decide that the United States should unambiguously express its interest in negotiating rapprochement with Cuba, how should the Administration proceed?

The natural way to begin undoing the embargo, which hopefully may even have occurred by the time this article appears, would be to lift coercive sanctions affecting third countries, sanctions all the more offensive now that the formerly multilateral character of the embargo has been ended by the OAS vote at San José. The President should determine that it is no longer in the national interest to deny foreign aid to nations which aid or trade with Cuba, or whose ships enter Cuban ports. Restrictions on bunkering in U.S. ports by foreign vessels engaged in trade with Cuba should also be dropped. Constraints against trade with Cuba by subsidiaries of U.S. corporations operating in foreign countries, already relaxed on an exceptional basis in cases involving Argentina and Canada, should now be removed entirely. But these welcome (if overdue) measures to end U.S. conflict with third countries will not be understood—in Havana, in Washington, or anywhere else—as clearly indicating a U.S. government desire to improve bilateral relations with Cuba;

they will only signify that the United States does not wish its Cuba policy to affect relations with other countries. Before direct negotiations to settle outstanding issues in U.S.-Cuban relations begin, Cuba can reasonably expect some evidence of American good will to match its own recent gestures, some indication that the U.S. government hopes that the results of negotiation with Cuba will permit eventual normalization.

Such an expression of official U.S. interest in improved relations with Cuba could come about in any of several ways. The Secretary of State could make a major public pronouncement on Cuba, or the President could do so. Kissinger could even show up in Havana as he did in Peking. A flamboyant display, however, would needlessly rile up domestic critics and might create false expectations of rapidly improved relations. A much more advisable tack would be for the Administration to signal, clearly but unobtrusively, that it seeks to begin serious negotiations with Cuba.

As Castro himself has suggested, our government could easily advance this process by making it legal for U.S. firms to sell food and medicine to Cuba, thereby ending a unilateral and gratuitous sanction imposed despite a specific exemption of these items in the 1964 OAS resolution. Castro has already said Cuba would regard such a gesture as a "positive act"; Cuba would probably respond to it, perhaps by releasing one or more of the U.S. citizens still held in Cuban jails for political crimes. The President might then undertake any or several of a whole spectrum of measures. He might, for instance, suspend the current travel restrictions on U.S. citizens bound for Cuba, restrictions of dubious legality and even less effectiveness, in any case. He could order that Treasury Department asset controls be modified to allow personal remittances and other modest financial transactions to take place. He could enable Cuban journalists from Prensa Latina, the Cuban-sponsored wire service, to work in Washington, presumably in return for a Cuban agreement to allow the major U.S. wire services to reopen their Havana offices. He could make it clear—as contradictory decisions in 1975 do not—that the United States would welcome cultural and athletic exchanges with Cuba.

All these measures—and others of similar scope—should be undertaken by the Ford Administration soon, before the 1976 electoral campaign makes such an initiative a hostage of the vociferous and geographically concentrated Cuban immigrant minority. Though such actions would probably be understood in Havana as an important earnest of the U.S. government's interest in normalization, they would not significantly weaken our government's leverage in detailed negotiations with Cuba on specific, bilateral issues. Cuba's main incentives to compromise—access to the American market for its exports and access to American goods on terms comparable to those on which products from other countries are available—would still be withheld by the United States, pending the outcome of direct negotiations.

A U.S. initiative to break the current impasse would enable this country to move toward normalizing its relations with Cuba without sacrificing any legitimate American interest. It would allow the next 18 months to be used constructively: to expand contacts, to broaden communications channels and patterns, to foster trust (or at least to reduce distrust), to assess more accurately the costs and benefits of normalization, and quietly to begin detailed negotiations. Some of the thorniest problems in U.S.-Cuban relations would probably not be resolved until after next year's Presidential election. Beginning the process now, however, would enable both countries to create some momentum toward settlement rather than needlessly deepening mutual resentment. Seeking peaceful acceptance of America's most recent revolution would be a worthy task for the United States during its bicentennial year.

PANAMA PARALYSIS

by Thomas M. Franck & Edward Weisband

After 10 years of on-again, off-again negotiations, beginning with the Johnson-Robles agreement of September 24, 1965, the United States and Panama have reached the "fish or cut bait" phase in efforts to rewrite the 1903 treaty cutting a 10-mile-wide swath—372 square miles run by the United States "as if sovereign" and "in perpetuity" —across the isthmus. But with agreement at hand, Congress appears to be balking.

Thirty-seven senators cosponsored a resolution that "The government of the United States should maintain and protect its sovereign rights and jurisdiction over the canal and zone, and should in no way cede, dilute, forfeit, negotiate, or transfer any of these sovereign rights...."[1] The House of Representatives, on June 26, 1975, voted by 246 to 164 to deny funds to "negotiate the surrender or relinquishment of United States rights in the Panama Canal." With great difficulty this was converted, in October, into a joint Senate-House "sense of Congress" resolution that the negotiators should "protect the vital interests of the United States in the Canal Zone."

Not only have the opponents of the treaty been first out of the starting gate, but they have entered an impressive and determined string of seasoned contenders. Congresswoman Leonor Sullivan, for example, chairs the House of Representatives' Committee on Merchant Marine and Fisheries which must report out the essential enabling legislation. Sullivan has made it clear that she will sit "forever" on any such bill. "I've told them again and again," she says, referring to the State Department, "the House will never enact a law to give away the

zone.... If the 1903 Hay-Bunau-Varilla Treaty isn't honored, no treaty is worth anything. They'll be wanting to renegotiate the Louisiana Purchase next." Among other potential opponents with key committee posts are Senators Sparkman, Eastland, Symington, and McClellan.

At least one opponent of a new treaty, Senator Barry Goldwater, has recognized that "getting their hopes up and then getting it killed is bound to cause trouble with Panama." Ambassador Ellsworth Bunker, the chief U.S. negotiator with Panama, agrees. If the treaty is rejected, he says, "we would likely find ourselves engaged in hostilities with an otherwise friendly country, a conflict that, in my view, the American people would not long accept."

Despite such warnings, the ritual preliminaries for a deadly U.S.-Panama game of "chicken" are already in place. President Omar Torrijos has recently declared that if his country's volatile students, radicals, and nationalists use violence against the zone— as they did in 1959 and 1964—"we will have two alternatives, to smash it or to lead it, and I'm not going to smash it." A substantial number of members of Congress, however, see this as a bluff. Some agree with Congressman Larry McDonald, that "these threats, if one could call them that, are coming from U.S. officials, not from any organizations in Panama. Apparently, some of our public officials will stoop to anything in their efforts to weaken the United States. As for Mr. Bunker, someone should remind him that he represents the United States of America and that his proper posture, particularly when confronting a country ruled by a Marxist-oriented military strongman, is proudly erect, not cringing on his belly."

In a small foretaste of confrontation, on September 23, 800 Panamanian students hurled Molotov cocktails and rocks at the U.S. embassy in Panama City. They were reacting to Secretary of State Kissinger's reported remark at a southern governors' con-

[1] *U.S. Senate Resolution 301, 93rd Congress, 2nd Session, March 29, 1974.*

ference that the United States must retain the right to defend the canal "unilaterally" and "indefinitely" (or, according to a later version, "for a long time"). This represents the continuing ambivalence of the administration, badgered by congressional hawks and fearing the growth of the Reagan-led right wing in a presidential election year.

The Two Options

Despite these ambiguities, there are now only two directions for the U.S.-Panamanian relationship to go. One leads toward a U.S. withdrawal—phased, to be sure, over years—from its three isthmian roles: as guardian of the Canal Zone, as commandant of the military bases and training schools, and as operator of the canal itself. This is the *de-escalation* option.

The other direction points toward a firm, unrelenting reassertion of Washington's intention to retain long-range control over all three U.S. roles in Panama. The exercise of this *escalation* option would have to be accompanied by the dispatch of enough additional military forces to deal decisively with any local rioting and attempts at sabotage. It might also involve a series of substantial carrots, such as the return of some "spare" lands and construction of a high-level bridge and a third-lock system, as well as other public works to help divert Panamanians from political to economic concerns.

In practice, there are no other alternatives. That is the hard fact from which President Ford tends to shrink. And the choice of alternatives can no longer be postponed or temporized away. Some authorities have called for the canal's "internationalization." This third option, however, is no longer viable. It has been rejected by the Panamanians, as has a related proposal to place the waterway under Latin-American, regional, or OAS (Organization of American States) control. Under pressure of Panamanian "whirlwind diplomacy" around their capitals, Latin-American states (a few, like Brazil, with less enthusiasm than meets the

eye) have fallen into step behind Panamanian claims to sole control. The Security Council, too, has demonstrated, during its March 1973 meetings in Panama, that there would be no significant support in the United Nations for any solution other than a bilaterally negotiated transfer from the United States to Panama. By the unprecedented step of re-electing Panama to the Security Council as representative of their region only two years after the expiration of its previous term, the Latin Americans have again given Panama the means to use this world forum to press for an unqualified acknowledgment of their sole sovereignty over the zone. Finally, the February 7, 1974 Kissinger-Tack Agreement on Principles set its sights on a bilateral solution in which, at a time to be agreed, "Panama will assume total responsibility for the operation of the canal. . . ." It is on this basis that the recent talks have proceeded between Foreign Minister Tack and Bunker. They have created a firm expectation that a decision will be made soon and in a bilateral framework.

A Bad Year

Ideally, 1976 is not a felicitous choice for the year of Panama. The U.S. withdrawal from Vietnam has rendered this country sore and preoccupied with its loss of credibility in the world. It has also left the State Department, and Kissinger in particular, with less clout to exert in Congress on behalf of a Panama treaty. Even among the Washington foreign policy establishment and the White House, in the words of one U.S. negotiator, "Panama is always sixteenth on any list of the 15 top issues." As a presidential election year, 1976 leaves the president and members of Congress particularly vulnerable to political passions. And passion, in this instance, is mainly the prerogative of those who oppose "giving away the canal." Most of these are southern Democrats and midwestern and southwestern Republicans who are the mainstay of President Ford's increasingly vulnerable right wing. Those Americans who see the need for satisfying what they recognize as a natural Panamanian desire for territorial integrity and decolonialization are, for the most part, liberal Democrats who are unlikely to vote for Ford no matter what his policy on Panama. Nor are they imbued with the kind of zealousness over this cause that manifests itself in public rallies and congressmen's mailboxes. Robert Dockery, staff counsel of the Senate Foreign Relations committee, has observed that "no year ever seems to be the year for Panama."

It appears that those within the Ford Administration who have favored postponing a final settlement until after the 1976 elections are getting their way. Six months of 1975 were frittered away by infighting between the State Department and the Department of Defense. When negotiations were resumed in September, Bunker returned to Panama with instructions which were bound to create another stand-off. The most hopeful timetable, now, does not provide for action on a treaty by Congress before November 1976. It is less clear that Panama's volatile students can be restrained that long unless there are good prospects for a highly favorable treaty.

The protracted negotiations have revealed a pattern for settlement which can protect essential U.S. interests while satisfying all but the most radical minority of Panamanians. Such a treaty, over a short transitional period, would phase out the quasi-sovereign status enjoyed by the United States in the zone, together with its incidents, such as commercial, judicial, and police services. The United States would yield title to the bulk, i.e., more than half, of zonal territory. A canal authority, probably an incorporated agency of the U.S. government but with increasing Panamanian participation, would run the canal for a fixed period, terminating around the end of the century, after which it would relinquish operating rights and titles to Panama. While they endure, these operating rights and titles would be immu-

nized by treaty—to the extent law can protect against politics—from premature Panamanian abrogation. The authority's senior officials would be subject only to limited Panamanian jurisdiction.

By separate but related treaty, there would continue to be U.S. bases in Panama, perhaps half a dozen in number, but fewer than at present, established and operated under lease and status-of-forces agreements very similar to other U.S. overseas base arrangements. This base agreement would run for a decade or slightly more beyond the end of the agreement governing U.S. operation of the canal itself. The United States and Panama would jointly undertake the defense of the canal. The Latin-American counterinsurgency training program in Panama would be phased out, implicitly if not explicitly. Tolls would be allowed to rise to give Panama annual revenues in the $50 million-plus range. While these are not all terms to which the parties have already agreed, a final treaty, if there is one, will probably not depart much from these basics.

A treaty cannot, however, come into effect until after a national plebiscite in Panama and until the U.S. Senate has given its "advice and consent" by two-thirds majority. In addition, since U.S. property is to be disposed of, the participation of the House of Representatives is probably necessary under Article II, Section 2 of the Constitution.[2] That these bodies will go along is far from a foregone conclusion. Except in a major crisis, congressional foreign policy tends to be made not by the "silent majority" but by small groups of congressmen representing committed minorities of Americans with deeply held convictions and intense loyalties to one side of an interest conflict. In the case of the Panama Canal, there is keen articulation by opponents of "surrender" which is not matched by the majority either of members or of citizens.

[2] *See* Disposal by Treaty of United States Property Rights in Panama, *Congressional Research Service, Library of Congress.*

The Panama Lobby

The Panama lobby in Congress and in the nation, which opposes such a treaty, consists of three interest groups and one amorphous but potent ideological constituency. Best organized among these are the labor groups like the Canal Zone Central Labor Union and Metal Trades Council (affiliated with the AFL-CIO), representing the preponderance of U.S. employees of the Canal Company and zone government, and the Panama Canal Pilots Association, which consists of approximately 200 U.S. and three Panamanian citizens. It is a much-quoted shibboleth on Capitol Hill that "the canal pilots won't work for the Panamanians." As for the U.S. employees of the zone government and Canal Company, Panama-ization presents them with the threat, at best, of loss of privileges and, at worst, with diminution of career prospects.

Second are transnational corporate interests. AIMS, the American Institute of Merchant Shipping, has a primary stake in keeping tolls low and the canal open, which is the status quo. U.S. corporate investors in the zone—such as ITT, which owns Central American Cables and Radio, Inc., as well as Transoceanic Communications, the zone-based communications system—are beginning to register their unease at the prospect of coming under direct Panamanian jurisdiction, although they are keeping a low profile.

The third organized interest group is the U.S. military establishment. At its periphery, this includes the Veterans of Foreign Wars. The key factor, however, is the Department of Defense—in particular the Department of the Army, which has traditionally had the main role in running the zone—and the Joint Chiefs of Staff. It has always been clear that Congress would never approve any treaty with Panama over the opposition of Defense and the Joint Chiefs of Staff and this, throughout the negotiations, has given them a sort of veto. This

was held carefully in reserve until late spring, then used very effectively.

That story of last summer's interdepartmental guerrilla warfare has been widely chronicled by the media, in large part because Defense strategy, masterminded by Army Secretary—and more recently Ford Presidential Campaign Manager—Howard Calloway, called for it to be played that way. While Bunker and Assistant Secretary William D. Rogers kept an agonized public silence in accordance with interdepartmental etiquette and a prior agreement, Defense emissaries and "spokesmen" began to appear everywhere—in *Washington Post* interviews and at National Security Council and congressional offices—expressing their concern that the treaty, as it was shaping up, would not protect the national defense interest. They fretted that State was willing to settle for a 25-year tenure while the Army needed 50 years plus a strong renewal option and that State was willing to concede land and water areas of the zone that the Army needed to defend and sustain itself. This was not the view of all, but only of some of the hawks in Defense who saw the issue in terms of presidential primaries.

The conflict over these issues was resolved in a series of National Security Council meetings in July and August, culminating in a new set of instructions personally approved by President Ford. The result, in the unanimous opinion of the scribes, was a famous victory for the State Department.[3]

On September 4, in a news event staged with the loving care of a Canossa, Assistant Secretary Rogers flew down to Panama with the chairman of the Joint Chiefs of Staff, General George S. Brown, and Deputy Secretary of Defense William P. Clements, Jr.,

---

[3] *For one such account see Stephen S. Rosenfeld, "The Panama Negotiations—A Close-Run Thing," Foreign Affairs. October 1975, pp. 10-11. Our analysis of these events, however, varies from that of the Rosenfeld article, which implies that Defense did not want a treaty with Panama and that the president's new instructions to Bunker in August constituted a victory for the State Department. We disagree with both of these assertions.*

for a carefully orchestrated one-day meeting with Torrijos. This culminated in a statement by Brown at Panama City airport: "I assured General Torrijos that the Joint Chiefs and the Department of Defense were committed to working out a new treaty and that we fully support Ambassador Bunker's efforts."

When Bunker returned to the talks in September, the Panamanians had high hopes, fanned by erroneous press reports, of that State Department victory. But the victory was really a compromise. And Bunker's cautious opening gambit—offering a 50-year base agreement with option to renew—seemed a terrible letdown. Since then, however, State has signaled that this is far from being its final offer and has urged the Panamanians to come back with an offer of their own.

Besides the specific interest groups there is a larger, amorphous ideological constituency opposed to the treaty. It is composed mainly of unorganized U.S. voters whose interest in the canal is primarily symbolic and who see its surrender as yet another retreat from superpower commitment. Much of this opposition comes from the South and Southwest, is confined to a certain generation, reflects the mystique of Teddy Roosevelt, and was learned in school by persons now in their forties and fifties who used the "imperial America" class of textbooks. The building of the canal, to some people, was the moon-walk of the 1910s. The staffs of members of Congress opposed to concessions insist that no subject engenders a more continuously heavy stream of mail overwhelmingly opposed to surrendering any of the legacy of McKinley and Roosevelt.

In addition to these interest groups lined up against the treaty, there is the ever present Kissinger Factor and the divinely ordained War Among the Branches. A prime source of congressional opposition to the direction of the current negotiations stems from the usual resentment felt by members at being excluded from the State and Defense Departments' bargaining with a foreign power. In 1967, after an earlier set of negotiations, it was bitterly pointed out that the draft treaties were not communicated to congressmen, while they were circulating freely on the streets of Panama City. In 1974 and 1975, similarly, U.S. negotiators —with the exception of the State-Defense imbroglio described above—have strictly adhered to their commitment to secrecy while the Panamanians have been less inhibited. As a result, even liberal members of Congress and pro-de-escalation staffers of congressional committees concerned with foreign relations complain that "Bunker has made no effort to keep us informed. When he does come up here, we arrange to hear him in secret session but he still tells us nothing." Most of what Congress knew about the negotiations—some of it inaccurate—was learned from published versions of interviews given by Foreign Minister Tack or official leaks in the Panamanian press. On September 24, Ambassador Gonzalez-Revilla, the deputy Panamanian negotiator, in an "off-the-record" discussion at the Council on Foreign Relations (which promptly found its way into *Washington Post* and *New York Times* news stories), detailed what had and what had not been agreed to date. Inevitably, these leaks put the direction of talks in a light most favorable to Panama, thereby further arousing the concern of Congress. This is accentuated by a notable and as yet inchoate coalition of anti-Kissinger and anti-secret diplomacy attitudes that unites the conservative and liberal wings of both Houses.

The antitreaty forces focus on the importance of the canal (1) to American trade and (2) to American defense. They argue that these interests are too important to be entrusted to the stewardship of an unstable foreign government. Protreaty advocates can rebut these assertions of the canal's importance and of the vulnerability of American interests. But ultimately, if the argument is to be won by the protreaty forces, it will have to be shifted to other, higher ground of their own choosing.

Trade

The trade issue raised by those who opposed de-escalation relies in part on an assertion that canal tolls will skyrocket if the United States does not retain firm control over the waterway's operations. One reply to this is that even with the United States still operating the canal, tolls—which remained virtually constant until last year despite the rise in almost all costs since the canal opened in 1914—will have to climb very substantially to permit reasonable upkeep and modernization as well as the inevitable increase in fixed annuities to Panama. The 20 per cent increase in tolls granted last year is only a beginning, since income still barely covers operations and maintenance and does not provide for improvements.

The proposed treaty does not envisage Panama supplanting the new Canal Company as toll-collector for approximately 25 years. But even if the power to fix charges were to revert to Panama tomorrow, the elasticity of tolls would still be limited. The real inhibitor of a toll increase is not U.S. control but the economics of the alternate routes, or the canal's "traffic sensitivity." In the case of United States intercoastal traffic as well as in the case of exports and imports beginning or terminating at either coast, the most obvious and commonly used alternative is transshipment across its own territory. For other cargo, the route around Cape Horn offers an option which becomes attractive either when a ship exceeds a certain tonnage or after tolls have increased above a threshold. Although the traffic sensitivity to toll increases varies from commodity to commodity, a recent expert study shows that when tolls are increased beyond 150 per cent, "the revenue impact of the higher toll rate is more than offset by the decline in traffic volume." For bananas, total predicted toll revenues decline after the charges are increased by only 25 per cent. For sugar,

iron ore, scrap metal, coal, and crude petroleum, the anticipated revenue shrinkage point is reached when tolls increase beyond 50 per cent. For seven other commodities that point is 100 per cent and for 10 more it is 150 per cent, or possibly higher.[4]

The Maritime Administration of the Department of Commerce points out that a 200 per cent increase in canal tolls would raise prices of products shipped via the canal by less than 5 per cent. A 75 per cent increase would cause a 1.8 per cent rise in commodity price, assuming demand remained constant.[5]

Rates are only one aspect of U.S. concern over the canal's availability for commercial shipping. Still, it is no longer the commercial lifeline—at least not for the United States—that it once was. It remains important, but its importance to other countries is far greater and is increasing. Three-quarters of Nicaraguan ocean cargo goes through the canal compared to about 17 per cent of U.S. seaborne commerce, putting America tenth in order of dependence on the route. In comparative terms, the canal is far more important to at least nine Latin-American states.[6] It is almost as important to Japan, South Vietnam, Taiwan, Korea, Mexico, and New Zealand as it is to the United States and it is of considerable, if smaller,

[4] *It has been pointed out that, at the 1972 level of tolls, a dry-bulk carrier of 12,500 dwt. could break even by sailing about 1,000 extra miles in order to avoid the canal tolls, but a 37,500 dwt. carrier could afford to travel an additional 1,600 miles and a 67,500 dwt. carrier, 3,200 miles. See J. E. Howell and Ezra Solomon,* The Economic Value of the Panama Canal, *prepared for the Panama Canal Company (Palo Alto, Calif.: International Research Associates, 1973), pp. 20-22, 23.*

[5] *U.S. Department of Commerce, Maritime Administration,* The Panama Canal in U.S. Foreign Trade: Impact of a Toll Increase and Facility Closure, *May 15, 1974, pp. 7-9.*

[6] *Ibid. Comparative percentages of cargo taken through the canal are as follows: Chile (34.3 per cent), Colombia (32.5 per cent), Costa Rica (27.2 per cent), Ecuador (51.4 per cent), El Salvador (66.4 per cent), Guatemala (30.9 per cent), Nicaragua (76.8 per cent), Panama (29.4 per cent), and Peru (41.3 per cent). The U.S. percentage is 16.8.*

importance to the Philippines, Canada, and a number of other Latin-American countries.[7] Further, since foreign trade constitutes only 10 per cent of U.S. gross national product (GNP), its vulnerability is even further diminished in comparison to Latin-American, Western European, and Asian states that must "trade or perish." Less than 1 per cent of our GNP passes through the canal.[8] The U.S. intercoastal trade, dominant in the canal's early days, now accounts for only 2.9 per cent of all cargo shipped through the canal.

This analysis suggests that collective bargaining with Panama by all canal users might be at least as effective as U.S. control in keeping the canal open, neutral, and economically viable. Certainly it is not only, or even primarily, the United States which ought to be concerned about toll stabilization and other terms of use. Panama, after all, needs the canal even more than its users. Its leaders have long referred to it as "our sole natural resource." Even if speculative mineral exploiting schemes pan out, the canal will remain central to Panama's economy for decades. And with Panama setting the tolls, the Latin-American, Japanese, and Western European user states would have a common interest with the United States in exerting leverage to keep tolls down rather than, as at present, being united with Panama in opposition to U.S. "colonialism."

Also, as the comparative dependence of the U.S. economy on the canal declines, so does the number of cargo vessels physically able to pass through it. Already, not only oil supertankers but many cargo ships carrying other bulk or containerized commodities are too large. The advantage of the larger ships is that their speed is such as to

cut the costs of the longer voyages on alternate routes. Thus, a considerable portion of the coal now shipped from the eastern United States to Japan travels in huge cargo ships via the Cape of Good Hope route at prices which are competitive per ton with the same load sent via Panama.

Still, the canal is certainly important to the U.S. economy, and if it were closed to shipping, as compared to merely being subject to a moderate rise in tolls, there would be a pronounced negative impact on the economy. The coal of West Virginia, the grain of the Middle West, the cotton and textiles of the Southeast, and the oil for the northeastern states remain significant users of the waterway. But closure of the canal to U.S. ships or cargo, for whatever reason, is conceivable only if Panama were prepared to go to war with Washington.

How Strategic A Value?

Is the canal a cornerstone of hemispheric defense strategy? This important issue breaks down into two others: How important is the canal itself to U.S. global naval strategy? How crucial is the Southern Command's (CINCSOUTH) headquarters base to U.S. strategic interests in Latin America?

The strategic value of the canal to the United States has rapidly diminished in recent years. The military itself assumes that in the event of a future war, the use of the canal would be denied the United States either by air attack or by sabotage. The present locks, dams, and power systems, a government study has found, "make the present canal a vulnerable target. In certain situations, the canal could be closed for two years."[9] This was, for a time, the principal argument in favor of building a new sea-level canal, which would be far more resistant to bombing or sabotage. That project, however, is now thought to be so fraught with ecological dangers and burdened with

[7] *Ibid.*

[8] *1973 figures based on statistics in statement of General David S. Parker, governor of the Panama Canal Zone and president of the Canal Company, in U.S. House of Representatives, Committee on Merchant Marine and Fisheries, 93rd Congress, 1st Session, Hearings on the Panama Canal, series no. 93-19, July 17, 1973, p. 3.*

[9] *Report of the Atlantic-Pacific Interoceanic Canal Study Commission, December 1, 1970 (Washington, D.C.: Government Printing Office, 1971), p. II-6.*

astronomical costs as to be excluded by both Washington and Panama.

U.S. bidexterity has also diminished the waterway's strategic coin. While the present canal was initially favored by Roosevelt because the Spanish-American War had demonstrated the need for naval mobility, the emergence since the start of World War II of virtually separate U.S. navies on each ocean has downgraded this consideration.[10] This is further evident from the construction of more than 24 U.S. aircraft carriers that cannot traverse it. During the Vietnam war the carriers *Enterprise, Independence, Boxer,* and *Annapolis* were deployed from the east coast but could not go via the isthmus. Nuclear submarines, too, cannot run the canal except by surfacing.

On the other hand, the Vietnam war did demonstrate the residual strategic importance of the canal, if not in moving naval vessels, then in transporting supplies. Ships that take the canal route rather than circumnavigating Cape Horn can save 8,000 miles. Between 1965 and 1970 (the years of maximum use), the number of U.S. warship transits rose from 284 to 1,068 before again declining. It has been estimated that closure of the Panama Canal "would approximately double the requirements for ships to support operations in the Pacific."[11] Nevertheless, the United States has increasingly switched to cross-continental land transport to bring strategic goods to the Pacific coast. The land transport option could seriously strain existing rail and road facilities in a large-scale emergency. On the other hand, if up to $10 billion were saved by not having to modernize the existing canal, or build a new one, some of this money could be spent on needed improvements in domestic pub-

lic transportation. More immediately, the resupply of U.S. forces in Korea and Japan is logistically better accomplished through the ports of Seattle and San Francisco.

The Defense Department is concerned not only with the canal as a logistic resource, but with many other defense facilities—$760 million worth—not directly related to the canal operation: airfields, dry docks, a communications and command center, and a jungle warfare school. But CINCSOUTH facilities are barely sufficient to defend the canal against Panamanians, let alone engage in hemispheric missions. The approximately 6,500 troops, including noncombat support forces, currently deployed in the canal area are insufficient to play a major role in a Central American military operation. They would certainly be unable to do so if they were simultaneously defending the whole zone against angry Panamanians. Ultimately, too, the only way for the United States to defend the canal against agitators is alongside the Panamanian troops.

Yet even the most avid congressional advocates of no surrender shy away from recommending large-scale military escalation—estimated at 50,000 to 100,000 U.S. troops —that would be required to make the Canal Zone riot-, sabotage-, and guerrilla-proof.

Any realistic appraisal of U.S. forces likely to be stationed in Panama must conclude that these forces can only be deployed as a tripwire, not as a Maginot line. A tripwire strategy involves the commitment of just enough forces, over just enough real estate, to ensure that a potential aggressor cannot achieve his objective (capturing the canal) without confronting the United States. A few thousand troops located in base areas— perhaps one at each end and one toward the middle of the canal—would be sufficient for that limited purpose. The aggressor could overrun the bases, but he would then have to deal with Washington's virtually unlimited retaliatory capability. Bases sufficient for this purpose are an integral part of the agreements now being negotiated with Panama.

---

[10] *"The Navy has always operated on the assumption that in a major war the Panama Canal would be denied them, and, in effect, the United States today possesses a two-ocean Navy"* [Panama: Canal Issues and Treaty Talks *(Washington, D.C.: Center for Strategic Studies, Georgetown University, 1967)*, p. 51].

[11] *Report of the Atlantic-Pacific Interoceanic Canal Study Commission, op. cit.,* p. II-5.

None of this is to deny the legal and practical validity of the argument made by critics of de-escalation that base lease agreements are subject to premature unilateral termination by the host country and that the effective use of leased bases can be restricted in specific crises (as happened, for example, when the Thai government objected to the use of U Tapao base during the rescue of the *Mayaguez*). Yet, it should also be recognized that, militarily, the strength or vulnerability of U.S. bases in Panama will first and always depend on the number and types of forces deployed and second on the acquiescence of the local population. And if our objective is to provide residual U.S. forces and reinforcements with a legal status that is defensible—morally, if possible, but with force, if necessary—against the possibility of reneging by Panama, then a better stand can surely be made on a clear, definitive, and openly arrived at 1976 base agreement that reconciles minimal U.S. and Panamanian strategic interests than on a 1903 treaty negotiated on Panama's behalf by a dubiously accredited Frenchman with a $40 million personal stake in its outcome, the meaning of which has been bitterly contested since 1904.

The Basic Issue

Proponents and opponents of the de-escalation option each essentially perceive the Panama Canal Zone quite differently. The pro-status quo forces see the zone as a continental parcel of U.S. territory, acquired in perpetuity like Hawaii or Puerto Rico, encumbered only by the obligation to return it to Panama in the unlikely event that the United States decides to give it away to anyone. But this is just a fancy way of saying the zone is a colony. It is run by the U.S. Army, has no elected representation in Washington and no legislature in the zone itself, and is not likely to acquire any. Why should we now doubt the necessity of decolonizing the zone? The British, French, Dutch, Belgian, Spanish, and, most recently, Portuguese empires have all been wound up—as was our own Philippine presence. Does the United States want to be perceived as the world's last colonial power, stubbornly clinging to an enclave which actually cuts an independent country in half and leaves it bereft of a single deep-water port of its own?

In his efforts to save the zone for the United States, Congressman Dan Flood has recently introduced legislation to give its U.S. inhabitants an elected delegate in Congress. But unlike Puerto Rico, which is similarly served, the zone is mostly inhabited by a small group of stateside government employees and military personnel who have been posted to the Panama Canal to do a job. They are not by any stretch of the imagination the stuff of which indigenous commonwealths are made.

The presence of U.S. Canal Company employees, support service operators, and 6,500 troops with an equal number of dependents in the Canal Zone—America's *pieds noirs*, living at a suburban stateside standard of living—creates friction in a Panamanian economy "just down the block" in which the per capita income is about $700. At the other end of the pay scale, U.S. minimum wage laws apply to local employees, thereby creating a different kind of distortion and tension. An unskilled Panamanian laborer in the U.S. zone must now be paid at a rate equal to that earned in Panama by a fully trained schoolteacher.

Against this may be set two facts. First, the level of U.S. aid to Panama has been the highest, per capita, of any country in the world and disbursements amounted to $227 million in 1972. More significantly, since 1936, successive U.S. presidents, often against the recommendations of their defense and commerce advisers, have sought to ameliorate and, most recently, to terminate the colonial relationship. The Hull-Alfaro agreement of 1939 and President Eisenhower's concessions in the 1955 Chapin-Fabrega agreement made some significant concessions to Panamanian sensitivity.

These were not, however, directed to the fundamental fact of a U.S. colony cutting Panama in half, focusing instead on the right of the army to intervene outside the zone in Panama, on the size of the annuity, and on the Canal Company's purchasing and commercial licensing policies: changes that were essentially cosmetic. By 1959, the anticolonial agitation to be found in any Third World area had begun in Panama. In 1964, students clashed with U.S. forces in the zone over efforts to fly the Panamanian flag alongside The Stars and Stripes. Panama called an emergency session of the OAS under the Rio Pact, alleging an "unprovoked armed attack."

Through the efforts of the OAS Peace Committee, diplomatic relations and negotiations were resumed on April 3, 1964. In a landmark concession, President Johnson, on December 18, 1964, instructed the U.S. negotiators to seek an entirely new agreement with Panama that would terminate the 1903 treaty and would "recognize the sovereignty of Panama" while seeking to retain, for a fixed period, U.S. rights to operate and protect the canal and to administer those areas essential to that limited purpose.

In the decade following President Johnson's recognition that there was a colonial regime, that it was a relic of an earlier era, and that it ought to be ended, there have been painstaking negotiations—and even more painful *lapses* in negotiations—in an effort to enunciate the elusive formula that would give the United States narrow, functional rights for a transitional period while returning to Panama the attributes and, increasingly, the functions of sovereignty. These efforts have now climaxed in the Bunker-Tack round of talks.

Whether one regards the purpose and direction of these talks benevolently depends, ultimately, on how one would prefer the United States to act in, and be perceived by, the world. It is this which, for more than a decade, has been the fundamental issue. And it is on this that protreaty advocates must now take their stand if a mutually acceptable treaty is to be negotiated and ratified by Congress within 24 months—the limit, in the opinion of most observers, for avoiding a bruising confrontation.

In such a confrontation, the United States could only lose—even if it won over Panama. It would appear to the whole world as yet another contest between justified nationalism and imperial America. No doubt the United States has important interests in the canal. But politics, the art of the possible, has demonstrated to the post-World War II world that essential interests can be protected without—often, nowadays, *only* without—recourse to colonialism. Real U.S. self-interest demands not that we teach Panama to mind the United States—they already know from decades of big-stick interventionism which is the stronger republic—but that we expand the underexploited but potentially large areas of interdependence.

Perhaps most important to the strategy of those who will work to enlist Congress and public opinion on the side of the de-escalation option is to move the debate away from the important but inconclusive concern with shipping costs, toll elasticity, and defense logistics toward this more basic issue. In the words of one senior Army Department negotiator, "For those of us who really care about the Army, My Lai was an awful blow. We know what that's done to our reputation. The last thing in the world we want now is to be ordered to start shooting into a crowd of Panamanians." Ultimately, what is at stake in the Panama debate is America's global role and image.

ATOMS FOR BRAZIL, DANGERS FOR ALL

by Norman Gall

The weight of Brazil in world affairs increases every day. In a world full of disturbances and contradictions, the conduct of your country, Senhor Minister, appears as a factor of stability and equilibrium.— *Toast by the West German foreign minister on the eve of the signing of the Brazil-German nuclear sales agreement, June 1975.*

The Deal

The 1975 nuclear deal between Brazil and West Germany is momentous in several ways. It is a major step toward diplomatic independence by two steadfast postwar allies of the United States in response to the upheavals in the world energy economy in the mid-1970s. It calls for the largest transfer ever made of nuclear technology to a developing country. This complex umbrella agreement threatens to establish a new kind of commercial rivalry for international sales of power reactors that could accelerate nuclear weapons proliferation in the final decades of this century. If fully implemented over the next 15 years, it would give the German reactor industry desperately needed export sales and fuel supplies. It also would meet Brazil's projected demand for atomic energy through 1990 and provide much of the technological base for Brazil to make nuclear weapons if she wished. The deal thus would satisfy the long-standing ambitions of both countries for greater nuclear "self-sufficiency" and would contribute toward realization of Brazil's dream of becoming a major power.

The Brazil-German agreement was negotiated in the months following the Indian nuclear explosion of May 1974. That event had a special psychological impact among developing countries, particularly Brazil and Argentina, the rival "near-nuclear" neighbors which both refused to sign the 1968 Treaty on Non-Proliferation of Nuclear Weapons (NPT). A *New York Times* editorial headlined "Nuclear Madness" spearheaded U.S. reaction to the deal. It called the agreement a "reckless move that could set off a nuclear arms race in Latin America, trigger the nuclear arming of a half-dozen nations elsewhere and endanger the security of the United States and the world as a whole."[1] The official Soviet reaction was more cautious in expressing concern for nuclear proliferation, reflecting Moscow's perennial suspicion of Germany's intentions in the nuclear field while avoiding language that might disrupt her own growing nuclear trade with Bonn. More than any other event in the development of commercial nuclear power, the Brazil-German deal has led to intense questioning of the safety and viability of the international industry as presently organized. Some of the more important issues were raised in a speech by Senator Abraham Ribicoff a few days after the accord became public knowledge:

Hard economic times and the high price of oil have combined to establish a desperate need to sell and a desperate need to buy nuclear power reactors. Nothing less than balanced international payments and energy self-sufficiency are at stake. The resulting cutthroat nuclear competition is leading to the spread of plutonium reprocessing and uranium enrichment facilities. The capability to produce nuclear explosives is spreading "like a plague" in the words of the Inspector General of the International Atomic Energy Agency, who is responsible for detecting the diversion of peaceful nuclear materials to weapons development. . . . In truth, the United States must assume a major share

---

[1] The New York Times, *June 13, 1975, p. 36.*

of the responsibility for the present nuclear proliferation problem. We pioneered the civilian nuclear power technology, made it available to other nations through our atoms for peace program, and still clearly dominate the worldwide nuclear power industry. Closer attention should have been given to safeguards over the years, particularly to safeguards conditions on the re-export of U.S. nuclear technology by nations like France and West Germany.[2]

Giant Reactors

The centerpiece of the deal is the sale to Brazil of between two to eight giant reactors, together worth from $2 billion to $8 billion, that would accelerate her nuclear energy program toward the goals of 10,000 megawatts of electricity generating capacity by 1990 and of producing 41 per cent of her total energy supply by 2010.

The basic design of the power plants to be built by the West German consortium Kraftwerk Union (KWU) was developed by Siemens—senior partner in KWU and Germany's largest producer of electrical equipment—under license from Westinghouse, the world's largest reactor manufacturer. Westinghouse suspended these licensing arrangements in 1970, after KWU was formed to compete with Westinghouse in the international market.

The agreement, signed in Bonn on June 27, 1975, provides for creation of several mixed companies for joint Brazil-German participation in all phases of the nuclear energy industry, from prospecting for uranium ore in Brazil to the construction of reactors and the manufacture of components. The deal also calls for intensive training of Brazilian professionals in nuclear technology and heavy participation by Brazilian

industry, which would enable Brazil eventually to become an exporter of nuclear fuels and equipment. The deal would generate contracts for some 300 German firms and "now assures for the first time the stability" of 13,000 jobs in KWU's own offices and factories. A leading German weekly observed that "the federal government already had invested DM 15 billion ($5 billion) in nuclear energy research out of tax moneys— of which at least half was for basic research —and now this was finally to pay off."[3]

To obtain these benefits for West Germany, Bonn has assumed the entire financial risk for the first two plants through a consortium of five big banks lending $1 billion at concessional interest rates. Half the debt will be financed at 7.25 per cent by the Kreditanstalt für Wiederaufbau, a development bank formed to distribute Marshall Plan aid. The Kreditanstalt will draw one-third of its contribution at 3 per cent interest from a special revolving fund left over from the Marshall Plan used to finance German exports.

The Dangers of the Deal

Bonn's commitment to provide Brazil with a uranium enrichment plant and a facility for reprocessing spent fuel, from which plutonium could then be extracted, raises a major political issue. These plants could be used, alternatively, for the preparation and recycling of reactor fuels, or for the production of nuclear weapons.

In response to widespread criticism of the deal's dangers, West Germany obtained Brazil's reluctant agreement to a framework for international inspection that goes far beyond the safeguards required by the International Atomic Energy Agency (IAEA) to detect any diversion of nuclear equipment or materials for weapons production. These safeguards would cover not only the life of

[2] *U.S., Congress, Senate, Congressional Record, 94th Cong., 1st sess., June 3, 1975, p. S9323. The first general disclosure of the deal came a few days earlier in Robert Gillette, "Nuclear Proliferation: India, Germany May Accelerate Process," Science, May 30, 1975. Also see Lewis H. Diuguid, "Brazil Nuclear Deal Raises U.S. Concern," Washington Post, June 1, 1975, p. 1.*

[3] *Heinz Michaels, "Querschüsse aus den USA," Die Zeit, June 20, 1975. Also see "Atomwirtschaft: 12,000,000 Mark für Deutschland," Wirtschaftswoche, June 27, 1975, p. 13.*

the agreement but also the useful life of all installations built under it and any application of technical know-how acquired from the Germans to any other nuclear facilities built in Brazil.

These new "know-how" safeguards, to be applied for the first time in the Brazil-German deal, apparently now are becoming standardized in international sales of nuclear technology as a result of an agreement reached, at U.S. initiative, by the principal supplier nations, known as the "Secret Seven," [4] at a series of secret meetings in London throughout 1975.

However, nobody seems to know how these technology safeguards will be implemented after enrichment and reprocessing plants with weapons-making potential are delivered to countries such as Brazil, whose military regime for the past decade has had a programmatic commitment to carrying out "peaceful" nuclear explosions. Since there is no intrinsic distinction between a "peaceful" and a military nuclear device, the spread of these plants throughout the world could create a series of de facto situations clearly beyond the control of the international inspection machinery. This machinery is operated by the underfinanced and understaffed IAEA, which is empowered only to report violations to the U.N. Security Council and has no enforcement mandate.

The text of the Brazil-German accord makes it contingent upon a safeguards agreement with the IAEA, "assuring that these nuclear materials, equipment, and installations, as well as the special fertile and fissionable materials produced in them, processed or used, and the respective technological information, are not used for nuclear weapons or other nuclear explosives." However, the semiofficial commentary published with the text in the Brazilian press said: "For Brazil, this does not represent a commitment to forgo nuclear devices in the future. . . . One can presume that this does not

rule out the possibility of Brazil developing her own technology based on knowledge acquired by Brazilian technicians who become familiarized, in time, with the jet-nozzle process." [5]

THE DEAL IN A NUTSHELL

> *Uranium exploration and mining:* Initial exploration of two areas totaling 73,000 square kilometers. Guaranteed delivery of 20 per cent of any ore to German utilities, with proportion increasing later. NUCLEBRAS (the new Brazilian state nuclear energy corporation) share, 51 per cent in joint company.

> *Uranium enrichment:* Construction in Germany of a pilot plant by 1981, with an industrial-scale plant to be built later in Brazil, using experimental jet-nozzle technique being developed by Germans. NUCLEBRAS share, 75 per cent.

> *Fuel fabrication:* Pilot plant, then commercial plant built by Germans. NUCLEBRAS share, 70 per cent.

> *Reprocessing of spent fuel:* Construction of pilot plant under technical assistance agreement between NUCLEBRAS and German consortium. NUCLEBRAS share, 100 per cent.

> *Power plants:* Two 1,300-megawatt pressurized water reactors by 1985, and option for six more by 1990, with increasing participation by Brazilian industry in construction and component manufacture to reach 70 per cent by 1980 and 90 per cent by 1990.

Looking beyond the dangers of nuclear weapons proliferation in exports of the "complete fuel cycle," the Brazil-German deal reflects the centrifugal forces in the postwar international power structure that have been gaining momentum in recent years. At the height of U.S. influence, the principal

---

[4] *The United States, Canada, France, Great Britain, Japan, the Soviet Union, and West Germany.*

[5] *From the Portuguese text of the agreement and commentaries published in* Jornal do Brasil, *June 28, 1975, p. 11.*

supports of the Western system were the American command of strategic nuclear weaponry, the role of the dollar in assuring monetary stability, and U.S. control of critical fuel supplies through the overseas petroleum reserves held by the major oil companies and through the commitment of the U.S. Atomic Energy Commission (AEC) to provide enriched uranium for the West's nuclear power plants. Now all of these elements of U.S. power have declined in importance, forcing adherents to this power, such as Brazil and West Germany, to make bargains for themselves in a much more uncertain world.

The Impact of the Energy Crisis

Brazil's nuclear deal with West Germany must be viewed in terms of the impact of the energy crisis on Brazil's rapid economic growth that has created a dominant role for her in South America. Under the pressures of the energy crisis, Brazil has reached into the South American heartland to make arrangements for critical energy supplies with two of her weaker neighbors, Bolivia and Paraguay. These two deals are for natural gas from Bolivia and for a huge binational hydroelectric dam, Itaipú, to be built jointly with Paraguay. Both were negotiated over the opposition of Brazil's traditional rival, Argentina, which during the 1950s and 1960s developed a long lead over Brazil in nuclear technology and has been suspected of attempting to fabricate nuclear weapons of her own.

While Brazil's ambitions and geopolitical rivalries will be discussed more fully later, it is worth stressing here that Brazil has been moving toward a new and still undefined role in world affairs in the tense climate created by the quadrupling of oil prices in 1973-1974. As the *developing* world's leading oil importer, Brazil has been in deep balance-of-payments trouble since the 1973 Middle East war. Consequently, she has adopted a new "ecumenical pragmatism" in her foreign policy by which she

has moved closer to the Arabs diplomatically and has sought to diversify her export markets and her sources of energy, technology, and foreign investments.

Explaining these policy departures in a lecture at Chatham House, London, in October 1975, Foreign Minister Antonio Azeredo de Silveira said: "During the cold war, a rigid alignment with the leader of the Western bloc was required of the nations of the developing world that share the basic values of the West. The reason for this or, if you prefer, the pretext was that the future of the entire system we belonged to was at stake and that unity was the price of survival." Observing that "these realities no longer apply to the final quarter of this century," Silveira explained that "an emergent power, with a wide range of interests in many fields, cannot allow rigid alignments, rooted in the past, to limit her action on the world stage." He voiced hope that the Brazil-German nuclear deal could lead to a "horizontal interdependence."

In Washington, the deal led to prolonged analysis of U.S.-Brazilian relations. Partly as a result of these deliberations, Secretary of State Kissinger visited Brasilia in February and signed an agreement committing the foreign ministers of the United States and Brazil to an annual exchange of visits for consultations on world problems, an arrangement that Brazil had sought actively for two years. At a dinner in his honor, Kissinger pronounced an official blessing over Brazil as ". . . a nation of greatness—a people taking their place in the front rank of nations. . . . My country welcomes Brazil's new role in world affairs."

The German Connection

The "horizontal interdependence" between Brazil and West Germany stems from the peculiar nature of Germany's own energy crisis. With no oil or uranium of her own, West Germany is now heavily dependent on petroleum imports and has staked her energy future on the world's largest per capita investment in nuclear power. This means construction of some 40 power stations that would raise the nuclear share of her electricity supply from 7 per cent in 1974 to 45 per cent in 1985, an increase from 4 million to 88 million tons per year coal equivalent.[6]

In implementing these plans, West Germany thus far has relied on supplies of enriched uranium sold by the U.S. government, the main nuclear fuel supplier to power plants throughout the non-Communist world. Consequently, West Germany's energy position was severely compromised by the one-two punch delivered in 1973-1974.

First came the oil price rises that accompanied the Arab boycott. Then came an important event that was little noticed in this country outside nuclear industry and government circles—the suspension by the AEC of the signing of all new contracts for future supplies of enriched uranium because, in the surge of reactor orders in the early 1970s, projected commercial demands for enriched uranium were outstripping the capacity of the three AEC enrichment plants (the newest of which was built in 1956). In addition, the AEC retroactively classified as "conditional" enrichment contracts for 45 foreign reactors scheduled to begin operation in the early 1980s, including two in Brazil and 10 in West Germany.[7] It is still not known who will supply the enriched uranium for the first two KWU plants.

Testifying that the enrichment cutback was a trigger to the Brazil-German deal, the top State Department science official told Congress: "We have run out of capacity. We saw that coming. We did not take action."[8] According to a spokesman for Westinghouse which is building Brazil's first nuclear power plant and was negotiating to build more:

> We thought . . . that we pretty well had that business locked up until the question of contracts between Brazil and the U.S. government for the slightly enriched uranium for fuel came to a sudden halt, and the Brazilians were denied firm contracts for the slightly enriched fuel, and at that point, any further industrial discussions between ourselves and the Brazilians ceased and Brazil started discussions with West Germany, with the results that were recently announced.[9]

While it is not at all clear that Westinghouse had Brazil's future reactor orders "locked up" by July 1974, many specialists see the U.S. cutoff of future enrichment commitments as having created both a reason and an opportunity for Brazil and West Germany to act together to implement separate strategic aims. Brazil has long expressed interest in "self-sufficiency" in the the nuclear fuel cycle for civilian and/or military purposes, while West Germany has wanted to make inroads into the fast-developing international nuclear energy market that has been dominated by U.S. manufacturers.

West Germany has been driven to search for new export markets and for critical fuel supplies by the loss of direct control of most of the world's known oil reserves by the major Anglo-American oil companies, and the inability of the U.S. government to maintain its open-ended commitment to fuel the world's nuclear power plants. This

[6] "West German Energy Outlook," The Petroleum Economist, *June 1975, p. 208.*

[7] *U.S., Congress, Joint Committee on Atomic Energy,* Future Structure of the Uranium Enrichment Industry: Hearings *(Washington, D.C.: U.S. Government Printing Office, 1974), pt. 3, vol. II, phase III, p. 1351. For a detailed and perceptive account of the international enrichment crisis in the 1970s, see Edward F. Wonder,* International Uranium Enrichment Cooperation: The American Case *(Ottawa: The Norman Patterson School of International Affairs, Carleton University, mimeograph, December 1975).*

[8] *Testimony by Myron B. Kratzer, acting assistant secretary, Bureau of Oceans and International Affairs, State Department, U.S., Congress, Senate, Committee on Foreign Relations, International Organization and Security Agreements:* Hearings, *July 22, 1975.*

[9] *Testimony by A. L. Bethel of Westinghouse, U.S., Congress, House, Committee on Interior and Insular Affairs,* International Proliferation of Nuclear Technology: Hearings, *July 22, 1975 (Washington, D.C.: Government Printing Office, 1975), pt. 3, p. 67.*

search has led Germany to act as a catalyst of the nationalist ambitions of such countries as Brazil, Iran, and South Africa in trading her technology for fuel supplies.[10]

West Germany's efforts to capture the Brazilian reactor market began in June 1968, shortly after Siemens won the Atucha I contract to build Latin America's first nuclear power plant in Argentina. Foreign Minister Willy Brandt, during a visit to Brazil, publicly expressed German interest in supplying Brazil with nuclear technology. A few months later a former vice minister of foreign affairs, Pio Correa, was hired as president of the Siemens subsidiary in Brazil. A bilateral agreement for scientific and technical cooperation was signed in 1969. A key role in these negotiations was played by the new president of NUCLEBRAS (the new Brazilian state nuclear energy corporation), Paulo Nogueira Batista, who then became the minister-counselor of the Brazilian embassy in Bonn to implement the accord.

Brazilian technicians were sent to Germany for training in nuclear engineering, and in 1971 a formal working relationship was established between Brazil's National Council for Nuclear Energy (CNEN) and the Center for Nuclear Research in Julich, whose representatives were to help in promoting exports of German nuclear technology. Visits of German scientists to Brazil under this agreement led to rumors, reported in the London *Sunday Times,* "of Germans conducting nuclear research in areas that would be ruled out if it were attempted on German soil." The Soviet defense ministry newspaper *Red Star* interpreted the scientific agreement as a German attempt to draw Brazil into its "atomic diplomatic game" and to encourage Brazil to reject the NPT.[11]

Apparently, intensive negotiations with the Germans did not begin until after the U.S. cutoff of future contracts for enriched uranium in July 1974. A number of important Germans visited Brazilia in mid-1974 on secret business, among them State Secretary of Technology Hans Hilgar Haunschild, former Defense Minister Franz Josef Strauss, and State Secretary for Foreign Affairs Hans George Sachs.[12] Agreement on the Brazil-German deal was reached on February 12, 1975. The U.S. ambassador in Bonn was informed a week later, and a general outline of the agreement filtered into the American trade press within a few days.[13]

Meanwhile, the 38-year-old head of the "international section" of the Julich nuclear research center, Klaus Scharmer, defended Germany's new relationship with Brazil:

> Brazil has the capacity—and will use it —to produce components and even build nuclear installations on her own. Only a partner that knows this aptitude can maintain fruitful contact for a long period. We thus saw that to try to sell installations to Brazil on a turnkey basis would be an unwise policy. We must combat the "development gap" that tends to grow between countries that are more and less developed. We must try to hasten the advance of the underdeveloped.[14]

U.S. Objections

The 1975 nuclear deal readily evokes memories of the U.S.-German rivalry for the Brazilian market that began before World War I and reached its climax during the arms race of the 1930s.[15] In both Ger-

[10] *See Robert Gerald Livingston, "Germany Steps Up,"* FOREIGN POLICY 22.

[11] *H. Jon Rosenbaum and Glenn M. Cooper, "Brazil and the Nuclear Proliferation Treaty,"* International Affairs, January 1970, p. 88.

[12] *Política Nuclear: Os projetos, as alternativas e o misterio,"* Visao, September 9, 1974, pp. 27-28.

[13] *The dates were given in* Frankfürter Allgemeine, *June 5, 1975. Translation from German Press Review, June 11, 1975, p. 3. First news of the negotiations appeared in* Nucleonics Week, February 20, 1975.

[14] *"Depois da vitóriapolítica, desafió talvez mais difícil,"* Visao, July 7, 1975, p. 16.

[15] *See Stanley J. Hilton,* Brazil and the Great Powers, 1930-1939: The Politics of Trade Rivalry *(Austin: University of Texas Press, 1975).*

many and Brazil, U.S. objections to the nuclear deal were widely interpreted as reflecting the disappointment of American suppliers who had sought the contract. While U.S. newspapers and politicians urged the Ford Administration to pressure Bonn into rescinding or modifying the Brazilian deal, Washington's negotiating position was severely undermined by its inability to offer other nations an alternate source of reactor fuel.

Chancellor Helmut Schmidt expressed surprise that the Brazil deal had not been mentioned by the Americans at a high level. Thus, two days before the accord was signed in Bonn, Schmidt told a press conference that "some of this exciteu discussion—some of it also in a segment of the American press —would appear rather clearly to go back to the very tangible interests of major industrial firms in the United States."

The German press took the same tack with much greater vehemence. "In order to get contracts the Americans fight in the international competition with heavy gloves," said the liberal, pro-Western *Die Zeit* of Hamburg. "No matter where a plant is being planned, American diplomats agitate as if they were employees of the American firms." One German official complained that "our strongest competitors are actually not Westinghouse or General Electric. The strongest competitor is the American Export-Import Bank.... Even when we try to lower the burden of interest through all sorts of tricks, the Eximbank comes in with 2 per cent less." [16]

Leading German papers claimed that American reactor salesmen in Iran, Yugoslavia, and Argentina spread rumors that KWU's financial difficulties would prevent it from making promised deliveries, and suggested that reliable supplies of reactor fuels might not be available if U.S.-built power plants were not ordered. Further questioning of American motives occurred in January 1975, while negotiations for the Brazilian deal were in their final stages, when the United States objected, in NATO councils, to a West German reactor export to the Soviet Union as part of a package deal that would have included Soviet sales of electricity to Germany. [17] A leading German economic weekly gave this view of the intensifying competition:

> With the Brazil deal, KWU is breaking into a new market that previously was firmly in the grip of U.S. companies. Westinghouse and GE are trying to protect their shrinking market position in various ways: hard sell by sales managers and U.S. government permission, wherever possible, to apply massive political pressure to those who issue the contracts. Just as the U.S. aircraft industry managed to check foreign airplane producers, the U.S. reactor industry is blocking competition from other countries. [18]

Geopolitics of Uranium

On top of the intensifying competition for export markets, the disorder in the international reactor industry has been compounded by the new uncertainty about the future U.S. capacity to export enriched uranium, thus creating a new geopolitics of uranium supplies. After the AEC cutoff in 1974 of new enrichment contracts, the Soviets have become important suppliers of enriched uranium to Western Europe. Moreover, the West Germans have been trying to diversify their sources of uranium by providing their own enrichment technology, the experimental Becker jet-nozzle process, to two potential uranium suppliers, Brazil and South Africa. The Germans are reported to have secretly assisted the South Africans, with exchanges of visits by key officials,

---

[16] *Heinz Michaels, "Querschüsse aus den USA," Die Zeit, June 20, 1975, and "Atomwirtschaft: 12,000,-000 Mark für Deutschland," Wirtschaftswoche, June 27, 1975, p. 13.*

[17] *The deal foundered over Soviet-German disagreement on Bonn's insistence that the electric power lines from the reactor pass through West Berlin en route to West Germany.*

[18] Wirtschaftswoche, *op. cit.*

to develop something very similar to the jet-nozzle technology the Germans will be providing Brazil under the new deal; in October 1975, a West German air force general was forced to resign when news leaked out of an undercover trip he made to South Africa that included a visit to a nuclear research center.[19] Two months later, *The Economist* reported that Iran, which is South Africa's main oil supplier and has an ambitious nuclear program of her own, may also finance commercial development of South Africa's jet-nozzle process in return for guaranteed supplies and access to the technology.

Similarly, one of the main hopes for both sides in the Brazil-German deal is that German geologists will help discover substantial uranium reserves that they believe to exist in Brazil. (While she has large proven deposits of thorium, a fertile material that can be made into reactor fuel and bomb material, no commercial technology has been developed so far for the use of thorium in power plants.)

Brazil has greatly intensified her uranium exploration since 1969 but with uncertain results. What was initially reported in mid-1975 to be a major find of 50,000 tons of uranium ore, in the pre-Cambrian rock of the Brazilian shield in the sprawling inland state of Goias, was modified two months later by an official estimate of only 1,500 tons. German geologists are now fanning out over the northern Amazon basin to seek new uranium deposits, with 80 per cent of their exploration expenses subsidized by Bonn. This is because Brazil's present proven reserves are far from enough to pay, in any significant degree, for the huge transfer of nuclear technology that is envisioned for the next 15 years.

Meanwhile, German firms have found valuable deposits in Namibia (South-West Africa) and are also exploring for uranium in Austria, Algeria, Australia, Canada, In-donesia, Nigeria, Spain, Switzerland, Togo, and the United States. Defending Bonn against criticism of the Brazil deal, Munich's leading newspaper observed that "the temporary export stop of the United States of uranium products made strikingly clear the dependence not only of the Federal Republic but also of the entire Western world on American fuel for nuclear reactors."[20]

Enrichment: The Gordian Knot

Uranium enrichment involves a scale of industrial activity without precedent. The U.S. government's Oak Ridge gaseous diffusion plant contains more than 1,500 machines, each the size of a railroad car, spread over more than 100 acres of factory floor. The electricity needed to drive these machines costs $500,000 a day. They are cooled by up to 90 million gallons of water daily, evaporating in huge clouds that form over the Tennessee Valley. To build such a plant today would cost $6 billion.

As long as these huge costs and the U.S. domination of gaseous diffusion technology prevented other nations from entering the business, the United States has been able to use her control of supplies of enriched uranium as a way to prevent nuclear proliferation. This leverage was applied by encouraging other nations to depend on U.S. enrichment services, on the condition that all fuels, and the plutonium therein, be monitored against diversion bilaterally or by international inspection. These controls have become less effective with the multiplication of reactors throughout the world and the spread of enrichment capacity, with new technologies, to other countries. The Brazil-German deal is the first major consequence of the accelerated scramble for alternate sources of reactor fuel, issuing from the inability of the United States to sign contracts that would commit U.S. sources to a major investment in expanded enrichment capacity.

[19] Robert Gillette, "*Uranium Enrichment: With Help South Africa Is Progressing,*" Science, June 13, 1975.

[20] Sueddeutsche Zeitung, *June 5, 1975.*

In seeking the "complete fuel cycle" in exchange for a commitment to export enriched uranium to West Germany, Brazil originally had asked Bonn to provide the new gas centrifuge technology, which is said to use much less energy than the gaseous diffusion process used in the United States. But this proposition was vetoed by the Dutch, who share control of the centrifuge process with Britain and West Germany as partners in URENCO, the European enrichment consortium, now building a centrifuge plant in the Netherlands.

Instead, the Brazilians had to settle for the experimental jet-nozzle process which is mechanically simpler than the two other technologies but consumes more electricity: nearly twice as much as the gaseous diffusion process and 20 times more than the centrifuge. While simpler mechanically than the other processes, the jet nozzle poses formidable technical problems of its own.

To separate the fissionable U-235 from the nonfissionable U-238 in gaseous form under enormous pressures, uranium hexafloride gas (mixed with hydrogen) is pumped through a long slit, forming a rapidly moving sheet of gas. The gas strikes a curved wall, where centrifugal forces carry the heavier U-238 (making up 99.3 per cent of the gas) to the outer surface of the sheet. The isotopes are separated along paring blades with tolerances of 0.00005 (five hundred-thousandths) of an inch that must remain accurate, stress-resistant, and stable under these pressures.

The jet nozzle process, in laboratory tests, has been so energy-intensive that only a few nations, such as Brazil or Switzerland, have enough cheap hydroelectric power to use it economically. Moreover, the industrial-scale engineering problems are still unsolved. The prospects of the jet nozzle competing with the centrifuge process in Europe were so dubious that in May 1974 Bonn's research minister ordered a cutoff of federal subsidies for development of the jet nozzle, only to have the order reversed under industrial and bureaucratic pressure. Development of the jet nozzle has continued as a technology for the export trade.[21]

One of the striking features of the deal is that NUCLEBRAS will actually finance development of the experimental German jet-nozzle enrichment process now in the pilot plant stage, into an industrial-scale operation. If sufficient uranium discoveries are made in Brazil, or if ore can be shipped economically from abroad, Brazil could become an important exporter of enriched uranium. But a huge commitment is needed to bring this technology into industrial production. Last year, for example, the South Africans disclosed that merely to bring their version of the jet-nozzle process to the pilot plant stage, they were employing 1,200 persons and had spent $148 million since 1970. Brazil has few scientists and technicians available for this scale of nuclear research. To build a full-scale enrichment plant in Brazil, an investment of billions of dollars would be needed. Her available human and financial resources are already overcommitted, and there must be serious doubts as to whether Brazil can sustain or justify such an effort on a process that is still unproven.

The International Reactor Industry

The increasing cost and uncertainty of oil supplies has stimulated ambitious plans in several countries for new atomic power plants that would increase the nuclear portion of the West's electrical generating capacity from 2 per cent to 15 per cent in 1985. But unexpected increases in both capital costs and time needed to build these plants have caused suspensions and cancellations of orders from utilities. The added capital outlays have tended to nullify the lower operating costs that are the nuclear plants'

[21] See Robert Gillette, "Nozzle Enrichment for Sale," *Science, May 30, 1975;* James J. Glackin, "The Dangerous Drift of Uranium Enrichment," Bulletin of the Atomic Scientists, *February 1976; and* Jonathan Kwitny, "Enriching Venture," The Wall Street Journal, *November 20, 1975.*

main commercial advantage. Inflation will be pushing the aggregate price tags of the West's nuclear power plants to between $1 trillion and $1.5 trillion by the early 1990s.[22]

At the same time, strong public opposition to nuclear power has spread from the United States to France, Germany, Japan, and Sweden, compounding the inflation and delay. Foreign demand for nuclear power plants has grown far faster than U.S. demand, with 50 per cent more nuclear generating capacity already existing abroad. Both U.S. and European reactor manufacturers have responded to inflation and delay at home by competing fiercely for export sales in third markets, especially in developing countries with authoritarian regimes that need not worry about public opposition.

According to separate projections by the IAEA and AEC, the market for nuclear power among developing nations is likely to be concentrated in a handful of countries. The IAEA estimated that more than half the installed nuclear generating capacity by the year 2000 will be absorbed by only four nations: Brazil, India, Iran, and Mexico, and that 70 per cent of the same market will be concentrated in eight countries.

However, a more detailed study subsequently commissioned by the AEC found even this limited market potential to be "too optimistic," due to extremely loose forecasts of electricity demand, ignorance of costs, shortages of foreign exchange, and the inability of many national electricity systems to absorb the output of large nuclear plants. This independent study, by Richard J. Barber Associates of Washington, stresses the importance of the sales push of companies and governments in developing this market:

Nuclear reactor system vendors have acknowledged, more or less openly, that many of the initial nuclear plants sold both domestically and internationally under "turnkey" arrangements were (and apparently still are, in the case of new reactor types) "loss leaders" for which the reported prices paid by utilities significantly understated the true cost of building the plants. Governments have clearly subsidized domestic and international power sales of their vendors by means of no-interest or low-interest loans, loan guarantees, absorption of research and development costs, preferential access to and pricing of fuels and reprocessing services, etc. The amount of such subsidies is often concealed, thus distorting the true cost of the power station. ... The German government, for example, underwrote the success of Siemens' sale to Argentina by giving the Argentine government a five year no-interest loan, a subsequent very low interest loan, and balance-of-payments considerations. France managed to sell a reactor unit in Spain in return for loans covering 90 per cent of its cost and agreeing to represent Spanish interests in the Common Market. It is common knowledge in nuclear industry circles that German, U.S., and Canadian vendors "lost their shirts" on their initial sales to Argentina, India, and Pakistan.

Until the Brazil-German deal was negotiated, there had been little official concern or public discussion as to the economic wisdom and military implications of the drive to export, and even give away, nuclear reactors.

The plutonium for India's 1974 nuclear explosion was diverted from the unsafeguarded "Cirus" research reactor donated by Canada in 1956, for which the AEC supplied heavy water. India's first nuclear power plant, built by General Electric (GE) was financed with a $74 million U.S. foreign aid loan at 0.75 per cent interest over 30 years after a 10-year initial grace period, with additional support coming from the AEC and the Ford and Rockefeller foundations.[23]

---

[22] "The Case Against Nuclear Power," The Economist, May 10, 1975, p. 84.

[23] Pan Heuristics, Moving Toward Life in a Nuclear Armed Crowd (unpublished report to the U.S. Arms Control and Disarmament Agency).

With her own scientific community building on the technological base provided by the United States and Canada, India has created an immense network of nuclear facilities of all types. The "Cirus" reactor is located at the Trombay laboratories, near Bombay, which alone employs 10,400 persons, including 2,400 scientists. During construction of the plutonium separation facility at Trombay, senior Indian scientists repeatedly visited the AEC reprocessing plant in Idaho, under the "Atoms for Peace" program, for extensive interviews with staff members on the technical problems of extracting plutonium from spent fuel. Today India manufactures her own rockets and solid fuel propellants, and plans to launch rockets by 1979 capable of putting a 1,200-kilogram payload into orbit, or of delivering nuclear warheads anywhere in Asia. India's example has not been lost on other ascendant powers. While several countries are now trying to acquire nuclear technology with bomb-making potential, Brazil and India are the only two developing countries carrying out space programs with their own launching facilities.[24]

However risky and unprofitable the export trade in nuclear technology now may seem, this is precisely the direction in which the industry keeps moving.[25] German and French reactor manufacturers, still marginal in the international industry, have fought for survival, seizing on the 1974 U.S. enrichment cutoff as an opportunity to win power plant sales by offering such "sweeteners"—with bomb-making potential—as the technology for uranium enrichment and for plutonium separation from spent fuel.

Competing U.S. firms cannot legally offer these "sweeteners," but the pressure for them to do so is very great as escalating costs and political complications have shrunk the domestic market: In 1975, only seven nuclear power plants were ordered in the United States, compared with 18 abroad, and a U.S. deal to build eight nuclear plants in Iran is stalled in a dispute over Iran's insistence on the right to reprocess her own spent fuel. In November 1975, the Shah told *Business Week*: "In atomic energy you are asking us for safeguards that are incompatible with our sovereignty, things that the French or the Germans would never dream of asking."[26]

Two months later, a Westinghouse representative complained to Congress: "The U.S. government is proposing to attach a permanent veto power over nuclear fuel processing in Iran, as a precondition for sale of U.S. nuclear reactors. Other vendors from Germany and France are already selling nuclear reactors to Iran without such conditions. The result is obvious—the U.S. has sold no reactors to Iran, despite an Iranian desire to buy a large number."[27]

These broader economic and political considerations make the implementation of the Brazil-German deal a critical indicator of the future course of the international reactor industry. The compulsion to export is deeply felt in this high-risk, capital-intensive, heavily-subsidized industry. The instability is such that even West Germany's huge "complete fuel cycle" deal with Brazil was

[24] Robert Gillette, "India: Into the Nuclear Club on Canada's Shoulders," Science, June 7, 1974. For a detailed Canadian account of India's nuclear development, see Barrie Morrison and Donald M. Page, "India's option: the nuclear route to achieve goal as world power," International Perspectives, July-August 1974.

[25] France, for example, arranged in 1975 to build reprocessing plants in South Korea and Pakistan. While the South Korean deal was canceled in early 1976, thanks largely to U.S. pressure on Seoul, the Pakistan deal subsequently was approved by the IAEA and is going through. Prime Minister Zulfikar Ali Bhutto has vowed that Pakistan would match India's nuclear capacity even if Pakistanis had "to eat grass" to mobilize the resources. Industry sources estimate that for a reprocessing plant to be economically viable for civilian uses, it must reprocess spent fuels from at least 20 reactors. Pakistan has only one nuclear power plant.

[26] "Recession's Impact on Iran: Interview with Shah Mohammad Reza Pahlavi," Business Week, November 17, 1975, p. 57.

[27] Testimony by Dwight J. Porter of Westinghouse, U.S., Congress, Senate, Government Operations Committee, Nuclear Proliferation: Hearings, January 29, 1976.

not enough to dissuade AEG Telefunken from trying to withdraw as Siemen's partner in KWU, citing 1974 losses of $287 million.[28] Explaining West Germany's overseas sales drive, a KWU spokesman told a Brazilian journalist:

> We have to export. KWU has the capacity for construction of six reactors a year, and would be very satisfied if it could build three of them in Germany now. We can't export to France or Spain because the American competition is very strong. We were able to sell one reactor each in Argentina, Holland, Austria, and Switzerland, and have begun to build two in Iran.[29]

However, nobody has determined the real cost of these exports, nor the real benefits likely to accrue to customers and suppliers, nor whether these big deals will provide any real guarantees for the industry against an increasingly uncertain future. Nor is it clear whether any economic gains could outweigh the mounting dangers of nuclear proliferation.

The Rivalry

While the world energy crisis and the instability of the international reactor industry created the conditions for the Brazil-German nuclear deal, Brazil's "great power" aspirations and the peculiar nature of her own energy crisis provided the incentives. Moreover, Brazil's nuclear rivalry with Argentina made the risks of not seizing upon this opportunity unacceptable from a military point of view.

Although achieving power and prestige in proportion to her size long has been a major aim of Brazilian foreign policy, these ambitions have only been taken seriously since the military seized power in April 1964. Tightly restricting mass consumption and civil liberties while providing incentives and guarantees that attracted large amounts of foreign investment, a succession of military regimes set the stage for the so-called Brazilian "miracle."

This was a surge of rapid economic development crowned by a growth rate averaging 10 per cent yearly in the 1968-1974 period, a "miracle" that was a conspicuous beneficiary of low oil prices and of the radical expansion of the world's money supply and trade in the postwar decades. As industrialization advanced by giant strides, Brazilians began to see themselves emerging from the role of a "key country" in the global strategy of the United States to become an important military-political force in their own right. During the visit to Washington in 1971 of President Emilio Garrastazu Medici (1969-1974), those aspirations were encouraged by President Nixon's oft-quoted blessing: "As Brazil goes, so goes South America."

While Brazil's relative geopolitical position has been strengthened greatly by the political disintegration of Argentina in the 1970s, Argentina one day could recover sufficiently to inhibit Brazilian maneuvers in South America. At the same time, the energy crisis has become a crucial factor in Brazil's future growth and influence. While Brazil today is the world's fifth-largest country in area and seventh-largest in population, there is no other continental nation so deficient in economically useful deposits of fossil fuels.

Brazil's main energy asset at present is the immense hydroelectric potential of her great rivers, which is being harnessed at an impressive rate. Hydroelectric production has increased thirteenfold over the past three decades and tripled since the mid-1960s, leading to fears that the water-flow potential near the major cities may be exhausted before the turn of the century. This is being given as the main economic justification for Brazil's embarking on an ambitious nuclear power program, even though electricity de-

---

[28] *"AEG to Pull Out of Kraftwerk Union, Either Partially or Completely,"* Nucleonics Week, *November 7, 1974, p. 1.*

[29] *"Depois da vitória. . . ."* Visao, op. cit., *p. 16.*

mand is unlikely to continue growing at the rate of recent decades. According to NUCLE-BRAS president Nogueira Batista:

> By 1980, our hydroelectric resources would be exhausted in the southeast and the Sao Francisco Valley. We will still have at that time only the hydroelectric potential of the Amazon (90,000 megawatts), a good deal of which is in the region's north (far from markets). . . . The fact is that the installation of our nuclear reactors near the centers of consumption will enable these energy resources to be used right there without costly and wasteful long-distance transmission.[30]

The Impact of India

The Indian nuclear explosion of May 1974 had a major impact in both Argentina and Brazil. For some time these two countries had viewed each other's activities in the nuclear field with suspicion. After May 1974 it became a topic of common table talk among the elites of both countries to speculate about who would get the bomb first. Indeed, the Argentine magazine *Estrategia* praised the Indian peaceful nuclear explosive (PNE) as showing "how an underdeveloped and technologically dependent country can attain objectives based exclusively on her own appreciation of the priorities of national defense." [31] The same article added:

> The projections of Brazil's demographic growth place Argentina at a disadvantage that will tend to widen markedly over the next 30 years. Despite all the distortions of her growth, Brazil will become an important power, causing Argentina, if she does not adopt pertinent policies, to find it increasingly difficult to overcome Brazil or even maintain a situation of relative equilibrium. . . . Argentina is, for the moment, ahead in nuclear technology. The Atucha power reactor, using

natural uranium, is now operational and the project for the new reactor in Rio Tercero assures [Argentina] an advantage for at least the medium term. . . . Argentina and Brazil both are theoretically capable of producing an atomic bomb. This would mean, above all, a *political* decision. [emphasis in original]

The present nuclear rivalry of Brazil and Argentina dates from the early postwar period. Initially, Brazil supported U.S. efforts to control the development of atomic energy by secretly agreeing in 1945 to limit her thorium exports to consignees "in the United States or . . . designated or approved by the United States" in return for annual U.S. purchases of specified amounts of thorium ore.[32] However, Brazil's rivalry with Argentina soon led both countries to try to acquire technology developed in the unsuccessful German atom bomb project.

Shortly after the Argentine National Commission for Atomic Energy (CNEA) was formed in 1950, President Juan Peron appointed Ronald Richter, an émigré Austrian nuclear physicist who had done fusion research in Nazi Germany, as director of a new research facility on a remote island in a lake in southern Argentina. The facility was launched with considerable publicity.[33] Twenty months before the first U.S. thermonuclear (hydrogen) explosion, Peron gave a press conference to tell the world: "On February 16, 1951, in the atomic energy pilot plant on the island of Huemul, in San Carlos de Bariloche, thermonuclear reactions were carried out under controlled conditions on a technical scale." Peron then turned the press conference over to Richter, who told the reporters: "I control the explosion. I make it increase or diminish at my

---

[30] *Mauricio Dias, "Entrevista: Paulo Nogueira Batista,"* Veja, *July 23, 1975.*

[31] *Luis Garasino, "Explosión Atómica en la India: Proyección Eventual en América Latina,"* Estrategia, *May-June 1974, p. 91 and p. 97.*

[32] *From a recently declassified document, in U.S. National Archives Record Group No. 77. For an account of Anglo-American efforts to control world uranium and thorium supplies, see Martin J. Sherwin,* A World Destroyed: The Atomic Bomb and the Grand Alliance, *(New York: Alfred A. Knopf, 1975), pp. 104-105.*

[33] *John R. Redick, "Nuclear Proliferation in Latin America," p. 7 (unpublished manuscript).*

desire."[34] Twenty months later, Richter was suddenly fired and jailed when Argentine scientists found that he was experimenting with gas discharges using high-voltage capacitors, an activity not unrelated to fusion research but falling far short of his claims.

A Secret Deal

These strange experiments in the south of Argentina may have led to a much more serious effort by Brazil to obtain German nuclear technology during the postwar allied military occupation. In 1953, Admiral Alvaro Alberto, the first president of Brazil's National Research Council, visited Germany and met with Paul Haarteck, Otto Hahn, and Wilhelm Groth, scientists who had played key roles in the abortive Nazi atom bomb projects. According to a recently published report, Groth, who pioneered the centrifugal enrichment process, told Alberto: "Allocate the necessary funds and we will make the prototypes. Then we'll all go to Brazil and make the equipment there."

A secret deal was made to ship three gas centrifuges for uranium enrichment to Brazil. Three Brazilian chemists were sent to Germany for special training in the handling of heavy gases, while Groth quietly ordered components from 14 different German factories. Alberto later told a parliamentary inquiry that "Germany was a country occupied by the victorious powers, and if it were discovered that they were planning to produce enriched uranium, this would lead to an international crisis."

The secret was uncovered only when the centrifuges were ready for shipment. After the machines were seized on orders from James Conant, U.S. high commissioner to Germany, the Brazilian government then turned to France in an attempt to obtain gaseous diffusion technology, again unsuccessfully. In a confidential memorandum to Brazil's national security council, the U.S. embassy in Rio "frankly" observed, that this "German adventure in Brazil . . . could be considered as a potential threat to the security of the United States and the Western Hemisphere."[35] The embassy also urged Alberto's dismissal, warning that "the subject of atomic energy is and may continue to effect [sic] the political and economic relations between Brazil and the United States."[36] Alberto, now a national hero and a pioneer of Brazil's shrewd policy of "specific compensation" (trading natural resources for technology), resigned his post in frustration in 1955.

The nuclear programs of Brazil and Argentina accelerated after 1955, when both countries signed agreements with the United States under the "Atoms for Peace" program, making available newly declassified scientific information and providing for the training of nuclear scientists and technicians. While Brazil obtained her first research reactors under this program, Argentina steadfastly pursued an independent nuclear development policy to avoid international controls where possible and dependence on the virtual U.S. monopoly over supplies of enriched uranium.

Argentina Moves Ahead

With her own uranium reserves, a large pool of trained manpower, and a relatively advanced industrial base, Argentina soon moved well ahead of other Latin American nations in developing a nuclear energy program. In 1958, Argentina became the first Latin American nation to operate a research reactor. In 1968, her CNEA began operating the region's first, and so far only, chemical

---

[34] *Text of press conference in* La Nación, *March 25, 1951, p. 1.*

[35] *While U.S. official documents concerning this episode are still classified, Portuguese translations of them have been published repeatedly in Brazil over the past two decades. I am quoting here from the texts translated in Juárez Távora,* Atomos para o Brasil *(Rio de Janeiro: Jose Olympio, 1958), p. 347.*

[36] *The English original is quoted in Moniz Bandeira,* Presenca dos Estados Unidos no Brasil *(Rio de Janeiro: Civilazacao Brasileira, 1973), p. 369n.*

processing plant—on a pilot scale—for reclaiming plutonium from spent reactor fuel, and in 1974 Argentina started up Latin America's first nuclear power plant.[37]

"The CNEA in 1957 made a fundamental decision: not to import research reactors but to build them in Argentina," the CNEA scientist Jorge Sabato wrote in a detailed account of Argentina's progress. "In this way we would not only have, in these reactors, a tool for training and research, but their construction would also allow us to develop our own capacity for nuclear engineering. . . . In 1957, the CNEA also decided not to import fuels. These should be manufactured in Argentina. And so it (gradually) occurred. The development of our own nuclear engineering capacity was very important in the realization of our own feasibility study for Atucha I,"[38] the 320 megawatt power plant, fueled with natural uranium, that went into operation in 1974 near Buenos Aires. By the early 1970s Argentina was operating six major centers for nuclear research and many of her scientists and engineers had received advanced training in the United States and Europe.

Argentina's nuclear program was developing so rapidly that the twelfth Pugwash Conference meeting in the Soviet Union in 1969 was told that Argentina was mobilizing her physicists to produce nuclear weapons within 15 years.[39]

In February 1968, the CNEA announced that it had chosen Siemens of West Germany from among 17 bidders from five nations to build the Atucha I nuclear power plant. Although U.S. suppliers had underbid the Germans, CNEA's choice of a system using natural uranium, rather than the enriched uranium fuel of U.S.-designed reactors, enabled the Argentines to employ their own uranium reserves and to do so without obligatory international controls.

Explaining Argentina's rejection of the U.S. bids, Sabato wrote that "the fundamental disadvantages of the enriched uranium design is that at the moment only one country (the United States) provides commercial uranium enrichment." Natural uranium reactors also have a military advantage over enriched uranium reactors: They are especially prolific in producing weapons-grade plutonium that can be separated chemically from spent fuel. Natural uranium reactors also are designed for frequent and easy replacement of fuel rods while the reactor is running, not feasible in enriched uranium plants, making inspection against secret diversion of plutonium for weapons production much more difficult.

The military implications of Argentina's decision to build a natural uranium power plant were not lost on the Brazilians. Early in 1974, while Atucha I was being readied for operation, a nuclear engineer published an article in Brazil's official military journal that has been widely and repeatedly quoted in the Argentine press. It said:

The Brazilian people need to be proud of their country for other, more serious reasons than football and carnival. International prestige is, evidently, a national objective. . . . The relationship between Security and Development is very well known. Undeniably, it will be impossible to be a power without the required military protection. A simple agreement like Itaipú would be impossible if one of our neighbors had 20 kilos of plutonium.[40]

The Argentines, meanwhile, have become deeply concerned over Itaipú, the world's largest hydroelectric dam, which the Brazilians are building, with some Paraguayan assistance, on the border of the two coun-

[37] Robert Gillette, "India and Argentina: Developing a Nuclear Affinity," Science, June 28, 1974, p. 1351.

[38] Jorge Sábato, "Energía Atómica en Argentina," Estudios Internacionales, October-December 1968, p. 342.

[39] Walter Sullivan, "Pugwash Parley in Sochi Told of Argentina's Nuclear Plans," The New York Times, October 27, 1969, p. 19.

[40] Elvé Montiero de Castro, "A Energia Nuclear no Brasil," A Defesa Nacional, January-February, 1974, p. 63.

tries. Itaipú is only about 10 miles north of the Argentine frontier in a region that, over the centuries, has been a theater of recurrent geopolitical rivalries, first between the Spanish and Portuguese empires and later between Argentina, Brazil, and Paraguay.

The dam has become a symbol in Argentina of Brazilian penetration and domination in areas of the continent where Argentina used to have great influence. Argentina opposed the Itaipú dam on grounds of environmental impact and international law, and has mustered majority support for her position at recent international conferences, but that has not affected the progress of the project.

The NPT

Argentina and Brazil refused to sign or ratify The Treaty on Non-Proliferation of Nuclear Weapons (NPT) on similar grounds. During the 1968 U.N. debate on the proposed NPT treaty, Argentina said she "cannot accept remaining subordinate to a continuing dependence on the great powers in nuclear technology for peaceful ends, especially when our country has laid the foundations for a nuclear technology needed for economic development." Coining a phrase that was subsequently heard often in the nuclear proliferation debates, the Argentine delegate said the NPT would "disarm the unarmed" while imposing no restrictions on the superpowers' arms race.[41] The Brazilians have seen the NPT as an attempt to "freeze" the international power structure to contain emergent powers such as Brazil.

Shortly after taking office, President Arthur da Costa e Silva argued: "The development of scientific research in the field of nuclear energy includes, inevitably, at a certain stage, the use of explosions; to veto access to the use of explosions would be equivalent to impeding the development of the peaceful uses of nuclear energy."[42] In December 1967, as Argentina's CNEA was preparing to announce its final decision on the design and contract for Atucha I, Costa e Silva approved a National Security Council report that recommended, as permanent objectives, "transfer of nuclear technology to our country; obtaining in the shortest time our independence in the production of nuclear fuels; creation of an infrastructure of support for the nuclear program; and formation and training of teams competent in the different (specialized) areas."[43] In 1967, Brazil's National Council for Nuclear Energy (CNEN) commissioned a study of the feasibility of building an atom bomb, concluding that such a project, if attempted, would take 15 years.[44]

Brazil's Nuclear Development

Brazil's nuclear development had been slowed by a number of false starts. At the end of the 1950s, President Juscelino Kubitschek (1956-1961) had decided on construction of a 150-200 megawatt power reactor using enriched uranium following the U.S. model that dominates the industry today. In 1961, however, the seven-month government of President Janio Quadros, in developing its independent foreign policy, reversed these plans and opted for a natural uranium reactor along the lines of the first reactors then being developed in France. This project continued under President João Goulart (1961-1964) as Brazilian technicians went to France for training and French nuclear engineers went to Brazil to begin preparations for construction of the

[41] *José María Ruda, "La posición argentina en cuanto al Tratado sobre la No Proliferación de las Armas Nucleares,"* Estrategia, *September-December 1970, January-February 1971, p. 79.*

[42] *Quoted in James W. Rowe, "Science and Politics in Brazil,"* in Kalman H. Silvert (ed.) The Social Reality of Scientific Myth *(New York: American Universities Field Staff, 1969), p. 91.*

[43] *Quoted in "Política Nuclear: Os projetos, as alternativas e o mistério,"* Visao, *September 9, 1974, p. 25.*

[44] *H. Jon Rosenbaum, "Brazil's Nuclear Aspirations,"* in Onkar Marwah an Schulz (ed.), Nuclear Proliferation and the Near-Nuclear Countries *(Cambridge, Mass.: Ballinger, 1975).*

reactor. However, this project was, in turn, cancelled by the military regime that seized power in 1964, while the French, a few years later, abandoned their efforts to develop a natural uranium reactor in favor of U.S. enriched uranium technology.

Subsequently, Brazil seriously weighed the possibility of buying a Canadian Candu natural uranium reactor of the type which is to be used in Argentina's second nuclear power plant and was used in India to "cook" the plutonium used in the 1974 nuclear explosion. Brazil also has repeatedly asked Westinghouse to help her develop a new technology to use her huge thorium reserves as reactor fuel, assisting the experiments of the Brazilian "Thorium Group" in Belo Horizonte. Westinghouse, a contractor to the U.S. Navy's classified research program to develop a reactor based on the thorium fuel cycle, declined Brazil's request on the grounds that it could not commit the resources to develop thorium technology, and because, as presently conceived, a power plant using thorium would need an initial charge of weapons-grade uranium, and would not be economically competitive.

Yet Brazil's quest for "self-sufficiency" has continued, through her 1972 contract with Westinghouse for her first nuclear power plant and, more importantly, through her giant deal with West Germany embracing the whole fuel cycle.

A Decisive Step

News of the Brazil-German deal had such a psychological impact in the Western Hemisphere that its main political effect may have been achieved long before the final details of the complex agreement are worked out and construction begins in 1977-1978 on the eight-year project to build the first two power plants. The commanding general of the First Army in Rio de Janeiro said the nuclear accord "constitutes a decisive step that reinforces the country's sovereignty," and predicted that Brazil would "be transformed into a great power." Foreign Minister Silveira, after signing the agreement, said that "Brazil has gained new technological and political status on the world scene with the nuclear agreement," adding: "Both of our two countries must pray that nobody throws an atomic bomb at our heads while we are working at carrying out these agreements. Because we won't be the ones to throw it."

Argentina's present inability to check Brazil's initiative in the nuclear field parallels her inability to counter Brazilian geopolitical initiatives in the interior of South America, and is easily understood in view of the political disorder that has escalated steadily over the past two decades in Argentina. Under these conditions, it is not surprising that Argentina's own nuclear program would be paralyzed by her present financial difficulties.[45] In addition, many of Argentina's nuclear scientists have left the country. Many are working now in Brazil. The former head of CNEA, Admiral Oscar A. Quihillalt, is now serving in Iran as adviser to the Shah's atomic energy commission at a reported monthly salary of $10,000, assisted by seven other Argentine specialists.

In July 1975, the present head of CNEA visited Tripoli to sign a nuclear cooperation agreement between Argentina and Libya, while at home Argentina is engaged in an expansion of her pilot facilities for the reprocessing of spent fuels. With reserves of trained manpower and critical energy supplies greater than Brazil's, Argentina's capacity for maneuver can only increase if the new regime stabilizes the country. An expanded nuclear program would have great symbolic value in such a comeback. The Argentine military's concern about the deal may be contained in *Estrategia's* admonition:

> Given the available facts, *it is possible to affirm that* [Brazil] *has taken the firm decision to join the Nuclear Club, that is,*

[45] See Mark Gayn, "No safeguards yet, Canada building A-plant in Argentina," The Toronto Star, *July 22, 1975, p. 1.*

to make an atom bomb under the concept of peaceful uses . . . the decision to manufacture the nuclear explosive and the opportunity, are critical for Argentina, since our neighbor's nuclear device, without a counterpoise, will affect our Security palpably and decidedly. (emphasis in original) [46]

The Future

This likely peril is being instituted by an ally in our backyard (while) the U.S. government is heavily committed in West Germany's backyard to defend them against a likely peril. . . . I say of all the countries in the world that should not have done it is West Germany. . . . The present government in Brazil may be very amenable to the United States. . . . But we are living in a changing world where governments are being toppled over day by day. How do we know that we will not have another Castro in some other country in Latin America? Once that happens and they have the facilities to make the bomb, then we have something else to worry about. . . . I might conclude by saying this: If this agreement goes through at this time in this fashion, it will make a mockery of the Monroe Doctrine.—*John O. Pastore (D., Rhode Island), chairman of the Joint Congressional Committee on Atomic Energy, on the Senate floor, June 3, 1975.*

The senatorial thunder that greeted the news of the Brazil-German deal seemed to treat it as a kind of stab in the back from two of the closest postwar allies of the United States, as well as one more sign of the erosion of U.S. power and influence. However, an outsider might have been surprised by the strange failure to foresee these developments by those statesmen who promoted "Atoms for Peace" and arranged for this torch to be passed from one generation to the next.

In January 1976, David E. Lilienthal, the AEC's first chairman (1947-1950), told

the senators that "we, the United States, our public agencies and our private manufacturers, have been and are the world's major proliferators." Not only did the United States let the genie out of the bottle, but her salesmen have proselytized the genie's magic powers as a "safe and cheap" source of energy supplies. While the Soviet Union has been far more responsible and cautious in purveying the "peaceful uses" of atomic energy, the U.S. government has, in the words of a Brookings Institution study by Jerome Kahan, "actively encouraged the sale abroad of U.S.-built reactors by providing extensive technical assistance, attractive financing through the Export-Import Bank, and long-term supplies of enriched fuel at stable prices. During this period, foreign firms entered into licensing arrangements with U.S. firms in order to acquire the capability to produce reactors."

In view of the results of these policies we might well ask, with Mark Twain, "Shall we go on conferring our Civilization upon the peoples that sit in darkness, or shall we give those poor things a rest? Shall we bang right ahead in our oldtime, loud, pious way, and commit the new century to the game; or shall we sober up and sit down and think it over first?"

Problems Ahead

There are problems ahead at every level —technical, strategic, political, and moral. Apart from the military potential of commercial nuclear power, the industry still must solve such problems as the long-term fuel shortage, safe disposal of large amounts of deadly radioactive waste materials, danger of terrorist theft of plutonium extracted from spent fuel, and rapid escalation of reactor construction costs.

As inflation and delay have raised the price of reactors from $300 per kilowatt of capacity in 1970 to $1,135 in 1975, the nuclear industry has been hit hard by recent cancellations of orders for at least 12 new power plants by U.S. utilities and post-

---

[46] *Juan E. Guglialmelli, "Y si Brasil fabrica la bomba atomica?" Estrategia, May-June 1975/July-August 1975, pp. 13-14.*

ponement of 133 more. Consequently, there are pressures for increased government subsidies, which is a hallowed tradition in the nuclear industry throughout the world.

At the same time, enormous capital investments will be required for the next phases of development of the U.S. nuclear industry, anticipated for the late 1970s. These would be the expansion of enrichment capacity and large-scale separation of plutonium from spent fuel rods to obtain additional reactor fuel. These new phases of the industry's development involve physical as well as financial risks that are becoming the focus of intense political debate.

". . . it would be worth considering restructuring the international industry into a single cartel-consortium of producing governments using a standardized reactor technology. . . ."

The Ford Administration has proposed federal guarantees of up to $8 billion for construction of uranium enrichment plants by private industry. The leading candidate for a franchise and guarantee for commercial use of this highly classified technology, presently restricted to a government monopoly, is Uranium Enrichment Associates (UEA), a consortium organized by Bechtel of San Francisco, the world's largest private engineering firm and a specialist in construction of nuclear power plants. In recent years, Bechtel has hired two former Nixon cabinet members, George Schultz and Casper Weinberger, as well as Robert Hollingsworth, a former AEC general manager.

Bechtel's salesmanship in the nuclear field led to one of the more picturesque diplomatic episodes to emerge from the Brazil-German deal. In April 1975, four State Department officials made a trip to Bonn, where they tried to persuade the Germans that enrichment technology should not be sold to Brazil because of the proliferation

danger. Upon their return they learned that Bechtel had offered Brazil the same kind of technology two weeks before in a last-ditch effort to stop the German deal.

In a letter to Brazilian Minister of Mines and Energy Shigeaki Ueki, dated March 21, 1975, a Bechtel executive had written: "There has been a most recent decision by the Energy Research and Development Administration [(ERDA) a successor agency to the disbanded AEC] to encourage UEA to seek potential sites for enrichment plants outside the U.S.A. One of the locations which is most promising is Brazil, with the abundant hydro potential in the Amazon Basin." Because of ERDA's support, the Bechtel letter added, UEA "can offer Brazil the entire gamut from development of the mine, ore processing, enrichment, fuel processing, through the design of and construction of the nuclear power plants themselves."

Because enrichment activities are confined by U.S. law to a government monopoly operating within the country, and exportation of classified technology is prohibited, the Brazilians previously had been turned down in repeated efforts to get U.S. help in developing their own enrichment capacity. Under State Department pressure, Bechtel withdrew its offer three weeks later, informing the Brazilians in a letter that "it develops that within some United States circles there has been some concern about misinterpretation."

In view of the enormous government subsidies given, one way or another, to private nuclear energy companies in industrialized countries, the Brazil-German deal shows that "businesslike" competition between these subsidized national companies really amounts to competition between the national governments themselves in a highly dangerous sphere of activity. Because of the military potential of the "peaceful" uses of atomic energy, many developing countries are lured into ordering nuclear power plants they cannot afford, which will lead to heavy downstream losses for the already hard-pressed international reactor industry. On the other hand, the desperate need to sell reactors will lead each manufacturer to satisfy clients' demands for "sweeteners" that can be used in weapons making, such as enrichment and reprocessing plants. This will turn each sale into an act of political and diplomatic significance for the client and his neighbors and, in effect, what may be regarded as a military alliance between buyer and seller, lasting at least as long—perhaps a decade or two—as the time needed for the facilities to be built and the manufacturer paid off.

In response to the Brazil-German deal, the U.S. proposed a standardization of the conditions of export sales of nuclear power plants. Foreigners viewed this initiative coolly. They saw it as a maneuver to deny them their first big chance to enter the international reactor business, and to preserve the commanding U.S. position in the field.

At the "Secret Seven" meetings in London of supplier nations, the United States sought agreement on prohibition of the export of reprocessing plants, except under rigidly prescribed conditions. However, U.S. sources later said that France and West Germany would agree only to consultations and safeguards inspection agreements before exporting sensitive equipment and materials. This would have the effect of fabricating a paper umbrella of unenforceable guarantees as a license to create a series of dangerous de facto situations throughout the world.

Who Owns Nuclear Technology?

Because of the fuzzy economics of the nuclear industry and its clear military potential, the illusion that these companies can be run as a "business" may soon evaporate. More and more questions will be raised about the wisdom of parceling out to competing sets of corporate executives a costly technology, developed at public expense, that owes its origin, and most proven use, to achievements in destruction and terror.

Apart from the bomb itself, the electricity-generating reactor was first developed for military purposes in the U.S. Navy's atomic submarine program. The submarine reactor was then "scaled up" to generate electricity commercially by Westinghouse and GE with research and development funds provided by the AEC. To the degree that further development of commercial nuclear energy is justified to prevent the collapse of industrial society, then much more rigid controls should be imposed to restrain the economic and military anomalies, which are in the nature of the beast, from getting out of hand.

Rather than continue to stimulate "free" competition in the nuclear industry, it would be worth considering restructuring the international industry into a single cartel-consortium of producing governments using a standardized reactor technology to minimize diversion of materials for weapons purposes, licensing technology and exporting power plants only under the strictest nonproliferation controls. The standardization of reactor technology, in addition, could significantly reduce costs.

Brazil's Energy Options

While Brazilian officials have spoken of building 63 nuclear power plants by the turn of the century, the deal with West Germany contains firm orders for only two reactors. The size of the initial commitment may reflect some uncertainty about the growth rate of Brazil's future energy demand and about the performance of the German contractors. But the real issue is Brazil's capacity to pay for per capita energy consumption approaching the level of the developed nations.

Brazil's impressive postwar growth was intimately related to the expansion of the world economy and the low price of oil, especially in the 1960s and early 1970s. The Cinderella Year of the Brazilian "miracle" was 1973, when the national product grew by 11.4 per cent. Imports, exports, and the internal money supply all grew by half and oil imports by 46 per cent in that one year.[47] The 1973 Middle East war signaled an abrupt slowdown in this expansion. Over the previous generation Brazil's energy budget had quadrupled, while shifting from a wood-burning to a predominantly oil-burning and hydroelectric economy.

But even with this growth, Brazil's per capita consumption of commercial energy, while 60 per cent greater than the developing countries as a whole, was less than one-third of the world average and one-tenth that of the industrialized nations.[48] Petroleum imports created roughly half the cumulative current account deficit of $14 billion that Brazil incurred in 1974-1975. Present plans call for Brazil to spend around $65 billion through 1985 to develop her own energy resources—mainly offshore oil and hydroelectric and nuclear power, but also including shale, coal, and various forms of solar energy. This $65 billion is roughly equivalent to her whole national product for the Cinderella Year of 1973.

One of the ironies paving Brazil's new nuclear road is that Brazil could easily become a theater of major technological breakthroughs in using nonconventional energy sources, especially solar energy. Apart from the fact that her deposits of oil-bearing shale are second in size only to those of the United States, Brazil is in an excellent position to use photosynthetic transformation of solar energy to produce liquid and gaseous fuels, such as alcohol, methane, and hydrogen, which are both light and easily transportable.

Brazil already has adopted a plan to mix alcohol and gasoline to run her automobiles, which she did three decades ago during the World War II shortages, and is developing a car engine fueled entirely by alcohol. The alcohol would come from sugar cane or from new plantations of cassava on soils of low fertility occupying just 1 per cent of Brazil's total area to meet the country's fuel needs. Some scientists now view the Amazon jungle, with the high density and humidity of its vegetation, as one of the world's most efficient natural systems for conversion of photosynthetic energy. They calculate that the Amazon biomass might be industrially converted into methane at costs competitive with today's oil prices.

Such innovations could be extremely beneficial and could be the focus of international support and cooperation. In an editorial written shortly after the Brazil-German deal was signed, *Science* magazine observed:

> It is to be hoped that in solving its own energy problems Brazil will come to choose to exert world leadership not in facilitating nuclear proliferation but in providing the tropical countries with examples of how best to harvest and utilize solar energy.[49]

Whose Responsibility?

The centrifugal forces operating in the international nuclear energy industry, which have made it possible for Brazil to become a vessel of nuclear proliferation and Argentine scientists to become roving agents of the same process, can only be checked if governments assume direct responsibility for the industry. The salesman's vision of commercial nuclear energy as a boon to mankind and, he hopes, to corporate profits must be discarded in favor of a view of nuclear power as a dangerous but necessary device to be used with great caution.

Since the U.S. government funded the research and development effort for commercial applications of nuclear power by American reactor manufacturers, who then transferred this technology under license to government-subsidized companies in Europe and Japan, these governments have a re-

---

[47] Petrobrás Annual Report, 1973, p. 29.

[48] World Energy Supplies: 1970-73, *United Nations Statistical Papers, Series J, No. 18, 1975, p. 19.*

[49] *Philip H. Abelson, "Energy Alternatives for Brazil,"* Science, August 8, 1975.

sponsibility for the "business" of nuclear energy. Indeed, the developing countries singled out by disarmament specialists as being in the "near-nuclear" class and acquiring nuclear technology with clear military potential—South Korea, Taiwan, Brazil, and Argentina—are the same ones to which the big U.S. and European private banks are most heavily overcommitted with shaky loans.[50]

Not only does this imply a Western subsidy to these countries of the huge expense of acquiring nuclear power under very loose terms in the past and present, it also means, for the future, an important source of potential leverage for financial as well as technological restrictions on nuclear proliferation.

Disarmament specialists argue, with reason, that controls on "horizontal" nuclear proliferation need the moral sanction that can only be supplied by controls on the "vertical" proliferation of the nuclear arms race between the superpowers. However, as a practical matter, the present structure of the international nuclear industry still makes it possible for "horizontal" proliferation to be controlled by the Western governments themselves.

Curiously, while the moral claim of developing countries for access to "peaceful" nuclear technology has its main juridical support in Article IV of the NPT, it is the nonsigners of the NPT, who exhibited weapon-making intentions or capacity, that are benefiting most from transfers of "peaceful" nuclear technology, often under concessionary or giveway financial terms.

The pressures to export nuclear technology are expected to escalate rapidly in coming years. Inflation, construction delays, and the mounting impact of suspensions and cancellations of reactor orders are rapidly shrinking the home markets for nuclear power plants in the principal industrialized countries.

In 1975, Westinghouse and GE *each* still had a share of the world market almost as large as all other producers combined. However, U.S. domestic orders for nuclear plants peaked in 1972-1973. Even before the suspensions and cancellations of the past year struck the industry, U.S. companies were capable of producing annually almost four times as many reactor pressure vessels and turbine-generator units as the United States would need in 1977.

At this critical moment, Germany emerged as a major competitor in the international nuclear market. Looking over its shoulder to the expected entry of French, Swedish, and Japanese competitors into the crowded and unstable world market, KWU is being driven to grab as many orders as it can before the competition becomes even more fierce and disorderly.

While Bonn's handling of the Brazil deal initially received virtually unanimous support from the German public in the face of U.S. criticism, some voices subsequently have been raised in West Germany to express concern for some of the deal's implications. "It may be that global expansion of the technology necessary for putting together bombs can no longer be prevented, that in the evil competition for nuclear customers the level of prohibition necessarily drops ever lower," *Der Spiegel* observed.[51] "But must the Federal Republic play the role of advance guard?" Karl Kaiser of the German Society for Foreign Policy, an adviser to the ruling Social Democrats, wrote in *Europa Archiv*:

On the commercial side of nuclear energy expansion we must ask ourselves whether the former policy of unrestricted nuclear know-how and power stations to developing countries should be pursued in the future.

If the international nuclear industry is to maintain its present scale of operations, government subsidies may have to increase rad-

[50] *See Ann Crittenden, "Loans Abroad Stir Worry,"* The New York Times, *January 15, 1976, p. 1.*

[51] Der Spiegel, *March 15, 1976, p. 73.*

ically and competition may become much dirtier. Too much money already has been invested in nuclear energy, and too many specialized careers have been developed by talented and well-paid technicians, for the industry, by itself, to accord anything but secondary priority to the security implications of its activities. Placed beside these economic stakes, the besieged industry seems to regard the prospect of local nuclear wars or accidents as small potatoes.

Ironically, the world has begun to forget the horror of smaller nuclear weapons. Leaders of developing nations widely regard them as symbols and instruments of power, forgetting that the military advantage of their possession, as well as the economic investment in their development, can be nullified rapidly by proliferation. The main strategic advantage of nuclear weapons lies in long-distance strikes requiring an elaborate delivery capability. In local nuclear wars between neighbors, neither party may escape without massive, lasting damage. A high U.S. official involved in the London negotiations among supplier countries recently remarked that the spread of nuclear weapons potential throughout the world, unfortunately, may not be stopped until the next city is destroyed. By that time, however, the spread of this destructive capability may be so extensive that efforts at control may no longer be possible.

In terms of both economic and military potential, the world is rapidly approaching a no-win situation in the development of commercial nuclear power. It is so burdened by inflation, capital shortages, political controversy, and uncertainties over future fuel supplies that, in the United States, *Science* magazine could recently observe: "The nuclear industry is in such trouble that many people are saying, with some truth, that a *de facto* moratorium on future nuclear development already exists." [52] If this paralysis

persists in the U.S. industry, it could spread to nuclear energy enterprises in other industrialized countries, which are experiencing comparable problems of their own. The international reactor industry would then be faced with a clear choice between subsidizing—i.e., giving away—exports of nuclear power plants to developing countries on an even greater scale than in the past in order to sustain industrial capacity at home, or scaling down the nuclear energy enterprise to much more manageable proportions.

In this connection, the liberal *Die Zeit*, in its defense of the Brazil-German deal, made two important observations. The first was: "The deceptive distinction between nuclear technology for 'peaceful' and for 'military' uses lies at the core of the nonproliferation policies. In reality this dividing line is almost irrelevant. Whoever achieves a high level of civilian technology is almost automatically on the threshhold of manufacture of nuclear weapons." [53] The second was a suggestion that, "if America were to dismount from its high horse of nuclear monopoly rights," i.e., the dominant U.S. market position, then a step toward closer integration of the industry's goals could be taken through formation of a "loose confederation" of supplier countries that could be known as "NUTEX" (Nuclear Technology Exporters).

This idea is similar to the more recent proposal by Senator Ribicoff for "a cooperative arrangement with other suppliers, including France and West Germany, that will guarantee each supplier a minimum market share of reactor exports." [54] Such an arrangement might be organized along the lines of Atomic Energy of Canada, Limited (AECL), the government company that acts as general contractor for the Candu reactor and parcels out business to the various component manufacturers.

---

[52] Luther J. Carter, "Energy Policy: Independence by 1985 May be Unreachable Without Btu Tax," Science, February 13, 1976, p. 548.

[53] Joachim Schwelein, "Heisses Geschäft mit dem Atomstrom," Die Zeit, June 27, 1975.

[54] Abraham A. Ribicoff, "Trading in Doom," The New York Times, March 26, 1976.

While this might require the United States to yield a larger share of the international reactor market to other countries, it could bring the compensating advantage of heading off the kind of trade wars that could lead to nuclear wars. It could promote sharing of the financial burdens of such costly undertaking as enrichment, research, and development, and the production of specialized components. It also could end the plague of "loss leader" giveaways of nuclear exports by establishing financial, technological, and safeguards standards for all sales and by placing final control of these transactions in the hands of an international directorate run by governments, which is where the responsibility belongs. The reactor export industry should become an international public utility.

The fact that the international community has been able to stop the use of certain chemical and biological weapons for more than a half-century offers hope that concerted action can still manage the nuclear trade. Any additional cost incurred by this kind of management would be the price of peace. The failure to pay this price may mean infinitely greater costs further down the road.

KENNEDY AND THE CUBAN CONNECTION

by Donald E. Schulz

Conspiracy theories are fashionable; sometimes even fruitful, as in the case of Watergate. So it should not be surprising that recent revelations of the Senate Intelligence Committee and other sources have resurrected a very old question—namely, what connection, if any, did the Castro government have with the assassination of John F. Kennedy?

A current speculation is that the Cuban dictator, having learned of CIA plots against his life, decided to strike back, returning violence for violence, with consequences that are now a matter of historical record. Indeed, the recent report of the task force headed by Senators Schweiker and Hart, while finding no hard facts to support this theory, did uncover some fascinating circumstantial evidence.[1]

We are told, for instance, of the June 1963 decision of the National Security Council's "Special Group" to step up subversive activities against the Havana government and of the subsequent renewal of CIA contacts with a high-level Cuban official, Rolando Cubelas (code-named AMLASH), who proposed the overthrow and assassination of Castro by means of an "inside job." We learn that shortly thereafter, Castro is-

[1] *U.S., Congress, Senate, Select Committee to Study Governmental Operations with Respect to Intelligence Activities, The Investigation of the Assassination of President John F. Kennedy: Performance of the Intelligence Agencies, Final Report, 94th Cong., 2d sess., 1976, Senate Rept. 94-755. Hereafter referred to as the Schweiker-Hart report. Unless otherwise specified, information in this article comes from the Schweiker-Hart report and U.S., Congress, Senate, Select Committee to Study Governmental Operations with Respect to Intelligence Activities, Alleged Assassination Plots Involving Foreign Leaders, An Interim Report, 94th Cong., 1st sess., 1975, Senate Rept. 94-465.*

sued a public warning that should U.S. leaders aid "terrorist plans to eliminate Cuban leaders, they themselves will not be safe." This threat, however, was ignored. CIA covert operations were escalated. On October 29, the head of the agency's Special Affairs Section, Desmond Fitzgerald, met with AMLASH. Presenting himself (inaccurately) as a "personal representative" of Attorney General Robert Kennedy, he informed the Cuban that the United States would back the proposed coup. On November 22, the very day that the American president was struck down on the streets of Dallas, a CIA case officer met once again with AMLASH to reassure him of U.S. support for the operation and confirm that explosives and rifles with telescopic sights would be provided. In addition, the Cuban was given a ballpoint pen, fashioned with a special hypodermic needle, which could be used to inject a lethal dose of poison into the intended victim if the opportunity arose.

Neither this nor previous assassination plots against Castro were ever made known to the Warren Commission. Indeed, the evidence strongly suggests that there was an overwhelming predisposition on the part of the White House, the Justice Department, the FBI, the CIA, and the commission itself to accept Lee Harvey Oswald as Kennedy's lone killer, without adequately investigating other hypotheses and leads that might have led to different conclusions.

Thus, almost immediately following the shooting, FBI Director J. Edgar Hoover, the Justice Department, and the White House exerted pressure on senior FBI officials to promptly complete their investigation and issue a factual report upholding the "lone assassin" thesis. In the words of Deputy Attorney General Nicholas Katzenbach:

> It is important that all of the facts surrounding President Kennedy's assassination be made public in a way which will satisfy people in the United States and abroad that all the facts have been told and that a statement to this effect be made now.

The public must be satisfied that Oswald was the assassin; that he did not have confederates who are still at large; and that the evidence was such that he would have been convicted at trial.

Speculation about Oswald's motivation ought to be cut off, and we should have some basis for rebutting thought that this was a Communist conspiracy or (as the Iron Curtain press is saying) a rightwing conspiracy to blame it on the Communists.

No doubt there was here a sincere belief that such findings were in the national interest. After all, the dangers of irresolution were obvious. Speculation, feeding on fear and grief, might inflame public opinion and drive the Johnson administration into taking some rash and hazardous action. Only the previous year, the United States and the Soviet Union had gone to the very brink of nuclear war over Cuba. There was little enthusiasm in Washington for repeating that scenario.

Although understandable, this attitude would taint the investigation with prejudice from the very beginning. The ensuing FBI inquiry would be handled primarily as a regular criminal case, its almost exclusive focus of attention being on Oswald. And while a massive array of data was compiled on the suspect's background, activities, contacts, and the specific act of assassination, nowhere is there evidence that a broader study was ever conducted to explore the possibility of a conspiracy, either foreign or domestic. The result, not surprisingly, was a report that mirrored the prevailing predispositions.

Moreover, once those conclusions were issued, the bureau's reputation was at stake. Hoover himself viewed the Warren Commission as an adversary. The chief justice, he felt, was "seeking to criticize" the FBI and "find gaps" in its inquiry. Needless to say, such defensive reactions were hardly conducive to a healthy working relationship. Technically speaking, the bureau fulfilled its responsibilities to the letter; it supplied the commission with the information requested. But it volunteered very little. And among the items that never reached Earl Warren's desk was a report on the CIA's assassination plots against Castro.

The CIA's performance was similarly suspect. A major difficulty was the extreme compartmentalization of knowledge within the bureaucracy. The desk officer who coordinated the initial investigation was not even aware of the AMLASH operation. Nor, for that matter, was the CIA director, John McCone. Furthermore, those who were aware weren't talking. Whether out of a desire to avoid another "Cuban flap," or to protect the agency from embarrassment and preserve the secrecy of its activities, or because of a failure to draw a connection between the AMLASH plot and the Kennedy assassination, neither the deputy director for plans, Richard Helms, nor Desmond Fitzgerald, nor the case officer assigned to AMLASH volunteered their knowledge to the authorities responsible for conducting the investigation. As a result, information that might well have become an "absolutely vital factor" in the inquiry—according to the desk officer who coordinated the CIA investigation—was never received. By the time the Warren Commission began to issue requests to the agency, the possibility of a "Cuban connection" had been effectively dismissed. Subsequent analyses were directed almost entirely toward the issue of Soviet involvement.

Neither the Warren Commission as a body nor its staff was ever given details of the CIA's Cuban activities. Ultimately, however, this was the responsibility of the commission itself. If its inquiry was flawed and incomplete, this must in large part be attributed to its own lack of imagination and initiative. At least one of its members, former CIA head Allen Dulles, was aware of the general nature of the covert operations being waged against the Castro regime. Assassination plots had been hatched during his own tenure as director, apparently with his

knowledge. Yet there is no evidence that he ever told his colleagues on the commission about those activities. Nor was the issue ever pursued in the commission's requests for information to the intelligence community—in spite of Oswald's known Cuban contacts and Castro's warning that U.S.-sponsored terrorism would bring retaliation.

In sum, if a CIA-FBI "coverup" deprived the Warren Commission of vital information, the latter's performance was also far from impeccable. And while the vice-presidential candidate from Pennsylvania may have gone a bit overboard when he declared that "there is no longer any reason to have faith in its picture of the Kennedy assassination," [2] at the very least it has been demonstrated that the investigatory process was seriously flawed.

Thus, the Senate Intelligence Committee, disbanded on May 31, 1976, recommended that its permanent successor, the Senate Select Committee on Intelligence, continue the inquiry in an effort to explore the leads that have been uncovered and resolve the troubling questions raised. Thus, the House of Representatives on September 17, 1976, voted to compose a special 12-member Committee on Assassinations to "conduct a full and complete investigation" into the deaths of John F. Kennedy and Martin Luther King. And so, apparently, we are to have a reopening of the case—at last.

A Tale of Two Dialogues

In light of these developments, it seems appropriate to recall a little-known campaign of accommodation launched on a covert basis by Washington and Havana in the weeks preceding that fateful day in November 1963. Actually, the origins of this tentative and ultimately ill-fated rapprochement may be traced back to the previous spring, when Castro, as part of a general reassessment of domestic and foreign policy, announced his readiness to normalize rela-

---

[2] *Statement by Senator Richard Schweiker cited in the* Columbus Citizen-Journal, *June 24, 1976.*

tions with the United States. The primary reason for this initiative was fairly obvious: Nikita Khrushchev, sobered by the chilling experience of the missile crisis, sorely in need of Western trade and technology to help bolster the hard-pressed Soviet economy, desired a reduction of international tension in preparation for a renewed campaign of détente. At the same time, Castro, increasingly dependent on his Muscovite sponsors, found himself obliged to embrace the banner of "peaceful coexistence" in order to secure the economic and military agreements that he needed to assure the continued survival and development of his revolution.

It was not until September, however, that this campaign began to bear fruit. At that time, William Attwood, a special adviser to the U.S. Delegation to the United Nations, informed Averell Harriman and Adlai Stevenson that he had received information from various sources that Castro was unhappy with Cuba's satellite status and was looking for a way out; in short, that he wanted an accommodation with the United States and was willing to make substantive concessions to get it. The message was passed on to the president, who approved the suggestion that a "discrete contact" be made with Carlos Lechuga, head of the Cuban Delegation to the United Nations. Subsequently, such communications were established and a series of meetings held between Attwood and Lechuga to discuss the prospect of negotiations.

In point of fact, by early November, Kennedy had decided to push toward an opening with Cuba in an attempt to take Castro out of the Soviet fold and erase the memory of the Bay of Pigs. Accordingly, a preliminary conference with Lechuga and René Vallejo, Fidel's personal physician and confidant, was sought at the United Nations in order to prepare an agenda for discussions. On November 18, this message was transmitted by telephone to Vallejo in Havana. Shortly thereafter, Lechuga was instructed to set forth such an agenda for

U.S. consideration. Ironically, due to a lag in communications these orders were received only on November 23, the day after Kennedy's assassination.[3]

But this was not the whole story. Even as these developments were unfolding, a second dialogue was taking place through an unofficial envoy—the French journalist, Jean Daniel. On October 24, Kennedy had received Daniel in the White House. The subject of conversation was Cuba. The president, it seems, had learned of the Frenchman's forthcoming visit to the island and had decided to seize the occasion to send Castro a message. In essence, this communication came down to a strong hint that the United States could learn to live with a Socialist Cuba in a "normalized" relationship *providing* certain conditions were met. What were those conditions? One, clearly, was an end to Castroite subversion. While expressing sympathy for Latin-American aspirations for justice and progress, Kennedy stressed that those goals would not be achieved through Marxist dictatorship. The United States had a special responsibility to the "Free World" to contain Communist expansionism. As long as the government in Havana continued to export revolution, the economic "blockade" of the island would remain in effect.

Beyond this, not much was definite. The American negotiating stance had not yet been worked out. Moreover, the president's position remained extremely delicate. Cuba was still a highly emotional issue. Even the State Department had serious qualms about the desirability of dealing with Castro. For obvious political reasons, Kennedy could not be too direct.

Nevertheless, Kennedy's remarks were suggestive enough to convince Daniel that Kennedy had had second thoughts about the efficacy of U.S. policy and was seeking a

---

[3] *William Attwood*, The Reds and the Blacks *(New York: Harper & Row, 1967), pp. 142-146; and Senate Select Committee, Alleged Assassination plots . . . , op. cit., pp. 173-174.*

change. He had come to accept the Cuban revolution as a fact of life. The clock would never again be turned back to the days of the Batista regime, when colonialism, economic exploitation, and national humiliation prevailed—with North American complicity. Kennedy acknowledged U.S. responsibility for much of what had happened. It was almost as though the United States had manufactured the Castro movement without even realizing it. Now it would have to pay. Indeed, the function of the Alliance for Progress would be to correct the vast accumulation of similar mistakes currently jeopardizing all of Latin America. The United States now had the chance to do as much good as it had done wrong in the past—providing, of course, that the area did not go Communist.

But could the United States tolerate "economic collectivism"? The issue, of course, had particular relevance for Cuba, and Daniel wanted to be quite sure of Kennedy's position. The reply: The United States already had accepted it—for instance, in Guinea and Yugoslavia. Only three days earlier, the president had had a "most positive" discussion with Marshal Tito. And the attempt to isolate the island economically? Was this a punishment or a political maneuver? Kennedy smiled. Was Daniel suggesting that the blockade was not politically effective? He would soon have the opportunity to see for himself. In any case, the main issue was Communist expansion. Castro had become a "Soviet agent" in Latin America. He had to be contained: "The continuation of the blockade depends on the continuation of subversive activities."

Thus, Daniel, bearing this message and an invitation to revisit the White House upon his return, set off for Cuba. There he found a proud, critical, yet remarkably receptive Castro. Indeed, during the course of a six-hour interview the *líder máximo* found occasion to praise the American president for his sincerity, realism, and "good ideas": Kennedy might yet become a greater leader

than Lincoln. He had come to appreciate "many things" over the past few months; might still understand that there could be "coexistence between Capitalists and Socialists, even in the Americas." For their part, Castro and his countrymen wanted nothing more than peace. They were not supplicants; they asked merely to be left alone to concentrate on the socio-economic tasks of the revolution. If the United States could accept Cuban socialism, then "everything can be restored to normalcy on the basis of mutual respect of sovereignty." The issue of subversion would not be an obstacle. Cubans would naturally "feel solidarity" with their revolutionary brethren in other lands. Ultimately, however, each nation had to determine its own destiny, and "if they choose other regimes than ours, this isn't our business."

That was two days prior to Kennedy's death.

Moreover, on the afternoon of November 22, Castro and Daniel resumed their conversation at the prime minister's summer residence on Varadero Beach. In the midst of the questioning, the telephone rang. The call was from the Cuban president, Osvaldo Dorticós, for Castro. The message: Kennedy had just been struck down in Dallas. It was not yet known whether he would live or die.

Stunned, Castro came back and sat down. Three times he repeated the words *"Es una mala noticia."* ("This is bad news.") He fell momentarily silent. Then the speculation began: There was an alarmingly large lunatic fringe in the United States. This could as easily be the work of a madman as a terrorist. Perhaps a Vietnamese? Or a member of the Ku Klux Klan? In any case, Kennedy might still survive. If so, his reelection would be assured. This last was said with visible satisfaction.

But this was not to be. Within a half hour, the news came over the radio: The president was dead.

Castro stood up. Now everything had changed, would have to be rethought. Kennedy, at least, had been an enemy to whom Cubans had become accustomed. Now the assassin would have to be found quickly, "otherwise, you watch and see, I know them, they will try to put the blame on us. . . ." [4]

This did not, of course, come to pass. In spite of an initial flurry of speculation— Oswald was soon discovered to be a Castro sympathizer with some rather tenuous links to the Fair Play for Cuba Committee—the Johnson administration was quick to embrace the "lone assassin" thesis. Subsequently, the Warren Commission was appointed not so much to get at the truth (the president himself would have preferred to stand on the FBI's report) as to stop the "rash of investigations" that was bound to occur should the nation remain unconvinced of Oswald's sole responsibility for these tragic developments.

Concessions for Survival

But what did all this mean? I have recounted the story of the Castro-Kennedy dialogues because it provides an important —perhaps crucial—frame of reference for congressional investigators and the public alike. It is not, of course, proof of innocence. But would Castro have been so intent on coming to terms with a man whom he was conspiring to kill? One may seriously doubt it.

In point of fact, the rapid collapse of the Cuban economy (the 1963 sugar harvest had come to only 2.8 million tons, compared to 4.8 million tons in 1962 and 6.7 million tons in 1961), aggravated by the devastation of Hurricane Flora that autumn, had made a concerted attempt at rapprochement virtually imperative. Castro was now more dependent than ever on his Muscovite sponsors. During his initial visit to the Soviet Union the previous spring, he had committed himself to a drastic modification of his ill-conceived program of rapid

industrialization. Thus, sugar would once again be given priority attention by Cuban economic planners. And the foreign exchange earned from its sale abroad would pave the way for the island's eventual industrialization.

By the same token, however, this meant that the Cubans would have to obtain premium prices and a guaranteed market for their product. And although the Soviets had consented to an increase in the price of their purchases for the current year, the kind of long-range agreement that Castro was seeking had not yet been worked out. Only in January 1964, with his return to the Soviet Union, would such an accord be reached. In exchange for Castro's support for "peaceful coexistence" and other matters (including an explicit pledge to "do everything necessary to re-establish goodneighbor relations between Cuba and the United States"), Khrushchev would agree to take 2.1 million tons of sugar in 1965 and a million more tons each successive year until a level of 5 million tons per annum was attained during 1968 to 1970, all at a price of six cents a pound. [5]

In retrospect, it seems unlikely that Castro would have jeopardized an arrangement so critical to the future of his revolution for the sake of a vendetta against Kennedy, especially when the latter was beginning to respond to his covert initiatives at rapprochement. Indeed, the available evidence suggests that Castro's courtship of the American president was motivated by more than the mere necessity of striking a bargain with Moscow. There was also a clear desire to see an end to the U.S. boycott which, in spite of occasional Cuban protests to the contrary, was seriously damaging the national economy. Thus, when Hurricane Flora passed through the southeastern part of the island in October, leaving more than 1,200 casualties and flooding some 2,500 acres of the country's best farmland, Castro

---

[4] *The testimony of Jean Daniel may be found in* The New Republic, *December 7, 14, 21 and 28, 1963.*

[5] *The text of the communique may be found in* Hoy, *January 23, 1964.*

seized the occasion to issue a public appeal to Washington to lift its sanctions.[6] To little avail. The official position of the State Department remained as inflexible as ever.

No doubt, there was some hope that the normalization of relations with the "colossus" would lead to Cuban participation in the Alliance for Progress. After all, hadn't Castro himself been the *true* father of the alliance? In May 1959, long before the two countries had broken ties, he had called on the United States to make a $30 billion commitment to a 10-year program of economic development for all of Latin America. His proposal had been the object of considerable ridicule. Later, of course, the Kennedy administration launched its own similar plan in an effort to keep the Castroite virus from spreading to other lands. Now, perhaps, the time was approaching when Cuba would be able to share in the wealth that was being redistributed. Hadn't Kennedy hinted as much in his conversation with Daniel? In any case, the renewal of relations would provide a welcome balance to dependency on the Soviet Union.

The courtship of the United States did not end abruptly with Kennedy's death. Castro continued his initiatives, this time in public view.[7] But it was too late. The assassination had terminated Washington's interest in accommodation. For political reasons of its own, the Johnson administration quickly retreated to an uncompromising cold war stance, demanding in effect that Castro divest himself of his dependence on the Soviet Union, even as it made

it impossible for him to do so by continuing its policy of isolating Cuba economically and politically from the so-called "Free World." Under these circumstances, Castro's enthusiasm for détente gradually waned, eventually disappearing altogether in the wake of American interventions in Vietnam and the Dominican Republic.

But that is another story. Our concern is with the opportunities, pressures, and constraints with which Castro had to contend during those fateful weeks prior to Kennedy's assassination. And what about Castro's alleged threats against the president? According to Associated Press reporter Daniel Harker, on the evening of September 7, Castro had held an impromptu, three-hour interview at the Brazilian embassy during which he issued the following warning: "We are prepared to fight them and answer in kind. United States leaders should think that if they are aiding terrorist plans to eliminate Cuban leaders, they themselves will not be safe." Moreover, the "CIA and other dreamers believe their hopes of an insurrection or a successful guerrilla war. They can go on dreaming forever."[8]

The gist of this communication has been confirmed by other sources.[9] The issue that remains is how to interpret it. The theory that has thus far dominated public discussion is that Castro found out about the AMLASH-CIA conspiracy and decided to retaliate in kind. My own opinion is somewhat different. I suggest that what was involved here was a simple exercise in deterrence. It is not unlikely that AMLASH had indeed been discovered, if he was not a double-agent to begin with. Even the CIA suspected that he was an unstable individual and a security risk. At the very least, he talked too much. Moreover, the timing of Castro's warning is especially suggestive. It was issued immediately following the resumption of the AMLASH connection, on

---

[6] *See the report on Castro's television appearance of October 21, in* Cuba Socialista, *November 1963 and his October 31 speech in the Foreign Broadcast Information Service's* Daily Report, *October 31, 1963.*

---

[7] *See, for instance, Castro's January 2, 1964 speech to the Cuban people, in* Revolucion, *January 3, 1964; the January 1964 Soviet-Cuban communique in* Hoy, *January 23, 1964; Castro's interview with Richard Eder, in* The New York Times, *July 6, 1964; Castro's speech of July 26, 1964, in the Foreign Broadcast Information Service's* Daily Report, *July 28, 1964; and Castro's news conference with foreign journalists in* Bohemia, *August 7, 1964.*

---

[8] Miami Herald, *September 9, 1963.*

---

[9] *Most notably, in the* Las Vegas Sun, *March 1, 1976.*

the very day in fact that CIA headquarters received word of the meeting. Castro's choice of the Brazilian embassy as the site of his remarks is similarly provocative. It had been in Brazil that AMLASH had met his U.S. contact. Was this a calculated attempt by Castro to let Washington know that he knew about the operation? At least some members of the Senate Intelligence Committee believed that it was.[10]

By the same token, however, the very fact that the threat was issued in public suggests the improbability of its actually being carried out. If Castro were going to have Kennedy assassinated would he broadcast it to the world? I think not. Certainly, he could have had few illusions as to the impact that such an act, openly proclaimed and recognized, would have had in the United States. The demand for retaliation would have been overwhelming. And although the revolution had survived the CIA-sponsored invasion at the Bay of Pigs, that had been a half-hearted affair conducted through Cuban surrogates. A full-scale onslaught by the U.S. marines was entirely another matter. In perspective, it seems rather unlikely that Castro would have invited such an attack, especially when he had the evidence of the missile crisis to consider. Clearly, the Soviets were not willing to lose Moscow in order to defend Havana.

A more probable interpretation is that the statement of September 7 was intended to deter the United States from pursuing the AMLASH operation and other subversive activities that were rapidly becoming a serious threat to Cuban internal security.[11] That the warning was ignored does not necessarily mean much. Bluff is often

a key element in deterrence. In any case, Castro could not have been sure that the United States would back AMLASH until at least October 29, when CIA agents met with the Cuban once again. And even then, their support was couched in such general terms that it was not at all clear whether the assassination would be permitted (Fitzgerald later claimed that he had informed AMLASH that the United States did not do such things) or technical assistance rendered. Only on November 22—too late to have affected the events in Dallas—would those issues be finally resolved.

Speculation and a Lead

Does all this mean that we may discount the possibility of a Cuban connection? The answer is no. For one thing, the evidence presented in these pages, though clearly outweighing anything that has thus far been offered in support of the retaliation hypothesis, remains circumstantial and inconclusive. If the events of recent years have taught us anything, it is that human beings —and governments—often behave in inconsistent and self-destructive ways. Assassination is a highly emotional issue, and Castro is excitable. Under other circumstances, it would not have been surprising had a threat on his life triggered a pre-emptive attack. And even under the very special conditions described above, it is not impossible that Castro did, wittingly or unwittingly, set in motion the machinery of retaliation. All that was really necessary was that Cuban security agents behave in much the same way as their North American counterparts—that is, semiautonomously, initiating and perpetuating cloak and dagger operations without the explicit authorization of their political superiors. If, due to a lack of political control and a prevailing atmosphere of cold war hostility, CIA agents could be engaged in an attempt on Castro's life at the very moment that the American president was secretly exploring the prospects for an accommodation, it is

---

[10] *This from a source close to the committee, cited in the* Columbus Dispatch, *June 21, 1976.*

[11] *The problem was especially acute in the Escambray mountains of central Cuba, where more than 1,000 guerrillas were waging a determined struggle—with CIA support. These and lesser uprisings throughout the island were eventually put down, but only after several years of struggle and considerable human and material cost.*

not difficult to imagine similar distortions occurring on the Cuban side. Might not some overzealous security officials have taken Castro's threat of September 7 for tacit authority to set up a "program of elimination"?

Moreover, it is important to remember that the "Cuban connection" refers not merely to Castroite involvement but also to the possibility that *anti-*Castro forces were responsible for the killing. After all, Oswald had had contacts with both sides. And certainly the exiles had reason to view Kennedy with bitterness. Promises had been betrayed. The thrust of official policy was no longer on "liberating" the island but rather on "containment"—that is, accepting the Castro regime as a fact of life and limiting the damage. Following the missile crisis, the CIA's covert operations had been reduced. Operation MONGOOSE, the plan to use Cuban dissidents and exiles to overthrow the government in Havana, had been terminated. And the FBI and other agencies had begun to bring their power to bear in a serious attempt to restrict the paramilitary adventures of the exiles. Inevitably, this shift toward opposition had given rise to heated emotions. Might such resentments have been translated into direct action against the president? By the same token, if his assassin could be established as a Castro agent, or at least a sympathizer, might this trigger a U.S. invasion and return the exiles to their homeland?[12]

But all this remains speculation. It is possible to imagine any number of scenarios that might have led to the fatal events of November 22. Hence, the importance of the leads uncovered by the Senate Intelligence Committee; for if they offer substantial new evidence or the promise that such evidence might emerge through further investigation, then clearly a major reopening of the inquiry is obligatory.

With this in mind, let us briefly examine the nature of these leads.

Certainly, the most sensational (not to say sensationalistic) of the lot is the case of "D," a Latin American who appeared at the U.S. embassy in Mexico City a few days after Kennedy's death with a story which, on the surface, would seem to lend strong support to the retaliation hypothesis. On September 18, it was asserted, "D" had been at the Cuban consulate, where he had seen Oswald receive $6,500 from two other men, one of whom was Cuban, and had overheard the trio discuss the forthcoming assassination. Subsequently, he had tried on several occasions to warn the American embassy, but to no avail. Eventually, he had been told to stop wasting his time.

This claim created quite a stir. The fact of the matter was that Oswald *had* been in Mexico City in late September and *had* visited the Cuban consulate (in an unsuccessful effort to obtain a Cuban travel visa). Was this mere coincidence? Again, recall the date of Castro's threat against U.S. leaders.

In retrospect, there is legitimate question about the way in which the ensuing inquiry was handled. The Schweiker-Hart report makes a convincing case that the FBI performance was an essentially negative effort, designed to discredit rather than objectively investigate "D"'s allegations. Nor was the CIA's inquiry immune from criticism. This was Mexican national territory. As such, it was the Mexican police who first interrogated the subject and extracted from him a written confession that his entire story was a fabrication. Later, however, when questioned by U.S. authorities, "D" claimed to have been pressured into making this retraction.[13]

Here, some doubt lingers. Was the CIA so anxious to avoid another "Cuban flap" that it too conducted a "negative" investigation? The Schweiker-Hart report does not

---

[12] *See, in particular, the arguments and evidence presented by Robert Sam Anson, in* They've Killed the President! *(New York: Bantam, 1975), pp. 246-74.*

[13] Report of the President's Commission on the Assassination of President John F. Kennedy *(Washington, D.C.: Government Printing Office, 1964), p. 308.*

go this far, but it does demonstrate that such a concern existed. Moreover, it suggests that the agency was very quick to write off "D"'s story once word of his retraction had been received. Thus, for instance, mention is made of information from a "sensitive and reliable source" that tended to confirm his initial testimony. This report was never satisfactorily explained, though it was later made available to the Warren Commission staff. Similarly, it is noted that on December 2, the Mexican station reported that it had reason to doubt its earlier conclusion that "D" was fabricating. By then, however, headquarters had lost interest.

Yet, loose ends notwithstanding, one must, in the final analysis, agree with the Warren Commission. There are simply too many contradictions to lend "D"'s story much credence. While his claim to have been pressured into a retraction by the Mexican police seems plausible enough, it must be noted that when he was subsequently given a polygraph test by U.S. authorities, the machine indicated that he was probably lying. Upon being informed of this finding, the subject once again altered his testimony, admitting in effect that he must have been "mistaken." Moreover, it was soon established that Oswald had been in New Orleans on September 18, the day that he was alleged to have been at the Cuban consulate in Mexico City.[14] (Though a story later came in changing that date to September 28, when he *was* in Mexico.) Furthermore, the telephone extension number that "D" claimed to have used in his efforts to warn the American embassy would not have given him the individual to whom he had allegedly spoken; in addition, no one at the embassy had any recollection of his calls. Finally, by his own account, part of the mysterious conversation at the Cuban consulate had been conducted in Spanish. Yet Oswald spoke little, if any, Spanish. That he could have participated in such an exchange would therefore seem rather doubtful.[15]

A More Promising Lead

A somewhat more promising lead involves the testimony of a certain Washington lawyer, whose underworld clients had been called upon by an unspecified government agency to participate in a project that was said to have the highest governmental approval. The objective of this program was the assassination of Castro. According to this version, the plot had nearly reached fruition when the Cuban dictator learned of it. By exerting pressure on captured subjects, he was able to find out the full details, whereupon he decided that "if that was the way . . . Kennedy wanted it, he too could engage in the same tactics." Thereafter, assassination teams were dispatched to the United States for the purpose of killing the President.

This story would seem to have some basis in reality. The lawyer's clients had apparently been involved in the CIA's early efforts to enlist mafia support against Castro. But that campaign had been terminated in February 1963, long before Kennedy's assassination. Moreover, the information which these individuals were said to possess with regard to the alleged Cuban retaliation was strictly hearsay—"feedback" provided by sources close to Castro, who had been placed there in order to carry out the original project. In fact, when these same clients were interviewed by the Senate Intelligence Committee they denied recollection of such information or of ever having discussed the matter with the lawyer.

Still, one cannot rule out their initial tale. There are obvious reasons (the foremost being self-preservation) why such men would not want to get involved with a Senate investigation of the underworld.

---

[14] Ibid., p. 308.

[15] It appears that "D" (real name, Gilberto Alvarado) was an agent of the Nicaraguan Intelligence Service. His intention in manufacturing this tale was to trigger U.S. action against Castro. Ibid., pp. 307-308.

By the same token, the mere fact that the CIA's mafia campaign had been terminated months prior to the assassination does not necessarily mean much. Covert operations often acquire lives of their own. In this case the mafia intermediary, John Rosselli, had simply broken off communication with his Cuban contacts without informing them that the $150,000 bounty placed on Castro's head had been withdrawn. Under such circumstances, the conspiracy could have remained operational long after it had been officially abandoned. And Castro's security forces, had they uncovered the plot, would presumably have had no way of knowing that it no longer enjoyed U.S. sponsorship.

But this is conjecture. The reluctance of the clients to repeat their story to Senate investigators suggests the difficulties likely to be encountered in any follow-up inquiry. Nevertheless, the effort must be made.

Two other less promising leads are the following:

On the evening of November 22, a Cubana airlines flight from Mexico City to Havana had been delayed five hours, awaiting the arrival of a mysterious passenger. At 10:30 PM, this individual arrived in a twin-engined aircraft and boarded the Cubana plane without passing through customs. Subsequently, he travelled to Cuba in the cockpit, avoiding identification by his fellow passengers and by Mexican authorities.

We also learn of a certain Cuban-American, a Castro sympathizer with connections with the Tampa Chapter of the Fair Play for Cuba Committee with which Oswald may also have had contact. On November 23, this person crossed the border from Texas to Mexico, eventually making his way to Havana via a Cubana airlines flight on which he was the sole passenger. Later, the CIA received a report that he was somehow "involved in the assassination."

With the exception of the story of the Washington lawyer, which only surfaced in 1967, information about these episodes

was in the possession of the intelligence community as early as December 1963. Yet, there is no evidence that the Warren Commisison was ever provided with the kind of data that would have enabled it to pursue these leads. Who were these individuals and why their strange behavior? The Senate Intelligence Committee's staff contacted the Federal Aviation Administration in an attempt to determine the origins of the twin-engined craft—without success. Records from that time period are no longer kept. As for the Cuban-American, when last heard he was living in Cuba, beyond the reach of U.S. investigators, spending much of his time playing dominoes. That was in September 1964.

In short, the task is formidable. Thirteen years have passed. Leads which once would have been relatively easy to pursue have long ago dried up. Key witnesses have died, disappeared, or are otherwise inaccessible. This is true even of our old friend AMLASH. In March 1966, Cubelas was sentenced to 25 years in prison for plotting Castro's assassination in league with the CIA. Only after a personal appeal for clemency by his intended victim did he manage to escape the death penalty.

Was AMLASH a double agent? There is some reason to think so. Certainly, he was a professional intriguer and opportunist of the first rank. In the early 1960s he had served as Castro's hatchet man at the University of Havana, where he rode around in big cars and lived the sweet life while presiding over the destruction of traditional academic freedoms. In the process, he had apparently acquired strong connections with Cuban intelligence and had begun to cooperate with it in various ways. (This, at least, was the testimony of AMWHIP, a Cuban exile who had been involved in the AMLASH operation from the beginning.) By mid-1965, the CIA considered the risk serious enough to terminate the entire affair. In the words of the chief of special affairs staff counterintelligence, "Fidel reportedly knew that this group was plotting against him and once enlisted its support. Hence, we cannot rule out the possibility of provocation."

Picture, if you will, the following scenario: Castro, having suffered through innumerable attempts on his life in the years since he came to power, suspected that at least some of these plots had the backing of the U.S. government. This was not illogical, in view of the CIA's vast ongoing campaign of violence and subversion against his regime. But he had no proof. The agency was not the only one interested in "eliminating" him. Elements of the underworld, the Cuban exile community, and the counterrevolutionary underground within Cuba itself were also involved in such activities. And the CIA had taken some care to cover its tracks (for instance, by using mafia figures to mediate its contacts with potential Cuban assassins) in order to prevent operations from being traced to their original source. Castro could not be certain of what he strongly suspected.

He decided to find out for sure. Cubelas had earlier established direct contact with CIA case officers. Now Castro would have him draw them out. In the process, he would discover not only whether the agency was involved in such schemes, but whether the Kennedys were aware of and had authorized these tactics.

Thus the resumption of the CIA-AMLASH connection and the latter's proposal for an "inside job," to include Castro's assassination. Thus, also, Cubelas' request for a personal meeting with Robert Kennedy to obtain assurance of U.S. support. And thus Castro's warning of September 7, a move calculated to deter the president and his brother from embracing the very plan that he himself was initiating.

Of course, it must be understood that the purpose of this trap would not have been to lure the Kennedys into engaging in assassinations but (1) to determine whether such operations were in fact part of U.S. policy and (2) to send the president a message that they would not be tolerated. At the same time, the stick of deterrence would be complimented by the carrot of conciliation, as Castro moved through Attwood and other channels to cultivate the soil of rapprochement.

Looking Ahead

The above scenario is largely conjecture. But even should its essential features prove accurate, it does not answer the central question at hand—namely, what happened *after* September 7?

Here, the Schweiker-Hart report is not much help. For all its value as a critique of the investigatory process through which the Warren Commission reached its conclusions, it fails to provide the hard evidence that would make the hypothesized Cuban connection more than fascinating speculation. Nor do the leads that have been uncovered appear to be all that promising. Too much time has passed. There is a strong suspicion that the case will never be satisfactorily resolved.

Hence the reluctance of some legislators to reopen the inquiry. After all, this is a highly emotional issue, with considerable potential for demagogic distortion. One can already discern the beginnings of a sensationalistic brand of journalism, thriving on a mixture of circumstantial evidence, allegation, speculation, and emotion.[16] No doubt a major follow-up investigation would add more fuel to the fire. And certainly no responsible public official would want to stir up potentially dangerous passions without good reason.

On the other hand, one also gets the impression that there is some concern that a serious reinvestigation might turn up something. Who knows, really, what might be found? What political processes set in motion? With what consequences? What, for instance, would be the reaction of the Amer-

---

[16] *I refer especially to the article by Hank Greenspun in the* Las Vegas Sun, *March 1, 1976, which received considerable national attention.*

ican public and the U.S. government should hard evidence actually be discovered linking Castro—or even pro-Castro Cubans—to Kennedy's death? And where would the Soviet Union and détente fit into the picture?

In short, it would be most convenient to pretend that the Schweiker-Hart report did not exist. Or at least to reduce such inquiries as may now be necessary to a mere "tying together of loose ends." Though Richard Sprague, chief council and staff director for the recently created House Committee on Assassinations, has vowed that "no document" and "no witnesses" will be beyond the reach of his probe, it remains to be seen whether he will be able to keep that promise. The committee's legislative authority ended with the last Congress, and the attempt to reconstitute it under new leadership has already run into heavy opposition.[17] (It seems there may be a conflict between the civil liberties of committee witnesses and some of the investigative techniques proposed by Sprague.)[18]

Moreover, even if these difficulties are worked out, there is still the matter of the budget. A study group of 170 persons has been requested at a two-year cost of some $13 million. According to Sprague, these are the "bare bones minimum" figures for the task at hand. Unlike the Warren Commission, the committee will not have the full-time services of more than 200 agents from the FBI, CIA, and Secret Service. Furthermore, it will be simultaneously conducting two separate investigations (one each for the Kennedy and Martin Luther King assassinations). Inevitably, its staff and budget will have to be formidable if a credible job

is to be done. Should the figures requested be significantly cut by the full House, the inquiry may be in trouble from its very inception.

My own opinion is that the case should be reopened, without blinders. We do not need another "negative" investigation, designed to discredit the leads that have been uncovered. Though it found no "smoking pistols," the Schweiker-Hart task force raised serious questions which should be honestly confronted. And even if our congressional sleuths do not come up with clear-cut findings of guilt and innocence, it would be reassuring to be able to believe that they had been open-minded and determined in their efforts. The issue is not only the Kennedy assassination but the integrity of the U.S. government. If, after all of the revelations made and questions raised by the old Senate Intelligence Committee, Congress should fail to meet its responsibilities, wouldn't there be good reason to wonder whether it too had become part of the "cover-up"?[19]

There will, of course, be risks and costs involved; there always are. But this is not 1964. Cold war tensions have abated considerably. The American public has had time to get over the trauma of the assassination. And the temper of the age, strongly anti-interventionist and self-critical, makes another invasion of Cuba improbable, even in the event that incriminating evidence is found. In short, it is difficult to imagine a major international crisis coming out of all this.

Moreover, recent reports out of Havana indicate that the Castro government is not nearly as apprehensive about these developments as might be supposed. Far from viewing a new inquiry as an obstacle to rapprochement or a prelude to and legitimization of future Yankee aggressions, Cuban

---

[17] *The outgoing chairman, Thomas Downing (D., Virginia), is retiring. The new chairman is expected to be Henry B. Gonzalez (D., Texas). Sprague is the Philadelphia attorney who drew national acclaim for resolving the Yablonski murder case and securing the conviction of United Mine Worker's President Tony Boyle.*

[18] *See David Burnham, "Assassination Panel Is Warned on Its Techniques," The New York Times, January 6, 1977.*

[19] *According to a recent Gallup poll, 80 per cent of the American public now believes that Oswald did not act alone; only 11 per cent still adheres to the "lone assassin" thesis; the remainder are undecided. The Washington Post, December 26, 1976.*

officials have stressed a desire that the case be reopened. Their suspicion is that a "Cuban connection" may very well be discovered. It is reasoned that the recent murders of Sam Giancana and John Rosselli might well be connected with their roles in the CIA-mafia plots against Castro. The feeling is strong (though no proof is offered) that there is a link between those intrigues, Cuban exile politics, and the Kennedy assassination.[20]

Regardless, the case is potentially explosive and will have to be handled with a keen sense of responsibility. It must be made very clear that we are only trying to get at the truth. Thus the importance of exploring all of the evidence, both that which supports the retaliation hypothesis and that which does not. I believe that there is a substantial body of reason and circumstantial evidence, admittedly inconclusive, that suggests that Castro was not directly responsible for the killing in the sense that he ordered it done.[21]

The possibility of indirect responsibility is another matter. It is not inconceivable that Cuban security agents or others in or sympathetic to the regime, inspired perhaps by Castro's rhetoric and threats against North American leaders, may have taken it upon themselves to "eliminate" the president. The whole poisonous atmosphere of hatred and fear that pervaded U.S.-Cuban relations during this period was highly conducive to such schemes. The possibility of exile involvement also cannot be overlooked. Thomas Downing, outgoing chairman of the House Committee on Assassinations, has recently come into possession of information that suggests that right-wing Cuban exiles may have sought the president's death in retaliation for his withdrawal of air support at the Bay of Pigs. These materials will bear close scrutiny.

In the end, the "lone assassin" thesis may very well be reconfirmed, for want of other evidence if nothing else. But this is far from certain. So by all means, let there be a reopening of the investigation. And let it be a serious one, designed to uncover new leads as well as follow up old ones. As with the discovery of the Watergate tapes, it may only take one good breakthrough to settle the whole issue. And even if that breakthrough never comes and the case is never resolved, we will have at least made the effort. That is surely worth something.

Then too, in the process, we will no doubt learn more about the conduct of U.S. foreign policy. One thing is certain: The Senate Intelligence Committee only skimmed the surface in its examination of our "secret war" against Castro. Just to set the record straight, the first proposal to enlist the CIA to assassinate Castro was made not in December 1959, as the Senate Select Committee has suggested, but some two-and-a-half years earlier, when the young Cuban guerrilla was still struggling for survival in the Sierra Maestra. The source: The U.S. Ambassador to Havana, Arthur Gardner. Fortunately for Castro, Fulgencio Batista, then president of the republic, declined the offer.[22] Perhaps, had he accepted, he would have remained in power longer than he did.

---

[20] *Alton Frye, "The JFK Assassination: Curiosity in Havana,"* Ibid., *September 12, 1976.*

---

[21] *This tentative conclusion, incidentally, is by no means shaken by the recent discovery of a J. Edgar Hoover memorandum quoting a "reliable informant" to the effect that Oswald had told Cuban officials during his September 1963 visit to the Mexico City consulate that he intended to kill Kennedy. According to the informant, this information came directly from Castro and was based on a report that Castro received from Mexico City. But this has been known for some time. In August 1967, Castro gave an interview to British journalist Comer Clark in which he revealed that Cuban officials had heard Oswald threaten Kennedy's life. Unfortunately, at the time Oswald's remarks had been discounted as the ravings of an unbalanced person. In point of fact, it seems that the Schweiker-Hart task force was aware of the Hoover memorandum and chose not to include it in its final report, since Castro had previously admitted this knowledge in public. Again, the question arises: If Castro were guilty, would he have drawn attention to himself by volunteering this information?* The New York Times, *November 14, 1976 and* Columbus Dispatch, *November 14, 1976.*

---

[22] *See Hugh Thomas,* Cuba: The Pursuit of Freedom *(New York: Harper & Row, 1971), p. 947.*

SOUTH AMERICA LOOKS AT DETENTE (SKEPTICALLY)

by Mariano Grondona

The word *détente* evokes opposite responses in liberal circles of the United States and Western Europe on the one hand, and in the military or semimilitary systems of the Southern Triangle of Latin America on the other. For the United States and for many in Europe, *détente* refers to a kind of hope: the possibility of constructing a positive and durable relationship between the democracies and totalitarian states, between capitalism and communism, that perhaps could evolve toward a final convergence of both systems into something resembling universal social democracy.

In the Southern Triangle of Latin America, which is inclining toward a striking political homogeneity, *détente* refers to a new potential for trade with the East, but also carries with it a measure of alarm and fear. In recent years, the nations of Latin America have experienced conflict which more than once has placed them in a state of crisis, and has raised the specter of Cuba. The anti-Communist regimes throughout Latin America consider *détente* an ideological cover for possible subversive penetration into their own societies. Or they sometimes regard it as U.S. abandonment of its less important allies.

Henry A. Kissinger provides an earlier example of this phenomenon of opposite responses in A World Restored, *in which he compares the views of the Austrian chancellor, Clemens von Metternich, "the*

continental statesman," with those of the British chancellor, Lord Castlereagh, "the insular statesman." They agreed on the necessity of Napoleon's defeat, but for distinctly different and almost opposing reasons. Castlereagh, says Kissinger, was not concerned about the kind of political system that the powers on the continent might choose—be it republican or monarchist, nationalist or imperialist— but that no single regime be able to acquire enough power to unite the European continent at the cost of England's pre-eminence. For Metternich, on the other hand, the type of political system adopted by each of the continental powers was of supreme importance. Seated atop the volcano of an Austrian Empire, suffering from the agitation of the two revolutionary ideologies of the time—liberalism and nationalism—Metternich could not allow this double ferment to boil over on all sides of his nation without the risk of internal turmoil.

Castlereagh and Metternich opposed Napoleon because he embodied a revolutionary stance. But the revolution that "the insular statesman" struggled against was purely international: alteration in the balance of power in Europe. The revolution that "the continental statesman" fought was the subversion of traditional values and principles started during the French Revolution and exported by Napoleon's troops. Metternich, who had no English Channel to protect him, was not only concerned about preserving the diplomatic status quo in Europe but also the political status quo in his own state.

The contradiction found in Castlereagh and Metternich is now being repeated in our own times. When international communism—that newfangled "Bonapartism" —makes an advance, it is perceived differently by the developed nations of the West than by the pro-Western sectors of developing nations. For the United States and Western Europe, the Allende rule in

Chile, guerrilla warfare in the Río de la Plata region, or the occupation of Angola, were viewed as threats solely to the extent that they constituted significant changes in the international balance favoring the great revolutionary power of the twentieth century. Latin-American and African anti-Communists did not react the same way. This is because those events and processes were threatening to the internal structure of their societies. Kissinger, a new Castlereagh, was able to negotiate Angola in exchange for some other advantage in some other part of the world. His own political system was not in immediate danger. For the anti-Communists in Angola, there was no other spot in the world that they could negotiate in exchange. For that reason, Metternich's philosophy is spreading among the pro-Western forces of Latin America and Africa, who are defending their own territory, their own system, and for whom no other watchword remains open but intransigence.

The governments of the Southern Triangle of Latin America have declared time and again that there is no holy alliance in their region against the influence of international communism. Nevertheless, in the Southern Triangle there still exists what we would call a "holy alliance situation"—mutual assistance among political regimes whose objection to Communist pressures is resolved not at the negotiating tables of the great powers but in actual confrontations, at times bloody.

Opposition between the two views of détente is made even more acute when the Latin-American regimes of the Southern Triangle, in order to fight against Communist penetration, sometimes restrict public freedoms in a way judged intolerable by the Northern Hemisphere. The paradox then arises that the most ardent defenders of what they consider pro-Western principles are criticized most by the Western capitals. Many believe that is what happened to Pinochet; the regimes in Brazil,

Bolivia, Uruguay, Paraguay, and Argentina are, to varying degrees, subject to the same fate.

Something similar happened between 1812 and 1822. Castlereagh, whose country was midway between the traditionalism of the Hapsburgs and the liberalism of the French, failed to agree ideologically with Metternich, who was much further to the right. The United States and especially Western Europe have absorbed different degrees of radicalism and socialism. They have moderate regimes, in the manner of Castlereagh's England, that can only look with reproach on the activity of the Latin-American right. In this case, history is repeating itself. The opposition between U.S. and European liberalism and the anti-Communist right that holds sway in the Southern Triangle of Latin America and in the south of Europe (another area where communism is not solely an "external" threat), parallels the contrast between the center of an international system that is secure and flexible, and its periphery where daily life takes on the aspect of a battlefield.

This contrast demands a detailed analysis, because it is the anti-Communist right, and not the liberal center left, that is taking over power in vast areas of Latin America.

A North-South Communications Gap

There is a communications gap between U.S. and European liberalism on the one hand and the predominant trends within the Southern Triangle of Latin America on the other. The relevant factors are:

1. None of the military or semimilitary regimes of the Southern Triangle has formally renounced democratic aspirations. However they all stress the necessity of establishing, prior to the full restoration of a democratic system, a series of preconditions, without which they think the system of elections and parties would quickly degenerate into demagogy or Marxism. These preconditions are: (a) establishment

of effective public law and order, and the subsequent elimination of subversive outbreaks, social disarray, and widespread disobedience of the law; (b) consolidation of the financial sector, based on control of inflation and of administrative chaos in state management; (c) establishment of a self-sustaining process of economic development; (d) reorganization of political parties and labor unions. For U.S. and Western liberals, these preconditions are no more than a pretext for indefinitely delaying the restoration of democracy. The Southern Triangle's reply is that in the North Atlantic area, democracy has been the result of a long process that first assured the given conditions for political authority and economic development under efficient monarchies and oligarchies, only later opening up to unrestricted participation by the masses. Latin America, according to this interpretation, is in the earlier stage of development.

2. From the standpoint of the Southern Triangle, democracy is an end, a goal. Democracy is built out of conditions in themselves authoritarian. From the Northern standpoint, democracy is an end, as well as a means. It is not just the best of available systems, but also the road leading to its own fulfillment. Democracy is like a muscle that is built up through exercise; it seems contradictory to attempt its foundation on nondemocratic premises.

3. As seen through the eyes of the Southern Triangle, the Communist movement follows a double tactical pathway. Vis-à-vis the developed and strong regimes, it is responsible and even scrupulous in the fulfillment of its obligations. On this level, the Soviet Union arouses interest as a country receiving technology and investment, and as a vast market for imports. In contrast, vis-à-vis "weaker" regimes, communism focuses on efforts to agitate and to penetrate. This is the dominant tactic in Latin America. For an Argentinean, for a Uruguayan, for a Chilean, the word

"communism" has connotations decidedly different than for an American or an Englishman. This is because the former sees one side of the coin and the latter, the reverse side. U.S. liberals view South American anticommunism as a type of McCarthyism; South American anti-Communists view détente as complacency and weakness.

4. This semantic wall applies not just to "democracy" and to "communism." It extends also to "socialism." To a supporter of the regimes in power in the Southern Triangle, the word "socialism" signifies "violence." It carries the same connotation for many Socialists of the region. Socialism is a firearm. It is taken or it is seized, but in any case, it implies that other word, "revolution." In the North, on the other hand, the word "socialism" is considered peaceful and evolutionary. It is interpreted in many cases as the final ripening of democracy in the direction of a more just, more humane, and more egalitarian society. Thus the paradox could arise that one and the same person, traveling in Switzerland and Argentina, might be considered a Socialist in one country and an anti-Socialist in the other, without undergoing any fundamental change in values.

5. According to northern liberals, time is working in favor of democracies. If they succeed in keeping the peace, they believe that internal evolution will lead the Soviet Union into harmonious existence with the West. Improvements in living standards in totalitarian states will compel them to gradually loosen political controls. Greater commercial and cultural relations between East and West will bring both systems closer to common political practices approaching the ideals of a social democracy.

The Southern Triangle's view on this matter is different. It is believed that the Soviet Union is a typical empire with an unlimited appetite for expansion. Its leaders, far from becoming "bourgeois" as a function of economic progress, will intensify their preparations for war, develop greater sophistication in exercising political control, and further penetrate the soft spots of the non-Communist world. But this process, apparent since the end of World War II, involves a logic of catastrophe. Just as Hitler did, Soviet Communist rulers only believe in power. The Western democracies provide only feeble verbal protests in opposition to such advances, just like Chamberlain and Daladier, four decades ago. The result will be comparable. At any time, Soviet totalitarianism will cross an invisible line, the line of maximum tolerance. No one knows what the analogue of Poland will be. But it will have one. The Western powers have lost all credibility as far as the Communist leaders are concerned. Their declarations may be forceful at times; their actions however are not. When they finally move from declarations to actions, it may be, as in 1939, too late.

6. The regimes of the Southern Triangle deem themselves bulwarks against Communist penetration. In this sense, they consider themselves staunch allies of the United States. In liberal circles, on the other hand, the opposite view is held. They regard the authoritarianism of the right just as much as that of the left as conspiring against the West's basic ideals. As a rightist regime, by its nature, nurtures a leftist reaction, far from reassuring the West, the regimes of the Southern Triangle are creating the conditions for just such a swing of the pendulum in the opposite direction. When liberal groups pressure the U.S. Congress to suspend military or economic aid to one of the countries of the Southern Triangle, the decision comes as a surprise for the leaders of that country. They ask if the United States is truly aware of its real allies. They reflect bitterly on this, and recall, without any great love or admiration for the superpower they are dealing with, what happened to others who believed themselves to be friends of the United States—the South Vietnamese, for example.

7. We have already seen how, during World War II, Western liberalism favored Marxism as a final option and opposed fascism. Stalin was an ally, and not Hitler. If faced with the same choice, the final option would undoubtedly be the reverse for the military or semi-military regimes of the Southern Triangle. This may also be true as far as the European and U.S. right are concerned. From the standpoint of the Southern Triangle, it is unjustifiable for the international press to pillory Pinochet, while praising Mao and forgiving Castro. It is also unfair to focus only on the violations of human rights in certain countries, without giving recognition to the progress being made in other fields. Such an attitude seems cynical, for while the American press and Congress condemn the regimes of the Southern Triangle, American businessmen, diplomats, and military men deal on an ever increasing scale with those countries. At the worst, the Southern Triangle is fearful that it might be abandoned by the United States if international conflicts so require. No one in that section of the world can forget Vietnam and Angola. It is believed that while the Soviet Union is an unwavering defender of the regimes that place themselves under its protection, this is not the case with the Western world. The Latin-American right suspects that the Western powers have lost their will to resist.

Moreover, Western liberalism is not at a loss for words when it comes to making denunciations. Any incident will serve to reinforce the notion that in the Southern Triangle, far from seeking democracy and fighting subversion, what is really being built up is a new totalitarian system. Thus, the Southern Triangle seems to be overstepping the boundaries of international legality, and, consequently, its rulers take on Nuremberg features.

To many, the gap between U.S. liberalism and southern anticommunism now appears beyond repair. Subjects such as détente and human rights make that gap evident. Diplomats and businessmen may be able to ignore its existence for practical purposes, but its existence and consistency is one of the central facts of inter-American relations. Only a substantial evolution toward the right in the United States or toward the left in the south could modify this divergence in viewpoints.

The conflicting viewpoints of the right-dominated Southern Triangle and U.S. liberalism does not necessarily hamper hemispheric relationships. The majority in the United States Congress, the press, the Democratic majority and the Republican minority represent U.S. liberalism. Other important U.S. institutions and groups, the business community, the Republican or Democratic right, and the military take a different view. As for the Department of State, its liberal leanings are well known; political discretion prevents it from carrying these leanings too far. Similarly, it cannot be overlooked that in the northern areas of Latin America there are regimes with strong leanings toward the liberal viewpoint, such as Mexico, Venezuela, Costa Rica, and Colombia. In the Southern Triangle itself, political parties out of power as well as university and press circles represent varying degrees of liberalism. Inter-American relations and Latin-European relations carry on in this sense a honeycomb of lines crossing each other; ideological alliances transcend national boundaries. There is no such thing as a single Latin America. Nor is there a single North America or Europe, or a single Argentina or Brazil. The problems of détente and human rights crisscross the West free of geographic, economic, or cultural boundaries.

Détente

Détente lends itself to a number of interpretations.

First of all, détente refers to the bilateral relations between the United States and the Soviet Union. Here is the crux of détente. But this aspect does not receive much special attention in Latin America. What worries the rightist circles is anything said about an advance in armaments by the Soviets; for such an advance is considered one more proof of how little disposed Westerners are to take up battle. But the problem of armaments is not a real issue in most of Latin America, in part because there is nothing that can be done south of the Rio Grande to resolve it. Local conflicts in the international arena outside the Latin-American region, such as in the Middle East or Korea, are also of minimal interest.

It is a well known and welcomed fact in all of Latin America that the relaxation of tensions between the Soviet Union and the United States has led to the proliferation of trade and mutual cooperation agreements in all directions. However, outside of brief periods such as the presidential terms of Velasco Alvarado in Peru and Allende in Chile, the main economic, financial, and commercial ties have kept expanding between the United States, Western Europe, Japan, and the Latin-American region.

Although bilateral U.S.-Soviet relations do not capture the attention of Latin Americans, this is not the case with regard to Cuba. In recent years, as a result of the development of leftist and left-of-center regimes in the region—Allende in Chile, Perón in Argentina, Velasco in Peru—Cuba regained a place in intraregional relations. A mini-détente between the United States and Cuba was apparently being contemplated. But Castro's military intervention in Angola produced a complete turnabout in the situation. In the Southern Triangle, it is believed without reservation that guerrillas are supported at least in part by Cuba. It is known that centers for training and outfitting guerrillas remain active on the island. The fact that Cuba may have turned into a military base for the open export of revolution to black Africa provokes fears of similar interventions on our continent.

On the other hand, it is hard for military regimes to maintain normal relations with

Castro's regime. Commercial trade between Cuba and Argentina, for example, is important; Cuba is the principal importer of Argentine automobile engines. The opening of this market led to a significant conflict over the stand of U.S. affiliates in Argentina, which had to decide between abiding by their own country's embargo and their host country's trade policy. With Cuba, it is much more difficult now to maintain the two-way street of ideological conflict and economic cooperation typical of relations with East-bloc countries. For most Latin-American countries, except Chile, it is not too much of a strain to trade with the Soviet Union. Cuba is too close for this type of exercise, and relations will worsen.

Cuban and Soviet penetration in Angola opened a new source of worry for Latin Americans, and, more particularly, the South Atlantic nations. The fact that international confrontation has now reached the southern part of Africa turns the South Atlantic—which until recently had been a forgotten sea—into a potential theater of war operations. Countries like Brazil and Argentina intend to capitalize on their strategic positions in order to be admitted as full or associate members of NATO. They hope to acquire a "Spanish position"— bulwarks in the rear guard of the Western defense system, just like Franco's Spain. They are confident that this position will allow them to enjoy a status that would be denied if all that mattered were democratic orthodoxy.

On another level, détente is only possible in a climate of ideological disarmament with the East. That disarmament has already occurred, at least in regard to U.S. liberalism and various forms of Western European socialism. An emphasis on human rights, pacifism, and antimilitarism create the political and ideological climate in the Northern Atlantic that allows for progress on the diplomatic and commercial road of détente. But this same climate has heightened tensions with the rightist regimes of the Southern Triangle of Latin America and, until recently, with those of Southern Europe —The Greece of the colonels, the Spain of Franco, the Portugal of Salazar and Caetano. There is a Social Democratic front in Europe, in power in countries like the United Kingdom, West Germany, Austria, and Portugal, which is applying considerable pressure in France. However, two important changes should be mentioned here. One is the defeat of the Socialists in Sweden, a country that has been in the vanguard in denouncing the rightist regimes. The other is the liberalization of Spain. Just as the change in Sweden may give the Latin-American right a better chance to breathe, the direction of change in Spain is a new cause for worry. Spain has played, and still plays, a significant role in Latin America. Imitation of Spain is a possibility. The political and economic experiences of individual Latin-American nations influence each other. We speak with great ease in this region about the Brazilian "model" or about the Peruvian one. Spain and Portugal are among the very few countries that enjoy the privilege of penetrating this process of emulation and imitation.

But the sheer vigor of the liberal and radical trends that give détente a marked ideological flavor could affect relations between Latin Americans themselves. We have already witnessed the breaking off of relations between Mexico and Chile and Venezuela and Uruguay. We have seen the cooling of relations between Mexico and Argentina and the interruption of the Andean integration process due to the opposition of Chile. These examples are not merely incidental. Ideological coexistence between a liberal North and a conservative South is becoming more and more difficult in this region. Until very recently, it was possible to prevent Latin-American political currents from halting the economic, diplomatic, and cultural convergence of the region. Today, ideological polarization is causing the erosion of political pluralism. A basic principle governing conduct between the Latin-American ruling bodies has been weakened.

There is a crusade in the wind in Latin America. Before very long, moderation could be replaced by intransigence. The nations of the Southern Triangle are closing their ranks when regional security and human rights are discussed. On the other hand, regimes of similar political coloration are accentuating their gestures of solidarity. At the recent meeting that the Organization of American States held in Santiago, Chile, the Southern Triangle voted unanimously to prevent any sanction against the host country. On the other hand, Argentina recently chose as its ambassador to Caracas a member of the Radical Party, attempting to salvage its relations with Venezuela— partly because the expansion of a third country, Brazil, brings together two opposing regimes with strong geopolitical ties.

Another relevant factor is the general impression that organized subversion is rapidly losing ground in the Southern Triangle. Even in countries like Argentina, where its outward manifestations are still considerable, it is believed to be a transient phenomenon—diminishing rather than expanding. In reality, in the Southern Triangle today, the problem is more the excesses of the repressive groups than those of the guerrillas. At the same time, there are signs of infiltration and agitation in the northern parts of Latin America, especially in Colombia. But this case, when considered along with others, raises the question of whether subversion is migrating from the South to the North. Its strategy would be to limit itself in the South to acts of attrition, especially through international denunciations, while more concentrated action is directed against the more open, penetrable regimes in the North of the region. If this assumption is confirmed, how would it affect the present ideological debate?

Until now, the U.S. government has been cautious in approving sanctions against the rightist regimes of the Southern Triangle —more so than certain European countries. Only Chile is on the blacklist, and then only up to a certain degree. But this has already created friction. For example, the temporary detainment of a U.S. priest created diplomatic difficulties between Argentina and the United States; the suspension of military aid to Uruguay was denounced by two high-placed generals of that country. Military aid to Argentina is under attack. These are small incidents, but they could be aggravated should present attitudes persist.

The outcome of the U.S. elections could influence the course of events of détente. No surprises were expected if Gerald Ford had won. But Jimmy Carter, in contrast, has been an unknown factor. We are told that in international affairs, he proposes to bring actions into line with principles— an attitude directly opposed to the pragmatism of Kissinger. But its consequences are difficult to foresee. The Ford-Kissinger policy was "soft on everybody"—on the Soviets, but also on the regimes of the Southern Triangle. Will Carter be "hard on everybody"? The fact is that neither the Soviets nor the regimes of the Southern Triangle are living up to the principles of U.S. democracy. What will it be like in a world where, at the same time, pressure is put on the Soviet Union and the Southern Triangle in defense of human rights? If concern for human rights becomes more crucial in U.S. policy toward the East, will it also make the regimes of the Southern Triangle less acceptable?

A Common Ground

I have devoted much of this article to investigating the differences between U.S. liberalism and the military regimes of the Southern Triangle in relation to détente. I would now like to raise the question of whether there is a possibility of finding a common ground for those two camps.

Two winds are blowing from the East. Soviet power is simultaneously a classical power and a revolutionary power. The Soviet state conducts itself like the rest of the states and maintains normal relations with them. The Soviet Communist Party continues insisting on ideological and political expansion; it is in this sense a destabilizing force.

Those who back détente have made an historical wager on the victory of the state over the party. They believe that if enough time is granted to this evolutionary process, the Soviet Union will behave more and more like a nation that is compatible with the community of nations and less and less like an empire ravenous for world conquest. A rough sketch of Pygmalion's vocation can be gathered from reading some of the speeches that Kissinger delivered during the recent election campaign. The United States, the former secretary of state believes, should show sufficient firmness and patience to get on with the "education" of the Soviet Union about the rules of living together in a civilized community of nations. Once that system has been formed, he will have his dream: a world like post-Napoleonic Europe, ready for 100 years of real peace.

The historical wager in favor of the state against the party is the first premise of the backers of détente. The second is ideological in nature. We might label it "the centrist analysis." The "center," which is opposed to leftist authoritarianism as much as it is to rightist authoritarianism, refuses, in this context, to "bend" either to one side or to the other. It rejects the suggestion that just because the rightist military regimes are anti-Communist, they can become allies. This would be "bending" the center toward the right. The center does not consider itself as a compromise or a crossroads between the left and right. Nor as a moderate form of anticommunism. It wants to be both anti-Communist and antidictatorial at the same time. Or better yet, antidictatorial in an absolute sense, wherever the dicta-

torship may come from. It believes that rightist military regimes are just as far from its ideology as Communist totalitarianism.

There is even what I have called a final option toward the left. This does not mean that authentic liberals and supporters of détente would accept, in the final extreme, Communist domination. It means that they would accept a renewal of the Grand Alliance of World War II, but not a reverse coalition with those whom they view as successors of Hitler and Mussolini.

This last assumption is not so much ideological as "vital"; a question of sensibilities. The supporters of détente acknowledge that Pygmalion does not limit himself to changing the person he seeks to educate. He too changes, to the point of falling in love with her! Some of those who back détente assume and accept the fact that if in the course of U.S.-Soviet coexistence, Soviet society will have to approach the Western ideal step by step, then Western society will also have to assimilate varied doses of socialism, until both are at a sufficiently close distance to encourage a sincere friendship. Along this line, one can see what Zbigniew Brzezinski and Samuel P. Huntington called the "theory of convergence"—rejecting it in their classic study, Political Power: USA/USSR.

At the heart of this theory there is something we would call "economicism," the supposition that in the final analysis, the economic structure of production determines political behavior. An excellent version of this hypothesis can be found in the well-known works of John Kenneth Galbraith. In this analysis, given the extent to which large corporations, under the control of "technostructures," direct not only the U.S. but also the Soviet economy, the political and international decisions of the two societies will in the end resemble each other and converge.

One final intellectual trend reinforces the supporters of détente; the thesis that ideologies are not as important as nationality. The Soviet Union, China, the United States, it is assumed, are "nations" with permanent objectives and interests above and beyond "ideologies" and "religions." Kissinger's pragmatism is positioned here. Following this approach, the international power game does not differ as much as widely believed from the games of centuries past. For that reason, China is at odds with the Soviet Union. For that reason, it is possible to build up once again a pluralistic international system through patient negotiations, a discreet show of face, mutual concessions and advantages. From this perspective, détente would be but a new manifestation of an art as old as the world: the art of diplomacy.

Two winds are blowing from the East. The supporters of détente are opting for one, its South American critics for the other. The latter maintain that the Soviet state is no more than a cover for the ideological imperialism of the party. To continue playing the game of détente is to grant time to ideological expansion until it may be too late. The South American hawks feel that the course of history will run not for but against Western ideals unless something is done to reverse the trend. From this point of view, what matters today are the left and right, not the center—a mere geometric point without substance of its own. For the center represents the desire not to choose, the refusal to confront reality, i.e., the constant advance of an empire pursuing ambitions at the expense of an "imperial republic"[1] which, like ancient Athens, prefers to continue being a republic rather than take possession of its empire.

The final option of the hawks points naturally toward rightist authoritarianism and not toward Marxism. Pygmalion, according to them, does not teach; to the contrary, he is infiltrated and manipulated. "Economicism" is unacceptable. Politics has

its own laws and cannot be reduced to economics. If the Soviet Union receives wheat and technological assistance thanks to détente, the result is not its conversion, its being "bourgeoisied," but rather a freeing of its resources to be used on a new push in armaments or revolution. New missiles or revolutionary aid to Angola are born out of the wheat. Finally, the hawks believe that ideas, not national interest in the classic sense, rule the world. Like it or not, Western nations are confronting the spread of a new secular religion, whose believers are motivated by fanaticism.

The inner ambivalence of the Soviet position (its peace-making and aggressive nature) not only instigates the debate between U.S. liberalism and the military regimes of the Southern Triangle, but also brings to life two incompatible mentalities, whose dialogue may be impossible in the final analysis. Conservatives and liberals everywhere have two different attitudes toward the world and history. A head-on clash between the two can be avoided as long as no issue ever obliges the one group to take a clear stand against the other. Détente is one of those issues. For this reason, in the United States as in the rest of the Americas, détente is an occasion for this latent disagreement to reveal itself. Conservatives and liberals discover that they cannot resolve their differences on détente through discussion.

Different scales of values are involved in this dispute. On one scale, order ranks first; on another, change ranks uppermost. While order is political, change is economic. Order is solid; its boundaries are fixed. Change is fluid; it suggests mixtures and combinations. Circumstances air either one or the other trend. In the Southern Triangle, the conservatives are triumphant because the wind of revolutionary aggression is blowing. In the Northern hemisphere, where the gentle breeze of trade and diplomacy is prevailing, doves fly more freely.

---

[1] *Raymond Aron*, République Impériale *(Paris: Calmann-Lévy, 1973).*

The polarization of positions between U.S. liberalism and the Southern Triangle has produced new tensions on the issue of détente. The advent of coexistence at the end of the 1950s and the beginning of the 1960s was well received by a Latin America where democratic reformism held sway. The Latin America of Frei, Frondizi, and Belaunde coincided with both the era and spirit of John F. Kennedy, Nikita Khrushchev, and Pope John XXIII. It was the time of the Alliance for Progress. The United States seemed capable of leadership then. But the era of détente of Nixon and Brezhnev, of Kissinger and Gromyko, had from the beginning another flavor—a flavor of diplomatic calculation and politics.

Likewise, the Latin America witnessing this had also changed. Peronism, Peruvianism, and the turnabout to the center-left in nations like Venezuela and Mexico, were taking the region toward a Third World outlook. Governments in Latin America today that are not anti-Communist and military are overwhelmingly partial to the Third World. But this has not resulted in enthusiasm for détente. The expansion of trade in all directions was praised, as was the elimination of ideological barriers to international competition. However, it is feared that if détente advances in the direction of alliance and friendship, it will lead to a division of the world into spheres of influence between the two superpowers. According to this hypothesis, Latin America would remain imprisoned within the grip of U.S. imperialism. According to this view, the true line dividing the world today does not run from North to South separating the East from the West, but rather from East to West separating the North from the South. Whatever the arrangement between the superpowers of the North, this cannot be good news for the South. Hegemonial arrangements would be made at its expense. To the extent that détente opens up this possibility, it is regarded with suspicion.

This prompts a final reflection upon the paradoxes of anti-Americanism in Latin America. If the campaign of liberals for détente and against rightist authoritarianism continues, if sanctions affecting nations like Chile and Uruguay for violation of human rights are extended, then the military regimes of the Southern Triangle acquiesce to varying amounts of anti-Americanism. They like to regard the United States as the bastion of the West. Yet when they observe its contacts with Moscow, its censuring of regimes that are combating communism within their own borders, there is a strong temptation for those in power today in the Southern Triangle to accuse U.S. leaders of abandoning their allies and of forsaking their historical role.

This development will not bring Third World currents any closer to the United States. They do not want alliance with the United States. Unlike the anti-Communists, they are not disillusioned pro-Americans. They want to free themselves totally from any and all influences, and they cannot accept the idea of a division of the world as a condition of détente. Finally, among those who push for sanctions against the regimes of the Southern Triangle, there are the theoreticians of dependence; Marxists or Communists who, for ideological reasons, identify the United States as their principal enemy. As was witnessed a few months ago in the subcommittee of the House Committee on International Relations, several of the principal Communist leaders of Argentina—natural enemies of the United States—testified on the violation of human rights by the Argentine military regime—presumably a friend of the United States. Carl Schmidt once said that one of the decisive problems of politics is to identify one's enemies with certainty. The least that can be said is that such a definition has not been attained between the U.S. Americans and the Latin Americans with respect to détente.

BRAZIL: THE END OF A BEAUTIFUL RELATIONSHIP

by Roger W. Fontaine

The dust has begun to settle, and in the distant haze I see the smoking ruin of a special relationship. The United States and Brazil have ended more than a century of close ties. The destruction followed a trumpet blast from the Carter administration consisting of two shrill notes: human rights and nonproliferation. The underlying motif: morality in foreign policy.

What have we done that's so bad, and why are the Brazilians so angry with us? To answer that properly, we must separate intentions from results. Then, perhaps, we can write ourselves a new policy, before the poisoned relations with Brazil extend into the next generation.

President Carter, whose intentions were lofty if not exactly modest, wanted to restore respect for human rights in Brazil and, more importantly, to prevent that country from acquiring a complete nuclear fuel cycle and hence the bomb. The objectives were laudable; the implementation is another, rather sad matter.

We have alienated a friend and old ally, and we did not get (nor will we likely get) what we sought in the first place. Worse, we have probably increased the chances that Brazil will select the nuclear option by the end of the century. That decision will be made by a generation of Brazilian leaders who have accepted Charles De Gaulle's warning: Don't trust the Americans if your greatness is at stake.

We have also bungled on the issue of human rights. The current trend in Brazil is toward more, not less, authoritarianism, and our ability to stem that disturbing development in Brasília has probably reached a postwar low.

The results of the Carter policy were foreseeable: nothing the Brazilians have done should come as a surprise. But those who make high-pitched moral pronouncements rarely let simple matters like consequences get in the way of their good and righteous cause.

A short history of our new policy toward Brazil should prove instructive. The president made the dangers of nuclear proliferation a central issue during the campaign, and Brazil was soon singled out as a leading target for criticism, because its 1975 agreement with West Germany was to provide the South American giant with a nuclear fuel cycle. The first move of the Carter administration was to place direct pressure on the Germans to cancel the agreement, commencing with Vice President Walter F. Mondale's trip to Bonn last January. That move had the effect of virtually canceling the "memorandum of understanding" which had been signed by the United States and Brazil less than a year earlier. The memorandum formally pledged regular consultations on economic, political, and technological issues affecting both countries, as well as the coordination of all policy in the international arena. Our new approach to nuclear proliferation, of course, fell within the scope of the agreement. The Rio de Janeiro newspaper, Jornal do Brasil, remarked at the time that a "memorandum is a record of things that cannot be forgotten."

The Carter administration, however, chose to forget, first ignoring the Brazilians and then, one month after the Mondale visit to Bonn, sending a State Department delegation to Brasília to demand that the West German agreement be modified. To be sure, the United States sweetened *this bitter pill with a promise of an "assured" supply of enriched uranium, but, not surprisingly, in light of today's tight supply situation, that offer was rejected by the Brazilians. It also confirmed a long-held Brazilian suspicion that the United States really wants to keep underdeveloped nations technologically dependent, while itself growing rich on the immensely profitable sale of enriched uranium. The Brazilians refused to discuss the matter, and the large American delegation headed home after one day of talks. A terse communiqué mentioned the stalemate and only vaguely hinted at a future meeting.*

A Heavy American Hand

Our achievements to date are: (1) We broke our word by not consulting the Brazilians, prior to the vice presidential trip to Germany, on a matter deemed vital to Brazil. Consequently, it is difficult to believe that the Brazilians will soon trust us again. It is equally doubtful that any prudent Mexican official, for example, will put much faith in his own country's special relationship with the United States. (2) We have succeeded in propelling the Brazilian nuclear program forward. Not only is the West German deal still intact, but a larger number of Brazilians are now convinced that the nuclear option is worth serious consideration. If by some slim chance we were able to cancel all or part of the Brazilian-West German nuclear accord, that would make the Brazilians even more determined to go ahead—by themselves if necessary, even though it would take them longer and cost more in real resources. That would have two additional unfortunate consequences: The new, independent program would not have to submit to any outside safeguards, unlike the present arrangement with Germany. And a nuclear and Gaullist Brazil would be much more inclined to develop a nuclear weapons system— something no responsible Brazilian official

now espouses—because the heavy American hand in this affair has only strengthened the cause of those hardliners who promote an ultranationalist nuclear policy.

The militants' simple message is: America stands in the way of future Brazilian grandeza. How? By keeping Brazil permanently dependent on, and inferior to, the United States, particularly in advanced technology. Recent developments confirm the worst suspicions and force others, who had given the United States the benefit of the doubt, into rethinking their own, more moderate, views.

One curious fallout of the new U.S. policy is Argentina's public support for the Brazilian position, which may lead to cooperation in nuclear development. That these two natural rivals should forge an atomic entente is not only ironic, but also avoidable. The Argentine nuclear program is more advanced than Brazil's, and its sources of foreign assistance perfectly complement those of its larger neighbor. Between the two nations, they know everyone in the nuclear trade. Neither one is bound by the nonproliferation treaty, nor by Latin America's version of that agreement, the Tlatelolco treaty.

Three Bad Assumptions

Poor policy is usually rooted in bad assumptions. I detect three of them: Brazil's nuclear program is susceptible to modification, because it is the brain child of a few local politicos who suffer from premature delusions of grandeur. The United States has to act the way it does, because there are no available alternatives. Brazil is susceptible to our influence, in part because of its recent economic difficulties.

The first miscalculation is probably the biggest. Brazil's nuclear policy is not simply a matter of prestige, although there exists in Brazil a current of nationalist feeling that is both volatile and widespread, as well as easily underestimated—possibly because it is less anti-American than that usually found south of the Río Bravo.

But prestige accounts for only a small part of Brazil's current nuclear strategy. At the heart of the rationale is worry over the country's future well-being, which in turn depends on the development of massive new energy resources by the end of the century. Fossil fuel and hydroelectric power will not be enough, since planners believe Brazil's requirements will rival those of any nation immediately below the superpower slot. According to their time schedule, nuclear power is the only way to fill the gap by the year 2000.

This conviction is reinforced by the fading of the so-called Brazilian miracle after the revolution in oil prices beginning in 1973. Brazil now imports 80 per cent of its fuel requirements, and only strenuous efforts to increase exports will erase the massive trade deficits the country has incurred. High fuel bills have slowed growth, and nuclear energy is believed to be vital if Brazil is to escape the economic strangle hold of foreign oil-producers.

The second assumption, that the United States has no other choice, is also wrong, provided that policy-makers are willing to exercise patience and persistence in following a different policy. The German-Brazilian accord might have unraveled by itself. Until we blundered into the china shop, serious doubt was arising about the quality of the goods being offered. Furthermore, given Brazil's pinched budget, there might have been a stretch-out or even cancellation of some parts of the agreement; American alternatives, if presented at the proper moment, might have been listened to in Brasília.

Presenting Brazil and West Germany with a carefully developed list of extra safeguards (which we could have offered to pay for) could have made diversion of weapons-grade plutonium all but impossible. There is evidence that both countries would have welcomed suggestions, at least until we poisoned the atmosphere.

Now, of course, national pride is at stake; public positions are chiseled in granite, and any suggestions from Brazil's former friend will be treated with suspicion, if not outright hostility. Indeed, the current regime may even accelerate development, despite current budget restraints, in order to prove Brazilian independence. It is an indication of our lost opportunity to recall that the Geisel administration, in direct contrast to its predecessor, had been trimming back the grand projects begun in the euphoric early 1970s.

That raises the last mistaken assumption —that thanks to their economic problems, Brazilians are under our thumb. This requires a reminder that making foreign policy involves more art than science. It may well have seemed in early 1977 that Brazil was vulnerable to pressure. That calculation, based on the 1974-1975 slowdown, was quite wrong, because the Brazilians are lucky. They are now in the process of fashioning a second economic miracle. Admittedly, the first one, which featured high growth rates (around 10 per cent a year) between 1967 and 1973, was not literally a miracle, that is an inexplicable event according to the economic laws of nature. The second one, however, comes closer to the type found in the New Testament, particularly in the story involving loaves and fishes. Demonstrating a perfectly elastic supply curve, like the one in Matthew, the Brazilians seem to come up with abundant supplies of new exports at good prices when others happen to falter momentarily. Thus, coffee, soybeans, and orange juice are propelling Brazil toward the number two position in world export of agricultural products. Two years ago, it was cotton and sugar. Two years from now it may well be a different list, but the cornucopia seems unlikely to fail.

All of this naturally breeds a certain amount of self-confidence among Brazilians. That self-confidence also helps to explain *their rude response to our other great cause of the moment, human rights. This prickly issue surfaced a week after the State Department mission returned, and it led to Brazil's cancellation of a quarter-century-old military agreement with the United States. It was not the most important military or security agreement the Brazilians could have revoked, but it was a warning that patience was wearing thin in Brasília. Moreover, no such step had been taken before, not even during the most difficult days of the Quadros and Goulart regimes.*

Lofty Intentions, Pure Ideals

The cancellation came after the release of the State Department's report on the state of human rights around the world, mandated by Congress to cover all countries with which the United States has military assistance programs, including Brazil. To soften the blow, the State Department sent the report to Brazil's foreign ministry before transmitting it to Capitol Hill. The ministry rejected the report out of hand and returned it to Washington. The stated reason was the by now familiar cry over American intervention in the internal affairs of another country. Perhaps. More certain is the fact that such reports have a highly patronizing tone, which many human rights advocates would have us eschew, except in the case of regimes they don't like.

The United States meant to do "good" in Brazil, but good intentions are not enough. A foreign policy based solely on a few, simple moral precepts can get even the most virtuous into trouble. Though Don Quixote charged across La Mancha with the loftiest of intentions and the purest of ideals, he succeeded only in battling windmills and scattering sheep. This is not to suggest that morality in foreign policy is per se a quixotic adventure. But the American operating moral code had better be well grounded in a reality that includes a mature understanding of *what is possible in a sinful world. Otherwise, we will end up wrecking windmills.*

Somehow, the Brazilians have not appreciated our efforts to make them better. Even the opposition party finds it difficult to be scolded as if they were naughty boys. The real anger goes deeper than that. The Brazilians do not appreciate being lumped together with the likes of Idi Amin and the current robber band running Ethiopia. Moreover, they dislike seeing a policy of hostility toward them matched by friendly overtures to the police states headquartered in Hanoi and Havana. Quite aside from bruised feelings, the fact is that official public criticism invariably drives the criticized nation into protests over interference in its internal affairs. And that in turn makes impossible the small, but often worthwhile, gains achieved through quiet diplomacy. Official U.S. criticism also strengthens those in Brazil whose commitments to any definition of human rights are less than fervent. At the same time, it in no way encourages the present leadership to take any further risks on behalf of "decompression."

Making Repairs

What happens next? The administration may choose to go forward and place more pressure on Brazil. If it does, relations will come close to the breaking point; the Brazilians have already said as much. Alternatively, the United States could decide to do nothing for a while (the present course of action) and simply let the kettle cool off.

In the meantime, can the special relationship be patched up? Will Brazil resume its place as first among equals in Latin America—a kind of proto-partner of the United States? That seems doubtful, at least for now. The truth is that Brazilians are not merely angry, they are bitter. Bitterness lingers. As Brazilians see it, they did enjoy a particularly close relationship with the United States.

Favors were exchanged over the years and a bank account of good will had steadily accumulated. Then suddenly, this year, shocked Brazilians discovered that account was empty, their only comfort a bank president lecturing them on the virtues of thrift.

Recently, relations have improved slightly. The United States has backed off its previous hardline position on nuclear proliferation, and Brazilians are openly relieved at Germany's continued intransigence on the issue. Letters have been exchanged between the White House and the Palacio do Planalto, and Carter has eased the pressure on Bonn. Terence Todman, assistant secretary for inter-American affairs, hinted recently that even the memorandum of understanding would be maintained in principle (although the second consultative meeting called for by the memorandum is now three months overdue). Finally, Mrs. Carter in her June visit made only the vaguest public references to the nuclear and human rights issues, alluding to misperceptions on both sides.

But the United States needs to do more than refrain from doing additional damage; it also needs to make repairs. Meanwhile, there is the lingering question: Has Don Quixote given up knight-errantry or merely reined in Rocinante for a breather?

One further aspect of recent American actions toward Brazil is disturbing. It has to do with priorities in the hemisphere. If the new American design really does include the assumption that drawing up an agreement favorable to tiny Panama is a major feature, while erasing others with big Brazil is merely a detail, then I suggest that design needs radically new engineering, as well as a different engineer.

MEXICO'S OPPORTUNITY: THE OIL BOOM

by George W. Grayson

You can divide the countries of the world into two types, the ones that have oil and the ones that do not. We have oil.—*José López Portillo*

As President José López Portillo completes his first year in office, he is witnessing the worst economic conditions in Mexico since the Great Depression. The post-World War II boom, which saw the country's Gross Domestic Product (GDP) shoot up 6 or 7 per cent annually, has ended. Population now grows faster than the economy. Mexico's 63 million inhabitants make it the world's tenth largest nation, and population is expected to double by 2000 when Mexico City—now third behind Tokyo and Shanghai—will be the planet's largest metropolis. This steep rise (3.2 per cent per year) means that half the country's inhabitants are under 15 years of age. Soon they will be elbowing their way into a labor force half of whose current number (17.5 million) already lacks work or is marginally employed. It also means that U.S. cities will continue to attract hundreds of thousands of "nondocumented" emigrants from Mexico, where 17 per cent of the people earn less than $75 a year and three out of 10 cannot afford a minimum balanced diet.

In an attempt to create jobs, boost incomes, and breathe life into the egalitarian goals of the 1910 revolution, Luis Echeverría, president from 1970 to 1976, encouraged public sector investment in everything from steel-making to skyscraper construction. He put particular emphasis on infrastructure projects requiring heavy capital goods imports. Because Mexico has one of the world's lowest taxation levels and because Mexican investors, alarmed by Echeverría's leftist rhetoric, spurned government securities, the development program was financed largely by an expansionary monetary policy and external borrowing.

"The oil companies delighted their American and European shareholders with fat dividend checks, but won few friends in Mexico."

The upshot was that the public debt rose fivefold to $20 billion under the mercurial Echeverría, while private sector indebtedness surpassed $7 billion. The burden of these loans, over half of them made by American financial institutions, becomes apparent when one remembers that the nation's GDP is only $79 billion. With the possible exception of Brazil, Mexico is the most debt-ridden country. A confluence of factors—the size of the debt, Mexico's propensity to import more than it exports, double-digit inflation, fear of political instability—brought massive capital flight, a halt to private investment, and two devaluations of the once-vaunted peso in late 1976.

Despite a recent surge in Mexican exports, a modest slowing of inflation, and a decrease in the capital flight, conditions remain grim. Nonetheless, López Portillo and his key advisers exude a quiet confidence that the floundering economy can be righted and the economic miracle of the 1950s and 1960s restored. This guarded optimism springs from the discovery of oil deposits as large as those in the Middle East, from which Mexico expects to earn nearly $20 billion by 1982.

Mexico's desperate need for foreign exchange and the United States' accelerating demand for foreign oil commend the exchange of U.S. dollars for Mexican petroleum. But four circumstances complicate this overtly sensible interchange: (1) a history of foreign exploitation of Mexican resources before the 1938 take-over of the major oil firms, (2) the constraints placed upon increased production by Mexico's national oil company and the union that dominates it, (3) Mexico's relations with the Organization of Petroleum Exporting Countries (OPEC) and pressures to ship refined products to a diversified market, and (4) the imperative of Washington's pursuing a policy that combines sensitivity to Mexico's sovereignty with an understanding of how Mexican oil can resolve problems confronting the two nations.

All's Well that Ends Well

With the price of natural gas having increased threefold in recent years, petroleum fourfold, and uranium sevenfold, the possession of energy reserves obviously enhances a nation's power. This was not the case 69 years ago, when entrepreneurs first discovered commercial quantities of oil in Mexico. Then, vital resources served as a magnet, attracting ruthless profit-seekers, avaricious transnational firms, and the diplomats and soldiers of major powers. Once these foreigners had wheedled, bribed, intimidated, and coerced local politicians and their praetorian guards, the resources fell under the sway of outsiders, offending Mexico's dignity and attenuating its sovereignty.

Such exploitation of Mexico occurred under the aegis of Porfirio Díaz, a venal dictator who ruled for 35 years after seizing power in 1876. Díaz believed in the inestimable value of technology, the advancement of his country through investment in mines, railroads, factories, and harbors, and the superiority of white men. (He showered himself with talcum to hide his Indian heritage.)

The vain strongman befriended two foreigners who pioneered the development of Mexico's petroleum. The first was Edward L. Doheny, a wily product of the rough-and-tumble American oil industry in which he had made a fortune. He began his quest for black gold near Tampico and in San Luis Potosí in 1892. Eight years later, he organized the Mexican Petroleum Company of California, explored widely, and spent about $3 million before drilling a gusher in the lake Santa Margarita in the Ebano region of San Luis Potosí.

The second entrepreneur was Weeman Pearson, whom Díaz lavishly paid to construct a drainage canal in Mexico City, a port in Vera Cruz, and a railroad in the Isthmus of Tehuantepec. The Yorkshire contractor found himself in Mexico in 1901, when the great Spindletop well sent a jet-black stream of oil 2,000 feet over Beaumont, Texas. Knowing that the geology in parts of Mexico was similar to that of Texas, Pearson invested nearly $25 million in exploration. In 1908, he founded the Mexican Eagle (Aguila) Company and shortly thereafter drilled the famous Dos Bocas well near Tampico, which initiated the first major stage in the production of Mexican petroleum.

Díaz encouraged both men's work, anxious to balance American against British interests, lest either become too strong. Fierce competition with Doheny notwithstanding, Pearson's Mexican Eagle Company—which boasted Díaz's son as a board member—became Mexico's pre-eminent producer. Winston Churchill contributed greatly to its success when in 1912, over strenuous opposition, he had the Royal Navy converted from coal- to oil-burning vessels. Thus the fleet glided into battle with the kaiser's *Kriegsflotte* propelled by American, Middle Eastern, and Mexican bunker oil.

Production soared from 10,000 barrels in 1901 to 3.9 million in 1908 to 193.4 million in 1921.

Output began declining in 1922. By this time, the productivity of the wells had diminished because of wasteful exploitation. The companies started to worry about their status under a viable government that might collect taxes and listen sympathetically to labor demands. The costs of production had begun to rise. And although the rate of well-drilling increased two-and-a-half times from 1921 to 1926, the majority of wells opened were dry as compared with a 62 per cent success rate before 1921.

The oil companies delighted their American and European shareholders with fat dividend checks, but won few friends in Mexico. They treated their holdings as foreign enclaves, sought the protection of their home governments, and arrogantly embroiled themselves in the host country's politics. These firms claimed not simply to hold 10- or 20-year concessions, but to own the mineral deposits that they exploited. The question of ownership constantly agitated relations between the corporations and the Mexican government.

While conditions improved somewhat in the 1930s, the petroleum workers endured physically exhausting work, squalid living conditions, low pay, and harsh discipline. The firms claimed that higher salaries and improved benefits were economically impossible to provide. Upon the election as president in 1933 of Lázaro Cárdenas, who promised to implement the social goals of the 1917 Constitution, the now unionized petroleum workers demanded better treatment by the oil companies. No doubt the companies could have made concessions, but they feared that demands would escalate and a dangerous precedent be set for their workers in other countries.

The ensuing conflict between the workers and the oil trusts is well known. It culminated at 10:00 PM on March 18, 1938, with a radio speech by the husky-voiced Cárdenas, who announced the expropriation of the 17 American and European corporations. While the labor conflict provided its catalyst and justification, the take-over was motivated by Cárdenas' desire to assert

Mexico's sovereignty after six decades in which the foreign firms had treated it as a fiefdom. President Franklin D. Roosevelt imposed a trade embargo on Mexico in retaliation for the expropriations.

How should the newly expropriated oil industy be run? For the Petroleum Workers Union (STPRM), the answer was simple: turn it over to the workers just as was done the year before with the nationalized railroads. Cárdenas rejected this approach because rail service had deteriorated under the union. Instead, he established a public corporation operated jointly by labor and government, with the latter boasting a majority of the appointments to its nine-member board of directors. Thus, on June 7, 1938, Petróleos Mexicanos (PEMEX) was formed.

The expropriation and related events shaped the development of Mexico's petroleum industry. First, PEMEX's Generation of '38—those dedicated engineers and managers who went to work for the newly formed public body—have consistently advocated conservation of Mexico's oil, lest production again plummet, as it did following the 1921 production peak. Second, despite the failure of Cárdenas to turn the industry over to the union, the *petroleros* (petroleum workers) enjoy excellent pay, generous benefits, and notable influence, especially in the hiring of PEMEX employees, as a result of their crucial role in keeping the oil industry operating immediately after expropriation. Third, because of resistance by the workers and the public at large, foreign capital has played a restricted role in Mexico's petroleum sector. Fourth, in accord with its original aims, PEMEX is expected to fulfill an important social mission: namely, supplying petroleum and related products at low prices to Mexican consumers.

"Sitting on a Sea of Oil"

The Aztecs discovered petroleum and used it before the Spaniards arrived in 1519.

They burned it as incense to their gods, calked their boats with it, applied it to their bodies as a medicine, and utilized it as a dye and glue. But not until May 1901 did the commercial exploitation of petroleum begin when Pearson discovered crude at Ebano. By the time of nationalization, five major areas were under production.

In addition to the Ebano deposits, the so-called Golden Lane (*Faja de Oro*), though accounting for only 13 per cent of output in 1940, had given Mexico a worldwide reputation between 1908 and 1921; the rich Poza Rica fields, discovered 100 miles south of Tampico by the Mexican Eagle Company in 1930, contributed over one-half of the country's output at the time of Cárdenas' decree; and deposits in the Isthmus of Tehuantepec produced 25 per cent of national yield in 1938.

"The Aztecs discovered petroleum and used it before the Spaniards arrived in 1519."

After expropriation, PEMEX opened a new Golden Lane field southwest of the original *Faja de Oro*, the San Andrés deposit, and the national company also found oil in both the eastern and western parts of the state of Tabasco, as well as in the Altamira area north of Tampico, oil located in the central part of the state of Veracruz, and prolific gas reserves near Reynosa in the northeast state of Tamaulipas.

Extremely large reserves existed in the southeastern states of Tabasco and Chiapas. Frank M. Porter, president of the American Petroleum Institute, urged Director-General Pascual Gutiérrez Roldán to drill deep wells in this area. Gutiérrez Roldán heeded this advice in the early 1960s, and the investment paid handsome dividends when production began, six years ago, in the rich Reforma area.

Although production in the Reforma area amounted to only 0.4 million barrels in 1972, by December 1973, 14 producing wells in these fields yielded 71,000 barrels per day, equivalent to 13 per cent of total production. During 1976, output in Tabasco and Chiapas averaged 451,276 barrels daily, giving rise to one-half the nation's output of oil, condensates, and natural gas (894,219). By December 1976, the Reforma yield had climbed to 515,982 barrels per day. High quality crude and exceptional productivity characterize the wells in this area. While the average well outside Reforma furnishes approximately 120 barrels each day, those in the Reforma average over 5,500 barrels.

The Chiapas and Tabasco fields are also rich in natural gas. Most wells in Mexico yield an average of 1,000 cubic feet per barrel, but the amount of gas associated with each barrel of oil in this new area approaches 6,000 cubic feet. According to *The Economist*, reserves exceed 20 trillion cubic feet.

Mainly as a result of the Reforma output, Antonio Dovalí Jaime, director-general of PEMEX from 1970 to 1976, announced that as of December 31, 1975, Mexico's proven reserves totaled 6,338 million barrels—just over 1 billion barrels higher than the proven reserves a decade before. Curious as to how reserves had increased only 20 per cent while production had nearly doubled over a 10-year period, president-elect López Portillo named a task force to investigate the size of Mexico's holdings. This group of experts concluded that proven reserves actually stood at 11,160 million barrels, a figure which Jorge Díaz Serrano—the chairman of the task force and López Portillo's choice to head PEMEX—announced in December 1976. One year later, PEMEX stated that proven reserves total 17 billion barrels.

Why had such low reserves been reported before the task force study? The most cogent answer is that the Generation of '38, which held many important posts in the national oil company until Díaz Serrano

made a number of new appointments, preferred a conservative figure lest Mexico once again become the focus of foreign aspirations. Many diplomats in Mexico City believe that not even Echeverría was informed of the large reserves because of his erratic behavior and flamboyant globe-trotting.

> "... the IMF ... has limited Mexico's foreign borrowing to $3 billion in 1977."

PEMEX claims proven, probable, and possible reserves of 120 billion barrels. No doubt this puffing is designed to secure foreign investment, credit, and political support. Still, a number of foreign geologists and petroleum engineers consider 17 billion barrels to be an implausibly low figure and believe that reserves really exceed 60 billion barrels. Four factors bolster their optimism. To begin with, only about 10 per cent of Mexico's geologically promising structures have been explored; serious exploration is just beginning in Chihuahua, Baja California, Sonora, Durango, and Nuevo León. Second, *Excelsior* has reported the discovery of new fields in Tabasco State that will help double current production. Third, Díaz Serrano has described as "gigantic" recently found oil and gas deposits in Coahuila and Tamaulipas. Finally, the official figure excludes reserves in the continental shelf, where "Chac-1" and "Bacab-1"—two remarkably productive wells found at a depth of approximately 15,000 feet in the Campeche sound—indicate the presence of a new oil-producing province. The offshore petroleum fields consist of 60 structures, of which 24 have been selected for exploitation in the next two years. Of 70 exploration wells drilled in 1976, 25 proved productive, for an extremely encouraging 31.6 per cent success rate; during the same period, 200 of 257 development wells furnished commercial quantities of oil and gas.

Although PEMEX officials prefer to talk about the 17 billion barrels of proven reserves, they have announced a six-year development program that confirms Díaz Serrano's belief that "we are sitting on a sea of oil." As he has stated, "We intend to drill 3,476 wells, 1,324 of which will be for exploration and 2,152 to develop the already discovered fields." The goal of this program is to double the production of crude oil and gas liquids to 2,243 million barrels per day, and increase exports five-fold to 1,100 million barrels per day.

It is anticipated that natural gas output will increase the current level of 2 billion to 4 billion cubic feet per day by 1982. The program also calls for a 100 per cent increase in the output of basic petrochemicals to 18.6 million tons annually, with an increase in the number of plants from 60 to 115.

According to Díaz Serrano, the ambitious goals of the six-year plan will require $15 billion in foreign exchange. Sales of petroleum and petroleum products will generate about one-half of this amount; the rest will be obtained through foreign borrowing. In light of the abundant reserves, Mexican leaders feel they can secure the required loans. International bankers showed their interest in Mexican oil by oversubscribing PEMEX's last two loans, each for $300 million.

So Many Constraints

Although executives in PEMEX's headquarters are optimistic, there are a number of constraints on Mexico's ability to achieve its production goals. Even though foreign lenders are well disposed toward PEMEX, the International Monetary Fund (IMF), alarmed at the nation's incredibly high foreign debt, has limited Mexico's foreign borrowing to $3 billion in 1977. Unless this limit is removed or raised, it could hinder PEMEX's well-laid plans, because the Mexican government must borrow money for many things, including current debt-ser-

vicing, other than oil. Still, PEMEX will probably find ways to obtain international credits without their counting against the IMF-imposed limit.

Another problem facing PEMEX is expanding domestic demand for petroleum—a demand that could diminish the exports so vitally needed to earn foreign exchange. The six-year plan contemplates a 7 per cent annual increase in domestic consumption, but Mexico's population is growing faster than that of any other major country, and the nation's appetite for energy seems insatiable.

Of all the constraints, the most important is the inefficiency of PEMEX, which J. Paul Getty once barbed as "the only oil company I have known that lost money." Whether PEMEX has operated in the red is unclear because, along with some 400 other public firms, its income and expenditures flow through the national treasury. This makes it virtually impossible to ascertain an accurate profit and loss status.

"Well-connected politicians often own . . . the trucking companies that transport PEMEX products. . . ."

We do know that financial and personal connections between companies and PEMEX executives have strongly influenced the award of equipment and service contracts and concessions to operate gas stations. Well-connected politicians often own both the trucking companies that transport PEMEX products and the country's handful of private petrochemical plants.

Like all Mexican public corporations, PEMEX has a bloated bureaucracy. In 1938, the company's 17,600 employees produced 38,818,213 barrels of petroleum, while 81,042 workers rendered 238,270,853 barrels in 1974. Despite the enormous capital investment in the petroleum sector, the greater efficiency of technology with which to extract, process, and transport oil and related products, and the incredible quantities of petroleum found in the Reforma area, the annual per capita productivity of the *petroleros* only increased from 2,206 to 2,940 barrels during this 36-year period. In the same time span, per capita productivity in the United States rose from 3,186 to 15,124, and in Venezuela from 2,735 to 37,356.

Political cronyism and pressure to secure jobs for relatives and cohorts partially explains the large number of employees. More important is the role of the powerful Petroleum Workers Union, which makes the Teamsters look like a bunch of Little Lord Fauntleroys. Hero of the 1938 expropriation, the union has won high wages for its members and the best fringe benefits in Mexico. For example, in 1974 PEMEX spent $745 per *petrolero* on education, medical services, housing, recreation, and miscellaneous items. This outlay marked a 393 per cent increase since 1960. The union also looks after the employees' families. Over 50 per cent of the individuals hired by PEMEX in 1976 were related to current workers. The postexpropriation esprit de corps among workers has long since vanished as corruption suffuses their well-funded union. In many locals, large payments are required to obtain jobs and win promotions, and, as evidenced by the recent murder of the STPRM's secretary-general, violence is often used to settle disputes.

While vested interests succeeded in gutting President Carter's energy program, the Mexican chief executive, who wields much greater influence relative to other power contenders, has begun to reorganize PEMEX. He demanded that union leaders limit wage requests to a 10 per cent increase and endorsed foreign participation in the development of Mexico's petroleum resources. That López Portillo has spoken loudly will help to remove—or, at least, weaken—the constraints on achieving the goals of his six-year plan. As a matter of fact, exports, expected to be only 153,000 barrels per day in 1977, reached 240,000 barrels per day by August 1.

Assuming constraints on increased production can be overcome, the prospect of so much oil in Mexico raises three key policy questions. Will the nation's love-hate relationship with the United States and its desire for greater economic independence from its affluent neighbor lead to membership in OPEC? Irrespective of international affiliations, will Mexico make good on pledges to diversify its export market and sell a smaller percentage of its oil to the United States? Will Mexican exports consist mostly of crude or refined products?

No Go on OPEC

Despite Mexico's vocal commitment to Third World economic solidarity vis-à-vis capitalist nations, no major government official, political party, or interest group has endorsed membership in OPEC. As a high STPRM official stated in an interview on May 30, 1977: "Our nation thrives on charting its own course in international affairs." Apart from fraternal ties with other developing states, Mexico differs from most of the 13 cartel members. The majority of these countries export one principal item—oil—whereas Mexico also earns substantial foreign exchange from tourism, silver, coffee, and farm products. In comparison with the 80 or 90 per cent of hard currency which it ordinarily generates for most OPEC members, oil accounted for less than 8 per cent of the value of Mexico's exports in 1976.

Even more significant, the cartel sprang up in 1970 in reaction to price manipulation by multinational corporations on which OPEC nations depended for the exploitation, refining, transportation, and marketing of their oil. In contrast, Mexico freed itself from similar foreign influence four decades ago by expropriating the companies that dominated its industry. Unlike the OPEC countries, Mexico boasts a national oil firm that has gained invaluable experience and know-how since 1938. While all OPEC members have now created state companies, these tend to specialize in the lifting of crude as compared with the fully integrated structure of PEMEX. Further, the Mexican Petroleum Institute, a research center and think-tank, has a number of patents to its credit, and PEMEX performs a high percentage of its own engineering, design work, and equipment production.

". . . the powerful Petroleum Workers Union . . . makes the Teamsters look like a bunch of Little Lord Fauntleroys."

Joining OPEC would expose Mexico both to anticartel criticism and the loss of export preferences under the 1974 U.S. Trade Reform Act. Washington has already imposed this sanction on OPEC members, including two Latin-American states (Venezuela and Ecuador.) While the developed countries can cushion the impact of higher energy costs through their pricing of manufactured goods, most less-developed nations enjoy no such hedge, and the sharp rise in oil prices since 1973 has ravaged their economies. Mexico would do well to remain outside the body responsible for this increase, especially if it wants to gain influence at the expense of Venezuela in Central America and the Caribbean, where OPEC prices have exacerbated economic problems.

In addition, the cartel has had increasing difficulty arriving at a common price, as evidenced in December 1976, when Saudi Arabia and the United Arab Emirates agreed to only a 5 per cent increase while the 11 other members committed themselves to a 15 per cent rise in export rates. Although the members finally hammered out a compromise, such differences may emerge in the future and, though unlikely, OPEC could shift from coordinating prices to setting production quotas. This possibility makes the cartel even less attractive to a new producer such as Mexico, which, if a member, could play but a minor role in influencing the organization's policy.

As a result, Mexico has simply dispatched wide-eyed observers to OPEC sessions and charged prices somewhat higher than those of the cartel ($13.40 per barrel versus $12.70). Saudi Arabia and some other Arab members are reportedly opposed to Mexican membership, in view of its present modest export level (240,000 barrels per day) and its vigorous courting of Israel, which purchases 10 per cent of this output. An interest in attracting American Jews as tourists helps explain closer Mexican-Israeli ties.

A "Sell-America" Policy

Where will Mexico sell the bulk of its hydrocarbons? Every oil-related official document carries a de rigeur paragraph about the maximum diversification of purchasers and a key cabinet member has emphasized that "Mexico will not commit itself to supplying the United States with petroleum." Yet, several factors strongly favor a "sell-America" policy.

First, Mexico is used to doing business with the United States, which accounted for 62.4 per cent of its imports and 56.2 per cent of its exports in 1976. Second, financing from American banks, holders of over half of the Mexican government's foreign debt, is crucial to PEMEX's $15 billion six-year development program. Third, despite the bitter expropriation struggle four decades ago, American firms—often with Mexican partners—have provided invaluable exploration, geological, and engineering assistance to PEMEX. A U.S. company is expected to win a contract to build 10 drilling platforms, each sustaining 12 wells, to permit concerted development of the Campeche continental shelf. Fourth, because of high production costs and the absence of a deep-water port for supertankers, Mexico can most profitably sell oil and natural gas to the United States, which will continue to receive 80 to 90 per cent of its exports.

Strict conservation methods could limit U.S. oil imports to 8 mbd (millions of barrels per day) in the early 1980s. But the Central Intelligence Agency is probably more realistic when it projects that demand (22.2 to 25.6 mbd) will probably outstrip domestic supply (10 to 11 mbd) by at least 11.2 mbd by 1985. Secure sources such as Mexico (1.5 mbd), Canada (32,000 bd) and the North Sea (300,000 bd) should provide almost one-fifth of American imports at that time.

Díaz Serrano, an unabashed admirer of American petroleum technology, dispelled lingering doubts about Mexico's sales pattern on May 30, 1977, when he announced plans for a 800-mile, 48-inch gas-duct linking the Reforma fields with the U.S. border. From the pipeline terminal in McAllen, Texas, the gas will flow through existing lines across the sunbelt and southern states. Delivery would jump from 50 mcf (thousand cubic feet) per day (equivalent to 10,000 barrels of crude) in 1977 to 2,000 mcf per day (400,000 barrels) or 3 per cent of total American consumption when the $1.6 billion line is completed. In early August, Mexico signed a letter of intent to sell large quantities of gas to six American companies, including Texas Eastern Transmission Corporation and Tenneco, Inc.

López Portillo Calls the Shots

PEMEX will manage the construction of the system, compared by Mexicans to the trans-Alaskan pipeline. The company's lack of experience with such a major undertaking means that the project, scheduled for completion in two years, will probably not be finished until 1980 or 1981. The Export-Import Bank has agreed to supply $590 million in loans and loan guarantees: the six American firms have discussed putting up $800 million. Before work begins, Mexico and the United States must agree on a price. PEMEX wants to peg the gas price to BTU equivalents of OPEC oil entering the U.S.

market ($2.60 per thousand cubic feet), an amount far above both the price of Canadian imported gas ($2.16) and that set in Carter's energy plan for domestic gas ($1.75). Negotiators are now working on a compromise.

Will Mexico sell mostly crude or refined products? Pressures are building for PEMEX to stimulate the economy and demonstrate its advanced status and technological *machismo* by exporting products. But López Portillo, who calls the shots, has emphasized the urgent need to move crude to galvanize his country's economic growth.

The imperative to earn hard currency springs from the current bleak economic conditions. In view of the huge investment required for refineries and the current worldwide surplus of refining capacity, more money can be made quickly by exporting crude. Consequently, PEMEX's recently published six-year investment program calls for a relative diminution in outlays for refining, while expenditures for drilling, production, and transportation rise.

Leftist politicians have attacked the government for selling Mexico's birthright to the United States. In fact, the current policy—staying out of OPEC, exporting to the United States, shipping crude—represents not capitulation to the Colossus of the North but a well-reasoned strategy to reduce Mexico's dependence on American and European banks and international lending agencies.[1]

What Next?

What policies will advance Mexico's economic interests, while satisfying U.S. security needs? In view of extreme sensitivity to outside interference in Mexican affairs, how can the United States and international financial agencies contribute to a rational policy?

---

[1] *For example, Francisco Ortiz Mendoza, leader of the Popular Socialist party's legislative faction, opposed the sale of natural gas to the United States, because it would "increase Mexican dependence."*

Immigration Control: The United States must act at once to stem the flow of illegal or "undocumented" Mexican immigrants to this country. At the very minimum, Carter's quasi-amnesty plan—permanent legal alien status for those who have lived in the United States since January 1, 1970, temporary legal alien status for those who entered between that date and January 1, 1977, and deportation of the rest—should be implemented.

At present the U.S.-Mexican border is the most traversed in the world and poses about as much of a barrier to illegal crossings as the Maginot Line. The Immigration and Naturalization Service has estimated that there are from 6 to 8 million people in the country illegally, 60 per cent of whom are from Mexico. Sharply reducing this flow is more a political than a technical problem.

"Leftist politicians have attacked the government for selling Mexico's birthright to the United States."

Many experts insist that a combination of methods—ubiquitous electronic sensing devices, spotlight-equipped helicopters, non-counterfeitable work cards, sturdy fencing, criminal penalties for employers knowingly hiring unlawful workers, expansion of the U.S. border patrol, etc.—will improve the situation. But Carter and Congress must grasp a nettle that is increasingly prickly— a resolute program could offend Hispanic-American voters who hold the political power balance in a half-dozen populous states.

Closing the border escape valve will force the Mexican government to confront difficult questions about Mexico's economic development. Action should be taken now because (1) future oil earnings can finance long overdue reforms, (2) postponing action will, in view of Mexico's population explosion, turn a flood into a tidal

wave within a decade, and (3) López Portillo offers moderate, enlightened leadership that may not be offered by his successor. Restricting the border flow is not intended to sensitize the president to Mexico's needs. He is well aware of the Herculean problems facing his country. But many powerful constituencies—key industrialists, professionals, bureaucrats, labor leaders, businessmen, and political chieftains—must understand that only by promulgating structural changes can they avert massive social unrest and continue to enjoy a reasonably comfortable life.

With 7 per cent of the American work force unemployed and four out of 10 black teenagers without jobs, it makes no sense for millions of foreign workers to enter the economy. Many aliens do fill jobs that now seem too menial or demeaning for Americans. But the nation's welfare system is in shambles, and the Carter administration has voiced a determination to get people off welfare rolls and onto work rolls. While city youth may not flock at once to asparagus fields or apple orchards, there is a growing body of research that suggests incentives can be found to attract Americans to jobs currently held by aliens.[2] Labor and civil rights leaders who decry the presence of foreign workers must be prepared to recruit their unemployed constituents for the jobs that would open when the unlawful emigration declines.

Mexico is a valuable ally with which relations are improving as evidenced by the creation of three bilateral working groups in the aftermath of López Portillo's February 1977 visit to Washington. Sensitivity and flexibility must accompany a new border policy. During a five- to 10-year transition period, temporary migration visas could be issued for limited periods to vital-

---

[2] *Sociologist R. Wayne Kernodle of the College of William and Mary, who has conducted extensive research on migrant workers on the eastern shore of Virginia, is convinced that Americans will work in food-gathering if the pay is decent and employment conditions are humane.*

ly needed workers. The quota for legal immigrants from Mexico should be increased to its September 1976 level of 62,000 each year. (It is now 40,000.)

Population Growth: The United States, both through bilateral contacts and international financial institutions such as the World Bank, should provide all the assistance possible to Mexico's nascent family planning program. Efforts over the past several years have reduced population growth from 3.6 to 3.2 per cent. Future population growth is unclear because of the large number of women just now reaching childbearing age. Family planning, more successful in urban centers, has barely touched many small cities, much less the countryside where families average 5.7 children (compared with 4.4 in urban areas). Mexico's oil earnings can finance a comprehensive rural family planning program.

Labor-Intensive Industry: Over one-third of Mexico's work force is currently unemployed or underemployed. In good times, the Mexican economy generates 300,000 jobs each year; during the recent recession, the figure may have fallen below 200,000.

Under President Robert McNamara, the World Bank has insisted that developing countries undertake vigorous population control programs as a prerequisite of major assistance. A similar requirement should be applied with respect to labor-intensive industry. Here the World Bank, along with other multilateral lending institutions, might recommend: (1) credit policies that promote labor-intensive production, (2) tax benefits for employers who create jobs, (3) a tax on capital gains and a higher levy on imported capital goods, (4) improvement of vocational education opportunities, and (5) restraint on unreasonable social benefits for workers that make machines more attractive to employers than human beings.

Meanwhile, the U.S. Agency for International Development and the Department of Commerce should offer Mexicans assistance in marketing items in developing countries. An often heard complaint is that even if a country makes a commitment to labor-intensive methods, appropriate technology is difficult to find or is simply unavailable. For this reason, the United States should support the creation of a special institute, under the aegis of the United Nations, whose mission would be to catalog existing labor-intensive technology, help develop new applications of this technology, and disseminate this information to interested countries.

To encourage the creation of jobs in Mexico, the United States has proposed establishing a $2 billion joint industrial development fund, the purpose of which would be to provide Mexican entrepreneurs with low-interest, long-term loans to establish light industry and labor-intensive agricultural projects in northern and central states beset by high unemployment.

". . . American shoe and textile manufacturers cannot stand a flood of Mexican goods."

Among labor-intensive activities that might be emphasized are speciality farm crops in northern Mexico; irrigation, soil conservation, and road-building projects throughout the nation; and food-processing, furniture, clothing, shoes, and leather goods in Guanajuato, Chihuahua, Michoacan, Zacatecas, and Jalisco—states that have generated more than half of the illegal immigrants apprehended since 1969.

Trade Policy: If Mexico embarks upon a serious program of labor-intensive production, and if it is willing to reduce the extreme protectionism it practices, the United States should facilitate the entry of more items into its market. Any move in this direction will cause organized labor to read the riot act to a Democratic administration just as it did 13 years ago to halt the "Bracero" program and as it has done with respect to the border-industry plan. However, AFL-CIO leaders must realize that although Mexico has stepped up the sale of goods north of the Rio Grande, it ran a $2 billion trade deficit with the United States in 1976, and that this strategically important country must be allowed to send more products to the United States in return for exporting fewer bodies.

In addition to placing more Mexican imports on the duty-free list, vexing practices such as the "seasonal tariff" on tomatoes should be relaxed. Already under heavy pressure from Asian imports, American shoe and textile manufacturers cannot stand a flood of Mexican goods. It may be necessary, therefore, to negotiate further limitations on imports from Hong Kong, Taiwan, and South Korea to give Mexico greater opportunities in the U.S. market. While favored relationships are frowned upon by the Office of the Special Trade Representative, self-interest dictates that Washington give a preference to Mexican wares to help defuse a potentially explosive situation in a country with which a 1,946-mile border is shared. Mexico is simply more important to American security than certain Asian nations.

It is naive to think that significant quantities of new shoe and textile imports can enter the U.S. market. These industries, now plagued by severe unemployment, generate strong protectionist pressure. Thus Mexico must cease protecting many manufacturers by shifting from quotas to tariffs on imports and identify other products for export to the United States. Under the General System of Preferences (GSP), the United States offers reduced tariffs on approximately 3,000 items exported by less-developed countries. Mexico has failed to take full advantage of this program. Its exporters often neglect to request the preference to which they are entitled, and there are no fewer than 500 GSP items that Mexico did not even attempt to export to America in 1976. Most important in this category were paper goods, dried fruits, metal products and chemicals.

Mexico must also look elsewhere for markets. It has signed trade accords with the European Economic Community and Brazil. Perhaps the best potential market for Mexican goods is Japan, whose 113 million inhabitants boast an average income of $4,000. U.S. ability to influence Japanese-Mexican relations is obviously limited. But if Washington is willing to recognize that the Japanese should play a role in the development of Mexican oil, this might entice Tokyo to look more favorably on Mexican goods. Washington and Mexico City might also consider a joint study of the Japanese market to determine appropriate exports.

Tax Reform: While exports must be encouraged, trade will not provide the engine for Mexico's economic growth. As López Portillo has emphasized, "It is essential to stress that our development depends on the productive efforts of the Mexicans themselves. . . ." The impetus can only come from within the country, by bringing more people into the market economy. At a time when many Third World nations are narrowing the gap between the rich and poor, this social fissure is deepening in Mexico, despite the country's rich array of resources, its position as one of the most advanced developing states, and the rapid advancement it has boasted—except for the last two years—since World War II. Even though politicians consistently trumpet the populist goals of the 1910 revolution, the position of the country's poorest 40 per cent has not improved materially since the overthrow of dictator Porfirio Díaz 67 years ago. As for the well-to-do, economist David Felix points out that while in 1950 the average income of the top 5 per cent of households was 22 times greater than that of the poorest 40 per cent, two decades later the multiplier had risen to 34.

To stimulate demand for domestic goods, income must be redistributed toward the 20 million Mexicans who occupy the base of the country's social pyramid as spectators rather than participants in the market economy. Petroleum sales will generate some of these moneys. Major tax reform is also required. (At 11.2 per cent of GDP, Mexico has one of the world's lowest payment records.) Given the economic uncertainty and the 35 to 40 per cent increase in production costs since devaluation, a major tax increase would raise the hackles of businessmen, possibly spurring capital flight. The most prudent move, therefore, should be to boost the yield from present rates, inasmuch as an additional 60,000 million pesos could be generated each year if the collection machinery were streamlined. For technical guidance on fiscal matters, international lending agencies, the Internal Revenue Service, and American universities could help. But increasing the payment of taxes by the affluent will require resolute political action by López Portillo.

Energy Conservation: Although Mexico has a great deal of petroleum, attention must be given to husbanding these reserves. The government now sets low energy prices, thereby encouraging energy- or capital-intensive production. Conservation practices such as highway speed limits, automobile mileage standards, efficiency criteria for appliances, and prudent electricity pricing techniques, should be encouraged. Technical assistance might come both from the increasingly conservation-minded Canadian and American experts and through the U.S.-Mexican working groups responsible for economic questions.

Energy Diversification: Because oil will last only a few decades, diversification of Mexican energy sources should be emphasized. There are major deposits of commercial grade coal in Coahuila, which provide 11.1 per cent of the nation's energy needs. Mexico is one of the only countries with identified geothermal resources, located near Mexicali on the U.S. border, which can easily be developed. But next to petroleum, Mexico's greatest potential lies in solar energy, to which López Portillo has shown a strong commitment. As one of the first countries to take part in the Solar Energy Project of the Organization of American States under the Mar del Plata Resolution of 1974, Mexico has purchased solar water pumps for arid areas in Sonora, Durango, San Luis Potosí, and northern Baja California. Also under investigation is the widespread use of solar photovoltaic cells for hot water heating and heat generation.

Abundant, pollution-free, self-renewing —solar power offers many advantages for a sun-drenched country like Mexico. One of its often overlooked benefits is decentralized power generation. Mexico could become a world leader both in petroleum production and in the advancement of nonconventional energy sources. Solar energy could also be used to produce liquid and gaseous fuels, such as alcohol, methane, and hydrogen. Success with solar energy might induce Mexico City's policy-makers to re-evaluate their fledgling nuclear program under which the first light-water reactor, Laguna Verde I in Vera Cruz State, will come on line around the end of the decade.

The United States and international agencies can provide modest assistance to Mexico. But Mexicans must manage their own development. Unless decisive political leadership is shown now, this ancient Aztec nation could find itself in the mid-twenty-first century with the same deformed economy, but it may have exhausted the abundant oil reserves with which to pursue the egalitarian ideals of the 1910 upheaval.

PANAMA TREATY TRAP

by Richard A. Falk

The new arrangements for the Panama Canal are regressive and unwise, if not utterly imperial. They make no genuine adjustment to changing international realities, and thus they are unlikely to remain acceptable to the Panamanian people for very long, nor should they.

In debating the new treaties, most American politicians presupposed the desirability of maximizing the U.S. role in running the canal for as long as possible and negotiable. Even supporters of the treaties rested their case on bedrock jingoism. The Senate Republican leader, Howard Baker of Tennessee, crowed that "building the Panama Canal was our 'moon shot' of the first decade of this century." And Senator Charles Percy (R.-Illinois), eager to dispel any illusion that he is an idealist, sought guidance by wondering aloud, in the midst of the treaty hearings, what Teddy Roosevelt would have wanted to do about the canal if he were still alive. Not to be outdone, Jimmy Carter ended his "fireside chat" about the canal in February with the astounding claim, undoubtedly correct, that a resurrected Teddy Roosevelt would have championed the new treaties; it is as if the imprimatur of the most ardently imperialist American president still remains an asset to persuade the country about what should be done in a controversial area of foreign policy.

The tone of advocacy was decisively set by spokesmen for the Carter administration, who argued, above all, that the United States can do everything under the 1977 treaties that it ever wanted to do under the 1903 arrangements.

These feelings about the Panama Canal demonstrate with unmistakable clarity that the United States has not yet outgrown imperialism. Indeed, the debate over the treaties was so narrow that it amounted to a conversation between rational imperialists who favor ratification and sentimental imperialists who oppose. Treaty rationalists argued that certain cosmetic adjustments were necessary to avoid anti-American turmoil in Panama, while the sentimentalists insisted that the symbols of the American presence in the canal were inseparable from substance. What is impressive, and depressing in its implications for other issues, is the consensus that framed the debate. Both sides believe in a perpetual American right to use force to uphold U.S. interests in the canal. All agree that this right includes the discretion to intervene in Panamanian internal affairs if Washington thinks that is necessary to assure the so-called neutrality of the canal.

"... the United States has not yet outgrown imperialism."

The narrowness of the debate reveals some truths about American attitudes toward the world that liberals, in particular, are reluctant to acknowledge. It is apparent that neither the worldwide movement against colonialism, which has succeeded virtually everywhere in recent decades, nor the trauma of Vietnam has changed the mentality of the American people or their elected representatives. Here is the United States, in the late 1970s, about to stumble into an open-ended commitment to intervene in a shaky Third World country, without even considering proprieties or costs.

At the same time, the United States has forced the Panamanian government to accept a bad bargain. Panama's current leadership agreed to the 1977 treaties principally because it is faced with a deteriorating and desperate economic situation and badly needs the economic sweetener that was added to the treaties by the American negotiators.

Panama's canal revenues under the 1977 treaties will depend on the volume of tonnage that passes through the locks. The best estimates are that Panama will increase its annual revenue from about $2.5 million to as much as $60 million, when and if the new treaties go into effect and until they expire at the end of 1999. Panama is only assured $10 million unconditionally each year and another $10 million from the surplus accumulated from operating revenues; the additional revenue projected for Panama is based on a per ton annuity that assumes a certain level of canal tonnage. These payments are far less than the revenues Panama would receive if the tolls were fixed, (as are Suez Canal tolls) largely by market considerations, rather than reflecting a policy of partially subsidizing international shipping interests. It is also far less than the $200 million per year that Panama had been demanding in the negotiations until last year, when it abruptly cut back its demands, apparently as a result of a deepening financial crisis that created a desperate need for some kind of immediate economic relief. More assured than the canal revenues, however, and directly helpful in meeting Panama's short-term crisis of foreign indebtedness, is an economic package accompanying the new treaties. Panama is to receive $295 million in U.S. loans and investment guarantees over the first five years, as well as $50 million in connection with arms purchases spread out over 10 years. These financial inducements are less than Panama had sought, and do not significantly alter the country's bleak economic outlook.

As the distinguished historian Walter LaFeber, of Cornell University, concludes,[1] "Only large canal revenues could rescue the governmental debt" and avoid an antigovernmental uprising in Panama. LaFeber believes that "... the rapidly deteriorating Panamanian economy and [General Omar]

---

[1] *Walter LeFeber*, The Panama Canal (*New York: Oxford University Press, 1978*), p. 202.

Torrijos' increasing dependence on outside private investors set the stage for the climactic negotiations of a new treaty during the summer of 1977."

Frustrated Nationalism

The new agreements are not likely to quell Panamanian nationalist demands for long and will probably make the United States the target of a continuing worldwide anticolonialist campaign. Indeed, the only way the new treaty regime can succeed is if the Panamanian government becomes even more repressive than it already is. The 30 per cent opposition to the treaty plebiscite in Panama, together with intense opposition to ratification among Panamanian nationalists across a wide political spectrum, indicates the degree to which the new arrangements are already unacceptable in that country. Even Torrijos, the leader of the Panamanian revolution, indicated his own misgivings at the September ceremony in Washington where he and Jimmy Carter signed the treaties. He drew a distinction between "two types of truths—logical truth and pleasant truth." Torrijos signed the treaties "in the name of logical truth," indicating that it was not pleasant to accept an arrangement that "does not enjoy the support of all our people, because the 23 years agreed upon as a transition period are 8,395 days, because while this agreement is in effect there will be military bases that make my country a strategic reprisal target, and because we are agreeing to a treaty of neutrality that places us under the protective umbrella of the Pentagon."

Supporters of the new treaties sometimes concede their colonialist features, but argue that they are a definite improvement over the 1903 Hay-Bunau-Varilla Treaty, that they are as progressive as American public opinion will tolerate at this time. Furthermore, they claim that unless Panamanian aspirations are at least partially satisfied, there could be a serious wave of anti-American violence, including possible sabotage of the canal. The new agreements, then, are held up as an example of politics as the art of the possible. This view assumes that a delay of 23 years before American troops leave Panama will prove acceptable, or that a regime of permanent protective custody administered from Washington is preferable to the present arrangement.

But the evidence is that Panamanian nationalists are neither satisfied nor appeased by the 1977 treaties. It is one thing to struggle against a colonial heritage that arose at the beginning of the century, but quite another to legitimate the colonial character of the relationship late in the twentieth century.

"The new agreements are not likely to quell Panamanian nationalist demands for long. . . ."

To dramatize his own protest, Leopoldo Aragón, a former political prisoner who was expelled from Panama by Torrijos, burned himself to death in Stockholm outside the American Embassy last September. One of the most widely known and respected Panamanian political figures, Miguel Antonio Bernal, also living abroad in exile, denounced the new treaties as "far from fulfilling the aspirations of the Panamanian people." Bernal argued that the new arrangements replace the "perpetuity imposed by force" in 1903 with a "legalized perpetuity." In an interview published by *Intercontinental Press* last September, he indicted the Torrijos regime for conferring such legality on the American presence and for creating a permanent American right of intervention: "We consider this as the most aberrant, disgraceful, and unacceptable type of perpetuity, as a stigma that this generation and future ones will be forced to bear, for it legalizes the American presence on our soil." Bernal reminded "the Panamanian and American governments, which have been working hand in glove, that the disappointment and dissatisfaction of a people can only

be followed by hatred and rebellion"; the treaties, he argued, represent "one of the worst concessions in Panamanian history, because they fly in the face of the struggle and sacrifices made by our people for 73 years."

These Panamanian reactions against the treaties gain additional credibility from the extent to which the 1977 agreements won support from individuals such as retired Admiral Elmo Zumwalt, former chief of naval operations, and William F. Buckley, the conservative commentator—that is, from individuals normally associated with an aggressive U.S. foreign policy that makes no sentimental or idealistic concessions to the Third World. It is clear that their support, as well as that of opposition figures like Gerald Ford or Henry Kissinger, is based on the conviction that, indeed, the new treaties effectively maintain—rather than transform—the American role with respect to the canal. That impression is also fostered by Deputy Secretary of State Warren Christopher's almost gleeful insistence that, "According to the joint chiefs, these treaties are not only as good as the existing arrangement in terms of our national security, they are far better."

One reason for confusion over the treaties is that Torrijos has successfully projected a leftist, nationalist image, especially in the United States. It is true that Torrijos built his political base by claiming nationalist and social reformist credentials. But these earlier features of his rule look largely opportunistic in retrospect, and his true political inclinations seem associated with personal power and wealth. Recently, he has drifted to the right, opening the country to promiscuous foreign investment, siphoning off a personal fortune for his family and coterie, compiling an abysmal human rights record, and alienating and repressing progressive elements in his own society.

As one Latin-American expert, Martin Needler, concluded months before the treaties were signed, the "odds are that Torrijos' leftism and nationalism will erode and the lineaments of a classic, personalistic Latin-American dictatorship not interfering with the social and economic status quo will emerge." Needler even suggested that Torrijos was following a path strikingly similar to that of the Cuban dictator Fulgencio Batista, who also started out as a populist reformer but moved rightward to satisfy personal greed and meet economic pressures. (It has often been theorized that given their similar historical and economic ties to the United States, whatever happens in Cuba will probably also happen eventually in Panama.)

To Intervene Or Not To Intervene

These concerns can be further clarified in relation to the issue of intervention, which people on all sides of the American debate concede to be the Achilles' heel of the 1977 agreements. On this point, the administration says one thing to reassure the Panamanians that their sovereignty is not being infringed upon, but quite another to reassure Americans that their rights will be preserved even after the removal of American troops in 1999. American senators insisted on being promised that the United States retain permanent, discretionary interventionary rights to uphold its interests in the canal. After the original negotiated text was agreed upon, various steps were taken to provide added reassurance for the American side, including the Carter-Torrijos "understanding" of October 14, 1977.

Torrijos has been much praised by American politicians for his flexibility in these respects. Of course, as the dictator of Panama, Torrijos need not obtain any genuine assent from Panamanian lawmakers to assure ratification. However, tilting the treaties even further in the American direction exposes their colonial features, thereby strengthening resentment in Panama.

As is well known, the nonintervention norm is practically synonymous for Latin Americans with sovereignty itself. To grant the United States a permanent, unilateral right to intervene in Panama on behalf of the canal's so-called neutrality is inconsistent with even moderate nationalist aspirations in Panama. Little wonder that Panamanian demonstrators against the treaty contended that Torrijos had accepted a colonial status for Panama, evidently renouncing the country's sovereign rights in exchange for a few Yankee dollars.

From the very beginning, administration spokesmen sought to quiet conservative critics of the treaties who complained that the right of intervention was ambiguous in the 1977 arrangements. They insisted that it was implicitly there. For instance, early in the hearings before the Senate Foreign Relations Committee, Secretary of Defense Harold Brown was asked by Senator Dick Stone (D.-Florida) whether the United States could intervene to deal with an internal situation in Panama that it believed might threaten the neutral operation of the canal. Brown replied that in his view, American officials would have "the right to take whatever action we considered necessary."

"Recently, [Torrijos] has drifted to the right, opening the country to promiscuous foreign investment. . . ."

The defense secretary added that this was what Torrijos had in mind at the signing ceremony when he said that Panama was placing itself "under the protective umbrella of the Pentagon." (Significantly, Torrijos went on to say that "this pact could, if not administered judiciously by future generations, become an instrument of permanent intervention.") Ambassador Sol Linowitz, one of the U.S. negotiators, also supported this view by telling the Foreign Relations Committee that there was "no limitation" on American rights; "there is nothing which says that that threat is to be limited to a particular type of threat."

Problems emerged when the Panamanian negotiators gave their own version of the U.S. role in Panama. Speaking before the National Assembly, Romulo Escobar, the chief Panamanian negotiator, claimed the American role did not extend to threats to the canal that arose out of problems of "internal order." Torrijos, also speaking in Panama, stated that the neutrality treaty meant that "if we are attacked by superior forces, the United States is obliged to come to our defense." Somewhat self-consciously, he explained that "a weak country like Panama needs the protection of a major power if we are attacked by superior forces." And he reassuringly added that nothing in the treaties gave the United States any right to take action on internal strife in Panama.

"The ambiguity of the canal treaties is vital to the bargain."

Although these two interpretations are contradictory in spirit, the treaty text is ambiguous enough to make them both plausible. Rational pro-treaty forces in the United States understood the necessity of the ambiguity. Buckley's *National Review* editorialized that its own pro-treaty position was premised on an unlimited, discretionary, American "right of intervention," but that it understood why such a right could not be spelled out. The U.S. intervention in the Dominican Republic in 1965, the conservative magazine pointed out, enabled American troops to quell a domestic threat of radicalism without Washington ever having to claim a formal right to intervene. On that occasion, the Organization of American States (OAS), under pressure, granted the United States an appropriate figleaf justification. In the Panama Canal context, *National Review* argued, future U.S. leaders must simply understand and act upon their right of intervention, whether the perceived threat is internal or external. Linowitz gave a revealing demonstration during

a White House press briefing of how some future international lawyer might deal with the touchy issue of intervention if the occasion arose:

Under what conditions would we intervene in the canal to protect the neutrality?

Linowitz: I don't like the word intervene. Under what conditions would we be in a position to move? The answer is if the permanent neutrality of the canal were jeopardized.

Who would decide that?

Linowitz: We would. Then the United States would be in the position to take such steps as might be deemed necessary.

It is worth recalling that none other than Ellsworth Bunker, the other negotiator of the canal treaties, reassured an OAS meeting of ministers of foreign affairs in 1965 that in the Dominican Republic, "We are not talking about intruding in the domestic affairs of other countries; we are talking simply about the elementary duty to save lives in a situation where there is no authority able to accept responsibility for primary law and order." One can easily imagine the rationale for a future intervention in Panama: "We are certainly not seeking to intervene in Panama's internal affairs, but only to uphold the neutrality of the canal, a responsibility enshrined in a treaty and beneficial for all states."

The interventionary right is further endorsed in the Carter-Torrijos "understanding," which confers upon the United States an unrestricted right to defend the "neutrality" of the canal without securing the prior assent of the Panamanian government. Yet the understanding also retains an element of ambiguity, by expressly stating that the neutrality treaty shall not be "interpreted as a right of intervention in the internal affairs of Panama."

Given potential developments in Panama, including the prospect of a turn to the left in Panamanian politics, this ambiguity might place future American leaders in a difficult, dangerous situation. It is worth recalling that the ambiguity in the Geneva accords of 1954 encouraged Hanoi and Washington to proceed, each on reasonable grounds, in contradictory directions that culminated in the Vietnam war. The North Vietnamese regarded the Geneva accords as settling the future of all of Vietnam after a two-year interval enabling an honorable French withdrawal. The Americans, on the other hand, construed the agreements as partitioning Vietnam into two states, thereby giving South Vietnam full sovereign rights to make whatever arrangements it saw fit to defend itself against internal and external enemies.

The Vietnam analogy is instructive in another respect. The United States converted the ambiguity into a commitment (to the Saigon regime) that soon took on a life of its own. It was widely argued that any refusal to uphold this commitment, however foolish the commitment might be, would damage the reputation of the United States as an ally and an alliance leader. In Panama, the commitment to defend the "neutrality" of the canal is also likely to assume a symbolic significance that could induce American leaders to honor it even when they realize it is foolish and costly to do so.

The ambiguity of the canal treaties is vital to the bargain. If it is resolved in Panama's favor, then the arrangements become unacceptable to the United States. This is easy to understand, because the main threat to American interests in the canal comes from the possibility of internal developments in Panama. The prospect of an external invasion by some other power seems remote to the point of irrelevance; and besides, in that eventuality, Panama would almost certainly welcome any U.S. help it could get.

Is There A Better Way?

But the surfacing of this dilemma raises some deep questions that have thus far been kept off the public agenda. The main question is whether it is feasible or beneficial for the United States to insist upon a colonial role for itself into the next century. Such a role seems bound to entangle the American government on the reactionary side of Panamanian politics, as well as to risk U.S. involvement in a series of unpopular, violent struggles. The situation in Panama is very unstable: rapid population growth, a highly inequitable distribution of wealth, growing unemployment, heavy foreign indebtedness, an adverse trade balance, and a long tradition of militant opposition politics.

Would it not be better and cheaper for the United States to leave the canal to the Panamanians? Have not the British been fortunate to be free since 1956 from the burdens and prerogatives associated with the administration of the Suez Canal? The Panamanians need canal revenues so badly that it is difficult to imagine why they would want to interfere with transit rights; and in the unlikely event of such interference, action appropriate to the circumstances could be taken whether authorized by treaty or not.

The new canal arrangements, although intended as a positive contribution to international peace and security, are an anachronism. Their only justification is a continuing insistence that the United States must dominate the Caribbean and the Gulf of Mexico area as a *"mare nostrum* of the United States."* (This was the argument recently advanced by Hanson Baldwin, formerly of *The New York Times*, in the *American Enterprise Institute Defense Review.*)

No less an authority on the American role in the world than George Kennan is sensitive to the drawbacks of going part way on the canal and proposes "turning the canal over entirely to the Panamanians." [2] Kennan is convinced that the canal is no longer militarily or commercially important enough for the United States to justify the burdens of joint administration and defense.

[2] *George F. Kennan*, The Cloud of Danger: Current Realities of American Foreign Policy *(Boston: Atlantic-Little, Brown, 1977)*.

In light of this geopolitical reality, he argues, it places the United States in an exposed, risky, and unpopular position to maintain its role. It is sad that Kennan's view, which proceeds from a rather conservative assessment of U.S. interests, has not been seriously considered. One could take his argument further and point out that it would not only be advantageous for the United States to end its special role in the canal, but it would also be a positive contribution to the construction of a viable system of world order.

Another option would be to seek the partial internationalization of responsibility for the Panama Canal. Panama could be given administrative control and the economic benefits, while the international community could be entrusted with the mission of assuring transit rights and neutral management. This mission could be assigned to the OAS, the United Nations, or even a newly created international entity with the power

---

". . . the foreign policy consensus [is] set by the Pentagon and the political right."

---

to propose whatever measures might be necessary to keep the waterway open, including forcible occupation. There is no assurance that internationalism would work in a period of crisis, but this doubt exists with all options. At least under an international scheme the United States would not be insisting on discredited prerogatives to act unilaterally; nor would it find itself burdened by a commitment of uncertain scope and application. Furthermore, the arrangement would uphold the principle that international waterways like the Panama Canal belong to the entire world community.

There is a precedent of sorts for such a step. After World War II, the United States proposed the internationalization of the waterways of Europe, including the Kiel Canal. Harry Truman, making this proposal

in a radio report to the nation on his return from the Berlin Conference in August 1945, said "we think this is important to the future peace and security of the world." This at least suggests that at one time the internationalization of other countries' canals and waterways was not alien to American official sensibilities. The only option, short of turning the canal over to the Panamanians or internationalizing it, that genuinely serves true American and world interests would be to modify the 1977 treaties by shortening the transition period, by renouncing any unilateral U.S. right to use force, and by giving Panama an option after U.S. withdrawal to terminate any arrangements of joint defense. It is evident from Torrijos' remarks on various occasions that he would much prefer a resolution that went further in according Panama full sovereign rights.

In a search for a Panama Canal arrangement that would be politically and morally palatable, both domestically and internationally, the United States has pressured the current Panamanian regime to assent to arrangements that create new problems without solving the old ones. But it is poor politics, and even worse morality, for those who consider themselves anti-imperialists to find their refuge, however tacitly, in the cause of rational imperialism.

In the end, the real question is whether the Carter administration could have done better. Was it truly trapped by the nostalgic affinity of the American people for the canal and by the political imperative of winning the support of the joint chiefs of staff? If so constrained that nothing more than the new arrangements could have been achieved, was it an exercise in benevolent statecraft to push ahead anyway at this time? These are difficult questions for which no convincing answers can be given. To some extent, we must await the judgment of history.

From the outset, the Carter administration seemed convinced that it had to build a center-right coalition to win support for the treaties, and that more liberal outlooks could be ignored. The constraints imposed by such a coalition induced an unstable and anachronistic arrangement for the canal. But the canal is probably not as much of a special case as some pretend, and a similar coalition-building process is at work across the whole spectrum of American foreign policy, including the international economic area, although with different sectors of society and bureaucracy playing the role that the joint chiefs played in the Panama context.

If this assessment is correct, it suggests that an American president is locked into the status quo to such an extent that it is virtually impossible to implement progressive reforms. This rigidity critically limits the capacity of even the most enlightened political leadership in this country to adjust to a changing world situation. It also suggests the need for fracturing the foreign policy consensus, whose terms of reference are set by the Pentagon and the political right.

LATIN AMERICA: A NOT-SO-SPECIAL RELATIONSHIP

by Abraham F. Lowenthal

Not since the heady days of John F. Kennedy and the Alliance for Progress has Washington lavished so much attention on Latin America. The president and his wife, the vice president, the secretary of state and his deputy, the secretary of the treasury, and the U.S. ambassador to the United Nations all visited the region during the Carter administration's first 18 months, traveling to a total of 17 different countries, many of them more than once. Terence A. Todman, Carter's original assistant secretary of state for inter-American affairs, managed to tour all the countries of the hemisphere before he became ambassador to Spain last July. The Panama Canal issue absorbed more high-level official energies than any other single foreign policy question during Carter's first year-and-a-half in office.

Will this vigorous initial concern with Latin America endure and eventually produce lasting positive results? Or will a familiar cycle be repeated—a burst of interest in Latin America complete with visits, speeches, and proclamations of new policies, followed by concrete decisions (or failures to decide) that weaken or even contradict the very policies just announced? Will basic problems go unaddressed, as has been the case so often in the past? The answers lie primarily in the economic realm. How the United States deals with fundamental economic issues will influence inter-American relations much more than any initiatives the Carter administration has taken so far.

It took former Secretary of State Henry Kissinger years to discover Latin America. The Carter administration, by contrast, began with an expressed concern for the region, stressed often by the president himself. His second major foreign policy address as president was to the Organization of American States, whose headquarters in Washington he has already visited three times (more than any previous president). The first visit by a chief of state to Washington after Carter took office was from Mexico's president, José López Portillo. President Carlos Andrés Pérez of Venezuela followed soon thereafter. In September 1977, 17 Latin American heads of state converged on Washington to witness the signing of the Panama Canal treaties. Each visiting chief executive met individually with Carter, who devoted the better part of a week to his visitors. Neglect, benign or otherwise, is no longer Washington's official approach to the nations of the Western Hemisphere.

Fewer Promises

The Carter administration has begun to reform the rhetoric and concepts of inter-American relations. Shopworn phrases like "Pan-American community" and "special relationship" are being largely abandoned, as Washington concedes that its treatment of Latin America and the Caribbean has often been discriminatory and one-sided. The United States is not again promising preferential treatment for Latin America. Instead, this administration has focused on the growing significance of key Latin American countries in dealing with a global agenda of issues equally important to North and South America. The Carter administration on the whole has been treating the countries of the Western Hemisphere as they wish to be treated—as individual, sovereign nations, each with interests of its own.

Under Carter, the U.S. government has also mustered the courage to tackle two thorny problems that previous administrations had avoided: Panama and Cuba. Even

after Kissinger and his colleagues turned their attention to these issues in 1974, they deliberately stopped short of measures that would have risked major domestic criticism. Candidate Jimmy Carter, too, was notably cautious on these matters during the 1976 presidential campaign. From the moment he took office, however, Carter committed himself to revising the troubled U.S. relationship with Panama by recognizing that country's sovereignty over the Canal Zone, and to moving, on a measured and reciprocal basis, toward renewed relations with President Fidel Castro's Cuba. By the time of his first National Security Council meeting, Carter had accorded the Panama Canal issue top billing. He rejected advice from inside

---

"It took . . . Henry Kissinger years to discover Latin America."

---

his administration and out to leave U.S.-Cuban relations alone until the Panama problem could be resolved. Instead, Washington began to press forward on both issues and even linked them to others—such as the recognition of Vietnam and initiatives to improve relations with Jamaica and Guyana—to demonstrate its acceptance of ideological diversity and its intention to deal with all nations, regardless of size or political bent, on the basis of mutual respect.

By negotiating new treaties with Panama and by successfully, if not always gracefully, pushing them through the arduous process of Senate ratification, President Carter accomplished a necessary task. And by establishing direct and public diplomatic contact with Cuba and expressing interest in an eventual resumption of full bilateral relations, the Carter administration ended an outmoded and self-defeating U.S. policy. Cuba's African involvements and the White House's somewhat irascible reaction to them have obviously complicated the process of eventual rapprochement between Washington and Havana. Whatever the course of

U.S.-Cuban relations, however, the United States has improved its own capacity for dealing with the challenges Cuba presents by abandoning its ossified stance of the 1960s and early 1970s.

Additionally, the Carter administration has moved away from broad, undifferentiated regional policies toward more carefully tailored bilateral and subregional approaches. This process of refining U.S. policy in the Western Hemisphere (to an extent, a return to the historical pattern disrupted by the sweeping generalities of the Alliance for Progress) had already made headway in previous years. For instance, the memorandum signed in 1976 by Kissinger and Brazilian Minister of Foreign Affairs Antonio Francisco Azeredo da Silveira set up special mechanisms for handling U.S.-Brazilian relations. The Carter administration has concentrated not only on Brazil, but also on Mexico, Venezuela, and the Caribbean. Brazil and Mexico account for one-fourth of all U.S. trade with less developed countries outside the Organization of Petroleum Exporting Countries; these two countries plus Venezuela account for almost 70 per cent of all U.S. trade with Latin America and well over half of U.S. investment in the hemisphere. All three countries warrant more high-level attention than they previously received, not only because of expanded U.S. investment and trade but also because of the enlarged international role they will play as middle-rank powers.

The Carter administration has also recognized the potential significance for the United States of improved relations with the countries and territories of the Caribbean, America's third border. Spurred by the impact of burgeoning immigration from the Caribbean, Washington is paying attention to the region's economic problems for the first time in years. Study missions and task forces have been created within the U.S. government to deal with Caribbean issues, and a multilateral consultative group has been convened under World Bank auspices to co-ordinate external development assistance. Caribbean development is finally being considered on its own merits, rather than solely within the narrowly defined terms of military security that dominated U.S. perceptions of the region—between periodic Marine landings—for generations.

No Carter administration policy affecting Latin America is as dramatically new as its stand on human rights. Kissinger seemed mostly indifferent, if not hostile, to this issue; this administration gives it pride of place. Despite contrary congressional instructions, the Ford administration generally supported loans by international financial institutions to nations that flagrantly violated human rights; the Carter administration has already opposed more than 25 such loans, mostly in Latin America. The United States was not previously a party to the Inter-American Convention on Human Rights;

"Carter has altered the U.S. reputation for automatically identifying with authoritarian regimes."

---

under Carter, Washington not only signed the agreement, but also persuaded several other countries to do so after years of delay. The United States has recently spearheaded efforts to strengthen substantially the budget, staff, and authority of the Inter-American Commission on Human Rights. And this administration has also found ways—through formal and informal meetings and other expressions of interest and sympathy—to build new links with democratic opposition groups throughout South and Central America and the Caribbean.

To an impressive degree, Carter has altered the U.S. reputation for automatically identifying with authoritarian regimes. Fundamental American values—particularly respect for human rights and a preference for constitutional democracy—have been forcefully reasserted. The lives of hundreds of people in several countries have improved, at least in part as a result of pressures from Washington. Significant numbers of political prisoners have been released in Chile and Haiti and some have been let go in several other countries, and lists of political prisoners have been made available in Argentina and Chile. Commissions to investigate human rights conditions have gained entry to several countries. Reports of the use of torture have decreased. Most important, perhaps, a mood of cautious hope has begun to grow that brutal repression is no longer being legitimated. And although the Carter administration's role in precipitating this year's outbreak of elections throughout Latin America and the Caribbean should not be exaggerated, it is fair to say that the United States has been consciously and effectively reinforcing this trend, particularly in Peru and the Dominican Republic.

The increased attention paid to the countries of Latin America and the Caribbean, the abandonment of paternalism, the recognition of Latin America's potential role in dealing with a broad global agenda, the priority given to key bilateral relationships, and the reassertion of fundamental national values as a guide for policy are all commendable changes. The administration also deserves praise for so far resisting the impulse toward military intervention that has so often marked Washington's approach to the region. The previous four American presidents all launched major interventions in Latin America within their first two years in office—the Guatemalan invasion of 1954, the Bay of Pigs fiasco of 1961, the Dominican intervention of 1965, and the massive efforts in 1970 to destabilize the Allende government in Chile. It is highly unlikely that any similar adventure is being carried out or contemplated by the Carter administration.

An Orgy of Attention

It is too soon, however, to conclude that the improvements Jimmy Carter and his team have introduced in U.S.-Latin American relations will be of lasting importance. Many of the toughest problems affecting the region—particularly items on the economic agenda—have yet to be seriously faced. Whether the administration's impressive start will ultimately amount to much depends critically on decisions and actions yet to be taken, as well as on trends and developments beyond any president's control.

The burst of high-level activity expended on Panama and Cuba, for example, may turn out to be insignificant, or even counterproductive, as a way to improve inter-American relations over the longer term. The orgy of official attention to Panama, in particular, may make it much harder to get high-level attention for economic issues. The administration's initiatives on the Panama and Cuba issues were unquestionably courageous efforts to remove troublesome political problems of the past. But as bridges to a "new era of inter-American cooperation," as President Carter and others have heralded them, they appear in danger of being left hanging, precisely because the underlying economic issues in hemispheric relations remain unresolved.

Despite its talk about the individuality of the respective countries of Latin America and the Caribbean, the Carter administration has been remarkably insensitive in several specific areas. U.S.-Brazilian relations deteriorated seriously in 1977 as a result of objective clashes of interest (some of them long-standing) and of early mistakes by the Carter team. Particularly damaging was Vice President Walter F. Mondale's highly publicized direct approach to West Germany concerning its sale of nuclear reprocessing technology to Brazil, an approach made prior to any direct U.S. discussion of the matter with the government of Brazil.

After a brief honeymoon between incoming administrations in the United States and in Mexico, U.S.-Mexican relations were also strained in 1977. The principal reason was the somewhat peremptory proposals by the United States for dealing with massive

Mexican immigration. A Carter plan calling for strict measures to control the flow of "undocumented immigrants" from Mexico was sent to Congress last August with little prior consultation with Mexican authorities —or, for that matter, with Mexican-Americans. It should have been obvious that a genuine jointly devised approach to this problem would be far more likely to succeed than a unilateral one. Moreover, it could have helped assure Mexican cooperation on other matters of shared concern, such as guaranteeing U.S. access to Mexico's huge reserves of natural gas and its projected reserves of petroleum.

Many Latin American and Carribbean countries have been hurt by individual U.S. decisions: to raise tariffs on imported sugar; to sell surplus tin from the government stockpile in order to lower the price; to grant or deny certain airline routes; and to tighten tax regulations on business exemptions for conventions abroad. The gap between announced policy and actual decisions is nowhere more notable than in U.S.-Caribbean relations. The administration's Caribbean initiative seems to be fizzling as specific choices have to be made. State Department and Agency for International Development recommendations for doubling U.S. government support for Caribbean development were turned down, first by the Office of Management and Budget and then, on appeal, by the president himself. Caribbean development has been officially accorded high priority, but an administration that has established so many priorities is unable to make such a commitment very meaningful.

Ghosts of Paternalism

Washington's new human rights policy is difficult to evaluate, because it is unclear how much emphasis is being placed on the policy's several distinct, and not always compatible, objectives. The policy is supposed to win renewed domestic trust in the government and its foreign policies, re-

take the ideological advantage from the Communist parties of Eastern and Western Europe, provide a legitimate basis for sustained U.S. government communication with those in opposition to authoritarian government, disassociate the United States from repressive regimes and their acts, and actually influence the treatment of individuals abroad. Contradictory signals abound, reflecting intra- and interdepartmental disputes within the U.S. government about ends and means, as well as different evaluations of external circumstances and trends. In the relatively uncharted domain of human rights, broad policy guidelines are necessarily abstract and often unenlightening. In practice, policy is defined case by case, country by country, loan by loan, and speech by speech through an iterative process in which the personal styles and ambitions of individual participants in the policy-making process are probably more influential than any other factor.

> **"Carter's record to date on North-South issues . . . has been mixed at best."**

As the human rights policy takes shape, several problems are emerging. Excessive expectations can easily be aroused, as in Nicaragua, risking eventual disillusionment. Heavy-handedness from abroad, no matter how noble the cause, can actually strengthen the domestic hold of repressive regimes, at least temporarily; this may have happened, for a time, in Chile. Policies fashioned to deal with one set of important problems—to fight inflation and stabilize economies, for instance—may contradict and even undermine efforts to promote civil and political liberties, as in Peru. Conversely, policies designed to protect individual rights may not only constrain the development of the countries denied credit by international financial institutions, but may also severely damage the institutions themselves. Vigorous implementation by Washington of the human rights policy in the Western Hemisphere can conjure up ghosts of the paternalist past. And, finally, the whole policy may be used perversely by a strange right-left alliance in Congress and U.S. society as a means of avoiding the resource transfers sought by Latin American and other Third World countries. These difficulties do not argue against a major U.S. concern for human rights, nor should they obscure what the policy has already accomplished. The policy's lasting impact, however, will depend to a considerable extent on how carefully this concern is calibrated. The danger is growing that exuberant and single-minded pursuit of human rights objectives may eventually produce its own backlash, turning officials away from the concern that these issues should always evoke.

But economic issues present the most vexing questions about the administration's policies toward Latin America. Unfortunately, Washington's desire to win Latin American cooperation on global problems is tangible only with regard to the issues the United States itself deems to be urgent: energy, monetary policy, and nonproliferation.

The issues that most deeply concern the majority of Latin American countries—improving access for middle-income countries to the markets, capital, and technology of the industrialized nations; increasing the amount and availability of concessional aid to the poorest countries; making the terms of international trade in commodities more predictable and more favorable to producers; and making multinational corporations more responsive to the interests of host countries —are accorded much lower priority. Unless these and similar North-South problems are confronted, the Carter administration's embrace of a so-called global approach may turn out to be an empty shell, addressing Latin America's principal concerns even less adequately than the old regional approaches.

Carter's record to date on North-South

issues—admittedly restricted by recession and adverse public opinion—has been mixed at best. The administration has sometimes succeeded in resisting strong protectionist pressures. But access to the markets of the United States and other industrialized countries is certainly not being significantly expanded, as it must be if Third World aspirations are to be accommodated. To many Latin Americans, the Multilateral Trade Negotiations under way in Geneva seem thus far largely unresponsive to their needs; industrialized countries are likely to secure greater benefits from trade liberalization than are less developed countries, at least in the short run. Even more troubling is the scheduled expiration in January 1979 of the waiver provisions of the Trade Act of 1974, which allow the secretary of the treasury to delay the application of countervailing duties to goods benefiting from favorable tax treatment in exporting countries. Unless agreement can be reached by January, any Latin American export to the United States currently receiving a government incentive will be subject to countervailing duties within 12 months of a U.S. manufacturer's complaint.

Developments on other North-South issues are not much more encouraging. Obtaining U.S. capital is becoming more difficult, not less, for most of the countries of Latin America and the Caribbean. Concessional aid is relevant only for a few poor countries in the hemisphere, but even they are getting little help from the United States. The administration's request for a 28 per cent increase in worldwide U.S. aid has been whittled down in the authorization and appropriation processes; even if the increase had been appropriated in full, it would still have been quite small in absolute terms and would have left the United States far below the U.N. objective that aid be equal to .7 per cent of a country's Gross National Product. Of course, much more credit is available to Latin American and Caribbean countries from international financial institutions, and this will continue to be the case if the U.S. Congress approves the necessary appropriations. But the debt service paid by nations in the Western Hemisphere on earlier loans now consumes 93 cents out of every dollar borrowed from the United States and the international lending institutions. Moreover, credit from private sources is rapidly drying up for precisely those countries that are in greatest financial difficulty—Peru and Guyana, for instance. The short time-horizon of commercial banks practically assures a perverse cycle of ever-deepening debt.[1]

Despite the Carter administration's rhetorical receptiveness to international commodity agreements, the main difference in this field between this government and its predecessors is that now many more officials are tied down either negotiating or preparing to do so.

Concrete results are sparse. The International Sugar Agreement has been concluded (though Senate ratification is uncertain); and a rubber agreement is being hammered out, but this commodity is of little interest in Latin America. Other negotiations—including those on copper—seem painfully slow and unpromising.

Aside from a few scattered statements, there is scant evidence that the U.S. government will pressure multinational corporations (MNCs) toward greater responsiveness to the needs of developing countries. Richard N. Cooper, under secretary of state for economic affairs, told a group of business executives that the U.S. government would henceforth remain neutral in disagreements between American companies and host countries rather than automatically taking the side of U.S. corporations. But the actual behavior of American embassies has not changed perceptibly. Indeed, the administration has not yet done anything to repeal two pieces of legislation—the Hickenlooper

Amendment first adopted in 1962 and the 1972 Gonzalez Amendment—which still threaten developing countries with U.S. government coercion on behalf of MNCs in cases of nationalization or expropriation.

Finally, little is being done, despite rhetoric to the contrary, to improve the terms governing technology transfers. President Carter's proposal, announced in Caracas last March, to establish a "new United States foundation for technological collaboration" was notable mainly for its complete omission of any further details.

The Carter administration's accomplishments in Latin American policy, then, are so far more style than substance. Attention is being paid to the region, but few problems have been resolved and several have not been tackled. The issues granted priority in Washington are the same as in the past. Rhetoric and tone have changed more than choices and actions. Emphasis has been placed on setting goals, more than on elaborating strategies to achieve them. The major innovations in U.S. policy have been in the most intangible arena, human rights. On matters of dollars and cents the Carter administration has so far produced only small change.

Initial skepticism may still be overcome as trade and tariff negotiations evolve, as specific commodity agreements are worked out, as actual investment disputes arise and are dealt with, as projects demanding increased resource transfers for the Caribbean and elsewhere are considered, and as the president's proposal to establish a foundation for technology is elaborated. No one who favors positive change should help make it unlikely by expressing too much pessimism.

It must be noted, however, that Carter has thus far repeated a familiar pattern.[2] Whether calling its approach a "Good

---

[1] See Albert Fishlow, et al, "The Third World: Public Debt, Private Profit," FOREIGN POLICY 30 (Spring 1978).

[2] For a more complete discussion of these issues, see Abraham F. Lowenthal and Gregory F. Treverton, "The Making of U.S. Policies Toward Latin America," Working Paper #5 (Washington, D.C.: Latin American Program, The Woodrow Wilson International Center for Scholars).

Neighbor Policy," an "Alliance for Progress," a "Mature Partnership," or a "New Dialogue," or pointedly eschewing rhetoric and labels, as Carter has done, one administration after another has promised to improve U.S.-Latin American relations. Always goaded by a period of tension in hemispheric relations, successive governments have inevitably announced reforms, pledged greater attention to the needs of the area, and vowed their support for Latin America's social and economic development. In earlier days the United States sometimes promised to help secure democracy in the region. "Human rights," rather than "democracy," is now the slogan, but the point is the same.

Rhetoric or Results

The next phase in this historic cycle, which the Carter administration may now be entering, has generally seen the newly expressed policy toward Latin America vitiated, or even contradicted, by U.S. government actions. Despite the promises that they will receive enhanced consideration, Latin American interests are slighted or contravened. Despite the pretense of consultation and negotiation, Latin Americans are the victims of unilateral decisions made in Washington or New York. Whatever the official rhetoric of cooperation, Latin Americans learn that private interests in the United States can use public instruments to achieve their will. Although Washington promises to help Latin American development, generous resource transfers from the United States often wind up tied to political concessions or special commercial privileges. Events of the past few months—the sugar tariff increases; Washington's decision to sell surplus tin despite the adverse impact on Bolivia; the threat to impose countervailing duties; the decision to curtail sharply the proposed Caribbean initiative; the unilateral proposals to deal with the problem of undocumented aliens—fit the classic mode.

What explains this persistent gap between each new administration's proclaimed Latin

American policy and the pattern of decisions, actions, and omissions that ultimately comprise the real policy? Why does the resolve of new administrations to improve inter-American relations so often come to naught, or to only a bit more?

Many of the U.S. government's decisions and actions affecting Latin America and inter-American relations result from initiatives in other policy arenas—foreign or domestic—with limited consideration, if any, given to their likely impact in the hemisphere. The many examples include the sugar and tin decisions; the policies regarding nuclear proliferation, arms transfers, and human rights; many provisions of tax law and its implementation; and a number of trade policy decisions. Actions of this sort

---

"It is much easier for the [U.S.] government to manage its relations with the Soviet Union or China than with Chile or Peru."

---

are often not significantly influenced by regional considerations or by the U.S. government personnel working on inter-American affairs. Those within the administration primarily concerned with inter-American relations may push hard for alternate policies. That they so often fail reflects the relative lack of priority accorded to the region.

A second point, often ignored, is that a multiplicity of nongovernmental entities and processes, which no administration can easily control, influence the shape of inter-American relations. These entities—multinational corporations, private banks, and labor unions, for example—operate within a structure strongly affected by past and present U.S. government decisions. Official policy can influence or constrain private actions, for U.S. citizens, individual or corporate, are rarely entirely oblivious to Washington's preference. Still, what the U.S. government decides to do, or not to do, in

Latin America cannot by itself alter the main impact of the United States. In a curious sense, it is much easier for the government to manage its relations with the Soviet Union or China than with Chile or Peru. Latin American and Caribbean countries are very strongly influenced by decisions taken by Exxon, the American Smelting and Refining Co. (ASARCO), United Brands, Citibank, Manufacturers Hanover Trust, or Chase Manhattan, to name just a few examples. And some of the main problems in inter-American relations—especially access to capital and technology—are issues over which the U.S. government has considerably less influence than nongovernmental actors.

A third reason for the contrast between announced intentions and subsequent actions has to do with the policy-making process itself. Each new administration brings to Washington a fresh cadre of officials determined to do better than their predecessors. They often bring with them concepts and policies forged by task forces and study groups. The new recruits draw on this background to draft policy directives and presidential speeches. In time, however, their influence is attenuated by the persistent pressures of special interests and sometimes by the passive resistance of the career bureaucracy.

Because private U.S. interest groups can pursue their particular objectives through many different channels in the executive branch and Congress, broad and consistent reforms of U.S. policy are hard to achieve. Any reform that penalizes a well-organized group—copper companies, sugar or citrus growers, shoe manufacturers, labor unions, or church groups—can usually be shelved or defeated by a coalition assembled within the highly fragmented structure of U.S. foreign policy-making. Even when the proposed reform promises to benefit U.S. society as a whole, the group likely to be injured can often prevent the reform's adoption. And even when a new policy is formally adopted, an administration must then en-

sure its full implementation at all levels of sharply divergent bureaucracies. The Treasury Department is often decisive in shaping and implementing U.S. policies on commercial and monetary matters; on export subsidies, countervailing duties, and other elements of trade policy; on the negotiation of commodity agreements and buffer stocks; on the behavior of international financial institutions; in short, on most of the substantive issues in contemporary inter-American relations. The Departments of Agriculture, Energy, Justice, and Commerce; the Export-Import Bank; the Civil Aeronautics Board —not to mention the Pentagon and the Central Intelligence Agency—all have direct influence on U.S. policies affecting Latin America. To ensure that all segments of the U.S. government will cooperate to pursue a new policy, an administration must be willing to give that policy significant priority. Constant monitoring, innovative coordination, and energetic implementation are required. That kind of priority is, and must be, rare.

New administrations also find it hard to follow through on proclaimed intentions because of the often underestimated and still growing role of Congress. Trade policy, human rights, arms transfer policy, agriculture policy, foreign aid, and other matters important in the hemisphere are today strongly influenced by Congress. Almost any new policy initiative must first run the gauntlet of congressional scrutiny, influenced by constituent pressures of all sorts, before it can be fully implemented. Few proposals survive this ordeal unscathed.

Constant Tension

Lasting improvements in U.S.-Latin American relations are difficult to achieve for three reasons that are more basic: the reality of declining but still remembered U.S. hegemony in the hemisphere, the emergence of sharp clashes of interests between the United States and the countries of Latin America and the Caribbean, and the absence of a coherent and widely accepted vision in Washington of how inter-American relations should be restructured to respond to these two changing facts of hemispheric life.

An overwhelming imbalance between the United States and the countries of Latin America and the Caribbean has long conditioned the realities of inter-American relations. Because the United States is so much bigger, richer, stronger, and more extensively involved around the world than any other country in the hemisphere, what is crucial for a Latin American nation may be of marginal significance in Washington. Moreover, what may appear to be mutually advantageous from Washington's perspective seems exploitative from a Latin American standpoint. Because so many in the United States still think of Latin America as a U.S. sphere of influence, an intolerable affront to sovereignty—like the reservation to the Panama Canal treaties introduced by Senator Dennis DeConcini (D.-Arizona), providing the United States with the permanent right to send its troops into Panama to protect the canal—can be approved with few qualms in the United States. The inevitable result of this continuing imbalance of power, real and perceived, is constant tension rooted in ambition, fear, jealousy, and resentment. As the bases for America's hegemonic presumption erode, tensions will probably not be relaxed but rather increased.[3]

During the next few years, a new Latin American assertiveness resulting from enhanced power and from changes in the composition of the area's leadership will exacerbate the tension. Traditional pro-American elites are being replaced all over the hemisphere by civilian and military technocrats, often of a nationalist bent. These new leaders, many of them trained in U.S. graduate schools, tend to identify their countries' interests independently of, and even in confrontation with, the United States. But

another important source of increased inter-American disagreement is the change in the focus of Latin American economies from inward-turned import substitution to outward-oriented export promotion. Most Latin American countries, except for the smallest, no longer care about obtaining bilateral concessional assistance from the United States. They, like other Third World countries, primarily seek new rules and practices that will improve their access to markets, capital, and technology in the industrialized world.

As Latin American and other Third World economies expand and as their export potential and their thirst for capital and technology grow, conflicts will inevitably arise between them and the industrialized countries. The specific issues will include commodities, tariffs, countervailing duties, debt management, technology transfers, the conservation and management of resources, the terms of capital and labor migration, and the formulation and management of international rules to govern these and other problems. As Brazil, Mexico, Venezuela, Argentina, and other Latin American countries strive to fulfill their potential, they will encounter a growing tendency of industrialized countries to defend the status quo through protectionism, preservation of existing international monetary arrangements, nonproliferation policies, and the like.

Consequently, to achieve a major and lasting improvement in its relations with Latin America, the United States will have to help establish a new international economic and political order within which the claims of Latin American and other aspiring powers are more fully accommodated.[4] A reformed international order would reconcile U.S. interests with those of Latin American and other Third World countries in

---

[3] *See Abraham F. Lowenthal, "The United States and Latin America: Ending the Hegemonic Presumption,"* Foreign Affairs, *October 1976.*

[4] *For an outline of such an order, see Albert Fishlow, "A New International Economic Order: What Kind?" in Fishlow, et al,* Rich and Poor Nations in the World Economy *(New York: McGraw-Hill, 1978).*

ways ultimately more favorable to Third World interests than under the existing order. More of the world's manufacturing would take place in the South, and painful adjustments would have to be accepted by the North. Increased benefits from international trade in raw materials and other primary products would accrue to the less industrialized countries. The advantages derived by the rich countries from prior accumulations of capital and technology would decrease. The present and prospective benefits from the world's commons—especially from the seabed and outer space—would be distributed in a more equitable manner. The rules and regimes affecting these and other international issues would be made in fora where the interests of the countries of Latin America, among others, would be protected. To a large extent market forces can be used to make the new international order work, but substantial structural change will be required to assure that markets operate in a world where leverage, influence, and rewards are not so unevenly distributed.

No administration to date has seriously attempted to change the structure of the international order, which has so overwhelmingly favored the United States. Economic concessions granted by Washington to Latin American countries and others have always been provided grudgingly in exchange for cooperation on specific political or strategic matters. Never has the United States sought to transform the very nature of its relationship with the rest of the hemisphere. If Jimmy Carter wants to inaugurate a truly new era in U.S.-Latin American relations, that is the challenge his administration must face.

PUERTO RICO: OUT OF THE COLONIAL CLOSET

by José A. Cabranes

The problem of Puerto Rico is colonialism, and decolonization stands at the front and center of the island's politics and its relations with the United States, now and for the foreseeable future.

Colonialism in Puerto Rico has been unique—"colonialism with the consent of the governed," it has often been called. So it is not surprising that the decolonization process there may have few counterparts or precedents elsewhere in the world. But that process may prove to be as difficult, confusing, and painful for all concerned—including U.S. policy makers—as any experienced by the European powers in Africa and Asia. The universal Puerto Rican longing for political change today presents the United States with a major domestic political dilemma and a serious foreign policy problem.

There is not yet a clear consensus among Puerto Ricans about the island's political future. There is, however, a very definite consensus about its present status as a "commonwealth": Things cannot remain as they are. Puerto Ricans must work toward a relationship with the mainland that will lift the enormous psychological burden of decades of dependency and political inferiority, enabling the island's 3.2 million people to live in peace under a permanent form of government.

None of Puerto Rico's political parties is happy with the commonwealth arrangement as it now stands. Advocates of both statehood and independence regard it as essentially colonial. As Oreste Ramos, a fervently pro-American conservative senator and leader of the dominant prostatehood New Progressive Party (NPP), recently told the U.N. Decolonization Committee, "the political inferiority inherent in Puerto Rico's present status is an insult to the national decorum of the United States and to the dignity of the people of Puerto Rico." Advocates of independence put the matter in less genteel terms.

Even the defenders of Puerto Rico's present status, formally adopted in 1952, now call for "a new dimension of sovereignty" that will give the island "the maximum plenitude of autonomy." A generation ago, the Popular Democratic Party (PDP) pronounced colonialism dead, proclaiming the birth of the *Estado Libre Asociado de Puerto Rico* (deliberately translated as "Commonwealth of Puerto Rico" rather than as "Free Associated State of Puerto Rico"). But at the United Nations, it recently joined unlikely companions—Cuba and its Socialist and Third World allies—to draw attention to its frustrated petitions to the United States for greater autonomy.

Puerto Rico's three historic political movements—supporting statehood, commonwealth status, and independence—are now all firmly committed to the vigorous pursuit of political change. A referendum on the island's status has been set for 1981 by the prostatehood administration of Governor Carlos Romero Barceló. Romero rejects the widespread belief that a statehood petition must be supported by an overwhelming majority of the voters in order to be taken seriously by Congress. He has an uncomplicated faith in the principle of majority rule and believes that statehood requires no greater mandate than a simple majority. Nevertheless, Romero's followers expect a surge of support for statehood, and possibly even a prostatehood majority in the 60-70 per cent range, especially if PDP traditionalists begin to fear that their leaders are heading toward something akin to independence. Romero is convinced that a Puerto Rican statehood petition would be accepted by the required ma-

jority of each house of Congress, but he unequivocally states that its rejection would compel him to support independence rather than see Puerto Rico endure indefinitely what he regards as the inequality and powerlessness of commonwealth status.

The proponents of a more viable commonwealth status, on the other hand, hope to stem the rising statehood tide and move the island toward a new and permanent relationship of "free association" with the United States. Meanwhile, the independence forces, confident that both of these political drives are pipe dreams that will be frustrated by Washington, expect eventually to be able to pick up the pieces and mobilize a disappointed people toward national sovereignty.

The collapse of support for the status quo, even among many original proponents of the island's commonwealth status, has polarized Puerto Rican society. Many of the island's citizens believe that an imminent political showdown will settle whether Puerto Rico, after 80 years under the American flag, will join the federal union or move toward significantly greater (or complete) freedom.

The Forbidden Word

Except among Puerto Rico's *independentistas*, the word "colonialism" has been absent from the political lexicon of U.S.-Puerto Rican relations for a generation. Determined to prove themselves trustworthy fellow citizens—Americans with a colorful heritage and language, but surely as American as apple pie—proponents of statehood and commonwealth status focused their campaigns for political change exclusively on Washington, avoided references to "colonialism," eschewed political identification with Third World peoples, and left the anticolonial arena of the United Nations to the small minority of independence advocates. Yet no word other than "colonialism" adequately describes the relationship between a powerful metropolitan state and an impoverished overseas dependency, disenfranchised from the formal lawmaking processes that shape its people's daily lives.

In 1978 the statehood forces and those seeking modification of the commonwealth arrangement came out of the colonial closet. Inspired in part by the directness of expression and the political achievements of blacks, chicanos, and even Puerto Ricans in the mainland United States, Puerto Ricans on the island have become more assertive and less deferential in expressing their political aspirations. Romero has unabashedly spoken of the "vestiges of colonialism" that exist in the current relationship, and the frustrated proponents of reformed commonwealth status have shown themselves less reluctant to use that forbidden word in speaking of Washington's failure to heed their pleas for a greater measure of self-government.

The statehood movement originally took root among the island's blacks and poor whites.

In a climactic two-week period in late August and early September, Puerto Rican leaders of every political stripe—including even Maurice A. Ferré, the Puerto Rican-born mayor of Miami—appeared before the U.N. Special Committee on Decolonization, dramatizing the widespread dissatisfaction with the status quo. In doing so, they effectively recognized the existence of an alternative forum for efforts to resolve the prolonged Puerto Rican identity crisis. They also shattered the delusion of a generation of U.S. policy makers that the question of Puerto Rico's political future is strictly an American domestic issue, a quaint political notion that is reminiscent of similar claims asserted by European colonial powers during U.N. anticolonial hearings in the 1950s.

Even Romero, who faithfully stated the traditional U.S. position "that intervention by [the U.N. committee] is neither necessary nor appropriate nor acceptable to the people of Puerto Rico," took the occasion of his ap-

pearance at the U.N. to observe that the principle of self-determination enshrined in the U.N. Charter "includes the right to pass from the status of free associated state [or commonwealth] to statehood as well as the right to pass from the status of free associated state to independence." Although he admitted that "vestiges of colonialism" endure in Puerto Rico, Romero nevertheless testified, as the State Department wished, that the U.N. had no business intervening as long as the Puerto Ricans had the capacity to initiate steps to change their political status.

Because the United States is not a member of the Decolonization Committee, the State Department had to work through sympathetic official participants, notably Australia. But for the first time it could not persuade the committee to put off formal action on the issue. On September 12, 1978, after the failure of compromise efforts by India and others, a resolution proposed by Cuba was adopted by a plurality composed of Socialist and Third World states but, significantly, without a single dissenting vote. In relatively muted terms, it criticized alleged U.S. violations of the Puerto Rican people's "national rights," endorsing independence and any form of "free association" between Puerto Rico and the United States based on "political equality" and a recognition of "the sovereignty of the people of Puerto Rico" under international law. It went on to note the widespread dissatisfaction on the island with the current political status. Importantly, the resolution omitted any direct reference to political integration or statehood as an acceptable political fate for the island.

Although officially ignored by the U.S. and Puerto Rican governments, the adoption of the resolution was a setback for American diplomacy. For decades, the matter of Puerto Rican political status was defined out of existence as a foreign policy concern, and a reexamination of U.S. policy at the U.N. was avoided, despite the evident pressures on the island for political change. Consequently, the willingness of so many mainstream Puerto

Rican leaders to appear before the Decolonization Committee this time around took U.S. diplomats by surprise. They were alarmed to find the leaders of the procommonwealth PDP openly supporting a Cuban draft resolution in an effort to embarrass the United States and the prostatehood forces.

The traditional U.S. hard-line position—that nothing but deferral of U.N. consideration was acceptable, that nothing but the status quo was tolerable—frustrated the efforts of representatives of all the Puerto Rican factions to negotiate a consensus resolution defining a projected process of "self-determination" for Puerto Rico. Accordingly, each of the political groups, except the statehooders, scrambled to consolidate committee support for its ideological position. The PDP's collaboration with the Cubans and the resulting adoption of the Cuban-drafted resolution unnecessarily discredited the United Nations in the eyes of the statehooders, perhaps precluding any conciliating role the organization might have been able to play in the island's future. It also made possible the labeling of Puerto Rican political parties as either pro-American or anti-American, severely aggravating political tensions and, by all accounts, greatly strengthening the hand of "pro-American" Romero in a political dogfight with his predecessor and rival, "anti-American" Rafael Hernández Colón.

Blessings of Civilization

If all this proves to be as much of a surprise to the American public as to the befuddled U.S. diplomats at the United Nations, it is only because, as Gloria Emerson aptly observed in writing about Vietnam, "We have always been a people who dropped the past and then could not remember where it had been put." The contemporary Puerto Rican political imbroglio is the legacy of what President William McKinley's secretary of state, John Hay, called the "splendid little war" against Spain in 1898 and the subsequent U.S. colonial experiment. The controversy accompanying U.S. intervention in the

Cuban civil war of that year led Congress to adopt a resolution offered by Colorado Senator Henry M. Teller disclaiming "any disposition or intention to exercise sovereignty" over Cuba and asserting the determination of the United States eventually to "leave the government and control of the island to its people." However, this self-denying resolution clearly did not apply to Spain's other colonies, including Puerto Rico.

The invasion and trouble-free occupation of Puerto Rico on July 25, 1898, were followed by a proclamation to the Puerto Rican people suggesting that the island would have a more direct and lasting link to the mainland American political system than that envisaged for Cuba. The proclamation, issued by the commander of U.S. forces in Puerto Rico, Major General Nelson A. Miles, asserted that the Americans, "bearing the banner of freedom" would "bestow upon [the Puerto Rican people] the immunities and blessings of the liberal institutions of our government . . . [and] the advantages and blessings of enlightened civilization."

That Puerto Rico would become part of a new empire was confirmed by the terms of the 1898 Paris peace treaty, under which Spain merely abandoned "all claim of sovereignty over and title to Cuba," but ceded Puerto Rico, Guam, and the Philippines to the United States. For the first time in American history, as American historian Julius W. Pratt wrote, "in a treaty acquiring territory for the United States, there was no promise of citizenship, . . .there was no promise, actual or implied, of statehood. The United States thereby acquired not 'territories' but possessions or 'dependencies' and became, in that sense, an 'imperial' power."

Political resistance to colonialism was widespread in the United States from the outset. The nonpartisan Anti-Imperialist League, organized even before the Treaty of Paris was signed, drew to its standard a wide variety of national leaders opposed to the annexation of territories that were given no hope of statehood in the American union.

Its opposition to government without the consent of the governed was echoed in Congress in 1900 when the Democratic minority of the House Ways and Means Committee asserted that U.S. policy toward Puerto Rico was "pure and simple imperialism . . . . It does not matter in which form territory is acquired, it is to be held under our Constitution with the object of finally being admitted into the Union as a State."

If you scratch the skin of any Puerto Rican . . . you will find an *independentista*.

Imperialism was described by Democratic candidate William Jennings Byran as the "paramount issue" of the 1900 presidential campaign, and with the electoral victory of McKinley and Theodore Roosevelt, the United States effectively joined the major European powers in the rush to empire. The following year, the Supreme Court blessed the colonial experiment in the celebrated Insular cases, in which the new territories were held not to be "foreign territory," but nevertheless not "a part of the United States" for all constitutional purposes. In the Court's view, Congress was empowered "to locally govern at discretion."

"Discretion" soon came to mean moving the Filipinos toward independence even as the Puerto Ricans were drawn increasingly into the U.S. fold. As early as 1900, congressional reports drew a distinction between Puerto Rico's "law-abiding and industrious" people, who were believed to be overwhelmingly white, and the oriental people of the Philippines, who had vigorously and "ungratefully" resisted American rule from the beginning by claiming the right to national independence. Characteristically, Representative Thomas Spight (D.-Mississippi), compared the Philippines and Puerto Rico by invoking geographical proximity, the alleged racial similarity of Puerto Ricans to white Americans, and the injunctions of the Monroe Doctrine. Puerto Rico could become part of the United States, and its people American citizens, he told the House in 1900, because Puerto Rico was located within a traditional American sphere of influence:

> Its people are, in the main, of Caucasian blood, knowing and appreciating the benefits of civilization, and are desirous of casting their lot with us . . . . Its proximity to our mainland, the character of its inhabitants, and the willingness with which they accept our sovereignty, together with the advantages—commercial, sanitary and strategic—all unite to enable us to make her an integral part of our domain.

Their collective naturalization by Congress in 1917 (the year after the Philippines was first promised its eventual independence) cemented a relationship under which the Puerto Ricans have endured the mixed blessings of colonial rule by a nation convinced of its decent intentions and embarrassed by the very notion of colonialism.

First under the "organic acts" passed by Congress in 1900 and 1917, and now under the 1952 commonwealth constitution adopted by its people, the form of Puerto Rico's local government has been patterned on those of mainland state governments. The current structure extends to the island all congressional legislation unless Congress chooses to make it "locally inapplicable." Although Puerto Ricans are exempt from paying federal income tax (enabling the island to attract mainland investments in recent years), local taxes there are as high as the combined federal and state levies in many states. Similarly, because the island's economy is wholly dependent on trade with the mainland, its cost of living is comparable to that of New York City. Yet Puerto Rico's people do not vote in presidential elections or elect any voting representatives to Congress. These circumstances once drove former Governor Luis A. Ferré to dub Puerto Rico "a one-armed state."

During the half century before Puerto

Ricans were first permitted to elect their own governor in 1948, the islanders benefited enormously from improvements in sanitation, public health, education, and public works. The price for this, acceptable to many in a land of frightful poverty, was political subordination, effective economic domination by mainland U.S. interests, and a deep, abiding sense of dependency and powerlessness.

Calling the American Bluff

From the beginning of the century, the island's politics have been shaped by the struggle of political parties advocating one of three basic options for political status: statehood, independence, or some intermediate objective ("self-government," "commonwealth," or, now, "free association").

The statehood movement originally took root among the island's blacks and poor whites, who sought rapid economic improvement and the protection of American democratic institutions from the island's creole elite. It is no coincidence that the founder of the statehood movement was a black physician and populist, Dr. José Celso Barbosa, who had studied medicine in Michigan during Reconstruction and was inspired by American institutions. The island's original labor and socialist movements were staunchly pro-American and allied to Barbosa's statehood party as well as Samuel Gompers's American Federation of Labor.

From the 1930s through the mid-1960s, the statehood movement fell under the control of some of the island's wealthiest and most conservative families. Its revival in the 1960s and 1970s is due not only to the growing identification with the mainland (resulting largely from migration and travel between the two places and the modernization of the island's society) but also to Romero's evocation of the Barbosa vision of statehood as an instrument for social and economic justice. In his 1973 book, *La estadidad es para los pobres,* Romero argues that only the relatively well-to-do need worry about paying federal taxes under statehood, while the great majority of Puerto Ricans would benefit from full participation in all federal aid programs. His NPP followers see no conflict between libertarian and egalitarian goals; in U.S. citizenship they find an implied promise of political equality in an American system liberal and pluralistic enough to incorporate a racially mixed, Spanish-speaking people who by and large have embraced American institutions and believe in U.S. national self-advertisements.

If the American rhetoric of eight decades has been a bluff, the statehood drive will call that bluff. Its goal is nothing more and nothing less than Puerto Rican power within the American system—the sort of power that comes from having two senators and seven or eight representatives in the U.S. Congress.

The boom built on cheap labor may be over forever.

The independence movement, on the other hand, has always been strongest in the middle and upper classes, especially in the bar, the universities, and related elites. Originally a conservative (and sometimes, at the margins, a cryptofascist) force, it is now largely a movement of the Left. Despite its electoral failures in recent years, the independence movement is far from dead. It was once a major political force on the island, and its appeals to Puerto Rican values and sense of national identity should not be underestimated.

Divided today between the democratic socialist Puerto Rico Independence Party (PIP) and the much smaller, Cuba-oriented Puerto Rican Socialist Party (PSP), the independence movement faces seemingly insurmountable obstacles. Decades of economic integration with the United States, coupled with a growing dependence on federal funds, impede separation. Moreover, profound popular faith in the social and economic merits of the U.S. political connection is compounded by an equally profound fear that a small, poor, and overpopulated island with few natural resources cannot hope to prosper on its own. Perhaps the greatest obstacle to the appeal of independence has been the absence since the 1940s of heavy-handed colonial administrators who could be readily blamed for the island's troubles.

Nevertheless, leaders of the independence movement believe they have an effective veto over any efforts to admit Puerto Rico into the union. Their confidence is based on the conviction that Congress will not admit a territory in which a significant proindependence minority, supported by an unknown number of antistatehood PDP members, would tenaciously resist "assimilation." Their strenuous resistance is their trump card, for, as civil libertarian Roger Baldwin once observed, if you scratch the skin of any Puerto Rican, no matter how enthusiastic an American citizen he may be, you will find an *independentista*. It is the hope of PIP and PSP leaders that in time U.S. rejection of other options will indeed abrade the skin of their compatriots.

Frustrated in elections at home, the *independentistas* have pressed their case in recent years before the U.N. Decolonization Committee, in an effort to embarrass the United States into moving the island toward independence. Urging that the General Assembly restore Puerto Rico to its list of "Non-Self-Governing Territories," they argue that Puerto Rico's removal from that list in 1953 by a plurality vote of the General Assembly merely reflected U.S. domination of the world body. Citing international law, they maintain that a colony cannot consent to the perpetuation of its colonial status; therefore, the U.N. should not accredit a form of government that does not meet its contemporary criteria for determining whether a territory has achieved what its Charter calls "a full measure of self-government."

The difficult-to-define middle ground between statehood and independence has invariably been the terrain of a broad coalition of pragmatists who place political power and economic problem solving above ideological preoccupation with abstract notions such as equality or freedom. The political base of the procommonwealth PDP, which held power virtually without interruption between 1940 and 1976, was in the Puerto Rican countryside. Its leadership, however, was composed largely of technocrats and middle-class professionals who have been joined in recent years by a new class of conservative industrialists and merchants spawned by Operation Bootstrap, the much-touted PDP economic development program.

Bread, Land, and Liberty

During the anticolonial period following World War II, the Philippines achieved its long-promised independence, and Puerto Rico moved toward commonwealth status. This ambiguous and little-understood political formula was devised by Luis Muñoz Marín, a brilliant, charismatic, bilingual nationalist whose reform-minded PDP originally won control of the island's legislature in 1940 with a commitment to "Bread, Land, and Liberty." Fearing the possible economic consequences of independence, Muñoz Marín steered his political movement toward a form of decolonization that would involve neither independence nor statehood—a "third road to freedom" granting Puerto Rico an island government organized under a locally adopted constitution. As far as Congress was concerned, the change from colony to commonwealth was more form than substance. The House report of June 19, 1950, flatly stated that the legislation launching the commonwealth arrangement "would not change Puerto Rico's fundamental political, social, and economic relationship to the United States."

The *Estado Libre Asociado de Puerto Rico* was neither a member of the union nor an independent nation. Nor did its inventors regard it as a way station to either status. A political arrangement based upon the principle of the consent of the governed (and therefore not "colonial"), it was expected to permit a desperately poor people to retain mutually advantageous economic ties with the United States without losing its national identity. Muñoz Marín acknowledged that commonwealth status was an "imperfect" solution to the island's colonial condition. To those who yearned for greater self-government, Muñoz Marín touted the flexibility of American constitutional formulas and indicated that the 1952 "compact" between Puerto Rico and the U.S. Congress could and would be amended in order to complete the job left undone by compromise.

The commonwealth idea was an authentic expression of the postwar American liberal worldview: a poor and racially mixed Third World community undergoing modernization as a result of the inventive application of American capital and American liberal ideology. Chief Justice Earl Warren euphorically proclaimed the commonwealth "perhaps the most notable of American political experiments in our lifetime."

The relationship was not without its benefits for the United States. By 1977 Puerto Rico's annual purchases from the mainland had soared to more than $3.9 billion; on a per capita basis, Puerto Rico ranked second to none as a purchaser of U.S. goods. Under Operation Bootstrap, American manufacturers alone had invested about $5 billion in Puerto Rico by 1976. Puerto Rican soldiers have served in every U.S. military engagement since the beginning of the century.

To some extent and for a time, the commonwealth idea worked. Between 1940 and 1977, the per capita annual personal income of Puerto Ricans increased from $118 to $2,472 (the highest in Spanish America), with the result that the island came to be touted as a "showcase of democracy" and an alternative to "Castroism."[1] It was only natural that when John F. Kennedy organized the Alliance for Progress, largely in response to the hemispheric challenge of Castro's revo-

lution, he tapped as its first director Teodoro Moscoso, the technocrat who had managed Operation Bootstrap.

If it had ever seemed a problem for American foreign policy, by the early 1960s Puerto Rico seemed so no longer. Like the Filipinos, the Puerto Ricans had apparently exercised their right to self-determination: They had obtained the political status they requested, they were prospering, and they seemed politically content.

But even as the United States eliminated Puerto Rico as a foreign policy concern, Cuba and Third World and Communist allies began in the mid-1960s to take up the cause of the independence movement. At the time, the strength of the commonwealth idea was beginning to erode. Yet the beneficiary of that erosion was not the independence movement, but rather the movement for statehood and political equality within the American system. The results of the island's quadrennial elections tell the story and reveal one source of the current confusion.

Puerto Rican General Election Results Since Commonwealth Began		
Party(ies) Favoring Commonwealth	Party(ies) Favoring Statehood	Party(ies) Favoring Independence
1952 67.0%	12.9%	18.9%
1956 62.5	25.0	12.5
1960 58.2	32.1	3.1
1964 59.4	34.7	2.7
1968 52.1	45.1	2.8
1972 51.4	44.0	4.5
1976 45.3	48.3	6.4

Note: *The political status question was not necessarily the chief campaign issue in these general elections. Percentages may not total 100 due to electoral participation of independent voters and parties not advocating a political status alternative.*

A 1967 plebiscite on political status gave 60.41 per cent of the vote to proponents of a reformed or "perfected" form of commonwealth status and 38.98 per cent to the statehood movement. The *independentistas* denounced the plebiscite as a nefarious political maneuver to win from Puerto Ricans an endorsement of their political impotence.

---

[1] *A classic example may be found in "Why Puerto Rico Thrives as Cuba Crumbles,"* U.S. News and World Report, *March 28, 1960.*

Complaining of persecution and poor phrasing of the ballot, they boycotted the polls: The independence option drew a mere .6 per cent of the vote.

In the 1976 general elections, the combined votes of the statehood and independence parties constituted a clear majority of the electorate, for the first time since the commonwealth came into being in 1952.

Although conventional wisdom has it that commonwealth status made possible Puerto Rico's economic miracle of the past quarter century, in fact the reverse is probably true. Puerto Rico's economic expansion made possible the islanders' toleration of a political relationship with the United States that was not fundamentally different from the overtly colonial status that preceded it. Freedom from federal taxation, an elected governor, local self-government, tax incentives for American industry, and the possibility of participating in federal aid programs all antedated the commonwealth.

As long as economic expansion and optimism lasted, the commonwealth idea prospered. But it has apparently failed to survive the economic contraction of recent years and the realization that the boom built on cheap labor may be over forever. The island, dependent on trade for its livelihood and on U.S. capital for its development, has been largely absorbed into the high-cost American economy and finds it increasingly difficult to hold its own against mainland and foreign competitors. In the mid-1970s the island's official unemployment rate reached over 22 per cent, the highest since Operation Bootstrap. Declining private investment coupled with rising public spending and a rapidly growing social welfare system brought the island close to financial collapse in 1975-1976. The magnitude of the crisis was overshadowed only by the more spectacular financial trauma of New York City.

A Welfare State, Made in the U.S.A.

The Puerto Rican sense of powerlessness and dissatisfaction has been deepened in re-

cent years by the fiscal austerity resulting from these massive financial difficulties and the increasing reliance on federal funds. As a result of efforts by procommonwealth and prostatehood administrations alike, the island has come to be included in a growing number of federal aid programs. Invoking the U.S. citizenship of the island's people and insisting upon treatment equal to that of citizens on the mainland, successive commonwealth governments have managed to increase total federal outlays to Puerto Rico from $767 million in 1970 to $3 billion in 1976. Oblivious to the long-term impact of the wholesale extension of federal programs to the island, the executive and legislative branches of the U.S. government—not the Puerto Ricans—have turned Puerto Rico into a veritable welfare state. Official Washington was largely unaware in 1974, for example, that extension of the food stamp program to the island would cost the U.S. Treasury nearly $600 million a year by 1976, about two-thirds of Puerto Rico's people being eligible to participate.

Recognizing shortcomings in the present political arrangement, the PDP has pledged to work to reform, "perfect," or "refine" the island's commonwealth status. For a generation it has talked of rewriting the 1952 compact with Congress to transfer to Puerto Rico many of the powers now exercised on the island by the federal government, including some or all jurisdiction over communications, labor relations, trade regulation, immigration, and environmental matters. Autonomists also argue for independent Puerto Rican membership in international technical and cultural institutions. A more wide-ranging proposed reform would grant Puerto Rico effective veto power over congressional legislation applicable to the island. These proposals were designed to strengthen Puerto Rican self-confidence and meet the criticism that commonwealth status sanctions virtually unlimited congressional government of Puerto Rico without the islanders' concurrence.

A number of these reforms were embodied in the "Compact of Permanent Union Between the United States and Puerto Rico," fashioned in 1975 by a joint commission appointed by Hernández Colón and Richard Nixon and designed partly to redeem the PDP's long-standing pledge to expand the island's self-government. The two most notable proposals for reform would have given Puerto Rico virtually complete control over minimum wages (to establish lower rates than on the mainland) and environmental regulation (to avoid mainland timetables for reaching various standards).

The compact was introduced in Congress in 1975 by the PDP's resident commissioner. But its passage was stalled by the Ford administration's indifference, objections by mainland labor and environmental lobbies, and the strenuous opposition of many vocal Puerto Ricans. The latter included the statehood movement, dissident autonomists who felt the compact was too moderate, and the independence movement.

The statehood movement broke new ground in the November 1976 general elections by sweeping the PDP from every major political office on the island and winning the resident commissionership in Washington. The NPP victory effectively killed the proposed compact, ending years of efforts to revive and fortify the commonwealth idea.

Perhaps more important, the coincident victories of the statehooders in Puerto Rico and Jimmy Carter in the United States led to the removal of the procommonwealth forces from national political party affairs. Prostatehood Democrats, members of the local chapter of Americans for Democratic Action, led by a young politician with the emblematic name of Franklin Delano López, were early allies of Carter, while the PDP-affiliated Democrats backed Senator Henry M. Jackson (D.-Washington). After the 1976 election, the NPP quickly moved to take over the official Democratic party of Puerto Rico. Statehooders have been affiliated with the mainland Republican party since the turn of the century, when the GOP was the home of the U.S. progressive movement and the party of America's black people. Although it was also the party of imperialism, it was the only U.S. political party that did not question the permanence of Puerto Rico's position in the American system. The local branch of the Democratic party had been identified with the PDP ever since Muñoz Marín asserted his control in mid-century. However, with the newly democratized Democratic primary rules, statehood advocates have now been able to take control of the Puerto Rican affiliates of both major parties, and they can be expected to seek commitments to statehood in both national party platforms in 1980.

Responding to demands by the López group, the Democratic National Committee unanimously decided in mid-1978 to hold a primary in Puerto Rico to determine control of the local Democratic organization. The prostatehood Democrats promised that, if victorious, they would hold a presidential primary in 1980 for the island's 22-delegate national convention slate. Now tentatively set for the same week in February 1980 as that of New Hampshire, the presidential primary promises to introduce the island's political status issue into national presidential politics. Because national party primaries are regarded by orthodox autonomists as a step toward eventual statehood, the PDP boycotted the 1978 party primary and all but abandoned its traditional informal ties to the national Democratic party. It then apparently accelerated its search for political arenas other than Washington for the assertion of its political claims.

A Bombshell and a Milestone

The U.S. response to Puerto Rican initiatives at the United Nations was ambiguous. Moving adroitly in July to pre-empt a possible international embarrassment, Carter issued a proclamation to the Puerto Rican people solemnly affirming the U.S. commitment to the principle of self-determination and pledging to "support, and urge the Congress to support, whatever decision the people of Puerto Rico reach" in the 1981 political status referendum. There was no suggestion that presidential support was conditioned in any way upon the size of the majority in the 1981 referendum.

To the few people in the United States who paid attention to Carter's proclamation, it was nothing more than a restatement of traditional American political values. To the Puerto Ricans, it was a political bombshell and a milestone of considerable significance. Carter had acknowledged that political change was possible and would have his personal support. He had thus deftly begun to move away from the policy of his predecessors, which was carefully limited to extolling the status quo. Dwight D. Eisenhower had stated his willingness to support independence if the Puerto Ricans opted for it, but only Gerald Ford, as a vacationing lame duck president, had ever expressed support for the statehood movement.

Another sign of subtle but tentative change in American policy appeared last August, when U.N. Ambassador Andrew Young issued a carefully worded statement saying that "the United States would do nothing to stand in the way of a decision by the Puerto Rican people to extend an invitation to the United Nations, the Organization of American States, or other appropriate international bodies to observe a referendum."

By now some of the major Puerto Rican groups that appeared before the United Nations regarded it as the only authoritative and disinterested body capable of guaranteeing the integrity and fairness of any process for political change. This fact was ignored by the officials charged with implementing U.S. policy. Their actions suggested that the Carter and Young statements had no substance beneath them, that American policy on the issue would follow the usual lines. Middle-level officials from the State Department and the National Security Council staff defined the short-range U.S. policy ob-

jective as little more than avoiding the appearance of being soft on Cuba at the United Nations. The longer-range policy objective was to safeguard the congressional appropriation for international organizations from the kind of backlash that followed the U.N. resolution condemning Zionism.

In their zeal not to appear soft on Cuba, U.S. diplomats failed to take the high ground at the United Nations. They discouraged the efforts of several Puerto Rican liberals to build a multiparty consensus on a framework for the projected decolonization process and on the advisability of requesting U.N. observers for the proposed referendum. Indeed, U.S. diplomats approached various Puerto Rican leaders who planned to appear at the United Nations, expressing the hope that they would go home. The tactic failed.

As the Decolonization Committee hearing progressed, it became apparent that the United States did not have the votes to obtain a postponement of action. At that stage the United States urged its surrogates on the committee to work toward a consensus resolution in order to prevent the possibility of a Cuban resolution and a U.S. defeat. But it was already too late, because the various Puerto Rican factions, particularly Hernández Colón's PDP, were openly irritated with U.S. tactics. The Cubans, seeking to avoid a major confrontation with the United States and yet wanting to satisfy their traditional friends in Puerto Rico, scaled down their original resolution and accommodated the interests of the procommonwealth forces, thereby assuring the tacit support or abstention of a number of states. As a result, the Cuban resolution was adopted by a vote of 10 states in favor and none against, with 12 abstentions and two states absent or not participating.[2]

---

[2] *Voting in favor of the Cuban resolution: Afghanistan, Bulgaria, Czechoslovakia, China, Ethiopia, Cuba, Iraq, Syria, Tanzania, and the USSR. Voting against the Cuban resolution: none. Abstaining: Australia, Chile, Fiji, India, Indonesia, Iran, Mali, Sierra Leone, Trinidad, Tunisia, Sweden, and Yugoslavia. Not participating: Congo (Brazzaville). Absent: Ivory Coast.*

If Washington won a victory by preventing a majority vote for the Cuban-sponsored resolution, it was surely a Pyrrhic victory. For by failing to promote discussion about a consensus resolution among Puerto Rican political parties, U.S. diplomats severely aggravated tensions and hostilities among them and possibly set the course for continuing difficulties at the United Nations. During the hectic caucusing at the U.N. meeting, the PDP forces feared that unless they directly and actively defended their plans for the commonwealth, the field would be left to the statehooders and *independentistas*, who might tacitly agree to discredit the commonwealth idea by placing Puerto Rico on the U.N. list of non-self-governing territories. That would have left only statehood or independence as acceptable results of the self-determination process. Thus, the PDP moved to pre-empt any such anticolonial alliance by establishing, instead, an "anti-annexationist" front with the proindependence PSP and its Cuban patrons.

The days when Washington could treat Puerto Rico with benign neglect are over.

At the United Nations it should have been possible to avoid what India's delegate called "the twilight zone of controversial legality" (the question of whether Puerto Rico should be put back on the U.N. list) by building a consensus around the three important new elements in the case: the call by the governor of Puerto Rico for a referendum in 1981; Carter's statement that he would support whatever status the Puerto Ricans might choose in that referendum; and Young's statement that the United States would not object to U.N. observation of the referendum.

Unfortunately, U.S. diplomats were simply unwilling to face the fact that the substance of the controversy is political change —decolonization—in Puerto Rico. Like previous administrations, they regarded the suggestion of decolonization as a stigma to be avoided rather than the key to a major political problem. The State Department preferred to stand behind the precedent of the 1953 U.N. General Assembly decision that eliminated Puerto Rico from its list of non-self-governing territories, despite the fact that U.N. practice has never honored precedent in such an obviously political matter.

American diplomats were unprepared to consider that Carter's pledge to support the outcome of the 1981 plebiscite offered an opportunity to develop an authoritative process for Puerto Ricans to exercise their acknowledged right to self-determination.

A Colonial Office?

U.S. inertia and political misconceptions have been reinforced by the unwillingness of successive administrations to place responsibility for a Puerto Rico policy in any particular federal department, whether concerned with domestic or foreign affairs. The establishment or designation of any such central office might imply the existence of significant problems in Puerto Rico or evoke memories of the old Division of Territories in the Interior Department (the American "colonial office"). As a result, it is difficult, if not impossible, for the U.S. government to react quickly and intelligently to fast-breaking political developments in Puerto Rico or to shape the direction of U.S. relations with the island.

Until now, any government expression of untraditional views on the subject of Puerto Rico's political status has been regarded as a form of U.S. pressure on the Puerto Ricans and therefore a deviation from the principle of self-determination—a principle apparently interpreted only to mean that the United States will be bound in advance to do whatever the Puerto Ricans decide. But whatever the conclusion of Puerto Rico's prolonged identity crisis, it will invariably affect the United States and its relations with the world community.

By defining the question of Puerto Rico's relations with the United States as an entirely Puerto Rican matter, Washington is largely giving up any chance of affecting the outcome in Puerto Rico. More important, the United States is missing an opportunity to help steer the decolonization process in a way that would reassure all political groups that the process is fair to all and valid in the eyes of the world community. Because neither the United Nations nor the United States is now in a position to advise the Puerto Ricans on how to conduct their decolonization process, the rules of the game will be determined by whatever political party holds the reins of power when it takes place. The results of this curious definition of self-determination may be internecine conflict among Puerto Rico's bitterly divided political groups, with unknown domestic and international political repercussions.

That there will be repercussions cannot be doubted. Approximately 2 million Puerto Ricans now live in the northern industrial cities of the United States. As U.S. citizens, they move freely between the island and the mainland, carrying with them the political anxieties of their compatriots at home. Moreover, the February 1980 Democratic presidential primary in Puerto Rico will draw national attention to the island's politics.

The absence of a U.S. political backlash against the Cuban victory at the United Nations was due only to happenstance. The New York City newspaper strike resulted in a virtual blackout of news about the proceedings of the U.N. Decolonization Committee meeting. Next time, there will be no such luck. The Puerto Ricans will be back at the United Nations in August 1979, and probably for every session of the committee until the island's political future is settled.

Jimmy Carter has recognized the possibility of political change in Puerto Rico and, for better or for worse, he has stimulated the forces of change there. Andrew Young has carefully avoided heavy-handed pronounce-ments that the matter falls exclusively within U.S. domestic jurisdiction and has left the door open to a fruitful U.N. role in the determination of Puerto Rico's future. Washington must now deal on a continuing basis with the major domestic and foreign policy problems raised by the need for political change in Puerto Rico. The first order of business is to identify the relevant players in the drama. All of the principals (including the *independentistas*) should be invited to describe the constitutional processes that would meet their individual expectations and to state their concerns about pending proposals. Even if the expectations of some groups seem unreasonable or foolish, it is vital that U.S. policy makers learn directly what these expectations are, if only to be able to comprehend future political maneuvers in Congress or the United Nations.

This straightforward approach would allay the suspicions of some Puerto Rican leaders, especially in the opposition, that only an incumbent Puerto Rican government can hope to have direct official contact with the federal government and that their own chances of being heard are limited to mysterious or clandestine contacts in Washington or to public disruptions there and at home.

In a quite different decolonization context, the British held constitutional conferences in London with representatives of all significant groups in a colony to discuss the process by which the colonial relationship would come to an end. Two basic ground rules governed the British practice: acceptance of the metropolitan state's authority and an effective agreement that the inevitable outcome would be independence. Neither of these applies to the current Puerto Rican situation. Nevertheless, the British experience and common sense recommend that the metropolitan state be well informed and in direct contact with all political groups in the territory.

At the very least, a new central coordinating office in Washington responsible for Puerto Rico could serve as a point of contact and a source of up-to-date information for the federal bureaucracy. But its larger objective should be to meet periodically with Puerto Rico's political leaders and to keep in close enough touch with the Puerto Rican political scene to make informed contingency plans for the decolonization process. The office could sponsor informal discussions about what it will take to make Puerto Rico a state, an independent republic, or an autonomous entity freely associated with the United States. It could also help chart a useful, if limited, role for the United Nations in Puerto Rico.

The United States and Puerto Rico would benefit from the common recognition that political change on the island is inevitable, that it is possible only through electoral processes, and that those processes will be devoid of legitimacy if significant groups repudiate or boycott them. The United States may not be able to point the Puerto Ricans in any particular direction, but it should be ready to identify and reinforce the elements of any consensus that may emerge in Puerto Rico. In the absence of a consensus on the process for decolonization, the possibility for violence in Puerto Rico and on the mainland looms ever larger. Many wary Puerto Ricans—fearing that mainland officials, preoccupied with their other problems, will ineptly handle Puerto Rican policy— have begun to invoke the specter of Belfast.

The days when Washington could treat Puerto Rico with benign neglect are over. U.S. policy makers must now give serious thought to the future of an 80-year-old relationship. If and when they organize to deal with political change on the island, they can expect to receive the blessings of the president, who expressed his sympathy with Puerto Rico's political isolation and powerlessness by telling Puerto Rican friends in 1976 that he understood their concerns because "I am from the deep South, and you are from the deep, deep South."

DATELINE NICARAGUA: THE END OF THE AFFAIR

by Richard R. Fagen

"**W**e will win," said the middle-aged woman standing on a street corner in Managua, "and they," she said, shifting her eyes toward a National Guardsman standing across the street, "will lose." The guardsman, Israeli automatic rifle at the ready, was patrolling a *barrio* (neighborhood) that a few days earlier had been under the control of the Sandinistas and now had been retaken by the National Guard. The modest rows of wood and concrete homes and small stores were pockmarked with bullets. Several had been completely destroyed by the aerial bombardment that preceded the ground attack. Spent 57mm shell casings marked "Made in U.S.A." lay in the gutters—along with discarded U.S. Army combat rations, half-eaten tins of peanut butter and beans and frankfurters. At the next intersection, a pile of corpses still smoldered. As the breeze shifted, people moved to avoid the downwind stench.

It was the middle of June 1979, and what the Sandinista National Liberation Front (FSLN) called the final offensive against the Somoza dynasty and the National Guard had already been under way for several weeks. As the Sandinistas and their supporters were careful to point out, what was happening in Nicaragua was a national insurrection, not a civil war. Fed up with more than four decades of tyrannical and brutal rule, the citizenry had revolted. Inspired but not necessarily directly led by the Sandinistas, thousands of young men and women had taken up whatever arms were at hand. Hundreds of thousands of other Nicaraguans helped in what way they could: by closing their shops and businesses during the general strike of June; by sheltering and supplying the multitude of *muchachos heróicos* (brave boys and girls), as the Sandinista militias are known; or simply by passing information or aiding in the myriad of other tasks necessary to keep the struggle going.

This national insurrection was not, of course, the first expression of the outrage of the Nicaraguan people and of the military and political capabilities of the FSLN. The uprising of September 1978, almost a national mutiny, was in some sense a dress rehearsal for 1979. Then, for three weeks Sandinista regular troops and militias battled the Guard in the provinces. They seized but were

---

"Bullets for breakfast, bullets for lunch, bullets for dinner, and bullets before going to bed."

---

not able to hold four important, middle-sized cities. If nothing else, September proved that Somoza and the Guard were more than willing to launch air attacks against the civilian population, drag young men and women out of their homes and shoot them in the street, and torture and murder persons suspected of belonging to or simply supporting the Sandinista movement. September also demonstrated to the FSLN that to succeed, an insurrection against Anastasio Somoza Debayle and the Guard would have to be countrywide, better armed and equipped, and tactically more sophisticated. Both the dynasty and the Sandinistas realized that the next round would be even bloodier, longer, and more definitive. History has borne them out.

History has also reaffirmed the seemingly infinite capacity of the U.S. government to misread and mismanage the situation. In the aftermath of September, this took the form of an ill-conceived and unsuccessful mediation between Somoza and the more pro-American sectors of the opposition under the auspices of the Organization of American States (OAS). In June 1979 it took the form

of Secretary of State Cyrus Vance's roundly rejected call in the OAS for a peace-keeping force, followed by an extended and byzantine series of attempts to pressure and manipulate the five-person Sandinista-backed provisional government into a regime more compatible with U.S. interests.

Plunder, Exploitation, and Brutality

If the autumn of 1978 and the summer of 1979 were the dress rehearsal and the staging of the final offensive against Somoza, the scripting of the drama goes back to the beginning of this century. In 1912, after three years of unsuccessful attempts by Washington to stabilize Nicaragua by political and diplomatic means after the flight of dictator José Santos Zelaya, the U.S. Marines were landed. At stake were the outstanding loans of U.S. and European creditors, and also the possibility of canal-building rights through southern Nicaragua. The Marines stayed for 13 years, withdrawing only temporarily to return again in 1926 for seven more years. Only in 1933 did the occupying troops finally depart, leaving in their stead the U.S.-created National Guard headed by General Anastasio Somoza García. For the next 46 years the Somoza family never relinquished direct command of the Guard, and seldom gave up the presidency—and then only to hand-picked subordinates. Meanwhile, the Somozas and a close coterie of associates empowered and enriched themselves to an extent considered exceptional even in an area noted for plunder, exploitation, and brutality.

Although the Marines fought for years against nationalist General César Augusto Sandino—after whom today's Sandinistas are named—they were never able fully to defeat his guerrilla army. But with the Marines gone, Somoza García struck an uneasy truce with the insurgent general in 1933. Shortly thereafter, Sandino was assassinated after a dinner of reconciliation with Somoza. For the next 22 years, the senior Somoza ruled Nicaragua as a personal fiefdom, with the Guard as his private army and enforcer and with the continuing support and approval of the United States.

The dynasty expanded. When Somoza García's second son, Anastasio Somoza Debayle (Tacho), graduated from West Point in 1946 as a 20-year-old, he was given an important post in the Guard. Somoza García was assassinated in 1956, and his eldest son Luís moved immediately into the presidency while Tacho stayed on as commander of the Guard. By 1967 Tacho had added president of the republic to his list of offices. Shortly thereafter, Luis died of natural causes. In best family fashion, Tacho subsequently appointed his son, Anastasio Somoza Portocarrero, commander of the Guard's elite training facility and assault brigade.

From the outset, the dynasty was welcomed in Washington as a solid pillar of pro-American and anticommunist strength in an otherwise troubled area. In 1954 Nicaragua was the main staging ground for the Central Intelligence Agency-sponsored invasion that overthrew the left-Nationalist government of President Jacobo Arbenz Guzmán in Guatemala. In 1961 the Somozas played a similar role in the staging of the CIA-organized Bay of Pigs invasion of Cuba. Nicaraguan troops participated in the U.S. occupation of the Dominican Republic in 1965, and the Somozas even offered to send the Guard to fight communism in the Far East, first in Korea and later in Vietnam. (Their offers were declined.)

Until the early 1970s, through Republican and Democratic administrations alike, the Washington-Managua alliance seemed unshakable. But cracks were opened after the earthquake that leveled much of central Managua in 1972. The Somoza family turned the nation's disaster to its own advantage by siphoning off relief funds and speculating in land and commercial properties, thus eroding much of its legitimacy with the Nicaraguan middle class and private sector. Although this was not yet evident to Washington, the domestic bases of support for the dynasty were beginning to crumble just as surely as the foundations of Managua's buildings had

crumbled when the earthquake's first tremors hit.

So close was the identification of Washington's interests with the continued rule of the Somozas, however, that little actually changed in the U.S. posture toward Nicaragua until the Carter administration took office. Aware that support for the dictator had been eroding among the Nicaraguan middle class and private sector, and hoist on Carter's campaign pledges to introduce human rights considerations into foreign policy decisions, Democratic policy makers acknowledged that some changes in the Nicaraguan situation were inevitable. On the other hand, the new administration also feared any alternative to Somoza that would not be firmly controlled by the most conservative of the anti-Somoza forces. Meanwhile, Somoza's powerful friends in the U.S. Congress and elsewhere were doing everything in their power—in the name of anticommunism and hemispheric stability—to insure that the four-decades-old policy of U.S. support for the dynasty continued. The now familiar confrontation between human rights rhetoric and the ideology and geopolitics of the Cold War entered early into the late 1970s debate on Nicaragua.

State of Siege

What gave bite to Washington's Cold War fears, of course, was the increasing importance of the Sandinista movement in the anti-Somoza struggle. Founded in 1962 as an anti-imperialist, revolutionary organization dedicated to overthrowing Somoza, the FSLN had only limited popular support and won no significant military victories during the first five years of its existence. It then turned its activities more to political work and the rural sector. It was not until 1974 that the FSLN again made headlines outside of Nicaragua when it took 12 members of Somoza's inner circle hostage at a Christmas party and exchanged them for 14 political prisoners. A state of siege was imposed by Somoza, repression increased, and the battle was joined in both city and countryside, although still only intermittently.

Even after the audacious Christmas assault, the Sandinistas still did not have widespread popular support. In fact, in 1975, in an acerbic internal debate over tactics, the FSLN split into two tendencies: The "Prolonged Popular War" tendency believed in the necessity of extensive political work, especially in rural areas; the "Proletarian Tendency" emphasized linkages to the urban working class. By 1976, a third tendency, known as *"Insurreccionistas"* or simply as *Terceristas* ("the third ones"), had emerged. The Insurrectionists were instrumental in forging links between the FSLN and middle class and business groups, and their leadership and statements tended to reflect social democratic ideas as opposed to the more Marxist orientations of the other two.

Only in 1977 did the situation begin to change. A group known as the Twelve was formed. Composed of influential businessmen, clergy, and intellectuals, it called openly for Nicaraguans to join the armed struggle to force Somoza's resignation. In October, responding in part to pressure from the United States, Somoza lifted martial law and censorship for the first time in three years. There was an immediate response: labor unrest, student demonstrations, a wave of disclosures in the local press, and armed attacks by the FSLN against several provincial towns.

Clearly alarmed by the escalation of armed activity in Nicaragua, the Carter administration redoubled its efforts to find a political solution dominated by persons it considered to be acceptable moderates. Key to this hope was Pedro Joaquín Chamorro, the editor and publisher of the opposition newspaper *La Prensa* and a long-time power in the Conservative party (the legal opposition party to Somoza's captive Liberal party). As founder of the Union for Democratic Liberation (UDEL), a political group encompassing a relatively wide spectrum of Nicaraguan opinion, Chamorro was firmly committed to a political strategy for getting rid of Somoza.

In January 1978, however, Chamorro was assassinated. Tens of thousands of Nicaraguans took to the streets to protest his murder, and within days a general strike and lock-out called by UDEL largely paralyzed the capital and other major cities. Again the Sandinistas struck, attacking National Guard garrisons, and again the dynasty's repression was fierce.

In May 1978 a centrist umbrella organization known as the Broad Opposition Front (FAO) was formed. Initially it included UDEL, the Twelve, business groups, various labor organizations, and traditional opposition parties. But yet again these Washington-backed sectors of the opposition lost the initiative when, on August 22, the Insurrectionists attacked and captured the National Palace while Somoza's rubber-stamp congress was in session. Exchanging their hostages for 59 colleagues in Somoza's jails, the Sandinistas staged a triumphal march to the airport through streets lined by thousands of cheering Nicaraguans. Another general strike ensued, and on September 9 the Sandinistas launched new attacks on National Guard garrisons in five provincial cities.

The events and the aftermath of that bloody September are well known: Thousands of young people, armed with pistols, small caliber rifles, and shotguns joined the regular Sandinista troops. The rebels captured four cities. The counterattacks by the Guard were swift, brutal, and eventually successful—at least militarily. Cities were bombed, civilians killed by the thousands, and young people executed by the hundreds. In Nicaragua, and in much of the rest of the hemisphere as well, there was an upwelling of revulsion against Somoza and the Guard.

The Carter administration's dilemmas were increased rather than diminished by the events of September. Overt support for Somoza was no longer a viable policy, especially after the Inter-American Commission on Human Rights published a strong condemnatory report on the actions of the Guard and the Somoza regime. As more and more sectors of the Nicaraguan opposition turned pro-Sandinista in the context of profound hatred of Somoza, the centrist, electoral, non-Sandinista solution so favored by the Carter administration became more difficult to find.

But this was not for lack of trying. Under the auspices of the OAS, a team composed of representatives from the Dominican Republic and Guatemala as well as William Bowdler, director of the State Department Bureau of Intelligence and Research, met for many weeks at the end of 1978 and the beginning of 1979 with Somoza and the opposition, represented by the FAO. The U.S. goal was to stitch together a solution to the Nicaraguan crisis that for all practical purposes excluded

The White House and intelligence agencies conducted a desperate search for a Cuba-Sandinista connection.

the Sandinistas. But Somoza ultimately rejected the national plebiscite that was proposed. The United States then tried to lever the FAO into accepting a compromise solution more acceptable to Somoza. Thoroughly disgusted, some of the FAO representatives walked out in protest.

The failure of the mediation was the overture to the June insurrection. Even while the mediation was in progress, the Sandinista-supported United People's Movement (MPU), composed of more than 20 student, labor, and neighborhood organizations, announced a decidedly conciliatory 12-point program for a post-Somoza Nicaragua. It included provisions for a substantial private sector in a reformed economy and guarantees of individual and political liberties. Then, during the first week in March, the three Sandinista tendencies—all of which had endorsed the MPU program—announced that they had agreed on a unified military command and strategy. By April there was fighting in the northern city of Estelí and elsewhere. During May, clashes between the Guard and the Sandinis-

tas were everyday occurrences. On June 4 the the general strike began.

Practically all commercial and professional activity in the country ground to a halt. Within days, *barrios* from one end of Managua to the other were in arms, sometimes fully under the control of the *muchachos*, at other times left in smoking ruins by the ground and air attacks of the National Guard. "We've had weeks of bullets," said an old man in Managua. "Bullets for breakfast, bullets for lunch, bullets for dinner, and bullets before going to bed. But after they bomb you, bullets mean nothing."

Yet under this rain of bullets and bombs, beginning in September of 1978 and continuing through the summer of 1979, an unprecedented alliance had been forged: Well-armed and well-trained Sandinista regulars, perhaps numbering no more than 2,000, had been joined by thousands of young men and women loosely organized into militias. These combatants were backed by hundreds of thousands of ordinary citizens in the cities and countryside and supported at least rhetorically by every important opposition group in the country. There had been nothing like it in the history of Nicaragua and few similar events in the entire history of the continent. The national insurrection against *Somocismo* (Somozaism) was a reality. Within a few weeks León, the largest city after Managua, was fully in Sandinista hands, as were a number of other important provincial towns. A well-equipped Sandinista column had entered southern Nicaragua from neighboring Costa Rica, and for the first time the possibility of a Sandinista military victory was being mentioned by otherwise cautious observers.

Crude Stratagems

It was in this context of massive insurrectional activity, significant military achievement by the Sandinistas, and brutal attacks by the National Guard that the OAS met in Washington during the third week in June. The almost unanimous rejection of Vance's proposals for a cease-fire and a peace-keeping force suggested how out of touch Washington was with Latin American positions on Nicaragua. Meanwhile, in an attempt to placate conservative opinion at home and to justify diplomatic and perhaps even military intervention, the White House and intelligence agencies conducted a desperate search for a Cuba-Sandinista connection. Hardliners in the Carter administration, particularly on the National Security Council staff, harbored the hope that if other sectors of U.S. and international opinion could be convinced that Cuba was supplying the Sandinistas with both arms and advisers—perhaps even combat troops—they would come to support much tougher measures against the Sandinistas.

But all of these maneuverings failed, and Washington was faced with the reality of a Sandinista-backed provisional government that to most other observers appeared quite moderate in both membership and program. Composed of Violeta Chamorro of the Conservative party (widow of the martyred *La Prensa* publisher), Alfonso Robelo of the FAO, Sergio Ramírez of the Twelve, Moisés Hassán of the MPU, and Daniel Ortega of the Insurrectionist tendency of the Sandinistas, the provisional government immediately received the stamp of approval from all important opposition forces in Nicaragua and increasingly won support from anti-Somoza governments in the hemisphere and elsewhere. However, three of its members were quickly labeled radicals or Marxists by the Carter administration, and a frenzied effort followed in late June and July to undercut the five-person junta. At first this was attempted by proposing negotiations between an interim government named by the Nicaraguan Congress and the already-named provisional group. When all sectors of the opposition rejected that plan, the United States tried to modify the provisional government directly through the addition of several more conservative members. This too was unanimously rejected by the Nicaraguan opposition.

As each crude strategem was revealed and then abandoned, impatience and hostility toward the United States mounted both inside and outside Nicaragua. In June the question on everyone's lips in Managua was, "Why doesn't the Carter administration break relations with Somoza now that it has admitted he has to go?" In July, when the administration tried—with some success—to enlist the aid of Venezuela, Costa Rica, and Panama in its machinations and then threatened to withhold support for reconstruction unless certain conditions were met, Reverend Miguel D'Escoto, the provisional government's foreign minister-designate, exploded in anger: "The only way to characterize this is blackmail. . . . They're trying to bargain with the blood of our people."

Twisted Perceptions

Explanations of the unerring capacity of the U.S. government to be months and even years late in recognizing Nicaraguan realities—and Washington's consistently applied pressure for the most conservative and ultimately unworkable solutions—seem at first glance rather obvious: Cold War perspectives coupled with the presence of Marxists in the Sandinista movement congealed into a pervasive fear of an other-than-pro-U.S. post-Somoza regime—a "second Cuba," in the words of the more intemperate. A beleaguered and unpopular president, despite often expressed concerns about human rights in foreign policy, was not about to take risks that might lead to further accusations of weakness in the face of communism, of losing Nicaragua. Geostrategic fears of Central American dominoes—or at least substantially increased pressure on neighboring dictatorships should Somoza fall—worried national security planners.

Forty-five years of official support for the Guard and the dynasty left deeply worn grooves in military and diplomatic bureaucracies and perspectives. A powerful web of congressional friends and right-wingers outside the Congress gave Somoza a Washington lobby enjoyed by few other tyrants. When all of these feelings and forces are interrelated and set against the background of more than a century of U.S. hegemony, intervention, and gunboat diplomacy in the Caribbean basin, the American actions seem understandable and predictable, if not forgivable.

But there is an additional, less obvious explanation for the Carter administration's inability to see the handwriting on the wall in Nicaragua—and elsewhere. Washington seems incapable of understanding the nature and implications of a popular insurrection against tyranny, its partly spontaneous, organic, and nonelitist character. Even after Iran, whenever rebellion breaks out anywhere, Washington sees disorder, chaos, and uncertainty—opportunities for the Communists. What is neither perceived nor understood is the logic of the insurrection, its mass character, its essential legitimacy, its order and architecture expressed in the willingness of tens of thousands to persevere, suffer, and die if necessary.

This failure to understand is total. At the height of the June insurrection, a high White House official said that the National Guard had to be retained in order to "preserve order," to "prevent anarchy." At the very moment he was speaking, the Guard was looting shops and businesses, bombing civilians, and executing unarmed young men and women in the streets. A national security bureaucracy that could still claim in the summer of 1979 that the Guard was essential to order in Nicaragua was not simply stupid or ill-informed. On the contrary, it was and remains an apparatus so twisted in its perceptions of reality as to be incapable of understanding the nature of the tyranny; the fusion of Sandinistas, ordinary Nicaraguans, and even the business and commercial sectors; and the massive insurrection that had resulted.

To have opposed and tried to disrupt this process of fusion—as the Carter administration did—must therefore be seen as a profoundly interventionist and self-defeating

policy. Wisdom, real concern for the people of Nicaragua, and even self-interest would have dictated an acknowledgment not only of the necessity to end Somoza's rule, but also of the need to accept and work with the political alliance created by the insurrection process itself. One of the most grotesque aspects of the U.S. reaction was that it took the televised execution of an American newsman, Bill Stewart of ABC, to jolt the White House into a new attitude.

The Sandinista movement—the provisional government, its program, its cabinet, the popular support one senses in the *barrios* —are all legitimate and representative expressions of the revolt of the Nicaraguan people

> **Washington seems incapable of understanding the nature and implications of a popular insurrection against tyranny.**

against the dynasty. Washington talked the language of representation and democracy but was unwilling to accept as legitimate the politics that were springing from the still-smoking ruins of decades of dictatorship.

In setting itself against these political forces and forms, the administration only succeeded in tarnishing its own less-than-sparkling reputation among democrats in Latin America, angering vast sectors of the Nicaraguan population, prolonging the bloodshed, possibly moving the center of political gravity in post-Somoza Nicaragua to the left, raising the costs of reconstruction, and further confirming suspicions that it—like all of its predecessors—is not ready to allow Latin Americans to solve their own problems.

Now that Somoza and a significant portion of his most culpable friends, collaborators, and relations are safely ensconced in the United States with their plundered millions, one hopes that Washington has learned at least a modest lesson: A people that fought for two decades against the Marines, and then for 46 years against the Somozas will not easily allow its future to be stamped "Made in U.S.A." Of course, the meddling can continue. American power makes that possible, as does Washington's continuing arrogance. But it is to be hoped that the power will now be otherwise used and the arrogance substantially checked.

More specifically, what does it mean to be both supportive and noninterventionist in post-Somoza Nicaragua? At a minimum, it means continuing and extending the nascent policy of correct diplomatic and political relations with the Nicaraguan Government of National Reconstruction. In the last few moments of Somoza's rule, when Washington realized that the FSLN was only weeks or perhaps days away from a military victory, the negotiated departure of Somoza and the peaceful installation of the provisional government suddenly became official policy. This path had clearly become, in the administration's eyes, the lesser of two evils.

Now it is crucial to transform the grudging and dearly won acceptance of the new government into something more substantial. Aid for reconstruction, in all of its forms, will be the short-run litmus test of this acceptance—not only emergency and humanitarian aid to help feed, shelter, and care for refugees and others, but also generosity of intent and action in lending institutions and political forums both at home and abroad. Ironically, the Sandinista victory has given the United States yet another chance in Nicaragua. Can this kind of support be given without imposing political and economic conditions that violate Nicaraguan sovereignty? Can the decades-old attempts to shape Nicaraguan outcomes be contained? If the old ways continue, there is little to be gained and much to lose. Not the least of the victims will be the last shreds of the administration's credibility as the defender of human rights and democracy in Latin America. More important will be the continuing victimization of more than 2 million Nicaraguans who now need peace, time, resources, and understanding as they strive to rebuild their shattered country.

DATELINE PERU: A SAGGING REVOLUTION

by Abraham F. Lowenthal

Revolutions are more often proclaimed than carried out, especially in Latin America. While profound transformations are taking place in countries as different as Iran, Nicaragua, Angola, and Zimbabwe, what has happened to Peru's once heralded revolution of 1968? Although the Peruvian experiment has suffered major disappointments, some fascinating shifts have occurred—shifts that may open the way to more substantial changes in the 1980s.

Almost 12 years—three presidential terms in Washington—have passed since Peru's armed forces surrounded the National Palace in Lima with tanks and ushered President Fernando Belaúnde Terry to the airport. Army General Juan Velasco Alvarado and his colleagues in khaki announced their intent then to transform Peru's basic economic and social structures, to end external domination (especially by the United States), to seek a third path to development that was neither capitalist nor communist, and even to change national values. They would create a "new Peruvian man," one dedicated to "solidarity, not individualism."

Skeptics who considered the Peruvian military's earnest rhetoric as just another empty pronouncement were soon jolted. Within a week Peru had expropriated the International Petroleum Co. (IPC), an Exxon subsidiary long prominent in the country's politics, whose legal status was high on the agenda of U.S.-Peruvian relations. Within a year the regime had decreed a sweeping agrarian reform, which redistributed not only the small amount of land held by the peasants but also the rich sugar and cotton estates along the coast and the vast *latifundia* of the highlands.

With a burst of laws and regulations, the Peruvian military undertook to reform production and distribution, labor-management relations, the role of foreign enterprise in Peru's economy, the state's role in the economy and the media, and the nation's international relationships. Special emphasis was given to moving the economy steadily away from capitalist principles toward a quasi-socialist model. A new "social property" sector of worker-managed firms was intended to become the predominant mode of economic organization. An "industrial community" was created in privately owned firms, a reform that would give workers an increased stake in corporate profits and a say in management. An ambitious educational reform promised to attack class and ethnic divisions in a country where more than half the population in six highland provinces still did not speak Spanish when the 1961 census was taken.

The educational reform and the state-controlled media would promote the country's new social values: cooperation, not competition; social conscience, not selfishness; and renewed national pride. The military government launched a new agency—the National System to Support Social Mobilization (SINAMOS)—with full fanfare to mobilize the previously nonparticipant sectors of Peru's fragmented society, to raise popular consciousness, and to channel the resulting energies into the national political process. And Peru became a major participant in various international forums, taking the leading role particularly on new international economic order issues.

Not surprisingly, the new Peruvian man is nowhere to be found in Lima today. The military regime will more likely be remembered in a generation for having extended the superhighway from Lima all the way to the beach, thus facilitating its use by the middle class, than for profoundly reshaping Peru's values. *Limeños* from the upper class still enjoy the bullfights at Acho, and those from the lower classes still trudge along in the colorful procession of the Señor de los Milagros. All are much more moved by such old traditions than by the new social relationships or concepts of property Peru's military and civilian ideologues tried vigorously but vainly to introduce. The social property sector has all but disappeared. The industrial community reform has been eviscerated. SINAMOS has been scuttled with little more than a whisper of protest. Lima's upper-crust private schools have survived the educational reform almost intact. The traditional parties that dominated Peru's politics before 1968 persist today, with their leadership and their programs mainly unchanged. New parties, new leaders, and new concepts are hard to discover. And Peru's international profile has receded almost to invisibility.

Discredited and Disdained

As should have been expected, 12 years of military rule have done little to alter Peru's underlying realities. The country remains largely unintegrated ethnically and even geographically, its terrain dramatically punctuated by the Andes and the Amazon. Its economy continues to depend largely on the export of mineral and agricultural products. Income distribution has not been radically affected: Studies show that almost all the redistribution has occurred within the wealthiest quarter of the population.

Peru is still an overwhelmingly poor country, although a few families are impressively rich. As one intellectual pointed out after the devastating 1970 earthquake, which took some 70,000 lives, many highland Peruvians live every day the realities outsiders seem to notice only after a natural disaster: makeshift housing, inadequate food, no schools, no potable water, no access to medical care, and utter isolation. The revolution has not much changed any of these grim facts. Indeed, Lima seems poorer than it was 10 years ago. Beggars and pitiful street merchants are now a much more common sight. Visual impressions are supported by evidence that tuberculosis and other diseases are on the increase, that infant mortality is climbing, and that the overall rate of per capita economic growth in the past decade has been negative.

External debt and inflation expanded much faster than production or exports, and Peru found its economy in a shambles by the late 1970s. The steps taken by the military to restore economic health—drastic efforts to reduce government spending, incentives to increase the export of products in sectors where Peru has a comparative advantage, attempts to curb inflation and to cut down on external borrowing—have led not only to the pains of retrenchment but also to the reinforcement of the historic structure of Peru's economy.

What has changed in Peru, and remarkably so, is the structure and distribution of power. The traditional landed families and their financial institutions have lost almost all their influence. Individuals who have had the agility to retain wealth and prominence are rare. Most of Peru's former oligarchs have fallen from unquestioned authority to oblivion or even ignominy. Precisely those Peruvians whom every foreign reporter necessarily contacted 15 years ago are now out of touch.

The major newspapers—*La Prensa* and *El Comercio*—that set the agenda and established the limits of debate in Peru for years have been destroyed by a combination of government expropriation, intimidation, and intervention. No major newspaper has replaced them. Radio and television, also taken over by the state, contribute precious little to public information. Rags, tabloids, and weekly news magazines have sprouted, but periodic government crackdowns prevent them from printing anything controversial. No publication successfully defines issues for discussion in Peru today.

The Catholic church, once very influential in Peru, is now barely visible. Its early identification with the military government and the emergence of militant liberation theology priests, sympathetic to the revolutionary left but distrusted by the church hierarchy and many of the faithful, have hurt its reputation and unity. As a result, the church in Peru today is quiet, careful, and without much force.

The presence and influence of the United States—both of the American embassy and of U.S. corporations and other institutions—are sharply reduced from the levels of 1968. Marcona, Cerro de Pasco, Grace, and International Telephone and Telegraph have all more or less gone the way of IPC. Other corporations, such as Chrysler, have been driven out by tough competition. The Ford Foundation, once influential in Peruvian university circles, has seen its office shrink and its budget dwindle. Few of the major development projects in the country involve the U.S. Agency for International Development; the Soviets, the West Germans, the Japanese, and even the Spanish, the Swiss, and the Swedes are more visible. The Soviet, West German, and Cuban embassies are more active in cultural affairs than the U.S. International Communication Agency. Cuban and Soviet airlines now serve Lima's splendid but desultory airport.

More important, the USSR is now Peru's major source for tanks and other weapons. From the 1940s through the 1960s, the United States enjoyed overwhelming influence in all aspects of Peru's politics and economy; by now it is an important but not exclusive external actor in Peru, much as it was before World War II. In a recent year, Peruvian trade with both the European Economic Community countries and with those of the Council for Mutual Economic Assistance was as large as that with the United States. This represented a striking change from the days when the United States dominated Peru's commerce. This relative drop of American influence is part of a general region-wide (if not universal) decline of U.S. political and economic hegemony, but Peru's rulers no doubt consciously speeded the process.

The Peruvian armed forces are the source

of governmental authority at the national and provincial levels. But the military is now discredited, widely disdained, and audibly accused of corruption and incompetence. Peru's officer corps is generally on the defensive, apparently eager to use the scheduled 1980 elections to escape from office and return to the barracks. Peruvians of all stripes who used to predict that the military would rule for a generation now expect a civilian government within a year.

The traditional political parties have survived, but they lack dynamism and authority. No party appears to be able to project a vision of Peru in the 1980s that excites the country's imagination as Belaúnde's did in the early 1960s. It used to be said by the party faithful that only the American Popular Revolutionary Alliance (APRA)—Peru's oldest and largest party, founded in the 1920s by Victor Raúl Haya de la Torre—could save Peru. Others, no doubt, thought that only the army could muster the clout to reform Peru or that only the revolutionary left could force real change. Now it seems that no party or institution has the confidence to reshape the country. It is plagued by a vacuum of legitimacy and authority, if not of power. Ironically, the chief electoral beneficiaries of the past 12 years of military rule appear to be APRA, Belaúnde and his supporters, and some guerrilla leaders of the early 1960s—the principal targets of the army's hostility in 1968.

Repositories of Power

Where has all the power gone? In part, it has gone to a new group of entrepreneurs who have made a great deal of money during the past 10 years, mainly in import substitution industries and in mining. Whole new fortunes have been created from the sharp rise in the price of silver, for example. New "first families"—nationally oriented, aggressive, and conspicuous—have emerged in Lima. These families lack the social prestige and the political connections of the traditional upper class, but they are beginning to express themselves politically through the media and special interest associations.

In part, power has gravitated to the extensive technocracy that has emerged as a result of the explosion of the state's role in Peru's economy. Hundreds of technocrats—military and civilian—now play a crucial role in managing the economy. Before 1968 the state's share of national investment was probably lower in Peru than in any comparable South American country. Taxes were collected by private banks that actually charged the government for the use of its own revenue. Planning was anathema, and state enterprises were avoided. All that has changed. Not only do investment and production figures reflect the state's importance, but the vast Peruvian public bureaucracy occupies building after building in Lima: Petroperu, Pescaperu, Mineroperu, Centromin-Peru, Electroperu, the sugar cooperatives, and so on. The reach of the state into various parts of daily life is now much more insistent and effective, if sometimes disruptive and often ineffectual.

However Peru's politics evolves in the next decade, the requirements of the national and the international economy will probably cause the new technocracy to retain and even expand its influence. An interesting question is whether APRA, the perennial party out of power for the last 40 years, would be willing and able, if it finally won power, to engage the loyalties and skills of the technocrats, or whether it would insist on parceling out government jobs to the party faithful.

A third source of power—and one of expanding significance—is the increasingly mobilized populace. Trade unions, although still heavily influenced by the parties, are far stronger than they were in the 1960s, despite efforts by the regime to weaken them. *Campesinos* lack a well-articulated structure, but their participation in and influence upon the national political process is greater than ever before in Peru's history. Industrial unions have been gaining sharply in membership, political strength, and militancy. The teachers' union almost brought the country to a standstill in 1978. Major strikes, demonstrations, and outbursts of violence have occurred frequently since February 1975. Many of these begin in the outlying provinces, some of them apparently quite spontaneously, suggesting that there is an antiestablishment constituency ready to be more fully mobilized.

Part of this potential, at least, made itself felt in the 1978 elections for the constituent assembly in which five leftist parties received over 31 per cent of the vote. This was an astonishing gain over the 6 per cent the various leftist parties registered in 1962 and the trivial backing they appeared to have before the election scheduled for 1969. Hugo Blanco, an almost legendary radical peasant leader, alone accounted for over a third of the leftist tally, a display less of personal charisma than of widespread disaffection with the established parties. Class tensions have heightened considerably in Peru during the past few years; even the aborted reforms have contributed to radicalizing important elements of Peru's society by raising consciousness and expectations.

The fourth significant repository of power in Peru, not new at all, is external to the country—the private and official international financial community. The disappearance for a time of the anchovy; the thwarted hopes of discovering large amounts of petroleum; the international recession; and misjudgments of various kinds—such as the decision to build a major pipeline across the Andes before determining how much oil it would actually carry —conspired severely to upset Peru's foreign exchange balance during the 1970s.

By the end of the decade most of the country's export receipts were being used to service the debt. The result—pressure on Peru from the private commercial banks and from the International Monetary Fund to introduce austerity and to balance the accounts—has sharply reduced Peru's room to maneuver. Ironically, a regime that began with a serious determination to reduce Peru's dependence on foreign countries and institutions, now presides over a country apparently further than ever from autonomy. If the prices of copper, cotton, iron, and sugar climb, Peru's economy will boom in the 1980s. If a large expansion occurs in the first years after civilian politicians return to power, democratic politics will surely be reinforced. If, on the other hand, prices for Peru's exports fall, painful austerity measures and sharp political repression can be expected. How Peru's economy and politics evolve depends more than ever on matters beyond Lima's control.

Despite America's declining presence in Peru, U.S. government policies can still influence the country's future. Whether or not the United States and Peru's other creditors are flexible about rescheduling the Peruvian debt will ease or exacerbate its adjustment pains. How the United States reacts to a wide range of international economic order issues will help determine the country's prospects for economic development. The same applies to American domestic economic policies, which will significantly affect the level of demand for Peru's exports in Western industrialized countries. Finally, the extent to which Washington continues to pursue its human rights policies will have a strong impact on the country's political future, particularly as the 1980 elections approach.

The ultimate result of Peru's experiment will not be known for several years. The combination of an increasingly mobilized populace, burgeoning leftist parties, severely weakened sources of established power and legitimacy, external obstacles—both real and imaginary—to national development, and the now much stronger central government is bound to be volatile in the years to come. What will result in the 1980s cannot be predicted, but it can be said that the chances for violent swings to the left or to the right are much greater than they were a decade ago. Peru's generals and colonels may not have achieved a successful revolution, but it may yet turn out that they have made one possible.

CENTRAL AMERICAN PARALYSIS

by Richard Millett

U.S. efforts to respond to revolutionary change in Central America resemble those of a fire brigade during the London blitz. American officials rush frantically from place to place, trying to contain the damage and save what they can of existing structures. But they seem unable to deal with the basic sources of their troubles. Problems abound: an incipient civil war in El Salvador, a flailing economy and a Marxist-influenced government in Nicaragua, increased political violence in Guatemala, and lagging economic and political development in Honduras and Costa Rica. To forge a policy capable of dealing with Central America, the United States must drastically revise its approach to the region.

When Jimmy Carter took office, any suggestion that Central American affairs would emerge as the primary U.S. policy concern in Latin America would have seemed absurd. Since the 1954 Central Intelligence Agency-sponsored overthrow of Guatemala's left-leaning government, the United States has largely ignored Central America. The important canal treaty negotiations with Panama received some attention, but Panama has few historic ties with Central America, and the State Department does not group Panamanian relations with Central American affairs.

The Office of Inter-American Affairs was in fact a State Department backwater, usually manned by undistinguished individuals with little, if any, experience in the area. Political upheavals, such as the 1969 Honduran-Salvadorian war, or natural disasters, such as the Nicaraguan and Guatemalan earthquakes, invoked occasional flurries of activity. But for the most part, U.S.-Central American relations were simple and controlled. If any region could have been safely ignored by the United States in early 1977, it was probably Central America.

Both economic and political realities supported this assumption. With underdeveloped, basically agricultural economies, the five small countries and their 20 million inhabitants hardly threatened U.S. interests. The total area of Central America is just over 163,000 square miles; the republics range in size from Nicaragua (57,200 square miles, about the size of Iowa) to El Salvador (8,100 square miles, just larger than New Jersey). Guatemala has the largest population (6.9 million), followed by El Salvador (4.5 million), Honduras (3.6 million), Nicaragua (2.6 million), and Costa Rica (2.2 million).

The republics are poor relative to the United States: Costa Rica, the most prosperous of the Central American states, had a gross domestic product (GDP) per capita estimated at only $1,540 in 1978; Honduras, with a 1978 GDP of $480 per capita, was the poorest. The prime exports of Central America—cotton, coffee, bananas, and meat—could be easily obtained elsewhere. The Panama Canal's declining importance to U.S. policy and scheduled transfer to Panama diminish the area's strategic significance.

Central American politics were equally unobtrusive. In the three northern republics—Honduras, Guatemala, and El Salvador—pro-Western military dominated the governments; in Nicaragua a 40-year-old family dynasty seemed firmly entrenched; and in Costa Rica, which had no army, democracy seemed to be flourishing. All five nations usually supported the United States in international forums. None had formal relations with Cuba or China. Only Costa Rica, after long debate, had established diplomatic relations with the Soviet Union.

The American Proconsul

While the United States gave low priority to Central American affairs, Central American leaders devoted much of their energy to predicting, interpreting, and adapting to U.S. goals and interests. This subordination placed American ambassadors in the region in a very special and, at times, awkward position. Their traditional role was described in a 1927 State Department memorandum by then Under Secretary of State Robert Olds:

> Our ministers accredited to the five little republics, stretching from the Mexican border to Panama . . . have been advisers whose advice has been accepted virtually as law in the capitals where they respectively reside. . . . We do control the destinies of Central America and we do so for the simple reason that the national interest absolutely dictates such a course. . . . Until now Central America has always understood that governments which we recognize and support stay in power, while those we do not recognize and support fall.

Dr. Mauricio Solaun, U.S. ambassador to Nicaragua from 1977 to 1979, found that Nicaraguans, at least, partially retained this perspective, with the army even "saluting the American ambassador as if he were a proconsul." Ironically, it was in Nicaragua that the U.S. loss of power in Central America first became evident.

Shortly after taking office, Carter pressured the regime of Nicaraguan dictator Anastasio Somoza Debayle and the military governments of El Salvador and Guatemala for improvements in human rights and expansion of political freedoms. In El Salvador and Guatemala, the most visible result was the angry cancellation of military assistance pacts with the United States. Somoza responded with cosmetic changes that elicited a complimentary letter from Carter in summer 1978; but when revolution broke out, Somoza abandoned all pretense of reform and returned to brute force to maintain his dictatorship.

To the surprise of virtually every politician and military officer in Central America, Somoza defied subsequent U.S. pressure to give up the presidency. Unwilling to resort to force, U.S. policy drifted for several months while Venezuela, Panama, and Costa Rica increased their support for the revolutionary Sandinistas.

The extent to which the United States had lost control over Central America became evident when the Sandinistas began their final offensive in late spring 1979. Not a single Central American nation supported the Carter administration's proposal for sending an inter-American peace force to Nicaragua. When the United States then approved an Organization of American States resolution calling for the replacement of Somoza with a totally new government, only Costa Rica, among the Central American republics, voted with the United States.

Many Central American moderates feel that the United States takes their problems seriously only when they begin killing one another in the streets.

By mid-July 1979, when Somoza fled to Miami and control of the nation passed to the Marxist-influenced Sandinista Liberation Front, old patterns of U.S.-Nicaraguan relations—and therefore U.S.-Central American relations—were destroyed. The heritage of U.S. supremacy collapsed with Somoza.

Nicaragua—once a kingpin of American operations in Central America—was now warmly disposed toward Cuba, deeply suspicious of the United States, and committed to radical change at home and a nonaligned position abroad. Within Central America, the Sandinista triumph frightened conservatives, who in turn directed sharp expressions of anger at the Carter administration. Facing growing, increasingly violent opposition from the left, military governments in El Salvador and Guatemala feared that Nicaragua would provide inspiration and arms to revolutionary groups at home. Honduras, where thousands of Somoza's troops had fled for refuge, faced the possibility of serious clashes along its long, poorly defended border with Nicaragua. Increased conflict seemed certain in Central America. The State Department was forced to begin developing a new policy in the midst of spreading turmoil.

Lost Credibility

At this point, U.S. influence in Central America was at its lowest level in this century. Carter's human rights policy and his refusal to intervene to prevent a Sandinista victory confused and alienated much of the right, including the military, but failed to diminish the suspicions and hostility of the left. Moderate reformists, such as Christian Democratic and Social Democratic parties, appeared to be losing ground as forces became increasingly polarized. Decimation of their leadership by ultrarightist hit squads further compounded their problems.

Inability to control violence and contain Marxist influence in a region only two hours flying time from Miami contributed to an image of U.S. weakness in dealing with Central America in particular and the Third World in general. While most U.S. officials involved with Latin America policy recognized the urgency of formulating an effective program for Central America, their ability to do so had been consistently constrained by domestic and foreign political realities. There was no quick or cheap way to overcome 25 years of neglect or to restore the credibility lost during the Nicaraguan crisis. High-level administrative attention to the region was easily diverted by problems in areas of greater strategic significance, such as the Persian Gulf; and the willingness of Congress to appropriate significant funds for any effort in Central America was questionable at best.

In formulating a response to Central America's new political environment, the Carter administration had three basic options. It could decide that the costs of attempting to reverse the revolutionary process so outweighed the region's actual worth that the United States should withdraw and, at least for the present, allow events to run their course. Fear of domestic political consequences should a second or third Cuba emerge miti-

gated strongly against this option. Or, the United States could help prop up existing governments with military assistance and support. This would mean abandoning the human rights content of Latin America policy and would require isolating and perhaps even trying to reverse the revolutionary process in Nicaragua. A possible upshot would be U.S. military intervention.

The final option was to promote and identify with the process of basic change within the region, hoping at the same time to preserve a fair degree of political and economic pluralism. While discarding the traditional client-state approach to Central America, this option would actively seek to restore a modicum of U.S. influence and insure that none of the republics became dependent upon nations hostile to U.S. interests.

With little public debate, the Carter administration apparently chose the last option. Then Assistant Secretary of State for Inter-American Affairs Viron P. Vaky summarized this approach in September 1979 testimony before the House Foreign Affairs Committee:

> . . . Defense of the status quo will not avoid change; it will only radicalize it. . . . Failure on our part to identify with the legitimate aspiration of the people in these countries, and with those democratic elements who seek peaceful, constructive change, respect for human rights and basic equity will put us on the wrong side of history.
>
> Our task therefore is how to work with our friends to guide and influence change, how to use our influence to promote justice, freedom and equity to mutual benefit—and thereby avoid insurgency and Communism. Nowhere will this task be more crucial than in Nicaragua.

Unfortunately, attempts to implement this approach have thus far failed. Administration efforts to restore credibility to U.S. policies and stability to Central America have been consistently overtaken by events or undermined by congressional budget cuts. This has been most notable in El Salvador, Central America's smallest nation.

Assaults and Kidnappings

Since the early 1930s, the armed forces have dominated Salvadorian politics. As the population density of this agricultural nation increased, pressures for basic social and economic reforms mounted. Urged on by the handful of powerful families that controlled the economy, the military responded by using massive fraud to deny the moderate Christian Democrats victory in the 1972 elections. Throughout the 1970s the government encouraged the rise of right-wing, paramilitary groups that terrorized peasant and labor organizations, destroyed the Christian Democratic party's infrastructure in the countryside, and even murdered socially active priests. These events, in turn, led to the steady growth of armed, radical forces on the left that financed their efforts through spectacular assaults and kidnappings. By fall 1979 the nation seemed on the verge of civil war.

Encouraged by the United States, younger army officers ousted the hard-line military government in October 1979 and replaced it with a military-civilian junta. Their proclaimed advocacy of democratic reforms attracted strong U.S. support. Caught between violence from both right and left the new regime never gained full control of internal politics. The first junta collapsed in January 1980 when its civilian members quit in protest of military opposition to basic reforms.

Christian Democratic participation in a second junta led to a split within that party. Nationalization of banks, adoption of a new labor code, and promulgation of a far-sweeping agrarian reform law have failed to appease left-wing opposition and have infuriated powerful forces on the right. Only strong, direct pressure from the United States prevented a February 1980 countercoup by angry conservatives. By spring 1980 El Salvador was clearly in danger of drifting into civil war, a process accelerated by the brutal murder of Archbishop Oscar Arnulfo Romero, a heroic spokesman for justice for most Salvadorians.

While not as dramatic, events in the rest of the isthmus have been almost as frustrating for American policy makers. Guatemala, where internal violence has escalated considerably in the past few months, is a case in point. For well over a decade, bloody conflicts between left-wing guerrillas and government troops—supplemented by private far-right terrorist organizations such as the Mano Blanca—have been a recurrent facet of Guatemalan life. By 1979 murders of moderate and leftist political leaders had become so common that even Vice President Francisco Villagrán Kramer declared that "death or exile is the fate of those who struggle for justice in Guatemala."

Three factors have helped the right maintain control of Guatemala. While the population is the largest in Central America, nearly half of Guatemala's citizens are Indians, traditionally outside of active politics and impervious to appeals from the left. Furthermore, Guatemala's Central American neighbors, El Salvador and Honduras, also were under firm military control, insulating Guatemala from external subversion. Finally, high coffee prices and conservative economic policies produced a strong economy that reduced middle-class discontent. The recent growth in domestic petroleum production, which could enable Guatemala to reach self-sufficiency in a few years, contributes to the financial well-being of the country.

In the past year, the first two factors have changed considerably, thereby threatening economic stability. For the first time, substantial elements of the Indian population have shown signs of supporting and even joining the guerrillas. In March 1980 a confrontation between stone-throwing Indian women and army troops resulted in the machine-gunning of several women and the bitter condemnation of the army by the normally conservative bishop of El Quiché. Growing opposition has undermined control of two heavily populated highlands departments, Huehuetenango and El Quiché, and has produced a sharp drop in army morale.

The turmoil in El Salvador has created

acute anxiety over regional stability, leading many Guatemalan officers to talk openly about staving off subversion at home by fighting revolution in El Salvador. Also, the dispute between Guatemala and Great Britain over governing rights of the small Central American territory of Belize has increased regional tension. To date, mounting problems in Guatemala have precluded any intervention, but right-wing groups have funneled aid to their Salvadorian counterparts.

Frustrated and angered, the Guatemalan right has purchased full-page advertisements in local newspapers to denounce what they view as a weak U.S. policy that encourages left-wing uprisings and to charge members of the Salvadorian junta with membership in the Communist party. Rumors of a possible coup by the far right within the military have begun to circulate. But nothing is likely to happen before the U.S. presidential elections in November: Many right-wing Guatemalan politicians and military officers fervently hope for a victory by Republican candidate Ronald Reagan, believing this would remove U.S. opposition to their continuing or even escalating violent repression of the left.

Corruption is most visible in Honduras, where every area commander recently received a Rolex watch and a Mercedes Benz.

Honduras and Costa Rica have escaped the violence and polarization found in the other nations, but both are plagued by accelerating inflation, mounting labor troubles, and weak political leadership. Prospects for stability in Honduras, Central America's least-developed nation, are further clouded by strong public resentment of the flagrant corruption in the higher military ranks. This outlook is somewhat offset by the surprisingly honest results of the April 1980 Constituent Assembly elections. Although left-wing parties were excluded, the Liberal party defeated the military's traditional ally, the National party, and

initiated a return to civilian rule. Overall, the mixture of reform and corruption makes difficult a balanced U.S. response.

Costa Rica's democratic traditions and its relatively advanced social programs help insulate it from the region's violence, but the consumerist orientation of its increasingly middle-class society makes it especially vulnerable to mounting economic problems. Those problems could reverse the usually cordial U.S.-Costa Rican relations.

Frenetic Search

Events beyond Central America also hamper efforts to forge an effective policy. Historically, the United States has not given consistent attention to the problems of small, poor nations. Many Costa Ricans saw the U.S. actions in the controversy over tuna-fishing rights as demonstration that the United States is more concerned with the interests of a few Californian fishermen than it is with the well-being and dignity of a small, democratic ally.

Crises in more vital areas divert American attention and resources and diminish any sense of urgency. Currently, Iran and Afghanistan overshadow Central America; they also reduce U.S. tolerance of foreign attacks on past American policies and promote domestic acceptance of possible U.S. military intervention. The priority given to issues in the 1980 U.S. elections further obscures efforts to develop a consistent Central American policy.

Establishing a responsive American policy is complicated by the administration's frequent inability to deliver promised aid. Nicaragua is a case in point. Despite efforts by Ambassador Lawrence A. Pezzullo and his staff, attempts to moderate the course of Nicaragua's revolution have enjoyed only limited success. A key element of the American approach was to be the demonstration that the United States could not only tolerate but also could actually support basic social and economic changes in Nicaragua. This required combining verbal assurances of support with significant amounts of reconstruction assistance. Other nations, notably Venezuela, Panama, and Costa Rica, were counted upon to promote political pluralism and reduce potential Cuban influence.

The initial scenario was optimistic. Congress quickly approved the reprogramming of over $8 million in emergency aid for Nicaragua. Other nations offered substantial credits, and multilateral agencies, such as the Inter-American Development Bank (IDB), began processing major new loans.

The recent situation is less hopeful. Rebuffed in initial efforts to moderate the revolution, Costa Rica, Panama, and to a lesser extent, Venezuela have reduced involvement in Nicaragua. The processing of IDB and other multilateral loans has slowed dramatically. U.S. government efforts to provide a $75 million aid package have been cramped by a seemingly endless series of congressional roadblocks. Originally projected for late 1979, this package has been the subject of sharp debate; amendments, highly objectionable to Nicaragua, have been added to the authorization bill. Finally, the entire appropriation has been further delayed by the congressional mood of budget slashing.

These setbacks contributed to growing demoralization within Nicaragua's private sector and increased suspicion among the Sandinista leadership that the United States will never really support a revolutionary regime in Central America. As a U.S. diplomat in Managua recently observed, "We could have done so much with that money just a few months ago, but we've wasted our best opportunities in this country."

Costa Rican political leader Rodrigo Madrigal Nieto suggests the creation of a mini-Marshall Plan for Central America. Current U.S. aid to the region now totals just over $100 million annually. Nieto's proposal would cost about $1 billion more a year. Given the high level of U.S. expenditures abroad, that increase is relatively modest. American election-year politics, however, preclude any move in this direction before

1981. Instead, the Carter administration promotes the newly founded Caribbean-Central American Action, a program headed by Governor Bob Graham of Florida and designed to enlist private support for the region. While the Action program might produce limited benefits for Costa Rica and perhaps Honduras, it is unlikely that private investors will respond generously to the current, unstable conditions in the other three republics. In the absence of any joint executive-congressional commitment, the confusion and resentment generated by U.S. efforts in Central America will likely continue.

The result is a chaotic American policy. U.S. programs in Central America are inconsistent, confused, and indecisive. Statements of policy and expressions of concern lack credibility. The repeated visits by Assistant Secretary of State for Inter-American Affairs William Bowdler are perceived more as frenetic searches for a way out of crises than as any indication of serious, long-range interest in the area's problems. Many Central American moderates feel that the United States takes their problems seriously only when they begin killing one another in the streets.

Washington's Dilemma

Recent events raise the critical but uncomfortable question of what the United States should do if a moderate response becomes impossible. That point was reached in Nicaragua in June 1979, but the State Department continued to advocate a moderate compromise until Somoza fled to Miami. The approach only exacerbated the problem of diminishing American credibility. A similar point may be rapidly approaching in El Salvador. By supporting the current junta as the only alternative to violent civil conflict, the Carter administration is identifying with social and economic policies well to the left of any previously espoused by the United States in that part of the world. Yet the Salvadorian far left continues to denounce U.S. policy.

Part of the American dilemma stems from lack of experience in mediating between moderate regimes and radical opposition. Whereas the United States has successfully resolved disputes between moderates and conservatives, as in the Dominican Republic in 1978, American intervention in conflicts such as the current one in El Salvador demands a new kind of diplomacy. Furthermore, as many Salvadorians repeatedly point out, foreign intervention in such conflicts usually accelerates the polarization process and ultimately drives both the home government and the outside power toward the right. Despite these difficulties, standing aside and letting events run their course is politically unacceptable to the Carter administration—especially given the possibility that the result might be an anti-American, Marxist regime.

In the past, the United States counted on Central American armies to defend American interests in that region. The history of U.S. military influence in Central America is long, and the ties are intimate. Paradoxically, in every Central American country except Costa Rica, which abolished its army over 30 years ago, the military has become a major problem for American policy making.

No army in Latin America had more officers and men trained in U.S. military schools, and none had a closer relationship with the United States than did Nicaragua's National Guard. Yet the guard became the corrupt instrument of the Somoza family. Its brutality drove thousands of Nicaraguans to join the Sandinistas, and its internal weaknesses ultimately led to its total destruction. Such an outcome surely challenges the rationale for American training and support of other nations' armed forces, especially now that El Salvador's security troops—once again, groomed by the United States—are threatened with a similar fate.

The U.S. government's proposals for supporting the Salvadorian junta include a request for increased military assistance, notably a $5.7 million package for improvements in training, transportation, and communications. This proposal invoked considerable criticism, including a letter to Carter from the late Archbishop Romero, who claimed that such assistance "instead of favoring greater justice and peace in El Salvador, undoubtedly will sharpen . . . the repression."

In Guatemala and Honduras, conditions within the armed forces pose similar challenges for U.S. policy makers. In both countries, hopes for peaceful reforms in human rights and political freedoms require the acquiescence, if not the active support, of the military. In each nation significant segments of the officer corps, especially at junior levels, are sympathetic to such changes. But the higher ranking officers seem allied with the oligarchy and, in Guatemala, committed to a policy of brutal repression that ultimately alienates the armed forces from the general population. Corruption is most visible in Honduras, where every area commander recently received a Rolex watch and a Mercedes Benz. Again, it is difficult to see how efforts by an external power can deal effectively with such problems.

U.S.-sponsored training programs could educate officers on how corruption and popular alienation eventually destroyed the pre-1959 Cuban army and the Nicaraguan National Guard, but in the immediate future there is little the United States can do beyond encouraging these forces to reform themselves. Until this happens, American support for these armies only associates the United States with repression and brutality.

"We have frequently mistaken the support of governments for the friendship of populations. . . ."

From the standpoint of American policy, the essential question in Central America is whether the United States can live with and perhaps even support revolution in its own back yard. Although the United States accommodated nations such as Mexico, the traditional answer in Central America has been a firm no. The Carter administration indicates a willingness to change this response, but with qualifications: only if Cuban influence is limited; only if an unspecified amount of pluralism is allowed; and only if each Central American country refrains from involvement in its neighbor's politics.

An Avenue of Escape

Remaining unspecified is what the American response could or should be if those guidelines are ignored and if revolution—particularly revolution directed against unpopular, repressive, military regimes—spreads throughout the region. Being forced to choose between acceptance of control over much of Central America by hostile forces and open intervention by American troops is the ultimate nightmare of American policy makers. While either option entails disastrous political consequences, current international and domestic political trends may tip the balance toward intervention. It might be impossible to find any effective option between doing nothing and sending in the Marines.

A concerned State Department recently tried to defuse the issue. In his April 8, 1980, speech on Central America, Bowdler pointedly remarked that "we will not use military force in situations where only domestic groups are in contention." This, however, leaves open the possibility of U.S. military intervention in response to perceived involvement by Cuba or any other outside power.

One possible avenue of escape from this dilemma would be to seek major involvement by others, such as Venezuela, Mexico, Western Europe, and even Japan, in efforts to stabilize and develop Central America. The U.S. government has already moved in this direction. Testifying before the Senate Foreign Relations Committee last December, Deputy Secretary of State Warren Christopher declared: "We need to try to find out how the Latin Americans think we should address the problems of Central America and their own problems. We don't approach it on a U.S.-dominated or know-it-all basis. I think that is a fundamental change in our attitude toward Central and South America."

Unfortunately, U.S. consultations with other countries on Central American problems are no more credible than direct U.S. relations with that region. Seeing little evidence of long-range planning or of a meaningful financial commitment and having no interest in overt association with frantic U.S. efforts at crisis management, most nations avoid direct involvement in the face of Central America's mounting turmoil.

Mexico has joined with its northern neighbor in support of the new Nicaraguan government but has criticized the U.S. position in El Salvador, where Mexican sympathies seem to lie with the left. Venezuela has been more directly involved with Central America, but U.S. efforts to coordinate policies with the administration of President Luis Herrera Campins are complicated by Herrera's close ties with the area's Christian Democratic parties. The United States is already suspected of favoring small parties of this type and cannot afford any closer links with a single minority political faction.

In Congress there is widespread consensus on the bankruptcy of traditional policies toward Central America. Senator Edward Zorinsky (D.-Nebraska), chairman of the Subcommittee on Western Hemisphere Affairs of the Senate Foreign Relations Committee declared that in dealing with the area, "the fundamental mistake we make . . . is to back governments or regimes which enjoy little or no popular support."

A similar stand was taken by Senator David Durenberger (R.-Minnesota), who told the Senate Foreign Relations Committee that U.S. policy in Central America had "too long been characterized by inattention, ignorance, a lack of concern, and a blind acceptance of the status quo." Durenberger added that "we have frequently mistaken the support of governments for the friendship of populations while many people in these regions have labored under the twin burdens of repression and poverty."

It is easier to recognize past mistakes than to correct them. A turnaround in U.S. policy requires positive commitment rather than continual obsession with fears of domestic political embarrassment and expanded Cuban influence. The current attitude produces a policy that is perceived as a holding action, designed to slow the rate of change but incapable of affecting the nature of that change. This type of policy generates little enthusiasm and attracts few capable followers.

A Failure to be Responsive

A recurrent fear expressed in discussions of contemporary Central America is a new variation of the old domino theory. Many observers argue that failure to limit Cuban influence in Nicaragua, to prevent radical victories in El Salvador and Guatemala, and to deal effectively with the economic problems of Honduras and Costa Rica, would deal an irreparable blow to U.S. prestige throughout the hemisphere. Capital flight would increase, moderate political factions would collapse, and hard-liners on the right would resort to all-out repression to maintain their power.

Although exaggerated, such scenarios contain an element of truth. Central America is a small community, and events in any one nation often affect developments in another. Thus, the governments of Honduras, El Salvador, and Costa Rica are already concerned about the impact on their populations of radio broadcasts originating from Nicaragua.

Such interdependence works both ways. The key challenge for U.S. policy is to offer a viable, pluralistic alternative to radical violence as a means of altering existing social and political structures and promoting economic development. Ideally, such an alternative would then influence neighboring states.

At the moment, the best location for this kind of effort is Honduras. The April elections restored Honduran faith in the domestic political process and probably halted the precipitate decline in the military's public image. The Carter administration has already indicated through diplomatic channels its hopes that the new Constituent Assembly will not limit election voting rights to assembly members but rather will open political participation to include the general population and the leftist parties excluded from April's voting. The United States has also encouraged the government, the military, and the assembly to work for honest and prompt direct elections for a new president and congress. Recent statements by the military and the major parties in Honduras suggest that this scenario may actually occur.

A hopeful U.S. government has attached requests for a Honduran package to current emergency aid proposals for Nicaragua and El Salvador. Unfortunately, the Honduran proposal is no exception to the rule that Central America aid packages are small, poorly focused, and contingent upon approval by a slow-moving Congress. In the case of the Honduran development package there is no assurance of any significant funding beyond the upcoming fiscal year. Moreover, the proposed assistance does not address such fundamental problems as access to American markets, terms of trade and technology transfer, or guaranteed energy supplies. Once again, U.S. rhetoric seems to outstrip its ability or willingness to commit American resources.

An example of the type of program which could restore American credibility and promote positive development throughout Central America is the current national literacy campaign in Nicaragua. Financed and inspired by Cuba, Nicaragua is endeavoring to eliminate nearly 50 per cent illiteracy in less than a year. Major U.S. assistance would make possible a similar effort in Honduras. A literacy project would mobilize national energies, especially among the youth; support future education programs in health, sanitation, and agriculture; and give both Honduras and the United States a badly needed sense of accomplishment. A literacy campaign in Honduras would also provide opportunities for cooperation with other regional powers in Central American development efforts.

Central America's problems are critical, and the time left for dealing with them in a peaceful, democratic manner is extremely short. Despite the polarization of internal politics and the lack of credibility in U.S. policy, positive elements do exist. Guatemala should soon be more than self-sufficient in petroleum. Honduras and Nicaragua have significant areas of undeveloped land, and Costa Rica, with its democratic traditions and high level of literacy, can draw on valuable human resources. Important support for reform could come from the Roman Catholic Church, whose energies in Central America are already devoted to promoting justice and human development.

Many Central Americans share the sentiments of a Costa Rican congressional leader who stated sadly that "the United States does not really care about Central America." What has been lacking is a definite commitment by the United States to support political and financial alternatives to the violent revolutions of the far left or the brutal repression by the entrenched right. Any verbal commitment by the president and Congress to the future development of Central America must be coupled with significant amounts of long-term economic assistance. In the conclusion of his April 8 address, Bowdler recognized the urgency of responding to the current situation in Central America: "Central America is in a critical period of its history. Our support for peaceful change can increase the likelihood that more democratic and equitable societies will evolve out of the present crisis. Conversely, our failure to be responsive can only help the enemies of freedom."

Unfortunately, if history offers any guide, it is that the United States will probably fail to be responsive. Domestic politics, budget concerns, and preoccupation with big-power politics may well keep the United States from making any serious commitment to Central America. If, after a century and a half of involvement in Central America, the United States can still offer no positive commitment to nonviolent and democratic development in that region, then its hopes for peace and justice in more remote areas are slim indeed.

AUTHORS

JOSE A. CABRANES, a federal judge with the U.S. District Court for Connecticut, was special counsel to the governor of Puerto Rico and administrator of the commonwealth's Washington office while the Popular Democratic Party was in power. He is the author of *Citizenship and the American Empire.*

RICHARD R. FAGEN, professor of political science at Stanford University, is the author of numerous works on comparative politics and Latin America and has been awarded research grants in Mexico, Cuba, and Nicaragua. He most recently co-edited *The Future of Central America: Policy Choices for the U.S. and Mexico* with Olga Pellicer.

RICHARD A. FALK, Albert G. Milbank Professor of International Law and Practice at Princeton University, sits on the editorial boards of *World Politics* and *The American Journal of International Law* and has written numerous books and articles on international law and national policy. His most recent book is *Human Rights and State Sovereignty.*

ROGER W. FONTAINE, senior staff member for the National Security Council, was director of Latin American Studies at the Center for Strategic and International Studies at Georgetown University. He is the author of many books, including *U.S.-Cuban Relations: A New, New Look.*

THOMAS M. FRANCK, professor of law and director of the Center for International Studies at New York University School of Law, was the director of the International Law Program of the Carnegie Endowment for International Peace. His most recent book is *Human Rights in Third World Perspective.*

NORMAN GALL, a contributing editor to *Forbes* magazine, was a senior associate at the Carnegie Endowment for International Peace from 1974 to 1977. During this time he engaged in a major study of Brazil, where he now resides. He has been writing about Latin American issues for various publications since 1961.

GEORGE W. GRAYSON, professor of government at the College of William and Mary, has served five terms in the Virginia House of Delegates. He is a contributing editor to the *Handbook of Latin American Studies* published by the Library of Congress and the author of *The Politics of Mexican Oil.*

MARIANO GRONDONA, professor of political science at the University of Buenos Aires and editor of the Latin American magazine *Vision,* is responsible for "Tiempo Nuevo," a political TV talk show in Argentina. In addition, he has written numerous articles and books on modern Argentina.

LAWRENCE E. HARRISON, visiting scholar at the Center for International Affairs, Harvard University, was with the Agency for International Development (AID) for more than 20 years, serving at AID missions in Costa Rica, the Dominican Republic, and Nicaragua. He is the author of *Underdevelopment Is a State of Mind.*

ROBERT LAPORTE, JR., acting director of the Institute of Public Administration at Pennsylvania State University, has served as a consultant to a number of government agencies. He has lectured and written extensively on Pakistan, India, and South America.

ABRAHAM F. LOWENTHAL, on leave at the Truman Institute of Hebrew University in Jerusalem, is secretary of the Latin American Program at the Woodrow Wilson International Center for Scholars in Washington, D.C. He was a lecturer at Princeton University, a consultant to the Commission on United States-Latin American Relations, and served as director of the April 1983 *Report of the Inter-American Dialogue.* The author of numerous books and articles, Lowenthal most recently co-edited *The Peruvian Experiment Reconsidered* with Cynthia McClintock.

RICHARD MILLETT, visiting professor at the Air War College, Maxwell AFB, Alabama, has written many articles about U.S. and Central American Policy. His most recent book is *The Restless Caribbean.*

JAMES PETRAS, visiting scholar at the Center for Mediterranean Studies in Athens, frequently lectures in South America and Europe and contributes to *Le Monde Diplomatique.* His most recent book is *Class, State, and Power in the Third World.*

DONALD E. SCHULZ, assistant professor of social sciences at the University of Tampa, Florida, has written many articles on Latin American and communist issues. He is currently working on two books, *Revolution and Counterrevolution in Central America and the Caribbean* and *The Cubans, the Soviet Union, and the United States.*

EDWARD WEISBAND, professor of political science and director of the Ph.D. Program in Public Policy Analysis at the State University of New York in Binghamton, is a frequent guest on television and radio programs concerning foreign affairs. He has written many books and articles dealing with national and international politics.

INDEX

Acción Democrática (AD) party (Venezuela), 26, 27, 28, 29, 33
AD. *See* Acción Democrática party
AEC. *See* Atomic Energy Commission
AECL. *See* Atomic Energy of Canada, Ltd.
AEG Telefunken (German company), 68
AFL-CIO. *See* American Federation of Labor-Congress of Industrial Organization
Agency for International Development, U.S. (AID), 13, 21, 118, 132, 160
AID. *See* Agency for International Development
AIMS. *See* American Institute of Merchant Shipping
Alberto, Alvaro, 70
Alcohol, 77, 120
Alessandri, Jorge, 11
Algeria, 64
Allende Gossens, Salvador, 10, 11, 12, 15, 16, 20, 28, 98
Alliance for Progress (1961), 3–5, 10, 21, 25, 27, 84, 86, 103, 128, 130, 135, 145
Alvarado, Gilberto. *See* "D"
Amazon Basin, 75, 77
American Enterprise Institute Defense Review, 126
American Federation of Labor-Congress of Industrial Organization (AFL-CIO), 119
American Institute of Merchant Shipping (AIMS), 50
American Petroleum Institute, 111
American Popular Revolutionary Alliance (APRA) (Peru), 161
Americans for Democratic Action, 147
American Smelting and Refining Co. (ASARCO), 136
AMLASH. *See* Cubelas, Rolando
AMWHIP (Cuban exile), 90
Anaconda mines (Chile), 11, 17, 19(table), 20
Anchovy disappearance, 162
Andean development bank, 27
Andean Group, 8, 11
Anderson, Jack, 10, 11
Anglo-Persian Oil Company. *See* British Petroleum
Angola, 95, 98, 99, 102
Annapolis (U.S. aircraft carrier), 54
Anti-Americanism. *See* Latin America, and the United States
Anti-Communists, 94, 95, 96, 101
Anti-Imperialist League, 141
APRA. *See* American Popular Revolutionary Alliance
Arab oil boycott (1973), 29, 30, 32, 60, 61
Aragón, Leopoldo, 123

Arbenz Guzmán, Jacobo, 153
Argentina, 95
  GNP, per capita, 6–7
  and Libya, 73
  military, 103
  nationalization in, 11
  and NATO, 99
  and nuclear power, 57, 66, 68, 69–70, 71, 72, 73, 77, 78, 105
  oil, 32–33
  political prisoners, 131
  size, 7
  and the United States, 6, 8, 11, 13, 20(table), 63, 70, 99, 100, 103
  and West Germany, 62, 66, 71
  See also under Brazil; Chile; Cuba; Mexico; Venezuela
ASARCO. *See* American Smelting and Refining Co.
Asian Development Bank, 18
Athabasca tar sands (Canada), 31
Atomic Energy Commission, U.S. (AEC), 60, 61, 63, 66, 67, 74, 76. *See also* Energy Research and Development Administration
Atomic Energy of Canada, Ltd. (AECL), 79
"Atoms for Peace" program, 67, 70, 74
Attwood, William, 83
Atucha I (Argentina), 62, 69, 71, 72
Australia, 64
Austria, 64, 99
Austrian Empire, 94
Authoritarianism, 97
Ayacucho, Battle of, anniversary (Peru), 28
Aztecs, 111

"Bacab-1" oil well (Mexico), 112
Bagasse, 41
Baja California (Mexico), 112, 120
Baker, Howard, 121
Baldwin, Hanson, 126
Baldwin, Robert, 144
Bananas, 52, 163
Banzer, Hugo, 13
Barber, Richard J., Associates, 66
Barbosa, José Celso, 143
Batista, Fulgencio, 37, 84, 93, 124
Bay of Pigs invasion (1961) (Cuba), 36, 83, 87, 93, 131, 153
Bechtel (U.S. company), 75
Becker jet-nozzle process, 63
Belaúnde Terry, Fernando, 103, 158, 161
Belize, 167
Bernal, Miguel Antonio, 123
Betancourt, Rómulo, 24, 25–26
Bethlehem Steel (U.S. company), 19(table), 33
Big Stick policy, 1, 56
Blanco, Hugo, 162
Boeing (U.S. company), 13
Bolivia, 28, 37, 95
  nationalization in, 11, 22, 34
  natural gas, 60
  oil, 33
  tin, 34
  and the United States, 6, 11, 12, 13, 22, 27
  See also under Brazil; Chile
Border-industry plan, 119
Bowdler, William, 155, 168, 170, 172

THE
SPHERE
OF SECRETS

Catherine Fisher

THE
SPHERE
OF SECRETS

Book Two of
The Oracle Prophecies

GREENWILLOW BOOKS
An Imprint of HarperCollins*Publishers*

The Sphere of Secrets

Copyright © 2005 by Catherine Fisher

First published in 2004 in Great Britain by Hodder Children's Books as *The Archon*
First published in 2005 in the United States by Greenwillow Books, an imprint of
HarperCollins Publishers

The right of Catherine Fisher to be identified as author of this work has been
asserted by her.

The text of this book is set in 11-point Galliard.

Library of Congress Cataloging-in-Publication Data

Fisher, Catherine.
The sphere of secrets / by Catherine Fisher.
  p. cm.
"Greenwillow Books."
"The second book of the Oracle Prophecies trilogy."
Summary: Together with Alexos, Seth, Oblek, and a fallen silver star, Mirany is
forced to continue the battle against the evil general Argelin.
ISBN 0-06-057161-6 (trade). ISBN 0-06-057162-4 (lib. bdg.)
[1. Fantasy.] I. Title.
PZ7.F4995Sp 2005 [Fic]—dc22 2004042436

10 9 8 7 6 5 4 3 2
First American Edition

 GREENWILLOW BOOKS

THE FIRST OFFERING
OF PEARLS

Last night I became a fish in the sea.

I swam deep, and my body rippled and quivered and the long barbs around my tiny mouth trailed and tickled.

Above me was the moon, huge and white. Below, the shells of oysters, half open, breathing. And inside them, tiny and shining, there were pearls, in which I saw the glimmer of my reflection.

Deep in the waters, beauty is made from pain. This is something gods should study.

She Sees Words on the Moon

So the rumors were true. And *these* were elephants.

Their enormous bodies amazed Mirany. In the evening heat they stood in a great semicircle, twelve beasts, tails swishing, vast ears rippling irritably against flies. On their backs were towers, real towers of wood with gaudy painted doors and windows, within which the dark-skinned merchants sat on jeweled palanquins tasseled with gold.

From her seat before the bridge, on the left side of the Speaker, she watched the animals through the twilight. A huge full moon hung over them, the Rain Queen's perfect mirror, its eerie light shimmering on the emptiness of the desert, the fires on the road, the black ramparts of the City of the Dead. A breeze drifted her mantle against her arm; someone's thin silver bracelets clinked. There was no other sound, except, far below, the endless splash of the sea against rocks.

The central elephant was lumbering forward. Its great feet, heavy with bangles, thudded into the soft sand, the swaying mass of silver chains on its neck and ears and back brilliant in the moonlight. It wore a scarlet harness of tiny bells and immense pearls, the largest dangling between its eyes, a fist-sized, priceless lump.

Behind the mask, Mirany licked sweat from her lips. The eyeholes restricted her view, but she could see the Speaker, Hermia, and the rest of the Nine, the girls sitting rigid as if in terror, their bronze masks smiling calmly as the enormous beast neared. Next to her in the line, Rhetia fidgeted. The tall girl was alert, watching the crowd. Her fingers, light as dust, touched Mirany's wrist. "He's looking at you," she whispered.

On his pale horse, Argelin should have been easy to find. But he sat in shadow, armor gleaming, the bodyguard of sixteen huge men that never left him now, armed and facing outward. Mirany smiled sourly. There were probably others in the crowd. The general was taking no chances. And yes, his helmeted eyes were turned her way. Quite suddenly she felt exposed, unprotected. But she was as safe here as anywhere, these days.

Hermia stood. Hurriedly, Mirany and the rest of the Nine rose with her, and as the elephant came closer over the cooling sand, the smiling masks glinted under their feathers and jeweled headdresses, all color draining in the pearly light.

The great beast reached the bridge, and bowed its head.

The smell of it was hot and rank, of dung and perfumes, and Mirany saw the myriad folds and wrinkles of its dusty skin, the sag of its belly as it lowered itself. She drew her breath in. For the elephant was kneeling before the Speaker. It knelt clumsily, and the thud of its great limbs in the sand sent vibrations across the wooden bridge. The rider, hidden behind the vast headdress, flicked a hand and spoke; the elephant lay right down and lifted its trunk; then it made a sound that chilled the night, a terrible brazen roar.

Hermia did not flinch, though one of the Nine— probably Chryse—made a moan of terror. Argelin's horse started nervously. The elephant looked along the crescent of the Nine. Its eye stopped at Mirany.

It recognizes you, the god remarked in her ear.

Recognizes?

As a friend. They are considered very wise, Mirany. Their memories are older than any other beast.

It has such small eyes, she thought, *deep-set and shrewd.* As she answered she seemed almost to be speaking to the animal. *Where have you been for so long? I thought I'd never hear you again.*

Gods have a world to run. I have been busy.

We need you! Things are going wrong.

From the wooden howdah on the elephant, a ladder unraveled and a man climbed down. He was tall and bearded, wearing a robe of white and gold, so stiff with pearls it looked almost rigid. He put his hands together and bowed over them.

"What is it you seek here?" Hermia's voice rang across the desert.

"I seek the wisdom of the Oracle. I seek to hear the words of the god."

"From what land have you traveled?"

The answer was solemn, and measured. "From the east where the sun rises. From the Islands of Pearl and Honey, over the deep sea we bring the gifts and request of the Emperor, the Exalted, the Wise One, to the Bright god of the Oracle."

The masked face nodded. "How have you prepared?"

"By fasting, by lustration, by purification. By three days of meditation. By washing three times in the silver pool."

"What is your name?"

"Jamil, Prince of Askelon, companion of the Peacock Throne."

Hermia raised her manicured hands. Crystals glinted from her fingernails. "The wisdom of the god is infinite," she said. "The day is auspicious, the hour a sacred hour. Enter the precinct of the Mouse Lord."

Formalities over, the Prince turned and beckoned, and two more men, identically dressed, climbed down from the elephants and joined him. Behind them, Argelin's line of soldiers closed up.

The pearl merchants took out jewel-handled swords and thrust them dramatically into the sand; then they walked forward to the bridge. Without a word Hermia swept around and led the Nine and the three strangers on to the Island. They had sailed in a week ago, a fleet of vast caravels that were anchored now in the harbor, all but blocking it. Their wives wore brilliant colors, their children bracelets of pearl. The whole population of the Port had been thronging the wharfs for days, fingering the bales of merchandise, the cloth, foodstuffs, gems, ivories, exotic fruits—bartering, stealing, arguing, tasting. Even on the Island Mirany's sleep had been broken by the bizarre trumpeting of the elephants, terrible and fascinating.

Walking now under the moon, she said in her mind, *Do you already know what they want to ask?*

I know.

And will she give them the right answer?

He laughed, a quiet sound. But all he said was, **The palace is full of such wonders, Mirany, and all for me. Music and silver gaming boards and food—such sweet tastes! And there are tiny fish in the garden pools with snouts and trailing whiskers!**

For an instant the voice was a boy's, full of delight. Mirany shook her head, dismayed. *Listen to me! Don't you know Oblek is missing?*

They had reached the stone doorway. It leaned, to the left of the path, and beyond it in the mothy dark were the steps that led up to the Oracle. The Procession halted and the Speaker turned. "The Bearer-of-the-God will attend me."

Mirany licked her lips and stepped out. For a second she and Hermia looked at each other, and behind the openmouthed mask the Speaker's glance was a flicker of hatred. Then they were climbing, the three strangers behind them. Everyone else waited on the path. The Oracle was forbidden to them, even to Argelin, though Mirany saw how he watched them, how, just for an instant, Hermia caught his eye.

The steps were ancient, and worn smooth. They wound in a coiling climb through thyme and artemisia and myrtle bushes, and in the darkness small beetles raced across the warm stones, and an owl hooted somewhere over on the Temple roof. Mirany was sweating in the mask, her breathing loud, and behind her the three men toiled in their heavy robes, the last one carrying a box of sandalwood that smelled sweet and attracted clouds of moths.

Are you still with me? Mirany thought.

There was no answer, and she frowned. She had offended him, then. He was touchy, she knew that.

As they came up on to the platform she felt the breeze that always blew up here from the sea. It flapped her light dress and Hermia's robes, and she breathed it gratefully, and saw the black, restless surface of the waves, moon-glittering to the horizon.

Hermia turned. Her voice was breathless and quiet. "Well, Men of the Pearls. This is the Oracle."

They stood together, as if wary. The moonlight made their stiff robes gleam. Prince Jamil's eyes flicked nervously at the stone platform, the ancient tree, the dark, barely visible pit beneath it. He took one step forward.

"Wait," Mirany said nervously. "You must wait for the Speaker to be ready."

Hermia spread her arms wide, and coming behind her, Mirany helped her off with the blue robe that was crusted with the crystals of the Rain Queen. Underneath, Hermia wore a simple white dress, belted at the waist. Her feet were bare. She turned her back to the men and took off the mask.

For a moment then, as Mirany searched for the Flask of Vision in the basket and held it out to her, she felt Hermia's hatred on her like heat, like the glare of some basilisk whose gaze could petrify. As their eyes met she knew it was happening, that terrible turning to stone, the stupid fear coming over her, making her small, nervous, fumbling. And then Hermia had drunk the liquid and put the mask back on, and the beautiful golden face was smiling at her.

She stepped back, cold.

Hermia crossed the platform. Small mists and coils of vapor rose between her and the men. At her feet, almost lost in the darkness, was the Oracle.

It was a pit of darkness. Smoke rose from it, and invisible fumes, and at its lip dark sulfurous crusts formed, faceted with basalt. It led deep into the earth, into the Underworld. It was the mouth the god spoke through. Looking at Hermia kneeling down, bending over it, Mirany smiled a secret smile behind the mask, thinking of the kingdom that lay down there, the place of the god's shadow, furnished with copies of the world's riches. Seth had told her about it.

Thinking of Seth made her frown. She hadn't seen him for weeks. Since he'd been promoted.

It may be he has other things to concern him now. The voice seemed amused.

Mirany snorted. *Apart from himself, you mean?* It wasn't fair. She knew that.

Hermia gasped. The strange weaving movements of her body had stopped; now she flung her head back and screamed, a horrific, savage sound that made even Mirany flinch. The merchants knelt hastily, the one with the box bowing right over, his forehead to the floor.

Convulsed, the Speaker swayed and fell to her knees. Then she cried out, a great wordless cry, a yell of wrath into the darkness. Hands splayed on the hot pavement, head down, she shivered and shuddered.

Very quietly Mirany turned to the men. "You must make your offering now. Don't go too close. Don't move too quickly."

The merchant gave her a glance; then he turned and said something in a curt language to the others. The one with the box opened it hastily; a waft of sandalwood and lavender drifted into the air. The Prince took a gift out and came forward.

He approached the Oracle warily, with exaggerated slowness. As he knelt the pearl-crusted robe buckled in stiff pleats, its rich embroidery scratching the stones, loud in the silence. Moths danced drunkenly in the fumes of the pit.

He held out his hands.

Mirany stared. Balanced on his spread palms was a perfect globe of silver, a polished shimmer of beauty. Lines were incised all over it, devices and symbols and what looked like writing, strange dense letters that she couldn't read, in tiny blocks of text. It was moon-sized, and in the pale light it seemed another orb of the sky, descended into his hands. As he raised it she sensed its weight, that it was solid, priceless.

"For you, Bright Lord. From the ancient treasury of the Emperors, we offer the Sphere of Secrets."

Carefully he lowered his hands into the miasma of the pit, and with a reluctance that Mirany shared, he opened them. The Sphere fell, like a flashing star. Far below they heard it rattle and tinkle. Then there was silence.

Hermia raised her head. She was sweating, her voice harsh, an effort. "What do you ask of the Oracle, Lord Jamil?"

The man sat back on his heels. He spoke quietly. "The Men of the Pearls seek the god's permission to pass through his land. We wish to send an expedition to the Mountains of the Moon."

The Speaker swayed. She murmured words, nonsense. Then she hissed, "For what purpose?"

"There are lodes of silver in the mountains. Long ago, before the time of the Archon Rasselon, there was an arrangement for our people to work them, and carry the metal back on camels to the Port. The work is dangerous, the desert desolate, but we want to attempt this trade again.

We will pay any dues the god requires, for his Temple, and his favor."

Silence.

Hermia shivered, curled tight into a ball. She hissed like a snake, and the merchant scrambled up and stepped back. He watched calmly.

Behind her mask, Mirany gave a cold smile. You had to admit, Hermia's act was impressive. Especially if you knew that there was nothing in the Flask of Vision but wine. Mirany knew, because she'd tasted it. Hermia was playing for time now, probably thinking fast of how much to demand. There would be a huge amount in tax for any trading agreement. Harbor dues, bribes. Argelin and the Temple would be rich.

So what's she waiting for?

The god's voice was somber. **Not for my words. And yet she has just seen them. You have all seen them.**

Where?

They were written on the silver globe.

Hermia was ready. Shaking, sweating, its hair uncurling, the gold mask lifted slowly and out of it a voice hissed, distorted, unrecognizable. Its words were forced out, as if in pain, as if from some great depth. "I have heard. I say this. The desert is mine. It is forbidden. Enter it and you will burn in my wrath. For the veins of the earth are sacred, the heights of the moon are holy. None shall tread them but I. The footsteps of men are a disease, and a curse."

Sudden spasms made Hermia's whole body heave and

shudder and then collapse; while the devastated merchants scrambled up and stared, Mirany ran forward and wrapped the blue robe over the Speaker. Then she turned, trying to hide her amazement. "The Oracle has spoken. You should go now. The Speaker will need to recover."

The dark bearded man spread his hands wide in appeal. "This is all we are to expect?"

"It seems clear. The god has refused."

"But . . ." He shook his head, controlling his anger with an effort. "We had hoped . . . surely the god will reconsider."

"I don't know." Mirany's voice was cold. All at once she hated herself for even being here, for being part of this. She wanted to blurt out that the god had said no such thing, that it had been only Hermia who answered. But she was in too much danger already. And any hint of trickery might even bring about war.

The merchant stared at her, eyes dark. Then he gave a slight bow, swept around and walked down the steps, his companions close behind him, their backs stiff with hauteur and dismay. When she was quite sure they were gone, Mirany breathed out, in utter relief. She took the mask off and felt the sweat on her face cool in the breeze. Then she turned.

Hermia was sitting up, hair askew, her angular face shadowed by the moon. She had the mask of the Speaker in her hands, its gold discs and ibis feathers tangled, the open mouth gaping and dark.

"Do you want me anymore?" Mirany muttered.

"Want you?" Hermia was hot, and triumphant. "If it were up to me you would have been reburied in the tomb, laws or no laws. Get out. Send Chryse up here."

Mirany didn't move, to her own surprise. "I expected the . . . god to grant their request."

"Did you? Well, the god speaks to me." Hermia looked at her directly. "Not you. You are still only Bearer, Mirany. And not even that for long, because the god will kill you soon, as he always does." She tucked a strand of hair away tidily. "Until that happens, you can put up with hearing me speak. And with knowing your poor little Archon has failed you."

Striding angrily down the steps, her dress brushing the thyme bushes into rank scent and clouds of midges, Mirany raged in despair. "Listen to her! What should I do? Nothing's changed, after all we did. The Oracle is still being betrayed. And why did she turn them down?"

A snake zigzagged across her path; she jumped back instantly. It looked at her and said, **Maybe others have an interest in the Mountains of the Moon.**

Others? Who?

But the snake had slid into the undergrowth and the night was silent.

Mirany stood still. Far below, the sea lapped the rocks at the cliff base. Cicadas rasped, a night chorus. She folded her arms and breathed deep. There was one thing she could do. If the words of the god were on the silver Sphere, then she would have to read them, even if they lay deep in the dark heart of the earth, in the caves and tunnels of the god's shadow.

It would mean talking to Seth, or finding Oblek.

She scowled. One would be too busy, ordering his hundred scribes about. And the other would be drunk.

She Lives among Spines and Thorns

The sun slanted in early to the Upper House. Already, an hour after dawn, with the Ritual finished and breakfast being served, the heat of it was starting to creep along the shaded terrace, under the awning that flapped in the sea air.

Up in the loggia, Mirany came out of her bedroom door and paused, looking down. There were two voices. Maybe three. One was Rhetia's and she was relieved about that. She walked along the marble corridor, past the beautiful remote statues of past Speakers, and down the steps into the courtyard. Rhetia looked up. The tall girl was wearing a black dress and a necklace of turquoise and silver; Mirany knew it had come from the merchants' stock. Samples of everything had been sent up to the Island, perfumes, jewelry, robes, for all the Nine. It hadn't done the Men of the Pearls much good. As she sat at the table she puzzled again about Hermia's refusal. Why forbid the Mountains of the Moon? No one ever went there. The desert was a furnace, the hills stark and barren. But if there really was silver, maybe Argelin had his own plans for it.

The tables were spread with oranges and figs and soft bread rolls, and the pale watered wine that came from Alenos. Mirany chose an orange and cut into it with a pearl-handled knife. Juice spurted, a ripe sharp scent. Quietly she said to Rhetia, "Where's Chryse?"

"With the Speaker. Where else?"

Mirany nodded. Since the Nine had found out for sure that Chryse—giggly, golden-haired Chryse—was Hermia's spy, since the terrible night of the Shadow, and the coming of the new Archon, a rift had developed in the sacred precinct. Seven against two. No one spoke to Chryse unless they had to. She pouted and threw tantrums and swam alone in the pool and avoided them all. Whether she was ashamed or just didn't care Mirany had no idea. Once she had thought she knew her. That had been a big mistake.

Rhetia glanced toward the other two girls. Her voice was low. "So what did the merchants want?"

"To set up a silver mining operation somewhere in the mountains."

"Nice. I'll bet the Speaker jumped at that."

Mirany swallowed a segment of orange. "No. She turned them down."

The tall girl gave her a sharp glance. "Why?"

"No idea. Unless—"

"Unless Argelin wants to run it himself, yes. Still, it seems odd. Why not get the pearl men to do all the work, provide slaves, camels, ships, and just cream off a profit from the top? No risks for him."

Rhetia was intelligent and arrogantly sure of herself. Mirany always felt small and dull next to her; she was used to it, and it wasn't as bad as when she'd first come here, but still it depressed her. She sensed the tall girl had a sort of grudging respect for her now, after everything that had happened, but they would never be real friends. Not like she'd been with Chryse.

She took some bread. Instantly Rhetia beckoned the servant from behind her chair. "Taste that for the Bearer."

"There's no need," Mirany muttered hopelessly.

"Don't be ridiculous. Give it to her."

The bread was a small roll, soft and fresh. With a bitter hatred of herself for being so weak, Mirany gave it to the servant, a thin dried-up woman called Kamli, probably Rhetia's slave. The woman's hands were callused and strong; she took the bread calmly, broke a corner off and chewed it. Her eyes met Mirany's; hot, Mirany looked down.

The woman said quietly, "It seems safe, holiness."

She handed the roll back. Mirany took it, miserable. "Thank you," she whispered.

The threat was real, she knew that. Hermia had sworn to destroy her, and even though by law the Nine could be harmed by no one, secret poison would never be proved.

For the last few months, especially at first, after her reinstatement, she had hardly dared to eat at all, except for fruit, which was probably safe. She'd got thinner. Oblek had made some sour joke about it and even the Archon had looked up from his latest pet and said, "Mirany, you do look pale."

But putting someone else's life at risk turned her sick. She ate the roll slowly, still wary. It tasted like ashes. How could things be like this! Nothing had changed! Alexos was Archon, yes, but she was in more danger than ever, and Oblek . . . Where was Oblek?

She stood quickly. "I'm going to the Palace."

Rhetia pared an apricot. "Take a litter. And a few guards." Then she said casually, "We could always use him, you know."

"Use him?"

"Prince Jamil." With a swift gesture she waved the slave away, tossed down the fruit, stood, and pulled Mirany aside into a cool white room facing out over the sea. Kicking the door shut she turned, her voice suddenly decisive. "Don't you see? We could explain to him that the Oracle is being abused. You could tell him what the god really says—that Hermia and Argelin are in it together."

"I don't—" Mirany began, aghast, but Rhetia ignored her.

"Our problem is that we have no forces! Argelin's soldiers mean he can do what he wants. There's no leader to stand against him. Now the Emperor is powerful. He has huge armies—cavalry, hoplites, elephants! Think of it,

Mirany! They could destroy Argelin, and then Hermia would have no support, and we could force her out. A new Speaker. A *real* Speaker!"

Mirany had backed to the window. Now she said, "You, of course."

"Yes, me! Why not?"

Mirany shook her head. She couldn't believe this. "You'd cause a war? Deliberately—"

"We need to get rid of Argelin. Don't be so prim, Mirany. I doubt there'd be much fighting. Just the threat would be enough."

"You don't know that. People would die!"

Rhetia shrugged. "Slaves. Soldiers. No one important."

Outside, a gull screamed in the blue air, like a cold omen. Mirany clasped her hands together to stop them shaking with anger. She was appalled and very, very scared. "You really believe that, don't you?"

Rhetia was pacing up and down, the black pleated hem of her dress gathering swirls of sandy dust. She seemed consumed with a triumphant excitement, turning her head and fixing Mirany with an irate stare. "Of course I do. Sometimes deaths are necessary. When she was young, my grandmother was a priestess, too, Mirany. Did I ever tell you that? In the Archon Horeb's time. She had an enemy called Alanta, a woman from a good house on the same island. Only one of them could come here, so they fought for the privilege."

"Fought?"

"With shield and spear."

"To the death?"

"Of course to the death!" Rhetia shook her head impatiently. "Sometimes you have to take your life in your hands, Mirany! The gods challenge us, and if we die we die. At least our cause is a good one. You know that more than anyone. And you know things can't stay as they are here for much longer. We have to look out for ourselves or end up choking on some poison. If it takes the threat of war to restore the Oracle, I'll do it. I'm not afraid of that."

Mirany turned and looked out at the sea. The blueness of it seemed deep and safe; she had a sudden desire to plunge into it and swim, anywhere, away from here. Instead she forced herself to turn back. "Listen to me." Her voice was quiet, and firm. "We say nothing to the pearl men—"

"That's utter—"

"*Listen to me!*" Furious now, she came and faced the tall girl. "There'll be no war and no battles and no smashed ships, do you hear me? That's not what the god wants."

"He's told you, I suppose," Rhetia said acidly.

"Yes, he's told me! There are other ways to do this, better ways—"

"We can't wait for the god! *We* have to act. The gods work through us!"

Mirany looked at her strangely. "Not always."

"What?"

"When the Archon was chosen. Who chose him, Rhetia? It wasn't you, because I saw you at the door of the house, and it wasn't Hermia, because you'd drugged her and left her here. So who was it wearing the Speaker's mask? That tall queenly woman in the robe of raindrops? I think you know as well as I do who it was."

Rhetia was silent. They had never talked about what had happened that night; the suspicion that the Rain Queen herself had come from her mystical garden to choose the Archon was almost a thing beyond saying. Now Rhetia seemed to lose some of her strength; there was a chair carved like a bird with open wings, and she went and sat in it, not looking at Mirany at all. After a moment she said, "I don't know what happened. I prayed, and then a sort of darkness came. When I woke up, I was lying there, on the stone platform, and the dawn had broken and everyone had gone. I ran all the way to the City. And yes, there was . . . someone else wearing the Speaker's robes."

For a moment then, they exchanged glances. Mirany said, "I'm going to find the Archon—"

"That little boy! What use is he?"

"I don't know. I don't know what use any of us are. But say nothing, Rhetia, to the merchants or anyone. Wait for me. Let the god do this the way he chooses."

She was halfway out of the door before Rhetia spoke again.

"I won't be poisoned. And I won't keep silent forever. If you're not with me, I'll do something without you. I will be Speaker, Mirany."

◆　◆　◆

As she walked hastily down the terraces of the processional road toward the bridge, Mirany shivered, despite the heat. As if things weren't bad enough! Rhetia had always been ambitious, and she was ruthless. She came from a long line of proud rulers and queens; she'd always resented Hermia and hated Argelin. But war!

Dimly, Mirany realized there was a stone in her sandal and stopped to unlace it. Kneeling on the stone road, the silence of the Island came up around her like a haze, and with it the heat rebounding off the smooth cobbles with a dazzling glare. Sweat broke out on her back. She wished she'd brought something to cover her arms.

The pause calmed her. When she had retied the strap and stood up again, she felt easier, as if some tension had loosened. In her mind she said, *Are you here?*

There was no answer, but as she walked on she felt the god was close, sensed that peculiar awareness of someone other that she was beginning to recognize.

The road was quiet. A few pilgrims to the Temple passed her, all on foot, some barefoot, loaded with offerings. They bowed, and she smiled back. Rhetia always ignored them, and Chryse would giggle behind their backs, but Mirany felt sorry for them, because usually they were desperate for the god's help, their children were sick or their crops had failed. Though the terrible drought had ended with the Archon's coming, the Two Lands were still dry as dust, the fields, as always, irrigated with the barest drips of water. It was well known that only the richer farmers could afford to pay

Argelin's taxes on water. His soldiers guarded all wells and oases and even had a guardpost on the dried-up bed of the river Draxis, which had ceased to flow generations ago.

At the bridge she crossed, looking down at the dolphins that always seemed to play there, in the warm shallows. There were two guards at the land end, Temple guards, and she nodded as they bowed to her, and then walked on quickly. She didn't trust any of them.

It was good to be walking, and off the Island. The desert spread out before her, shimmering with heat, rocky and spined with thorny bushes, hissing with insects. A pungent stink of cow dung came from somewhere, though the road was kept scrupulously swept, and away to her left the dark facade of the City of the Dead rose up, the seated silhouettes of the Archons that lined its battlements black against the piercing blue sky. Flicking off mosquitoes, she thought of Seth.

Argelin had been very, very clever. There was no doubt.

Two weeks after the new Archon had been chosen, Seth had been promoted. From fourth assistant archivist to second. He'd been delirious with happiness, and disbelief. And since then he had been so busy with his contracts and lists and plans and invoices that she had barely seen him. Why bother having someone killed when you could work them to death?

The Port wall loomed ahead of her, its gate open. Before that she turned off the main road, down a track lined with myrtle trees. Here on the highest point of the great cliff that tumbled down to the sea, was the Archon's Palace.

A white, gleaming building, its terraces and corridors rose above the drowned volcano. Precious trees grew in its gardens, watered by fountains, an unheard of luxury. As she came in through the gates she saw the fountains were running and splashing, great torrents of water gushing from urns held under the arms of solemn statues, a whole row of them, silent and identical, beautiful young girls. Yellow roses scented the air. Beyond, in the courtyards that skirted the kitchens, the Archon's army of servants worked, the bustle and clatter of pans coming up from below, the smell of garlic making Mirany's mouth water. On the trees lemons grew, almost ripe, and under the olive groves nets were hung to catch the falling fruit. She passed the new aviaries with their thousand colorful birds, parakeets and macaws and hummingbirds and birds of paradise, finches with plumed tails and scarlet beaks—a cacaphony of chirrups and song and fluttering wings. Once the new Archon had come, every ship in the Port had brought him gifts. Because of the rain. And his youth.

Mirany entered the house.

It was cool, the marble floors so smooth that she slipped off her gritty sandals and walked barefoot. The ornamental pool in the atrium had a bench and a pile of pictured scrolls beside it; she dipped her toes in the lukewarm water and padded from room to room, leaving a trail of wet prints.

"Archon?" she called. "Alexos?"

He was only ten, but the god was in him. Everything, all their plans, all their lives, depended on him. And yet Argelin had known how to deal with him, too.

Every room was full. With toys, with carved models of animals that roared and walked and growled, with board games and bats and balls and conjuring tricks and spinning tops. There was a great model of a theater, presented by the actors' guild, with tiny people to make up the audience and a set of actors with removable masks and a whole library of play scripts. In the room at the foot of the stairs she found chests of clothes and expensive fabrics, all strewn about, scattered with the half-eaten rind of a melon. Spilled raisins made a trail through the halls and galleries. Small animals scattered as she came by, a rat, a gerbil, furry things like guinea pigs, whole litters of them. In one room a great reptile slept on a branch in a cage; the cage was heated by underground piping and the creature sat immobile, its scales lurid green, its eye a coned stare. She wasn't even sure it was alive until its tongue darted out and snapped up a fly, an instant of terrifying speed.

There was no one anywhere. Trying another door, she found it jammed; shoving it wide, a table toppled on the other side, spread with fruit, some eaten. Putting her head around, she said, "Archon?"

The room was dim, the windows filmed with silk. Something chirred; a green slither zigzagged across the floor toward her, hissing. Hastily she jumped back and slammed the door.

He had everything a boy could want. The whole Palace was a child's paradise. When the rain had come, the people had been beside themselves with joy; every well in the town had brimmed full, every duct and pipe and barrel had been filled. Next morning there had been queues of people from here right back to the Port, bringing quinces and damsons and precious plums, gold coins and silks, rings and tunics, musical instruments, animals of every species, a million scrolls of tales and stories. And above all, toys. He had all the toys in the world and no one to play with them with. He had stood on the roof in his gold mask and waved his gratitude, a tiny silent figure.

She came to some stairs and looked up. "Alexos! Where are you? It's Mirany."

No one could speak to the Archon, no one see his face. But they had ignored that, she and Seth and Oblek. Oblek had sworn not even death would separate him from the boy, had marched in and sat down and defied any soldier to remove him. Argelin hadn't even tried. Instead, that night, he had started sending the wine.

Casks of it.

Sweet wines and red wines and vintages from Paros. Distilled spirits in amphorae from the ships of merchants, brought from beyond the sea. Honeyed meads and beers brewed from hops.

For the cellar of the Archon.

Oh yes, she thought acidly, climbing the wide marble staircase, Argelin had known just how to deal with them all.

He had given them what they wanted. Their secret dreams.

Except her. He didn't know what she wanted.

It would take a god to know that.

She stopped on the fourth step. "Where are you?"

In the jungle chamber, Mirany.

There was a great door to her left, brass, with the sign of the Scorpion embossed on it in copper. She creaked it open and slid in.

It had once been a room. Now it was a forest, carpeted in turf, great trees rising to its ceiling, creepers and branches crowding it. Through the open windows butterflies flew in, attracted by the nectar that dripped from exotic flowers, and flocks of tiny, brilliant birds cheeped and swooped overhead. There were monkeys of all sorts, baboons and tiny gray ones with babies hanging to their bellies, and longtailed lemurs that swung and screeched and somersaulted with a crash through the foliage. And there was Alexos, hanging upside down from his knees, feeding pieces of apple to a chimp as big as himself.

"Mirany!"

"For god's sake," she said in terror. "You'll fall!"

"No. I'm good at it. Watch me with Eno!" He swung, and the small brown monkey that was his favorite jumped onto his back with a chatter, and then the boy was swarming down a rope feet first, then to a branch, then somersaulting down and down to land on the grass at her side, breathless and dishevelled. "See?"

He was taller. His face was red and heated and full of

mischief but its beauty was the beauty of the god. In sudden despair she sat down on the withering turf and put her arms around her knees. "Is he back? Has there been any sign of him?"

"No." The boy looked at her, and his happiness faded. He crouched down. "I've had the servants look everywhere."

"In the cellar?"

"We looked there first. He was here two days ago, Mirany, because he had the harp out and was playing it, such sad songs, like he used to sing for me years ago, before I was young. Then we played hide-and-seek and something happened and I never got around to finding him." He frowned. "Poor Oblek. It's all my fault."

"Your fault?"

"Don't you see, it's because he can't make the songs anymore. It makes him sad. I promised him that when I was Archon, we would go on a great quest to find the place that songs come from. But I forgot, Mirany, because there were all these lovely things to play with and the ceremonies and the children to put my hands on and cure, and being carried in a litter and waving at all the people. I forgot about the songs. And I think he may have gone to look for them on his own."

She shook her head. "Not without telling us."

He watched her carefully. "You think Argelin has got him."

"He tried to kill Argelin. Argelin would have been

watching this palace. If Oblek stepped outside, they would be waiting for him."

In a scared silence, they watched two lemurs scream over an apricot. Then Alexos stood up. "Mirany, there's something else you have to do. Tonight. You have to go down into the Kingdom of Shadows and speak with my brother."

"Kreon?"

"I dreamed of him. He stood in the dark and held a Sphere in his hands, a Sphere of Secrets, and he said, 'Brother. This is waiting for you. Send for it.'"

Alexos took her fingers, and his hand was cold. "There were mountains all around us, Mirany, in my dream. Ice mountains. Silver mountains. And the Sphere in his hands grew and grew till it filled all the night, and the mountains opened for it to go inside. And there was writing on it. And it was the moon!"

HE GETS MORE THAN HE BARGAINED FOR

"It's from *what?*"

"A unicorn." The trader laid the long, spiral horn in Seth's hands. "Animal like a horse. Lives far in the west. Beyond the ends of the earth."

Seth turned the thing, wondering. "If it lives beyond the ends of the earth, how did you get it?"

The man winked. "One way and another. Things get traded, passed on. See these? They're called thunderstones. Have one in your house and it'll never be hit by lightning. They come from deep in the rocks."

Seth picked one out of the pile. A small coiled animal, made of stone. Its ridges were like the shell of some sea creature. "How much?" he ventured.

"Sixty. The bagful."

"Forty."

"Fifty."

Seth nodded and added it to the list, a few skillful strokes of the stylus. "As for the unicorn's horn, what's it good for?"

"Medicine." The man leaned on the prow of his boat, its siren figurehead drawn high on the rocky beach. "They powder it, the doctors and the sibyls. Deals with all sorts of complaints. Wind, belly gripes, ulcers. Good for women." He winked again. "You know."

Seth didn't know and wasn't sure he wanted to. But he thought he could sell it on and nodded.

"That all?"

"Everything, scribe. Unless—" The trader glanced around at the slaves, saw they were back on board and came so close that Seth could smell his breath. "Unless you want something special."

"Special?"

"Rare. Precious. Not to be found more than once in a lifetime."

Seth sighed. He should have been expecting this. The biggest con. Always left till last. "Don't tell me. The egg of the phoenix. No, a hippogriff that flies. Or dragon's teeth, and if you sow them an army springs up from the soil."

The trader stepped back. His tanned, leathery face, burned almost black, looked sour. "Go on, scribe, make fun of me. You're an educated lad. All that writing and figuring and learning piled up inside you. But maybe there are things even you don't know about. Things from the gods themselves."

Seth nodded with a superior smile. "I'm sure. So what is it?"

The trader wiped his hands on his tunic. For a moment he seemed absorbed in the task. Then he looked up. "It's a star, master."

"A *star*?"

"That's right." The man faced him solemnly.

"Oh, come on." Seth gave a short laugh. "Do I look that stupid? How did you get it? Prop a ladder against the sky and climb up?"

He didn't have time for this. The cart should have been back at the warehouse an hour ago; the trader had been late, and the goods needed to be under cover before the next duty roster started. If the overseer found out he was bringing smuggled goods into the City, that would be another cut he'd have to pay out of the profits.

The trader ignored the sarcasm. He yelled something to one of the slaves on deck, a few words in some island dialect. The man went below, and the trader turned back. "Three nights ago," he said quietly, "we were out at sea, between the Heclades and the reefs of Scorya. A bit tricky there, so I was steering. A fine night, before the moon rose, all the stars bright, the Hunter, and the Dogs, and the Scorpion. And then there was a flash, a streak of light from the Scorpion's tail, and something scorched down and fell into the sea—splash!—just off the bow."

The slave was trudging up the beach. Irritated, Seth said, "If you're trying to sell me some scrappy chunk of stone . . ."

The trader turned and took a bundle from the slave. "No stone. When we leaned over the side we could see it, shining, far below the waves. Anton dived for it, as he does for pearls. Take a look, scribe. Surely your Archon would want to buy a star."

He was tugging back the folds of the old wrapping. As the cloth fell open his face was lit with a sudden brilliance that made him narrow his eyes; he looked up at Seth in triumph.

Seth stared. He was so astonished that for a fatal moment he even let it show. In the man's hands, deep in the filthy rag, a point of light burned. White and fierce, a glassy crystal, it blazed; he could even see the faint shadow of the trader thrown by it on the sand. Nearby, the slave lingered, as if unable to tear himself away.

Seth breathed out. He licked his lips, said hoarsely, "Is it hot?"

"No. We were afraid it would burn, but it's cool. Take it, scribe."

Carefully, the fragile crystal was placed in his hands. He narrowed his eyes against the light, caught a faint metallic smell, not unpleasant. He shook his head. "The philosophers say the stars are studded in the outermost sphere of the sky."

"Maybe one came loose. What else can it be? It's small enough, as you see." The trader turned, saw the slave, and jerked his head sourly. When the man had gone, he took a shrewd look at Seth's face and said, "Of course, it costs."

Seth looked up. Everything was blurred; rainbow spots of color dazzled him. He flipped the cloth over the brilliance and nodded, arranging the folds. "I had no doubt it would."

They eyed each other. The trader began. "Five hundred staters."

Seth shrugged, elaborately careless. "Out of the question."

"For a star?"

"For ten stars." He put it back in the man's hands. "Besides, what would I do with it?"

They both knew he wanted it.

The trader looked thoughtful. "As I said, the Archon's favor—"

"I'm already a friend of the Archon." Seth tallied the bill rapidly, brought a purse out of his pocket and began to count over coins.

"Lord Argelin—"

"I doubt a star would amuse him."

"The Nine—"

"Are also friends of mine." Tugging the purse strings shut, Seth pocketed it. He gave a shout to the impatient slaves; two of them immediately grabbed the handles of the cart and began to drag it along the steep track up to the road. If they were quick they'd get it back in time.

The trader sighed. "Four hundred, then. As a favor. Though I could get six on the open market."

"Then take it to the Port, and pay Argelin's commission, and the auctioneer's cut, and the taxes. . . ."

They were silent. Until the trader shook his head bitterly. "You're too cocky, son. That will bring you down one day. That and your greed."

Seth shrugged. "My price is two hundred. I've only got your word for what it is."

"You can *see* what it is." Exasperated, the trader glanced at the tide. "All right. All right. Two fifty. Or I try elsewhere."

Seth considered, but it was only a pretense and they both knew it. "Done." He took the purse out and counted a hundred staters. "Take that. Send a man to the City tomorrow and ask for the Office of Plans. I'm second archivist. He'll get the rest then." Forestalling protest, he held his hand up. "I don't have any more on me. I wasn't expecting stars."

Reluctantly, the trader held out the fragile bundle. As he took it Seth felt a faint tingle of power through the cloth, just as he had in saying "second archivist," in that elaborately offhand way. They shook hands; the man shouted to his slaves; the boat began to be pushed off the beach. Seth turned and scrambled quickly up the rocks to the track at the top of the low cliff, soft sand slithering under his sandals. At the top he turned; the ship was already afloat, one sail jerking up, a few ropes rattling through hawsers. Slightly breathless, he watched it catch the wind, the white cloth flapping and filling.

Only then did he allow himself to look down at the bundle in his hands. Crouching on the ground, he slipped the loose scarf from his neck, carefully lifted the star from its rags and replaced it in the soft fabric. Its white brilliance astonished him. Alexos would adore it. And when he got tired of it, Seth had no doubt he could sell it on for at least twice the price. A shining star! Making its own light in the dark! He threw the flea-infested rags away and tucked the new tight bundle inside his tunic. It was the bargain of a lifetime! He grinned, rubbing sweat from his hair. And yes, he'd got it cheap.

Standing, he saw the land was already almost dark. Far to the west, over the mountains, the sun was setting, making the distant peaks pinnacles of gloom, their shadows vast. Lights were lit in the Port; he could see the expensive houses up on the very top of the vertical terraces with their kindled torches blazing. One day he and Pa and Telia would live up there. They'd already moved out of the potters' quarter. That was a start.

The cart was too far ahead to hear by now, and the vast silence of the desert fell suddenly around him. The wind had dropped, only the faintest breeze creaking stiff branches of trees dead from thirst. It was three leagues to the Port, and no one lived out here but the odd goatherd.

Seth walked quickly. The goods would be useful. Most he would sell to various officials in the City and pocket the profit. Some Pa could trade in the markets. Altogether he was counting on a few hundred from this, enough for the rent for the new house—

He stopped.

Ahead, on the road, someone was coming toward him. The scuffling run, the loud gasping of a breathless man.

Instantly Seth drew the knife from his boot and stepped off the track, behind the dark fleshy leaves of a huge agave. Bandits! There were said to be plenty out in the desert, and if they'd been watching the trading they'd know he had money. Cursing himself for sending the slaves off, he licked dry lips and tried to breathe without shuddering.

The footsteps were fast, and then there was a slither and a gasp as if the man had fallen and dragged himself hastily up. Maybe this was someone running from fear. If so, Seth thought coldly, the best thing to do would be stay hidden and let him go by. There was no point in getting killed for some stranger.

Slowly he crouched, making himself small. The vast leathery leaves were cold against his hands; the knife seemed brittle and he tried to imagine himself using it, but the thought turned him cold. In the agave grove it was very dark; he sensed that the man had drawn level with him, a rustle among the leaves. Then the shadow stopped, gasping and cursing and bent over. A big man, heavy. From a bag slung on his shoulder he pulled out something that swished; now his head tilted as he drank from it. The sour smell of expensive wine made Seth stare.

Maybe he moved. Made some sound.

The stranger whipped around.

Absolutely still, Seth stopped breathing. And then he realized, with a terrible dread, that he was not hidden.

There was light, leaking from somewhere, the faintest silvery radiance, and it was growing, and because of it the man could see him.

The star!

The stranger lunged in, grabbed him with a vast hand and hauled him out. Immediately Seth stabbed with the knife, but a meaty fist twisted it expertly out of his grip and clamped itself over his mouth.

"Shut it, ink boy. It's me, Oblek."

Oblek. The thought was a soaking relief. And in the star radiance, he could see the familiar bald head, the ugly gap-toothed leer. The hand came away; he could breathe. "What are you—"

"Listen. They're after me. Since I came out of the Port. Two, maybe three."

"Thieves?"

"Argelin's heavies."

"Where?"

"Just behind. Thought I was finished, but now . . ." He clapped Seth on the back with a staggering blow. "Grab that stylus parer of yours and get ready. Two of us should see them off."

Seth stepped back, his hands open. "Not me. I'm not in this." He could hear them coming, horses, too, the clank of weapons. More than one.

The musician's small eyes were cold. "Seth—"

"No! Don't you see? I have to think of Pa, and Telia. If anything happened to me—"

"I saved your life once. You owe me." The words were so quiet the approaching rumble almost drowned them.

"Just run!" Seth hissed. "You'll have a chance!"

Oblek didn't move. He looked disgusted. "I hauled you back up that pit in the tomb. I should have let you fall. All you care about is profit, and your own stinking skin. Your father was right."

"My father?"

Oblek spat, and turned. "What he said about you once." He snorted with contempt and looked sidelong. "Get lost. I don't need a weak-kneed boy. I just wish Mirany could see what a useless piece of dung you are."

A shout. Oblek had his knife in one hand, Seth's in the other. He drew himself up.

Furious, Seth stepped back.

"You heard," Oblek growled. "Run away. Bury yourself in parchment and coins."

"You can still escape! Come with me!"

"Why should I?" The big man raised his head and glared at the approaching riders. "What's the point when the songs don't come anymore?"

Two men, with spears, bending low over the saddle. Oblek opened his arms and screamed, an agony of fury, "Here I am, you scum! Come on. Kill me! *Kill me!*"

With a sickening thud one of them struck at him. Seth turned and ran, ducking, breathless into the spiny growth, stumbling into a foxhole and out, never looking back, hating himself. Behind on the road the yells and catcalls of the fight burst out, the clang of metal, a screech of pain. But what chance was there, he thought, almost sobbing with fury, against spears and swords? Oblek was crazy, demented, always had been, from the beginning. Why should he be expected to die as well?

Rounding a scatter of rocks, he fell full length over one and lay with the breath thumped out of him, the tiny hardness that was the star bruising his ribs. Something scuttled over his neck, and slid off. Chest heaving, he rolled over.

The night was quiet.

Far above him were the stars, thousands of them, brilliant over the desert and he could smell smoke, and the crushed spines of tiny aromatic herbs under his body.

Voices. A laugh. The clink of a sheathed sword.

Oblek hadn't lasted long.

Had they killed him, though? Or were they taking him back to Argelin? All in all, that was more likely. The general would want to finish this himself. With his own hands.

As the thought flashed through him, Seth jerked over, scrambled up and ran. He raced heedless through the underbrush and scrub of the desert, keeping low, back toward the Port. There was a place where the road ran right along the edge of the cliff, the treacherous crumbling rim of the drowned volcano that formed the entire bay. They'd have to pass it. That would be the place.

He skidded to a halt just in time; before he knew it there was only sea below him, black, glinting with reflected light. Hurriedly he kicked tinder-dry branches together, hauled a dead branch across the track, picked up another and weighed it in his hands. It crumbled at the edges. Not much of a weapon.

They were coming already. He slid into the shadows on the land side of the path, crouched down, alert, something almost like joy filling him. His hands shook on the worm-ridden wood.

Oblek was alive. The soldiers had him tied and were half dragging him along on a rope behind one of the horses. Whenever he managed to scramble up, they jerked the rope and he fell again. The men laughed. One of them drank from the wine flask.

Seth prayed the musician had some strength left. He couldn't do this alone. *And you,* he thought angrily to the god, *what about you? Can't you help us?*

I have sent you a star. What more do you want?

Not a voice. Just his own mind, thinking. Was this what Mirany meant when she said the god spoke to her? He took a deep breath, rummaged for the tied bundle, tore it open with his teeth. Light spilled out, a thread of it. He stuffed the scarf back over it.

"What was *that?*"

The soldiers slowed. Then the first came on, pacing slowly, the horse flicking its mane, whickering with nerves. As it passed him, Seth swallowed, knew quite definitely he was too terrified ever to move.

Then he leaped out.

The horse sidestepped, shied; he was up and had the soldier by the arm and had dragged him down before the uproar broke out behind him; the soft branch came down on the man's skull with a thud that sickened him, then he spun and whipped out the star.

"Oblek!" he screamed.

The night shattered. Brilliance blazed from his hand; dimly beyond he saw the other horse rear up in panic, heard Oblek yell fiercely. Something struck him on the arm; he turned, slashing wildly. A spear whistled past him, hit a rock, sent a vast clatter of stones and half the path over the cliffside; scrambling back, Seth saw the soldier seconds before the sword flashed out, and could only dive to the side, the star falling out of his hands and rolling to the cliff edge. He scrambled after it, his fingers clutching desperately among rubble and dust; then the man was on him, a staggering weight, and a blow cracked one side of his face. Spitting blood, Seth kicked and yelled, heaved him off, saw his eyes for a second, his raised blade. Then Oblek came from nowhere, grabbed the man, swung him around, punched him in the stomach, and hurled him off the cliff.

After the shrill scream the night was unbelievably quiet.

One horse stood nearby, its reins trailing. The other had run, probably not far. Seth picked himself up unsteadily. "Did I kill him?"

"You couldn't kill a flea." Oblek bent and examined the man Seth had clubbed. "He's coming around." He shoved his arms under the man's shoulders and hauled him to the cliff edge.

"No!" Face numb, Seth could barely manage the words. "Let him be!"

Oblek barely paused. "We can't leave witnesses. They saw you."

"They just saw light! Please, Oblek! I came back for you. You owe me that."

The big man glared at him, a silent disgust. Then he dropped the soldier like a sack on the path. For a second Seth still thought he would roll the man over, but all he did was bend down and rifle his pockets. Taking the sword and a knife and some coins, he stood up. "You'd better be sure of that, ink boy. Because if he did see you, you can say good-bye to your cozy job."

He crossed to the cliff edge then, and picked up the star.

"What in the god's name is this?"

Seth snatched it. "It's mine. Come on. We've got to get out of here." He wrapped the star and shoved it inside his tunic, Oblek's small astonished eyes watching every glimmer.

"It shines."

"I'll explain later. I bought it." He looked up, froze.

The soldier was on his feet.

There was no time to yell. The man shoved; Oblek was thrust forward, arms out, past Seth. He howled as he fell, the rope, still around his waist, snaking over the cliff edge after him, an unraveling too rapid to see, so that Seth fell on it, and grabbed, and the sudden jerk tangled him, burned his hands, whipped him away.

Feetfirst, he plummeted, turning in the air.

Into rocks and spray and horror.

Into the black smack of the sea.

THE SECOND OFFERING
OF A FALLEN STAR

I don't remember when I first touched water.
Billions of eons ago.

I was hot and burning, a child in a fever, and
all at once there was this other, this wetness, a
cool hand on my forehead.

Possibly I'm not much of a god, because it was
the Rain Queen who brought life, dragging it in
the train of her dress. Plants grew, oceans swelled.
Creatures swam in her folds and crawled from her
hems.

Before she came there was no life.
And no death.

He Selects a Dangerous Master

Death was a terrible place. It churned with salt and sand and it roared in his ears. It clutched at him and sank with him, shoved him down, held its great hand over his mouth.

Seth was tangled in it like rope.

Somewhere inside him a bubble was growing, a huge membrane swelling as if it would burst him wide, webbing his open mouth, a scream that could never be screamed. Just as he knew it would kill him, he was hauled up into an explosion of air and darkness and the smell of fish and a gasping vomit.

"Hang on to me, I said!" Oblek's roar was choked and bubbled. Then he yelled, "Can't you swim?"

"No." Seth barely got the word out before swallowing a mouthful of sea. He choked in nose and throat.

"God!" Oblek's bulk maneuvered under him; he gripped frantically on sodden clothes, a fat, slippery arm.

The musician's voice was grim with humor. "Didn't teach you that in the City, then? All that learning? All those notes and scribbles? Not much use now. Any kid in the harbor can swim!"

"Shut up." Seth was terrified. There was nothing below him. Nothing but water, dark and deep and deadly. *Nothing.*

With a huge effort, Oblek's body turned. His feet splashed. He seemed to be lying on his back, a great whale in the water. "Let go a bit," he gasped. "You're strangling me."

Seth couldn't. He dare not. Water lapped against his lips, flooded his ears. Around him it shimmered with faint phosphorescence; he saw things flicker in it, fish, anemones. Something nibbled at his neck.

More splashing. "There," Oblek grunted. "A ship. See it?"

Breathless, Seth managed, "I thought life . . . wasn't worth living?"

The big man seemed to laugh. "Maybe something changed."

Even Seth could see it now, swinging around into his view. A huge ship, so huge it could never be real. A ship of the gods, blazing with light, music drifting from it. A ship to carry the dead.

With a great convulsion of water, Oblek began to swim. Seth gasped, grabbed again; he was tugged along, choking under the sudden wash, into water perfumed with rose and sandalwood, petals floating on its surface. Then the prow was looming over them. In the dark it seemed monstrous, a gaudy woman who sneered, her hair a mass of snakes, her breast wooden, festooned with weed. Torches blazed over her, ladders rattled, a flotilla of row boats clattered and bobbed around her. The roar of her passing sent waves right over Seth's face.

A half-eaten pasty hurtled down and hit the water next to Oblek.

"Hey!" the musician roared. "Down here!"

Seth was numb with exhaustion. He knew his hands were slipping. He was saturated with water; his stomach retched it; it blinded his eyes. The yells and calls, splash of ropes, jerk of hands grabbing him seemed oddly distant, things happening far away to somebody else. The sea clung to him, sucked him back, poured out of his clothes. Shivering, he was dragged out, his feet placed on a swaying ladder, rung after rung. Then someone heaved him onto a soft woolen floor that he knelt on and clutched tight, head down, coughing, sick.

His ears popped.

Music soared. Cymbals and drums, a sitar, other brazen sounds. Terror drained out of him, ran through the very pores of his skin. He opened his eyes.

The ship really was vast. The whole deck was roofed with silk; it rippled like a series of pavilions, carpeted with finest rugs, the warm night scented with spices. There were people everywhere.

"What's going on?" he gasped.

"Our High One gives hospitality to your general. Many people come. Rich people. Big party."

The thin sailor who had hauled him up looked uneasily at the mess on the carpet.

Seth almost choked. "Did he say 'general'? *Argelin's here?*"

Oblek was leaning wearily on the rail. He shrugged. "Out of the frying pan, eh?"

"You're bleeding."

"And you're half drowned. We're in great shape." He turned to the sailor. "We borrow boat. Quick. Yes?"

But they were already attracting attention. The music stopped; there was applause and a crowd of flute girls trooped out from the pavilion, looking hot and thirsty and wearing blue costumes of flimsy silk. Behind them the doors of the upper deck were flung open, and crowds of partygoers wandered after them into the evening air, drinking and laughing and talking and eating, brilliant groups of men in richly woven tunics and fine robes, the women's dresses embroidered and glinting with gems.

Oblek groaned, scratching seaweed off his soaked neck. "Too late."

The bright people dazzled. Their eyes were painted and outlined in kohl; their elaborate wigs glistened with thousands of braided strands. On necks and arms precious stones gleamed. Wide lapis collars of blue and gold reflected the lights; the smell of perfume was overpowering. A red-lipped woman who stared over at Seth wore spiraling gold armlets that snaked from shoulder to elbow. She said something and laughed. Heads turned to look.

He still felt sick, and could barely manage to stand. "We've got to get out of this!" In the lighted pavilion behind, he could see Argelin. The general stood with Prince Jamil's merchants and their wives, his bodyguards at a discreet distance. There were others, too, dignitaries from the City, the Chief Embalmer, the Lord of the Council of Tombs. Seth wondered if the Nine were here, and his heart leaped. Could Mirany get them away?

"Who the hell are you? Where are your invitations?"

This was all they needed. An ephebe, young, in a fresh dress uniform.

Seth glanced at Oblek. "We don't have invitations," he said quietly, keeping his eyes down. "We're just servants."

"Servants are supposed to wait in the boats."

"I fell overboard."

They were surrounded now. A group of grinning young dandies had come to listen, arms around the flute girls. Several were obviously drunk. "Should've swum around the ship all night," one remarked. The others roared.

Seth felt Oblek move closer.

"What about him?"

"He pulled me out."

The ephebe gave Oblek a hard look. Then he asked the question Seth had been dreading.

"Whose servants?"

Argelin's group was coming toward the entrance. Seth

licked dry lips. He gave a rapid glance around, at the smirking faces, the brilliant crowd. Then he looked again.

"*His,*" he said quietly.

Everyone turned.

The man at the back was leaning against the ship's rail, a tall, elegant figure, robed in a fine green robe. His fair hair was elaborately tied back; he wore a delicate collar of silver and his manicured hands held a goblet of wine. He drank from it calmly.

"Is that true, my lord?" The ephebe's voice was distinctly more respectful.

Under kohled lashes the tall man glanced at Oblek. Then at Seth. His eyes were strangely long, almond shaped, dangerous as a desert animal's. Seth held the gaze for a tense moment, fingers gripped tight together.

Then the man straightened and came forward. "I'm afraid so, Officer," he said, his voice aristocratic and bored. Folding his arms he snapped, "What happened, *slave?*"

"There was a . . . wave, Master." Seth had to grit his teeth to stop shivering. "I fell in. O-Oblios saved me."

"A waste of his time, I would say." The tall man turned to the ephebe. "I have never had such a worthless slave. Look at him! Soaked, seasick, good for nothing."

"You should sell him, lord." The ephebe had lost interest. He bowed and pushed through the partygoers. Seth breathed out with bitter relief. Now they could get away! But the tall man drank his wine and turned gracefully to the crowd.

"What an excellent idea!" He smiled, his eyes cold. "Maybe I will. Who'll bid me for him? Alia, my dear, make me an offer."

The red-lipped woman giggled. "Two staters."

"Two? Not nearly enough. After all, he's young and pretty."

Seth risked a glance at Oblek. The big man glowered, alert. They both knew the Jackal was playing with them.

He might be some lord, but he was also a tomb thief, the leader of the most notorious gang in the Port. They knew that, but it was Seth's guess no one else here did, and that unspoken threat of betrayal was all he and Oblek had to defend themselves.

"Three!" some old man announced. The flute girls on his arm laughed.

The Jackal gave Seth a sidelong glance. "That may indeed be all he's worth."

Seth stepped forward. "For the god's sake," he murmured. *"Argelin."*

The general had come out of the pavilion. His smooth face and razored dark beard were clear through the crowd; he wore a bronze breastplate that gleamed. No paint, no jewelry. Instead he surveyed the foppish crowd with cold distaste.

Instantly Seth ducked away.

The crowd bowed; the Jackal stepped back. "My boat is at the stern ladder," he said without looking around. "Get into it. Wait for me."

Seth didn't hesitate. Argelin knew them too well. Oblek was already lost in the crowd; for a hefty man he could move quickly and without fuss when he wanted to. He also seemed to know where the stern ladder was; Seth had no idea.

Argelin was leaving, it seemed. He drew the merchant lord away from the crowd; Seth, scrambling over the side, caught his voice.

". . . for your hospitality, Prince Jamil. As for the pronouncement of the Oracle, what can I say? No man understands the god."

The dark-bearded man nodded gravely. "It was a great disappointment to us. You know that."

"I am sorry for it."

"So you would inform me, then, if there was any gift, any . . . offering that might be made."

"To change the god's mind?" Argelin smiled.

They looked at each other for a long moment.

The Pearl Prince's eyes were dark and steady. "Anything," he said quietly.

Argelin's smile had faded. Now he said, "Thank you. But who am I to have any influence with a god?"

Prince Jamil did not flicker. "You are the general. You're a friend of the Speaker. I'm sure, if *you really wished it*, you could intercede."

For a moment, Argelin's calmness was almost lost. Instead he laughed, a humorless sound. "Your estimate of me is far too generous. I cannot help you."

Seth listened, clinging on like a spider. Argelin turned

toward him and he ducked. From the swaying ladder he heard Jamil say, "I have, of course, sent to inform the Emperor of our failure."

Argelin paused, his bronze armor gleaming. "You're not leaving, then?"

"Oh no. Not as yet." The merchant spread polite hands; his red silk robe flowed like flames. "We'll finish trading, buying and selling. My friends and their wives are eager to tour the sights of your great land. The City, the tombs and statues of the Archons. Perhaps even an expedition to the famous Animals in the desert."

Oblek tugged Seth's legs. He kicked him off, impatient. The general's face had darkened.

"Be careful."

"Careful?"

"Of the desert. It's the haunt of thieves and jackals."

"I have many armed servants, General."

Argelin nodded. "Indeed. But it is also waterless and a wilderness. Snakes and scorpions infest it. And did the god not say to you that those who enter it would burn in his wrath?"

The dark-bearded man put his hands together, fingertips to fingertips. His face was grave. "He did. But I had thought, my lord, that no one knew that message but the priestess and my companions."

The silence was charged. A faint flush came to Argelin's face as he realized his mistake, but when he spoke, his voice was almost mocking.

"Good night, Lord Jamil."

Seth was jerked down; breathless he fell into the boat. "Come on!" Oblek growled.

The boat bobbed, almost capsizing with the uneven weight. As Seth grabbed hold of it in terror, he found that it was cushioned, with a gaudy tented roof of mauve silk, the side curtains drawn so no one could see in. Lanterns hung over the side, shiny zigzags reflecting in the sea.

A black man at the oars glared at them. Beside him, armed and astonished, sat the red-haired man Seth remembered only too well. The Fox.

Oblek collapsed onto the frail bench. "Well," he said sourly. "Don't look so pleased to see us."

The slither of a long hooked blade out of its sheath was his only answer; just then the boat dipped again as the Jackal dropped lightly down and ducked inside.

"Row," he snapped. "Quickly."

Seth grabbed on to the closest thing; it was Oblek's arm. The sudden choppy motion turned his stomach over. He closed his eyes; Oblek laughed and jerked away. "Poor ink boy. Wishes he was at his safe little desk, eh?"

Calmly the Jackal sat and stretched out long legs. Then he leaned forward and considered them both. "I'm afraid this is our night's haul, Fox."

"Nothing else? The jewels?"

"Change of plan. I've told the others. It's all off."

Aghast, the Fox stared. "God's teeth! The planning. Getting the others on. All that work!"

"Wasted." The Jackal's cold eyes watched Seth. "All wasted."

Knife-sharp, the Fox spat. "I've waited for this, chief." He was glaring at Seth in fury. "We'll cut their tongues out, then we'll tie them together and drop them over the side. They can drown in each other's arms."

Oblek leered. "You with me, ugly."

Before the Fox could roar, the Jackal had reached out and caught Seth and hauled him close, face-to-face. "I think that's a very good idea. You betrayed us, scribe, at Sostris's tomb. And what happened to my reward for helping your precious Archon? We had a bargain—you never kept it."

Sweat ran down Seth's back. "Things haven't worked out."

"You surprise me."

"It's true! The Archon's got no power. He's just a boy—"

"And crazy, as I recall. But you seem to have done well enough out of him. This tunic cost a few staters." He flicked at it; at the touch, his face changed. Before Seth could pull away, the thief's quick fingers had darted in and snatched the wrapped packet out. He leaned back, curious. "What's this?"

"Don't open it!"

As soon as the words were out, Seth knew it was the stupidest thing he could have said. The Jackal raised an amused eyebrow at his men. Carefully, he unwrapped the star.

Brilliance shot across his face. He jerked back; the oarsman stopped, swearing in awe.

After a moment, his long eyes bright with the radiance, he asked again, wondering, "What *is* this?"

"A star." Seth was sullen. He knew what was coming, and it came.

The Jackal nodded calmly. "A star."

"It fell out of the sky."

"Did it now. Excellent. It will more than make up for the little enterprise you blundered into tonight." He rewrapped it, hiding the light. "Consider it an advance on your debt."

Seth tried to answer. Instead he squirmed hastily around and was sick over the side, retching uncontrollably outside the purple hangings. The rower grinned and the Fox gave a bark of laughter. Oblek smirked.

"Dear me," the Jackal said mildly. "Perhaps we'd better wait till we get ashore before I tell you what I want from you."

"Us?" Oblek said.

"You. And your Archon and the little priestess."

Seth wiped streaming eyes. His voice was a croak. "We'll pay you, don't worry. Alexos has money."

"I want more than money." The Jackal spoke with perfect clarity. "In order to get his beloved musician back with his ears and fingers still attached, the Archon might consider helping in a little scheme I have in mind."

"What scheme?"

The thief fingered the star, loosing a sliver of silver. He looked sidelong at Seth. "Something is going on," he said softly. "Something strange."

"Strange? Where?"

Over the muted splash of the oars, the Jackal's voice was a whisper. "In the Mountains of the Moon."

SHE RETURNS TO THE KINGDOM OF SHADOW

The City of the Dead brooded over the desert.

As the Archon's litter swayed on the bearers' shoulders Mirany held up a corner of one of the filmy curtains and looked out at the grim black bastions of the towering wall, the great statues of the Archons. Two hundred and sixty-nine of them, every Archon in unbroken line back to the legendary Sargon himself, immense hands on immense knees, staring out to sea. While the Archons kept their everlasting watch it was said that no enemy could defeat the Two Lands. And below, deep in the tombs, their bodies lay, emptied and preserved in gleaming carapaces of gold and lapis, coffined within nine coffins, wrapped and beautiful, nested in by scorpions, eaten by beetles.

Mirany bit her lip. Dropping the curtain she sank back on the red seat, palms flat on each side against the gentle swaying. The *tombs*. She dreaded going down into them again.

Since the terrible night of the Shadow, when she had been buried alive for betrayal of the Oracle, she had never been back to the City. The Island was dangerous, but at least it was bright, its white buildings full of sunlight, its flowers scarlet and scented. The City was a warren of dust and tunnels, a labyrinth of buildings housing clerks and scribes and painters and goldsmiths, millions of slaves, sinister masked embalmers. The peculiar smells of its corridors haunted her sleep. Sometimes now she would wake at night, breathless, desperate for air, would sit up quickly in the fine bed with its delicate hangings, would climb out just to see her dim face in the bronze mirror.

Her hair was growing; it was almost as long as it had been before. But something else had gone—a timid trust she had once had in people, like Chryse, who had betrayed her. And in the Island. She knew now that there was evil even there, that anything could happen, even among the Nine.

The thought made her remember Rhetia, and she rubbed one eye wearily. What could she do about Rhetia?

"Holiness?"

The litter had been lowered so gently she had barely noticed. Now the leading slave had opened the curtain and was looking inside. "We're at the gate of the City."

"Thank you."

She swung her legs out, the man taking her hand briefly, the loosest of touches. Was it allowed for slaves to touch the Nine? She had no real idea. There was still so much she didn't know. Standing, she felt the pleats of her dress swish around her ankles. Above, three huge black blocks of polished marble formed the gate.

"We'll wait for you here, holiness."

Mirany looked at him, alarmed. "That won't be necessary. I'll be going back to the Island from here."

"But you can't walk the road at night." The slave looked appalled. "The Archon said we were to look after you."

The other five were listening, one adjusting the bindings on his hands. In the warm darkness an owl hooted in the desert.

The man was right. And yet Mirany was certain that one of these men, maybe more, would be in Argelin's pay. The general would be told she'd come here. She didn't want him to know any more.

"The City has plenty of litters. I'll arrange for one to take me back to the Island." Her voice was quiet, though she tried to make it commanding, as Rhetia would have done. "There's no need for you to wait. The Archon will understand."

She turned, as if that was the end of the matter, and walked under the gateway. A faint scent of artemisia drifted from the bushes outside. Without looking back, she sensed the men's dismay, then heard their voices, the creak of the empty litter as they swung it up.

They were going.

She allowed herself a tight smile of victory.

On the other side of the gate two guards gave a hasty

salute, and then she was striding across the vast plaza that was the central square of the City. At its heart, black against the stars, rose the ziggurat, the stepped pyramid of sacrifice she had climbed only once. Around it, dark facades now, were the houses of mourning, locked and emptied. They would not be used again until Alexos' death. The thought of that gave her a jolt of horror. She told herself it was years away, but there was no way of being sure. The Archon's fate was to be a sacrifice. If it was necessary he would give his life for the people. That was the promise he had made.

Her sandals made a tap-tap on the dusty stones. There were few people around. Dark shapes ran into corners; one darted close in front of her, and she stopped with a stifled gasp, then let out her breath crossly. Cats. The City was infested with them. Oddly big and black, they bred and fought and padded in the buildings and workshops, watched green-eyed in the dark tunnels. Walking on, her heart thudding, she said quietly, "Is that you, Bright One? Are you hiding in cats now?"

There was no answer.

The god was not here. She was quite alone.

The Office of Plans took some finding. The corridors were sparingly lit with dim lamps, but few people were in them this late at night. A woman cleaner Mirany timidly asked insisted on taking her to the place herself, but it was awkward, as she would only walk behind, eyes down, clutching her wooden bucket, muttering at each corner,

"Left here, please, holiness. Right, if you please, ma'am. Sorry, down these steps . . ."

Finally, almost bowing to the floor, she groped for a bronze-bound door and edged it open.

"Thank you so much." Mirany slid past, but the woman raised her head and said abruptly, "Holiness, please . . . You know the god, you talk to him, don't you?"

After a second, Mirany nodded. The woman was a slave, probably ignorant as to who was who among the Nine. Perhaps she thought Mirany was the Speaker.

"Then . . . I know it's not my place to ask . . . but it's my son. He's ill. It's a cough, and sores around his mouth. Please ask the god to make him well."

"I will. But you must also ask him yourself."

"Me?" For a second the woman raised astonished eyes. "I'm a slave, holiness. I can't talk to a god."

"You can and should. Does the boy have medicines? A doctor?"

She knew what the answer would be. A quick shake of the head confirmed it.

"Then I'll make sure he gets them. What's your name?"

"Khety."

"Stay here," Mirany said quietly. "Wait. I may need you."

The office was a new place for her. She was astonished at the hundreds of desks. Even at this hour, half of them had scribes huddled over parchment, writing hastily, so intently that some of them barely noticed her swish past.

She walked down the airless rows of the cavernous room and wondered how Seth could bear to work here. But then he had no choice. Not everyone could enjoy the luxuries of the Island.

Ink blotched the sandy floor, splashes of rainbow color. In each wall thousands of scrolls were stuffed into pigeonholes, tags hanging. Others were piled in great wheeled baskets. The air was stifling; she breathed particles of parchment, fibers, dust; scraps of gold leaf drifted in the shafts of light. The whispers of styli scratched and scrabbled all around her.

At the far end the overseer sat at a high dais. He looked up and saw her only when she'd almost reached him, and scrambled off his stool in such a panic it fell behind him with a resounding smack.

Every head lifted.

Red-faced, Mirany whispered, "I'm looking for the second assistant archivist. Seth. Is he here?"

The overseer was instantly curious. "No, holiness."

"Do you know where I can find him?"

"His room maybe."

"Where is that?"

"Oh, you can't . . . Forgive me, lady. It wouldn't be right. I'll send someone."

A scribe was dispatched; in minutes he was back, hot. "Not there, holiness."

Mirany had been afraid of this. He was always so busy lately, always up to something! Aware that the men were watching, she tried to look unruffled. "Thank you. It's not important."

"Is he . . . in some trouble?" The overseer glanced fiercely over her shoulder; pens scratched instantly.

"No. I just . . . wanted to speak to him." It was weak, but she couldn't think of a reason. "Thank you." She was saying that too often.

The walk back between the dingy desks seemed endless, but Mirany was thinking hard. She could have asked the overseer where to find Kreon, but that would have caused even more attention, and someone would have passed it on. Seth had told her that everyone in the City thought Kreon was just a weak-minded slave. It was safest not even to mention him. She had hoped Seth would find him. Now it would have to be her.

Outside, the woman Khety was sitting on the upturned bucket. She scrambled up, anxious.

"Listen," Mirany said firmly. "I want to find a man who works in this part of the City. A caretaker. His name is Kreon."

The woman stared. "That one? Holiness, I know him. A great lanky man all white as paper. He's half crazy."

"Where will I find him?"

"You never know. Here, there. He never goes outside though. It hurts his eyes."

Mirany nodded, impatient. "He must have some place . . ."

Khety shrugged. The whisper that answered was not hers.

Below.

A prickle of sweat touched Mirany's neck. "Below?"

In the tombs, Mirany. Where you spoke to me before. In the shadows.

The slave stared. "You said something, holiness?"

"A light. I need a lamp." There was one on the wall; she took it quickly and checked the oil in the reservoir. Enough for an hour or more. "Where are the nearest stairs down to the tombs?"

"Nearby. But—"

"Show me."

At the end of the next corridor was a bronze gate in the shape of a vast scorpion, floor to ceiling. Khety put her bucket and cloths down and moved apologetically ahead; she opened a grille, a smaller door in the scorpion's thorax. Beyond it was darkness, a faint stirring of warm air.

"The Gate of Kyros, holiness. It goes down to the first levels at least."

Mirany raised the lamp. For a moment both their shadows glimmered, vast and indistinct on the corridor roof. It took Mirany a great effort to say, "Thank you. I'll go on alone from here."

The woman looked relieved, then cunning. "It's all about the god, isn't it. Some of the old women say his shadow wanders the underground halls, that he talks to the dead Archons down there. Once or twice, when I've been working alone, near the stairs, I've heard them. Their voices, muffled and strange. And music."

Music? In a flash Mirany wondered if Oblek was hiding with Kreon; the idea was a vivid relief. "Yes, it's about the god." She turned. "I want you to promise you'll tell no one where I'm going. Understand? And I'll arrange the medicines for your son."

It sounded like blackmail. But the woman just nodded, her face careworn, closed up.

Mirany clambered through the metal grille. The stairs were shallow and broad, well trodden. Without another word she started down them, her shadow at her heels, holding the lamp out, but beyond its small circle the darkness was impenetrable, thick as velvet, muffling all sound.

Down. Down. When she glanced back, even the faint glimmer of the corridor was gone. She was breathing loudly, too loudly; she made herself stop, listen to her heart thudding. There was no need to worry. There was plenty of air; and she could go back up anytime. She was the Bearer-of-the-God, and one of the Nine. She was not going to panic.

Head up, she strode on down. It was as if the earth was rising up around her; the plastered walls became stone, and then soil, and a strong earthy dryness began to must the air. She felt a faint fur of dust on her lips.

At the bottom, the tunnel walls were close; they had once been painted. Rows of wedge-shaped letters ran in blocks; a frieze showed the Rain Queen standing over the desert, water running from her hands and cloak. Below, the great shapes of the Animals waited, mouths wide. The plaster was ancient and much of it was cracked. Lumps had fallen; they crunched under her feet. She made her way cautiously along to a junction of tunnels, and paused. Five mysterious openings gaped before her.

She took two steps farther and stopped.

A draft came out of one of the tunnels, guttering the small lamp flame; Mirany cupped her hand around it, suddenly terrified. Beyond, in the dark, something detached itself from blackness and moved. She whirled toward it instantly.

"Who's there? Is that you?"

The darkness had cool hands. One came around and clamped over her lips, firm and smooth as a snake's skin. The lamp was blown out.

"Quiet, lady," a voice whispered close to her ear. "You're being followed."

THE SUN IS DRYING US OUT

He drew her back noiselessly. If it <u>hadn't been</u> for his cold hands on her mouth and shoulder, she wouldn't have known anyone was there. The blackness was complete; she had no idea in what direction she was facing.

A tickle in her ear. Words formed out of wisps of draft. "Take my hand."

She could breathe; his fingers came and gripped hers. Then he was leading her into nowhere.

She tried not to stumble, to gasp. At each step she flinched, terrified of walking into the tunnel wall, her hand out in front, groping, though she felt somehow this was a vacuum, a great emptiness in the earth. When the tips of her fingers brushed dusty plaster, the relief was immense, a sudden grounding. In an instant knowledge came back; she knew again what was up and down, what was forward and back.

"This way," the shadow whispered. "Don't be scared."

Kreon moved without hesitation, a creature that stopped and clambered without weight or substance. In the Book of Guidance she had heard scribes read of animal spirits who led the dead Archons along the Way—the Monkey, the Jackal, the Spider—each a guide and a danger. For a disordered second she felt as if one of them had hold of her hand, that she grasped a paw, the jointed pincer of a scorpion.

Then she jolted against him and realized he had stopped.

"From here we can see who's coming behind." He was crouching; his fingers groped for her wrist and drew her gently downward. "I have many spy holes and watching places."

Dust fell. Small stones slithered.

In the wall, a light showed, a faint glimmer of reflected lamplight. She saw a small hole, no bigger than a cherry. His darkness blocked it, then drew back. He seemed to turn to her; she saw his sharp profile, a wry, twisted smile. "Well. Take a look."

She leaned forward, hands among the rubble.

The spy hole looked down into a dim place, one of the tunnels they had just come through. Someone was groping along the tunnel wall, outstretched hand grasping a lamp. The figure was cloaked, but familiar, an overstrong scent of attar of roses rising from the peach-colored robe.

Mirany stared in disbelief. "It *can't* be."

The flames just below her guttered. The figure turned; Mirany saw a pretty, slightly plump face. Delicate blond hair.

"Mirany!" the girl whispered. "Come back! It's me!"

"Is she one of the Nine?" Kreon's voice was a breath.

"Chryse! The one who betrayed me—Hermia's spy. I'd never have thought she had the nerve to come down here alone."

He seemed to smile. "Her nerve is gone. She's terrified."

That seemed true. Chryse had come to the junction of passages and seemed too scared to venture into any. She sank down. "Oh *Mirany*," she wailed. "Where did you go?"

Mirany drew back. "Don't be fooled by her helpless act. I was, for far too long. What do we do with her?"

"Leave her awhile. I don't want her to see me, or the Sphere. Come quickly."

They didn't go far. Down steps, around a twisting corner, over a pile of rubble into a wider space. When he said, "You can light your lamp now," his voice echoed, as if the roof was far above.

When the tinderbox had finally rasped out a flame and the wick had caught, she put the lamp on the floor and stood back. Yellow light steadied, expanded into radiance.

She saw a painted chamber, every inch of its vast vaulted roof a colored extravaganza of blue and orange, gold and saffron. The Rain Queen had her arms wide, and the arms were wings, and the whole ceiling was her spread cloak.

From it hung pearls, thousands of real pearls, pale and creamy, some strung in long chains one below another, reaching down to where Mirany stood, so that she felt as if a shower of rain had been petrified in the air around her, each water drop solid and perfect, hanging, never reaching the ground.

Kreon stood among them, arms folded, his weak eyes watching her. A lanky man, as Khety had said, his skin dead white, his long hair bone bleached, straggly over his shoulders, his tunic patched on one sleeve. She had met him only once before, when he and Alexos had talked to each other in the strange language of the gods. And maybe once in her vision, where the god and his shadow had fought each other before the world began.

"How's my little brother?" His voice was dry.

She swallowed. "Well. Except that Oblek is missing."

"He told me. He and I speak in our dreams. Having a god inside us, we need each other." He looked around and pulled up a wooden stool and sat down, knees huddled up. He gestured for her to do the same.

There was a chair and a table, but no other furniture in the chamber. The wicker creaked as she sat; it was old, and frayed. "Where is this?"

"The tomb of Koltos." He looked around. "Robbed, as you can see. Many centuries ago."

"How did they get in?"

"The same way as we did. There."

In the corner a great hole had been hacked in the wall.

Beyond it was darkness. Mirany stared, appalled. "Did they steal everything? Where's the Archon's body?"

"Safe." He watched her closely, his smile secret. "I have places, Mirany, far below. The Fourth Dynasty tombs were made too close to the surface—many have been robbed. But thieves only want treasure. Over the years I have removed the bodies of the Archons, carried them deep into the earth. Don't fear for them. This is my kingdom and I guard it well."

She nodded, thinking of what Seth had told her of the great cavern of copies below the shaft of the Oracle. That reminded her. "We don't have much time. Alexos said you had something for us, and it sounds to me like the Sphere of Secrets. The god told me—"

"I am his shadow, Mirany." He leaned back, his face webbed with drifting pearl shade. "I know about the Sphere."

Between them on the table was a wooden stand, covered in a ragged cloth that looked as if it had been used to wash floors. Putting out a pale hand, he drew it aside. "And yes, I've brought it for you."

The pearl rain tinkled and clinked. On the stand a silver globe reflected it. Mirany stood up and lifted the Sphere from the stand. It was heavy. Solid, maybe. The writing she had glimpsed before was elaborate, cut into the metal, tiny blocks of text, and now she saw them close; the hieroglyphs seemed like those on old scrolls she had seen crumbling in the library on the Island, forgotten and mouse eaten. The lines and devices seemed like a map, linked; the symbols of animals, triangles, three small stars. Looking up she felt the reflection lighting her face. "What is it?"

Kreon shrugged. "An ancient device, full of power. It will need to be read, and doubtless it will show you the way."

"To where?"

He grimaced, a lopsided, humorless smile. "To what you desire. Or is that too dangerous a place to go?"

She sat slowly. "It may be. We all seem to want such different things. Rhetia wants to be Speaker. Oblek wants songs. Seth wants to be rich."

"And you?"

Now it was her turn to shrug, her warm fingers making cloudy marks on the cold silver. "I don't know. I suppose for everything to be sorted out. For everyone to be happy."

He leaned forward, suddenly tense. "Not even a god could do that. Not without paying a very great price. Mirany, listen to me now. You and Alexos brought the people rain from the Rain Queen's garden, but nothing has changed. We need a more permanent outpouring, as it was before the rivers died. Down here, where the night never ends, I lie awake and listen. I hear the land drying out, Mirany. I hear its rustles and shifts, its dessication, how the roots of the crops shrivel. I hear the slow crack of stones, the jackals gnawing bones that lie in the desert, the soft flesh turning to leather. I hear ants and the scorpions. Sometimes even, I hear people's dreams, how they dissolve, are evaporated, so that when they wake they've forgotten what they were, except the children, who cry. The sun is drying us out, all our life, so that a great thirst is always inside us." He stood up and walked, impatient, the pearls clinking and dragging against him, over his shoulders. "We need water that comes from deep, from the roots of earth, a great river. A deluge."

Abruptly he turned. "Do you know why they call this the Two Lands?"

"No."

"One is the land above, of the living. The other below, of the dead. Those two realms are linked, through the Oracle, but the Oracle is tainted by treason, like a poisoned well, and you need to find another drinking place, Mirany. A well of miracles."

He turned his head, listening. "You must go. Your little friend is crying. Whatever you do, don't let her see the Sphere." He came and took it from her, wrapping it carefully in the cloth. "The scribe, Seth. He can read all the old letters. He may be able to decipher this, but be careful. He's arrogant and greedy. He's not sure yet who he is."

Mirany took the bundle back. As he held aside the hanging strings of pearls for her, she picked up the lamp and looked back at him. "What about you?" she asked, curious. "Down here, alone in the dark. What is it you desire?"

He stepped back into shadows. "What I already have," he whispered. *"Nothing."*

• • ◆

Chryse screeched and leaped to her feet. The kohl around her eyes was a streaming mess. "Oh Mirany," she sobbed. "Where have you been? It is you, is it?"

"Of course it's me," Mirany snapped, striding out of the dark. She stopped, intensely irritated. "Why are you following me, Chryse? Couldn't Hermia get anyone more competent than you? How did you know where I was?"

"I made an old woman tell me. And I'm not following you." Chryse sniffed. "At least, not for them. I've finished with Hermia. It's just 'Do this, do that.' As if I was a slave, not one of the Nine. None of the others will speak to me. No one likes me anymore."

Mirany walked past her into the dark, trying to remember Kreon's directions. "Are you surprised? You tried to get me killed. They're all afraid they'll be next."

Breathless, Chryse stumbled after her. "Wait, Mirany. Please."

Mirany stopped so suddenly the blond girl nearly fell over.

"I'm waiting."

"I've changed. I'm not like that anymore. I want to be on your side."

"My side?"

"The god's side. You hear him. Hermia doesn't. She makes it up, I know that. So I've decided, Mirany." Her tearstained face was ridiculously determined. For a moment Mirany let the flame light play on the childish blue eyes.

"How can I ever trust you, Chryse?" she whispered.

Chryse dabbed her face. "I knew you'd say that. I'll show you. I've made up my mind. I'm your friend now and I'll show you."

Silent, Mirany walked on and climbed the steps. They seemed endless, and at the top there were the passageways to negotiate, and out in the windy plaza a litter to find, slaves to rouse. So it wasn't until they were being carried toward the bridge that she could bring herself to speak to Chryse again.

"Rhetia won't believe you."

"I don't care a toss about Rhetia." Already smug, Chryse was reapplying her makeup with the help of a small mirror. "Rhetia's not you. I always liked you, Mirany, even when you first came and everyone else laughed at you. We were friends. I just thought you were going against the god, but now that Alexos is Archon, I know you weren't. So it must be all right, mustn't it?" She closed the mirror and looked up, quite satisfied. For a second Mirany was sour with disbelief. And yet it wasn't that simple. It could all be true. Chryse always looked out for herself, and would have no compunctions about changing sides as often as would suit her.

Perhaps doubt showed in her eyes. Chryse smiled and settled her dress. "And now," she said comfortably, "why ever did you go down in those horrible tombs? And when are you going to tell me what's in that bag?"

"I'm not." Mirany's fingers gripped the cloth.

The litter lurched, stopped, then tipped violently to the left. Chryse gasped, grabbing the tassels. There were voices, yelling. Then the curtains were whisked aside and a man looked in. He was well wrapped, only a single eye showing, a gleaming knife in each hand.

Chryse screamed, a piercing terror.

The man shoved a piece of parchment into Mirany's hand, made a mock bow, and said, "Be there." Then he was gone.

Outside, there was panic. The litter was almost dropped; the slaves crowded in. "Holinesses, are you all right?"

"They were bandits—"

"There were ten of them—"

"Twelve—"

Chryse was rigid. "Why didn't they rob us?"

Mirany laid the note down slowly. "Because they've already got something of ours."

"What?"

"Oblek. They've got Oblek."

THE THIRD OFFERING
OF GOLDEN APPLES

Can a god commit a crime?

Once, long ago, I came to a place where all the dreams of the world were stored.

Dreams of music, of the joys of children, the poems not yet written, old women's hoarded memories. They were all there, lying in heaps around the cave.

Take nothing away, the Rain Queen warned me. She set monsters and many-headed dragons to guard the entrance.

I could not help it. I stole three golden apples.

They were so small!

But I never found the cave again.

It Has Been Centuries
Since I Gazed into Its Depths

"Where is she?" Seth paced the turquoise floor impatiently. He felt trapped in a great jewel; the walls and ceiling were complex facets of blue glass. His own reflections marched toward and away from him, upside down, anxious.

Alexos, feeding the monkey, said mildly, "Running up the stairs. I wish you'd keep still, Seth. It's making Eno giddy."

Seth glared at him. Then the door opened and Mirany stumbled in.

He hadn't seen her for weeks. She never came near the City, and nowadays he rarely left there, because being second assistant archivist meant a lot more work than he'd imagined. She looked different, he realized. Flushed and hot, but more assured. Not the timid girl he'd first met. To his surprise it was he who felt shy. To cover it he made his voice gruff.

"You know about Oblek?"

She looked at him, drew breath, and said, "Yes. Hello, Archon."

"Hello, Mirany. I'm sure Seth doesn't mean to be rude. He's worried." The boy let the monkey drop down and turned to them, his perfect face clouded. "So am I. They won't hurt Oblek, will they? Seth says the Jackal has kidnapped him."

She glanced at Seth. "He's safer with them than wandering around the Port. Look. They sent me this note." She held it out; Seth came and took it, awkwardly. Blue images of himself moved alongside him, over and under him.

The parchment was good quality. The writing was the Jackal's; he recognized it.

WE HAVE THE MUSICIAN. ARGELIN WILL NOT FIND HIM. BE AT THE PALACE OF THE ARCHON AT NOON.

It wasn't signed.

"Well." Mirany crossed to the canopied balcony and sat on the window seat, glancing out at the blue sea and the shimmering white buildings of the Island. "What's been going on?"

"It's very exciting." Alexos came and sprawled on his stomach on the shiny floor, feet in the air. "Seth found Oblek and they had a fight with some soldiers. Then they fell off the cliff."

Her eyes widened, a flash of alarm. "Off a cliff! Were you hurt?"

"No." Seth had caught it though; she still cared what

happened to him. He sat in the Archon's chair, leaning back. His voice relaxed; he waved a hand easily. "Oblek was, a bit. We swam, but the currents were strong and dragged us out into the bay. We would have been in trouble if the ship hadn't picked us up."

Mirany looked relieved. "It's a good thing you can swim! Most scribes can't."

He shrugged, red. "I had to keep Oblek up. He was . . . in a bad way."

"Tell her about the Jackal," Alexos said impatiently.

Seth nodded, modest. "The ship was one of the pearl men's fleet, a great caravel. There was a banquet going on aboard—Argelin was there and I was terrified he'd see us. So we pretended to be slaves. Of the Jackal."

"How?" The note of admiration warmed him.

"He's some sort of lord. I think we interrupted a theft he had planned, but he went along with us, though I should have known he'd have his reasons. When we got to the Port his men dragged us through the streets into some cellar. I don't know where—we had sacks over our heads."

Alexos giggled. "I'll bet you looked really silly."

Seth glared and turned back to Mirany. "I thought he was our friend," she said thoughtfully.

"He's a thief, Mirany. Ruthless. He says we owe him for getting Alexos into the ninth house. The cellar was full of his people, cutthroats, smugglers, women. Oblek settled right in. There's plenty of drink and he says they won't hurt him.

The Jackal has some scheme—he'll only speak to the Archon, and said to expect him. When I said that no one spoke to the Archon, he laughed. The next thing I knew I was bundled out, dragged down a few streets, and dumped."

Mirany frowned. "You think he's coming here? How?"

"I don't know."

Alexos shook his head. "Argelin has guards all around the building. They'll know."

A knock on the door startled them.

Alexos rolled over. Then he said, "Come in."

The palace steward. Looking terrified. For a second Seth knew the Jackal would walk in behind him with a knife in his back, but the man's words were even more unexpected.

"Lord Argelin is here," he whispered.

Seth jumped up. With a rustle Mirany came in from the balcony; glancing at her he saw she was pale.

"Be careful," she whispered.

Argelin was already in the room. He wore dark bronze armor and a red mantle; his smooth beard was immaculately shaved. A scent of tamarisk drifted around him. He took in Seth and Mirany with one rapid look, then gave a mock bow to Alexos. "My Lord Archon."

Alexos bowed back gravely. "General. This is a big surprise."

"I'm sure."

"Won't you sit down? Fetch a chair, Seth."

Argelin smiled. "I'm not staying. I just came to bring you some unfortunate news."

He waited, so Alexos had to say, "What news?" And then he smiled again, a cold pleasure that chilled Seth.

"The drunken, foul-mouthed musician . . ."

"Oblek?"

"Is dead."

There was an acute silence. Argelin dusted the chair with a glove and sat, leaning forward. "He was found by a patrol out on the cliffs and captured, but a fight ensued. He killed one of my men, and then was thrown over the cliff. No trace of his body has been found, but you know, *Lord Archon*, how the current is out in that bay, how deep and dark the water is."

They were too calm, Mirany thought. They should be more stricken. He might guess.

But Argelin leaned back, as if the shocked stillness satisfied him.

Alexos got up and walked out onto the balcony. Above him the canopy flapped in the hot wind. His back to them, he spoke quietly.

The water has opened her arms to him, then.

Mirany stiffened. Seth saw how she glanced at him, how the turquoise room seemed all at once to be moving around them, as if they were in a bubble, sinking, deep, the waves above them.

Argelin glanced around; a slight frown creased his face. "No loss. He owed his life to the god, after all. The god has taken it."

Alexos turned. With two steps he was across the room and looking straight into Argelin's eyes.

I am the god, Lord General.

For a moment his voice echoed, immensely old, through all the ages of the earth. Then it was a boy's, petulant. "And Oblek was my friend. I liked him."

Argelin stood. "You have two friends left." His dark eyes moved to Mirany. "For the time being. Look after them a little better, Mouse Lord."

At the door he paused and glanced at Seth. But he went out without another word.

Mirany breathed out tension. "He enjoyed that. You could see."

"So did I," said the man leaning inside the balcony.

She gasped; Seth grabbed Alexos, pulled him back.

"It's a sad thing," the Jackal remarked, ducking his head under the canopy as he came in, "that a thief is more feared than a tyrant."

"How did you get in here?"

"Over the roofs, down the terraces." Winding a thin rope around his waist, he put a foot on the chair Argelin had used and slid a narrow blade into his boot. "Your security is lax, mad child. Anyone could get in."

Astonished, they stared at him, but he surveyed the room curiously with his long eyes, noting the crystal walls, the carved balustrade of glass that hung over the gardens below.

"Fascinating. Is this a solid jewel?"

"It's the most secret chamber." Alexos came out from behind Seth. "No one can listen through the walls here."

"And they do that, do they?"

The boy nodded, wide eyed.

The Jackal raised an eyebrow. "There are drawbacks, then, in being a god." He pulled the chair up and sat astride it. "So Argelin thinks the man who tried to murder him is dead. I could show him otherwise."

"What do you want?" Mirany whispered. Despite what Alexos had said, she couldn't help glancing at the door. Seth noticed. He crossed the room, opened the blue crystal panel, and glanced out.

The white loggia stretched empty, all its filmy hangings moving in the breeze.

"No one."

The Jackal had found a jug of water. He poured from it into a chased silver goblet and drank.

Then he said, "What you owe. Without me, you would be dead, girl, and this mad boy would be herding goats and picking lice out of his hair. Remember that."

Alexos came and sat by him calmly. "That's true," he said. "Isn't it, Seth?"

The Jackal took another drink. His grin was amused; his long eyes slid from Alexos to Mirany. Then he said, "Listen. Three months ago, on the day of the second seedsetting, a patrol of Argelin's men were out in the desert, beyond the Oasis of Katra. They saw something dark crawling among the dunes, and when they came up to it, they found it was a man. The burned, dried-out remains of a man. He was barely sane, his skin blackened and flyblown, burrowed by sandworms, his tongue swollen, his eyes blind. They carried him back to the Port, but it was clear he would not live. He was put into a litter and taken to Argelin's headquarters, at dead of night, under heavy guard. No one was told, no reports were made, no forms filled out. A doctor Argelin trusts was sent for. The man's very existence was kept secret."

"So how do you know?" Seth asked suspiciously.

The tomb thief's smile was unruffled. "My people know everything. Go everywhere."

"Even Argelin's guardhouse?"

"Quiet, Seth." Mirany was alert. It annoyed him, but she didn't seem to notice. "Go on."

"Thank you, holiness." The Jackal drank, taking his time. "Well, when he was conscious, the traveler gasped out his story. It seems he was the last survivor of a secret expedition Argelin had sent out months earlier: seventeen men, camels, a wagon. They had left two days after the Choosing of the Archon. Since then nothing had been heard of them. Argelin had probably written the whole thing off."

"Expedition to where?" Mirany said quietly.

There was a suppressed excitement in her voice. *She knows something about this*, Seth thought.

The Jackal obviously thought so, too. He looked at her thoughtfully. "To the Mountains of the Moon, lady."

"For the silver!"

He was silent. Then he said, "Indeed, long ago there were silver mines in those highlands. Before the Archon Rasselon and the great drying up of the rivers. It seems certain that Argelin had plans to try and reopen the trade for himself."

She shook her head. "Not only him. Prince Jamil wants the same."

Outside, the canopy flapped. Warm air moved through the blue jeweled room.

"How do you know?" Seth asked.

"That's what he asked the Oracle. But the god—that is, Hermia—told him he couldn't enter the desert. Argelin must have told her what to say."

"I'm not surprised." The Jackal's voice was dry. "Because what is hidden in the mountains turns out to be more precious than silver."

"*More* precious?"

"Much more. The survivor gabbled, in his delerium. About great gates, a city, animals that talk. About the Well of Songs."

Mirany turned, her skin prickling. Alexos had lifted his head, was staring at the man in delight, his dark eyes shining. **The Well of Songs! It has been centuries since I gazed into its depths.**

Was it spoken aloud? The Jackal glanced at the door quickly. "The very same. The mystic Well of legend. But what really shocked Argelin to the core was the small bag they found strapped under the man's rags. It contained five tiny lumps of ore. Argelin had it tested. It was gold. Pure, incorruptible, yellow, priceless gold."

Seth was silent. In the blue-faceted room of crystal only

the waves could be heard, far below at the foot of the cliffs, and a gull, far out on the water, screaming.

"Gold," Alexos breathed.

The Jackal sipped the water. "Gold, little mad one."

"But he doesn't know where," Mirany said. "Surely the mountains are so vast he could never find it. . . ."

"Surely, holiness, you are wrong." Suddenly the tomb thief had lost all his amusement; his face was tense, his eyes sidelong. "Think of what it means for him. He has to find it, because gold will bring him everything. He will buy mercenaries, artillery, power. He will no longer need the Oracle or the Nine. Argelin will make himself more than General. He will make himself king."

Placing the cup on the table, he sat back and watched them, the mockery coming back into his voice as if he could not keep it out.

"Who knows. He might even decide he can do without the god."

SHE SEES THE SIGNS IN HIS FACE

Mirany gave the steward her best glare. "The Archon is busy," she snapped. "Not to be disturbed."

"But he always wants to see new gifts, lady. A deputation has come from the Guild of Music Box Makers."

She bit her lip. "Thank them for the gifts. Show them somewhere, give them refreshments. They know no one can see the Archon."

The steward bowed, looked harassed, and backed off.

Mirany closed the door and leaned her back against it, breathing out with relief. Her dress was damp with sweat.

The Jackal stepped out of hiding and sheathed the knife. "Very good. I've said before that you're wasted on the Island."

Alexos was cross-legged on the floor, the monkey on his shoulder. "All right," he said as if the interruption had never happened, "so there's gold. But the Well! I remember the Well, Mirany. So high, so remote. Hidden in a cave in the snows of the highest pinnacle. The water is deep and fresh and icy. Whoever drinks of it tastes the god's joy!"

She came and knelt by him. "When did you go there?"

"All the Archons went once. Xamian. Darios. Rasselon went, but he was the last, because he stole the three golden apples from the Rain Queen, and she was so cross that she hid the Well and withdrew the rivers. They shriveled up, all of them, even the great Draxis. Since then, some of the Archons have searched for the Well. None of them found it. . . ."

"You will." The Jackal had come back to the chair. "I intend to get to the gold before Argelin, and there's only one way. You, little crazy one, are to make a great proclamation. That the Archon Alexos will revert to the ancient custom of his predecessors. That he will make the Pilgrimage of Suffering to search for the Well of Songs, and expiate the sin of Rasselon. Unmasked, barefoot, with only a small group of chosen companions." He sat gracefully. "Of which I, needless to say, will be one."

Seth came in from the balcony. "You're the one who's crazy. It's a journey into death! You said yourself only one man survived."

"They did not have the Archon." The thief's strange eyes watched Alexos. "*The Archon who can turn stones into water.*"

Silence.

Until Seth said tightly, "How did you know about that?"

The Jackal laughed his cold laugh. "The musician talks a lot when he's drunk. And believe me, we keep him drunk."

The monkey chattered and ran to Mirany, who picked it up. "This is about more than gold," she said slowly.

"Is it?"

"I think so."

The Jackal looked at her. After a moment he said to Seth, "On the ship. Why did you think I wouldn't give you away?"

"Because I'd talk. And because you enjoy risks."

The tall man stood and strode to the balcony. His back was stiff, his fair hair tied back.

"Astute. A scribe's close scrutiny. Yes, I take risks. Risk is all that keeps me alive." Looking out at the Island, he said, "My family was once among the most exalted here, did you know that?"

"No," Mirany whispered.

"Years ago, before the Council of Fifty was dissolved. Before Argelin came to power, before lists of dissident men were posted on street corners, before wives and children disappeared, before heads adorned the spikes of the Desert Gate. My father was rich, and respected. We had a great house on the cliff top, cool marble floors, fountains. Now sand covers it; bats haunt its ruin."

He turned to Mirany and crouched, so that his face was

level with hers, his long hands on her wrists. "I remember how they broke down the doors, how my father was cut down in the courtyard, how my mother screamed, how her sons were dragged away. I remember how the fountains ran red."

She was silenced. His look flickered; something dark came and went in him. But he drew back, and she saw how he breathed in, how his hands were steady.

"I was too young then to be a threat. And by now Argelin has forgotten me. He sees a painted princeling, effete, short of money, a scrounger of invitations to every play and party, with a taste for antiques and pretty women. A man who lives on others, a man without honor. All that I allow him to see." He turned to Alexos. "But below the bright desert lie the tombs. Ghost-haunted, dark, piled high with forbidden treasure. And there's not one thief in the Port who does not fear the Jackal, not one pimp, cutpurse, rogue, or beggar with painted sores who does not know that name. Argelin thinks he rules, but the Underworld is mine. The streets, the opium dens, the hidden store places, the nests of pickpockets. Like the god's shadow, I haunt him silently." His face was edged with blue light. As if he'd said too much, alertness came back to him; he glanced sharply around.

Seth said, "Don't you have enough gold?"

"Not to infiltrate the army. But now I will." Abruptly he walked over to the balcony, glanced over, then up. "Do as I say, Archon. Set up the pilgrimage. We'll find your Well, any well, and I'll gain us enough to bring Argelin crashing down." He glanced over. "I'll be awaiting your proclamation. And remember, so will Oblek."

With a lithe vault he swung himself up onto the blue glass balustrade, feet balanced. "Though he may not want to come back."

Alexos said, "You won't hurt him?"

"Hurt him?" The Jackal tensed, ready. "Why bother? He'll drink himself to death."

Then he jumped.

Mirany gasped, but already the man was gone, hauling himself lightly up the carved cornices of the building, slithering on to the flat roof. She ran over and looked up. A few flakes of dislodged plaster fell on her face. The sky was blue and empty.

"And how does he think," Seth muttered angrily behind her, "that we can find the Well or some seam of gold in a range of mountains thousands of miles long?"

Mirany pulled herself back into the room. "Alexos knows the way."

The boy looked unhappy. "I don't. I've never found it again, Mirany."

"Then we'll have to use this."

She went over and brought it out of the bag she had placed in the corner, and held it out, her eyes never leaving Seth's face. She saw what she had expected, that flicker of amazement, of desire. Unmistakable.

"What is that?" he breathed.

"The Sphere of Secrets." She handed it to Alexos; his

thin hands clutched it tight. "The merchants brought it as an offering to the god. It needs to be deciphered. Kreon says it's a map of the way to all we desire. The Well of Songs."

Seth reached out, impatient, and snatched it as if he couldn't wait any longer. He held it up, turned it, fascinated. "The text is archaic. Pre-Second Dynasty at least. They used a half-syllabic, half-symbolic alphabet— I've seen it on scrolls in the Room of the Crocodiles."

"Can you read it?" Alexos asked, anxious.

"Odd words. *The road . . . gates of . . . Beware . . .* I'd need to get it back to the City and work on it."

"The City!" Mirany said. "Would it be safe?"

He looked at her. "As safe as on the Island."

He was right, of course. She had had to sleep with the bag that contained it tied to her hand in bed. Chryse had been in her room after the dawn Ritual; when Mirany had come back from breakfast the blond girl had been sliding breathlessly out. "Looking for you," she'd said.

There was no safety in the Upper House.

Seth's eyes were bright with pleasure. "It shouldn't take long. There are word lists there, translations."

"You won't show anyone?"

"Of course not." Preoccupied, he barely listened. The silver Sphere glimmered in his hands.

She glanced at Alexos; the boy smiled at her, and then reached out and gently patted her arm, an old man's reassurance. "Don't worry, Mirany," he whispered. "It will be quite safe with Seth."

"And what about you?" she said. "Going into the desert? Into that terrible desolation?"

He shrugged. For a second, bleakness filled his eyes, ancient and anguished. "I was Rasselon. It was all my fault. How long has it been since the rivers dried up?"

"I don't know," she mumbled.

He nodded, then brightened and grasped her hand. "Let's go and see my new presents," he said.

She thought of that elaborate music box later, the way it had played tune after tune, and how he had danced happily around it with the monkey screeching. She thought of it as she stood in the stifling heat behind the smiling mask of the Bearer-of-the-God, with Chryse fidgeting beside her and the great bronze bowl in her arms. There was a scorpion in it, just one, and it sat motionless in the bottom, its tail rigid and quivering. She had no idea if it was the god. When she asked, no one answered. But there was music here, too, a harsh brazen clamor of cymbals and zithers and horns, and the scorpion crouched, seemingly flattened by the noise. Tense, she waited for it to scuttle, then flipped it expertly back into the bowl. She was calm, licking salty lips. Being Bearer demanded constant concentration.

Around her, on the steps of the Temple, the evening was hot, the light of the setting sun a red furnace that burned them all. Hermia had spread the last of the great scarlet silks down the marble slabs; now she knelt and bowed down to the ground, the open-mouthed mask touching the rippling cloth.

"Scorpion Lord, Bright One," she said clearly, her voice ringing. "Your people wait. Your sun burns. Your land scorches. Your day ends. On the feast of your Reconciliation with the Shadow, bless the fevered and the thirsty, those who suffer."

The scorpion's tiny pincers scratched the bronze. It seemed to explore the incised lines of decoration. Mirany felt sweat run down her forehead. Her arms ached.

Hermia sat back on her heels, and behind her, the Nine came forward, forming a semicircle, and beyond them the people crowded, the sick, carried on stretchers, limping, hobbling, children, aged.

Argelin's soldiers kept them back, a firm line of armored men, spears crossed. Behind them, in elaborate litters, the aristocracy watched, the guildsmen and eminences of the City, the scented actors, the polite, curious merchants. Prince Jamil was there; she saw him through the eye slits, sitting in the shade of a great canopy. Then he stood, and she knew the Archon had come.

Risking a glance, she turned her head to the Temple.

Alexos stood on the highest step. For a second, in that garish light, she felt sure that the statue of the god within had stepped down from its pedestal and come out here. But the sun dazzle blinded her; when he stepped down she saw it was only him, a tall thin boy in a white tunic, with the gold mask on his face, the beautiful grave mask of the god, his dark hair almost hidden by its feathers and looped hanging crystals. He raised one hand and beckoned.

Behind the Nine, Argelin nodded. His guards separated, making a gap in the line, an avenue of spears. Slowly, the people began to stumble up.

These were the ones who would have been able to pay. She knew very well that anyone who wanted to get near the Archon would have had to bribe not only the general, but his officers, and probably the scribe of accession, and maybe even something for the Island coffers. Those who couldn't pay were at the back, and stood no chance. From their wails and cries, they knew it.

Argelin was on his white horse, his bodyguard standing around him. She saw how he watched Hermia, covertly, and there was a preoccupied, moody look about him.

The sick stood in a row, and Alexos moved along them. From here she couldn't see, but she knew he was touching them, his frail hands on their suppurating sores, on their ulcers and fractured limbs, their fevered faces. Silent, masked, he was the god and the god was their last hope. Gulls cried over him, high in the warm air. Stillness fell, the sun descending, the distant mountains flushed with its light. For a moment the peaks caught her attention; the highest glimmered white, cleft and unscalable. Was there a Well up there, a place like Kreon had spoken of, untainted, a pure Oracle between the lands of the living and the dead?

The faintest touch nuzzled against her thumb. She glanced down and froze.

The scorpion was balanced on the rim of the bowl.

Beside her, she felt Chryse's utter stillness.

"Don't do this!" she breathed. "If this is you, don't kill me. Not yet. Not here!"

To serve the god means treading the edge of death, Mirany.

"I know. But you need me!"

There is so much suffering here. Look at it, Mirany. Do they expect me to cure all of them, to take away all that brings them to me? If they were not hurting, would they even remember I existed?"

She took a careful breath. "They want to live. I want to live."

But the garden of the Rain Queen is so much better. You know. You've seen it.

"Please. My friends are here."

I thought you were different, Mirany. The voice sounded peeved. *But you're just like all the rest of them.*

A gust of wind fluttered her dress. The scorpion fell with a scutter, sliding helplessly down into the depths of the polished metal. Mirany closed her eyes; her whole body ached with tension.

"Thank you," she breathed.

There was no answer.

Except that a great cry came from the line of sick. One of them jerked back, screamed.

Hermia stood quickly; behind her Argelin barked an order and soldiers raced up the steps, but the Archon held up his hand and they slowed, reluctant.

It was a woman, and she was sobbing now. She was holding out her hands to the crowd, and she screamed, "I'm cured! The god has cured me! *I'm cured!*"

The crowd went wild. They surged forward, breaking the cordon, a great wave of people racing up the steps. Argelin yelled, furious.

"Mirany!" Chryse gasped. "Quickly!"

The Nine clustered together on the scarlet silks. Below her she saw all the crowd's thousand faces, all the hope, the excitement, the terror. It came at her like a wave and she almost stumbled, but the soldiers had regrouped; savagely they beat and forced the people back, and the front rows were crushed and screaming until a voice said, "Keep still, all of you."

A clear, petulant voice.

A voice that came from the golden mask of the Archon.

Mirany licked her lips. The crowd fell totally silent. Their astonishment was huge. The Archon never spoke. His voice was never heard until the day he gave up his life. The only voice the god had was the Speaker's, but now Hermia was standing still, and judging by her stiffness, as astounded as any.

"I have something to say to you, and I know it's against the rules. But the rules only go back a little way, and I can remember when there were none, and the

Archon spoke freely to his people. When I talked to you, even without a mask."

A stir in the crowd. Argelin had dismounted; he was pushing desperately forward, his men shoving people aside.

Alexos had noticed; his voice quickened. "We've become separated; it's all gone wrong somehow, hasn't it? What use is an Archon who only helps you by dying? So I've decided. I'm going to put things right."

Argelin had almost reached the steps. *Quick!* Mirany thought.

"I proclaim, here and now, in front of all of you, that I intend to make the great pilgrimage of the Archons, to make the journey that each Archon made, centuries ago."

She moved.

As the general leaped up the steps she stepped right in front of him, blocking his way. The bronze bowl clinked against his breastplate; the scorpion scrabbled up the side. For a split second of horror, he stood still.

And Alexos cried, "I will make the journey to the Well of Songs. I will drink of the water, and bring it back for you, from beyond death and the desert. **I will make the rivers flow and the crops grow for you. I will save you, my people.**"

There was silence. Then a swelling, an indrawing of breath, a great ragged cheering that went on and on, a clatter of shields, a chorus of rattles and zithers and drums.

Mirany gasped. Argelin had grasped the bronze bowl with his gloved hands; he looked at her in fury over it.

"This is all your doing," he whispered, his voice lost in the uproar.

Every Journey Begins with a Toll

"Why you?" Pa said shortly.

"Because the Archon has his closest friends with him."

"And that's you, is it?"

Seth shrugged. "I helped bring him here."

Telia picked husks out of her barley bread. "I don't want you to go," she said, scowling. "There are scorpions and monsters in the desert."

"There are scorpions and monsters everywhere." Seth sat on the wooden stool beside her. Seeing her alarm, he said quietly, "Don't worry. I'll be back in a few weeks."

She tossed the bread down and turned away from him, leaning her elbows on the white windowsill. "You're never here anyway," she said.

Despite himself, it hurt him. His father shook his head and went to the door. "Pity your Archon friend can't help her," he muttered. "I don't suppose you've even remembered to ask him."

Hot, Seth watched Telia's stiff back. She was five now, still too small, a fretful, sickly child. Last year in the terrible drought she had had a fever for weeks. Now he thought there were times when her mind went blank, when for a few seconds she didn't hear or see anything, forgot what people said to her.

"I'm sorry I haven't been here," he said quietly. "It's hard work, being second assistant archivist. There's such a lot to do." On the windowsill were red geraniums. Beyond, roof below roof, the white buildings of the Port tumbled, their labyrinthine alleys and stairs winding down to the noise and scurry of the harbor. It was airier up here, a cooler house than the last. He felt a brief pride that he had been able to afford the rent.

"But you go to see the Archon." Telia turned. "And that girl."

"She's not—"

"And now you're going for miles and miles and miles."

"I have to go!"

She had dark hair, cut straight across her eyes, like his mother's had been. For a moment the memory brought a swell of sadness that startled him. His mother had died bearing Telia, and now none of them talked about her. He usually kept her image out of his head, the endless scrolls and invoices and plans and contracts filling up the empty space. But now he was tired, had been working all night in the deserted scroll vaults of the City by one guttering lantern, painstakingly translating the text on the silver Sphere, and the memories crept in.

Suddenly the house cat jumped onto the sill. Telia reached up and patted it; it arched and rubbed against her hand. "Tammy loves me," she said accusingly.

Seth couldn't stand this. He lifted her on to his lap. "Listen. I'll bring you presents from the Palace. Toys and nice clothes. I'll be back before you've even noticed I've gone."

Her dark eyes were unblinking. "Are you going right now?"

"Yes." It wasn't true; the Archon would leave after nightfall, at moonrise, according to tradition, but Seth knew he wouldn't be back here before then. "Will you kiss me?"

She gave him a small wet kiss under the ear, then scrambled down. "Bye, Seth."

He looked after her at the swaying door curtain, feeling numb and depressed. "Good-bye, Telia," he whispered.

His father came in with a canvas bag. "Spare tunics. Boots. Small sword. Ointments. A cloak, because it's bitter out there at night. And some money."

A small bag of coins. Seth went red. "I don't need money. You keep that."

"Got plenty, have you?"

"Enough. You'll need it for Telia."

Sour, his father nodded. "Her dowry. If she lives long enough."

"Pa—"

"Have you even asked the priestess yet, about getting her onto the Island? Or do all your big concerns put us right out of your mind?"

He took a breath. "Not yet."

His father nodded, that I-knew-it grimness Seth loathed, and then he burst out, "What use is it creeping to the Archon! A boy, without power! You should have got onto Argelin's staff, years ago. I always said so. We'd be a damn sight better off."

White-faced, Seth stared at him. Then he picked up the bag and stalked to the door. He thought he wouldn't be able to get the words out, but at the door he stopped. Without looking around, he said, "I'll see you, then."

A chair scraped the floor. "Let's hope so," his father said acidly.

There was a woman singing on the corner of the leatherworkers' street; the high echoes of her voice bounced off the tenements, mingled with the stink of tanned skin, the acid from the vats catching in Seth's throat, stinging his eyes. For a moment the street blurred; he wiped his face hastily with the back of his hand and hurried on, almost running down the steps, ducking between the lines of stiff hides.

What else did they want from him! He worked his fingers to the bone for them, hour after hour, cheated and bribed and schemed for them! Bitter self-pity welled up in him, and a sort of furious, hurt despair that made him want to fling the canvas bag down the steps and kick it all the way to the harbor. Pa! What did he know about the way things worked, the struggle to be promoted, to be noticed, to get out of the teeming throng of slaves and workers and scribes and to be someone more, to be looked up to, to earn enough! Did they think he just had to ask Mirany and Telia would be whisked to the Island?

Coming under the arch at the end of the street, he allowed himself a grim smile. Maybe that was his own fault. Too much boasting . . . *My friend the Archon . . . Mirany can't really manage without me . . .* He turned into a small piazza and ducked under the shady portico. All right, he'd ask. Though Mirany was in no position to help.

The fist came from nowhere. It was a crack of agony in his stomach; he was down gasping for breath, doubled up. The second blow over the back of his head was almost a relief, its black dizziness something he could fall into. But they yanked him to his feet and made him stagger, fended him off. His face was gripped, twisted up.

Through the shock and pain a voice said, "Sure it's him?"

"It's him. Cocky little beggar."

He groped for his bag, but they had it. As the red throb in his head receded he could see them, and a new terror tingled down his spine. Argelin's men. A small squad, six men. They lined up around him, said, "Move," and marched, and he had to keep up, shoved roughly in the back whenever he stumbled.

Down the steep streets the patrol hurried, past shops shuttered from the midday heat and a tethered dog that barked, maddened by thirst, through the tunnels below the water tower of Horeb and by the fountains it had once fed, the dolphins and naiads cavorting in a dry basin, their stone torsos cracked and baking. Seth's whole body ached. His throat was parched; he swallowed and tried to think. What did Argelin want with him?

They thought Oblek was dead. The other soldier from the ambush must have recognized him. Instantly he started to plan. What could he offer? "Listen," he croaked. "Do yourselves a favor. You've got the wrong man."

"Shut it." The optio glared back.

"I can pay. Don't take me in. You never found me."

They didn't even slow down. Obviously they could see he wouldn't pay enough. He concentrated instead on getting his breath back, standing upright. He was sure his knee was bleeding.

The fast march took them through deserted streets. Anyone in the way stepped aside quickly. Seth covered his face and head with his mantle. He didn't want anyone from the Office of Plans to see this. Stupid, as he probably would never go back there.

And then in a second of panic he thought of the Sphere. It was well hidden, down in the City, stashed at the back of one of the myriad of pigeonholes where the plans of the Archons' tombs fragmented into dust over centuries. But if he was executed or imprisoned, Mirany would never find it.

The Well of Songs would be lost, and Alexos and the Jackal and Oblek would wander in the desert till they died.

Fish-stink. The rattle of ropes, slap of sails. Even in the midday heat the harbor was a place of movement, the breeze shaking and slapping every canopy, the gulls screaming and wheeling over the tip of discarded innards, crabshells, hideous inedible deep-sea creatures.

The general's headquarters was a stark, forbidding building. Once up the steps and past the door guards, there was a wide atrium swarming with people; he had been here before, and he remembered the day he had first met Mirany, and how she had insisted on seeing Oblek. Could she do that for him? Would anyone even know where he was?

The squad dispersed; papers were signed. His bag was roughly searched and the sword taken; then the contents were stuffed back. He was glad he hadn't brought the money, because that would have gone, too. The optio grabbed him, turned him, searched him with careless efficiency, signed another paper, and said, "Follow me. Don't try anything."

They went down some stairs. The place was bigger than he'd thought, made of some dark stone. Corridors led back, lined with doorways, mostly closed, some with grilles in. Cells, he guessed. Sweat broke out on him. Would they torture him?

Down again. The air grew cooler, dimmer. He realized with a shiver of surprise that the building must run back below the houses and streets stacked above it, even into the soft volcanic rock of the cliffs. Masonry began to become patchy; he could see the walls were strangely twisted basalt, glassy and fused at some unguessable heat. A vast round urn full of water stood outside a bronze door, and incense burned before a small statue of the Rain Queen set in a niche in the glittering black wall.

"Wait."

The optio knocked and went in. In seconds he was back. He jerked his head.

Mouth dry, Seth stepped back. "Listen—" he mumbled. Instead the optio shoved him inside.

He had expected a small cell, but the width and splendor of the room he stumbled into made him draw a breath of silent astonishment. It might be underground, but every wall was painted and hung with rich hangings. Tripods of bronze held expensive red-figure vases from the Cascades; a tiger-skin rug was sprawled on the marble floor, its vast jaw gaping. Myriad lamps hung from the roof, bronze and gold and crystal, each bearing a flame that flickered, and an enormous circular mirror reflected them so that the chamber blazed with light.

A round table in the room's center was spread with papers and documents, some held down by lemons taken from a heap in a colorful majolica bowl. Beside the table was a striped day couch, with a woman sitting on it. Leaning on the table, his hands spread on the papers, was Argelin.

"Come closer." He stood upright, watching.

Seth stepped in.

"You didn't expect me." Argelin folded his arms. He was not wearing armor, but a robe of dark red, edged with a gold stripe. His narrow strip of beard and dark hair glistened with oil. "That's good. I've come to think you clever enough to foresee what I'd do."

Seth was baffled, but he tried not to let it show. "Not that clever," he muttered.

The woman was mantled, but she pulled it back. As he'd expected, it was Hermia. The Speaker wore a white pleated dress and her hair was elaborately coiled. She smelled of lavender and some musky perfume, and she stood up, looking at him calmly, a close scrutiny that made him want to squirm, but he held still.

"Clever enough," she said at last, "to plot with a priestess to plant your own candidate in the Archon's Palace."

He said nothing. He had to find out what was going on here.

"Sit down," Argelin said softly.

For a moment Seth thought it was addressed to Hermia, but they were both looking at him. He came around the table and sat on the striped couch. His knee was a scab of blood, he noticed.

Argelin propped himself on the table. He said, "I won't waste time. I'm offering you a quaestorship. A thousand staters a year, but of course you can treble that by your own dealings; as long as the correct taxes come in, I turn a blind eye."

"A quaestorship!" Seth was too stunned even to think properly. That meant one of the elite squad of tax gatherers. The quaestors—there were twelve of them—were the general's agents in the Port, running the whole vast operation of debt collecting, taxation, tolls. They made thousands in bribes. It was an offer that made no sense.

Argelin was amused. "You look a little overwhelmed. Did you think your current promotion was an accident?"

Seth shrugged. "No, but—"

"I obtained it. As a taste for you of what I can offer. You're ambitious. You don't want to spend all your life moldering among the scrolls as a second assistant archivist."

Hermia was watching, her angular face alert. He said slowly, "What do I have to do?"

Argelin smiled, came around the table and picked up a lemon from a pile of papers. He tossed it from hand to hand. "Well. First I want to know who put it into the mind of that boy to announce this unlikely expedition. Was it the priestess Mirany?"

Seth licked his lips. "No. At least . . . no, I don't think so. I don't get to know much of these things. I'm a scribe, that's all. They don't tell me."

"Don't they?" Argelin said smoothly. "The boy must have got it from somewhere."

"The god?"

Hermia glared at him.

"Well, he *is* the Archon."

"Is he?" she hissed. "If I could be sure of that—"

"When did he first speak of it?" Argelin interrupted abruptly. Hermia transferred her glare to him, but before she could say anything, Seth made up his mind. He had to sound assured. If they thought he was lying he'd lose everything. But he couldn't mention the Jackal. The Jackal was as lethal as Argelin, and he was caught between them.

"The day of the announcement. He's got this idea in his head about the Well of Songs. I don't know where he got it, but he's all excited about going there. Something about the water of the Well being pure and filling you with joy. You heard what he said, about bringing it back for the people."

"I heard what he said." Argelin placed the lemon carefully on a parchment. "This is the only reason?"

"As far as I know."

"Nothing else? About discoveries in the mountains? Has he had secret messages from the pearl merchants?"

Seth was sweating. "Look, I just don't know—"

Hermia stepped in front of him. "Yesterday the Bearer visited the City of the Dead. She asked for you. She brought something away with her. What was it?"

They were both attacking him. He fought for a clear mind. "I don't know. I wasn't there."

"A small wrapped object. Heavy. She took it to the Archon's Palace and you *were* there."

He looked down. He felt tired and bruised. "It was . . . a sphere."

Argelin looked at Hermia. He came close; something changed in his voice. "A sphere?"

"Made of silver. It was old."

"Where did she get it?"

"I don't know." He felt as if a great pressure was forcing down on him. Desperately he wished for water, cool air.

"Was it inscribed?"

"Yes." A whisper.

Argelin nodded. "They would have given it to you to decipher. The boy is illiterate and the girl little better. Have you read it?"

Hopeless, he nodded. A brief memory of Mirany holding up the Sphere came into his mind. He saw, quite suddenly, what he hadn't let himself see then, that she had been watching him. Testing him. And he knew he had given himself away, his leap of greedy interest—she had seen that. She hadn't really wanted to give him the Sphere.

Her mistrust filled him with anger. Defiant, he looked up. "It's a series of directions for finding water in the desert, and a map to the Well of Songs." He stood, took a ewer from the table and poured, his hands shaking, so that a few drops splashed on the papers. Then he drank, while they watched. When he'd finished, he put the cup down deliberately. "Is that what you want, for me to give it to you, so that they die of thirst out there, Alexos, all of them?

Or to alter the instructions, lead them into desolate places? Is that what you want for your quaestorship?"

Argelin smiled. He went and sat on the couch and said mildly, "No. What I want is for them to follow the map. If there are dangers, the Archon can find them first. But you will be my spy. You will give a copy of the map to the officer that takes you back to the City. He will stand over you until you complete it. I, too, wish to know the way to the Well of Songs."

He seemed pleased, glanced at Hermia. But the Speaker's face was cold. She said, "There are too many unanswered questions here. Prince Jamil will be furious. The Oracle has forbidden him the desert, and yet others go there."

"Not at all. No one can go while the Archon makes his pilgrimage."

"And there's the boy. If he really is the Archon—"

"None of that matters," Argelin said quietly, taking her hand."

"*It matters to me!*" She shrugged him off, stalked across the room. All at once Seth sensed they had almost forgotten him; it was each other they were tormenting, and it was an old uneasiness, renewed.

Argelin stood. His face had darkened; he turned to Seth quickly. "Listen to me. Once you have found the Well of Songs, *you will make sure that the Archon does not return.*"

Seth couldn't breathe. A splinter of terror stabbed him. "I'm not a killer."

"Oh, you'll be surprised at how easy it is. A fall from some high rock. Poison. An unfortunate accident. Don't try to betray me, or to double-cross me. Your father and sister remain here, and I assure you I'll have no hesitation in visiting my anger on them. Two more slaves for the market; who knows where they might end up? And when you get back—alone—your office awaits. Work well for me and your career is made. Now go."

Seth glanced at Hermia. Her face was closed but her eyes glittered with anger; she gave him one sharp look.

He turned away and walked to the door.

Outside, as its heaviness slid shut behind him, he closed his eyes and shivered, his whole body wet with sweat. His knees felt weak. He looked at the image of the Rain Queen and then up the corridor and nodded bitterly, crushed with a despair that seared into his soul.

"Well, Pa," he whispered into the darkness. "It seems you've finally got what you wanted."

THE FOURTH OFFERING
OF A LOCK OF HAIR

I turned the apples into stars, white as diamond, blue as sapphire, red as ruby. I hid them in the sky and they were lost among billions.

And the rivers dried up.

I was Rasselon, and in his body I wandered my Palace in silence. I saw the fish gasp in the shrinking pools, the flamingos peck at dry stream beds, the crops withering, the flies on the children's faces.

Shame scorches fiercer than the sun.

I have spent lifetimes searching for the Well.

What must I do to find it again?

She Does Not Whisper in His Ear

The sun burned. Its setting scarlet flamed on the Mountains of the Moon, and on the long slender syrinxes of the musicians below on the road.

It burned on the mask of the Archon, and all the sky to the west was a furnace, and the sea a moving gloom of purples and twilight blues.

As Mirany linked hands with the Nine, she saw, from a corner of the eye slit, that a dolphin leaped from the waves, its tail flashing as it submerged, and then another and another, a whole school of them, each a wet gleam of red.

In the center of the sacred circle, Alexos stood. Before him was the dark pit of the Oracle, its faint vapors rising, its jagged sides crystallized with sulfur and basalt.

Alexos knelt. The Archon's mask was almost too big for him, its gold and feathers and hanging lapis, but he used both hands and lifted it off carefully, and she saw his face was hot, his black hair tousled.

He blew the hair from his eyes and laid the mask down.

Silent, their dresses rippling in the wind, the Nine began to intone the chant. It was archaic and crude, a lament not made of words but sounds, the hiss of the cicada, the croon of the owl, the rattle of the scorpion. As the sounds rose the wind gathered them; the Nine stamped their feet, moved in a slow swaying ripple, and the steams from the Oracle drifted and hung, and Mirany felt their acrid power as she breathed them in. Monkeys chattered in the circle, and she could see them, slipping between Chryse and Ixaca, one clutching Ixaca's skirt, and snakes, too, a whole heaving knot of them spilled from the pit and unkinked and tangled on the stone pavement. There were flying things, birds and bats and harpies, human faced, and as she stepped the endless steps she saw how, among the hissing throng, Alexos was calmly cutting a lock of his hair, how he knelt and cast it into the pit.

"An offering from myself to myself," he whispered. "From the light to the dark. From the sound to the silence. From the living to the dead."

Giddy with the fumes, Mirany knew the cut ends of hair were falling, falling down and down into the earth, and out here they were falling on her, too, a drift of dusty rain from the cloudy twilight. It pattered on the stones, a brief drizzle, one of the infrequent downpours since the Archon had come, but not heavy, not enough to fill the irrigation channels in the fields.

Alexos stood. He took his sandals off and tied them around his neck and gripped the wooden staff that the Speaker held out to him. For a moment their eyes met, his dark ones and Hermia's steel-bright gaze; then Mirany saw how the Speaker's mask turned sideways, as if she would whisper something to him. But no words came. Instead, she stepped back into the dance.

Slowly, the sounds died. The Nine stood in silence. The flame in the sky had almost gone; a cool wind gusted in from the sea.

Mirany was strangely breathless; things moved in the corners of her eyes. Small creatures brushed past her legs. Out of the air a tiny cloud of fireflies came and danced.

Alexos said, "I begin my journey here, even as I will end it here. I, Rasselon and Horeb, Antinius and Alexos, Archon once and to come, God-on-earth, Bright Lord, Mouse Lord, Rider of the Sun, begin my journey. I will drink from the Well of Songs. Until I return, pray for me."

A tall boy in a white tunic, he stood simply in the dimness. And one by one the Nine turned away, turned outward, a circle with their backs to him, and as he walked away from them down the broad steps and along the circling path of cobbles, she knew he was passing under the stone door and coming into the road, and that all the people of the Island would be there, a double row, all with their backs turned to the road, for who could see the Archon unmasked?

From here she could see them, and the soldiers lining

the bridge, and beyond that, crowding the road to the desert, hundreds of the people of the Port, some carrying torches that guttered and sparked. As Hermia led the Nine down after him and they walked back to the Temple, a sort of sadness seemed to swamp her, a terrible anxiety for the lonely figure on the endless road between the ranks of turned backs.

"Cheer up," Chryse whispered happily. "He'll be back."

Mirany glared at her. "As if you're concerned."

"I do have feelings, Mirany." Chryse's blue eyes glanced from the mask of the Taster.

"Yes, about what's for supper and what dress you'll wear tomorrow."

"That's not fair—"

Mirany turned on her, tugging her own mask off as they crossed the threshold of the Lower House. "Yes it is! I wish you'd stop all this, Chryse. I can't trust you; I'll never trust you! Never again."

Chryse's eyes had tears in them. But she took her mask off and smiled. "Not even if I tell you a secret?"

"I don't want to hear it." She set off walking quickly up to the Temple precinct. She wanted to see Alexos for as long as she could. But Chryse ran after her.

"You will! It's about Hermia and Argelin. They've had an argument."

"They've had arguments before." The Temple rose above them, a dark facade against the stars. She hurried up the worn steps.

"Yes, but not like this!" Chryse stopped, breathless.

"Oh wait, Mirany! Listen to me. Just give me a chance!"

Mirany stopped. She didn't turn around, but waited for Chryse to catch up. Then, with an effort, she said, "Well?"

"It was really serious, Mirany, lots of shouting. It was about the Archon. Hermia is starting to believe that Alexos is the real Archon after all. She doesn't tell me much, but I think it might have started when he brought the rain. And because of the Rain Queen choosing him, though I'm not sure Hermia believes that, because she was drugged at the time anyway."

The warm wind fluttered Mirany's dress around her ankles. She said, "And she's told Argelin?"

"No! She's not that stupid. At least I don't think she has. But he knows. And now Alexos has gone away into the desert and I think she's afraid what might happen. Did you see how she went to whisper to him? I wonder what she wanted to say!"

"So do I," Mirany said thoughtfully. Turning, she strained her eyes to see him, but the tiny flames of the torches on the bridge were too bright, the people too far away.

Rhetia was coming up the steps.

"Oh, not her! I'm going," Chryse said quickly. "She hates me." She ran down past the taller girl, but Rhetia didn't even turn her head, as if Chryse had no more importance than the moths that danced in the twilight.

At the top she stood next to Mirany, looking out at the road. "What did that little trollop want?"

Mirany sighed. "She says she's on our side now."

Rhetia spared her a sarcastic glance. "Don't tell me you believe that."

"Not really. But—"

"*Mirany!* You're so soft! She's getting to you, after all she did. Forget her; anything she tells you is just for a purpose. And don't tell her anything yourself."

Mirany was silent. Which of them was more dangerous, she thought—sly Chryse, or Rhetia with her ambition and a ruthlessness that might bring about war? She stole a sidelong glance at the tall girl, her folded arms, her confidence that seemed even more self-possessed than usual.

"What have you done?" she said quietly.

Rhetia grinned. Then she tapped the side of her nose.

Alarmed now, Mirany hissed, "What have you done, Rhetia? Have you spoken to Jamil! I told you not to!"

Rhetia turned back to the distant, dispersing figures on the road. "Let's just say Argelin's going to get a big surprise. Very soon."

Chilled, Mirany hugged her arms around herself, that sudden anxiety surging back, for Alexos, for Seth, for Oblek. *Be careful!* she thought. *Be careful.*

The first sliver of the moon was rising over the sea. Through the ragged clouds it threw a glimmer on the water like the scrawl of a child's crayon.

I will be very careful, Mirany, the moon said in her ear.

Seth got to the bridge late and had to force his way through the crowds. He was bone-weary; it had taken all afternoon to copy the text from the Sphere with Argelin's man checking every letter. Now, with the excitement of the crowd, the festival air, the torches and sausage sellers, the outskirts of the throng seemed like a harvest gathering, or some festival of wild joy.

But as he made his way through to the road, people were more silent. And then he saw a small figure in the distance and knew the Archon was coming. Instantly people turned around, shielding their eyes and faces. Even the soldiers turned, awkward with their great oval shields and the long ceremonial spears, a clatter of bronze that moved relentlessly along the line, each man turning after the other. Tokens were cast on the path before the Archon; flowers and small miniature paintings of loved ones, written blessings on folded strips of lead, scented streamers of bright cloth. Alexos' small bare feet padded around them; he walked quickly, looking curiously at the objects, at the mantled backs and shoulders of the people.

And for a second Seth had a terrible desire to do as they did. To cover his face and turn away and let Alexos walk past him. To stop this descent into treachery right now, so that he could get to the harbor and ship out, anywhere, away from it.

But Pa and Telia would be here. And Alexos had stopped.

Seth realized everyone around had turned away; their eyes slid to him, sidelong, astonished.

Alexos said, "Seth? Are you coming?"

Seth licked dry lips. "Of course I am," he said gruffly.

A mile from the bridge the Archon stopped again. In the hushed remains of the crowd a tall man stood waiting, only his eyes showing above the mantle that was wound around his face and hair. He was dressed for a journey and had a pack on his back. His arms were folded. He waited patiently. Alexos pointed. "You."

The Jackal stepped out. The rising moon sent his frail shadow down the road. Together, the three of them walked on.

The crowd grew thinner. Once past the last few hovels, in the scrub at the desert edge there were only lepers, huddled at a distance, having nothing to throw.

"Blessings on you, boy," one called, his voice cracked and hoarse.

"Move back," the nearest soldier growled, raising his spear. Alexos stopped. "Let them be." Raising his voice, he called, "I'll bring you back songs, I promise."

They murmured, dissatisfied. Seth pulled Alexos on. "The Archon should never be heard," he muttered.

"I told you, I'm going to change all that." Alexos shook his head earnestly. "When I get back, it will all be different, Seth. It will be like it was long ago. Before Argelin. Like the great age of the Second Dynasty, before the rivers died."

The Jackal nodded, amused. "That will take some doing," he murmured.

There were no more people. Only soldiers, a bronze

line of them stretching to the last milepost beyond the City of the Dead, its towering facade a dark horizon to their right, the vast seated Archons black against the stars.

"My statue will be just there," Alexos said thoughtfully. "There on the end where the line stops. It won't look like me. None of them look like me."

Seth was sweating. He stumbled; Alexos waited for him kindly.

"Were you all mad," the Jackal asked politely, "and made Archon by conspirators?"

"Oh no. I was found in many different ways. Once by being lifted up by a bird, snatched from the cradle. Once by being born during an eclipse. I can't remember them all." He sighed. "I wish I could have seen my mother in the crowd. You did send her the money, Seth?"

"Yes."

The Jackal glanced at him sidelong. "You're quiet. Missing your desk already?"

Seth didn't answer.

The last soldier swung his spear in a salute, and after him the road was empty. As they walked on the silence of the desert gathered, the faint scuttle of tiny invisible creatures suddenly loud, their own footsteps echoing.

On each side the scrubland was gray and formless, a void of shadow. Stunted juniper bushes made small stands of darkness, and the air seemed to vibrate with bats and the heat that rebounded from the cooling rocks.

The Jackal drew his long knife and said, "We should be wary from the start. There are many animals in the desert, and many dangers. You, scribe, keep to the rear. I'll go a little ahead."

Before Seth could answer or protest, he strode off, pulling the covering from his head. At once Alexos whispered, "Did you read the Sphere, Seth?"

"I read it. Mirany was right; it's the map to the Well. I've got it safe, don't worry. But don't tell him."

Alexos glanced at the Jackal's back. "You think he'd take it and go by himself?"

"Who knows what he'd do. As long as he thinks you might know the way, you're safe." *But not from me,* he thought, and almost stumbled again.

Instantly the Jackal stopped.

Seth came up close. "What is it?"

"Someone. In the shadows." His voice was calm. Ahead a solitary olive tree hung over, almost bent to the ground. Something clinked in its tangle.

Then out of the dark a low call came, eerie, the cry of some ground-nesting bird. Seth breathed out, but to his amazement the sound was repeated, this time from the Jackal, a soft sly whistle.

Two shadows came rustling out of the tree. *Ambush,* Seth thought, and grabbed at his sword, but the voice that roared across the rocky track froze him instantly.

"Archon!"

"Oblek!" With a laugh of delight Alexos was running;

the big man caught him up and swung him around, giddy against the stars.

"Did you think I wasn't coming with you? To the Well of Songs itself!"

Breathless, Alexos grabbed him and steadied himself. "I told you, Oblek! I told you we'd go one day."

The big man clapped an arm around him and pulled him tight. "So you did, old friend. And now I'm with you there's nothing can harm you. Nothing and no one."

Defiant, he looked at the Jackal, and Seth, and the scornful figure of the Fox, squatting on his heels, his striped robe bristling with weapons. "All of you remember that."

The Jackal smiled his cool smile. "So nice to have us all together again," he said acidly.

The First Stirrings of Unease

Mirany was in the middle of fastening her new pearl necklace when she remembered. It came back to her like a flash of light, like a touch of the god. *The slave woman's son!* How could she have forgotten!

Chryse put her head around the door. "Hermia says hurry up. The litters are all waiting. I'm going on ahead with Ixaca." She had gone before Mirany could speak, still staring horrified at herself in the polished bronze mirror. What if the boy had died? She'd promised medicines and sent nothing!

She flung the necklace down, ran out onto the loggia and down the white stairs at the end. Ignoring the waiting litters, she vaulted the low stone wall and dived into the rooms below, where the girls who served the Nine cooked and washed and scoured. This afternoon was the dedication of a new shrine in the Port, the sacrifice of a goat to be

buried in the foundations. The shrine was being paid for by
the Guild of Barley Growers, whose crops had failed again,
for the second year in a row. All the Nine should be there.
But this was so important!

"Genet." She caught the floury arm of a woman.
"Where is she?"

"There, holiness, but you shouldn't—"

The girl was turning a spit at the fire; a row of birds
were dripping fat. Mirany said, "Genet, listen to me. Leave
that, this is urgent. I want you to get blankets, some food—
broth, nourishing stuff—and a warm mantle from the
storeroom. Small, for a boy."

"Lady—"

"It's *urgent*. Go to Sehen and tell him I said he's to give
you a box of ointments—you know what to take. The boy
has a cough and sores around the mouth. You're to take
them straight away to the City, to a cleaning woman called
Khety. She works at the Office of Plans. I promised her."
She frowned. "Tell her I'm sorry it's so late."

The girl stood, after a glance at the woman who was
baking.

"A cleaning woman?"

"That's right."

She nodded, bemused. "I'll go now, holiness."

All at once Mirany sensed that her request was interfering
with all sorts of duty rosters and hierarchies. She backed out
hastily. "Thank you. I'm really grateful . . . really." Turning,
she bumped into an old woman; she recognized her as

Rhetia's servant, the one who had tasted the bread for her. The woman had a jug of wine in her hand, as if she had just come from the cellar. Mirany stared at it. It looked cool and fresh, and vine leaves kept the lip clear of flies.

"Who's that for?"

The old woman looked at her. "My mistress."

"The Nine are going to the Port." But as she said it, like a cold shiver, the truth came to her.

"Not the Lady Rhetia. She feels a little unwell." Even the servant didn't sound convinced.

Barely hearing her, Mirany shoved past, raced up the steps to the courtyard. One litter was left, the slaves sitting in the shade. "Wait," she snapped, then took a breath and walked quickly to the Upper House.

It was silent.

The white loggia with its statues looked cool and remote. From an open window a fine gauze curtain drifted in the sea breeze. Bees buzzed in the roses below.

Voices.

They were coming from Rhetia's room, and one of them was deep. A man's.

It was strictly forbidden for men even to be in the precinct. Mirany slipped her sandals off and padded barefoot on the cool marble. Argelin came here. But this wasn't him.

Reaching Rhetia's door she waited, staring at the word CUPBEARER in gold and the scorpion above it. The door was tightly shut.

Mirany put her cheek against it, feeling the fine grain.

It was cedarwood and smelled sweet. Rhetia's voice was so close it startled her. "I assure you, I know this is so. It's been so for several years. There are people who are starting to get tired of tyranny and deceit."

"Including yourself?" The voice was grave and deep. Mirany closed her eyes. She knew it was Prince Jamil's.

"Including me. You may have heard of what happened two months ago."

"At the Archon's Choosing?" There was a pause, then, "Rumors reached the Empire. That the choice was not Argelin's."

"He was wrongfooted by a group of . . . associates. People who know the true intentions of the god."

"Also including yourself."

"Led by myself."

"The god has spoken to you?"

Rhetia's dress rustled. Then she said quietly. "He has spoken to me from the Oracle."

Mirany jerked her head back and stared at the door. Rhetia's nerve! It appalled her.

At the end of the corridor she was aware of the servant woman, holding the jug, watching her. Waving her away would be no use; she'd tell Rhetia later that Mirany had been listening. Embarrassed, on a hot impulse, she opened the door and walked in.

Rhetia was sitting near the window, the pearl merchant on a zebra-skin stool. Both stood in alarm.

"What are you doing here!" Rhetia snapped.

Mirany decided to be very controlled. "I should be asking that. Aren't you going to introduce me?"

Rhetia took a breath of fury, but she said, "Prince, this is the Lady Mirany. Bearer-of-the-God."

He bowed. "Holiness. I think we have met before."

"One of the *associates* Rhetia mentioned." She watched his face. It was calm, gave nothing away.

As the door opened and the servant woman brought in the wine, there was an uneasy silence. The woman poured carefully, into two cups, then said, "Shall I bring another cup, holiness?"

"No," Mirany said, knowing the question had been for Rhetia.

As soon as the woman had gone she sat on the couch and said, "Prince Jamil, I'm sorry your expedition was forbidden. But I think you should be very careful about—"

He lowered his body, massive under the encrusted robes. "Lady, if the Oracle is corrupt, this is a matter of vast importance to all the world. The Oracle is the world's center. Every ruler trusts the words of the god. Any breath of scandal, any hint of corruption must be cleansed away. The god, if no one else, would demand it of us."

Mirany felt despair settle on her. She felt very small, very powerless. Things were racing away from her. The Pearl Prince looked on her kindly, as if she was a little girl. "Holiness, I understand your fear. But I must communicate this news to the Emperor."

"Don't," she said sharply.

He stopped, frowning. "Lady—"

"Don't." Ignoring Rhetia's scowl, she stood up. "Your army is vast, your chariots and elephants and infantry. Here in the Two Lands we have very little. The country is destitute from years of drought, and only trade in salt and the pilgrims to the Oracle keep us alive. If you spread this . . . rumor, you won't need a war to destroy us." She came up to him, and though he was sitting, his face was level with hers, a dark, grave face. "Don't tell anyone. Defy Argelin if you want. Go into the desert. Go to the mountains and start your silver trade. Leave the cleansing of the Oracle to us."

"Mirany." Rhetia was icy with anger. "You're meddling in things you don't understand here."

Prince Jamil held up his hand. Then he stood. "I will consider what you have told me," he said, and he was saying it to Mirany. He glanced at Rhetia. "And your concerns, holiness, I will consider and send you word."

At the door he turned to them. "It may not be possible to act without many deaths. Are you prepared for that?"

"Yes," Rhetia said calmly. "If the god wills it."

When he was gone, they both sat in silence. Mirany expected an outburst, but Rhetia just stood up after a moment and went to the window, looking out. "I suppose it's a little late to go to the shrine now," she said thoughtfully.

Astounded, Mirany stared at her back. "I asked you not to tell him! What have you started!"

Rhetia turned. Her anger was cold and remote. "One of my slaves died this morning. After merely tasting one segment of an orange here in my room. It seemed fresh, but when I looked I found a tiny hole where a sharp needle had pierced it. It was poisoned, Mirany."

Chilled, Mirany clasped both hands together. "Hermia?"

"Who else?" She turned, her back straight, her head held proud. "War has begun, Mirany. And I didn't start it."

They reached the Oasis of Katra about an hour after midnight. Alexos was tired out and had been riding on Oblek's back for the last few miles. Seth felt footsore already, his calves aching and the sand gritty in his boots. He scowled to himself. He wasn't used to so much walking, and it would get worse. He was a scribe. Scribes sat at desks.

The oasis was a darkness ahead, lit with the dull red glimmers of campfires. There were always people here; it was the last watering place before the arid country, and it marked the crossroads where the road turned northwest, to the salt plains. Caravans of nomads worked this route all year, long strings of camels that brought salt and opals and some forms of crystal down to the Port. Seth had often seen them; browned, dried-up men, all in black, their wives rarely unveiled. They spoke a strange dialect and had strange ideas. He had even heard they had their own gods.

The Jackal stopped. "Now," he said, "be wary. Tell no one who we are or where we go."

Oblek scowled. "We're not stupid."

"That's a matter of opinion." The tomb thief turned to Seth, the moon slanting obliquely on his face. "There will be men here who might know something of the mountains."

"We don't need them. We know the way."

The Jackal's long eyes watched him. "I'm pleased to hear it."

"Let me down," Alexos said sleepily. He slid to the ground and pushed his dark hair back.

They walked on, a tight group. There were trees at the oasis, Seth realized. He could see the fringes of their branches against the stars, tall pines and cypresses. Coming closer, he smiled with surprise, because the smell of the place rolled toward him over the desolation, a sweet smell of mingled flower scents and crushed grass and the dung of animals. A dog barked, sharp and anxious. Figures moved before the fires.

"Stand still, strangers."

From the shadow of the trees on the left a man emerged, another behind him. The first man held a chain and on it were three great dogs, of a kind Seth had never seen, black faced and heavily muscled. The beasts broke out into a low ferocious growling that terrified him, pulling their handler after them. If he let go, Seth thought—

"Where are you from?"

The Jackal stood, alert. "The Port. Traveling west. Is there room here for another group?"

"If you don't have pox, or vermin." The man in front spoke, and as he came out into the moonlight Seth heard Alexos gasp in horror, and his own stomach gave a squeamish lurch.

One side of the man's face was a pitted mass of scars and seared skin; his left eye was blank, his whole cheek as if it had once melted and reset.

If the Jackal was shocked, it did not show by one flicker. "We have no pox, friend. Show us where we can make our camp, and we'll be no bother to you."

The scarred man walked forward. "There are over a hundred of us, lord, so I doubt you could be."

Lord, Seth thought. The Jackal had altered his voice, but not enough. It might be a bad mistake. As they followed the man past the guard dogs and into the dimness under the trees, Seth rubbed his face wearily with one palm. He was desperate to sleep.

There were tents pitched under the trees, many of them, wide leather structures. Camels were tethered beside them in long rows, and their curious aloof faces watched him as he stumbled by. Some men still sat around campfires. As the strangers passed they stared impassively, their eyes red glimmers, the smoke of their pipes fragrant.

"You have tents?"

Oblek shrugged. "No. Ours is a pilgrimage. We walk light."

"Then you may use a spare one of ours, if you wish. It contains only grain sacks."

"Thank you," the Jackal said graciously.

The burned man nodded, a grim nod. "Not at all, lord." He showed them the leather structure, and the Fox dived in first, tossed a few things around, then thrust his ugly head out of the door flap.

"Safe, chief."

The Jackal turned. "We will only be here one night."

"If the god wills. But the desert has her own moods."

"The weather?"

"There may be a dust storm. It should be brief."

Oblek had a hand on Alexos' shoulder; he thrust him down and into the dark opening. "What do we call you?" he growled.

The nomad turned his scarred face away. From the other side, he looked normal, a handsome man. "My name is Hared. Once leader of this tribe."

He took three steps away, then turned back. "May the god give you a good sleep," he said quietly. "And may you give us your blessing, Lord Archon."

Alexos was crouched in the tent door. He reached out and gripped Oblek's knife as it whipped out of the sheath. For a moment he and the nomad looked at each other in the scented darkness, and when he spoke his voice was old, and cool as the stars.

You have it, my son.

A Private Matter

It had to be a girl.

Lying awake in the morning he realized that, because a girl would have the best chance of getting right up to Mirany and giving her the note. It lay warm in his hand under the blanket, carefully written in thin graphite strokes. PA AND TELIA IN DANGER. GET THEM TO THE ISLAND. PLEASE. She could read, maybe not that well, but well enough. But he had to get the note to her, and only the nomads were going the right way.

Hared had been right about the dust storm. Seth could hear it now, a peculiar dry rustle against the leathery sides of the tent, even over the grunt and whistle of Oblek's snores. Carefully, he raised his head.

The Jackal's blanket was empty, neatly folded. The Fox too was missing, but Alexos lay curled up, only the top of his hair visible, and the big man was sprawled next to him, flat on his back. Seth crept out from his blanket, pulled on his boots and pushed the note carefully down inside, next to the knife he kept there. Then he put his head out of the tent.

The oasis was a maelstrom of red. There was no air but a swirling mass of dust, gritty in his eyes and tasting oddly salty on his lips. He pulled the mantle tight around his face and crawled out.

There were trees, many of them, and under them a glint of water; he made toward it eagerly, head down. A small pool, its surface scummed with redness. Camels leaned and drank from it, one wary eye on him.

"Boy!" The voice was indistinct, muffled. He turned and saw an old man beckoning him toward a larger structure than most, with smoke coming from its top.

Seth stumbled over.

The man grabbed him and pulled him inside. "Drink in here," he growled. "More comfortable than lying on your face in the dirt."

Breathless, Seth uncovered his face. "Thanks," he muttered.

It was some sort of communal gathering place, and there were plenty of people inside. In one corner a fire burned and a kid had been spitted over it; the meat was still raw but the stink of fat clouded the high roof. A circle of women sat near it; he thought they were sewing, or weaving, but their hands moved so expertly among the dark wools and intricate frames of hanging weights that he wasn't really sure how the bright cloth was being made. They glanced at him, and he went red, and they laughed, light, scornful giggles. He could see why the nomads kept them veiled in the Port, because they were beautiful, dark haired, dark eyed, and garlanded with ropes of crystals.

"They're all married," the old man said.

Seth turned in alarm. "No disrespect."

"Then keep your eyes to yourself. The food is this way."

There was plenty. Jugs of water and watered wine, and olives, figs, cheese, a hard, seeded bread. Seth ate hungrily. "Where is everyone? All the men?"

"Saddling up. Taking the tents down. We leave for the Port as soon as the weather settles."

Seth chewed a fig thoughtfully. "What do you do, when you get there?"

The old man spat and laughed. He had few teeth left; he moistened his bread in a dish of water and then slurped at it. "Pay the general's taxes! He takes half, at least. Then we have the business of unloading onto the ship, if our contact is in port. Haggling. Bartering."

"Do you go," Seth asked quietly, "anywhere near the Island?"

"Sometimes Hared's wife goes, or the other women. They give an offering to the Temple. He wants a son but his wife . . . well . . ." He shook his head sourly. "If you ask me, he should get another."

"Which is she?" It was a risk, but he kept his voice faintly bored.

"The one with the long earrings."

She was young, Seth thought. Not much older than Mirany. Glancing at her, he saw her raise her head and look back at him; for a few seconds their eyes met. She didn't giggle, and her smile faded. After a moment she looked away.

Seth gazed around the tent. A few men smoked and played some sort of dice game on the other side of the fire, but they were absorbed and barely looked up. Of the Jackal there was no sign. Nervous, he said, "Where are my friends?"

"The tall lord, he's with Hared. Buying supplies." The old man looked at him curiously, eyes bright. "You didn't bring a lot with you."

"The Archon has to travel without anything. To live on what the god brings us."

The old man nodded. "But you must take water. West, toward the mountains, there's very little."

Seth thought of the silver globe in his bag. For a moment he was afraid it might already have been stolen, but then Oblek was sleeping right over it. It would take an earthquake to move him. "Have you been that way? What is out there, in the desert?"

The old man settled more comfortably on the worn rug. With a sudden sinking feeling Seth recognized that smug look. Now he'd get an hour of traveler's tales, about crawling for days without water and giant scorpions and birds with wings of metal. He should never have asked.

The old man said, "I've heard things. Passed down, from father to son. The tribe holds the memory of the desert. West of here, the road turns, but there is a track that leads the way you want to go. Very faint, often sand blown. It's marked with a rock, with an image of the Rain Queen carved in it, so old that her face is smooth now."

Seth nodded. That was on the map.

"After that, for a day southwest, there is scrub. Look out for small desert rats; they make good eating. The ground rises slowly. You will come to a place of dead trees, if you keep the star of the Archon directly ahead of you. Beyond the dead trees, a way beyond, is the first Animal."

Seth glanced back at the women; one of them had made a joke and they were all laughing, a merry uproar that made one of the dice players look over and mutter something.

"What are the Animals?" he asked absently. "Who made them?"

The old man shrugged. "I have seen the first, but only from a distance, from a hillside. Their true shape can only be seen from above, so that makes it clear that it was the god who drew them on the desert. There is a tale that says when the god was young he wanted a place to play, so he made a great ocean of sand and built hills and palaces and populated them with monsters."

"Monsters."

"You will see. The Animals he drew with his finger in the sand. Don't halt near them at night, or when the moon is waxing." He mused, remembering. "When I saw the first one, the great cat, it shone in the moonlight."

He ate the last of the bread, then drank the water in the dish. Licking it dry, he put it into a pocket in his robe and said, "But the Archon . . . he knows."

"He's only a boy."

"He is the god. He has walked this path a hundred times. One day he will find it again, the Well of Songs. They say it lies high in a sacred cave. There he will make amends for his theft." Suddenly he stood, said, "Eat. I'll be back. An old man's bladder is weak."

Alone, Seth took an olive stone from his mouth and tossed it down. Then, deliberately, he turned to the circle of women and kept his voice low. "May I speak with you?"

He said it to the young one, but there was no chance of getting her on her own. It would have to be all of them, a huge risk. Startled, the girl looked at him, then flashed a glance beyond to the dice players. They were counting coins and arguing.

"It isn't permitted," she said quietly.

"Please. I . . . the Archon needs your help." He took out the letter quickly, before the men saw. "The Archon needs this parchment to be taken secretly to the Island, and to be given into the hands of the Bearer-of-the-God. *No one else.*" He held it out to her, but she made no move to take it. One of the other women said, "What does it say?"

"That is hidden."

"He is the god. He can speak through the Oracle."

None of them were weaving now, though they kept the looms clacking, the sound covering their words. He saw how they looked at the letter, intrigued. None of them would be able to read it.

"To the Speaker, yes. But this is to the Bearer. A private matter. Please, I need you to take it."

Ignoring the others, he looked at her. "Only a woman can do this. Your husband need not know. No one need know."

Her fingers came up from the wool; they were long and slim and the nails had been painted darkest red. She took the letter from him and looked down at it, at the seal stamped with the signet of his office, the snake and scorpion of the City of the Dead. Then she looked up at him. Her voice was almost a whisper. "I need something in return."

Seth glanced at the other women. Each one watched him, all merriment gone.

"I need a son." Her hands came over the letter and touched his; he almost jerked back at their warmth. "My husband . . . you've seen him. The scarred man."

Seth nodded. He was old enough to be her father, he thought.

She licked her lips. "He is kind. He was burned in a great fire, in one of the black tar pits. His honor is destroyed, and he is not able to be the father of the tribe now, because a leader must be without disfigurement, and beautiful. Like the Archon." She looked down. "Hared was beautiful once, they say."

The dice players threw again. The sound made her uneasy; her eyes darted that way. "To restore his honor he and I must have a son, or he will put me aside. Ask the Archon to send me a son. Then I will take your letter."

The door curtain lifted. Seth crushed the parchment into her fingers, murmured, "I will," and turned and snatched up the water jug, pouring with a shaky hand. He didn't look up but could hear men coming in; they came and sat around him, and when he drank, he saw the Fox leering at him and the Jackal sitting with Hared, red dust drifting from them at every move.

"Where's the musician?" The Fox took the jug from him.

"Asleep."

The Jackal glanced over. "Get back there, Fox. Bring them here."

"Think they'll run off?" Seth was agitated; he was listening to the murmur of the women behind him, the clacking the looms made. Hared was murmuring to his wife; then the scarred man came over and sat. Seth made room for him.

The Jackal watched Seth with his strange gaze. Then he said, "We have purchased some grain, water, and fruit. The storm is subsiding and in a short time, according to our friends here, it will be safe to leave."

Seth nodded, preoccupied.

"Is anything wrong?"

"No." He tried to sound normal; the Jackal missed very little. "Well, maybe I'm concerned. Alexos . . . he's only ten. This will be a terrible ordeal for the strongest of us."

The tomb thief drank, his fair hair long on his shoulders. "Worry about yourself. A scribe doesn't get a lot of exercise."

"My brains do." Seth was annoyed. "And you'll need them."

"As I remember," the Jackal said icily, "your cleverness consists mostly of treachery."

"And yours of dishonesty."

Hared was watching them, a faint astonishment on his marred face. "Are you not friends?" he said quietly. "It is folly to go into the desert together unless you trust each other. In the desert men have only one another. It's a place that strips away everything and lays a man's soul bare."

Seth looked away. The Jackal said calmly, "Let's hope, then, that it doesn't prove too much for us."

The old man was coming back, and behind him, sleepy and tousled, was Alexos, and Oblek, looking grumpy. The women stopped their looms and watched the Archon. Something new came into their faces as they saw him, a tenderness, a consciousness. The girl who was Hared's wife seemed to have tears in her eyes.

Alexos sat down and took some figs. "These are my favorites," he said happily.

Oblek poured wine, downed the whole cup and poured again. His hands were shaking, the skin on his face and bald skull pitted and scabbed. His small eyes were puffy, his clothes soiled.

The Jackal watched him. "There'll be no wine in the desert."

"Except what I can carry."

"We carry water, fat man. Water and only water."

"Yes, Oblek." Alexos turned to him sternly. "You mustn't take any wine. It's not good for you, and it spoils your playing."

The big man looked at him, then blearily reached over and ruffled his hair. "I'd better drink as much as I can now then. As for my playing, old friend, it's finished. The songs are drowned."

"We'll find them." Alexos looked at Hared thoughtfully. "Thank you for your kindness. My blessing is on you and on your people, and on your children."

The man turned his good eye to him. "I have no children," he said bleakly.

Alexos shrugged. "This is a crossroads," he said. "There are all sorts of ways from here."

Into the puzzled silence the Fox put his red head around the door flap. "Storm's over, chief," he said. "We can go."

They each had a heavy burden of food and water, except the Archon, who had nothing except the staff that the Speaker had given him. He played with it now, teasing the chained dogs who barked joyfully and even rolled over for him. Seth envied him, pulling on the pack and adjusting the straps. Its weight crippled him. The thought of slogging under a burning sun with it filled him with dread, but there was no point in complaining. The Fox, he knew, was waiting for him to do just that, so he kept an obstinate silence.

Hared said, "Good luck and the Rain Queen go with you, and the favor of the Shadow."

"Shadows," the Jackal remarked dryly, "are just what we need."

He set off, walking quickly, and Oblek and the Fox tramped after him, and Alexos waved and said, "Goodbye!" and ran barefoot ahead, using the staff to vault stones.

Seth took a few steps and looked back. The women had come out of the tent and were watching; he saw the young one, her face half veiled, and their eyes met. He would speak to Alexos, but what could Alexos do? The letter was a secret. For a moment he thought about telling the others about it. Why not? Why not tell them Argelin was blackmailing him, threatening his family? He turned, and trudged away from the despair in the girl's eyes. He knew why not. The reason was that he could barely admit it even to himself. The reason was that if nothing else happened, he would have to do what the general wanted.

And if the Jackal or Oblek found out, they would slit his throat.

After a while he looked back again, but the camp was deserted. In front of him the land was dust red, a sere, parched, shimmering silence.

He hitched up the pack that was already an ache in his shoulders, and trudged on, dispirited. Into the desert.

THE FIFTH OFFERING
OF THE SPILLED WINE

There is a world all around these people that they know nothing of.

In this world the land contorts into the shapes of great beasts, and trees are women, and the stars fall like ripe fruit. The only ones who see this are the poets and the singers, and when they forget, they grow unhappy, and search for the Well.

For whoever drinks of the Well becomes like a god, knowing the truth of dreams.

I am worried, though, about such knowledge. Such knowledge is dangerous.

And the Well, therefore, must be guarded.

SHE SEES THE COSMOS CRUMBLE

Mirany.

The voice was a whisper. ***Come outside and look, Mirany! Come and see.***

She opened her eyes and looked around the silent room. It was bright with a silvery moonlight and there was no sound in it at all but the far off wash of the sea.

Alert, she sat up slowly, her eyes going to every corner, her hand to the knife she always kept under the pillow.

"Is that you?"

Who else? I have something I want you to see. Go out on the terrace. It will be safe. I promise.

She felt strange, a weak light-headed hunger. For days she had been eating nothing but fruit and eggs, things that would be difficult to tamper with, she had thought, but since the death of Rhetia's slave she had been almost too scared to touch anything. She and Rhetia had their food prepared separately now by trusted servants, who then had to taste it first themselves, but even so, Mirany knew that death was close. Maybe Seth would get back to find a new Bearer, a new hierarchy altogether.

No one will see. Look back, Mirany.

Halfway into her tunic she glanced behind and almost screamed. A great terror surged through her; she had to clutch her own mouth. In the bed, lying curled and fast asleep, another Mirany lay, as if she herself was a ghost, a wraith that had risen up from her own body.

Don't be scared. That's not you. You are you.

"Am I dead?"

He seemed to laugh, a happy sound. *I was going to do that, but you were so scared before. So I've brought you into the world of the gods, just for a while. Now come outside.*

She felt dizzy, but her hands and feet were cold, her body as solid and real as before, she was sure. The dry skin on her heel where her sandal chafed still itched. So she couldn't be dead. Crossing to the door, she opened it a slit and peered out.

The loggia was silent, striped with moonlight. The statues of the Speakers gazed out to sea, their faces throwing elongated slants of blackness. The nearest one turned to her and the face was marble, cool and curious. Sure now this was a dream, Mirany stepped out.

The floor was cold under her bare feet, and it was wet, running with water. The water was running down the facade of the Upper House like a waterfall, a glinting, splashing stream, rainbow-tinted with spray.

Below, the rest of the precinct was in darkness, except that in the shadowy courtyard, bats were flitting, and a few of the Temple cats slept in small furry heaps.

"Is it real water?" She cupped some, put it to her lips.

As real as anything is real. It runs here always but when you are awake you don't see it. Look up. To the right of the moon.

The sky was black, the stars brilliant. Small dark flickers across them showed where the bats darted and swooped after invisible insects. Mirany waited. "I don't see anything."

This is the way it starts, Mirany. The way wars and wonders are prefigured. With the falling of stars and portents in the sky. Look.

A flash. It shot across the blackness and she gasped, as if it had seared her sight. And instantly the night was full of falling stars, a vast shower of tiny bursting meteors that made a silver rain high over the Temple roof, completely silent, an extravaganza of brilliance.

"The stars are falling!" She gasped. "All of them?"

Not all. The three I stole must plummet to earth. One is already here. Now the others are coming...

Two scorches of light, out of the east. They flashed in front of her, and after them came sound, a terrible tearing, a rumble that made the very walls and terrace of the house shake, so that one of the statues toppled and smashed, an explosion of smithereens.

Doors opened. Someone shouted. A guard dog howled.

Two stars fell. Low over the roof they swished, out into the desert, far to the west. In their wake the meteor shower fell like rain, and it *was* rain, she thought, a silver wetness that fell into the sea and coated the surface, gleaming on the flying fish as they leaped, on the vast leviathans and monsters that rose up from the depths, hideous whiskered mermen, beautiful naiads who stared at the sky.

Rhetia's door was flung open; the tall girl ran out. She took no notice of Mirany, her upturned face lit with radiance. She looked amazed, then exultant, a fierce delight that chilled Mirany.

"Can she see me?"

No one sees you. But it is time to go back.

"They fell in the desert. Does that mean—"

Seth has one. They must find the others, or my theft can never be remedied. There have been so many thefts, Mirany. From the living and the dead. Go back now.

She opened her eyes. Rhetia was shaking her hard. "Come and see! The stars are falling! It's a sign, Mirany, a great sign!"

Mirany sat up, dizzy. Her face was stinging, as if from some great radiance. And the soles of her feet were wet.

Two miles past the rock that marked the trail, the Jackal made his move.

Oblek was at the back; he stopped, scratched, turned his back, fumbled with the pack. Before he could get the flask to his lips, an agile arm slid around his neck and jerked; the point of a knife was thrust into his back. Oblek swore, furious, swung like a bear. "Seth! Treachery!"

Seth didn't move.

The Fox ducked, gripped his left arm expertly and twisted it up. The musician howled with rage and agony.

"Well." The Jackal turned and strolled back. "Just as I thought."

He took the flask and sniffed the lip. Then, very slowly, he tipped it and let the wine pour in a slow heartbreaking trickle onto the stony track. It lay in the dust for a moment in glistening globules.

Oblek gave a great jerk; the Fox gripped him tighter. "You scum!" the musician raged. "Poxed, backstabbing, bastard scum!"

The Jackal didn't flinch. He tossed the empty flask down. "It's for your own good. Tell him, Archon."

"He's right, Oblek," Alexos said sadly. "I told you not to bring it."

"Is there any more?" the tomb thief demanded.

"*No!*"

"Fox."

With one movement the Fox kicked Oblek's pack over, the Jackal picked it up and rummaged through it thoroughly, ignoring the stream of curses Oblek hurled at him. But when he pulled the second flask out, the musician fell silent. The Jackal looked at him straight.

"No!" Oblek said hoarsely. He turned to Alexos. "Old

friend, listen to me. One flask! That's all. In all this desert! We might be dying of thirst soon, we might be desperate for it. Don't let him." He licked his lips, watching the Jackal. "Don't let him!"

Seth had never seen such a change. Oblek was terrified, the bluff, reckless man brought down to abject despair. Alexos shuffled. But when he looked up, his eyes were innocent and without mercy. "He's got to, Oblek."

"Indeed," the Jackal said, breaking the seal. "We have no choice. The nomad was right when he said the desert strips a man bare. We have to trust one another out here. Our lives will depend on that."

Oblek didn't answer. His body slumped; the Fox let him go and he almost fell forward, his small eyes fixed on the stream of wine that emptied with a wet gurgle onto the sand. It sank in and was gone.

For a moment no one said anything. Seth was tense, waiting for an outburst, a fight. But Oblek seemed too stunned. He stepped forward, picked up his pack, and swung it on. Then he walked past them all, staring straight ahead, saying nothing even to Alexos. He seemed smaller, as if something had been knocked out of him.

The Fox sheathed his knife and came over. "It's only the start, chief."

"I know." The Jackal stared after the big man. "Watch him. He's your responsibility."

The Fox gave a grimace, his toothless mouth downturned. "Nursemaid, me."

"He'll need one."

The one-eyed thief nodded, settling the knife back into his belt of weapons. "And if he gets to be too much trouble?"

The Jackal gave a glance toward Seth and Alexos. "We leave him somewhere, Fox. We leave him for the vultures."

"It's a good thing you don't mean that," Alexos said, walking on, "or I might get cross."

"Oh, I mean it"—the tall thief bowed gracefully— "*holiness.*"

Seth was sure he did. Alexos was safe while they thought he knew the way, but he and Oblek were expendable, and should watch each other's backs, though the big man was too absorbed in his despair to be relied on. Coming last along the track, Seth trudged into the hot afternoon, head down, footsore. Already the skin of his face was being burned by the sun; he had taken to winding cloth over his lips and cheeks, but his eyes were almost blinded by the glare from the pale desert sands, the shimmering tricks the heat played. As the old man had warned, for the last day the ground had risen slowly in a smooth, seemingly endless slope, a gritty track with some sort of rock under it, and rocks on each side. Yesterday they had passed the dead trees, a parched and dessicated forest of trunks bleached to pale gray, so tinder dry and frail that barely any strength was needed to snap them off, but at least last night they had made a great fire; then first the Jackal had kept watch while the others slept, and then the Fox. Seth had meant to keep an eye on them both, but he'd been so weary he'd sunk into a deep sleep and Alexos had woken him before dawn by sitting on his chest. The plan was to start early and sleep out the hottest part of the day in any shade they could find, though shade was a rare thing out here, and would get rarer.

Trudging at the back, Seth looked around. The desert was not bare. Small scrubby plants still grew, their leaves fleshy and thick. There were holes too, scrapes and burrows, though he'd seen none of the rats the old man mentioned. Maybe they only came out at night.

Insects plagued him, buzzing around his face. He brushed them off, watching the others as they walked ahead.

Oblek was far in front, stumbling with a dogged ferocity. Alexos chatted to the Jackal, the tall thief walking easily. Then the Fox kept alert watch, of the sky, the distant hills, sometimes turning back to glance at Seth.

He couldn't help thinking about it.

How he would do it, if he had to. If there was no choice left. Alexos was eager to explore; he poked holes, grubbed under cacti. Everything fascinated him. It would be so easy, too easy, to push him, let slippery rocks or quicksand do the evil deed. But even as he thought it he was revolted, furious at himself. He liked Alexos. The boy was strange and friendly and totally without guile. And it wouldn't stop there, because there was Oblek, and even the Jackal, though Seth couldn't work out how the Jackal would react, not if they'd already found the Well. Even if they hadn't, it was he, Seth, who had the Sphere.

He realized he was weary, worn out with the worry of it. Surely he could outwit Argelin! He tried to make himself confident, lifted his head, thought of the way they'd got Alexos to be Archon, despite everything! He was Seth! The plotter, the one who knew all the dodges! And yes, once Mirany got the letter, Pa and Telia would be safe.

On the Island.

He frowned. For a moment he had the distinct idea that the Island was as dangerous as the desert. Maybe worse.

They were an unheroic group, to set out on such a quest. Thieves and madmen and conspirators. None of them trusted the others. Stumbling, he wished Mirany was here. Though maybe she didn't trust him that much either.

At the height of the sun they stopped, though the only shelter in the desolation was a thicket of spiny cacti. Alexos crawled in and went to sleep straight away. The Fox checked the ground scrupulously for scorpions, then drank and curled up, three of his knives stuck upright in the sand, ready.

The Jackal gave Oblek a dry smile. "Feeling better?"

The musician was red-eyed. His hands shook. "Drop dead."

The tall man nodded. "Take care with the water. Ration yourself."

Oblek looked at him murderously over the water flask. "Don't worry. When mine runs out, there's yours."

The Jackal glanced at Seth, then leaned back on one elbow. "Go to sleep, fat man," he said calmly.

Everyone slept, or so Seth thought. But hours later, when a stone in his back made him groan and turn over, he opened his eyes and saw that the Jackal was on his feet, standing out in the heat with his back to them, looking at the mountains. There was a rigidity in his stance that was disturbing, the way his face was raised to the distant peaks, the faint breeze moving his hair. He turned, as if he'd sensed someone watching. Seth closed his eyes instantly. When he opened them again, the Jackal was sitting, his back against the heaped packs. His strange gaze scanned the wasted land.

Late in the afternoon they packed up and walked on, into the abrupt night, a darkness that rose up out of the land before them, though the high peaks still shone with light for a while, as if up there lay the country of the gods. As darkness deepened, the desert cooled, the insects giving place to moths and clouds of mosquitoes that hung and clustered and danced over certain spots. A breeze sprang up, and then dropped just before midnight, leaving a tense stillness that made the Jackal pause and look up at the sky.

"Chief?"

"Wait, Fox. Listen."

They stood in a tight group, Oblek with an arm around the boy. The night seemed so silent Seth thought he could hear the faint slithers of sand in the burrow mouths.

"I'll set a few traps, if you're stopping," the Fox said hopefully.

The Jackal gazed east. His voice was a whisper of awe. "Archon?" he said, "What are you doing to the sky?"

Alexos stopped yawning. Eyes wide, he stared. The sky was a sudden explosion of falling lights, a cascade of brilliance. Under its splendor, Seth felt cold terror creep into his heart.

"I'm not doing it," Alexos gasped. "At least I don't think I am. Look at it, Seth!"

The shooting stars scorched and crackled, sudden streaks almost too fast to see, outlining the watchers' faces with silver; Oblek's great head shiny with sweat and starlight.

And last of all, in a great rush, two stars came loose and fell, with a rumble and crack of thunder so low that the desert shook, and Seth dived to the sand, feeling the others crash beside him. Molten flame burned; they felt heat scorch over them.

Amazed, they watched the stars flare into the dark mountains.

A distant concussion shook the world.

Then there was silence.

After a while, pushing himself up on his elbows, the Jackal brushed sand from his face. "More falling stars. This is a good portent, I hope." He picked himself up, an elegant shadow, his long hair glinting. He had made a good effort at keeping his voice calm; but Seth knew he was more shaken than he wanted to show.

Sore, Seth scrambled halfway to his knees. And then his

fingers clutched in the cold sand. The brilliance of the
meteor shower lit the desert for miles ahead. In its radiance
he saw eerie lines, ghostly and faint, whirls and tangles of
phosphorescence scrawled on the desert, a great spread of
them, intertwining and linking as if some huge secret
symbol had been marked out by a giant finger, and as he
turned he saw it was all around them, that they had walked
blindly into the heart of it.

"*What is that?*" he breathed.

It was Oblek who answered, his voice thick with disuse.
"Don't they teach you anything in your precious scrolls, ink
boy? This is the first of the great Animals." He put his arm
around Alexos' shoulders uneasily.

"This is the Lion."

HE COULDN'T CARE LESS

"It has to be done." Alexos was earnest. "As Archon, I have to walk the ritual path of the Lion, and that means even if it takes all day. So now we've had something to eat I'll start. All right?"

Seth shook his head. "Why bother? Why not just go past it?"

"It wouldn't be right, Seth. This is why I've come. Otherwise the Lion will come padding after us, and there'll be trouble. I have to talk to it."

It was useless, Seth knew. Once Alexos had an idea, he stuck to it. He glanced at the Jackal, who was picking meat from the last tiny bones of the desert rat. "Start when you want," the tall man said. "Just don't expect us to wait around."

Alexos put both hands on his hips and drew himself up. "I wouldn't advise you to cross me, thief king," he said, his voice echoing in the emptiness. "Remember who I am."

"Oh, I remember." The Jackal wiped his fingers on a square of cloth. "The mad child who says he knows the way to the Well of Songs."

"Which makes me the god."

"If you say so." He stood and began to put things into the pack. Then he said to the Fox, "The moon will rise soon and there are about five more hours of darkness. I think we should use them. We can stop and sleep when the sun gets too hot."

"You're not listening to me!" Alexos stamped his foot in fury. "Stop talking as if I wasn't here! Tell him, Oblek."

Oblek scowled. "Leave the boy alone," he muttered without conviction. He sat where he had slumped when the fire had been lit, silent and morose. He had eaten nothing. His head hung, as if it was heavy. Now he took another mouthful of water from the emptying flask; Seth noticed how his hands trembled helplessly.

The Jackal noticed, too. Alexos gave him one glare, then turned and walked to the nearest of the strange lines. Seth went after him. The lines seemed to be formed of some lighter material. He scuffed at one with his foot, and it glinted even in the starlight, like powdered crystal, crushed glass.

Alexos stepped onto the line and began to follow it, as if it was a path. With a careful, upright walk he paced the twisting line, his bare feet on the cool gritty stuff. The line snaked on itself, spiraled like a maze. To follow it around the vast outline of the Lion would take hours, Seth thought. He went back and picked up his pack.

The Jackal strode straight across the desert, ignoring the lines, and the Fox came behind with Oblek. The big man trudged without looking to right or left.

"Come on," the tall thief called.

Alexos took no notice. He tiptoed steadily, arms out, along the pale lines of the god's outline.

The Jackal said, "Get him."

"Get him yourself," Seth muttered.

The thief's long eyes looked at him. Then he went over, grabbed Alexos and swung him off his feet. The boy gave a yelp. "No! Leave me—I've got to do this."

He kicked, but the Jackal had him firmly around the waist. "Your being mad was quite amusing in the Port," he said mildly, "but this is no place to start playing games."

"But I'm the god!"

"Indeed. Well, strike me dead with a thunderbolt and go back to your fun."

"Oblek!" Alexos was distraught, but the musician had plodded far ahead; if he heard, he didn't turn around.

"I'm afraid Oblek is suffering a little frustration of his own just now." The Jackal looked after him, over the boy's back.

"Put me down!" The Archon was struggling so much, Seth thought he would choke himself.

"Let him be," he said quietly.

"If I do," the Jackal said sternly, "he walks with me. No

running off." He let the boy down but kept a firm grip of his arm. "I don't want to tie you up, but I will." He strode off; with a jerk Alexos was yanked after him, after one wild look back.

"This is a mistake," he said, his voice full of fury, his eyes wet. "And you'll regret it. The Lion is following us now."

"What a pity," the Jackal said, acid. "The god will just have to deal with it, won't he?"

They walked for hours, into a darkness that paled behind them. The ground grew softer, the bushes sparse. Finally Alexos was so tired the Jackal had to carry him, asleep on his back, and Seth and the others took turns with two packs, an unbearable weight.

The desert was strange at night. The sky was immense, and there were stars in it that Seth had never seen before, brilliant reds and blues, millions of stars. He knew the names of some of the constellations, of the Scorpion and the Running Man, and the Rain Queen's Necklace, but even the familiar shapes seemed lost in the welter of glittering points of light. He stared at them until his neck ached, and at the mountains ahead, black pinnacles that seemed no nearer than they did from the walls of the City. How could four men and a boy ever reach them? No one had come back from the mountains since the rivers had dried. He must be mad, even being out here.

His feet ached. The muscles of his calves felt stretched,

the constant slither of the fine sand tugging at them. His back and shoulders were an agony of stooped bruising. Sand was in his eyes and rubbing them made it worse; it was in his hair and nostrils and even caked the folds of the scarf over his mouth. And he was so thirsty. A mouthful at a time, every precious swallow, the water in the leather flask was going down. There would be a time, he thought wryly, when he would be praying to have its weight crushing him again.

The Fox stopped and waited for him. "I'll take the pack, pretty boy."

"I can manage."

"Sure. But we take turns."

Teeth gritted with effort, Seth heaved the thing off. The relief was huge; his own pack felt like nothing. He grabbed the straps and helped the Fox on with it; the one-eyed man was wiry and swung it onto one shoulder as if it was nothing.

Then the Fox turned on his heel. "What was that?"

"Where?"

"A sound. Listen."

They waited, unmoving in the dark. Behind them the desert stretched into mists and glimmers, a faint wispiness that seemed to emanate from the ground. It hung, a layer of gray, closing in.

"I didn't hear anything," Seth said at last. "What did it sound like?"

The Fox's one eye stared into the mist. "A stone rattling." After a second he said, "Maybe I was wrong."

"Trouble?" Far ahead, the Jackal was waiting.

"Nothing, chief." But under his breath he said to Seth, "Keep your eyes open. This is bandit country."

They walked faster. Seth was uneasy, not wanting to be at the back anymore. The predawn chilliness grew, the mist creeping after them, prowling around the spiny bushes, slinking low. He began to hear sounds, a clink, a shuffle. Sand slithered; a whisper of moving crystals. Something touched his ankle.

Seth stopped. He turned and saw the mist was almost up to him, sand-gray and silent. There was movement in it, a shape that loomed and padded. He took a leap back and opened his mouth but before he could yell the fog stuffed itself in, choking him, rolled over him and was all around; instantly he lost direction, blind.

"Oblek!" he gasped.

Someone answered, muffled. He crouched, hands in the grit. It was out there. He could hear it, its paws soft on the stony unstable ground, its great body lithe. Cold with sweat, he scrambled around. It was behind, in front, everywhere. He groped for his knife and drew it; it was wet with condensation. The mist was breathing on the blade, becoming a maned beast putting its face into his, licking him with a soft tongue of cloud, slashing a paw out and rolling him over so that he yelled and screamed and scrabbled backward, into spines and cacti.

"Oblek! Jackal!"

The mist split. Tawny rays like whiskers seamed it, an

eye of gold opened in it. Dazzled, he put a hand up to protect his sight, saw a sudden fan of brilliant yellow rays pierce the fog, turning it amber, dissolving it, thinning it. His body grew a long spindly shadow, and so did a rock nearby, and the stump of a dead tree, and far, far ahead, frighteningly far, the sun was rising over an empty horizon.

A touch on his shoulder made him jump; the Jackal was there, armed, and the others, watching.

"What did you see?" the tall man asked quietly.

Seth ran a hand over his face. His voice sounded scared and hoarse. "A lion. In the mist."

"A lion."

"I saw it."

"I told you." Alexos looked bone weary but he folded his thin arms. "You should have let me talk to it."

The Jackal nodded slowly. "So now we are pursued by demons." The sunlight lit his face; he turned away from it. "For some of us, that's not new."

"What does it want?" the Fox said. He caught the Jackal's eye. "I mean . . . not that—"

"To stop us." Alexos glared at him. "To consume us."

"No problem." The Jackal walked on grimly. "We can always tether the fat man to the sand. He should make quite a meal, even for a lion made of fog and fear."

"It was *there*," Seth growled, still shaken.

"Of course it was. In your head. What do you say, musician?"

Oblek looked up. His eyes were vacant; he had to force his cracked lips to speak. "I couldn't care less," he croaked.

"Exactly." The Jackal turned. "Nor could I. Now we walk. Fast. The foothills are still far away, and we must find water in the next two days, or we die out here. That's our real danger, not mirages and dreams." He grabbed his pack from the Fox and hauled it on, his elongated shadow stretching toward the hills. "Come on."

Alexos came and walked by Seth. "I believe you, Seth," he said. "It's back there, snuffling." He glanced behind, at the empty land. "And look at our footsteps. So easy to follow." His voice lowered. "What does the Sphere say?"

"That the first beast *must be appeased for its nature is anger, and it prowls in the mind and its jealousies are claws.* There was something else about *flowers* but I couldn't translate a few phrases, they were too worn." Seth raised his head, struck by a sudden doubt. "There's something wrong here. If the Jackal thinks you know the way to the Well he must believe you are the god. And yet he obviously doesn't." He looked up. "You don't think he could know about the Sphere?"

"How?"

Seth's mind was working rapidly. "He has a spy in—" For a moment, a heartstopping moment, he almost said, "*Argelin's headquarters,*" and bit his tongue. "All sorts of places. Maybe he knew Mirany brought it to you." It sounded lame. But if the Jackal knew about the Sphere, why not just take it and go? *And if he knew about the Sphere, did he know about Seth's orders?*

"Then we'd better be careful," the boy said gravely.

"You're right," Seth muttered. Suddenly he swung the pack down, rummaged in the secret compartment he had made in the bottom, and took out the parchment with the translation of the Sphere's script on it. He read it quickly.

"What are you going to do?"

"Destroy it. The Sphere will tell them nothing. They'll need me alive."

Alexos nodded. "Good idea. If you can remember it."

"I'll remember." He memorized it quickly—not difficult, as he'd been working on it for so many hours. Then he tore the parchment into tiny shreds and scattered them on the desert, watching the Jackal's tall back.

There was silence for a few paces. Then Seth licked sore lips. "Archon—"

"What?"

"The nomad woman. She asked me to ask you for a son for her."

"That would be nice," Alexos said dreamily.

"And . . . I mean, I know you're the god. I saw you change the stones . . . and bring rain. So, if you are, you must be able to help her. And you must know . . . things . . ."

It was useless. Alexos was using his staff to vault stones. He seemed quite unconcerned at anything Seth was saying. "I know things."

"About me?"

Alexos laughed. "I know you're clever, Seth."

He closed his eyes. "Clever."

"And you're my friend." He ran on, toward Oblek.

Seth looked at his thin body in the dirty white tunic, the bare feet, the dark tousled hair. "Beware of your friends then," he whispered.

By noon they were all worn out. The sun had crawled overhead, a molten inferno. Its glare was a weight; they bowed under it. But there was no shelter, though the Fox scouted a little way ahead, his keen eye the only visible feature of his wrapped face. They had entered a dry valley of slithering stones, as if a watercourse might once have run there, centuries ago. But now nothing grew in the merciless heat, and the whole landscape shimmered and blurred without even a breeze to relieve the scorching furnace.

Seth drank a few mouthfuls of warm water and crouched. "We've got to stop."

"Not here." The Jackal's lips were crusted with sand. "No shade."

"Then we'll have to do without. Alexos is worn out."

The tomb thief looked at the boy, already asleep. "Cover him or he'll burn."

Oblek took a cloak from his pack and spread it over Alexos, then pulled out the flask and drank thirstily. Water dripped down his chin, his great throat working.

"Take it easy," Seth whispered.

Oblek's small eyes were lit with smothered fury. His face was scabbed, and the scarf he wore around his head made him seem like an outcast, a leper. "Leave it to me," he growled. "We'll have water enough, the Archon and me. Soon."

Finally, they had to sleep in the burning sun. Curled under his spread cloak, Seth sweated. Tiny sand flies hopped on his nose and cheeks, on his tightly closed eyelids. He was stifling in an oven, but he slept, too weary to care.

A murmur woke him.

A stifled gasp, almost of fear.

He opened his eyes, lifted the edge of the cloak and peered out. Light dazzled him, the sand surface red hot as his fingers sank in it.

He saw the Jackal, sleeping a little way off. The man was well wrapped, and lay on his side, but wasn't still. His body twitched, as if he was crawled over by ants, and as Seth stared, the thief gave a low sharp cry of pain, his eyes opened, and he sat up with a convulsive gasp, glancing around.

For a second he looked haggard and lost, totally unlike himself. Then he rubbed his face and drew up his long knees and sat, breathing hard, recovering. The Fox came and crouched, and gave him the water flask. They talked, so quietly Seth couldn't catch any of it. The Jackal drank, and then laughed, a shaky, mocking sound. He stood up, brushing sand off, and the Fox lay down in his place.

Seth lowered the edge of his cloak and lay in the dark, thoughtful. A nightmare. Not the sort of thing he would have expected the Jackal to suffer from. For a moment there, a brief second, the tomb thief had been afraid.

Seth turned over. Drowsily he thought of Pa and Telia. Had the message got to Mirany? Could she do anything? As he drifted back into sleep, the desert stirred under him. He realized with strange clarity that he was lying curled against its great warm flank, that its body itched with lice, its hills and valleys were muscles and bone under a fur of shifting sand. He told himself he should get up and shout a warning.

But it purred in his ear, and he slept.

Yelling.

A furious roar.

Instantly he had the knife out, was up, flinging off the cloak.

He had slept too long. The sun had sunk, the sky to the west a dull copper red, ominous. All the dry valley had blossomed. It had become a sea of rustling yellow flowers, stiff crisp growths that had sprouted and shot up and burst into seed in some bizarrely rapid lifetime, triggered by who knows what—a breeze, a drop in temperature, the levels of light? All before him, high as his chest, acres of crisp flowers made tiny jerky movements. Seed pods cracked, petals dried even as he looked at them, detached, dropped.

And in the heart of the brilliant crop, the Jackal and

Oblek were fighting. A roaring, crashing, vicious struggle, with Alexos yelling anxiously and the Fox holding him well back. Seeds and fluff made a cloud; through it Seth ran to see Oblek's great arms around the thinner man, how he hefted him off the ground, flung him down, crushed him. But the Jackal was lithe; he twisted in the bruising grip, jerked, elbowed Oblek in the stomach. As the big man lurched, he was out, behind him, one stringy arm around his neck, choking.

Oblek roared and floundered. Alexos screeched. "Don't hurt him! He doesn't know what he's doing!"

Waist-deep in the dessicating sunflowers, destruction raged. Oblek was too strong; he broke out, his face red with fury, his broad hands clawing the Jackal's arms, punching him hard, once, again, with a clumsy blind retribution.

Seth gasped, "What happened?"

"Fool tried to steal our water. Stay clear." But the Fox pushed the Archon at Seth and moved in, alert, a knife in each hand.

"They'll kill him." Alexos was white, his eyes wide with terror. "Don't let them kill him, Seth."

Hesitant, Seth gripped dry flower heads with both hands. He was a scribe. Scribes had no idea how to fight. But he could feel it overwhelm him, that vicious heady anger, and as the Jackal reeled and the Fox went in hard against Oblek he dived in, too, not even sure who he was fighting for, wanting only to hurt, to attack. Grabbing the big man's arm, he twisted; Oblek yelled and flung him off so easily he crashed into the stiff flower stalks with all the breath knocked out of him. Scrambling up, he saw the Fox's knife slash down, embed in the sand an inch from Oblek's eye; then the musician was pinned, the Jackal bruised and worn, coming from behind and stamping hard on his arm, kneeling on him. The tomb thief glanced up, his yellow eyes cat bright.

"Do it!" he snarled.

"No!"

It was as if the desert screamed. A roar from everywhere, a huge voice, a rumble.

The earth shook, boulders dislodged and rolled.

Alexos spread his hands wide. *"I will not permit this."*

They stared at him. He was white with fury.

"I told you to let me speak with the Lion. The Lion is here, we walk on his back. The Lion is inside you! His anger is yours. And mine!"

Around him, in great circles radiating from his feet, the flowers were dying, their brief lives over; they crisped slowly, curled, bowed, fell to fragments. And as they crumbled Seth saw the desert floor was crawling with life, beetles and rats and scorpions and ants, tiny flitting lizards, scuttling spiders of enormous size, feeding on the seeds and one another, ferociously killing.

Alexos twisted east, the way they had come. He hissed, *"Let them see you."*

And as the millions of flowers crumpled, Seth saw the Lion. It was enormous, its great paws the outcrops of hills, its body the valley sides. A vast slab of projecting rock turned and was its head, the muzzle wired with thick whiskers, the eyes amber, their black pupils growing crevices that widened as they stared at him.

In the silence the only sounds were tiny scrabbles, the dried-out flowers falling, Oblek's breath, a hissed curse from the Fox.

The Lion watched. Its tail flicked. When it spoke, its voice was the slither of gravel. "They dishonored my form and your journey. I should devour them."

"They are sorry," Alexos said quietly. And then, "I'll make sure they look more carefully now. That they honor the signs." He walked forward, a boy in a dirty tunic, until he was below the beast, its nearest paw higher than his head, its claws gleaming. "I promise you that, because I am the Archon, and they are only men. They don't know anything. They didn't know about you."

The Lion opened its mouth and roared. Or maybe it was just a landslip, the last rays of light making the hills glow.

Because at that instant the sun sank behind the Mountains of the Moon, and there was no lion.

She Is Hindered in Her Quest

The elephants had walked down in a long line, each holding the tail of the beast in front. Now they waded into the sea, foam curling around their great thighs. Gulls cried over them, amazed. The animals sprayed one another with salt water; their keepers scrubbed them with long brushes. Urchins from the Port whooped and splashed in the shallows, keeping a safe distance, and the wash of the disturbed water sent moored boats lurching and their ropes dipping and dripping, taut.

Chryse moved a little farther into the shade and said, "I wonder if they drink through those trunks. I mean those are their noses, aren't they?"

Mirany leaned on the white balustrade and looked down. "I suppose." She wasn't looking at the elephants. Beyond them, some of the merchant ships had sailed out to sea. Others were unmoving, gathered like a fleet. Surely they must have heard from the Emperor by now. Something was happening; she saw running sailors, sails being hastily dropped. Could they be going home?

"They are, you know." Chryse touched her own snub nose. "It must be horrible."

"Chryse, for the god's sake!" Mirany glared around at her. "Haven't you got anything to do?"

The blond girl shrugged. "I've swum and had lunch and had my toes painted. What else is there?" Then an alertness came over her face, and she edged closer. "Why? What's going to happen? Have you heard from the Archon?"

"No." She said it quickly.

"Not even through the Oracle?"

Chryse's voice was oddly smug. Mirany gave her an irritated glare. "Not even through the Oracle."

"That's a pity. Because I have."

Mirany turned. "What?" For a shattering second she thought Chryse meant the god had spoken to her. She felt a pain like indrawn breath, a shocking jealousy. Then she thought, why shouldn't he speak to her? Even her?

"It was yesterday." Chryse sat on the white marble bench and smoothed her dress. "After the dawn Ritual. You and snobby Rhetia had gone off on your own, as you always do now, and I was last out. There were pilgrims there, you know, like there usually are. Wealthy ones, with offerings. I was going past them when a woman stepped out and said, 'Holiness?'"

She glanced up under her lashes, saw Mirany's stare, and smiled. "I said, 'Yes?' and she looked all around, as if she wanted to see if anyone was listening. One of those really pretty desert women, Mirany, and her hair was so glossy and her lips so red. What do they use for that, do you think?"

"I haven't the faintest idea." Mirany came and stood over her.

"Well, you can't get it in the market. Anyway, there were other women with her, so she must have been important. She said, 'You are the Bearer-of-the-God, aren't you?' I don't know why she thought that. Someone else must have pointed me out, and got it wrong. I mean, with the masks on . . . So I said yes."

"Chryse." Mirany was tight with fury. *"What have you done?"*

Unperturbed, the blue eyes met hers. "In fact, I did you a favor, Mirany. Because if I hadn't taken it Hermia might have got her hands on it."

"It?"

"The letter."

It was no use screaming at her. Mirany made herself take a deep breath. Ominously quiet, she said, "What letter?"

Chryse smiled. "Well, I'm telling you. I had to hide it, you see. This woman, she put her hand out of her robe— she had lots of those fabulous silver bangles—and she held it out. 'He said I had to give it only to you,' she said. She sounded really scared. So I took it. It had a seal on. I said 'Thank you,' and she said, 'Tell him, tell the Archon, that he has done something wonderful for me. Hared and I are so happy.' There were tears in her eyes, Mirany. I don't know who Hared is."

"And the letter?"

"I told you it's hidden. I've got a secret place." She was so smug Mirany wanted to grab her arm and twist it behind her back.

Instead she sat hopelessly on the bench and said, "What do you want for it, Chryse?"

Chryse smiled happily. "That's what I like about you, Mirany, you know how things work. But all I want is to show you that I'm on your side. For you to trust me. I could have given the letter to Hermia, after all."

"You might already have done that. Did you open it?"

Chryse pouted. "Yes."

"What's it about?"

"I don't know! I couldn't read it."

Mirany nodded. Chryse couldn't read at all, she was sure. "Did you show it to anyone?"

"Oh of course not, Mirany! So is it a deal?"

What choice did she have? "Yes."

"And you'll have your breakfast with me from now on, just to prove it?"

She might be arranging her own death. But she had to see the letter. "Yes! Now give it to me."

They ran to the Lower House, and Chryse made her

stay out in the courtyard, well away from the building. Scarlet flowers made a bower there, and the bees hummed in them as she waited impatiently. A servant hurried by, carrying plates of sweetmeats. Mirany caught her arm.

"What's happening?"

"The Pearl Prince is due to visit the Speaker, holiness."

Surprised, Mirany nodded; just then Chryse came out, looking slightly flustered. "I've got it."

She held out the parchment. It was very small, and grubby. The seal was broken but Mirany recognized the emblems of the City, and when she opened it, she saw the letters were Seth's, carefully drawn, as if he'd been afraid she couldn't read them.

PA AND TELIA IN DANGER. GET THEM TO THE ISLAND. PLEASE.

"You've had this since yesterday! Why didn't you give it to me before!"

Chryse looked surprised. "Is it that important?"

Mirany swore, a word she had heard Oblek use, then tore the note rapidly into tiny pieces and dropped them into the incense burner, poking them down until she was sure they were burned to ashes.

"Well?" Chryse said expectantly.

"Something Seth wants done."

"Oh Mirany, you *promised*—"

"I'll tell you! As soon as I've done it."

There was no time to waste. It was urgent; she knew that by the small word at the end. *Please*. It sounded scared.

Not a bit like Seth. Leaving Chryse to follow or not, she ran hastily down and found six litter bearers; when the litter was ready, Chryse was first in.

"Where are we going?"

"The Port. Don't talk. I want to think."

She told the men to hurry, but the road was hot and crowded with fruit carriers and donkeys and pilgrims. All the way she fretted. Why was his father suddenly in danger? From Argelin? And to get them on to the Island was too risky, even for the little girl. Hermia would know at once. She frowned and shook her head; he had no idea, *no idea at all*, how things were for her. The only place where they would be safe was with Kreon. She would have to get them to the City and down into the tombs. There was nowhere else.

She hadn't been to his new house and was surprised to find how high up it was. Impatient, she gripped the seat as the bearers lurched around corners, asked the way, avoided strewn rubbish, climbed the hot steep streets. Finally the litter wouldn't fit under an arch in the narrow alley so she jumped out and ran, yelling at Chryse to come, racing up steps and through the winding lanes, filthy with refuse, higher and higher into the stifling tangle of white cramped buildings, hurtling around the last corner till she stopped so suddenly Chryse almost thudded into her.

This was the house. One of Argelin's guards leaned outside the door.

After a moment she whispered, "Wait here," and walked forward. The soldier glanced at her.

"The family that lives here," she said, breathless. "The man, the little girl. Can I speak with them?"

"They've gone," the guard said laconically. He obviously had no idea who she was.

"Gone where?"

He gave her a leer and sucked his teeth. "Argelin's dungeons, darling. They've been arrested."

"She showed it to Hermia."

Eight of the Nine sat in a circle with Chryse in the middle. She was already crying, and Rhetia had barely started. The tall girl stood over her, threatening. "She must have. She had the note for a day. Enough time for a message to Argelin and for the soldiers to go in. You just can't trust her, Mirany! You should know that by now."

"I didn't!" Chryse sobbed. "I didn't, I didn't, I didn't!"

"She's no airhead, though she wants you to think so." Rhetia looked at the blond huddle coldly. "I used to think that. She's dangerous." She turned to the others. "What do we do with her?"

Mirany stood by the window, uneasy. She felt hot and worried and angry. Seth had begged her to help and she'd let him down. But still she said, "She gave me the letter. If she was in Hermia's pay, why do that? Why not just lose it? I'd never have known it existed."

"Yes!" Chryse's kohl-streaked face shot up in hope. "That's right!"

"It's all part of her game. Use the message to arrest

these people, then use it to insinuate herself into your trust."
Rhetia shrugged, already bored. "It's obvious, Mirany." She
turned. "I think we should punish her. The punishment of
exclusion."

Chryse wailed with misery.

Mirany turned to the window. No one could lay a finger
on the Nine in theory, though she knew Rhetia might have
incited some of the others, Ixaca, maybe, to agree to have
Chryse poisoned. So exclusion was probably better, but
Chryse might not think so. No one would speak with her,
eat with her, touch her. All her possessions would be
broken, her necklaces unstrung, her perfumes spilled on the
floor, her dresses torn. Catty comments would be
constantly made in her hearing, and when she finally lost
her temper and screamed out, they would hold her down
and Rhetia or one of the others would slap her, or punch
her where the bruises wouldn't show. And it would go on
and on. Mirany knew; she had had a week of it once, when
she first came. She had cried herself to sleep every night,
desperate for home. For someone like Chryse, who only
wanted to be liked, to be part of everything, it would be
unbearable.

Mirany turned. "No. You need all our votes for that and
I won't be part of it. It's petty and spiteful and it will only
drive her back to Hermia. Besides, Rhetia, you want her
excluded for yourself, not for us. You want it in case she
finds out about your war."

There was an appalled stillness. A gull gave a long

mournful cry out over the waves. Mirany had no idea how much the others knew, but their faces were wary, fascinated.

Chryse, tears forgotten, whispered, "What war?"

Mirany looked at Rhetia. The tall girl was watching her intently. She would not lower herself to plead, even threaten. But under her loosely coiled hair, her eyes were cold.

Mirany looked down. Then she said, "Rhetia has told Prince Jamil that the Oracle is corrupt. She has asked him for armed forces to use against Argelin and Hermia."

A split second of utter disbelief. Then Chryse jumped up. "And she calls *me* a traitor!"

"Is it true?" Ixaca, the Anointer, was on her feet.

"Yes." Rhetia was calm. "It's true. We all know the Oracle is being betrayed, and I'm doing something about it. I intend to be Speaker. All of you, if you still want to keep your places, will back me."

But all the time her eyes were on Mirany.

Mirany licked dry lips. She was so tense she thought she would scream, but she said, "I'm going to Hermia."

Chryse stared. "Why?"

"To try and stop this. If she stepped down. If she accepted Rhetia as Speaker—"

Rhetia took a step forward. "She won't. And if you do that, Mirany, if you dare do that, then you've lost us. All of us. You'll be on your own, caught between sides."

It was a moment of pure fear. Because it was true. Seth was gone, and Alexos and Oblek, and now the Nine were against her, and Hermia would still hate her. There was no one in all the world to help her.

Except me.

Mirany jumped. His voice was so quiet, so sad. But it gave her something, an uprising of courage. She nodded. "I know that," she said, and was answering both of them. And then she turned and walked out.

There was a slave dressing Hermia's hair, but Mirany said, "Leave us, please." The girl looked at the Speaker; Hermia nodded and the girl went. Slowly, Hermia stood, as if she could tell by Mirany's rigidity, by the way her hands were clenched, what was coming.

But all she said was, "You should be dressing for Prince Jamil's visit."

"I doubt he'll be here." Mirany looked up. "Hermia, I know you hate me. For everything that's happened, for getting Alexos to be Archon, for the things I've said to you. But now I've come to warn you—"

"Warn me?"

"To beg you, then, to stand down. To let us have a new Speaker. You're almost the age to leave. If you don't—"

Hermia laughed, a harsh, uneasy sound. "Are you threatening me?" She came forward, suddenly vengeful. "You, who think you can hear the god? Who think you know what the god wants?" She smiled, cold, the careful curls dark on her white skin. "I thought that once, Mirany. When I was young and naive, I thought I knew what the god wanted, but then I realized it was my own voice, my own desires. When I became Speaker, I thought it would change. That the Oracle would pulsate with sound, roar with a great voice."

Her fingers picked up an ivory comb, turning it over. "That first day I was so terrified I could hardly breathe. Some city in the east had sent to know if they should invade their enemy's territory. I put the question, and then I waited."

She turned. "Can you imagine how that feels? That silence? The pit with its fumes, an open mouth out of which nothing comes? Nothing. The slow horror of realizing that these men with their foreheads on the pavement are waiting for an answer, now, immediately? That a thousand Speakers before you heard his voice, or said they did? That no one will ever know how many of them were lying? *Or will know if you should lie?*"

Shocked, Mirany stood silent. She had never seen Hermia so agitated. The Speaker's eyes darted to her.

"You would have failed. Many would. I didn't. Because the next thought, almost as breathtaking, almost as exultant, was that the fate of cities, of the lives of men and women was in my hands. That whole empires could rise and fall by what I said, that kings could be deposed and that a woman would look for her lost ring in the right place, that farmers would grow the crops I told them, merchants voyage to the ends of the world if I gave them permission. Me!"

She took a breath, her eyes bright, laying the comb

down with a click. "That power is intoxicating, Mirany. I will not leave the Oracle, not for you, not even for Argelin. And not for anything Rhetia thinks she can do."

"You know?"

"I know there's some conspiracy with the Pearl Prince. The general knows."

Mirany stepped forward. "You can stop it. The Oracle—"

"So you want me to say the god requires my retirement?" She laughed, cold. "You, so keen to cleanse the Oracle, want it to speak what you want. What a hypocrite you are, Mirany."

"And the Archon?"

She asked it quietly. It fell into a clamor of disturbed gulls, of distant voices.

Hermia raised her head and gave Mirany an uneasy look. Finally she said, "I'm sorry about the Archon."

"Sorry?" Mirany went cold.

"I had started to think that perhaps you were right about the boy. There is something . . . was something . . ."

The bleakness of her voice made Mirany come forward and catch her arm, a grip so hard she frightened herself. "*What do you mean, 'was'*? What's happened to Alexos?"

Hermia pulled away. "It is the fate of the Archon," she whispered, "to be sacrificed for his people. Especially if he is the god."

The door crashed open. Six bodyguards marched in,

fully armed. Behind them Argelin stalked, hot with haste, his armor dusty, his cloak red as blood.

Hermia turned. "What's happening? How dare you! . . ."

"I dare, lady, because the root of treachery turns out to be here."

"Here!" Wrathful, she faced him. "Are you accusing me?"

His smooth face was calm. "You rule the Nine."

"You know I'm not responsible for anything Rhetia does." For a moment they faced each other, in stony mistrust. Then, as if something was reassured in her, Hermia stepped close to him and her voice softened. "What is it? What's happened?"

His tension broke; he waved a gloved hand at the window.

Mirany looked, and gasped.

The sea was blue, but not empty. Rank on rank of galleys rose and fell on the smooth waves, caravels and slave ships, quinqueremes of banked oars, a great flagship with the Emperor's blazon of a ruby horse galloping across it. Alarmed clouds of gulls screamed over them, and beyond, in the Port, was chaos, the uproar of hasty defenses, fleeing people, spilled fish, the dragging out of great defensive catapults along the stone quays.

"Jamil's ships slipped out to join them, without the wretched elephants," Argelin said bleakly. "The Port is blockaded and I've closed every gate in the wall. The City is barricaded, but the Island is defenseless. You must come back with me, where you'll be safe."

"No." She flickered a glance at Mirany. "My duty is here. I will not abandon the Oracle."

"Hermia, I haven't got enough troops—"

"The god will protect his own."

He put a hand out and touched her arm, and then, as she stiffened, quickly withdrew it. "So be it," he said coldly. "But the rest of the Nine will be under house arrest. Anyone who tries to leave will be killed. The time for caution is finished." He glanced at Mirany. "I suppose you're happy now. Blood will flow in the streets because of you."

She swallowed, dry with fear.

He leaned forward, his face dark with fury. "Am I so terrible, lady, am I so relentless, for my downfall to be worth so much?"

THE SIXTH OFFERING
OF A SCATTERING OF FEATHERS

There are many things they think I want.

Thousands of gifts come to me. Birds, creatures, emeralds, silver. What can you give a god, who already has everything?

My shadow wants nothing, the darkness. The Rain Queen dispenses her life-giving arts for no reward.

But I have thought about it, and there are things I want. Your heart and mind. The three stars.

Not to be left alone.

THEIR NEEDS TORMENT THEM

There had been the Monkey, and now the Spider. Tiny in
the distance, Alexos walked the winding paths, a patient,
plodding figure.

"What does he think about?" the Fox rasped, "out
there?"

Seth shook his head. It was too painful to speak. They
were down to one gulp of water each every three hours, and
his tongue was swollen, his throat choked with dust,
swallowing a terrible effort, and yet he kept wanting to do
it, having to stop himself.

According to the Sphere, the next water hole was two
hours west. He had to get them to it. Or Alexos did.

The Archon turned, pacing back. Once he fell and Seth
stood, alarmed, but Alexos picked himself up and
completed the track, his small feet stumbling with
weariness. Then he came and sat by Oblek.

Silent, the Jackal handed him the water. He drank carefully, one tiny swallow.

Oblek's red eyes watched, bloodshot and sore. For two days he had hardly spoken, dragging himself along. When he slept, he sweated and cried out; even now he was darting scared glances at the dimming landscape, his eyes dull, terrified. Things were out there, he had whispered to Seth. Following him. Demons and dogs with great eyes. Dead men, crawling, unraveling.

Seth knew it was the heat and the mirages, and above all the drink, or lack of it. Oblek was drying out; his body craved wine and the lack of it tormented him, the heat and thirst deranging his mind. They'd be better off without him, Seth thought sourly, and it might come to that, because he could barely stumble now.

Without a word, the Jackal stood and looked around. Wearily, they followed him.

The Animals were appeased, at least. Alexos had insisted on walking their outlines, talking to them, burying a small lock of hair at the threshold of each. Seth rubbed the sandpaper skin on his face and remembered the Lion, the anger it had infected them with. They had seen nothing alive since then, not even a beetle. Now the mountains loomed large; he could make out individual valleys and peaks, though at dawn and dusk the topmost heights were lost in mist. Sometimes a white glimmer tantalized him. Was that snow up there? He had never seen snow, only read of it in old travelers' tales. Solid water. It hardly seemed possible.

They walked.

Over hours, the journey became an agony. Each step burned. There was no end to it. Under their stumbling feet the ground was hard and cracked, a vast salt plain brilliant with encrusted crystals. Only their eyes were uncovered, and even those they had to protect with their hands, blinded.

Mirages moved with them, of distant misty trees, of a shimmer of light on water; three times the Fox had to drag Oblek back from them. The musician rambled, talking nonsense. The water was gone.

The world was a shimmering furnace and Seth trudged across it, with not enough moisture in him even to sweat anymore. Stories and snatches of baby rhymes floated through his dissolving memory. He forgot where he was, who he was.

He forgot everything except staggering, one foot before the other.

And the unbearable, choking thirst.

And then, this place.

It stank. A bitter, raw stench that caught in the throat and made him cough. The desert had sunk into a great depression, and as they stumbled down, the floor of it became sticky, oozing a dark stuff that clotted and couldn't be wiped off. In places it had gathered into pools of thick black murk, too viscous and slow to be called liquid, though it flowed, if you watched it long enough. Bubbles rose to the surface, taking long minutes.

In front of him, Oblek stopped. He tore the wrappings off his face. "There!" he screeched. His great hand grabbed at Seth, hot and shaking. "See it! Look at it!"

Whatever the musician saw was terrifying him. Seth swayed with weariness. From the pools, fumes rose, acrid. Peculiar blue fire flickered over the surfaces, and every few seconds the whole quagmire gave a great belch and fat bubbles splatted, as if something down there had turned over. Could anything live in that? If so, Seth didn't want to see it.

"Demons!" Walking backward, Oblek seemed to notice the pools for the first time. He stumbled, fell on his knees in the oily mess, then saw the stuff on him and tried to rub it off, terrified. "Archon! Save me! I can smell them, Archon, the birds with metal wings, the fat coiled snakes! Look, they're creeping toward me. Archon!"

The Jackal pulled the covering from his face; his eyes were gritty with sand. "He's finished," he said, his voice a rasp.

"No." Alexos looked bone weary. He barely had the strength to talk. "There's nothing there, Oblek, and we have to get out of here. There's water ahead. Very close."

Oblek didn't seem to hear. "Leave me," he moaned. "Let me stay here. The birds are out there. I can smell them."

"That's this black oil—"

"Or I'll go back. Shall I?" Oblek looked up, his face lit by a manic cunning. "Back to the Port? It won't take me long. An hour. I'll go back and get us water. Wine."

The Jackal and the Fox exchanged glances. Then the tomb thief pulled Alexos away. "Come on," he said.

"I'm not leaving him." With a jerk Alexos stood his ground. "I'm not."

"He can't go on. Even you can see that. His mind's gone, and he's dangerous."

"He won't hurt me."

The Jackal frowned. "Boy, he'd cut your throat for a glass of wine."

"I won't leave him. Tell them, Seth."

Seth sucked dry lips. Getting the words out was agony, and gazing down at Oblek's pitiful huddle made him feel despair. To his own surprise he said, "The water's close. We can get him that far, between us."

The Jackal made no move. Then he smiled his cold smile. "Well. The desert does bring out hidden things, scribe."

"And hidden names, Lord Osarkon."

That surprised him. He couldn't hide the flicker in his eyes; Seth felt glad.

"So you've done some research. Is there a file on me, in the City of the Dead?"

"On your family. Their tombs. One of them was Archon, long ago."

"The worst Archon. Rasselon."

"Even he would not have left a man to die in the desert."

The Jackal eyed him coldly. "What do you owe the fat man?"

"He caught me once. When I was falling."

Oblek, behind, gave a grunt of memory. For a moment he looked at Seth and something of the old fierce light was in his eyes.

The Jackal shrugged, came forward and put his arm under Oblek's, a firm grip. Seth closed in to help. Together they hauled the big man to his feet, dragged his arms over their shoulders.

"Lead on, boy," the Jackal said sourly. "You've got an hour, no more, to find water. Or we lie down and die."

But the oily landscape clogged them, slowed them down. Mists and fumes dimmed even the sun, and breathing them left everyone sick and dizzy. Staggering along, Seth prayed Alexos could remember the directions he'd whispered to him a few hours ago, to keep the cleft in the mountains ahead, to watch for the rising ground, the scatter of cacti.

But after another hour of blazing heat they had barely escaped the oil field, and there were no cacti, and Alexos collapsed on hands and knees and sobbed.

Seth stared at the desert. If the spring had dried . . .

"What's that?" The Fox pointed.

Birds.

They were high, soaring on thermals.

The Jackal was clutching his side, looking up. "Is that the place?"

Alexos glanced at Seth; Seth gave a nod, tiny. But the Jackal saw it. Instantly he let Oblek drop and drew a sword, a bright, lethal blade.

"Chief?" The Fox had two knives out instantly.

The tall man came and leveled his blade at Seth's neck, lifting his chin with it. The sharp edge was warm; he felt the sting of a cut.

"Tell me," the Jackal croaked, "what is going on here."

"Nothing."

He gasped. With a swift slash the strap of his bag was cut; it fell and the Jackal kicked it over.

"Search that."

In seconds the Fox had the Sphere out; he threw it and the Jackal caught it one-handed. He stared. "First a star. Now the moon itself! What else are you lunatics hiding from me?"

"Filthy thief," Oblek growled. "If I could get on my feet—"

The Jackal ignored him. He sheathed the knife and examined the Sphere rapidly, his fingers touching the incised letters. "Very old. A map?"

Grudging, Seth nodded, rubbing his neck. It was sore, nicked open.

"To the Well, no doubt. You've read it. Where's the translation?"

Seth was silent. The tomb thief raised an eyebrow. "Would you believe this, Fox? He's holding out on us again. Just like last time." He came up close. "I suppose you've memorized this, too?"

"It's no good to you without me."

"No? What if I can read it, too?"

A flicker of panic must have crossed his face; the Jackal laughed painfully.

"I was educated, *scribe*, by better masters than ever taught you. I may not be so practiced, but I think I can decipher this. Here, look, is where we are." He touched the signs for the oil field, the cramped wedge-shaped letters, the device of the trapped vulture that it had taken Seth ages to work out.

"And this hieroglyph at the edge is the spring."

He looked up. "The landscape has dried. There have been centuries of drought since this was made. But it may still be here."

Half an hour later, with Oblek in a shuddering stupor and Alexos curled up beside him, Seth straightened the agony of his weary back. "I've found it!"

The Fox leaped into the pit, grabbed the wooden spade and worked frantically. Limp with relief, Seth climbed out and knelt on the burning sand, his hands raw. All the time he had been digging, the Jackal had sat and watched him, and even now the man's long eyes did not turn away, his fingers tight on the Sphere.

"Water, chief."

The hollow was barely knee deep, but the bottom was sludgy. Already the sandy mess was dark; as Seth watched, a slow pool accumulated. The Fox scooped some up carefully, tasted it, then spat. "Fresh. But it will take time to settle."

"Widen the hole. We'll need to fill every container."

That took another hour. Maddened, burning with thirst, they waited for the sand to settle out of the water hole. The sun had set; far to the west the birds they had seen earlier circled against the foothills. Alexos was watching them.

"Those aren't birds," he said suddenly.

The Jackal chewed a dried olive. "Indeed?"

"They are people with wings."

The Fox snorted.

"Don't you believe me?" Alexos looked at him, surprised. "I'm the Archon. I know things."

"You don't even know where your brains are, goat boy."

Alexos scowled. "He believes me."

He pointed to the Jackal, who tried to swallow the last of the olive and failed. "Indeed, Fox, he's right. I do begin to believe. The last Archon was a crazy old fool. He may well be reborn in this boy."

The Fox grinned, but Alexos knelt up in the sand. **"That's not what I meant,"** he said quietly. **"And you know it."**

Night had come. Quite suddenly its relief was all around them. The Jackal and Alexos faced each other; when he spoke again, the thief's voice was dry. "For a moment that time, when the rain came, I will admit that perhaps I thought . . . I *wondered* if you might not be the Archon in truth. But the god does not use thieves and fat musicians and lying scribes to work out his purpose. I do not think I am such an instrument of destiny."

"Everyone," Alexos said gravely, "is used by the gods, Lord Osarkon."

"Even the lowest of the low? Even those who rob the dead?"

Alexos watched him, his flawless face calm. "Do you hate yourself so much? Is it the dead that you dream of? Do they torment you, at night, in the dark?"

The Fox went rigid. Even Oblek watched, his bleary eyes fascinated.

After a moment the Jackal brought his face close to the boy's, his long eyes dangerous. "What do you know about that?"

"I know what it is to suffer remorse. I stole the golden apples."

"Remorse?" The Jackal managed a smile. "For what? Do the dead miss their treasures? Do they resent the water and food that can be bought with their jewels?"

"You know they do."

The thief's eyes almost flinched. Seth thought he would lash out, strike the boy, but instead he whispered, "I have thought it. Sometimes."

"Their footsteps haunt your dreams."

"The god must know."

"I do, my son."

"Then take them away, holiness. I beg you, take their weight off my soul, and I'll gladly believe you are the god.

Show me your powers. Cleanse me of guilt. I want to believe." There was a look in his eyes Seth had never seen there before, a hollow pain. Then he straightened, it slid away, and he said languidly, "And while you're about it, why not make the desert into an orchard full of balbal trees."

The Fox wheezed a grin. Partly of relief, Seth thought.

"You're making fun of me," Alexos said sulkily.

"If you're the god you know exactly what I'm doing, and will do." He stashed the silver globe carefully in his bag. "So I need have no fears for your safety, need I?"

A slurp interrupted him. Lying full-length on the sand, Oblek was lapping at the water like a dog.

Hours later, deep in exhausted sleep that lulled and held him like a warm cocoon, Seth saw the water hole flood. All night as he slept the water had risen, and now it gushed over the sides, the sandy edges crumbling, plopping in, and it spread on the surface of the desert, a great lake shining under the moon.

And on the lake there were ships, a whole flotilla of warships of all sizes, and they were sailing toward him, their sails full though the wind had dropped. Heavy keels ground on to the shore.

Mirany was next to him, and she said, "I came in a ship like that from Mylos."

He nodded.

Soldiers were leaping from the boats, men in the intricate armor of the Emperor. Elephants trumpeted, and all around the waters were thick with leaping dolphins, flying fish, and nereids.

"What will you do?" he whispered anxiously.

She shook her head. "I don't know, Seth. I don't know whose side I'm on anymore. There's only me left, all alone."

And the fleet was gone and she was on a rock, a tiny rock in the empty sea, and he was drifting away from her, the current taking him, and he couldn't swim, and he was drowning.

"Oblek!" he gasped, but there was no answer.

Far below, deep beneath his feet, Oblek's bloated, drowned face stared up at him.

He woke.

Someone had hold of his arm, was shaking him urgently.

Wiping sweat from his face, he rolled over.

"Seth," Alexos said. "Listen. What did he mean, earlier, when he said a star?"

"What?"

"The Jackal. What did he mean? He said, 'first a star and now the moon.' What star?"

Seth let his forehead sink back onto the softness of his cloak. He felt utterly worn out, his hands still raw from the digging. "Will you go to sleep!" he growled.

"It's important!" Alexos sounded almost distraught. "Please!"

"A star. I bought it. He took it." The words were

mumbled into the darkness, the warm delicious oblivion that was closing over him.

"A real star?"

"Ask him—the Jackal."

And he was asleep again. Until the tiny distant voice said, "I can't. He's gone."

For a full second Seth lay without moving. Then he opened his eyes.

"Who's gone?"

"Both of them."

With a jerk he rolled, sat up, stared. Then he swore, and leaped to his feet.

Oblek was snoring by the water hole. Two full packs lay beside him.

All around, in all the silent, predawn wilderness, nothing moved. A faint pink light showed in the east. To the west the mountains shone, their pinnacles bright. And the desert was empty, to every horizon.

Freedom Is Bought and Sold

The terms were clear.

The Port was to surrender, disarm, and hand over Argelin. Once the Emperor had installed a satrap, the Oracle was to be ritually purged. A new Speaker would be appointed. "By Jamil," Chryse said breathlessly, "because you can bet he'll be this satrap thingy."

Mirany nodded, impatient. "They don't seem to realize Argelin won't let anyone hand him over. What else?"

"Tribute. Five million staters, paid to the Emperor. What if they put some foreign woman in as Speaker, Mirany!" Appalled, she gripped the seat as the litter lurched.

Despite their house arrest, Argelin had sent a sudden order for the Nine to be brought to the theater. Mirany wondered what he and Hermia were planning.

"Argelin will fight," she said.

Chryse nodded. "The guards outside the Lower House

were changed at noon. The ones coming up from the Port were full of it. A man in a boat brought the letter with the terms in. Argelin set fire to it in front of everyone. He had the messenger stripped of all his jewels and clothes, had his ears cut off and sent him back in rags, and said that was all the tribute Prince Jamil would get from the Two Lands. Then he ordered the bombardment."

She could hear that for herself. The great catapults on the quay had been working all morning, the clatter of their winding gear clear even from the Island, the whizz and hiss and loop of the released rope, the splash as the stone balls plunged into the sea, the sizzle and stink of burning pitch.

"But it's useless," Chryse said, looking wide-eyed through the window, "because the fleet is keeping well out of range."

"Then he should save his ammunition." Mirany fidgeted with the mask on her knee. She knew a siege, however short, would be a disaster. The Emperor's ships were blockading the Port. Nothing else could get in or out, and this was a land that lived only on its imports. Little grew here, and the land was arid. At their backs was only the endless desert. In a few days the shortages would begin. Hunger, fighting. Without the traders, the people of the Port would starve and the thousands of clerks and workers in the City would have no pay. She dared not think about the riots that would bring.

As the litter lurched hurriedly through the marketplace she saw panic had already begun. Peering between the curtains, she glimpsed empty stalls, anxious queues, soldiers everywhere. Prices had shot up; sacks of grain were selling for three times their worth, and a woman was screaming curses at one stall owner, who had three huge slaves at his back. But people would pay it. Food would be hoarded like jewels now, the scraps thrown away last week dug up from midden heaps.

"What about us?" Chryse whispered. "Will the offerings still come?"

"I don't know. For a while. But the Island is better off." After all, it was the only green place for miles, she thought. Olives grew there and lemons, and oranges. The granaries under the Temple were always full. But how long before starvation drove these people there?

Then she grabbed the balsa frame of the litter and screamed, "Stop! *Stop! Now!*"

The six slaves jerked to a standstill; the central one turned awkwardly. "Holiness?"

She jumped out, thrusting the Bearer's mask into Chryse's hands. "Hold that."

"Where are you going? Oh Mirany, the soldiers! . . ."

She pulled the mantle over her head. "Quick. Give me your jewelry, Chryse."

"*What!*"

"Now!" She snatched the rings as Chryse tugged them off reluctantly, then whipped the earrings from her ears. Chryse screeched. "Not those!"

"Wait here." She grabbed the slave's arm. "Keep the

curtains closed." Then she was racing across the littered square, between dogs fighting over scraps and donkey dung and the snaking food queues. She stopped, glancing around. She had seen him. Where were they!

Then a flicker of bronze caught her eye.

Two soldiers were marching him down to the slave market. Pa had a rope around his wrists, the other end looped around the soldier's shoulder, but at least he wasn't chained. Mirany sped after them.

They turned a corner, and by the time she had caught up they had entered a small white stairway that led down to the next terrace. An arch spanned the alley, with a few red flowers growing in a tiny barred window above it.

"Wait! Wait! The god commands it!"

The guards turned. One lifted his spear, but when he saw she was alone, he lowered it, reluctant, then dropped his eyes. The other, more insolent, stared straight at her.

"Do you know who I am?" she said rapidly.

"One of the Nine."

"The Bearer. The Bearer-of-the-God." She stepped right up to him; he was young and hard eyed and she had no idea how to handle him. *Help me*, she thought. *I need you to help me now.*

The guard made a jerk with his head. It might have been a nod.

"This man. There's been a change of plan. You're to hand him over to me."

Pa was standing very still, carefully not looking at her.

The guards exchanged a glance. "We were told—"

"It doesn't matter what you were told." She drew herself up, lifted her chin. "*I'm* telling you now. He comes with me."

The guard holding the spear licked his lips. She was sure of him, but the other one only stared, and it wasn't a stare she liked. He said, "That's more than we know. Argelin wants him sold. We're ordered to bring back the money as proof."

She nodded. His eyes did not leave hers. "So you see how it is."

"Then I'll buy him."

It was too quick; she was betraying her haste, her fear. Seth could have done it, the pretend reluctance, the holding out for a price. But there wasn't time; if soldiers came looking for her—

She held out the jewelry, her own, and Chryse's.

Despite his care, the guard's eyes went wide.

"We're not—"

"From you. I'll buy him from you. All this, for you. Sell some of it, give Argelin the coins. Keep the rest. It's the price of ten slaves. But it must be now, and it must be secret."

Pa's hand tightened on the rope. For a moment there was a silence filled only with gull cries. Then the soldier moved. He grabbed the jewels, slapped the end of the rope into her hand.

Instantly Pa turned and ran, Mirany close behind. Rounding back into the square, he yelled, "Where's Telia? Have you got Telia?"

"The litter. Over there."

Chryse was standing; the slaves had put the litter down. As Mirany ran up they gaped, but she shoved Pa inside and screamed at Chryse, "Get in! Quickly!"

Hastily the slaves bent and heaved. The extra weight slowed them, so Chryse put her head out and snapped, "Hurry up. We're late."

Breathless, Mirany lay back on the soft bench. Opposite, Pa crumpled.

"Where is Telia?"

"I don't know! He asked me to look after you. When I got to your house you were gone."

"Argelin had us arrested." Pa was watching her. He looked drawn, his face haggard. "I don't know why." Then he said, "They must be using us to get at him. They took Telia away this morning. Where is she? What are they doing to her!" His voice was an agony.

Mirany pulled the mask over her face. Her voice came out muffled, echoing. "I promise you. We'll find her."

The tracks were clear. They led west, and Seth trudged in them. Beside him Oblek plodded, the pack on his back. Alexos wandered wearily out to the right.

The wind that had risen hissed sand at them, a searing heat. It had taken hours to fill all the leather bottles with the sandy water, and all the time Oblek had cursed the Jackal, his house, his parents, his parents' parents. Despite the empty sands, none of them could really believe he and

Fox had gone. Seth found himself gazing out, shading his eyes, watching for them.

Finally, when they realized it was true, the arguments had started. Seth had suggested that they turn back, and Alexos had insisted on going on.

"We'll never get him to the Well!"

"But it's Oblek we're going for, Seth. It's Oblek who needs the songs!"

It had only ended when the big man had put a hand down on the sand, heaved himself up, and swung the pack on his back. Then he had looked down at Seth.

Something had changed. His eyes were steady—sore and red from grit, but steady—they no longer searched out demons, and his hands were less shaky. He pulled himself upright and wrapped the scarf around his face and head, shoving it into the neck of his filthy tunic. Then he took the short sword the Fox had left thrust into the sand and felt the edge of it with his thumb. His voice was raw and rough with disuse. "I owe you, ink boy."

"I owed you. Twice."

The musician nodded. "He would have left me. As it is, there's water, food. He's given us the chance to go back. If you want to, go. You might get through."

"Not long ago you were desperate to—"

"Not long ago I was out of my head. Now I feel like death, can't stop shaking, my legs are jelly and small red maggots feel like they're crawling inside my skin. But I'm Oblek again. And I'm not going back or taking mercy from any tomb rat." He tried to fold his arms. "Once I was a musician. The best, the rarest. I've tasted life without that and it stinks. I won't be dried up, scribe, I won't be without the songs. Whatever's out here, I'll get through it if I have to crawl every inch of the way." He glanced down at Alexos. "So take me to your magic Well, old friend."

Now, hours later, Seth watched him. He had to admit the big man was tough. The raging heat was enough to kill anyone, but Oblek had the shakes and was barely out of delirium, a descent into some personal hell Seth could only guess at. The Jackal had been wrong to write him off. He scowled. The tomb thief had the Sphere and didn't need them. But they had their own journey to finish.

Oblek glanced over. His voice was raw. "Need to drink."

Seth nodded.

They crouched. There was no shelter, no rocks, no growth. The Jackal's tracks were lost on the desiccated ground.

The leather bottle moved from hand to hand, their eyes fixed on it as each sipped. Oblek licked a drop carefully from his burned lips. "Tell me the route. If something happened to you—"

Seth shrugged. Then he whispered, "We've passed the region of the Animals. There are others: a vast Beetle and a thing that looks like a crocodile, but they're far to the north and our path doesn't cross them." Just as well. The Sphere had said of the Beetle, "*This is the beast of decay and the redemption of corruption. Its power resides in the inmost places, in the films and mildews of entombment, in the contagions of pestilence."*

Its revenge, if unappeased, might have been horrific.

"Then?" Oblek rasped his chin. His hands were shaking; he clenched them.

"Difficult. The text was worn. Something about the migration of birds overhead—roosting places." He scratched peeling skin from his knee. There had been another word, too, but he wanted to keep it to himself.

"Tell us," Alexos said quietly.

Seth looked up, alarmed. He swallowed. "A hieroglyph. It took hours of searching old scrolls to decipher it. There's a syllabary written in Sretheb's time."

"What the hell did it mean?" Oblek growled.

Seth frowned. Then he said, "Devouring. Eating alive."

They were silent. "Might it mean a place where there's food?" Oblek muttered.

He shrugged. None of them really believed that.

Alexos said, "Could the Jackal have read that sign?"

Seth was savagely scornful. "No chance. He's full of himself, but even I had to search for hours."

"*Even* you." Oblek nodded. Looking out at the shimmering land, he brooded. "He shouldn't have left us. I'll tell that to his princely face before I smash it in pieces."

"Now that's the old Oblek."

The Archon was looking up, at a faint circling spot far in the west. "Birds?" Seth asked.

"Not birds." The boy looked at him, one of his closed secret looks. Then he said, "I think they've escaped. From his dreams."

The theater was packed. Every seat, the curving stone benches crammed with men, women, scribes, sailors, traders, whores, ranks of slaves standing at the top. The roar of the noise and the clatter of Argelin's guards as they kept order astonished Mirany; it rang down onto the stage as if the steep hillside penned it in, a babel of fear. Inside her mask all the voices reverberated; drops of sweat tickled her forehead. When the soldiers all crossed their spears in a clashing tight phalanx around the stage, it sounded like cymbals, announcing the performance.

The Nine sat on perfectly arranged stools, silver gilt. A brazier burned in the center, and behind it an image of the god looked into a mirror; twin opposing faces of purest white marble.

Alexos. What had Hermia meant about Alexos?

She was standing now, tall and regal, and the crowd fell silent as Argelin climbed the steps to stand opposite her.

The rest of the Nine stood, with a rustle of white, the feathers and looped lapis of their headdresses clinking, their calm smiling masks facing the crowd. High overhead in the empty blue sky, three birds circled.

Argelin bowed courteously to the Speaker, then turned to the crowd. "Citizens. We are under attack. Our land is threatened with invasion from a great empire, stronger than we are, with more ships and more weapons. Our trade is cut off, and the Port beseiged, all because the Princes of Pearl desire to control the greatest treasure of our lands. The mouthpiece of the god himself."

The acoustics were perfect; he barely had to lift his voice. Silence answered him, the faintest murmur of his own words journeying around the topmost tier.

The breeze raised frail edges of mantles and robes.

"They want surrender. They want to rule and tax and sell you all into their slavery. They want the power to tell the world what the god says. I say, they will never have that power. The Oracle will teach us the way to win this battle. The god will save his people!"

A cheer. Ragged and uncertain, but then the soldiers roared and the theater rang with voices. Argelin watched, his smooth face calm, his narrow beard perfectly trimmed. *An actor*, Mirany thought. A great actor who knew his audience feared him. He held out his hand; the noise subsided.

"They want you to hand me over to them. If you want that, I'll go. You have only to say the word."

Utter silence, except for a tiny squirm of scorn from Rhetia. Nobody moved; it was as if the crowd was frozen in terror, as if the slightest movement might condemn them. Argelin's eyes scanned the rows; the soldiers watched, impassive.

They're all too scared to breathe, Mirany thought.

You have a mask to hide behind, remember.

She almost gasped with surprise. Chryse's eyes in the mask slot shot to her.

You! You don't want me to speak, do you? Not here, in front of all these?

You could. "Give yourself up!" you could cry. People might join in, stamp, clap. The bolder ones. You could call his bluff, Mirany.

The silence was terrible. She felt it smother her. The god's voice was grave and cold. **No. So don't feel such scorn for them, Mirany, because they're all just like you.**

Argelin bowed. Then he looked up again. "Your trust, friends, honors me." There was the faintest scorn there, but she heard it, and Rhetia heard it, too. The Cupbearer took a small step forward.

The rest of the Nine froze.

Hermia turned quickly, raised her hands, tossed a cloud of incense on the burner; it cracked and spat, fragrant smoke rose.

She breathed it in, arms wide. Argelin stepped back. "Tell us, Speaker-to-the-God. What does the Oracle advise? For the Oracle is here, wherever you are. The god is here, and only you can hear him."

Mirany turned. Rhetia was very still, a stillness that might move.

Don't let her!

I cannot stop her. But I think she will not take a risk. She thinks Argelin will lose this war.

Will he?

Quiet, Mirany. I can't hear myself speak.

Hermia was swaying, the openmouthed mask making tiny gasping sounds. Chryse and Ixaca hovered behind, in case she fell. Argelin said, "Bright One, Lord of the Sun, Mouse Lord, Scorpion King. Advise us."

Words came from the mouth. The whole theater heard them, echoing. They said, **"A sacrifice. Give me the most precious thing you have."**

"They killed something?"

In the dimness Seth was kneeling, examining the hollows in the sand. "Maybe. This is blood. And look, feathers."

"With what?" Oblek growled. "Fox had no bow." The big man had his arms wrapped tight around himself. He was sweating uncontrollably.

"Maybe it flew down. On some carrion."

Alexos had the feathers. He was looking at them close, his dark eyes fascinated by the barbs, how they linked and unlinked, his long fingers smoothing them so no gap appeared. "But these aren't from one sort of bird, Seth. There are all different sorts."

Seth stood. His shadow stood with him, stretching out up the dunes of soft sand that had been clogging their way since noon. Now it was night, as suddenly as ever, the moon low over the mountains.

He reached out and touched them. Small yellow

feathers. One long white-and-black one, broken. A handful of gray fluff. Pink plumes from some flamingo.

"And here, look." Alexos was tugging something out of the sand. "These are from gulls."

"No gulls in the filthy desert."

"No, Oblek, I know that. And look at this."

It was the corner of a piece of cloth. The boy tugged, and it came out of the sand so suddenly he fell back, and it was dark red and striped, a gaudy rag. Silent, they stared at it, the great tears slashed through it, the bloodstains. It was Oblek who said, "Fox was wearing that. Around his head."

Seth put a hand down and turned it over. There was a lot of blood.

"What sort of bird can do this?" he whispered.

Alexos looked up suddenly. Far to the west, almost hidden against the range of the mountains, something dark flapped.

"Whatever it is," he breathed, "it's coming back."

They had dressed her in a white robe with feathers to trim it.

Through the eye slits Mirany saw her brought up the steps, through a cloud of released doves that burst like a fluttering white pain from the baskets the soldiers opened. *Telia.*

Someone in the crowd gave a howl like a dog. If it was Pa, she prayed they would hold him back.

The little girl stood quietly and turned to confront the

crowd. Her face was calm, with that intense concentration Mirany had noticed sometimes, and she looked out at the sea of people without fear.

Argelin came and put his hand on her shoulder; she looked up at him gravely. He led her to the stone altar, and lifted her onto it; her bare feet hung over the side.

Then he turned to Hermia. "Bright One. The Archon is not here. He cannot give his life for the people. So we bring you another in his place."

Small Things Crammed Together

The bird was enormous.

Its wingspan seemed almost too great to keep it in the sky; it hung motionless on the currents of air, idly turning over the searing heat that came off the land. Then it soared down.

Slowly it zigzagged, its eyes never leaving the disturbed surface, the scattered feathers, the bloodstained cloth. All around the place the sand was humped and heaped, as if some great fight had happened, and hollows that were footprints led there and stopped.

The bird's fierce scrutiny was unwavering. Its talons waited, tight below its body. In all the night land nothing moved, not a mouse, not a beetle. There was nothing, anywhere, for miles.

What can we do? Mirany asked.

We?

We have to do something! He asked me to look after her— don't you see, this is all my fault! She wanted to cry out, to leap up and scream. The thought of Seth was an agony.

That's silly, Mirany. Lots of people act together. Chryse didn't give you the letter; Argelin arrested them. People always think their own actions are so important. He sounded almost sulky. Appalled, she thought, "You're not going to accept her?"

There was silence. Then, *That's another thing. People always think they know what's best.*

Smoke, and incense. The rising heat of thousands watching, the heat of the day stored in the stone benches, the flagged stage. She clenched her fingers.

"I won't let them do this."

Telia was watching her, dark eyes under a ragged fringe. Argelin turned and nodded; a slave came forward and helped the girl lie down, quite calmly. She had probably been drugged. All at once it struck Mirany like a wave of heat that Hermia had helped to plan this, that he and Hermia had things all worked out.

The Speaker came forward with unsteady, dragging steps. A scent of dark spices hung around her, her headdress seemed too heavy, her graceful neck bowed. She placed both hands on the altar and looked up, the glint of her eyes watching the crowd like a hawk. . . .

"I accept your offering, my people. And, believe me, I will save you."

Cheering roared down. Real, this time, a raw, hoarse savagery of relief. Behind it, unmistakable, the rattle and whip of the artillery down on the quays.

They think it's you speaking. Mirany was trembling with anger. *Why don't you show them—*

Why don't you? he whispered.

The bird circled. Its beak was long, a hooked horror.

It rose high, swooped, circled again.

Every instinct told it its prey was there, but the desert was huge and something had shuffled far to the east, a scuttle and scrape, a tiny vibration of paws.

It turned, flapped. Was gone.

In silence the wilderness was unchanging under the moon. Then it erupted.

An arm flailed from the sand, another, a spitting face. Seth gasped huge mouthfuls of air, spat out the hollow straw, heaved armfuls of sandy weight off his belly and legs. "Oblek!" he yelled, but the mound beside him had already opened; like one of the dead the musician rose from it coughing, streaming with sand, his face and body forming out of shapeless terrifying masses. Seth knelt up, blinded. He scraped hair from his face, groped, felt for Alexos.

"Archon! It's gone! It's safe!"

A meaty hand shoved him aside. Oblek forced fingers into the heap, grasped for the boy's body, paused, dug again, hard. "Alexos?"

He glanced at Seth, a flash of disbelief. Then they were both digging, flinging sand aside, hands wide, churning the desert till Seth leaped up and stared around, at the emptiness.

Oblek's roar was an agony of terror. "Archon! *Where are you!*"

The bronze bowl was empty; it lay at Mirany's feet, and though she had stood at the Oracle for long minutes this morning, nothing had crawled into it. But Hermia must have thought of that. Because as she stood over Telia her hands were not empty; she held a sharp curved knife, its haft beaded with emeralds and pearls, its bronze blade serrated.

Mirany stood in a terror of cold sweat. If she objected she had no doubt she might get half a dozen words out; then the soldiers would close in and it would be announced the lady had fainted. She glanced at Rhetia; the tall girl stood rigid. Would she let this happen? Probably. Rhetia was ruthless; if Hermia made a sacrifice and the war was still lost then what easier way to prove she did not have the god's favor, to turn the people against her? Rhetia didn't care about one small girl.

But I do. And you'll help, won't you? I know you will.

He was silent. So she lifted her chin, squared her shoulders, and stepped forward.

"Wait!"

It was a small word, but it rang. Shocked by the noise it made, she jerked in fear, her own command returning at her from every side, sharp, angry, fierce.

The Speaker's mask turned instantly; Argelin's face was edged with red light.

Before they could snap orders, she said it again. "Wait!" And then like a sudden peace flooding her, the moon came out and shone on them all, a gold light and she knew he was behind her, at the back of the stage on the high arch where the god appeared at the end of all the plays. She knew it from their faces, the soldiers' rigidity, the way the front rows were standing stricken, then kneeling, a ripple of awe that seemed to go right around the theater, up and up into the highest seats like a wind through a cornfield.

She turned. "The god is here," she said, her voice high and clear. "The god."

He did not move at first. Instead he looked out at the people, a tall figure, his tunic white, his face masked and as beautiful as the statue in the Temple, as pure, with that hurt look in his eyes she saw there every morning. The only light on him was the moon, and it caught his hair as he walked swiftly down the steps past her, past Hermia's frozen awe to the altar, as he caught Telia's hand, forcing her to stand, and then he lifted her onto his shoulder, and she sat there, sleepy, rubbing her eyes.

The silence was full of sound. Not the bombardment, not anymore, but birds, rows of crowded birds singing at night when they should never sing. Full of the cries of disturbed gulls, the gathering of millions of insects, whining and crackling as they crawled out of stones and crevices, of the skitter of mice. And the cats had come, the million mongrel scrawny cats of the Port, running in under doors, over lintels, sneaking under the feet of soldiers, their eyes green as emeralds. All the god's life was scurrying and hurrying toward him. And most of all, the scorpions.

Argelin hissed a curse; Chryse breathed a stifled, petrified sob.

For the stage around them was moving, crawling, alive. The moonlight caught carapace and claw, a jointed, stilted scramble. Out of holes they came and chinks in the stonework, from under benches and flags and marble columns. They fell from chiseled acanthus architraves, from the roof, from the pediment where the Rain Queen sat, her stone face calm. Red and gold and black, tiny, huge as lobsters, the scorpions attended their lord.

No one on the stage dared move a muscle.

And the god said, **There will be death, if you want death. There will be peace, if you want peace. All I can do is put back the apples I once stole, and show you the way to the Well, so you may drink. And yes, if you wish it, to make the rivers flow again.**

He put Telia down gently, next to Ixaca, who grabbed her hand. Then, ignoring the slithering scorpions, his bare feet walked to Hermia.

Mask to mask, they looked at each other, only their eyes visible in the gleaming metal.

"Who are you?" she whispered.

Hear me, Speaker. Don't shut me out.

Stricken, she stared at him. "Can it be you?"

No sacrifice. Not until I return, and then, if there's need, it will be me. As for who I am, you know that. He turned away, walked to the back of the stage and paused at the exit, perfectly lit, perfectly timed, like an actor. **Don't be scared, Hermia. You've known it for a long time now.**

"Seth. Tell me about the star."

Seth jumped, turning like a cat. Alexos was sitting by the water pack, legs crossed.

"Where did you come from?"

"I dug myself out." The boy looked at them both strangely. "Did you think I was suffocated?"

Gray with sand, Oblek stared at him. Then he swallowed, and rasped a hand over his face.

"Why did the Jackal say he had a star?"

Seth glanced at the musician. They both knew the boy had not been there an instant ago. Oblek reached unsteadily for the water, saying nothing. After a glance at the sky, Seth let himself sit slowly down.

"I bought the star as a gift for you," he said huskily. "The Jackal took it. He has it with him."

"It fell? Like the others?"

"Into the sea."

"Then that's the three." His dark eyes lit up. "Don't you see, the three apples I turned into stars? I thought I'd fixed them securely, but they came loose and now they're here, and we have to take them with us." He nodded, happily.

Oblek muttered, "Old friend. Where in the god's name have you been?"

Alexos looked at him, puzzled. "I've been here, Oblek, haven't I?"

The musician licked burned lips. "Not here. We looked for you. We were worried for you."

He was watching the boy with a fear Seth had never seen before. Oblek's eyes slid to him; he said, "When the bird was gone, you weren't in the place we buried you."

Lightly, Alexos shrugged. He stood up. "I was talking to Mirany. She's looking after Telia, Seth."

Horrified, Seth felt the blood drain from his face. "Is she?" he breathed.

"Yes. Like you asked." Alexos smiled his grave smile. "Let's hurry, shall we? I want to catch up with the Jackal. I want my star."

Neither of them said anything else. Three shadows, they walked in silence under the moon, alert for the sweeping hunter in the sky. Wrapped in a long thin mantle, Seth thought quickly. If he knew about the letter, what else did he know? About Argelin's orders? What was going on behind them? Were Argelin's men following? There had been no sign of them. And what sort of bird was it that was as huge as that? Had it killed the Jackal? Would they stumble on bones soon, half eaten by sand crabs, picked clean?

"Seth."

It was Oblek's rumble, and the big man had stopped, ahead.

For an instant of cold fear, Seth knew that was exactly

what he'd found, and was surprised at his own dread. What good had the Jackal ever done him?

But the musician just pointed. "What's that?"

The land had been rising for miles. Now, black against the starry sky, a building rose. Walls, turrets, a broken battlement. At first he thought it was perched on a crag, a towering outcrop of the Mountains of the Moon, and then as his eyes adjusted, he saw that the whole rock was fortified, what had seemed stone was crumbling battlements, the whole mass of towers and minarets so broken it was hard to tell what was rock and what masonry. It looked black, but the sinking moon glinted on slabs, making them glimmer.

As they stared, the sky paled. Behind them, leagues away, lifetimes away, over the Island and the Port and the sea, over the City of the Dead, the sun was rising.

Seth gasped. "It's covered with people."

"Not people. Small things. Crammed together." Under his hand, Oblek's small eyes were screwed up against the dusty wind. "Millions of them."

Alexos nodded. "Birds," he said simply.

Lights were lit, torches, all around the arena. They drove the scorpions back into the dark and the insects away and the cats back to the houses. The people were a different matter; they clustered around the lights, talking, weeping, going over and over the events of the vision, the message, as if, Mirany thought, it had all been some bizarre performance. Maybe it had. Argelin had withdrawn, his bodyguard closing around him, and though he had given Hermia one concerned look, she had not returned it. In fact she had swept out without a word to anyone, had rushed into her litter and closed the door in Chryse's face when the girl had tried to join her.

Disturbed, the rest of the Nine looked at one another.

Mirany took her mask off and blew hair from her eyes. She went and took Telia's hand. "Do you recognize me?"

"You're that girl. Seth's friend."

"Mirany."

"He likes you." Telia watched Pa hurtle down the steep stone steps. He grabbed her and held her tight. When he looked up, his face was years older. But all he said was, "Where can we go?"

Mirany thought quickly. "The City. Use Seth's pass. Find a cleaning woman called Khety and tell her I sent you. She's to take you to Kreon. Stay with him."

"The albino?"

"He's . . . more than that. He'll know you're coming."

Pa looked beyond, at the impatient soldiers. "What about you?"

"I'm more use where I am. Go quickly!"

He nodded and hustled the child away. At the bottom of the steps he turned back. "I can never thank you enough. He came because of you."

She was almost too tired to answer him. Then, from the Port, as he ran, came a great crash, a roar of voices, a sound she had never heard before, clashing bronze, a raw-throated, terrible rumble. The optio grabbed her instantly. "Lady! Hurry!"

Half flung into the litter, she felt it swing up and the men begin to run. "What is it? What's happened?"

Her face alight, Rhetia had the curtains open. Flames flickered red on her skin, and her face was joyous.

"Jamil's attacking," she whispered.

THE SEVENTH OFFERING
OF A BLUE EGG

Don't think the gods are strong. We are frailer than you.

How easily we are forgotten! Faith in us is fragile; we depend on you for it, and how fickle you are.

You have made gods of trees and birds and strange demons; you've worshipped stones and spun a million mythologies about us. You have laughed at us in your strength and prayed desperately to us in your weakness.

I hold the world like a blue sphere in both my hands, but one cry from you pierces me, and I cannot destroy it.

Gods are children before you.

A Nest of Horrors

Finches, he decided, stepping cautiously under the arch.

Millions and millions of finches, lovebirds, parrots, macaws, sparrows, species he didn't know, species blown miles off course, species with plumes and long tails that looked as if they belonged in stories with djinns and white-skinned princesses.

They covered the ruined city, a feathered layer always stirring, the uproar of their chirruping and fighting and rearranging ringing in the ancient tumbled stones, the blown hills of sand. The ground was white with droppings; as Seth walked his boots sank into a gummy mess, accumulated over centuries. The air stank, too. Oblek had his face well wrapped; only Alexos seemed not to mind, trying to entice finches onto his arm with a fragment of hard bread.

The birds watched them, beady eyed. The tiny bodies were crushed into long lines on sills and roofs, some this way, some that, hanging on, falling off, fluttering, pecking, a never-ending motion.

The city seemed empty but for them.

At a hanging gate Oblek paused. He glanced around it carefully, then waved Seth on. The farther they went the more ominous the city became; they had been climbing its smashed streets and plazas for at least an hour, the sun already making the brown brick walls too hot to touch.

"Keep up!" Seth glanced back at Alexos.

"So many birds, Seth! What do they all eat?"

It was a good question. Nothing grew here; there was no sign of water. Above them the ruined buildings rose to the heights of the crag. Empty, dust-deep rooms, their roofs gone, columns that rose alone, statues of broken torsos, giant-sized, dessicated by the desert wind. As they crawled under the remains of one, Seth looked up at it. A leg and body in a short tunic, and at its back a great shattered stump of rock. The smashed pieces all around it were a barricade they had to climb over; as one slid under his feet Seth staggered, and putting his hand down, he turned the stone. It was carved with feathers. Close together, huge. A wing. Beyond that there was no doubt. A double line of vast winged beings squatted on both sides of the paved road. None had faces; it was as if some revenging army had stormed through centuries ago, tearing everything down, smashing the faces of bizarre deities.

"Are they gods?" he whispered.

Oblek shrugged; they looked at Alexos. Tiny below a black basalt figure, his face looked pale and weary. "If they are, Seth, let's hope they have no worshippers."

All the way up to the citadel the dark headless masses crouched, their wings furled. Up here the wind gusted hot from the desert. High up, one dot circled.

"Would the Jackal come here?" Oblek muttered.

"The Sphere says the way leads through. There's a well marked. They'd look for it."

"If they're still alive."

The inner gateway was massed with birds. Thousands of eyes watched them approach, a restlessness that grew noisier, more frantic.

"Keep to one side," Seth whispered. "Don't disturb them."

Oblek's small eyes moved from side to side. "You first," he breathed.

Seth glared at him, then took a step toward the darkness of the arch. As he walked the stench grew worse, the road coated with white. He had to pick his way, small careful steps, utterly silent, and above him as the gateway loomed, the birds seemed a weight smothering his mind, an intent, breathless scrutiny. He was closer now, and there was a path, a way through the rubble. Stones had been lifted aside, cleared. Then, on the dusty track over a heap of shattered debris, he saw them.

Silent, he glanced back at Oblek and pointed.

Footprints. Boots, maybe two men, maybe more, and around them, others. Bare feet. Strangely shaped. The toes long, almost hooked, an odd spur jutting from the heel.

He heard Oblek's indrawn breath.

It was nothing, barely a sound, but it was enough. A bird squawked, fluttered. Another took off, startled, and in an instant they were all rising, a mass of panicking, screaming beaks, of wings that clashed and beat in urgent, mindless terror.

"Get down!" Oblek grabbed the Archon and flung him onto the path, one hand protecting the boy's head, the other beating off the wings and beaks. Seth dived under the arch, the air already a swirl of frantic bodies, crashing themselves to death against stonework, diving at his hair and face, tearing his hands as he curled into a terrified knot. The noise was unbearable; he knew that all down the streets they had climbed, all down the city in a ripple of screaming frenzy the birds were rising, a vast multicolored alarm for whoever lived here. Because someone did. Or something.

"In here!" Seth screeched.

Oblek tried to get up, but the birds slashed at him. Doubled over, arms around Alexos, he cursed and swore and staggered toward the arch, and Seth leaned out and grabbed him; they all tumbled in together, bruised, stinging with cuts. Birds were flying everywhere, uncontrolled, slamming themselves into the confusing curves of the arch, desperate to get out. Jerking back from a savage slash at his eyes, Seth felt something hard give behind him; he turned instantly.

A door.

He shoved at it; rubble blocked it but it shifted. Then Oblek was there, and with a heave he had the door open and they scrambled through. Steps led up, into darkness, and without stopping they ran up them, only slowing gradually as the racket fell away below and the clamor of their own breath and shuffles became the only sounds.

Then Oblek stopped and slid down the walls, breathless. "God," he managed.

Seth bent over the pain in his side. Then he sat, too.

Alexos was crying, a silent awed fear. He had a scratch on his face, but that was all. The backs of Oblek's hands were raw, torn by the birds' terror and menace. Seth felt he was one mass of bruises, dry as dust, his throat caked with sand. Taking a flask of water out, he downed some gratefully. Then he passed it over. Silent, Oblek's shaky hands took it without spilling a drop. When the big man had drunk, he shook his head, dust scattering from sweat-coated skin. "What nest of horrors have we walked into?"

After a while, Seth looked up.

The stairs led into dimness. Far up, a slant of sunlight angled down from some window, a brilliant rod of light. A bird fluttered into it, then out. It was cooler here, as if the walls were thick enough to keep out the scorching heat.

"There's no point going back down. If we keep up this way, we should come out at some upper level. We need to keep climbing now, to find another gate."

Oblek heaved himself up. "No point tiptoeing, either. Are you all right, Archon?"

"I don't like it here, Oblek."

"Nor do I, old friend."

"There are creatures here. Like the birds. Full of frenzy."

Oblek put a huge arm around him. The boy looked up, his grave face dirty. "I love you, Oblek," he said suddenly.

"And I love you, old friend. When we get back I'll make such songs for you as you'll never have heard in all your thousand lifetimes. Now, let's move on. This is no place to linger."

The stairs were wide. On the first landing broken doors led to rooms, most of them empty—the ones with no roof aswirl with birds. They explored a long corridor where the rags of curtains that might once have been red drifted in drafts. The whole place was empty, and silent, except for the screeches of macaws and parrots, distant now.

Then Alexos stopped. His hand tightened in Oblek's. "I can hear voices," he whispered.

The litter rocked. Mirany held on desperately. "They'll drop us!" she gasped.

They were at the gate of the City; the guards yelled a

warning and the litter went down with a thump. Rhetia was out in seconds.

"Open this gate!"

"Lady, are you mad?"

"*Open it!* The Nine must return to the Island."

The gate commander looked around helplessly. "The Port is under attack!"

"All the more reason for us not to be here." Rhetia advanced on him fiercely. "Or do you want to be the one responsible for our deaths!" When he hesitated, she drew herself up. Mirany saw her triumphant smile. "Open it," the man said sullenly.

Behind him, the guards ran to the great wooden bars. Without waiting for the litter, Rhetia slid through as soon as the gates were ajar, and Mirany ran after her. The desert was hot and silent. Behind them, from the area of the harbor, came the clash of swords. Mirany wondered where the invaders had landed, and if the wall was breached. Racing after Rhetia, she saw the black palisade of the City of the Dead over the desolate ground, the statues of the great Archons tawny in the afternoon light. A jackal ran, head down, then stopped and looked back at her.

She ran after Rhetia, thinking, *Where are you, Seth?* And as they passed the gardens of the Archon's villa she thought of all the animals in there, the jungle of monkeys and gifts. *And where are you, Bright Lord?*

This time, there was no answer.

Then Rhetia stopped and looked back. Behind them the gate was opening again. A few figures flitted through, in flimsy dresses. They walked, upright and with dignity, along the sandy road. Mirany caught at a stitch in her side. "Hermia."

Rhetia scowled. "I thought she might be too scared."

"Not her. Don't underestimate her."

The Speaker strode up to them. She was pale, her nose long and straight under her eyes, the manicured perfection of her eyebrows. Despite the heat her hair stayed in its elaborate coils. But there was something different. Hermia was shaken, Mirany realized. Like the Port, her defenses had been broken.

But she faced up to Rhetia. "Cupbearer. You and the Bearer will walk behind me."

Rhetia was cold. "I didn't think you would come. After what he said to you."

The Speaker came close. Eye to eye, the two were matched in height, in cold anger. For a moment Mirany thought Hermia would strike. Instead her voice came, precise and chiseled with wrath. "I am the Speaker. Not you. The Port is unimportant. What Jamil wants is the Oracle and only we can deny him that. Not by violence. But by silence." She nodded calmly. "We won't let the whole land burn for your ambitions, Rhetia. We, the Nine, will stand together. We will keep the angry silence of the god. Before Argelin, before Jamil. Until there is an end to this." She glanced at Ixaca and Gaia, who closed in.

Behind them Chryse watched, wide-eyed and flushed with excitement. "We all have to stand together. Are you with us?"

Rhetia stepped back. She glanced at Mirany, at all of them. The she looked down at the crowding ships, the pall of smoke rising over the Port.

"For now," she muttered.

The words were louder. Strange harsh words. Seth crawled under the last of the red curtains and found Oblek blocking him; the musician inched aside, then pointed with a stubby finger.

Seth bit his lip. Beside him, he could feel Alexos' astonishment.

They were high on a narrow balcony. Below was a vast hall, its wall pierced with windows so that sunlight slanted across it, barring everything with stripes of heat.

In the center on a stone platform was a bizarre construction, rickety and intricate. It seemed to be made of wood, pieces of brittle twig woven together, hundreds of them. Where had they come from, because the nearest trees were miles across the desert?

"It's a nest," Alexos breathed.

Seth stared. A nest. But for no bird. Because a staircase had been built up to it, a winding, patchwork contraption, leading through the teetering layers of wood, the pieces of jaojao bough nailed together to a top-heavy mass of broken chairs and tables, splintered screens, bed legs and slabs of mahogany and teak from precious carved objects. And high on the top, reclining among pillows and cushions and down and billions upon billions of feathers, was a figure that turned his heart chill.

Gigantic, bloated, she sprawled on the incongruous bed. Her robe was feathered, and her mask a hideous black and red, beaked with an eagle's cruel beak. Her fingers seemed swollen; even from here he could see each one was tied with elaborately knotted strings, red and blue and yellow, and the same strings were woven in her dank, greasy hair. She held a fan, made of some dark skin, and she fanned herself with it idly as she spoke in a throaty, cold voice.

It was the Jackal she was speaking to.

Seth's eyes widened. The tomb thief looked terrible. His pale hair had come loose, and there was a cut right down his face. The Fox was worse, crouching on the floor in obvious pain as if he couldn't even drag himself upright. They were in some sort of cage, made of pieces of white ivory, or perhaps bone. Bone. Seth swallowed. They looked like human bones.

Around, there were men. They wore the hideous bird masks, and clothes stitched with feathers, but they were men, and they were armed with spears tipped with what looked like stone or some vitreous sharpened mineral.

Oblek scratched. Then he breathed, "Now who's in trouble, thief lord?"

The Jackal gripped the bars of the cage. "I had no knowledge," he was saying tensely, "of your religion, or your rituals. We had no idea that birds were sacred here. We were simply trying to obtain food."

"You are thieves."

Even from here they could see the Jackal raise an eyebrow. "Not at all," he snapped.

Oblek allowed himself a grin. "Lying scum."

"You attempted to kill the High One. Then you came here and we know why. You seek the star. You will not find it."

Alexos wriggled up beside Seth. "The star! One of those that fell."

"And now"—the woman held up her hand—"we have yours."

It gleamed in her hand, a white shaft of pure light. Seth scowled, thinking of the hundred and fifty staters he still owed for it, and the Archon gave a small breath of recognition. "So long," he whispered. "So long since I've seen it."

The Jackal spread his fine hands. "I assure you, madam, one star is enough for anyone."

It was the wrong thing to say. The bird-men closed in angrily. The woman held up her hand. Her voice was very strange, an oily sound, as if something had been done to her throat.

"The High One has devoured the star."

"Birds," Seth muttered. "She means that vast bird."

"Condor?"

"Something similar."

"Eats more than carrion, then, I'll bet." Oblek was looking around the hall, noting a doorway in the corner, another opening high in the east wall.

"It can't have!" Alexos looked devastated.

The Jackal said, "We mean no disrespect. Keep the star. All we ask is to go free." His voice was taut, but Seth had to admire his composure. He must know perfectly well there was no chance.

A sound, glutinous and sinister. The woman was laughing. She nodded her head to the bird-men. Then she said, "Your souls will be free. On the wind, high in the sky, as will your rags of flesh. Wherever the High One takes them . . ."

Jerkily, with a lurch that made the Jackal stagger, the cage began to rise. The Fox gave a howl of fear, stifled at the Jackal's wrathful glare. The tall man pulled himself upright. "On your feet, Fox," he muttered. "After all our years of pillaging him, death is finally getting his own back."

Seth squirmed. "We can't leave them," he argued against the silence.

Oblek wriggled back. "We could."

"*No!*" Alexos breathed, and the big man tugged his hair. "Only joking, old friend." He grinned. "If anyone finishes that scum off it'll be me. That's the only reason we're bothering, understand."

Alexos nodded, grave. "Of course it is, Oblek."

The woman stood. It was a great effort, as if she hardly ever rose from the bed, and there was a great depression where she had lain, in the feathers. Something pale glimmered among the down. Seth stared. "What is that?"

Alexos' dark eyes went wide. Then he said, "It's an egg."

HE SPOKE TO ME FACE-TO-FACE

The egg was enormous, as long as Seth's arm. It was palest blue with odd splotches, and it nestled in the warm down and the woman covered it carefully, piling cushions and coverings on top. Then, awkward and clumsy, she began to descend the stairs.

"She *incubates* it?" Oblek looked amazed, then disgusted. "They think birds are gods and they hatch their eggs?"

"One bird. That huge one." Seth looked around quickly. "We have to cut the cage down. The bird will come through that opening in the wall." He turned quickly. "Archon, can you help? Can you do something?"

"Of course I can," Alexos said eagerly. "Anything you want."

"I mean . . ." Seth glanced at Oblek. "Something . . . magical."

The boy frowned. When he looked up, his eyes were

dark and his voice echoed slightly in the closed spaces.

"Is it fair for one god to work against another?"

"In the stories it happens all the time," Seth said, unwavering.

"I don't write the stories, Seth." He looked up, worried. "But I think the bird is coming."

The cage was high now, swinging below the vaulted roof. The two men waited, watching the window, glancing down at the floor. Seth knew the Jackal was calculating the jump, planning. Below, the bird-men and their queen moved back, and for the first time he saw that the floor down there was ankle deep with the same gooey whiteness that clotted all the fortress, splashed and dribbled under the great beam that crossed the roof.

From outside, a harsh eerie squawk turned him cold.

"Oblek. Find a way down and deal with the spearmen."

"All of them?"

"Unless you want to climb across and cut the rope."

Oblek leaned out and looked at the thin ledge along the wall. Then he clapped Seth on the shoulder. "All yours, ink boy," he said, and was gone, squirming back with Alexos ahead of him. Seth licked dry lips.

He put one leg over the balcony, and then the other, hands gripping tight on the corroding metal. Then he lowered himself onto the ledge, his foot stretched, feeling for it. The stonework seemed safe, but as it took his weight he felt its edges crumble, and he clung desperately to the bars of the balcony, silent, summoning up courage.

Then he let go, grabbed at stone.

Below him, in dimness, the hall was darkening. Torches were being extinguished, and a faint smoke began to rise around him, the familiar smell of incense. A hasty breath of it made him want to cough; he choked it down. Then, sliding his feet, splayed against the smoke-stained wall, he edged toward the cage.

The Fox was praying, gabbling words, over and over. The Jackal was on his knees, too, but when Seth could spare another glance, he saw the thief was working intently at the complex knotting that held the cage door, his long fingers swiftly unweaving the ropes.

Something blocked the bars of light, a great flapping.

Seth clung on, staring, horrified.

The bird flew past outside, so close he saw its cruel hooked beak. It was no vulture. There was a creature in old legends called the roc. Maybe this was it.

A yell made him grip tight, turn his head.

They had seen him. One of the bird-warriors pointed; the woman snapped something and the man grabbed his spear, drawing his arm back deliberately, taking careful aim. The Jackal stared; Seth glimpsed his utter surprise.

The spear whooshed. It smacked into the stonework just to his left and clattered down; sparks fell into his hair. Instantly he stretched his arm out, gripped, and hauled himself a few feet farther, his back and shoulders tense against the impact of the next flung point that would skewer him to the wall.

His hand slid, wet with sweat. He knew if he moved he'd fall; then the Jackal yelled, "Come on, Seth! Come on!" and he heaved himself up, the dark stone crumbling and soft against his cheek, arms trembling with effort.

Out of the corner of his eye he saw the spearmen aim again, knew he was dead, and instantly, with a roar that jerked their eyes away in shock, Oblek was down there, his sword sweeping, crashing into them, sharp pieces of stone being flung from behind him. One caught a spearman in the face; he went down. Oblek's weight sent another crashing.

"Seth!" The Jackal was close, gripping the bone framework. For a second their eyes met, an exchange of astonishment and hope, then his hands slithered, he screeched, grabbed, and with a wrenching of all his muscles had the rope in its brackets in the wall.

"Cut it!" The Fox was up now, hands bunched in fists. "Quick, boy! *The bird!*"

It was squeezing in, rustling its vast body through the window. A fierce-eyed head, the hooked beak, great talons of dark yellow that made horrible scrabblings on the stones of the sill. Below, the bird-people fought to hold Oblek, their vast queen standing back. And her arms were wide and she was singing, a wordless song of clicks and trills, an alien music rising to a racket of harsh screeches. Mesmerized, the bird listened, one golden eye fixed on her.

Seth had the knife from his boot. Desperately he

worked it across the hemp fibers; the rope was thick, twisted tight.

The woman ended her song. She and the bird watched each other. Then, with a swiftness that made the Fox screech and the Jackal swear, the bird dragged the rest of its huge body through and flapped with a draft and crack of vast wings to the beam.

One strand snapped. The cage jolted, the men toppled.

Oblek yelled below, a cacophony of blows and fury. The bird leaned forward. One claw grabbed the cage. Then its beak opened; it pecked viciously at the Jackal.

He flung himself back, flattened against the rear wall. Expertly, instantly, the bird twisted it, pecked again; the men hurling themselves away, stumbling. "God! Boy!" the Fox howled. Sweat in his eyes, his arms an agony of aching, Seth hacked at the rope. The fibers dwindled, frayed, untwisted. Then, with a terrible crack that flung him back with a cry of terror, they snapped.

The cage fell. It hit the ground and smashed open; Seth grabbed the wall, missed, fell after it into a blackness that rose up and smacked into him, a winded, gasping, softness under him, that growled, "Get off me! Quickly!"

The Jackal was already up, lithe and sudden. He grabbed a spear, and as the bird spread its wings and screamed down he stabbed upward, a rain of dust falling around him like snow. "Get Fox!" he yelled, but Seth was already struggling up, shoved aside by Oblek.

Startled by the stabbing spear, the bird screeched again.

In the wreckage of the cage the Fox was crawling; Oblek had one great arm around him. Seth snatched up another spear, swinging to face the woman.

She took off her mask. Her face was too small, hidden in rolls of fat, her hair razored short. She blazed with fury and defiance; he was frozen by her malevolence, unable to move.

The Jackal had no such problem. He swiveled and ran to her, grabbing the hand that clutched the star, twisting it viciously; she struck him hard in the face, a stunning blow. For a second it knocked him back. Then he brought the spear up into her chest.

"Give it to me!" His voice was cold as ice.

"Leave it!" Oblek yelled.

The Jackal's long eyes did not flicker.

She knew her danger. With a glare at her men picking themselves up, she slowly held out the star, a brilliant glitter on her palm.

"May it be cursed, and you with it."

"Too late, lady." The Jackal took it quickly. "I'm afraid I already am."

"*Seth!*" Oblek's roar.

Seth turned, saw the bird just too late. Its talon grabbed at him; he leaped with a gasp of terror, felt the slash of iron claws down his side, collapsed. The bird-men were on him instantly, one tugging the spear from his sore hands. They were kicking him, Oblek was yelling, wading in, but they were outnumbered, and he knew it was over.

Until a high clear voice rang out over the chaos.

"Stand still! All of you!"

Seth shoved a man off, stared up.

Alexos was standing above them, carefully balanced, on top of the rickety nest. In both hands he held the blue egg.

"Stand still," he said quietly. "Or I smash it."

The Nine crossed the bridge in a body.

Hermia turned to the guards. "Leave this place. You will be needed in the Port now."

"Lady—"

"Do as I say. We'll guard the Oracle ourselves."

Torn between reluctance and the terrifying sounds of battle from the Port, the men eyed one another. Without another word they raced down the desert road. Hermia turned and strode on. The Nine walked silently, each struggling with her fears. Mirany bit her dry lips and wished desperately that Seth was here, and Alexos. The boy was unpredictable and strange, but he was the Archon and the power of the god was in him. She even missed Oblek, his blunt, obtuse violence. Looking at Hermia's straight back, she felt useless, because there were too many plots here, a network of intrigue, a silent maneuvering for power. It was trickier than any battle. She had no idea whom to trust anymore.

At the precinct everything was in chaos. The slaves were building frail barricades of furniture; some of the women were just sitting and weeping. Hermia stood on the loggia and spoke to them all in a crisp voice.

"There is no need to panic. This is the Island, and you are safer here than anywhere. Everything will go on precisely as normal. I will have no interruption in the rites, no insult offered to the god. Those ridiculous defenses will be dismantled and the furniture replaced immediately. Koret"—she turned imperiously to the steward—"have a sentinel placed on the Temple roof. I want constant reports about what is happening in the Port."

Does she love Argelin? Mirany thought. *Is she terrified for him?*

"Preparations will resume for the evening meal. I will address all the Nine at sunset." She turned, the light breeze rippling the fine pleats of her red robe. "Now I wish to speak to the Bearer, privately. Bring rosewater and sherbet to my room."

She swept away down the marble corridor. In Mirany's ear Rhetia breathed, "Be careful. She's planning something."

The Speaker's room was bright and cool, muslin curtains drifting in the warm breeze. Hermia sat in a gilded chair while a slave reverently placed the openmouthed mask on its stand, arranging the feathers, the strands of gold discs. Koret came in and placed a brass inlaid tray with two red cups and a flask. There was a gilt plate of tiny fresh figs. Mirany suddenly realized she was so hungry she wanted to eat them all. It would probably be safe. Hermia wouldn't poison her here.

Without moving, Hermia looked at her. Her eyes were

dark, her face edged with tension, the perfect curls of her hair dusty from the road. Then she reached out and poured from the long-necked jug and handed a cup to Mirany.

They both drank. The liquid was sweet and thick, fragrant with oranges.

Hermia held the cup and stared down into it. "Mirany, I don't know what is happening."

Astounded, Mirany was silent.

"Today, at the theater, I saw him. We all saw him. He spoke to me face-to-face and I heard him as I've never heard him before." She looked up. "It terrified me."

It was an admission Mirany could hardly believe she was hearing. She muttered, "We were all—"

"You weren't. I looked at you, and you were amazed, but not afraid. Because you know him, Mirany, and I don't." She put the cup back on the tray with a click and linked her fingers. Her gaze was direct and cold. "I have made an unforgivable mistake. I've come to see that you were right about Alexos, and I was wrong. He is the God-in-the-World. His safety is vital. His quest for the Well must succeed. Do you have any way of communicating with him?"

Breathless, Mirany's hands clutched the cup. "Sometimes. That is . . . I talk to the god. He isn't always here . . . at least, he doesn't always answer." She stopped, aware of Hermia's scrutiny, of the glimmer of bewilderment, almost of pain. "I can never be sure," she said gently. "But the god is in Alexos."

"Yes. I think he is." Hermia stood up, drawing herself to her full height. "And so I must ask you to warn him."

Mirany's heart thudded. "*Warn him!* Of what?"

"There is a plot to kill the Archon. Argelin desires that he never return."

In the silence only a gull cried outside the window. Mirany tried to shape the words. It was an effort, but only a whisper came out. "Who is to kill him?"

She couldn't think it. She wouldn't. But the fear in the note he had sent rang in her mind, the word *please* like something undigested, impossible to swallow.

"The scribe. I believe Argelin has his family." Hermia watched her carefully.

Mirany shook her head, numb. "Even . . . He wouldn't . . ."

"There were other inducements. A quaestorship."

Mirany glanced up, her eyes wide.

Hermia nodded. "Now you *are* afraid," she said.

The woman's mouth opened in horror.

No one moved; even the great bird had flapped back to its perch and now preened irritably under one enormous wing.

Slowly, Alexos held the egg up. Its weight made his arms tremble; the bird-queen bit her lip.

"Boy!" she hissed. "Take care!"

The Jackal said, "Back to the doorway. Come on, Alexos. Bring it!"

Step by step, Alexos came down the stairs. The bird-men hovered, terrified behind their masks, but none of them dared make any move.

"Go free." The woman opened her arms quickly. "Leave! No one will hinder you. But lay down the unborn."

"Not yet." The Jackal's voice was urgent. "Bring it here. Take your time."

Alexos nodded, his face set in concentration. Sweat dripped into his eyes, he wiped at them with an arm.

"Old friend," Oblek moaned, "be careful."

He was halfway down. The nest creaked and rustled; parts of it jerked. Above him the great bird stared, its attention caught. It spread its wings; before Seth could yell a warning, it had launched itself, sailing down.

Alexos glanced up, twisted, ducked. His foot slipped; he grabbed at the rail with a yell.

The egg fell out of his hands.

Appalled, frozen, they all watched it fall, a slow, terrible arc down and down through the dusty sunslashed darkness of the vast hall, and as it hit the floor the fracture was in their own bones and skulls, setting Seth's teeth on edge, dislocating his mind—the woman's high scream and the crack of the thick shell, as it shattered on the stones.

THEY SWEAR TO KEEP THE SILENCE

No one moved. Then Alexos gave a great cry of pain, an anguish that cut Seth like a knife. Instantly he ran, climbing up to the boy, leaping the mess on the floor.

Alexos was white with shock. "I killed it," he breathed.

Seth snatched him up. "It's all right. It wasn't your fault."

The eggshell lay in pieces, ridged and jagged. From inside it a colorless fluid oozed; a wet gangly wing projected. Seth carried Alexos away from it and turned his head in disgust. Then something caught his eye.

"Look!"

But Alexos was sobbing.

Seth jumped, bent over the ruined shell. Ignoring the spear that jabbed his neck, he gently reached in and picked up the glimmering object that lay among the pieces and held it up, brilliant in his fingers. It was a star, blue as sapphire—

"The second star!" The Jackal had been grabbed and was flat against the wall, but his astonishment was clear. "It was in the egg?"

"Kill them." The woman's voice was hoarse with grief. "Kill them now."

"*No!* Wait."

Alexos turned, tears streaming down his face. He took a breath, then said, "This is my fault, not theirs. If anyone has to die, it should be me."

Seth's heart gave a great leap. For a second he thought, *If they do it, I won't have to,* and then he hated himself with a hatred that burned like fire. He turned fiercely on the boy. "That's rubbish! Do something about it. You're the god, aren't you? You make things happen, make things live and die. Show them who you are."

"He's right." Oblek looked at the woman. "Show her what a proper god really is."

Alexos looked at them, hope lighting his face. "Should I?"

He glanced down at the broken egg, then up at the bird. It sat motionless, unblinking eyes on him, as if he was a small morsel of prey far below. "I'm sorry," he said earnestly. "This should never have happened. I'll do what I can, but there are things that can never be put together again, moments that can never be repeated."

The bird screeched, a harsh sound.

Alexos knelt among the wreckage of the egg. He looked up at the woman. "If I succeed, will you let us go?"

"Who are you?" she whispered, her voice choked.

He did not answer. Instead he put his frail hand into the mess and stroked the twisted limb of the unborn chick, the gentlest of touches. From the corner of one eye, Seth saw the Jackal's tension. Oblek waited, patient, faintly smiling.

"Be alive. Be reborn, who was never born. Because gods are always born in strangeness, in impossible ways."

A feather moved. Or was it the breeze?

Seth stepped closer.

"I call you. From the Rain Queen's garden, where the trees are always in leaf. Where streams drip into cool pools and dragonflies flit. From where you sit in the topmost branches."

It moved. The woman put a hand over her mouth. A shiver, a jerking of limbs.

"They need you. They need us. Because without us they are empty and hollow and they turn on each other. They need us to blame and to curse. To love. To destroy."

It was staggering up. Ugly wings splayed, the bald head lifted on its scrawny neck. The chick opened its beak. A faint squawk rang through the hall.

Alexos scrambled back. He looked at the woman and his face was weary, with dark hollows under his eyes.

"I give you your divinity back."

Then he looked at Seth, a long look. *"Divinity,"* he said, *"is fragile."*

Seth went cold; at the same time the Jackal shoved back

his guards, took the second star from Seth, and strode to where his pack lay across the room. He hauled it on, threw another to Oblek, and dragged up the injured Fox. "Now we leave," the Jackal said briskly. "Before they get any more ideas."

Oblek crossed to Alexos. "Come, old friend. Come with us."

The boy turned to him. "I feel so tired, Oblek." He sighed.

"Then I'll carry you. Oblek will carry you all the way to the Well." Picking him up easily, the big man followed the others out of the hall. Seth hurried after them.

"Wait."

He turned at the door. The woman was standing over the chick, watching its ungainly movements. Above her the great bird eyed its offspring critically.

"We have something else of yours."

"Something else?"

"A silver egg. With markings on its surface. We took it from the tall man."

The Sphere. He stared at her.

"Do you wish for it back? You are a dangerous people, we can see that, when even your children perform miracles. Maybe you are gods yourselves. We no longer wish to be enemies with you." The woman beckoned a bird-man. "Fetch it."

He started toward the nest, but Seth said, "No." He licked his lips. "Keep it. As our gift to you." He turned and was almost out the doorway before he turned back.

"It will never hatch into anything, though."

The woman put her mask on, and its black-and-red beak turned sidelong to him. "Who knows what the gods can do?" its voice murmured.

Running after the others, he grinned to himself. Without the Sphere the Jackal could never leave them behind again. From now on, only he knew the way.

No one obstructed them. All the gates were open, the doors wide, the streets of ruined statues silent and still. By the time they climbed to the top of the destroyed network of towers and toppled pylons, the sun had long since set behind the mountains, and the myriad birds that flocked overhead in dark clouds, swooping and rising and falling, had settled into deafening chirruping rest on the headless images. At a stroke, as one, they fell silent.

Night had come.

The road was silent, the stars overhead brilliant. Mirany had run as far and fast as she could; now she hobbled along, a stone in her sandal, a pain in her side. No time to stop for either of them. She felt like crying, but she wouldn't, because she wouldn't believe it. Seth was ambitious but he would never hurt Alexos. Surely! But as she clutched her side and smelled the artemisia and lavender that lined the road, the knowledge deep inside was that she couldn't be sure, not of him, not of Chryse, not of Rhetia. She only trusted the god, and the god was not answering her, and his silence filled her with terror.

Besides, gods were unpredictable. You never knew what they would do.

The stone door leaned in the warm twilight; she ducked under it and followed the spiral path through a drift of moths. Cicadas chorused all around her, the voice of heat, and far off the waves hissed on the beach. Smoke and noise rolled from the Port. She had no idea what was happening down there.

When she came to the stone steps, she climbed them and stood at the top, on the flat platform. From here the sea stretched to the horizon, black and gently heaving. She turned, saw the outline of the Mountains of the Moon, their ghostly pinnacles against the stars. How high was Seth, and the others? Had they found the Well, or the Jackal his gold? Or were they already dead of thirst in the wilderness, still shapes crawled over by ants?

She shook the thought away and crossed to the Oracle.

In the shadow of its guardian stone, the pit opened.

"Listen to me," she said. "Listen!" She leaned down, lay on her stomach, her hair in her eyes. Then she put her face into the misty darkness and screamed. "Kreon! Listen to me!"

She had no idea if he could hear her. Seth had said the chamber was far down, that voices came muffled and broken, but surely no one had shouted like this, hung so far into the smoke, been so terrified. It was making her dizzy; her eyes blurred and she closed them. "Warn Alexos! Seth has been ordered to kill him. *Can you hear me?* Show me you can hear me!" Why didn't he answer her? Where was the voice in her head when she needed it?

Behind, from the precinct, came the soft shimmer of a gong, the signal for the meeting of the Nine. It was to be held here, so she had time. "Kreon," she moaned. "Please!"

Something scrabbled.

She jerked back instantly, knowing it would be a scorpion.

Its pincers came out, and then all of it, a large red creature, claws held high, and it ran at her as if she had called it. And if the god was in his creatures then she had, she supposed. It gleamed in the starlight.

Mirany took a breath. Edging closer, holding her skirt above her knees in a tight handful, she wondered if the fumes of the pit had not gone to her head, twisted her brain and eyesight. Because the scorpion had something tied around it.

She went and found the bronze bowl and held it out, brim to the floor. As they always did, the scorpion came close, attracted by the reflections perhaps, the shimmering of its own jerky movements. As soon as it was in, she stood, letting it slide helplessly down to the bottom, looking at it closely.

A bracelet. Thin and cheap and obviously well worn. Very small, a little girl's ornament. Mirany felt a flood of relief. It was Telia's; she always wore it. Telia and Pa were safe below, in the Kingdom of the Shadow. Then her gaze froze in horror. She had told them about Seth—had they heard? What were they thinking?

She clutched the bowl tightly, hearing feet race up the steps behind her.

Rhetia had a dark mantle around her shoulders. She was breathless. "I knew you were here! What's going on? What are you up to?"

Mirany sighed. "Do we all have to be plotting against one another?" Suddenly furious, all the pent-up anger churning inside her, she walked up to the tall girl and let it rage out. "You and Jamil, Hermia and Argelin, what's the difference between you? Lies from the Oracle and tyranny over the people. You used to be so proud, Rhetia, and yet you stoop to treachery now! You said your only loyalty was to the Oracle, but it isn't, it's to yourself! Is ambition worth so much?" Her voice was shaking; she turned away and yelled it at the Mountains of the Moon. "Is it worth killing for?"

There was silence. Then Rhetia said quietly, "You and I were never friends, were we? But I heard the Oracle once, and it said your name."

Mirany swung back. "Don't you *dare* say you're doing all this for me!" she snarled.

Rhetia raised her eyebrows. "Then I won't. But don't you see—you say you can hear the god. I don't know if I can—I've only spoken once to the Oracle, and the answer was that I woke up hours later and found that the Rain Queen had taken my place. I want to hear him, Mirany. I

want that power, that knowledge. So when I become
Speaker, you can stay as Bearer and we'll work together. But
only if Jamil wins. If that doesn't happen, if Argelin wins,
then neither of us will be left alive."

Wary, Mirany stared at her. "You really mean that, don't
you?"

Rhetia looked sour. "I may have made some compromises, but I don't lie." She turned. "The others are coming."

They were already here, Ixaca and Callia, Gaia looking
worried, Persis, the tall new girl, Tethys. Last of all came
Chryse, slightly breathless, wearing a pink robe, and behind
her, Hermia. None of them were masked.

They stood in an open-ended circle around the pit. The
girls who had barely seen it before flicked awed glances at
its ominous darkness.

Hermia looked around. "The news from the Port is
uncertain. The attack was repulsed by the general's men
and the attackers seem to have been driven back to their
ships. Several streets are still burning. I don't know how
many died."

The warm wind moved between them, billowing skirts,
soft with the smells of roses and thyme.

"I have decided on a plan to ensure there will be no
more violence." Hermia fixed each of them with her firm
gaze. "We withhold the Oracle. Each of us will swear that
the Silence of the god's anger will descend until there is a
truce. Whatever the threat to ourselves, we stand together,
unbroken. Do you agree?"

"Yes," Rhetia said firmly. If Hermia was surprised she didn't let it show. She looked at Mirany, who placed the bronze bowl carefully in the center of the circle.

Rhetia put her hand boldly on the rim. The scorpion froze, its sting raised and quivering.

"I swear to keep the Silence," she said, her voice firm.

Each of the girls did the same, hesitant, eyes fixed on the scorpion and its strange collar, ready to jerk away if it should move. Mirany swore with them. Last of all came Chryse.

The blond girl was wide eyed with horror. "I can't!" she breathed.

"Move slowly," Mirany whispered.

Chryse's fingers reached out; she gasped, "I swear to keep the Silence," and snatched them back with a shriek as the scorpion burst into life and raced toward her.

Only Mirany noticed that not even the tips of her manicured nails had touched the bronze rim.

Hermia nodded. "Thank you, all of you. This loyalty to the god comforts me. Jamil claims this war to be over the truth of the Oracle. Argelin says it's about trade and silver." She raised her head suddenly. "Now we'll see."

Lights. A glow of red torches, the crackle of resin. Between the olive trees the flames approached, the harsh clatter of metal behind them.

"Soldiers, here!" Rhetia turned instantly on the Speaker. "Is this some treachery?"

"Not on my part." Hermia watched, intent, her mouth hard.

The soldiers made a double line up the steps and crossed their spears. Some made furtive signs with their fingers, warding the god's wrath; others cast quick nervous glances at the black pit. Hermia stepped forward, her voice cold with fury. "Who sent for you? How dare you come to this place!"

"I brought them." Argelin climbed the steps, looking weary. His bronze helmet covered most of his face; only his eyes gleamed, his beard untrimmed. He stopped and faced the Nine.

"It's convenient to have you all here."

"Do you need a bodyguard with *us* now?" Hermia's voice was icy.

"With some of you, lady, I've needed one for a long time."

He was looking at Mirany. Then he turned. "As you may have heard, the attack is over. This time we held them off. The Desert Gate was overrun, but my men stormed it and recovered it. The enemy has returned to his ships. Next time we may not be so fortunate. I need money, Hermia. I need to buy mercenaries, melt down stores of metals, force the merchants and aristocrats to pay for repairs. Many of them would secretly be pleased if I lost this war. The fools think the Emperor would tax them less."

Hermia watched him closely. "I don't see what we can do."

"You have storerooms of grain and food and treasure, of offerings to the god. I need them now, or we're lost."

She nodded, impatient. "Take them. But the food must be distributed free to the people."

He stepped closer. "That's not all. The Oracle must speak. You must tell everyone the god confirms I'm the only one who can save the Port. He must order them to obey me in every instance." He reached out and took her hands, the moonlight slanting on the bronze of his armor. "In fact the Oracle must declare I am to be crowned king."

The Nine stood in appalled silence. Only Hermia seemed calm, without surprise, and as she watched the Speaker, Mirany knew that the pair of them had discussed this before, that they had planned this moment together.

Rhetia must have thought so, too. She was cold with fury; she opened her mouth but Hermia had already answered. "King? Not Archon?"

He almost smiled. "We already have an Archon."

She nodded. "Yes. And to be Archon might require the giving of your life."

"I would be willing to give it." His smile had faded.

"This land has never had any king but the god." Hermia's eyes never left Argelin's face.

He dropped her hands. "These are desperate times." A slight impatience had crept into his voice.

"Indeed they are, Lord General." She nodded, manicured nails tapping her ornate necklace of lapis and jade.

"So you . . . the god will speak?" He was alarmed now, Mirany thought. He sensed danger. As if suddenly tired of pretense, he took a step back, lifted his helmet off. One small cut bled on his chin. "Stop teasing me, Hermia. What's wrong with you? We agreed—"

"Things have changed." She looked at him, a calm, unflinching look.

"Changed? How?"

"The god appeared. You saw him. We all heard him. Now the god decrees that the Oracle will be silent. There will be no words from him until a peace is made." She came forward and touched his face, wiping the blood from it with the edge of her sleeve, and he let her, staring at her in a disbelieving wonder that left Mirany cold.

"You would do this to me?"

"I must."

After a second he said, "I loved you, Hermia."

She didn't flinch. "I thought so, my lord."

"Our alliance—"

She smiled at him with perfect calm. "Our alliance is dissolved," she said.

THE EIGHTH OFFERING
OF SILENCE

Men don't know what the stars are for.

Nor the rainbow, or the rose.

Last night I lay on my back in the desert and counted the stars. Each one is mine, a point of light, a reminder.

Each one was carefully considered; its color, its heat, the part it plays in the story. Even when I closed my eyes I could see them, because the stars are tiny and can fall into my eyes like dust.

I was so tired with the journey that I cried.

The Rain Queen sang me to sleep.

THEY ARE PURSUED BY DREAMS

They were three days into the mountains.

After the bird city the landscape had fragmented, become a broken, shattered uprearing of red rock, a rusty landscape. The redness came off on their hands as they climbed; they breathed it into their noses and mouths. Oblek's bald head was finger smudged; Alexos' tunic was filthy with smears.

But it was wonderfully cooler. Up here there were breezes, and as they clambered over the sharp scree that slid underfoot, headgear was pulled off and rolled into packs, and finally the Jackal hauled himself up to the top of one splintered cliff face and stood there, taking in great breaths of air.

He stared down over the desert. "I can see the Animals," he called. "Huge shapes, clear from up here."

Wedged in a chimney of rock, Oblek struggled and swore. "As long as they're not coming after us."

The Jackal's fair hair streamed in the high wind. "Nothing is coming after us," he said firmly. Seth glanced up, caught by something in his voice. The Fox looked, too, then saw Seth notice him and glanced away.

Alexos, who always climbed nimbly, was sitting cross-legged on the cliff, picking insects from his tunic. "Did you think Argelin would be coming?"

Seth went cold. "After the gold? How would he know the way?"

"I expect he has ways, Seth."

"No one. No people, no camels, no caravans, no ferocious birds." The Jackal turned away.

"We are all alone, at the ends of the earth."

It certainly felt like that. Pulling himself up beside the tomb thief, Seth rubbed his scraped hands together and looked down. The desert was a wasteland of palest gray; it stretched far away to the horizon, to a blue vagueness that might be the sea, or the sky, or the place where the two joined and the great serpent encircled the world, biting its own tail. And yes, he could see the Animals, and he drew a long breath of astonishment at them, for from up here the complexities of the shapes were amazing, sprawled over the sand, and there were other lines, hundreds of them, crisscrossing the desert, and vast scrawls that looked like words, miles wide. They had journeyed across a landscape of stories without being able to read any of them, or even known they were there.

"A book of the gods," Seth muttered.

The Jackal nodded, his long eyes narrowed against the glare. "Indeed. Over the pages of which we crawl like flies." He glanced up at Alexos. "Does he know what they say, I wonder?"

Seth was silent. Since the bird had come back to life, none of them had felt easy with Alexos, even though the boy was just the same, eager and curious, tiring himself out so that Oblek had to carry him on his back for miles. It was fear, he thought. Of what lived inside the boy. Of what it could do. In the Archon's Palace, or on the Island with its complex rituals, the god was contained, a being propitiated with gifts, controlled by rites, spoken with formally through the Oracle. But out here there were no rites and no rules of behavior. Out here the god was wild and free and dangerous and no one knew what he would do next. And the only way of talking with him was face-to-face.

"Ask him."

The Jackal gave his wry smile. "I confess to you, scribe, I dare not. Such beings are best left to your friend, the priestess Mirany. Gold is all that concerns me."

He turned south, gazing into the distance.

"What's that?" Seth pointed. A dry watercourse lay below them. It descended from the hills somewhere to the west, a dry crack, its ridged tributaries like veins in the land. It ran directly toward the sea.

"The Draxis. The river that once ran to the Port." He frowned down at it. "When the Archon Rasselon stole the golden apples, the Rain Queen dried the river."

"Your ancestor. So he was a thief, too, then?"

The Jackal gave him a cold look. "We're all thieves. Our crimes pursue us and our descendants. Even though we think we can flee them." He turned abruptly.

Seth stayed, watching the shadows lengthen.

Mirany. He wondered what was happening to her. Whether Pa and Telia were safe. He couldn't even ask Alexos, because of the reason why they were in danger. But the god would know anyway . . . wouldn't he, if he was a god? The old arguments circled in his mind. Weary, he turned away.

They camped under an overhang a little farther up. This high, the nights were very cold; there was little to make a fire from, but the Fox foraged and came back with branches from a dead tree; he was an expert fire maker and Seth was glad of him. They ate dried olives and drank some of the precious water; the last source was past; they had three days' supply left and the next water would be at the Well itself, if they ever found it.

The Jackal stretched his long legs. "Well," he said softly. "Perhaps we should know how far away we are from our goal, Lord Archon."

Alexos yawned. "I don't know. We'll find it when we find it."

Oblek grinned. The Jackal looked sourly at Seth. "And the keeper of the lost Sphere's secrets? What has he to say?"

"That we keep climbing toward the highest peak, the one with the cleft top."

"The one the sun goes inside," Oblek rumbled.

"Inside, or behind."

The musician sucked a sour olive. "There must be a great chasm. Burning. The sun descends into it and the god's horses drag it across the Underworld. That's right, old friend?"

"If you like, Oblek."

"But the sun sets in different places through the year. So does the moon." The voice was the Fox's, dry and sharp, and Seth looked at him with surprise.

"Does it?"

The one-eyed thief spat. "That's a scribe for you! Never lifts his nose from his grubby scrolls."

"A very big chasm then." The Jackal looked at Oblek. "A split at the world's end."

The big man spat out a stone. "Say what you want to say, Lord Jackal."

The Jackal raised an eyebrow. He leaned elegantly against the rocks. "You are more perceptive than you seem, aren't you? And yet it seems hard to think of you as a musician."

"He's a good one," Seth muttered. Oblek looked surprised.

The Jackal nodded. "What I have not said, then, is that Fox and I are . . . touched . . . that you felt you needed to rescue us." He sipped water. "We would have escaped without you, of course, but your help was appreciated."

Oblek snorted. "Maybe we should have waited and watched how."

"You might have learned something."

"The way to be eaten with dignity."

The Jackal's long eyes were expressionless. "Do I possibly detect some doubt?"

"You slimy ungrateful scum. We should have let that overgrown gull peck your innards out." But Oblek's voice was mild, and Alexos was grinning.

Then Seth said, "Where are the stars?"

"Oh yes!" Alexos sat up. "My stars!"

"*My* stars." But the tomb thief pulled the pack over and took them out, unwrapping them both. Light streamed from them, white and blue, unearthly brilliance. Alexos reached over and touched one; the glimmer lit the edges of his face, making his eyes dark. "They are so beautiful!"

He looked up. "But there's a third. We have to find it."

"I agree with you. But if you think you're tossing these into any well," the Jackal said, wrapping them quickly, "then you're mistaken, Archon. These belong to me, and if we find no gold, they may be my only profit." He looked at the boy. "What exactly do you want them for?"

Alexos took a deep breath. He seemed reluctant. Finally he said, "The Well is guarded."

Silence. Then Fox muttered, "By what?"

"Terrible beings."

"Beings?"

"Supernatural creatures of great power."

Fox was swearing under his breath; Oblek said quietly, "Why didn't you tell us this before, old friend?"

Alexos lay down and pulled a blanket over himself. He tucked the edges in tidily. "I didn't want to scare you, Oblek."

Dismayed, they all watched him close his eyes.

The Jackal's voice was acid. "How very typical of a god."

That night Seth dreamed of the Rain Queen. She walked down between the rows of desks in the Office of Plans, and her dress dripped and splashed, and trickles of water ran away between the paving stones. She put her hand on the scroll he was working on, and her fingers were wet, bound with strips of seaweed, ringed with coral and gold, braceleted with the polished shells of cowries.

He looked up, holding the quill tight.

Her face was just like Mirany's. But her hair was long, and curled over her shoulders.

"I have work to do," he said quietly.

"Work you do not wish to accomplish." She caught hold of his wrist and forced him to stand. Her grip was icy and slippery. "Come with me."

They went out into the City, and up onto the battlements. Above them the stone Archons rose; the Rain Queen led him along the row to the statue of Rasselon, and they climbed the steps and stood on the knees of the great figure, its torso towering above them, its vast face and sculpted eyes looking toward the mountains.

"If he could weep," she whispered, "he would weep a river for his people."

"Stone can't weep."

"No?" She smiled. "I can make stone weep. I can squeeze and contract and shatter mountains. I can slip along the veins of the world, make the desert blossom, make dry land a garden. I can make springs rise in the wilderness. If you only ask me."

"Is my father safe?" he whispered. "Is Mirany safe?"

The Rain Queen put her finger on her lips and smiled, and his heart sank, because he knew she wouldn't tell him. Instead she said, "Look at him. His flesh is gone to ice." For a horrible second he thought she meant Pa, and then he saw she was looking at Rasselon.

The statue glimmered. All at once it was nothing but ice, a frozen mass, honeycombed with holes and tunnels of meltwater, the whole thing collapsing slowly inward, crumpling, dripping, sliding, the fingers shrunk to stubs, the face slowly smoothing out to a featureless slab.

"Remorse is a mountain of glass," she whispered, her lips cool at his ear. "Slippery, impossible to climb. But at its heart is a star of fire."

And he saw it, deep within the figure, entombed in ice, a burning, brilliant point of red light. He put out his hand to it, but felt only the cold slippery surface of the Archon's body.

And the Archon's hand took his and held it tight.

The Jackal seemed to be dreaming, too. Watching the man's long body twitch, Oblek sucked a dry pebble and said, "Should we wake him?"

The Fox shrugged, wrapped in blankets. "Let him sleep. If he wakes in the middle of it, he remembers."

The musician nodded. "I had such nightmares, in the desert. Walked in delirium. Things crawled beside me, monsters, beasts, women I'd known, men I'd betrayed." He gave a wry grunt, feeding the fire with sticks. "Neither of us has lived a good life, Fox."

The red-haired man rubbed his face with one palm. "Few men do. But at least if you betray the living, they don't haunt you."

Oblek turned, curious. "And the dead do?"

"They do." He looked at the Jackal. "They haunt the chief. Too thin-skinned, these aristocrats. After the first few tombs most of us get used to it. The smell, the silence, the foul air, though that can make you see things, in the corners of your eye. Movements. Rustles. Mostly it's just a question of how to get the goods out, avoiding traps . . . hellish, some of them. I've seen a man cut in pieces by a rusty contraption that came spinning out of a wall. Right in front of me, he was."

He grinned and spat. "He had a fine burial. The chief was so furious he had the old Archon thrown out of the coffin and Melas put in it. Buried like a king. But him, he's never got used to it. Not the bodies, not that. It's the thieving, robbing the dead. It's as if when he decided to turn against his class, he deliberately made himself the lowest of the low, gave himself a name of a beast that everyone detests. As if he hates himself. So he gets nightmares."

"He sees them?" Oblek asked.

"Who knows? Rarely talks about it. He sees something. Calls them the Furies. Like those tin-winged beasts in the plays."

The fire crackled. As if he heard it, the Jackal murmured and rolled in his sleep.

The Fox frowned. "One day, he says, they'll catch up with him. Believe me, in that cage I thought they had."

The door opened; a servant came in with a tray and placed it on the small brass table. Behind her a soldier stood, spear at the ready.

Mirany jumped up. "Sophia! What's happening?"

The girl gave her a dumb, hopeless shrug.

"She can't talk to you. Orders." The soldier waved the girl out hurriedly.

Mirany glared. "This is an absolute disgrace! Don't you know who I *am*! I *demand* to see the Speaker—"

The door slammed. The key turned. She was raging at emptiness.

Sick at heart she sank onto the bed and stared at the window. Like the other, it was barred with planks of wood, nailed roughly across. Thin shafts of sunlight slanted in, and a trapped butterfly fluttered to find an exit. She pulled a shawl around her, miserable.

The Nine had been locked in their rooms for two days. The only time she had seen the others had been at the dawn Ritual, which had to go on, but then each of them was masked and guarded so closely that it was impossible to pass any message, or even whisper.

But Hermia's voice had been strong as she spoke the ritual words, as if that was the only way she could show them nothing had changed, that the Silence was unbroken.

Mirany wandered over to the tray. She didn't want to eat, but at least it was something to do. Boredom was killing her.

She took a piece of cheese and nibbled it. This couldn't go on. Argelin's fury at Hermia had been terrible; he had raged and cursed and had almost gone to strike her, but all the time Hermia had been calm. There would be no more words from the god, she had said, until a truce was called.

They were all agreed. They would all stand together.

Mirany wondered. Some of the girls would; others were weak. Chryse. What was Chryse doing, locked all alone in her room, without anyone to giggle with?

She tossed the cheese down, picked up the soft bread and broke it open.

A small piece of papyrus fell out.

Mirany stared at it in amazement, then grabbed it and unfolded it quickly.

MIRANY. HE'S TRYING TO DIVIDE US. HE'S ASKED ME TO BE SPEAKER. I TOLD HIM NOT ON HIS TERMS. HE SAID HERMIA WOULD HAVE AN ACCIDENT. HE'S SCARED OF LOSING EVERYTHING. DON'T TRUST HIM. BE STRONG, MIRANY. KEEP THE SILENCE. I'VE SENT TO JAMIL. HE'LL COME.

It was signed RHETIA.

Mirany read it twice. She didn't know if it was genuine, or some trick of Argelin's, but it sounded only too real. Rhetia was clever, and her slaves were loyal. But to refuse to be Speaker! Something she wanted so much! Mirany admired her then, though she'd always admired Rhetia, her strength, her assumption that she was always right. It must be useful to be so sure of yourself.

Footsteps. In the loggia.

Instantly Mirany crushed the message in her hands and shoved it into her underclothes. As she whirled around the door opened; Koret, the tall steward, came in and bowed.

"Lady Mirany."

Breathless, she said, "What? Are we free?"

He gave a covert glance behind him; she saw the terrace was crowded with an armed phalanx.

"I'm afraid not, lady. Lord Argelin wants to see you."

It was a mountain of ice, just as the Rain Queen had said. Seth and Alexos stared up at it, the smoothness of its sides, the sheer, unclimbable slopes. Hearing the others scramble behind, Alexos turned.

"Look at this! Look, Oblek!"

The Jackal pushed past them. Carefully picking his way forward, he climbed over the splintered shards of sharp material that jutted out, then he squatted, and looked at them intently.

"It looks like glass."

"Ice," Fox said, dubious.

Oblek shook his head. "We're not high enough."

The Jackal stared up. "This is not old. This is recent."

The whole landscape had been smashed, seared, melted and re-formed. Some tremendous heat had vitrified it, made jagged cliffs, torn great holes in the world. The face of the Mountains of the Moon had been pulverized and re-formed, and not of rock, but of some blackened and carbon-coated unbreakable mineral.

The Jackal knelt. He rubbed the black coating from the surface, smelled it, licked it. Then his long fingers explored the seams and fissures of the stuff, its curious facets, the shining planes. "Fox. Your knife, please."

The one-eyed thief chose the sharpest and most delicate weapon and held it out; the Jackal took it near the end of the blade and scratched the surface. No mark appeared; the bronze made no impact. Then he tried to prize out a piece, but the blade bent and the Fox fidgeted, so he withdrew it and handed it back without a word, straightening and rubbing his hands clean on his tunic.

"I told you. Glass." Oblek sounded sour. "And how in the god's name are we going to climb it?"

The Jackal looked sidelong at Seth. His eyes had a strange look in them, and his fair hair drifted in the upland breeze. "Congratulations," he said quietly.

"On what?"

"We are all very rich. We are wealthier men than the Emperor himself, though we can never spend a stater of it."

He looked up at the sheer tilted mass of the mountain, and then, quickly, at Alexos. "Perhaps the god knows what I mean."

Alexos took a deep breath. He looked uneasy, Seth thought.

"Do you know?"

Alexos shrugged. "I know the mountain is very hard."

"Hard?" Oblek came and put an arm around him. "I could tell you that, Archon."

The truth came to Seth like a blow. "He means it's made of diamond, Oblek. A great solid diamond."

In the utter silence a faint wind flapped the Fox's striped robe.

There was nothing any of them could say.

If There Was No Oracle . . .

The Island was unrecognizable. A barricade had been dragged to block the bridge, and the road had guards on it. Every building in the precinct was barred, with soldiers at the entrances; even the vast doors of the Temple had been forced shut, something no one had seen within living memory.

No one walked or laughed in the gardens. The pool was empty, its salt water unchanged for days so that a scum of oil and petals lay on it. The servants seemed to have been moved out; the terraces were deserted and in the hot air scarlet flowers hung thirsty and unwatered. Insects buzzed around her; she brushed them off, glad of the welcome heat of the sunlight on her arms and face after days in the shuttered room.

The phalanx closed around her; they walked up the steps to the highest terrace below the Temple, overlooking

the Port. It seemed as though Argelin had set up some sort
of headquarters here; she saw him sitting under an awning
in a bronze chair belonging to Hermia, a desk in front of
him littered with plans. Men came and went, messengers
racing, officers with reports.

While she waited, she glanced down at the Port.

Jamil's ships hung over their still reflections, waiting,
out of range. He wouldn't wait much longer. They would
be short of water and food, despite the raid. Soon there
would be an all-out attack, and the Port would fall.

"Lady." The optio waved her forward.

Mirany straightened. She felt grubby, wished she'd put
the white dress on, looked a bit more dignified. Her hair
needed arranging, too. Nervous, she pushed it out of her
eyes.

Argelin rose, looked at her, then waved the guards
away. They withdrew to a discreet distance; he turned on
the optio. "No one else. Until I say."

"General—"

"Whatever it is, deal with it yourself!"

He turned her roughly, and she pulled herself free.
Then he walked to the balcony and stood looking down
over the sea. Not knowing what else to do, she followed
him.

"I should burn this place," he muttered.

Appalled, she stared at his back. He swung around. "If
there was no Oracle and no Nine, *I* would be the one to be
listened to."

"You can't burn the god."

"What use is a god if no one can hear him? I think I might do it, Lady Mirany."

"Even you . . . the people would rise up—"

"Oh, I'd blame it on Prince Jamil, of course. It might even help me. The people would tear his soldiers to pieces with their bare hands. Then, after the invasion is repulsed, a new Nine." He licked his lips. A fine sweat glistened on his forehead and beard.

"What's to stop me, Mirany?"

"The Archon—"

He laughed then, a harsh laugh. "The Archon is almost certainly dead by now and there will be no search for another. I will be Archon and general all in one, and yes, king."

"And Hermia?"

His face darkened. "She has condemned herself. I always thought she was strong; I knew there was something in her I could never reach, but this obstinacy, this sudden treachery surprises me. We worked so well together."

Mirany's arms were burning in the sun. She drew her mantle up, rigid with fear. He looked at her. "As for you and me, no love has been lost between us, has it, lady? At every turn you've been the one who hindered me. Now things have come to this. I need a Speaker I can trust."

"Do you?" she breathed.

He smiled smoothly. "You know I do. And I've chosen one."

She swallowed. Bewildered, she said, "You can't—" But he stopped her with a gesture. Then he pointed behind her. She turned.

Down the terrace a girl was sitting on the balustrade, a blond girl in a new pink dress, feeding the tame doves. She looked up and waved happily. "Oh Mirany! I knew you'd see sense!"

Mirany felt sick.

"Do you see?" Argelin said calmly, pouring wine from a gilt jug and adding a splash of water.

Numb, she nodded. He held out the cup, and she took it and drank thirstily, not even noticing.

"I need someone who will do exactly what I tell her, when I tell her, and maybe there she is. Pretty little Chryse. She didn't take much convincing, I have to say. Not the cleverest of girls, not like you, or the acid Lady Rhetia, but with a certain sly intelligence. She knows what is best for her. I'll have no trouble with her as Speaker."

Mirany put the cup down. "You think not?" she said quietly.

Argelin glanced over. "No."

"Then you'd be wrong." She smiled at him coldly. "I know Chryse better. She serves the winning side, whoever they are. If you lost the war, she'd betray you to Jamil without blinking. She'd tell him the Oracle demanded your death. Believe me."

The general drank. "He won't win."

"He has the Empire behind him. Defeat these ships and

more will come. You can't keep them out. Only the god can end this, and Chryse doesn't hear the god."

"I don't want her to."

She nodded and took a big chance. "And you don't really want her as Speaker, either, do you? Even you don't trust her."

Annoyed, he clanged the goblet down onto the tray. A soldier glanced across, nervous. Argelin glared at her. "No. I don't. She's a self-serving little bitch. But you see, there is no one else. Unless, as I say, all the Nine perish in some unfortunate fire."

He wants it to be you, Mirany. He's trying to threaten you.

The voice was so unexpected she almost gasped with shock; and then relief flooded her.

Where have you been?

Busy. With eggs and diamonds and stars.

She turned, looking down over the blue sea. *What do I do? I can't let it be Chryse!*

Do you trust me, Mirany?

She nodded briefly.

Then do exactly what I say. Tell him you will be the new Speaker.

Her hands gripped the white marble of the balustrade. It was smooth and cool. The god's words felt like a great pain inside her; she thought of the oath they had all sworn on the bronze bowl, of Rhetia's scribbled letter. Be strong. Keep the Silence. They would think she had betrayed them.

I can't! I can't!

I can't force you, Mirany. I just want to see if you trust me.

"Well?" Argelin was watching her curiously. "You must know what I'm offering you."

"Why me? You said yourself—"

"Because I trust you not to order my death if it comes to that. Any of the others would. And because the others believe what you say, that you hear the god. That may or may not be true, but your pronouncements will have a certain . . . integrity."

He came and stood over her, tall. "You will be Speaker and you will announce that the Archon is lost, that I am now king. The rest of the Nine will be unharmed, if you agree, though a new girl will be needed and I will select her. The Temple and the Island will not be burned, and the Oracle will remain pure. Hermia will be kept in safety. Should you make any proclamation that we have not agreed on beforehand, she will be killed and the Oracle will be destroyed. You understand?"

"She'd be a hostage? You'd do that, to her?"

Argelin's voice was harsh. "She would have done it to me."

"But you loved her."

His dark eyes glanced at her. "Perhaps I still do. Love is not easy to understand."

She certainly didn't understand it.

Was she betraying them? Was she saving them? She had

no idea anymore. But there was only one voice that had ever mattered and that was the voice of the god, wherever it led.

She looked up, past Argelin, at Chryse.

"Send her back inside." Lifting her chin, she faced him. "From now on, I will be the Speaker."

Seth hung on the rope. His feet slipped and slithered on the glassy slope, though he'd taken his boots off to get a better grip. Above, the Jackal leaned back, amused. "Come on! I would have thought clawing your way up was what you did best!" Somewhere beyond, the Fox hauled and grunted a laugh, the rope taut around the pinnacle.

Seth swore. His hands were raw. He'd never be able to use a stylus again. Below, horribly far, Oblek was shouting encouragement at him, and inches from his face the sun glinted in beautiful, brilliant rainbows in the powdery heart of the diamond rock. He was climbing all he had ever desired in the world.

He made a last great effort, pushed off, hauled arm over arm. His muscles throbbed; his arms were jelly. Scrambling up the sheer cliff made his knees ache; he knew he could never take another step, and yet each one came, and finally the Jackal's long arm leaned over and grabbed him by the tunic, hauling him up in an ungainly sprawling heap.

"Good. Get the rope off," the thief said briskly. He looked over the edge. "You next, boy!"

Disbelieving, Seth shrugged out of the noose. "I nearly fell down there."

"Rubbish." Fox checked the knots, flung it over. "You did fairly well for a scribbler of tax bills."

Seth nursed his sore hands. For a moment he almost felt pleased at the praise; then a sudden fury came over him. *Tax bills.* When he was a quaestor he'd have such respect. . . . But he would never be a quaestor if Alexos went home.

The boy was climbing now. Easily and lightly he clambered up the diamond mountain, as Fox had done. None of them could climb like the Jackal, though; his meticulous ascent with the rope over his shoulder had been unbelievable, a finding of cracks and crannies that were barely visible, a reckless sprawling and dragging of his body up the overhangs and fissures of the vast cliff.

"Take your time." The Jackal leaned over. "Fox, get the spare. This may not hold the big man." Fox rummaged in the sacks. He tossed out a knife, an empty flask.

For a second Seth was alone by the tethered rope. It jerked slightly as the boy climbed, a small, impatient juddering around the diamond spike that held it.

"Nearly there." The Jackal leaned over. "I've nearly got you."

Seth stooped. The knife lay at his feet; he scooped it up. Its blade gleamed; it was sharp. Fascinated, he brought it close to the rope.

Now.

He'd never get another chance like this. The handle was warm; it felt rough in his sore palms. Fox had his back to him; he gripped the weapon tight, thinking of Pa, of Telia. Where were they? If he could know they were safe, just know that!

Tell me that, he thought. *Tell me! Or I'll kill you.*

The only answer was silence.

Save yourself! Just tell me!

Nothing.

Slowly, his hand shaking with reluctance, praying for someone to see, yell at him, he brought the blade to the rope. It was worn, fraying. It would take so little.

"Seth!" The Jackal's quiet voice made him jump in terror. *"What are you doing?"*

The rope snapped with a whiplash that slapped him right across the chest; he was flung hard against the Jackal. The thief slithered; gasped, "Fox!" Then he went over the edge.

Chryse stared openmouthed. "It's not fair! It was going to be me."

Mirany wanted to slap her. "I can't believe you! To side with him!"

"Oh Mirany!" The blond girl stepped back. "Isn't that just what you're doing? Of course, I'd just have pretended to side with him, but I wouldn't have really meant it. I just wanted to get out of that wretched room. As soon as I was Speaker, I'd have made a big silence, just like Hermia. And I'd have tried on all her robes."

Suddenly Mirany felt giddy. It was as if she was staring

down some vast precipice; she sank onto the stone bench. "Get me some water, Chryse."

Chryse pulled a face. "I suppose you think you can give me orders now—"

"Just get it!"

Wide-eyed, Chryse stared. Then she went.

Mirany looked down at the sea. *What's happening?*

I'm falling.

She could feel that. Emptiness below and above. One hand, gripping tight.

Hold me, Mirany! Gods can't fall, can they?

He sounded lost, terrified. His voice was so faint she barely heard it. She stretched her hand out quickly, over the marble balustrade. Gulls whirled about her. She held his hand; it was small, and gripped her tight. There was no weight but there was his fear, and she held on to it in the sudden storm of white birds that screamed and flew around her, of the papers whirling from Argelin's desk, the shouts, the flapping awning, Chryse's screech as she grabbed her windswept dress.

And out in the bay the ships rocked and tugged at their anchors, the elephants in their makeshift corrals on the beach trumpeting in terror.

"Don't fall!" she whispered. "If you fall, where will we all be?"

Seth dropped the knife and dived; as the Jackal clawed at rock he grabbed his arm, was almost pulled over the edge himself by the weight. Then the Fox had him around the waist, screaming curses in his ear.

Half over the cliff, Seth hung on. Below, the Jackal turned in space, with his other hand clinging on to Alexos. Far below, Oblek's terrified face was a blur of agony.

"Pull!" The Fox heaved back. Seth scrabbled, but the weight of the boy and the man seemed immense, as if the earth wanted them, as if it exerted a terrible power to drag them down.

"Help me!" Seth gasped.

Shouldn't a god be able to save himself?

And then something happened. Someone was there. A grip. It was light and strong and far away, but it took some of the pain out of his shoulders, and he dragged, and the Jackal's hand jerked, grabbed, had the rope. Slowly, as if out of some great abyss, they heaved the tomb thief up, and Seth leaned down his agonizingly stretched arm and grabbed Alexos, too, and in seconds the whole tangled mass of them were somehow over the rim and breathless, Alexos curled in a shuddering heap, the Jackal's hand bleeding, Seth trembling in every limb, icy with sweat.

The knife was lying by the edge. He stared at it.

Then he pushed his hair back with both hands, got up, and walked away. He felt sick and weak and yet there was something that he knew now, knew for certain.

There would be no quaestorship.

"It's not over, scribe." The Fox sounded dry. "We've got to get the big fellow up next."

Seth didn't answer. He raised his eyes and looked up at the mountain rising above him, its pulverized, scorched slopes, the great cleft at its peak, where high winds drifted a faint plume of snow crystals.

Close behind, the Jackal's voice said, "It seems I have to thank you again."

"You held on to the boy."

"Instinct. One can hardly let a god fall." After a second he said, "What happened?"

"Nothing. It snapped." Then, "Will you tell Oblek?"

"You must tell him."

Seth didn't answer. His gaze was intent, focused. "I see that now."

The Jackal sounded curious. "Up there? What can you see?"

Seth was hoarse with weariness, shuddering with cold and relief. He wrapped his arms around himself and turned. "I can see the star. The third star."

How Can You Say No to a God?

It was deep inside.

The star had smashed into the mountain and carved a great swathe through it, a collision that must have instantly vaporized rock, scorched a great wound that opened before them like a road, wide and smooth, still smoking.

It led them in. Wary, the Jackal stalked ahead, a tall shape in the bewilderment of half-seen images, of reflections, the smooth walls of the tunnel transparent, so that they could see ghosts of themselves, and boulders embedded in the crystal. Tiny insects were held in there, and seams of minerals, maybe even gold, because the Jackal stopped a long time at one, his hands flat against the sides, long eyes intent. Then he'd shrugged and walked on. "Too far in," he'd muttered, almost to himself.

Seth said, "You'll never get it out."

The tomb thief glanced at him thoughtfully. "Perhaps

the Lady Mirany was right. Perhaps the gold was only ever an excuse. Fox has a pocketful of diamond chips instead."

Oblek carried Alexos. Since the fall the boy had seemed worn out and listless; now he clung contentedly on to the big man's back, one cheek against his bald head, hugging him around the neck. As they walked Oblek hummed, a small sound that murmured and reverberated.

The tunnel through the diamond world was silent. The walls were a million shades of blue, the blues of the sea and the sky, of eggshell and distant cloud, of lapis lazuli and sapphire, of the watery robe of the Rain Queen, its waves and monsoon and storms. The blue of a small toy cart Seth had made once for Telia. Of the robe Mirany had worn when she came out of the tomb.

It sloped upward, steeper, so that the Jackal had to lean back and give Oblek his hand, and the musician leered a grin, breathless with the weight of the boy. Holes swelled and grew, interconnected; they walked in a honeycomb of exploded hillside, a great rock sponge.

But the star was so small to have done all this, Seth thought.

It burned, inside the mountain. For hours now they had inched and scrambled toward it, and its color was red, a coppery hot molten heat. As they approached, the porous rock became purple, shades of violet, scarlet. He could feel heat on his face and hands, a fierce blaze holding him back. Now they'd come this close to it, how could they touch it? How could they bear that pain?

At the end of the tunnel the Jackal paused. A thousand glittering movements paused with him; they saw a small chamber, the size of a room, faceted, polished to a gem by the terrible forces of the star crash. And on the floor, glowing red as a cinder, the third star waited for them.

They had arranged her hair and now they brought her the robe. She had seen Hermia wear it many times. Now she would wear it.

She stood up, the dress of finest white pleated linen falling smooth. Numb, without emotion, she held out her arms.

The Rain Queen's robe was so heavy. It was blue and it swished like the sea, and the million crystal raindrops sewn on to its surface swung in unison, each with a rainbow in its heart.

She turned. The slave fastened it, not looking at her.

None of the slaves looked at her, or spoke.

That was part of the ritual, Koret had said. Full moon, high tide, and silence. Not to be looked at, not to eat, not to be spoken with. Twelve hours sleeping alone in the Temple. Bathed from head to foot in the three lustral enclosures, of sea water in the black basalt, fresh water in the rose-colored marble, distilled precious rainwater in the last, the gold bath, so small the water had barely reached to her chin.

Once Hermia had done all this. Where was she? What was she thinking now? Mirany shivered. The wrath of the Nine would be unbearable.

The anointing with nine oils, the nine rings, the nine frail collars of silver, she let them all happen to her. She smelled differently, her skin felt strange. "It's still me," she said desperately, a blurted thought, but there was no answer. There had been no answer since the small hand had slid out of hers. **Trust me,** he had said, but she was terrified now; she wanted to call out, "Stop! I've changed my mind!" If he didn't speak to her again, would she have to pretend all her life? Would she become just another Hermia?

She turned.

The dark eyes of the Speaker's mask looked across at her from its stand, the looped crystals, the feathers and lapis, the beautiful calm face, coiled serpents carved on its cheekbones. Small breezes stirred in its open mouth.

"I never thought it would be you who'd be the traitor, Mirany."

For a startled moment she thought the venomous whisper was the god's.

Until she turned to face Rhetia.

Mirany!

Seth turned.

Alexos had mumbled the word; now the boy opened his eyes, slid down unsteadily. Seeing them stare, he wiped his face sleepily with his hand. "We've got to hurry."

"Is she in trouble?"

As if he didn't hear, Alexos pointed to the star. "There it is, Lord Jackal. If you want it, pick it up."

The tomb thief said, "It's red hot, Archon. Even you can feel that."

"It won't hurt you. I promise."

The Jackal took a step up close. The fiery glow lit his face as he bent down; they could see the heat in the air shimmer. The star was a coal, burning. He reached out, then drew back. "I'd rather keep my fingers," he said dryly. "I tend to find them useful."

Alexos turned. "You have to get it then, Seth."

Seth came up to the boy. But all he said was, "First, will you tell them, or will I?"

"No one need tell them." Alexos looked unhappy.

"Tell us what?" Oblek growled.

Seth scowled. But he clenched his hands and said, "Argelin made me an offer before we left. Of a quaestorship."

The Jackal didn't move, but an instant wariness slid into his eyes. "In return for what?"

"The way here. And for the Archon never to return."

For a second no one moved. Then Oblek drew the boy to him. "You treacherous scum. You accepted?"

Seth shrugged, weary. "You can't refuse the general."

The Jackal was watching him carefully. "We knew you'd been picked up. No other inducements? No threats?"

He licked dry lips. "My father. My sister."

They were silent. Then Oblek growled, "You should have let me kill Argelin, Archon."

Seth looked up, all the fear of weeks flooding him in an instant of agony. "Are they safe? Can you tell me if they're safe?"

Alexos looked at the floor. "If people knew everything, Seth, they'd have no use for gods. Besides, the Oracle is silent." He sounded sad.

"You knew, old friend?"

The boy looked up. "Mirany warned me."

That devastated Seth. He avoided Oblek's eyes, but the big man said, "Did you think about it?"

Seth looked at the Jackal. The thief's animal eyes watched him, but he said nothing.

"Yes. I thought. I held the knife over the rope. For a minute, I would have cut it. Then it snapped, and everything else snapped with it." He looked up, hot with shame and despair. "If you want to punish me, do it! If you want me to leave, I'll leave."

No one spoke. Till Alexos said patiently, "Oh Seth! They don't want that and neither do I. You know what to do. The Rain Queen explained."

Seth swallowed. Then he nodded, turned, and walked up to the star. The heat from it was appalling, the rock around it still sizzling. He bent and forced his fingers to close over it; he picked it up, and it was cold and pure in his hands. They all looked at its red fire.

"I will pay Argelin back," he whispered fiercely, "if he touches Telia."

◆　◆　◆

"Would you prefer it was Chryse?" Mirany's brazen defiance surprised herself. She marched up to the tall girl. "Because that was the only choice. Chryse, who'd do everything he told her, who'd sell us all for a new bracelet or the latest shawl. Would you really prefer her?"

"Don't be ridiculous. You swore!"

"I swore to keep Silence. I'll keep that oath."

"How can you? He's got Hermia as a hostage. The Island is heaped with dry tinder. If the ceremony doesn't go well, if the Oracle doesn't say he's to be king, I don't know what he'll do. I really think he'd destroy the precinct, Mirany! He doesn't care about the god's anger. The only person he ever cared about was Hermia."

She nodded, trying to think. "I know. I know!" She looked up. "What about Jamil? Can you still contact him, tell him what's happening?"

Rhetia scowled. "One of his conditions was that the Speaker should change. You've done that." She sounded disgusted.

Mirany was silent. Then she turned away and folded her arms, looking at herself in the long bronze mirror. Suddenly all she felt was astonishment. "Look at me. Mousy Mirany from Mylos. I can't recognize myself. I think if my father was here he wouldn't know me." She turned. "I don't want this, Rhetia, but the god told me to do it. *He told me.* How can you say no to the god?"

Her voice was choked; she didn't want to cry so she stopped abruptly.

Rhetia frowned. "You can't," she said harshly. "I suppose."

On the other side of the chamber the mountain was seamed with cracks; they climbed through one out into the night air. Seth looked upward. About a hundred feet above them the cleft pinnacle was white with frost; before it, was a steep slope of scree, dusted with snow. His breath made clouds in the air. He had never been so high, so bitterly cold.

"I know where we are!" Alexos' cry was a murmur of joy. "I've been here before!" He caught the big man's hand and dragged him up the unstable rocks. "This is it, Oblek! We're nearly there! I can hear the Well of Songs!"

"In that case, old friend, take care!" Oblek held the boy still. "Let me go first."

"I want you to, Oblek." Proudly, Alexos pushed the musician forward. "After all, I've brought you all this way."

"You've brought *me*!" Oblek began to climb, his ugly face wry. "I admit at some points I was a liability, but I've done some carrying myself, Archon."

"Of course you have. I couldn't have done it without you. All of you." And then Alexos stopped, his face in an instant a picture of bewilderment and dismay. "Oh! Wait! *Wait.*"

They looked at him. "What?" the Jackal snapped.

"I've just realized . . . there are only three stars." He held out his hands and then crumpled onto the rocks, knees up. He looked as if he was going to cry. After a moment Oblek came back and put an arm around him. "Explain, little god."

Eyes dark with tears, Alexos sobbed. Then he gasped out hopeless words. "There are four of you, aren't there, so there'll be four guardians. And we've only got three stars!"

Oblek looked at the Jackal. The tall man crouched. His fingers drew the boy's hands down from his face.

"The stars are weapons?"

"Sort of." Alexos sniffed, tears running down his face. "But don't you see, one of you won't have one! One of you won't have anything at all!"

THE NINTH OFFERING
OF A LIFE

A god is born, but doesn't die.

He changes shapes and bodies, moves from one mask to another.

Sometimes I am so quiet you would not know I was here; at other times I rage and thunder.

Gods are rivers, that flow into the sea and never end.

Stories, that begin and tangle and interweave and are all one.

The sun, that rises and sets and rises.

Which is why we come among you. To know what grief is. What love is.

HE LEAVES HIMSELF UNARMED

The Speaker was always anointed and masked at the Caves of the Python.

Huge and dark, they pierced the low cliffs that had once been the banks of the river Draxis before it had dried. They were sacred places, never entered except at the time of a new Speaker or at the Speaker's death, and they led far back into darkness. In the entrance cavern, the largest of them, the god had been born, so the story went, millennia ago, the god of light and darkness, sun and shadow. For a thousand years the Rain Queen had worked on the living rock, water dripping and eroding it, wearing it away, until in the morning of the world it had cracked with a great crack, and the god had emerged in three forms, first as a scorpion, small and red, then as a snake, sinuous, a ripple of scales, and finally as a boy, beautiful, naked, wriggling his head and shoulders out, then heaving himself up and standing at the cave mouth. He called, and the sun rose, far over the sea, and he held out his arms to its heat and smiled. And behind him out of the crack climbed his shadow, tall and thin and without color, and it stood at his shoulder, silent.

The crack was still there. Small candles always burned around it; withered flowers were placed on it, brought by expectant mothers and given to the custodian of the shrine.

Now the Nine—or Eight of them—stood waiting in a circle around it, silent, masked, their calm metal faces smiling at each other, and behind each mask all their anger and bewilderment and disbelief. Chryse had her arms folded, and Rhetia stood behind her. One of the girls was new, but from out here Mirany hardly knew which one.

She walked slowly, because the robe was heavy.

It was night, and the moon was full. Its early splendor glinted in the crystal drops; they clicked and slid and clattered. The path up to the cave was lined with soldiers, all silent. Above, along the tops of the cliffs, watch fires burned, and the people waited. She had thought they would be fewer, that they wouldn't dare to come out from the relative safety of the Port walls, but there they were, quiet crowds of women, sailors, beggars, merchants, looking down as she walked. She could smell the rank stink of the elephants, sense their restlessness in the corrals close by on the beach, and beyond the reach of artillery, far out at sea, the lights of Jamil's ships besieged the world with a ring of glimmers.

Mirany pushed hair out of her eyes. Even curled and

brushed into elaborate coils it was stubbornly coming loose. Her new sandals were stiff and the path was rough, slippery like scree. It twisted among stunted bushes of artemisia and gorse; a lizard slipped sinuously away, and beyond the crackle of the fires and the soft slap of waves, the night rasped with the song of cicadas. She thought of her first time as Bearer. It seemed so much longer than a few months ago.

"I've told you what I'll do," she whispered urgently. "Is that right? Is that what you want?"

He wasn't here.

He was far away, and not listening to her.

"You should be here. You should be everywhere!" She felt light-headed with hunger, worn with the weight of the robe. She slipped, and caught at a bush to steady herself; clouds of moths rose around her.

Argelin loomed out of the dark. He held out his hand.

She ignored it, straightened, and walked up into the cave.

A small fire burned in a brazier, but apart from that, the great cavern was dark. Breathless, she paused in the entrance, and looked back. Below lay the dry watercourse, cracked in the heat. Behind her Argelin whispered, his lips close to her ear, "Go in. Stand by the god's birthplace. And remember what I want. The fate of the Oracle lies with you."

It was so cold. He had never thought there could be so much cold. The very rock was frozen; as he scrambled up, his hands stuck to it, his knees were bruised by it. Above them the cave opened, a darkness at the top of the world, and he took a breath and looked around, at the Fox toiling at his left, at all the other peaks, white and unknown, stretching into the distance on each side. Far away, like a stater in the sky, the moon hung, perfectly round. It would be hanging like that over the Island, and the Port and the City. He wondered if Mirany was watching it now.

Ahead, like a black spider, the Jackal climbed easily. He wore no pack; all the gear had been left at the foot of the slope, because Alexos had said they should take nothing but themselves to the Well. No weapons. Only the stars.

As he climbed the last part of the slope he thought of what the Jackal had done. The thief had stood and looked at Seth. "Keep the red star. You need it."

"Two of them are mine," Seth had muttered sourly. "I paid two hundred and fifty staters for the first one."

"A good bargain." The tall man had nodded. "Now I have them. However, I think I feel generous. Fox!"

The Fox had thrown him the pack; out of it he took the first star and unwrapped it. Its white fire had dazzled them as he held it up. Then, lightly, he had thrown it to Oblek.

Caught off guard, the musician's nimble hands barely caught it. Then he said, "Why me?"

"You also need all the help you can get."

Oblek sneered. "And you don't?"

The tomb thief smiled, his animal eyes bright. Then he had taken out the second star, the blue one. He had looked over at the Fox.

"Don't fear for me, chief." The one-eyed man tapped the row of weapons thrust into his belt. "No beast or stinking demon gets the better of me."

"I fear, Fox, that even your knives won't cut what we have to face here. Besides, the boy says to leave them behind."

"That's right," Alexos said gravely. "You must, Fox."

"Do we listen to boys now?" the small man growled.

The Jackal shrugged. "We listen to the god."

The Fox had thrown all the knives down in disgust. Then the Jackal had held out the blue star.

"I can't take that! You're the boss."

"Then I give the orders. And I don't lead my men into anything I can't handle myself. Take it."

"Chief—"

"Take it. You can watch my back."

"That leaves you unarmed."

The Jackal folded his arms. "Of all of you," he said evenly, "I am the fittest, lithest, most intelligent, and most well bred. It's a logical choice."

"And the most pigheaded," Oblek had muttered.

But the Fox had taken the blue star.

And now Seth clambered upright, breathless, at the threshold of the cave. The four of them stood there, shoulder to shoulder, and Alexos pushed between and went a little ahead, two steps into the darkness.

Before them they saw the Well of Songs.

She looked down at the birthplace of the god.

There have always been cracks and passages in the earth, he had said to her once. **Gods move along them, up from the Underworld, from the streams and the darkness.**

Like the Oracle. Like the Well the Archon had set out to find.

This one was wide and jagged. She looked down at it and knelt, and bowed her forehead to the ground, the stiff robe rustling. "We will begin," she whispered.

Then she lifted her head and turned quickly. "But first, remove the weapons."

Uneasy, the soldiers glanced at Argelin.

Mirany kept her face calm. "This is a sacred place and a sacred time. It will not be polluted by instruments of death; it is a place of birth. Get them out of here."

Argelin gave a brusque jerk of his head. The soldiers dumped their spears hastily in a heap; the optio snatched them up and removed them. She turned, meeting his eyes. "And you, my Lord General."

He looked at her with rigid control; then he took the sword from his belt and threw it out of the cave. Behind him, like a small ripple, others did the same; she saw in the shadows the dignitaries from the City of the Dead, a few merchants, the most important moneylenders, his officers.

Witnesses, no doubt. Carefully chosen.

And Hermia was with them.

Mirany took a sudden startled breath.

Hermia wore black, a long robe of it. She had removed all her jewelry and undone her hair; she wore no kohl on her eyes and her lips were pale. But her eyes were alive with anger, and she stood tall, her intelligent face tightly controlled. Mirany felt a thrill of fear; sweat broke out on her back. The new Speaker was always masked by her predecessor; she had forgotten that.

And Hermia would kill her rather than do it.

She stood slowly.

This was it. The time had come and nothing had happened to save her. Was the god waiting to see if she trusted him? She turned and opened her arms, the droplets clattering. Drums and rattles began to beat softly, in some corner. She took a breath to speak the words of the Opening.

Instead, someone shouted.

Argelin turned, instantly alert. His guards closed around him.

One man appeared on the path to the cave. He was bearded and dressed in a red robe; he carried a heavy box, and before the men could grab him, he laid it down cautiously and scrambled up.

"A gift of truce."

"Truce?" Argelin stared. "From Jamil?"

"From my lord the Prince."

"How? There's no truce."

Mirany turned. "Yes there is, Lord General. As from now. During the Making of the Speaker, violence is forbidden." Before he could answer, she turned back. "Has your prince come? Is he here?"

"He waits below, lady."

"Then let him come up."

Ignoring Argelin's gasp of fury, she watched the Pearl Prince darken the entrance to the cave. His retinue followed, men clothed in cloth-of-gold and silks, and everywhere the gleam of pearls.

He bowed to her, and to the Nine. "I had your message. That the first of our Emperor's conditions was fulfilled. That the Speaker was renewed." His dark eyes watched her gravely. "This is so?"

"If the god wants it," she said quietly.

"Then if I witness this, there will be peace. Because the cause of the dispute was not trade, or my Lord Argelin's rule, but the pollution of the Oracle. The Oracle is for everyone. That is what we believe."

Mirany nodded. Without another word she began the prayer of Opening, and the voices of the Nine joined hesitantly with her. The moon was high now, its light filling the cave with a frosty luminescence, glinting on embedded crystals high in the walls, causing a faint mistiness to seem to rise from the great crack in the floor.

When the prayer was over, she stepped close to the brink of it and looked down.

Water.

Was that what she saw down there?

Was it water?

Steam rose from the Well, steps led down to it. It was huge, a sacred pool of hot, shimmering water, and statues stood waist high in it, and it was green and unknowably deep. In the cave walls around it, ferns grew, their fronds uncurling, and yellow-green algae powdered the glistening rock walls. Water steamed and condensed and dripped. Ancient wooden shapes, once carved, leaned from cracks; withered remnants of dessicated wreaths were on the side of the pool. And there were masks.

They hung on poles in the water, rotting faces that watched the strangers. As the steam drifted, Seth saw their eyeholes and cheekbones were bark and wood, paper and silver, corroded copper, tainted bronze. The masks of all the Archons until Rasselon, until the Well had been lost.

It was a quiet place. Only irregular drips into the pool broke its silence.

They came farther in, warily. The warmth was wonderful; he unwound the rags from his face and breathed it in, felt it thaw his numbed limbs.

"What now?" he whispered.

The cave took his words; it rolled them and muttered them, made them come back at him from behind, a low sonorous rumble that caused a row of drops to vibrate and spatter. The Fox eyed the entrance nervously.

Alexos went forward. He put both hands on the lip of

the great pool and leaned over, into its steams and heat. "It's been so long since I was here!" he whispered.

The Jackal came beside him. "Where are these fearsome guardians, Archon?"

The boy's face turned to them. To their surprise they saw tears in his eyes; as he turned back one rolled down his cheek and fell into the water. "Come and see, Seth, all of you."

Seth glanced at Oblek. He put his hands on the crumbling rock; it was worn smooth, oiled with iron red sediments. Then he looked down.

The water steamed. He saw its greenness open, as if the Archon's tear had opened a hole, a darkness swelling before the four of them, clearing the Well.

A face looked up at Seth. It was handsome and burned by the sun, its eyes alert and amused, but it was a mask, and behind it darkness lurked, a terror, an emptiness. He jerked back instantly. The face was his own.

Oblek, rigid, was staring into the pool.

"What are these, Archon?" he breathed, his voice raw with horror.

"The guardians, Oblek."

"They've always been here?"

"Oh no. We brought them with us." The boy looked at the Fox's disgusted stare, at the Jackal, who was looking into the pool without a flicker.

The water heaved. It bubbled and surged. Seth jumped back, dragged Oblek away; Alexos leaped hastily up onto a rock ledge. Out of the green depths came a pair of hands, agile, ink stained, Seth's own hands. They grasped the brim and hauled, and out of the water came a creature that wore his own face like a mask, dripping with steaming water, plastered with weed.

Beside it rose a thing like Oblek, vast and bloated and murderous, and a Fox-masked creature, cruel and shifty. And last of all crawled a slender, tall shape, its long animal eyes cunning and cold, totally without mercy.

The Jackal stepped back.

Without a word, the four of them faced themselves.

SPEAKER TO SPEAKER

They faced each other, Speaker and Speaker. Hermia carried the mask, its gold discs and ibis feathers draped over her arms, its perfect face with the incised cheekbones gazing fixedly at the shadows in the depths of the cave.

Mirany was very still. She knew suddenly that if Hermia put the mask on her, they would have changed places. She would have become false to the Oracle, a speaker of lies. *Help me*, she breathed. *Without you I'm just as bad as she is.*

But her words only returned to her, fractured and echoing, from ancient depths.

Hermia should have raised the mask. Instead she raised her voice.

"Before the new Speaker is masked, I have something to say."

The Nine tensed; Argelin looked furious. She raised a

manicured finger and pointed it straight at him. "I denounce this man. This man has plotted to have the Archon murdered." She turned, shouting it out, so that it rang in the caves, and the people heard it clearly out on the cliffs. "He bribed one of the Archon's companions to murder him. I saw and heard. I give witness before the god."

People were murmuring; outside, someone shouted. Here in the cave everyone stared at Argelin. The bodyguards glanced at one another, tense.

The general stood very still. Faint beads of sweat broke out on his face, but he stayed calm.

"The *ex*-Speaker is obviously overwrought," he murmured.

"This is a terrible accusation." Jamil came forward, and from the shadows behind him, Rhetia's voice. "If it's true, the god will take his revenge."

"Revenge?" Argelin smiled coldly. "For what? He can always find himself another body. Isn't that what gods do?" He eyed them all. "But the Speaker doesn't speak the truth. She only has her own voice. Isn't that the reason we're all here?"

He walked up to her, his voice low and mocking. "Even if it could be true, Hermia, what will any of you do about it? I rule. The army follows me. Every weapon is under my control. Look out there. Even now, my enemies are burning."

Jamil tensed. Then he turned, shoving men aside, and swore.

In the darkness of the harbor, bright flames flickered. Smoke rose against the moon. On the beach the elephants trumpeted wildly in panic.

Mirany put her hand to her lips. Fire ships!

"You've sent fire ships into my fleet! Are you crazy?" Jamil whirled, but Argelin's men grabbed him and his retinue instantly. The general smiled coldly. "Yes, my lord. *From up here, you can watch it burn.*"

How can you fight against yourself? Every move was countered, every punch blocked. The creature that was himself had Seth by both wrists; it wrenched him to the ground, clamping both hands over his mouth, smothering him, laughing at him. It had no being, was air and water, felt no pain. But it could kill him, and he yelled and screamed at it, struggled, kicked, bit. Somewhere in the cavern Oblek was wrestling with a vast drunken shadow, and the Fox circled warily around his own slyness. Only the Jackal and his reflection stood calm, eyeing each other. They might even have been talking.

Alexos jumped down and crouched by the pool. His fingers trailed in the water. "I should be in here, too," he said.

Far below, as if it peeped through a tiny hole, one giant eye looked up at him.

Jamil was pale with fury. "When the Emperor hears—"

"Your fleet can flee. If they have sense they will."

"They'll never leave me behind."

"Those ships are packed with pitch. The wind is driving them out to sea. They'll leave you, Pearl Prince, and I'll keep you as my hostage." Argelin faced the bigger man. "And if the Emperor wants his precious nephew back, he can make terms. With me, and with the god." He whirled around on Hermia. "Now mask the new Speaker and be silent! Nothing you can say interests me anymore. Nothing!"

Hermia looked at Mirany, and then at the Nine. For a second, Mirany felt sorry for her. Then Hermia lifted her head and the mask, but instead of fitting it onto Mirany's face she fitted it onto her own, and spoke through it, and the voice that came out was running and liquid and strange. It said, "Indeed, my lord. Then you will not mind me speaking about your dream."

Argelin stared. Then he hissed, "Get that off her."

No one moved. Hermia raised her hand and touched his face. "Last night," she whispered, "you dreamed of the Rain Queen. You dreamed she caught hold of your hands like this. She caught hold of you and drew you down, under the waters. Oh, you fought, and you struggled and tried to scream, but she stopped your mouth with water, she choked your lungs and dragged you into the depths. She drowned you, my lord. And you woke wet with sweat, gasping. Knowing you were dead."

She reached out and kissed him. But only the icy mask touched his face.

Argelin was white.

Mirany felt something finger her ankle, cold. She glanced down, then gasped.

Water was welling from the crack in the rock.

The star was useless. A lump of cold rock. He shoved his reflection away and dragged it out, but what did he do with it? "Archon!" he screamed. "Help me!"

From the corner of his eye he saw the boy gazing into the Well. He held the star up. "Do I throw it? Is that it?"

His reflection laughed. "Throw it? When did you throw anything away? It's ruby, worth a fortune, Seth. Buy yourself with it."

"No—"

"Buy Pa and Telia! Buy Mirany!"

"It's not . . . I'm not—"

"You are. You know you are." It had his hand, was prizing the star away. "You know all about yourself. You would have killed the boy, if you could have got away with it. That knife, over that rope? You wanted it to snap. You wanted it to fray—"

"*No!*"

He shoved it aside. "Give me the star," it whispered, head on one side, the cocky way everyone always hated, and he knew they did, that was why he did it. "Give it to me."

Seth licked his lips. Then he nodded.

And he hurled the star at his own face. Like a flash it

went through himself, a searing pain that made him cry out, as if he truly was that other, and then with a hiss the star splashed into the pool, was gone.

No one stood opposite him. He felt empty.

He felt as if he had thrown himself away.

Argelin grabbed the mask and tore it from Hermia. He was shaking with wrath. Her face was flushed; a light shone in her eyes.

He thrust the mask at Mirany. "Put it on."

She didn't move.

"Put it on!"

But Mirany ignored him. Turning to Hermia she said quietly, *"It's been so long since we were here, together, you and I."*

The Well surged and boiled. "Throw the stars in! Oblek!" Seth roared.

The musician and his image staggered close to the brink. With a vast effort one gave the other a great backhanded blow; the water bubbled and instantly Oblek was alone. He crumpled, then leered up at Seth in triumph. "Nobody gets the better of me," he gasped. "Not even my stinking wastrel self."

The Fox was in trouble. As his shadow held him down he yelled and screamed, squirming desperately. The blue star rolled from his pocket and Seth darted in and snatched it up; then he hurled it into the Well.

There was nothing but the Fox, sprawled on the wet rock.

"Now nothing remains but the final offering," Alexos said. He stood, and then leaped up onto the brim of the Well. *"You must take whom you choose, Rain Queen. You always make the choice. And I will never steal it from you, as I did once."*

Argelin whipped around. "Get the weapons. I'll end this here."

A soldier ran out.

Instantly Mirany looked at Hermia; the tall woman snatched the mask, raised it, and put it firmly and carefully onto Mirany's face, so that darkness came over her eyes; the cold bronze was icy against her cheekbones. She could feel the god inside her; his scorn welled up and overflowed, and despite the vow of Silence he spoke through her impatiently.

"Did you think you could kill me, Argelin? Did you think you could kill a god? I am alive, and I say this. You will not be king. You will never be king. Destroy my sanctuary and defile the Oracle, and you'll still hear me. I will speak in your dreams. Beware the one who will stand face to face with you. Who can withstand the scorpion that crawls within, or the snake that coils at his own heart?"

The Jackal folded his arms.

"Do you really expect me to fight you? I have no weapons against you."

His masked image smiled a cold smile; he knew it well. "The others behave crudely. You react differently, I expected that. You know me better."

The Jackal nodded. He stepped forward. "And they're afraid. But I am not afraid of you."

"You hate me. You hate yourself."

"I hate what Argelin has made me."

"No one made you into a thief except yourself."

Their voices were so alike, Seth barely knew which one spoke.

"You're a desert, a wilderness. I've descended into the depths of you. I've dug into you through sand and barrenness. I've found a desiccated corpse wrapped in golden trappings, with a fine voice and fair hair, pampered, and painted. Around it I've seen treasures piled, all of them rotting and settling, falling to pieces, except the hard bright gems, the gold."

"And I've seen the dead following you like rats. Their hatred was never as fearsome as mine. As yours."

He had no idea which was which. Both were real, both the same man, standing in the waist-deep steams of the Well. And the water surged and boiled as the stars erupted in its heart, and Alexos jumped down and said, "Quickly, Oblek. Help him. He can't escape on his own."

"Help him? Why should I help him?" Oblek was still. "He left us to die in the desert, Archon. Have you forgotten that?"

"And you want revenge? Take it now. Save him, Oblek. He'll never forgive you."

Seth gasped. The Jackal's reflection had caught hold of the tomb thief, had dragged him struggling toward the Well. They stood at its edge; then the image leaped up onto the brim.

"End it here," it said. "For both of us."

It reached out; slowly, the Jackal took its hand and stepped up. Close, face-to-face, they stood on the very brink of the Well.

Seth moved. With a sudden decision he hauled himself up on the lip of the Well. He shoved the reflected creature aside, grabbing the man's arm. "Don't listen to it! Stand still!"

The water was a mirage. The Well was empty, a pit.

It descended endlessly into the earth, and—so far below they were only pinpoints of light—the three stars still plummeted, and for a second he was dizzy with that fall, as if down there was something that dragged at him, something huge and terrible, beyond the circles of the world. Then, he screamed. The creature had leaped at his back; its fine fingers clawed him. Something stabbed him, once, twice. He staggered, stunned with pain.

The Jackal grabbed him, flung him at Oblek; Seth fell with a shaft of agony that shot through him like fire; as Oblek caught him he saw the Jackal strike.

He struck with contempt, and fury, a blow at his own being, wresting the diamond sliver from the thing's hands, flinging it into the pit.

The creature screeched. It crumpled into nothing, into a withered mask and dessicated bones, a whisper of fair hair that dissolved into dust. Then it fell.

The Jackal staggered.

For a moment he was white with fatigue, as if he would crumple, too, as if some terrible duel had ended and drained him dry. Fox held him tight, on the edge of the abyss.

Behind them, with a great hiss and roar, the Well of Songs overflowed.

"Archon!"

Almost lost in the steam, Oblek's yell cut Seth to the quick. He tried to move. Pain jabbed through him. His own blood clouded the water. As the blackness closed, it had Oblek's voice.

"Seth's dying!" it whispered.

Argelin turned. The optio ran in with an armful of weapons; instantly the general grabbed a sword and whirled back. Water was surging out of the ground; the cave was awash.

Rhetia gasped. "The cave's flooding! Where's it coming from?"

Someone sobbed. People backed to the entrance. The circle of the Nine broke up.

Argelin leveled the sword at Mirany's throat. His face was pale and fevered, his eyes cold glints. "I should have done this long ago. There will be no Archon anymore, and no Speaker. I'll burn the Oracle and kill anyone who objects!" His voice was taut with rage. "If you want silence, then you can have silence. Forever, and ever!"

He drew his arm back. The sword whipped, through moonlight.

Whom Shall I Speak Through Now?

"Oblek!"

A scream, out of ancient nightmare. For an instant it rooted them all in terror; then Alexos was on his knees by Seth, rocking, gasping.

"Help him!" The big man grabbed him. "Archon!"

The boy looked up at him, his beautiful face distorted with anguish.

"Whom shall I speak through now?" he whispered.

Mirany had no time to scream. The sword slashed; she knew its buckling agony, the burst of blood, but at the same time Hermia was there; Hermia was in front of her, the shudder was Hermia's, the cry was hers, the blood was hers.

The sword cut deep into the Speaker's breast; she fell with a tiny gasp. Chryse was screaming hysterically. Mirany scrambled up, her dress spattered. She was numb, barely knew that Rhetia had hold of her, was yelling, "Out! All of you get out! Now!"

The cave was a river. It was gushing from the rocks, lifting the edges of Hermia's dress, swirling around Argelin's knees as he knelt beside her.

Frozen, Mirany and Rhetia watched him crumple, as if some terrible invisible force crushed him, his hands reaching out hesitantly to Hermia's face, her hair. When he touched her a shock went through him; they felt it.

"Hermia!" His voice was blank, disbelieving. *"Hermia!"*

The Speaker's eyes opened; she tried to catch at him, and he snatched her up. Blood streaked the rising water.

"Don't leave me," he whispered.

She breathed sounds, barely heard. "The Oracle . . . spare the Oracle."

He shook his head, in anguish. "You always cared more for the Oracle than me! Always!"

Frantically he wiped the blood away, making it worse, spreading it everywhere. "Why did you interfere? Why did you move? God knows I would never have hurt you—"

She smiled weakly. "I was the Rain Queen. Just for a moment . . . I spoke . . . her words. You heard me."

"I heard you."

"We should not have become enemies."

"We never were." He gathered her up and her eyes closed, her head slipping to one side. "Stay with me, Hermia. I need you!"

She whispered, "I can see . . . the garden."

Mirany swallowed. Beside her, Rhetia took a step back.

For a long moment Argelin seemed not to realize she was dead. He held her as the waters rose, lifting her out of the surging flood. When he finally raised his face, Mirany saw he was fighting for control, a terrible, rigid control.

Unsteady with Hermia's weight, he staggered up, her long skirts dripping.

He looked at them over her body.

His agony was worse than any threat.

The water was cold. It dripped between his lips and he drank it, and it was sweet.

It filled him.

It was light, a golden liquid. He felt it fill him like strength, like music.

It sang in his heart, a song that he knew, that he'd always known, and had forgotten. A song Telia hummed sometimes, playing with her doll, on hot afternoons.

A song his mother had sung.

He opened his eyes. He was propped up, surrounded by blurred faces. Somewhere, the Jackal's voice sounded incredulous. "The bleeding has stopped."

Seth pulled himself upright. He was aching and sore and the sound of the song was in his ears. He said, "Someone died. Was it me? Was it Mirany? *What's happened?*"

"She's dead," the boy whispered.

They stared, stricken. Seth took a shuddering breath, numb, not believing what he'd heard.

"She can't be! Why did you let her die!" he raged, grabbing Alexos and wrenching him around. "Don't you care! Don't you care about her at all!"

Oblek said, "Leave him! He's brought you back from the dead!" But Alexos reached out and touched Seth with his frail hand, and it was like the touch of a leaf, so light, and for one unaccountable minute it was his mother's touch, long lost.

"It's not Mirany, Seth. It's Hermia. Hermia is dead and Mirany is the Speaker now. Just as you wanted it to be."

Stunned, Seth stared at him. Then he whispered, "You make it sound as though I made it happen."

The Jackal said calmly, "Whatever it is, we can't do anything. If you want to drink of this magic Well, Oblek, drink, before we drown."

The Well surged.

Backing, they saw the water was black, as if nothing was there, as if a steaming nothingness was pouring out, a wide pool of darkness, and as Seth felt it surge around his feet, the Jackal yanked him up. "Can you walk?"

"I'm fine."

The tomb thief looked shaken. "You should be dead."

Alexos said, "Drink it, Oblek! All of you! Quickly!"

Part of the side wall collapsed; a great gush of darkness roared out. It was hot around their ankles; in seconds it had risen to a raging outpouring, sweeping stones aside, cascading out of the cave mouth. Hastily Oblek bent and scooped up some in his hands; nothing was there, but he drank and drank, and Alexos sniffed and watched him, and then with one of those sudden changes of mood that turned Seth to ice, the boy was laughing. "Does it taste nice?"

Oblek swallowed. "Foul as sulfur. Will it really give me songs?"

"As many as you can sing, Oblek." He smiled, proud. "Just like you used to."

To Seth's amazement the Fox was drinking, too, gulping handfuls as if he could never get enough of the black water; it ran from his fingers.

"You, too, Lord Jackal."

The thief eyed the cauldron of darkness warily. "I don't trust magic, Archon."

"It's not magic." Alexos caught his arm, pulled him to the brim. "Please. We've come all this way and you must be thirsty."

The tall man looked down at the boy. "I am thirsty," he said quietly.

"Then don't hesitate. Or it will be too late."

The Jackal turned. He dipped his fine hands in and drank delicately. But he had time for only one mouthful. Then the earth shuddered; the cave shook.

He jerked back. "Move!" he yelled. "Now!"

◆ ◆ ◆

The earth shuddered. Everyone had fled; now Argelin waded to the cave mouth. He yelled, "Bring them!" The guards struggled back, water to their waists.

"Up here. Quickly." Mirany tugged the Speaker's mask off and pulled Rhetia after her up onto a higher ledge at the back of the cave. Already the water was too deep to get to the entrance. Across the torrent the soldiers looked at them hopelessly. "Jump in!" one yelled. "We'll get you out!"

"He's right. There's no choice." Rhetia moved; Mirany held her tight. "Look. Look outside."

The Draxis was rising. It was welling out of the earth, snapping brittle fences, ravaging waste fields of dried-up lemons and olives. A raging torrent, it foamed and bubbled, pouring from somewhere far upstream, and a thousand things were carried along in it, buildings and stones and birds and dead rats, and she saw it thicken and fill its ancient watercourse, foaming into the sea, a great dark wash of sediment clouding the pure blue ocean.

Argelin backed away from it but it surged around him, over him. He gave a gasp of terror, then yelled, "No! I won't let her go!" But the water had fingers; it dragged Hermia from his arms, pulled her deep, took her far into the depths.

"Leave her with me!" he screamed. "Leave her!"

But all around him the Rain Queen's fury surged.

"He'll be swept away!" Mirany gasped. She could feel the water's anger, its pent-up vengeance. But Jamil had yelled, and now in reply a strange trumpeting thudded the earth, and she saw the elephants had broken free and were strung out in a great linked line, trunk to tail. The first knelt; Jamil grabbed Argelin and thrust him toward the beast. Then they were aloft, the great animal's strength holding itself steady.

Argelin looked back, into the cave. The soldiers were scrambling out.

"We're trapped," Rhetia hissed, "and he knows it. He's leaving us here."

"More than that." Mirany had understood that look, seen how he called up to the cliff top, one savage command.

Then the elephants lumbered away.

Water hit them like a wall. Hot and steaming, it gushed out of the cave and swept them along with it, until Oblek grabbed an outcrop of rock and hauled himself up to the cleft pinnacle of the mountain top, reaching down and plucking the Archon out of the flood with one mighty jerk. The boy whooped with delight, dangling above the waters. Seth and Fox climbed out and the Jackal came after them; on top of the rocks they sat shivering, staring in disbelief at the river that had come from nowhere.

"We did it!" Alexos cried happily. "We brought the river back! Isn't it beautiful, Oblek?"

The big man grinned. "A miracle, old friend."

It roared down the mountain. Stones and boulders were rolled in it, a red flood, and already they could see it surging far below, out into the dry watercourse of the Draxis, raging toward the sea. Downstream the waters would crash like a wall, Seth thought, sweeping away dead trees until the thunder of their coming would bring everyone in the Port running out of their houses. Because the god's act was a danger and a wonder, and to some it brought life, and to others death. To Hermia. And was Mirany really the Speaker now?

The Jackal was standing, staring east. Far off, the sky was alight, streaked with pink. As the sun rose, the desert flushed with splendor, the new water glinting, a streak of fire fingering out, filling tributaries, streambeds, drowning flat cracked slabs of scorched rock.

Seth stood next to him. "It'll be chaos down there," he whispered.

"We'll drown," Rhetia breathed.

Mirany scrambled back from the black torrent. "Where are you?" she gasped. "Come quickly!"

His answer was pleased and happy.

We have drunk from the Well of Songs.

"And the river?"

The golden apples are returned. It seems the Rain Queen has forgiven us.

For a moment, even as the water came above her waist, she laughed, knowing the god's voice was back with her. Until she saw that Rhetia had heard it, too, saw her wide-eyed stare into the back of the cave.

He was standing in the shadows. He was tall and thin, his hair white, his skin drained of color. He held out his narrow hand and beckoned them quickly. *"Mirany. Come with me. Hurry."*

Mirany pushed Rhetia. "Move!"

"Is he—?"

"Just hurry!"

The cave ledge led back, into darkness. The Speaker's mask under her arm, Mirany waded after Kreon, seeing his silhouette flicker in front of her. Once she slipped and went under with a choked scream, because the water was black and steamed, as if it had surged from somewhere incredibly deep. Ahead, Rhetia was chest deep, breathless. Then, above the great crack, Kreon stopped. "This is the only way out."

Rhetia could still manage to snort with scorn. "Down! Are you crazy?"

"The caves lead to tunnels that link with the tombs. This whole area is a honeycomb, centuries old. The water will not fill them." He looked at them sadly. "You have to come with me now, Mirany. It's the only safe place until the Archon returns. Argelin has killed the Speaker, and the god's wrath will fall on him. Nothing will be the same."

"But Mirany's the Speaker. Why should we skulk in the tombs?"

"There's nowhere else." He looked beyond her. "Do you see?"

Smoke was rising from the Island. In the dawn light it

was a black column, and it went straight up, like the smoke from a pyre.

"He's done it." Rhetia gasped as the water reached her face. *"He's destroyed the Oracle!"*

The sun was rising; its light touched the cave wall above them. Kreon looked away quickly. "We must go."

The crack was deeply drowned. He lowered himself in, took a deep breath and was gone, the blackness covering him.

Rhetia said, "Good luck. Jump with me."

Over the sea, over the surge of the new river, the sun was rising. Its light flooded Mirany's eyes.

Hermia was dead and she was Speaker. But a Speaker in the darkness, exiled, outlawed.

"They'll be back," she whispered.

Rhetia shrugged. "What can they do? A boy and a fat musician and a scribe."

"And a jackal." Mirany looked down at the mask, its empty eyes filling with water, the darkness pouring through its open mouth. "They can defeat Argelin. For Hermia's sake."

Rhetia grabbed her. "Hermia wouldn't want him defeated. That's the worst thing."

Mirany slipped, losing balance. Then she raised her head and spoke to the sun.

"Don't be long. Things will be terrible now."

She took a deep breath.

Together, they jumped.